I0760788

Published by Imdalind Press

Cover Design by JVArts
Interior Design and Art by Duck&Bicycle

Production Management by Imdalind Press

ISBN : 978-1-949725-69-8
978-1-949725-70-4
Printed in USA
This Edition, November 2012, 2021
Ruby Edition, October 2022, 2024

KISS OF EMBERS AND TREACHERY

EXTENDED VOLUME, BOOKS 1-3

THE IMDALIND RUBY COLLECTION
BOOK ONE

REBECCA ETHINGTON

CONTENTS

KISS OF FIRE

EYES OF EMBER

SCORCHED TREACHERY

To My Grandmother—
Who loved to read and loved to hear my stories.
You always told me I could write, and strangely enough it turns out I can!

To My Papa—
Who taught me what true love really is.

PRONUNCIATION GUIDE

CHARACHTERS

Joclyn - /Jaw:s:lyn/

Ryland - /Rye-lan:d/

Wynifred - /Winifred/
Wyn - /Win/

Ilyan - /ill-ee-yawn/

THE WORLD

Imdalind - /Im-dahl-in:d/

Skřítek - /skr̝̊iːtɛk/

Trpaslík - /trpasliːk/

Víly - /viːlɪ/

Drak - /drah:k/

Silnỳ - /sil:nee/

Drevo - /drey:vo/

Vymàzat - /vee:mah:zaht/

Zêlství - /zɛl:str̝̊iː/

Tȍuha - /to:hah/

Zmizêt - /zmiːzɛt/

Svazovat - /svah:so:vaht/

další v příkazu - /dalʃiː v pr̝̊i:kah:zoo/

Děkuji - /dee:koo:jhi/

PRONUNCIATION GUIDE

Ahoj - /Ah:ahj/

Štít - /st:i:ht/

zánik - /zah:n:eek/

Mi Lasko - /Me Lah:s:ko/

Zlomený - /zlo:me:knee/

Omezující stone - /zah:n:eek/

EXTENDED RUBY EDITION

KISS of FIRE

IMDALIND SERIES BOOK ONE

REBECCA ETHINGTON

PROLOGUE

The heavy boom of the knock on the door pulled her out of sleep with a jerk. She sat upright, heart pumping, flesh heating, as she looked to the door. Her mind went to war, to battle, to an invading army that she would have to face and she felt her magic flare, the heat of it thrumming through her as though she would simply explode in flames and take them all down with her. It took far too long for her to realize that the sound was not an invading army and instead was nothing more than the incessant knocking that hadn't woken her husband up.

The large man didn't even stir.

Frustrating, considering the knock was clearly meant for him. It was always for him, especially this late at night when only one person would be up and wandering through the underground cave tunnels that made up their home.

Only one person would knock so loud they would risk waking everyone else around them up, although in this part of the caves that wasn't so much of a risk. The caves of Imdalind used to be full of Skříteks and Trpaslíks, of all the magic wielders of the world. But now they sat empty, too many lost to the centuries long war over magic that had been slowly wiping them all out.

He was knocking louder now. Why he didn't just barge in was beyond her.

"Get up, you big lug," she hissed, pushing her husband's shoulder.

No response.

Just more knocking.

Looked like there was only one option.

Sliding out from the warm covers, she raced to the door, opening it wide just as the man on the other side of the door was about to knock again.

It was exactly who she had thought it was. The last blood born ruler of the Skříteks, and the one they had chosen to lead them.

The King of Imdalind, and of all magic

Even if he didn't look like it, not right then anyway.

A King didn't usually wear torn jeans and a wrinkled t-shirt. A Trpaslík didn't usually wear a flowery nightgown either; yet she was. The only Trpaslík in all of Imdalind, facing the king.

"My Lord." She dipped her head and curtseyed, or tried to, she had never been one for formalities. His responding smirk said as much. "I'll go wake, Ta--"

She didn't get to finish before the King's wide hand wrapped around her forearm, holding her in place.

"No. It's you I need." His voice was deep with that powerful rumble that made him more of a King than his parentage ever would.

"Me? Why do you want *me*?" The shock jolted the last of the sleep out of her system.

"Someone has come to us with news," he continued, still rumbling as he stared at her with blue eyes that seemed to be glowing in the dark. She could have sworn she saw them flash with the powerful pull of his magic as he said the last few words. The words that had pulled him here to wake her. "We found her."

"You found her?" All of the heat in her veins turned to ice. She was the sole carrier of the fabled fire magic, but right then she could have been standing in a blizzard with the chill that moved up her spine.

They had found her. The Chosen. No wonder the King was so excited. He didn't just seem to be glowing, he was glowing.

"But we have been looking..." she could barely get the words out, it had been so long since that sight was given, since the prophecy had promised of her arrival. "We have been looking for her for centuries."

"Yes," he breathed out airily. "And I have just been given word of her existence."

"By who?" She knew she shouldn't have asked him, it was not her place, but thankfully he just bounced on his toes and smiled.

"From a very reliable source. He is going to lead us to her; I need you to help me get her out."

"Me? Why?" She took a step closer, shutting the door behind them. Her husband should know this, he was the King's second in command after all, but there was something about the way was bouncing on his toes... he looked like a love sick teenager. "Just go take her. Get rid of her parents and bring her back home. You've done it before."

They had. For centuries they had sought out the Chosen, not just to find the girl who had been seen in sight, but to protect them. They had taken the children who were marked with magic and brought them to Imdalind for safe keeping; that was until the Víly's had all disappeared, then there were no more children to find.

Until now.

"It's not that simple. She is not a child. She has seen almost seventeen years."

The fire in her veins flared.

"Seventeen?" How could that be? They were not the only ones looking for her. How had she survived so long?

It wasn't possible.

"Yes. We don't have much time. *He* might already be there." The giddy joy in his voice took a dark turn, those blue eyes flashing darkly as she felt his magic flare in the air, that powerful strain that made him king, nearly sucking the oxygen from the space.

Although, that might have been more from who the King was talking about.

Who *he* was.

"No." Just the thought of being near him... being near any of them. Her magic flared again, hot flames licking against her fingers as though she would burn them to a crisp right then.

"I expect you to be on your best behavior; and kill whomever I say, when I say." The King's voice was level, his manic excitement leaving as the oxygen level returned to normal.

At least that she could do, and gladly.

Unable to hide the smile, she nodded in understanding; not that there was any point in fighting him. The King returned the gesture before turning and striding down the hall, his steps echoing against the stone floor of the long cave corridor. It was only then she realized that he was not wearing shoes.

King of Imdalind, indeed.

"We leave at dawn." His voice echoed around the stone hallway as he yelled back to her, the darkness of night swallowing him up.

She did not move, however, she stood in the door frame, biting her lip as she started into the swallowing darkness of the caves that were her home. The caves that were built by the earth magic of the Trpaslíks long before this war even started. Now she was the last of her kind here, the last of her magic fighting beside this king. Perhaps, if they truly had found her all of that would change.

They had found the girl they had been looking for. The girl that could end everything. Now if only they could be fast enough to save her.

If only they could be the ones to get there first.

Because if *he* was already there. If *he* had already found her... then it would be too late for all of them.

And this war over magic was already over.

CHAPTER 1
JOCLYN

My longboard clicked rhythmically down the sidewalk as I moved. The warm wind of early summer tugged against my dark hoodie, pulling at the long strands of black hair that had fallen out of my hood. I didn't like traveling in front of the houses in this part of the neighborhood. I normally took the back alley, but today, some road crews were working on pot-holes and I had to make my trip in front of the giant mansions that littered the hills of the east side of the city.

The rich ladies, with their upturned noses, liked to look out their windows at me as if I were somehow infecting their perfect little world with a contagious disease. They looked at me like I was poor—which I was—a menace—which I wasn't—and like there was something wrong with me—which I wasn't even sure of. Normally, I would laugh at their response to me, but I didn't like them taking so much notice. Chances were, they would complain to my mother's boss and she would get in trouble, again. It wasn't my fault the road crews decided to work on the alley, but it's not like "His Grace" would care.

My mother had worked as Edmund LaRue's cook for almost ten years now, having taken the job after my father took off when I was five. Mr. LaRue—or King Edmund as I called him—was an arrogant, greedy, self-righteous man who ruled over everyone like a medieval lord. He probably had more secrets than rooms in his house, if that were even possible. However, as much as I despised him, he paid my mother well, so I didn't complain.

I jumped off my longboard as I reached his house. If King Edmund heard the clicking of it against the sidewalk, he might throw another fit; that is, of course, if Mrs. Nose-Against-The-Window hadn't already put in a call. I looked up the long driveway as I stepped in front of the gate. Only the gray Rolls-Royce lay parked against the side of the house, causing my heart to fall—no bright yellow Lotus. Ryland wasn't home yet.

I hopped back on my longboard to roll down the side of the house; my somewhat good mood dashed by the absence of my best friend. Who cared if King Edmund got mad at me for making a racket?

I crashed into the kitchen, the slam of the door disrupting the 70s music that my mother and Mette, the LaRue's baker, were listening to. Plopping myself onto one of the many bar stools surrounding the long work surfaces, I placed my head on my arms and covered my face as much as I could with my hood.

"Happy Birthday, Joclyn!" My mom was beaming. I only grunted as I attempted to burrow into my hoodie more. "How was school?"

"Fine," I answered into the countertop.

"Fancy that," Mette said in her rich, Irish accent. "She can disappear into that table. Must be a trick learned when one turns seventeen."

I grumbled nonsense at them again and covered my head with my arms, trying to ignore the laughter of the two women.

"Not funny," I growled.

"Hello, in there! Joclyn, can you hear me?" My mother lifted the side of my hood as she called into it, and I tried not to smile. "Well, I think she's done it! She has melded into the sweatshirt and become one with it."

"That will make it easier to wash her, that will."

"Not funny." I tried not to sound amused, but I don't think it worked. My mother snorted so loudly it reverberated off the pristine marble countertops.

"I'll just throw her in the washing machine, then a little bleach, *lots* of detergent, and the skateboard can go in the dumpster."

"Hey! It's a longboard, and it's the only way I get around! Unless you bought me a car. Did you buy me a car?" I shot up like a light, my face breaking out into an eager grin.

"There she is," Mom laughed, throwing a present at me. "Happy Birthday, honey! Sorry, no car this year."

"She lives. She lives. Praise the Lord! I thought for a second we would have to call a priest to exorcize her from the sweater," Mette laughed, her red bun bobbing on top of her large, round head. "Happy Birthday, dearie."

My mom nudged the present at me again, prompting me to open it. Her eyes were sparkling with that eager anticipation she always got about gift-giving. The package was a good size, but lumpy and squishy. Clothes. Clothing had been an issue with my mother and me since that darned mark showed up behind my ear and chased my dad away.

Even twelve years later I could still recall the pain from that moment. A shimmer of blue glitter, intense pain, and then I had been in a coma for five months. No one knew what had happened. I was fine, except that my eyes had changed from green to a colorless silver, and a small mark had appeared behind my right ear. It was the size of a penny, the skin vivid red and raised like a brand with a small indistinguishable figure standing out in vivid black.

My dad was convinced it meant something more, and left because of it. Yet another reason I preferred to hide the mark, and myself.

She thought I should show the world how beautiful I was. I guess she might be right; I could be seen as the epitome of the fair-skinned, dark-haired ethereal beauty. My mom fawned over my bone structure and perfectly-formed eyebrows that just grew that way. But, when I looked in the mirror, I only saw a skinny girl with stringy hair and dark circled eyes. 'Not quite good enough'. My mom obviously saw something different. She liked to give me blue shirts to highlight my black hair, or green belts to set off the silver of my eyes, or so she said. All I saw were vivid colors or an obvious lack of fabric that would make me stand out.

For years my mom kept trying to convince herself that my choice of baggy, dark-colored clothes was a stage that I would outgrow. I always found a way to hide myself; I kept my black hair long and falling in a sheet around my face, my clothes always dark and at least a size too big. It was all done in a way to help me blend in so people wouldn't notice me. I felt comfortable inside my safety shield, hoping that no one could see me or figure out what was wrong with me. When the Goth kids showed up at school, it worked to my advantage. My mom, for once, thought I was trying to be cool, but I wasn't overly emotional like they appeared to be. I just wanted to disappear.

"Go on," Mom prodded. "Open it."

I sighed before ripping off the paper. It was a deep red shirt, embroidered with some beads and fabric flowers. There was no denying it was pretty. It even looked like one of the things I wished I could wear, if only I felt comfortable doing so.

"Just try it on, Joclyn." My mom danced around in her white kitchen shoes, smiling big enough I could see her teeth. How in the world could I say no to that?

I dragged my feet all the way to the bathroom, the red shirt sticking out of the arm of the hoodie my hands were hiding in. I put on the shirt, cursing the fact that my mother could tell what size I was even through my purposely too big clothes. It was snug, but not too tight.

I stared at myself in the mirror for a second, looking through the tunnel of dark hair. I looked so different in the shirt, almost pretty. Without thinking, I pulled my hair up into a ponytail, just to see what it would look like, but the mark stood out so vividly; its ugly shape stuck out right behind and below my right ear. I pulled my hair around the side of my neck. The low twist covered it easily, but I still didn't trust it. Part of me wished I could dress like this, but I could never tell my mother that.

"Come on, Joclyn! We want to see."

I had looked in the mirror a second too long, trying to figure out a way to get out of this. Even if I said it was too small, my mom would insist I show her anyway. Best to get it over with. I sighed before leaving the bathroom, knowing that Mette and my mom would fawn over me. I closed my eyes so that I wouldn't have to see my mom dance around with excitement again. The door clicked open, and I stood there, eyes closed, waiting for it to come.

"Oh, Joclyn," my mom said, "it's beautiful." I didn't need to have my eyes closed, I could hear the soles of her non-slip shoes squeak against the floor as she danced in joy.

"Mom, don't..." I pleaded, but I knew it was useless.

"That color... with your hair... Oh, please wear it to dinner tonight, without that darn sweatshirt," she added. I could feel her tug on the hoodie, but I hung on to it for dear life.

"Mom. No." My eyes snapped open in my attempt to retort, and I froze. Ryland stood right in front of me, a huge grin on his face. My jaw dropped as my heart went into overdrive.

Ryland LaRue was the son of my mother's boss. Ry was two years older than me and stood a good head taller. We had been friends since my mother first started this job, playing together in the kitchen and hiding on the grounds of the estate. Ryland would always be my very best friend, but lately, it was hard to see past his dark, curly hair, crystalline blue eyes and 'private school Rugby muscles' without feeling like my heart was getting restarted. This heart-slamming was for a different reason though: he hadn't seen me wear anything other than a hoodie since I hit puberty. I felt uncomfortable, and Ryland's appreciative grin wasn't helping matters much.

Mette and my mother broke out into huge bouts of laughter at their little joke. The look of surprise on my face must have been hysterical. Rather than join along, as part of me wished to, I squeaked and moved to put my hoodie back on. I slid into it as quickly as I could without revealing my scar. I had kept it hidden from Ryland for this long, thanks to Band-Aids and carefully-placed hoods or hair; I didn't need him seeing it now. It would only give him a reason to run away.

"Ah, come on, Jos... It's pretty," Ryland pleaded.

"No," I spoke as sternly as I could, turning to repeat the word to my mother who was in stitches with Mette against the confection mixer. My mother's laughter stopped.

"Joclyn, you have to wear it tonight," she pleaded. "Your grandmother bought you a matching skirt."

"Skirt?" I gasped. There was no way they were getting me into a skirt. Although, I could tell by the look on my mom's face that I was trapped. My birthday dinner was the only time of the year I saw my father's parents. It would break their heart if I said no.

"Ugh. Fine. Fine!" I snapped, ignoring my mother's look of triumph before rounding on Ryland, one finger pointed into his face. "One word of this to anyone, even mentioning it to me, Ry, and I will kill you."

"Uh huh," he laughed, his blue eyes rolling. "What are you going to do, Jos? Hide from me? It does look very pretty on you, you know."

"Ryland LaRue, so help me..."

"Yeah, yeah, I got ya." He smiled, grabbing my hand that was still pointed in his face. "Come on. I'll have her back in an hour, Mrs. Despain."

"Better make it two, Ryland. I don't need her moping around while I try to get the chicken broiled." My mother smiled so brightly that I could have almost guessed what was on her mind. More gifts.

"No problem, Mrs. D."

"Oh, and Joclyn," my mom's voice called after us. I turned back to her, halting Ryland's departure. "Please try to avoid Edmund and Timothy. I think my job has been threatened enough for one week." She smiled, but it was half-hearted. She was always the first to get in trouble over my friendship with Ryland.

I nodded in understanding before Ry pulled me out of the kitchen and into the servants' quarters. We gained the usual snickers and side-glances as we scampered past the many rooms occupied by the live-in staff, heading to the back corridors that the servants used to move around the massive house.

At first, our friendship had been tolerated by Edmund, but a few years ago that had started to change and we had been labeled as unacceptable. Then last year, we were told we were not supposed to be friends at all. Ryland had been warned and threatened by his father to stay away from me, while my mother had been under constant "warning" of losing her job. I wasn't surprised. To *King* Edmund I was nothing more than a dirty peasant. We probably should have taken it seriously, but Ryland insisted everything was okay, so my mother and I followed his lead.

We entered the upper hall where Ryland's bedroom sat, the door just ahead of us on the left. I kept my eyes straight ahead, smiling like a loon. That was until an unusually short man in a three-piece suit with a thick, neatly-trimmed beard turned the corner to face us. I jumped behind Ryland, not needing his arm to move me there. I knew that man, and I hated him.

Timothy Vincent was the Vice President of Ryland's family's company, Imdalind Forging. He was responsible for the metal-forging method that had made them their millions. Timothy was also the man who reprimanded my mother on a weekly basis about my continued relationship with Ryland. He caught sight of us and moved forward quickly, an even angrier scowl than usual carved into his face. Timothy always made me uncomfortable, even on his best days.

"Ryland, we have been looking for you."

My heart sank. *We*. That could only mean one thing.

A deeper gait entered the hall, and I moved further behind Ry. I didn't have to see Edmund LaRue to know what he looked like. In many ways, Ryland could be described as his father's clone, but instead of the mop of loose curls Ryland had, Edmund kept his hair short and slicked back in a gentle wave. Where Ryland's eyes were the warm and welcoming color of the depths of the ocean, Edmund's were as cold and distant as the polar ice caps. They always cut into me with a frigid, poisonous edge that made my insides repulse.

I sank into Ryland's back, my face pressing against his polo shirt in an attempt to hide. His muscles were tense and strained.

Ryland's hand reached back and found the tips of my fingers that stuck out from the cuff of my hoodie. He squeezed my fingers between his in an attempt to reassure me. As always, his touch warmed my body, the tingling warmth shooting right to my stomach.

"Ryland! I am so glad we found you. I would like to move our lesson to an hour after dinner." Edmund's voice was laced with a false endearment that shook my bones. His statement was not a question, but a command.

Ryland had been taking lessons with his father since he was twelve. Ry had always insisted it was some fencing thing, but the way they talked about it always made it seem so sinister, like they were going to take over the world. Who knew? Maybe they were. Corporate drama was a little out of my league.

"Yes, Father, that's fine. I will meet you in the court." Ryland's voice was distant and diplomatic. When he talked like this, he reminded me of the heir to the multi-million dollar company he was, not my energetic, fun-loving best friend.

"Ryland," Timothy spoke slowly, dragging out his syllables, and I knew he was going to address our friendship. I shifted my weight, cursing the dark hoodie that stuck out from behind my hiding place. "I am so glad to see you have taken our advice about your choice of friends." Timothy's voice seemed hopeful, odd, seeing as how I stood right here.

I attempted to draw the fabric closer to my body. Being so close to both of them made me almost, dare I say it, scared.

"I have expressed my opinion on this multiple times, Timothy. Please do not make me repeat it." Ryland stood a little straighter as he attempted to end the conversation.

"Now, now, Ryland. We don't need any of that." Edmund's voice lacked any warmth. "After all, I would hate for your attitude to be the cause of a downfall."

I cringed. Was he talking about me, or about my mother? Edmund had never before said anything so bold when I was within ear-shot; it was almost like he couldn't see me. That, in itself, was a ridiculous thought; Ryland wasn't broad enough to hide behind, even with all his muscle.

"You know my terms in regards to that, Father." I could see Edmund's expensive penny loafers slide against the white carpet. I shifted my weight, scared he was moving to get a better look at me.

"So it would seem. Well, at least now I won't have to dismiss her mother, or worse. We just can't have anything spoiling my perfect son, now, can we?" Edmund's body shifted as he moved closer. Ryland's fingers pressed harder against my own.

"No, Father." There was a pause and then Edmund's shiny leather shoes stepped away from us down the hall. Timothy's shoes followed

Edmund's hesitantly, like they were waiting for something else to happen before he turned the corner.

We moved the last few steps quickly, darting into Ryland's spacious room before either of them had a chance to return.

Ryland's bedroom was roughly the size of my entire apartment. The giant rectangular space was separated down the middle on the left side by a long wall that housed a kitchenette on one side and Ryland's massive entertainment system on the other. The other half of the room contained his oversized bed that still sported the colored blankets we had used to make forts when we were little kids. Behind it all was a bathroom and a closet the size of a small motor home that contained far too many clothes for someone who went to a school that required uniforms.

I went to the high cabinet next to the entertainment center where he kept the chocolate before plopping down on his bed to enjoy a Mounds Bar. Ryland locked the door behind him, just in case his father or the servants decided to get nosey, and turned on some brainless TV show as he went.

"I hate them, you know. Hate," I spat sourly, ripping the wrapper off the candy.

"That's a strong word, Jos."

"I know, but don't you think they deserve it? Saying all that about how I am going to ruin you, talking about me like I was not even there. It's like they couldn't even see me."

"Maybe they couldn't," Ryland said almost inaudibly.

"Ha, ha, ha, very funny, Ry." I paused at the curious glance Ryland gave me. "They wouldn't hurt anyone because of me, would they?"

"I wouldn't put it past them," Ry grumbled as he leaned against the wall his TV was mounted to.

My head jerked up. "They would?" Not cool.

"Don't worry so much, Jos. I wouldn't let them, even if they tried. If I could get them to be nice to you, I would, but I can't. Either way, you don't need to worry about it. You only have to deal with them for the rest of the year. I get him for my entire life."

I sighed and the candy bar fell untouched to my lap. I didn't like the daily reminders that Ryland was leaving overseas for college in just a few months' time. Oxford, a huge giant ocean away. I tried to push the information to the back of my mind. I would be lucky if I ever saw him again.

"So, did you get the role?" Ryland asked eagerly, plopping down beside me, his obvious change in subject managed as smoothly as possible.

"No, of course not. The role went to Cynthia McFadden, not that anyone was really surprised."

"What? You read the role perfectly!"

"Well, I did here in your bedroom. In the school gymnasium, I'm not sure the drama teacher could hear my monologue over the catcalls about my lack of hygiene..." I hoped that didn't sound too bitter.

Cynthia had brought half the football team with her and they had quite a fun time jeering at anyone who auditioned for the same role as the cheerleader. I thought I had done a good job, even with the jocks yelling at me to bathe or brush my hair, but Ms. Flowers didn't think so.

"What role did you get then?" His silky voice was calm and eager.

"None."

"None? You would have been cast as Ophelia without question if you had auditioned at my school."

I couldn't help but laugh. "Of course I would have. You go to an all boys' school!"

"I guess you're right. But Michael Aliente has been eyeing that role for years now; you might have had your work cut out for you."

"Well, I don't think I could beat Michael; he's way too good at those monologues." We laughed, the thought of tiny Michael in a long Shakespearean gown bringing tears to my eyes.

"Do you want me to do something? I could make a phone call..."

"No!" I snapped. He had said it with only good intentions, but his face moved from concern to shock. My fast-beating heart plummeted; I didn't mean to offend him. "I mean, no, thank you. Cynthia will be great in the role, though she may come off as more of a floozy than a crazy girl, but, whatever."

"That's not what I meant, Jos. I meant about the guys teasing you. I could always pick you up from school in the Lotus; that would stop them in their tracks."

"They would only say I paid you." I smiled at him. I loved Ryland when he got like this; he was an incredibly caring guy.

He didn't return the smile. Instead, he looked at me as if I had just sold his precious car, to buy a longboard made of solid gold. "Joclyn, I don't like them making fun of you, especially when they say things that are not true. I mean, really! *You,* not bathe. I can smell your shampoo from a mile away."

"How do you know that's not just the perfume I use to cover up the almighty stench?"

"Joclyn."

"Ryland." My glare was no match for his; his blue eyes cut into me. "It's all right, really. It's not like there's anything you can do."

"I have a full Rugby team who would gladly fight for your honor."

"What, do we live in 1740 now?" I laughed. He didn't. Strangely enough, he was serious. "You would fight the Eagles' Landing football team for my 'honor'?"

He nodded.

I was beginning to feel uncomfortable. "Why? I mean, no one cares about me. I disappear in that school. They only said those things because they couldn't even remember who I was. I only auditioned because it was part of my grade..."

"I care about you, Jos, and I don't want people talking about you like that." My heart sputtered before I turned to him, making sure the mark below my ear remained covered.

"That's why you're my best friend, Ry, because you care. You are the only one who knows me." I smiled at him in a desperate attempt to convey that I was okay, that the name-calling didn't hurt, even if it did. I could tell he wasn't buying it. He could always see through my looks. "I'm fine, Ryland. Honest."

I waited, but he didn't say anything. I could just see him barging into my school with a dozen other guys in dark blue blazers. Ugh.

"Ry, I am asking you as nicely as I can manage to not do anything. I can handle it; you don't always have to protect me." I tried to put as much energy into my voice as I could. I am not sure it worked.

"All right, I won't do anything. It's just a crappy way to spend your birthday."

"That's okay. I got a great shirt, soon to be skirt-combo out of it, which I will never wear. So, no harm done."

"You know, you really should wear..."

"Don't start, Ryland," I said, falling back on his bed.

"You just need the right accessories, is all." He spoke quite calmly as he placed a small wrapped box on my chest. I sat up, letting the box fall into my lap.

"What? Are you asking me to marry you?" I scoffed at the words, but I still couldn't take my eyes off the box.

"Hell, no! I have been engaged to Cynthia McFadden for years. Didn't you know?" He pushed into my shoulder, almost knocking me over. "Just open it."

I moved back to a sitting position like a weeble toy. I couldn't say anything; the richest guy in the state had just given me a jewelry box.

Part of me didn't want it, but the girl inside of me forced my fingers to rip the paper off.

The box was black velvet, soft to the touch. I caressed it like the box itself was the gift before opening it to reveal an inside of soft black silk. Nestled into the shiny fabric was a teardrop-shaped ruby the size of my thumbnail. The beautiful jewel was suspended from a silver wire that wrapped around the Ruby in swirls and spirals that joined it to the thin silver chain. I could only stare at it. I knew without asking that the ruby was real. The necklace was worth more than my mother made in a year.

"Do you like it?" Ryland's voice was soft, entertained by my reaction as he chuckled at my solitary head-bob of a response. He grabbed the necklace out of the box and moved to place it around my neck.

"Sorry it's not a car," he laughed, "but your mom wanted to give you a full new outfit for your birthday and forced—eh, recruited me to help. I thought this would set off the diamonds in your eyes. I think she will do anything to get you out of those hoodies and jeans."

I looked down at the necklace that now hung around my neck, my voice coming back. I moved my hair out from under the chain, careful not to show that dreaded mark.

"Besides," Ryland continued, "you can always wear your new outfit under a hoodie and then your mom can still feel like she won." I couldn't help but laugh, though, I also felt like crying. I had never received anything so beautiful, something that I instantly loved. Darn my girl emotions! One tear had leaked out.

"Thank you, Ryland. It's beautiful. I love it." My voice did not get above a whisper.

"You know, Jos, you're more of a girl than you let on. I'm just glad I am the one who gets to see it." With that, Ryland kissed my forehead. I thought my heart might explode.

I hadn't had a birthday this good, ever.

CHAPTER 2
JOCLYN

That all ended with dinner.

We always met my grandparents at the same place; a little Mexican dive called La Fea Gato. La Fea Gato was in Sunnyvale, perfectly distanced between our two houses, so we each had to drive an hour to meet for dinner. After having done it for eleven years, it wasn't a big deal. I even had a favorite dish on the menu and spent the majority of the hour drive dreaming of Chile Verde rather than listening to my mom dote over how pretty I looked, and how big the rock Ryland had given me was.

At first, she had attempted to pull my hair up, but I had put my foot down, startling poor Mette with a wail she had never heard come out of me before. I didn't care how much my mom promised that the mark was barely noticeable, or that scars were fashionable; mine was staying hidden. In the end, I had brushed my dark hair out until it hung down to my waist like a sheet.

We arrived at the restaurant late, nearly tripping over an old man at the entrance in our rush to the table to allow my grandmother her obligatory time to ogle over how much I had grown or changed. We all knew it was an act; my grandparents only came out of respect for my mother's wishes. I never saw them any other time.

My grandmother was a round woman with gray hair that she always wore in a bun. Her appearance suggested that she would be wearing a flowered apron, smiling and selling butter rolls rather than wearing business suits with the severe look she always had. My grandfather had always been quiet and somewhat reserved, but today he seemed downright cranky, and greeted my mother and me with a curt head-nod. My grandmother didn't seem to notice and looked me over quickly before shoving a bright pink parcel into my hands.

I tried my hardest to smile at the impending skirt, but I was not sure it worked. My mom's iron grip dug into my arm as she prompted me to open it. Even though it was obvious no one wanted to be there, my mom was still going to try her hardest to make this work.

The tape came off easily, as if it had been rewrapped, and an atrocious red and black plaid skirt tumbled onto my lap, followed by a small black bag that would hold only a wallet, if I was lucky. I looked at them both as happily as I could before being shooed off to the bathroom where I held the skirt up against my new shirt. They didn't match. I was going to look like a style-defunct school girl. Of course, they all declared I looked wonderful anyway. I could have worn a stuffed chicken and it would have received the same reaction. My frustration and irritation were turning into uncontrollable laughter.

Once the food came, I bowed out of the conversation, and my grandmother seemed to lose her lackluster interest in me. I focused on my food as my mother and grandmother chattered away about work and neighbors, and aunts, uncles and cousins I had never seen. I caught snippets of information about Uncle Robert's new wife and Cousin Becky's new—scandalous—tattoo, not taking anything in. The taste of chilies and guacamole consumed me so much that I was unaware of my grandmother's question until my mother tapped my leg.

"Joclyn?" she asked, repeating her question, "how is school?"

"Fine," I said, hoping I didn't have to elaborate. There wasn't much more that I could say about school, so we sat in uncomfortable silence.

"Excuse me. I have to go to the restroom." Mom spoke as normally as she could, although it was obvious she left in order to give us all time to talk.

My grandparents had nothing to say without my mom there, so I sat staring at the last of my empanada and listened to the clink of dishes and bits of conversation around me.

"Don't open the bag until you get home." My grandfather's rough voice made me jump.

"Excuse me?" I asked, taken back.

"The bag. Don't open it until you get home. There's a letter from your father in it." I think I may have leaped a few inches out of the booth. The words "your father" were never spoken, least of all by his own parents.

"My father?" I spoke much louder than I had anticipated, my heart beating a million miles an hour. "You've seen him?"

My grandfather leaned forward, but my grandmother looked at him so sharply, even I felt uncomfortable with her gaze. My grandfather shrank back against the booth.

"Yes, dear." Her voice was falsely sweet. "Your father asked us to give that letter to you. And we agreed."

"You've seen my father," I repeated again, although I wasn't sure if I felt joy, anger or excitement at this. Each emotion was there, but they didn't stop swirling around each other; my stomach turned into a bowl of butterflies.

"Yes," my grandfather supplied, ignoring a second look from Grandma. "He came by just the other day wanting to see you. He had a birthday gift for you, so we put it in that bag so you could have it. But don't open it here; I don't know if your poor mother's heart can handle hearing a single word from him."

"He wanted to see me...?"

"Yes, followed us here, no doubt. Poor lad seemed desperate..." Grandma cut Grandpa off with one stern look and he sank back in his chair, looking crabby again. I didn't notice, though; I had begun spinning around in my chair in a futile attempt to look for my father. I knew it was pointless. I wasn't even sure I knew what he looked like anymore. Any man here could be him. That one had his eyebrows, another had his nose. Of course I had pictures, but they were from so long ago. Besides, it was hard to recognize someone from a twelve-year-old photograph.

"You might want to make sure his gift has been properly paid for, dear. I wouldn't be surprised if he stole it. I am not sure my poor son has had more than two coins to rub together in a while."

I stopped my frantic search to face my grandmother. Her face was somewhat hard and disappointed now. I wanted to hear more, to ask her what she meant, but my mother slid back into her chair, announcing herself to be full.

The car ride home was quiet, unlike either of us. The little black bag sat on my lap as if it were a bomb waiting to go off. I didn't want to look at it, but couldn't keep from stealing glances. I tried counting the stars, the fence posts, the houses. Nothing worked, my eyes kept floating back to the bag.

"So, Joclyn...?" My mom's voice came out of nowhere. "Did you have a good birthday?" I looked down at my mismatched clothes, at the beautiful necklace, and smiled.

"Yeah, Mom. I did. Thanks for everything."

"You should wear that outfit tomorrow."

"Not going to happen, Mom."

"Why not?" she whined, offended.

"Well, I would get mugged for the necklace and tortured for my mismatched clothes." My mom looked down at my outfit as I gestured toward it, her face breaking into a gigantic smile.

"It does look bad, doesn't it?" she sighed. "I thought your grandmother would have more style sense—"

"Well, if you limit her to pencil skirts, she does great," I scoffed.

"At least the bag is cute." Her comment was innocent enough, but it stopped me dead in my tracks, the smile draining from my face. All I could do was nod and stare at it.

It was cute, but I couldn't stop thinking about what could be inside. Any other person who had been abandoned by their father would throw it away without a second thought. Yet, I was drawn to it.

He had left because of my mark. Maybe the letter would tell me something about it, maybe he had found something out, or maybe it was a plea for us to let him come home. I couldn't stop thinking about the possibilities, my heart beating uncomfortably at each one. If I was smart, I would have just thrown it away.

When I got home, I ran to my room with only a hurried goodnight to my mom. A shower would have to wait, changing would wait. I ripped open the bag and dumped the contents on my white bedspread. A small dirty package and a piece of paper fell out, each one leaving gray grease marks on the spots they hit. I looked at them—the package or the letter? I opted for the package; get the gift out of the way so I could focus on the letter.

I grabbed the small crumpled paper and began un-wrinkling it into a flat mass. There, amongst the dirty folds, sat a pure white marble; it almost looked like a pearl. I looked at it in disbelief. How could my wayward, possibly homeless, father afford to give me a pearl. It must be fake. I knew there was something to do with teeth to be able to tell if it was real and so I reached out to grab it with the full intention of biting it in half. However, the second my fingers came in contact with it, a shock of white-hot heat seared through my arm. I jumped back, cursing. What in the world had my father sent me?

I stepped closer to my bed, stopping as my head spun on my shoulders, my vision tracking and my stomach heaving. I steadied myself, waiting for the spinning to slow and cursing whatever food poisoning I had gotten at the restaurant.

I looked everywhere for the bead, but the white pearl no longer lay in the dirty wrapper; instead, one of deep purple had taken its place. I moved the dirty paper around, and I searched over my bedspread, but no other pearl—of any color—could be found. Luckily, when I grabbed the purple bead, no shock moved up my arm, though the small marble was very warm. I couldn't help but be a little mad; it seemed like a cruel joke for a renegade father to send his daughter something that zaps her.

I placed the purple bead back on the wrapper and picked up the letter. Silly really, whatever was going to hurt me the most was going to be written on the page. I opened it, a shaky breath flowing out of me.

My Dearest Jocelyn:

Great, he doesn't even know how to spell my name right.

My Dearest Jocelyn:

I write this letter in the hopes that my parents will deliver it to you, and find you well. Happy Birthday!! I can't believe that twelve years have passed since I last saw you. I am sure you have grown into a beautiful young woman. Do you have a lot of boyfriends? Tell them to be careful or your dad will get them.

I was torn between laughter and frustration; it seemed odd for a man I hadn't seen in so long to be giving me advice on how to threaten boys. I almost put the letter down; maybe I should have.

I hope you are doing well in school and not giving your mom much trouble.

I know I have not been a good father. I would apologize, but I know I would not gain your forgiveness, and in truth, I do not want it. I would have taken you with me if your mother had not hidden you from me. You probably don't even remember that day; I suppose it is better that way.

I do need you to know what I have found, and why I left. I knew there was something more to your mark than the doctors could tell us. When I was in college, a young man by the name of Thom, who was in one of my classes, had something similar; and one day we found him gone, his dorm room trashed.

I was so afraid that the same would happen to you, that you would be taken from me, my precious daughter. And so, when your mom would not listen, I left to find proof. And I found it, Jocelyn!

Your mark is special; it is magical. Your mark means you can do magic. They call it Koosa! It took many years, but I found a group of people who find those with marks such as yours and save them from the people who took my friend from college. I do not want you to disappear. I only hope that those who would harm you haven't already found you.

The people I found gave me a rock to give to you. They call it a birthstone. It will help them find you. All you have to do is touch it and it will call to them, and lead them to you. Isn't that wonderful? I found a way to save you! I am told it may hurt when you touch the stone, so please be careful. But, touch it as soon as you can so you can be saved, and I can see you again.

Love Always,

Your Father, Jeffery Despain

I read it once, then again, and again. Then I cried for at least twenty minutes. My poor father! The smart, beautiful man that my mother had fallen in love with had lost his mind. He was talking about magic like it was real and referring me to cults so that I could be saved. I think I cried myself to sleep, clutching the necklace Ryland had given me in one hand and the cursed bead my father had given me in the other.

CHAPTER 3
JOCLYN

Nothing could have stopped the nightmares I had that night. They began the second I closed my eyes and did not leave until the moment my restless night ended. Every aspect of the letter came to haunt me in one terrifying race for my life. I moved from being chased by a homeless man with sharp jagged teeth who was covered in rags, to being surrounded by extraordinarily tall people dressed all in white. No matter how fast I ran, I couldn't get away from any of them. I ran through the silent dream in a trance, my body tense and terrified.

When I woke up, I felt like I hadn't slept at all. My body was heavy and numb from emotional and mental exertion. My chest hurt with every breath, each movement straining sore muscles. I lay in bed for a long time, drifting in and out of sleep, having decided that I wasn't going to school that day. The nightmares didn't return, but I slept fitfully, my subconscious afraid of being haunted.

By about three in the afternoon, my body felt better, like I was recovering from a small head cold rather than feeling like I had been hit by a large load of bricks. Not being able to ignore the call of nature any longer, I trudged to the bathroom. It was odd how ill my body felt, almost like I had caught some strange body-ache bug. As much as I wanted to blame food poisoning for my illness, I wasn't sick enough, and blaming body-aches on a pearl-like bead was downright silly. I tried to convince myself my problem wasn't physical, only emotional. Who would have thought that a delusional letter from my father would have affected me so much? I collapsed back on my bed, my head throbbing with the collision.

My phone buzzed as a call came in. I reached for it, assuming it to be my mom checking in on me. I was shocked to see Ry's name and a picture of us on top of his car on the caller ID. Ryland never called. Of course, we saw each other every day so there was never a need, but it was still odd. I stared at his name until the ringer stopped and the system sent him to voicemail. I could have answered and told him I was sick, but knowing Ry, he would be able to hear the lie in my voice, or even worse, he would rush over to check on me.

I sighed, my chest aching with the movement. I hadn't changed since the birthday party; I had fallen asleep wearing the odd outfit I had been provided during dinner, the necklace Ryland gave me still hanging from around my neck. The ruby lay against my white sheet, looking like a drop of blood. I touched it with my fingertips, surprised by its warmth. The sincerity of the gift still surprised me, and staring at it stirred up a whole range of emotions that clashed with the bone-crushing depression I felt. I rolled over and lost myself in my thick comforter, falling asleep again.

I woke-up a few hours later, the light of day leaving my room, my mother's hand pressed to my forehead.

"What hurts?" she asked, her hand moving to feel my glands.

"Everything," I whispered.

"Hmm. Well, you don't have a fever, so it's probably just a head cold. Can you eat?"

I shook my head no. Even if I had wanted to eat, I doubted anything would stay down. Mom clicked her tongue at me, a sure sign she didn't believe me.

"You'll need to get liquids down, though. I wouldn't want you to get too sick."

I mumbled something in agreement.

"You're just lucky it's a Friday, that way you have the whole weekend to recover." She stood and headed to the kitchen of our small apartment.

I could hear her banging around in search of cups. My mother spent so much time in the LaRue's kitchen that she often forgot where things were in our home. I guess that's why I spent so much time there as well. When I was here, I was always alone. You would think I would be used to it, but it just made me feel more forgotten.

"Mette had to go out of town for some family thing," my mom yelled from the kitchen. "I have to pick up her shift tomorrow, but Edmund and Ryland will be out tomorrow night, so I should be home early."

I shifted my weight and my torso filled with deep tissue pain again. I mumbled at her and rolled over, my phone buzzing again.

"You better get that," Mom sighed as she sat next to me, my body rolling into her.

"It's just Ryland. I'll see him on Monday."

"He's worried, Joclyn. It's not like you to avoid him." The parental scolding was dripping off her voice.

"Just tell him I'm sick."

"You're not sick, Joclyn."

I knew she didn't believe me.

"Now, are you going to tell him, or am I?"

I didn't move to the phone. I heard the click as she picked it up and began pressing buttons. I jumped up in anger, my body protesting my sudden movements.

"Mom!" I shrieked, "Give it back!"

"Not until you tell me what's really wrong." She continued to click buttons, staring me down out of the corner of her eye.

What could I tell her? I couldn't tell her the truth; the truth would break her heart. Besides, how does one say 'Dad's gone crazy, thinks I am a witch, referred me to a cult, and sent me a rock that hurt me' without both of us breaking out in tears? Our eyes locked together as my mind scattered around, trying to find something to tell her. She snapped my phone shut, handing it to me as she sat back down next to me.

"Are you going to tell me what's going on now?" she asked, draping her arm across my shoulders. I leaned into her, the soft parental contact relaxing me.

I hesitated, a frustrated breath shaking my chest as it left my body. I braced myself for whatever would come—yelling, screaming, crying—and prepared to tell her a limited form of the truth.

"It's Dad," I said. Her arm stiffened around my shoulders, her eyes glossing over as she looked straight forward.

I sighed, regretting my decision.

"He came and saw Grandma and Grandpa," I rushed on, "but he didn't want to see me." I knew my voice would betray the lie, but hoped that her stunned silence would cover it.

My mom's arm was rigid and stiff against my shoulder; it felt like a dead weight holding me down. I knew I was wrong to say anything, but now that I had begun, I couldn't take it back. I didn't know what else to say. We sat in silence for much longer than felt comfortable, my mom's arm relaxing around me as she came back to herself.

"At least he's alive." She spoke barely above a whisper.

"What?" I said, loud and accusatory.

She turned to me, her eyes glistening with threatening tears. I felt my stomach tighten. I had spent the last twenty-four hours in a paralyzing depression caused by my psychotic father, and here my mother sat, crying for his safety. My blood began to rise in a slow boil as frustration mixed with disappointment in a way I had never experienced before.

"He left us, Mom," I said. "He doesn't matter."

"Oh, honey." I could hear the longing in her voice, and I shied away from her. "I know it must be so hard for you to understand; you are still so young."

"I'm seventeen, not seven. I understand he left us. What more is there?" I could feel my anger rising in me. Most of the time I could squash down my outrage, but this time, I didn't want to. This time, I wanted to feel it. I wanted to yell, and I wanted everything that had been balling up in me to come crashing out. I needed it to.

"There is a lot more, sweetheart; more than I think I could ever make you understand." Her voice was pleading, and it only set me off more.

"Try me," I growled.

She hesitated, our eyes locked as she tried to gauge how much she could tell me and how I would respond, just as I had done to her a few moments ago.

Her arm moved back around my shoulders, pulling me into an awkward side-hug. "When I met your father, we were in college. We were young and he was dashing." She sighed and looked away, lost in her memories.

"Some people say young love is fleeting, but I think that's wrong. I think young love is perfect. It's pure and full of hope and desire, but it's more than that. Young love—true love—changes you. It's like something deep down inside you grows and becomes part of the other person. It only takes a moment, but in that one fleeting glance of space and time, you change. You want to be with that person, and with no one else."

My fuming began to lessen. I had never heard my mother talk like this before, her voice was so soft and light. The way she spoke, I could see my parents meeting, the love she would have had in her eyes. My anger began to lull.

"That's how it was when I met your father. I couldn't be without him, and in that one moment, when he first kissed me, I knew I never had to be. He was mine, and I was his. I know it sounds crazy, and you don't have to believe me, but I still feel that way for him. I love him, Joclyn.

Even though he left us, I still love him. I think you do, too. That's why it hurts so much that he didn't want to see you." She scanned me as she pleaded for me to understand.

I knew she was right, but at the same time, she was so very wrong. He did want to see me. He had sent me a gift and tracked me down. What hurt so much, what had broken my heart, and why I was so angry, was that he had betrayed me. He had used my blasted mark against me, told the world, and created some fabricated story that turned me into a science project.

"So, you're happy he's alive, and not mad because you still love him?" I could feel the bile rising in my throat.

"Honey, I—"

"No! That's not okay, Mom. He left us. He left *you*. He saw his broken daughter and bailed so he wouldn't have to fix her. He didn't even care enough to try! Where was his love for me? Where was his commitment to either of us?" The bottled emotions of eleven years returned and came flooding out of me in a rush, my tongue barely able to form words through the threatening tears.

"Joclyn! Don't say that. He thinks he left out of love—"

"Which only proves that he didn't love us! That he didn't care."

"But he does," she pleaded. "Don't you see? He came to your grandparents; he asked about both of us, I'm sure. It only proves that he does love us; he does care."

This time, I kept my anger in check. This time, I slowed my heartbeat. I had to; I couldn't tell my mother the truth. Her words were so desperate. The truth that she had somehow been waiting for him to return all this time made me sick to my stomach. I glanced toward the garbage can where the ripped-up letter laid, the weight of my lie feeling like lead in my gut. I stood up, the forgotten cell phone tumbling to the ground.

"I need to take a shower." I felt numb as I walked away. My small breakthrough had opened up a chasm of forgotten pain and heartache that I didn't want to revisit. Before I even hit the bathroom, I felt the tears fall. They splashed down my cheeks in warm trails that welcomed more.

I turned on the hot water, hoping my mother wouldn't hear my sobs, hoping the tears would take away all the pain. I stepped into the overly-hot water, burning my skin before I could turn it down and then curled up on the floor of the tub, the water from the shower pouring over me. Only then did I open my hand. The tiny purple bead sat in my palm, glistening as the water ran over it. It shimmered and sparkled as the color danced and changed. No matter how much I wanted to throw it down the drain to be lost forever, I knew I couldn't. This stupid thing would always serve as a reminder of what I had lost, and what my mother had so foolishly let slip away.

CHAPTER 4
RYLAND

The sun hadn't even risen yet, but the hallways were already filled with Trpaslíks. The burly men and women darting in and out of doors and racing through the hallways like angry workers. You would think they were house staff if you didn't look too closely. They were nothing more than my father's minions.

I had never understood how Trpaslíks had come to be loyal to my father, or how all of magic had broken apart. I had never been privy to that information. And it wasn't as though any of them were going to tell me. They hustled around in various states of panic, darting from door to door and dodging out of my way as I bolted toward the large door at the end of the hall.

I would rather be in bed, but I was smarter than to argue with my father's summons, especially when those summons came from Cail.

The murderous man had a penchant for torture, for bloodletting, and all of the things that my father had spent so many years striving to make me an expert in. It had never taken, but it wasn't like my father truly needed me, anyway. Not when he had Cail. As my fathers most favored subject, Cail had more authority than I did, and much more of a temper.

A door to my right swung open and two warm bodies stormed out in a panic, one of which slammed into my side, sending me into the opposite wall. I grunted, keeping myself upright as the light fixture to my right rattled as some dark magic flew from the Trpaslíks hand in what was obviously supposed to be a warning.

"Watch where you are going you ba--" The man had been ready to berate me, until he saw exactly who he was talking to. His eyes widened in panic and he stumbled back, his focus instantly darting down to the ground as he and his companion moved into the bow that they were required to give me.

I nearly rolled my eyes, it was such an old tradition, made for people who actually cared about birthright and order and ruling everyone.

People like my father.

"I am so sorry, Prince Ryland," he stuttered, still bowing. You would think my father and I had the same temper with how he was reacting. "I did not see you. I beg your forgiveness."

"Yeah, yeah. Okay, whatever," I yawned, waving the guy off as I continued my shuffle toward my father's office.

The poor guy was still bowing and mumbling apologies as I walked away, rubbing the spot where my shoulder had slammed into the wall. Everyone else cleared an even wider path from me, like I was going to bark at them in my half-awake state.

I wish they would all stop treating me like they did my father. Yet another thing I hated about my role in all of this. I didn't want to hurt people. I didn't want to be like him. I simply didn't have another choice.

Stifling my yawn, I pulled the muscles in my back into tight lines as I faced the door, raising my hand to knock. And then froze.

"I don't care who you have to kill to find them. I want them in my possession before the end of the week." My father's voice was clear through the old wood, the hundred year old architecture rattling with the force. I could practically see him sitting in that massive oak chair he used like a throne, leaning over a desk that was just as old.

I didn't need to hear the answering voice to know who else was in there with him, and who was making a sound like a wounded dog.

"We are trying, my lord. We don't even know if the report is true, it's been years since we've even heard a whisper of the existence of The Chosen Child, and to hear that *he* has surfaced again." Timothy, my father's right hand man. To anyone looking in he ran my father's company, the forging company that had been built on the backs of Trpaslíks and their magic. Timothy's Trpaslíks. He had been their leader centuries before the rift in magic began, Timothy and his son Cail. Now they groveled at my father's feet.

As did everyone else.

You could not miss the sniveling obedience in Timothy's voice as he kowtowed to my father, the high pitched whine almost convincing. The guy was a manipulative bastard and this was no exception. I glanced back. The hall was nearly empty now. No one left to overhear them but me. I took a step forward, turning my ear toward the door.

My father always kept me in the dark. So, the more information I could get on my own, the better off I was.

The safer I was.

I would need that, for me, for Joclyn, and for whatever ridiculous reason I had been pulled out of bed to be shoved before my father.

"Which is why you should be trying harder, yes?" I could barely hear my father now, the low threat was one I had heard many times. It usually preceded some kind of explosion, either magical or physical. "I have already asked once, I have sent out my best hunters, if I have to ask again..."

"You won't have to ask again," Timothy replied, his voice lowering darkly as menace dripped from him. "I have all my best men on it. We will find him. We will bring them to you."

"Good." My father's voice was like a fuse growing lower. "Because if I lose this, after searching for all this time, you will not see the next day!"

And there was the explosion. He yelled like a crack of a whip, the bang that followed clearly something exploding under the powerful pull of his magic that I could smell drift through the wood. Iron and smoke.

I should have knocked before this. I had no idea what he had summoned me for, but what they were talking about seemed more important than entering the room when he wasn't pissed off.

But then again, he was always pissed off.

"Hear anything interesting, Ryland?" All of the muscles in my back straightened as a grease filled voice hissed right in my ear, the heat of his rancid breath racing over my neck. I forced myself not to shiver as the familiar scent of Timothy's sniveling son bathed the air and overturned my stomach.

Cail.

I should have known he would have followed me here after dragging me out of bed.

"Besides your slimy voice in my ear?" I stepped back, not that it would cover the fact that I had been caught eavesdropping. "No."

Cail's wicked smile barely even twitched at my jab, only to fall as my father's voice raised through the door again.

"I want them in my possession, Timothy! I want them now!"

"Sounds like your daddy is in trouble," I jabbed Cail further, not that anything could penetrate the guy's malice.

"My *daddy* has better things to do than be your father's errand boy." His lip curled in the way it always did, as though he finally caught scent of himself and realized he had put an entire bottle of his foul cologne on.

"Isn't that what you two are here for? To run our errands?" I knew it was more than that, but I didn't know exactly what. I just knew that my father trusted them more than me. More than anyone.

"Again, little bastard, you know nothing."

He wasn't wrong, my father kept me in the dark unless he had some job for me, some person for me to hunt down and use all those vile skills he had trained me in on. Compared to Cail, I truly knew nothing. But I kept my mouth shut, even if it was just out of spite and refusing to acknowledge just how right he was.

Cail had worked as the head of my father's security for centuries before I was born. Not that he looked it, he barely looked a few years older than I did. He was shorter than me by a few inches, his dark auburn hair mixing with his black eyes and darkening his color so that he looked like a supervillain in all the movies Jos liked. He was dangerous enough to be.

Most of his appearance was thanks to his Trpaslíks lineage, the shorter squatter people were always darker in complexion, possibly spent their years underground, or the strength of their earth magic that they were known for.

They were a stark contrast from the tall willowy Skříteks who always wore their hair long and braided and wielded magic and skill that was more fit to battle and wars than to breaking rocks. Two of the four branches of magic, the other two having been lost to time. Well, at least one of them had–

"What are you doing here?" Cail snapped, pulling me out of my thoughts and back to the hallways and the yelling that was now echoing through the door.

"You told me to come here, Cail."

"You know what I mean," he was snarling, leaning into me again so that I was fairly certain I would choke on the smell of him.

"Who are they looking for, Cail? Have they truly found a Chosen?" I watched Cail carefully, I already knew he wouldn't tell me. Cail liked playing with his food.

"Even better." My father was still wailing as Cail reached around me and opened the door, the large wooden panel swinging wide and sending a plume of smoke into the hall. My father truly had lost his temper.

My father, Edmund LaRue, sat behind the ancient desk just as I knew he would be. Timothy was on his knees on the other side, the carpet so worn below him that he had clearly chosen that exact spot to grovel on more than one occasion. The second the door opened my father slammed his fist into the desk, both Timothy and I jumping at the thud that sent yet another wave of smoke through the air. Cail just smiled.

"Your son, sir," Cail said, nodding his head to the enraged man before he casually leaned against the wall like a 50's gangster. He had the black leather jacket for it, all he was missing was a switchblade.

"Father." I nodded once, his blue eyes twisting to me for only a second before returning back to Timothy.

"Get out of here, Timothy. Get this done."

"It will be." Timothy rose to his feet, that sniveling pout instantly replaced by a strong jaw as he turned and strutted out without giving me more than a glance. You would think he would be more careful to hide the act that he put on around my father from me, except he knew as well as I did just how little my father valued me.

The door had barely shut before my father turned on me. I straightened my back, refusing to look away from him as I felt my blood heat, my magic prickling and flaring over my skin.

Rage, power, defiance. Each emotion coursed through me with the single glare from my father, the fury tingling in the tips of my fingers. But I held it back.

Waiting.

"Lose something, Father?" I should have been more careful in my question, but I also knew he wouldn't divulge the information willingly anyway. It may have been better to be in the dark, but being on my toes in this place was far more important.

His eyes narrowed slightly as he glared at me, making it clear he knew exactly what I was doing. I just grinned, careful to keep my magic restrained and hopefully undetected.

"More like something has been returned to me," he said after a moment, his usual look of distrust fixed right on me. "I want you and Cail to retrieve it."

I nearly jumped out of my skin at his command. My father never sent Cail and I out on mission together for anything good, in fact the only reason he sent me out with Cail was to 'harden me up' with all the death and destruction that followed that man wherever he went.

It had been over a year since he had sent Cail and I out on a task together. In fact, after the incident in Greece a few summers ago I doubted he would have sent me out again, which I would have preferred. I had hoped that that part of my worth to my father had been eliminated.

"Isn't that what you have all these minions for?" I asked, trying to sidestep him. I had no interest in going on a mission with Cail, or discovering how much bloodshed would be involved in that. With how Cail was grinning I could tell it would be too much for my liking.

"I have minions to keep the Skřítek scum out of our realm! I have them to keep that... that... monster from controlling magic." He didn't say his name, but he didn't have to, we all knew who we were talking about. The self-proclaimed king of the Skřítek's. It was my father's title, even if his army was made up of Trpaslíks.

"But you Ryland, you are my greatest weapon, built to do my bidding. Besides, if I didn't have you do my bidding, then why do I have you? Why did I breed you and mold you into... this."

He grinned in the twisted way he always did when he looked at me, not like his son, but as the weapon he spent so many years building. My magic trilled up my arms in the anger that I was trying so hard to keep under control.

I may not have been the blood hungry monster that Cail was, but I was strong, and had never failed him yet. Even if every time I succeeded I felt as though another piece of my soul was turning black and moldy.

"What are we retrieving?" I asked, best not to push it further, not with the mood he was in.

"Never mind what, Cail will keep that information. But we need your skills, Ryland." He wrote something on a piece of paper and stood, extending it out to me. "The person I seek was last seen here. Track them, and return him to me."

"Him?"

"Do not concern yourself with such little things, Ryland. You will know it when you see them, when you feel their magic. It is a possession that was lost from me, and I would like it returned." He was talking about this person, this him, as if he was trying to protect it. The look in his eyes, however, was too hungry for that.

It sent a new wave of panic through me. There was something, some *he* that used to be his that was lost, and I had been the one to lose it. But that had been years ago, there wasn't any way that creature was resurfacing now.

You would think a Víly would be smarter than to return to the monster who kept him enslaved for ages. The tiny winged creature was the last of his kind, the last carrier of his kind of magic. If that was what he was sending me to find then I had to find a way to get him off his trail.

"How can I track it if I don't know what it is?"

My father's eyes flashed bright blue, the short fuse of his relit. "You have been trained better than that, Ryland. Just do what I ask."

Cail's dark chuckle rumbled as I stepped forward. He loved watching me be put into my place, and I knew I was just feeding into it and giving him exactly what I wanted, but I couldn't stop myself.

"Is it a Chosen? Is it the last one?" I took the paper, watching him for signs of explosion. He just smiled.

"Find them, Ryland." So much for getting any more answers. There was no arguing with him, his dark eyes were already flashing in warning of what would happen if I did.

Even standing here I could feel the heat of his magic wave off him, that powerful wall of his power that made him so dangerous. That made him the King.

I didn't even bow as Cail was already shuffling me out, my father still glaring with a silent warning of what would happen should we fail. The door had only barely shut behind us when I finally glanced at the paper in my hand:

La Fea Gato, Sunnyvale

"The ugly cat?"

"It's a restaurant," Cail provided, guiding me down the hall to the stairs that would take us to the roof.

"So we are not hunting an ugly cat?" I knew getting information out of Cail would never work, the man was a locked box and would sooner kill you than share things he had in that mind of his, but I had to try.

"Don't be an idiot, Ryland," Cail snapped, waving his hand and sending the door in front of us slamming open, revealing the roof and the quickly lightening sky of dawn.

"It's a Chosen, then." Not that I ever thought it was a cat, but hunting a Chosen was the only thing that made sense, especially given what I had overheard.

"Once again, Ryland, you are wrong." Cail turned on me, the slight breeze tugging on our hair as he stepped so close I could smell his breath. "We hunt a man, or rather we hunt the bastard that started it all, and the one your father will use to end it."

I just blinked at him. I knew Cail wouldn't give me more than that, and his smile seemed to suggest that this prize was somehow better than the last Chosen, the one that had been prophesied and that they had spent generations searching for. The one I had been trained to kill if only to keep my father on his throne, and to keep him in control of magic.

So, it could be the last Vîly then. After all, that creature had been responsible for the start of all of this in one way. He had created my father, the first of the Chosen Children, and the first true King of Imdalind. And, in a way, the Vîly had created me too; a monstrosity of magic and power that my father had created to help him regain his crown.

My gut tightened, no matter who it was that we were seeking, it was leading us down a path that I didn't think any of us were ready to pursue.

I didn't get a chance to ask before Cail turned and jumped off the back side of the roof and into the air, leaving me no choice but to follow.

CHAPTER 5
RYLAND

"She's not here, Ryland."

Angela and Mette were bustling around the expansive kitchen that was nestled into the corner of the estate, preparing who knows what for the never ending line of food that was required to feed the army of people my father stored in this place. It was far too much for just my father and I, which I had heard Angela remark on more than one occasion. I wasn't even sure if they knew exactly how many people they were feeding. Or even how many people were in this fortress.

I had no interest in telling them. I had no interest in doing anything other than avoiding my father. Of course, if Jos wasn't here that was going to make this a whole lot worse.

"I know. I just need... is there any coffee left?" I sunk into one of the barstools, which caused quite a few heads to turn, mostly from the younger, prettier kitchen staff who had probably been warned I should be avoided at all costs. I guess without Jos around they assumed that any rule regarding that was a moot point.

The fools. Jos would always be the exception to the rule, even if the rule was put in place because of her.

"Just a bit, m'dear. But I can always make ya more, you look like the dead." Mette was grinning, pouring a massive mug of coffee before she shuffled back to the pastries that she was pulling in and out of ovens like a dance.

"I feel like the dead." Everything ached, and my head throbbed from lack of sleep and a depleted store of magic. Even sipping on the coffee wasn't helping. I hadn't slept since yesterday morning when Cail had dragged me out of bed and into my father's office. We hadn't stopped moving, in our hunt for the mysterious 'no one' that my father demanded we find either. We had gone to the restaurant to find it empty, only a few kitchen staff left to clean and prep for the next day. Mariachi music streamed through the open side door that Cail had walked right through, demanding answers as I sniffed around, searching for the magic that he swore I would feel.

And I did, in a booth near the center of the restaurant and by the front door. The dark tangy aroma of it burned my nose, the zing of power that was behind it different from anything I had felt.

There was power there, yes, but it was a power I had never felt before.

It wasn't Skřítek or Trpaslík, and it certainly wasn't Víly.

I had tracked it the best we could, following it as it arrived, as it confronted something, as it lingered, and as it finally left. And then, we had followed it all night.

Nothing.

Our clear failure was stressful enough, and the impending beating my father would give me as punishment was only making the knot of nerves that had settled low in my gut worse. Add the fact that Joclyn was only responding to my texts to say she was sick had left me in a web of stress. I was fairly certain snakes had taken up residence in my stomach. I was actually amazed I could keep this coffee down.

With my father's threats and warnings about failure bumping around in my mind it was creating all sorts of horrifying scenarios in which my father did something to Jos while I was out of town in retaliation for any possible failure. It wouldn't be the first time he had done something like that. Thankfully her mother was here, that should have been enough to calm me.

Almost.

I tried to take another sip of coffee, only to have my hand shake. I set the cup back down before I got any on my shirt.

"How do you feel?" Joclyn's mother, Angela, bustled over as I set the mug down, her hand flying to my forehead, and then the side of my neck. "You don't have a fever. Any body aches?"

I forced myself to take a sip if only to hide the clench that was rising through my chest. Angela has always been the closest thing to a mother I knew. Somehow that made everything harder.

"I just haven't slept well, Mrs. D." How I longed to tell her everything that had happened, tell her how I failed at everything. Tell her how I hated my father, how she should leave because of him, but I was selfish, and I didn't want to lose this.

It always felt weird when she gave a crap about me. She was the only one who ever did.

I hated to think what my father would do when I finally reported to him that we had returned empty handed. If Cail didn't beat me to it.

Either way, I had every intention of hiding here as long as I could.

"Maybe I just have what Jos has--"

"Jos is not sick," Mrs. D chuckled as she cut me off. I nearly spilled my coffee with how quick I jumped, something that earned me a look from both Mette and Angela. Angela folded her arms giving me that look of frustration that she usually only reserved for Jos and my heart clenched again. Thankfully, Mette only chuckled and went back to her pastry dance.

"She's not?"

"Well, unless you gave her Mono and you both are trying to cover it up." Again with the look, although this time it was for another reason. It was lucky I wasn't drinking my coffee, although I choked on air instead so it barely mattered.

"I would have to kiss her to give her that, wouldn't I?" I said between coughs as I tried to catch my breath. "Hell, I would have to kiss someone in the first place to get it."

I had said that last part under my breath, but Mette heard anyway.

"Don't be foolin' us, boy," she turned a flour covered hand at me as she began to laugh again. "With a mug like that you probably have lines of lasses under the bleachers."

I only chuckled and shook my head, she really knew nothing about me, or the school I went to. Or me at all. It had always just been Jos for me. I had met other girls at parties, or the children of Trpaslíks who were trying to get their daughters married to a Prince, but they were all the same. Shallow, flippant. They didn't really care about me, just the money or the crown that I offered them.

Jos was... she was the only one I had ever dreamed about kissing.

"So, she's not sick. Just avoiding me," I moaned into my coffee, avoiding Mette's need for gossip.

"Not just you," Angela slid a bacon sandwich across the counter to me. "Something happened on her birthday."

Darn it. I sat up, moving right back into clutching my mug if only to keep it from shaking. I really was on edge, I never reacted this way. Spending so much time with Cail had fried my nerves.

"Do you think it was the necklace? I was worried it was too much..." Because giving the girl you were in love with a giant ruby necklace when you were still in the friend stage would always be too much. Thank goodness she didn't know what the necklace really was.

"No." She shook her head. "Dinner with her father's parents is always an ordeal."

She pressed her lips together and went back to her work, she was clearly hiding something, but I wasn't going to pry. Jos would tell me when she was ready.

"It must be hard to see them."

"Yes... I mean, no." Now I lifted an eyebrow at her. She signed and instantly began busying herself with the potatoes that she was prepping for some spiced dish. "It's probably just the food. That Mexican restaurant has always been a bit of a dive."

Okay, Angela was clearly hiding something. I wanted to ask, but I also didn't want to be the friend that pried into my best friends' life via her mother. I respected all of them more than that.

I cared for Jos more than that.

I would just have to head over there after I finished my sandwich. I would rather see Jos than speak to my father anyway, and it would keep me away from him and his wrath before my rugby game tonight. Prolonging our meeting and any punishment he had planned for me until after the match.

"You all still go to that same place?" Mette asked as I stuffed my face with bacon. "La Fea Gato?"

"Yeah--"

For the second time in ten minutes I jumped, although this time I not only sent a splash of coffee over the countertops, I also managed to choke on the piece of bacon I had just stuffed myself with. Everyone turned to stare.

"Ryland!" Angela was already patting me on my back as I gasped for air. "What in the world?"

"La Fea Gato?" I gasped, still hacking up bits of bacon as I avoided her question. "That place in Sunnyvale?"

"Yes," she stretched out the word as she looked from me to Mette and back again in clear concern. They were both looking at me as though I had lost it. Perhaps I had.

"You were there yesterday?" The sound of my heart was a thunder in my ears as I stared at her, as I ran through the path of the magic I had felt and tried to ascertain if I had sensed Joclyn anywhere in there. I hadn't, if only because Joclyn was mortal. There was nothing to sense. Just that dark magic, that had just so happened to be there at the same time as her.

"We go there every year," Angela said, looking from me to Metta again before going back to work, having clearly decided that I would survive and possibly only losing my mind. "And I guarantee that their food is not worth choking over."

"It's not that, it's..." I paused, looking from Angela, to Mette, to every other pair of eyes in that massive kitchen that were trying to make it look as though they were not staring at me. "I was just there last night. It's just weird you were there." Luckily everyone else was starting to look away. "I heard there was an incident there early in the evening. I hope everything was okay while you were there."

I really hated asking, I hated more using Angela or Joclyn as some kind of informants, but if they were there, they might have seen something that could possibly help me avoid the beating from my father that was surely coming.

Angela gave me another very curious look before she turned from the potatoes to the broccoli, still giving me side glances.

"We were fine, but there was no incident. Other than Jos getting a really terrible skirt." She chuckled to herself, the sound echoing in my head. "Nothing happened while we were there, anyway. Must have happened after we left."

Thank God for that.

I sat back and picked at more of the sandwich, mulling over what I was missing and what in the world my father had me looking for. 'The bastard who started it all' could only mean one thing, although the magic didn't match what I had learned was his. But if they didn't see any explosions or oddities while they were there then maybe he wasn't there, just near there. I would have to go back, check the businesses around it again. There were plenty of panhandlers around, and if it was just a sighting...

"You avoiding something, Ryland?" Angela asked, putting a pastry on my plate as she leaned over the table to me.

"Just enjoying your delicious food, Mrs. D."

"So, you're not avoiding the raging man on the second floor that I was just informed is screaming for you?"

True panic wrapped around my spine, every inch of skin beginning to ache and throb in memory of what was coming. I swallowed, my shoulders pulling together uncomfortably as my blood began to heat.

"I think I will go check in on Jos." I stood, but Angela was already holding something out to me.

"Stay as long as you need." It took me a second to realize what she was holding.

It was a house key, an extra key. There was something comforting about the key that buzzed through me as I took it. This small little thing that probably meant nothing to her, was warm and soft and felt like a whole world to me.

"Just do me a favor and don't do anything stupid."

"Trust me Mrs. D, the only stupid thing I'm doing is trying to be like my father."

She gave me a weird look, but I just shook my head and pocketed the key, ducking out of the backdoor and away from my father's rage.

I gave the house one last look, the same feelings buzzing around my head as they had for the last few months. I wasn't safe here. Joclyn and her mother weren't safe here. I wanted to keep them close, I didn't want to lose them, but it was proving harder and harder to keep them safe.

I was fooling myself if I didn't think the time for action wasn't approaching at a rapid rate.

I would have to choose.

I opened my hand, skin and blood heating as a spark of light formed there, the beam growing until I sent it away, letting it lead me to Joclyn.

To the necklace that I had given her.

The necklace that I had embedded with a piece of me to protect her, a svazovat. It was that that I was beginning to think my father's men had felt in the restaurant that night and misinterpreted it for something more.

Something worse.

Keeping her safe was going to be harder than I thought.

My mother had always warned me not to fall in love.

My mother was right.

CHAPTER 6
JOCLYN

I woke around midday on Saturday to the rhythmic knocking that Ryland had used as his signature since he was fourteen. I sighed in frustration. He had been here a few times before, and his visits always made me uncomfortable. Ryland grew up in a two hundred thousand square foot mansion; I grew up in an apartment that was smaller than his bedroom.

I listened to the incessant knocking for a minute more before grumbling and rolling out of bed. My body didn't hurt as much, but I still felt stiff and heavy. I straightened out, cursing beads, Mexican food, and useless fathers for my illness.

I had fallen asleep right after my shower last night, meaning my hair had dried as I slept, resulting in an endless tangle of black hair. I flattened it around my right ear as much as I could, making sure the mark was covered, then threw a hoodie on over my cami and shuffled to the door with cartoon dog pajamas dragging on the floor around my ankles. I yanked the door open and walked away, leaving it ajar so he could let himself in.

"Good morning!" Ryland's voice was loud and happy, as always. He bounded in, slammed the door and threw his arms around my waist, lifting me up in an attempt to tackle me to the ground.

"Put me down!" I pounded on his hands, trying not to smile. It was no use; his grip only tightened around my midsection. "I'm going to hurl!"

He dropped me and came around in front of me, inspecting the probability. He smiled at me impishly, sending my stomach into a pattern reminiscent of a roller coaster.

"Doesn't look like it to me." His blue eyes sparkled, his smile widening to a grin. He was enjoying this game too much.

"I'm sick, remember."

"Not according to your mother, you little faker." He smiled wider and tweaked my nose. My stomach did another flip at his touch.

"Traitor," I mumbled as I shuffled to the kitchen. Ryland bounded behind me, full of more energy than usual.

"Well, I had to get my information somewhere, seeing as someone wouldn't return my calls." He raised a brow at me as he settled into one of the two kitchen chairs, crossing his legs regally and looking out of place sitting at the tiny table at the end of our galley kitchen.

"Yeah, sorry about that. Sick or not, I did sleep all day yesterday." I pulled down a box of Fruit Loops and a bowl, carrying them and the milk over to the table where he sat. I could feel his eyes on me the entire time.

"People only sleep like that when they're sick. You okay?"

"I'm fine," I lied. His eyes widened in disbelief.

"Do you want some?" I shook the box of cereal at him, trying to break his gaze.

He shook his head and continued to look at me. "You know, when I was ten, I snuck into the kitchen and had some Fruit Loops from the box your mom used to keep in there for you..."

"And?"

"They were disgusting!" He made a face like he still remembered the sugar-sweet taste and it revolted him. I couldn't help but laugh; the idea of Fruit Loops being disgusting was funny to me. Of course, Ryland had been raised on a higher class of food, so it made sense.

I looked up to find him studying me. "What?"

"I'm worried about you. Are you okay?"

"I'm fine." I stuck a spoonful of cereal in my mouth, making it clear I didn't want to elaborate.

Ryland leaned forward and exhaled. "That's obviously a lie, Jos."

I ignored him, and continued to scarf down my cereal at an inhuman rate.

"I was worried," Ryland continued, his voice low, "that after I gave you the necklace, you thought I was looking at you differently, that you thought I wanted to be more than friends... that I scared you..." His voice trailed off and I dropped my spoon into the bowl. We stared at each other.

I had no idea how to respond. I felt hollow at his words. Somewhere, deep inside, I knew he was right; I did feel that way. It was obvious he was trying to make it clear that we were friends and nothing else. I sighed, knowing that I did, in fact, feel something more for him, but now I felt guilty, too. I should never have let myself feel that way. Ryland was my best friend, and somehow I had let my feelings change without even realizing it. It almost seemed like a betrayal of trust.

"No, Ryland, it wasn't that at all!" I tried to force a smile. "I love the necklace, but I know we're... I mean, I understand..." I looked up to him in a desperate attempt to find the right words and felt my heart sputter again.

He was looking at me, the bright blue depths of his eyes boring into mine with a look I had never seen before. His face screwed up in a heart-stopping half-smile that revealed a tiny dimple. I could feel my face fall again.

I grabbed the necklace from underneath my sweater and tried to screw my face back into a smile rather than the shocked disappointment I was sure I displayed. "I can give it back, Ryland. It's okay."

Ryland's hands shot across the small table to land on mine, hindering my intent to remove it. "No, Jos," he whispered, "I don't ever want you to take it off. Can you promise me that? That you will never take it off?"

He was dead serious. I don't know why, but the weight of his words settled on my chest, it warmed everything.

I nodded, and his smile widened. He kept his hand on mine, his gaze smoldering me before I broke away and went to staring at my bowl of ever mushier Fruit Loops.

"So, what *is* wrong?"

I chanced a glance at him before returning to stare at my cereal. I didn't know what to tell him, or even how much. After my mother's reaction, I worried he would blow me off, too. I sighed and poked at a mushy red ring of cereal in my bowl.

"Joclyn, you can tell me," he said, his voice low and comforting.

I felt that familiar wave of relaxing warmth I always got from Ryland, my resolve returning.

"My father," I said.

"Your father?" His confusion was understandable. We never talked about my father, just as we never talked about his mother. They were both kind of taboo topics.

"He sent me a letter for my birthday." I decided that I could be more truthful with Ryland than with my mother. I still had to keep some key details from him; he had no idea about my ugly mark, and I didn't want him to find out. "But don't tell my mother," I added. "I only told her he made contact with my grandparents."

"What did the letter say?" Here, again, was something I couldn't answer with the full truth. I focused on his dark curly hair, not wanting to look at him again, worried I would lose myself in his eyes for yet another time.

"He referred me to a cult." I dropped my head into my hands as the desperation over everything that had happened since Thursday night came crashing down on me. I needed to pull it together.

"Oh, Jos, I am so sorry." I heard his chair scrape against the linoleum as he rushed over to me and gathered me in his arms, moving into my chair and sitting me on his lap. His strong arms wrapped around me, pressing me into his chest.

I buried my face in his shirt, the smell of bonfires and a million rugby practices consuming me. I could hear the steady thrumming of his heart as it echoed through my head, the rhythm calm and soothing. It did more than mend my frayed emotions; it told me it was okay to feel them. His arms held me tightly, his rough hands moving over my back. He moved his head to rest on mine, surrounding me with a blanket of warmth, love and comfort. Only, that blanket was Ryland.

My heart rate didn't increase; instead it steadied as my emotions evened out. Ryland's touch was some sort of perfect drug that took all my pains and worries away. We stayed like that until my Fruit Loops had become a rainbow mush. Even though my frayed emotions had calmed, I didn't want to move; I felt so comfortable against him. I could tell he didn't want to move either; his arms held me, his tense muscles making a comfortable pillow. I sighed into him and he rotated his head to kiss the top of mine.

His lips brushed against my hair, his hot breath sending a warm tickle of joy down my spine, and I shivered. His chest heaved as he laughed, the sound echoing through my ears. My stomach tensed into a tightly wound basket as his lips began trailing across my head toward my temple. He breathed against the skin there, and the basket inside of me snapped. I jumped up out of his arms, leaving him looking lost, sitting alone in the chair. Necklace or no, he had just made it clear that our relationship had to be purely platonic, and I didn't like the summersault my stomach was now doing.

"I have to get dressed," I sputtered as I fled from the room, my head spinning.

I moved the few steps to my room and shut the door behind me. I stood there, my back to the door as my heart rate steadied. I wasn't sure what had just happened. Okay, that was a lie; I knew exactly what had happened. Had I not jumped up, Ry would have kissed me. My stomach did a joyful swoop at the thought. Did I want him—Ryland LaRue, my best friend—to kiss me? I pictured myself kissing him, his hands against my face, his soft lips pressed against mine. I slid to the floor as my legs forgot how to support me. Obviously, I did. I really, really did.

This was bad.

"Are you okay in there?" I jumped to my feet at Ryland's voice right outside my door.

"Yeah, I'll be just a minute."

"Can I watch Demo TV?" Ryland asked, his reference to my lack of cable making me smile.

"Yeah."

"Cool."

I grabbed one of my few pairs of jeans, some ballet flats, and a different cami before rushing across the hall to the bathroom. After taming my bed-head, and brushing my teeth and scrubbing my face, I stood still, looking in the mirror. I needed to make sure I didn't let this get out of control.

As I looked at myself, I was once again caught with that fantasy of us wrapped in an embrace, arms and legs tangled together from head to toe. I shook my head, wiping the image from my mind. He was leaving in a few months; best to keep him as my best friend.

I dressed and left the bathroom to find Ryland perched at the end of the couch, his legs bouncing up and down.

"You're wired," I pointed out.

"State Rugby finals tonight. My nerves are displaying themselves in some sort of super-charged state." I couldn't help but smile at him, his legs didn't seem to stop moving, even though he was sitting.

"Save it for the field, 'kay?"

"That's the plan, but it doesn't seem to be working."

I walked over and sat next to him, intending to watch whatever he had engrossed himself in, but his leg spasms were vibrating the whole couch.

"Knock it off. I feel like I'm in a blender." I pushed him sideways with all my strength, but he hardly moved. He only started shaking more, making odd buzzing noises in an attempt to mimic a blender.

I laughed before sliding off the couch to get away from him. His buzzing sounds grew as he followed me onto the floor, his large form toppling me over to smother me in his weird body-blender. I screeched through my hysterical laughter and slammed my elbow into his side in a desperate attempt to get him off me. He stopped shaking as he rolled away to lie beside me. We laid on the floor, side by side, our arms and legs pressed together as our laughter died out.

"Will you come with me tonight?" he asked, his voice sounding nervous for some reason.

"To your Rugby game?" I asked, my voice still chuckling as the last of the laughter escaped me.

"Yeah, you can be my lucky charm. Maybe I'll score the winning goal. Besides, it'll be good for you to stop moping around this place." He turned his head and winked at me. I was hit with the same vision again: his hand against the small of my back, his face pressed against mine. I sighed, nodding my head yes in defeat. I was in big trouble.

CHAPTER 7
JOCLYN

Ryland drove us to the Rugby game a few hours later—after making me endure two hours of infomercials that he found hysterical. To the standard middle class, things like Oxy-Clean and exercise videos were practical; to Ryland, they were hysterical ideas that no one would ever utilize. I just rolled my eyes at him. Sometimes, his innocence of everyone's normal existence was irritating, not endearing. Watching infomercials, he learned about rotisserie roasters and paint sprayers, and almost bought a leopard print Snuggie, insisting that I needed one.

It wasn't until we pulled into the parking lot at Whittier Academy that I began to second-guess my decision to come with him.

Ryland pulled his Lotus into a spot close to the locker rooms where a variety of other expensive cars were clustered. His canary yellow car looked a bit out of place next to all the black—while equally-expensive vehicles—surrounding us. I got out and leaned against the back while Ryland extracted his duffle bag from the small shelf behind the seats.

The campus of Whittier Academy was acre after acre of tall broadleaf trees with large flagstone buildings tucked among them. From the parking lot, I could see the large stadium, a few tennis courts and a neatly cut field next to a stable. Set away from the sporting arena was the first of what I could only assume were academic buildings or dorms, but nothing was labeled, so I couldn't be sure.

The whole campus had been taken care of with absolute perfection.

The trees were groomed, each hedge squared. The ivy growing up the side of the building trailed through the stone with eerie precision. Even the long stretch of cobblestone road we traveled seemed to be cared for with extreme diligence. The whole facility screamed wealth and privilege. I felt like a blob of dirt on its sparkling floors.

I shoved all of my hair into my hoodie, making sure my right ear and the mark were covered, and then smoothed out my dirty jeans as I tried to cover up my flaws. Somehow, growing up with Ryland, being with him every day, I never felt out of place; but, being here at his school, I could feel the gap between us widen.

He walked toward me with his rugged strut, and I sank against the car, trying for the first time since I was five to disappear from Ryland.

"What's up, Jos?" he asked, wrapping his fingers around my elbow. "Are you okay?"

"Yes... I mean, no... I mean..." He smiled at me and I felt my insides melt. "I don't belong here, Ry. This isn't my world."

"What do you mean, this isn't your world? You are part of *my* world, so you do belong here." His grin widened as he led me away from his car. My giddy, high-school-crush butterflies came out of nowhere just because he had referred to me as belonging.

"You gonna sit on the front row and cheer me on?" he asked, although I could tell by his tone he already knew the answer.

"Ha ha. No. I will, however, give you the loudest feminine yell from somewhere near the middle."

"That's my girl." He reached over and rumpled my hair like a dog's, ruining my perfectly placed hood. I gave him a spiteful look as I fixed his handiwork, but he only grinned at me before running off to join his team.

I watched him before turning around when some of the other boys began asking about me. Although I couldn't stop their ogling, I could at least pretend to ignore it.

I had moved about halfway up the stadium seats when a large, inclined roof caught my attention. Without even thinking about it, I changed directions toward the enclosed announcer's booth. It was covered in the same smooth flagstone as the other buildings, but it was the roof that called to me. The deeply angled slope extended high above the field, giving the perfect vantage point.

I jumped up about three feet and hoisted myself onto the red asphalt tiles. I loved being so high for the same reason I loved that our apartment was on the third floor with a big open window where I could sit for hours. From up here, I could watch over everyone; I could see what was going on and feel a part of it without the worry of someone else thinking something was wrong with me. What I loved the most, though, was the way the wind moved across my face, tickling my sun-starved skin. The powerful energy of the wind pushed against me, moving into me. It was lucky I was sane, because part of my soul wanted to take off into the air and soar away.

I sat perched on top of the booth; legs dangling on either side of the A-shaped roof, watching both teams run drills on opposite sides of the field. Ryland's team wore deep blue shorts and matching shirts, each one emblazoned with a giant dragon spewing a perfect line of fire. The dragon wasn't the school mascot, however; it was the logo of Ryland's father's company, Imdalind Forging. Being around Ryland so much, I often forgot how large his family's company was and how much it had a hand in everything Ryland did.

After about an hour of drills and prep, the crowd began to file in. When the slow trickle became a steadier flow I decided it was time to leave my roost, so I wouldn't get in trouble. I moved my way down the steep slant of red asphalt shingles, freezing in place when a hot trickle moved up my spine. I looked up, afraid some bird had decided to humiliate me, but stopped halfway at the sight of Edmund strolling into the stands.

He wore all black, his good looks accentuated by a heavy leather jacket and diminished by his usual scowl. I glued my body to the roof. Okay, I *really* shouldn't be there.

Edmund was accompanied by a shorter boy who appeared to be about Ryland's age, but given his height, it was hard to tell. His features were rough and rounded, giving him an odd child-like quality that didn't fit him at all. He had unkempt, deep-red hair and eyes so dark that, from my distance, looked almost black.

I sought out Ryland, fully prepared to glare daggers at him, only to find his face panicked as he looked back and forth between his father and me. I guess Edmund's appearance was a surprise for him, too.

Ryland looked at me one last time before he turned and began signaling his father down. I took Ry's distraction at full value and dropped the remaining six feet before rushing to find a seat that was, hopefully, far enough away.

I dodged through the growing throng of people, my femininity becoming apparent. I was one of a sprinkling of girls surrounded by the over-rambunctious boys of Whittier Academy, most in their bright blue blazers, even though it was a Saturday. I dodged through them, trying to avoid the catcalls that had started the second I had been noticed in the stands.

Oh, the joys of being among boys stuck in an all-boy school. Any time they even got around a girl, the hormones came out like crazed tiger cubs surrounded by fresh meat. Luckily, Tyler Brand, one of Ryland's friends I had met a few times, found me as I darted around, inviting me to sit next to him and his friends. I was still noticed far more than I was comfortable with and part of me wished I could sit alone; but with Edmund so close, it just wasn't safe.

I slid closer to Tyler and his group, attempting to make polite conversation; all the while, I kept looking around to find out where Edmund and the mysterious boy were going to sit. I had forgotten how hard it was to keep up a conversation with anyone other than Ryland. I tried to interject as much as I could, but I kept tripping over my words and making awkward comments. Before long, the group began to look at me with the expression I knew all too well: the look that said they knew something was just a bit off about me. Eventually, I gave up and sat back, making sure my hair covered my mark so it wouldn't give them another thing to dislike about me.

Edmund had chosen a seat in the front row about two sections over, the red-headed boy still right beside him. The boy looked almost protective, like he was supposed to be Edmunds's bodyguard. I had never seen him before, so I guess he could be. What bothered me the most about him was that he kept standing and looking at the crowd. It wasn't the casual glance for trouble; it was the deep stare of someone who was searching for something or someone. Several times his look lingered in my direction, and I felt my spine stiffen uncomfortably.

Even with the mysterious boy's continued stares, the game went by quickly, and I found myself enjoying it more than I had thought I would. I couldn't help but join in with the crowd's excited screams and cheers; their excitement was infectious, and before long, I was smiling from ear to ear. Ryland was right; a good Rugby game was the pick-me-up I needed. The Whittier Academy team made a scramble toward their line and I got swept up in the screams and hollers of hundreds of boys, anticipation of another goal resonating through everyone.

Ryland's team had the ball, passing it from teammate to teammate as they ran down the pitch. The ball got to Ryland, only for him to be tackled roughly by the opposing team when two players lunged at him, sending him backward into three more. All five members and Ryland went down in a spectacular heap of bodies. The ball continued on;

however, it took a moment before Ryland stood again, a bit of blood dripping from a cut on his lip.

I stood in worry. I must have looked ridiculous because I heard Tyler laugh beside me.

"He's fine," he yelled over the roar of the crowd. "It's normal."

I nodded as I looked back to the field to see that Ryland had already run to rejoin the play. I had seen a few of these tackles during this game alone, but it still seemed rough, given that the players wore no padding. I sat down; aware that Edmund's bodyguard was staring in my direction again.

Ryland jostled back into place among the running bodies. The ball quickly passed to him, but this time, he avoided all of the other players as he weaved around each of them. Once he passed them, the wide expanse of field lay before him. He took off in a dead run toward the goal line, his strong legs pumping him forward until he reached the other end of the field for a glorious goal. Our side of the stadium erupted as Ryland turned around in a sort of victory salute.

"26 – 19, with one minute left. We are the State Champs!" Tyler yelled, drowning out the voice of the announcer who tried in vain to say that Ryland had scored the winning points.

Ryland continued to dance and move about as the members from his team surrounded him. He sought me out before blowing a kiss in my direction. I looked around for who his gesture was aimed at before turning back to him in shock. What a dangerous thing to do with his father right there. I wasn't sure if I should be overjoyed or scared. My eyes locked with his, as my heart stuttered to a stop before he turned and ran back onto the field. I couldn't bring myself to move.

"I didn't know you and Ryland were like that," Tyler yelled suggestively in my ear.

My mind clicked back into action and I turned to face him. "What?"

"You know. I didn't know he loved you." He stretched out his vowels in a taunt. I stared at him, unsure of what to say. I looked away from Tyler, not wanting to give him the glory of an answer. I was confused about what I would say anyway.

The finality of the game explained the excitement level of the crowd. Everyone was yelling at the top of their lungs, jumping up and down. Banners of blue and silver waved all around me as the boys began the deep booming war-cry that was the signature of their team. I couldn't help but join in, knowing my petite voice wouldn't even be heard among them.

The ending whistle sounded and the stands emptied as the occupants rushed the field. The banners multiplied, and the screaming and yelling increased in amplitude—if that was possible. I was swept up with them in the excitement, forgetting that Ryland's father was still in such close proximity. I didn't care, though; I wanted to find Ryland somewhere in the crowd and throw myself in his arms and congratulate him.

I made it about halfway to the field before a sharp pain shot into my chest, causing me to stop short. It felt like I had been burned. My hand moved to the pain, shocked to feel Ryland's necklace red hot under my sweater. As soon as my hand made contact with it, the heat left it, taking the pain away. I looked at my hand and sweater, expecting to see welts or scorch marks, but nothing was there. I continued to stand in place as the crowd jostled me around in their attempts to pass my stationary form.

One perfectly placed shoulder was all it took to take me down. The force of the jolt sent me down hard. I threw my hands out in front of me, but not in time. My knee hit first, meeting the hard asphalt of the track that surrounded the field, a jolt of pain surging through my leg. My hands hit next, sliding against the asphalt in a deep grind that rattled my wrists. I winced with the pain that moved through my joints, waiting for my brain to catch up with me. A warm, stinging sensation spread across my knee, a telltale sign I was bleeding.

The bodies flowed past me in a steady stream I could barely see through. Knees, feet and legs jostled me around, digging my injured joints further into the ground. I looked around for some form of safety from them.

I had just caught sight of the home team's benches when a giant tug grew out of my chest; it felt like someone had grabbed the necklace in an attempt to pull me toward safety. I followed the inward pull, my hand fluttering around my sweater to shoo away whatever was pulling at me.

I pulled myself onto the bleachers, the changing angle sending a sharp sting through my knee. My jeans had ripped, revealing a couple of bleeding cuts. My mom was going to kill me; I only had a few pairs of jeans and we couldn't afford to buy a new pair right now.

I winced as I removed the loose bits of asphalt from my knee and the palms of my hands; my hands had small scrapes, but no blood was drawn. With the asphalt gone, the cuts on my knee didn't look so bad, but they still stung. I screwed up my face in irritation, resigning myself to sit there until the crowd thinned out and Ryland found me.

I had only sat still a moment before Ryland burst through the rambunctious crowd in front of me, his brow furrowed in worry. His chin was dribbled in dry blood, his battered lip now swollen and blue. He looked at me before catching sight of my knee and dropping down to inspect it.

"Are you all right? I got here as quickly as I could." His hands hovered around my knee before deciding the jeans were a lost cause. He reached out, obviously intent on ripping them more.

"No, don't!" I pleaded.

"What?"

"I need these jeans, Ry." I hoped he would catch my meaning without my having to profess my poverty.

"I'll buy you some more." He smiled shyly before pulling his hands apart, ripping the jeans down to the seam.

Great, my mom was definitely going to kill me now. They weren't even patchable. I highly doubted she would let Ryland actually buy me a pair of new jeans, either. The cuts weren't even that bad; they just liked to bleed a lot.

"Did you see me fall?" I asked, wondering what he had meant before.

Ryland looked up at me, a confused look on his face.

"You got here 'as quickly as you could'?" I asked, repeating his phrasing.

He still sat at my feet, trying to find something to stop the bleeding.

"Yeah, I was standing over there," he said, jutting his chin in the direction he came from.

He looked around a bit, as if he were looking for someone rather than something. Seeming not to find anyone specific, he sighed and removed his Rugby jersey.

My heart stopped. His muscles rippled as he removed the shirt, sweat glistening off every part of him. I should have been disgusted, but I couldn't tear my dumbfounded stare away from him. His muscles were more spectacular than I would have expected: large defined shapes—dare I say—chiseled into his skin. He had a large bandage wrapped around his right shoulder, as if he was nursing an injury. I didn't know that he had been hurt, though; he normally told me about these things. The whole image of him standing before me was like a bad cover on a romance novel. I forced myself to look away as he wrapped the shirt around my knee.

"It's not the most sanitary, but it will work for now." He tied the shirt before sweeping me up in his arms, careful to hold me away from his sweaty body.

"Ry! Put me down! I can walk!"

He looked at me out of the corner of his eye, a small smile playing at the edge of his lips as he carried me out of the stadium.

I looked behind us, seeing the horde of people jumping and cheering, and felt a pang of guilt.

"You're going to miss your party," I whispered, knowing the pleading was evident in my voice.

He didn't slow his pace, but his jaw hardened and his hold on me tightened.

"Don't worry about it." His voice was controlled.

"Ry, it's your senior year; you just won State. *You*. You scored the final points. You need to be there!"

He didn't respond as he set me in the passenger seat of his bright yellow Lotus.

"Okay, how about I take you home and then I'll come back? I just want to make sure you're all right."

"I can stay, Ryland," I pleaded. "It's just a little cut."

"It's not safe for you here." He shut the door behind me and walked around the car. I turned my head toward the party. I wanted to stay, too, whether it was 'safe' or not.

"What do you mean, it's not safe? Is it because your dad showed up?"

He threw the car in reverse, ignoring my question.

"Ryland?"

"It's just... Private school guys tend to drink a lot and I don't want you to get hurt."

It seemed like the lamest excuse I had ever heard. My forehead must have wrinkled in surprise, because Ryland laughed and then reached over to smooth my forehead with his thumb.

"You think I can't fend off a bunch of drunken brats?" I was affronted. I may come off as timid, but I could defend myself. Or, at least, I hoped I could.

I hadn't actually had the chance to prove that.

"I know you can't," he replied.

"Have some faith in me, Ry." I don't know why, but my pride bristled.

Ryland looked at me with obvious concern. "Drinking, drugs. We are all just spoiled boys. You shouldn't be around that."

"We?" I asked, hoping he wasn't counting himself among them.

"Just trust me, 'kay? I know it kinda sucks, but I want to protect you." His comment was odd; it still made no sense why I couldn't stay.

"Protect me?"

"Yes, Jos. There are just some people that you shouldn't be around."

His voice seemed distant and far away, as if he were thinking about something different. I opened my mouth to say something, but I blew off the idea of asking any more questions. He was set in his thoughts and not likely to respond.

He drove far too fast, his car weaving in and out of traffic in a mad rush to get back to my tiny apartment. We didn't go to my house though; we went to his. He pulled through the large wrought-iron gates, speeding back to the door by the kitchen. His sporty Lotus looked ridiculous next to my mom's rusty station wagon, and I couldn't help but laugh out loud.

I moved to get out of the car, but Ryland rushed around and picked me up before I could stand. The car ride had rid his skin of the glistening sweat, and he now held me close to his chest. The warmth from his skin seeped through my sweater and spread over my skin comfortably.

"I can walk, Ry," I protested, albeit half-heartedly. He smiled down at me as he walked across the parking lot and into the kitchen that was empty except for my mother.

"What happened?" my mom asked, her eyes bugging out of her head.

"She fell on some asphalt and cut her knee. I need to get back, but wanted to make sure she was okay first," he explained to her, his eyes never leaving mine. I heard my mom exclaim and rush out of the kitchen, presumably for a first-aid kit.

Ryland lowered me to the barstool I usually sat on. His movements were slow and controlled, his face lingering near mine for longer than was necessary. I was overwhelmed by his smell as he shifted, his face inches from mine. I swallowed, my mind filled with images of our interlocked lips; I didn't push them away this time.

Ryland lifted his hand to my face, resting it against my jawline as his thumb caressed my cheek. I was so confused. Wasn't it just this morning he had worried that I had gotten the wrong idea from the necklace? Wasn't it just this morning that he told me he just wanted to be friends? Wasn't it? My heart beat uncomfortably in my chest as he moved his head toward mine, his eyes darting down to my lips before returning to capture my gaze. My mom cleared her throat behind me, and we both jumped.

"See you on Monday, Jos," Ryland smiled at me before turning and rushing out the door.

I sat still, in shock, feeling like I was robbed of something important I stared at the door as I tried to wade through an endless sea of confusion.

My mom huffed and came over to me, first-aid kit in hand. "You can't have him, you know?" Her voice was a calm whisper. She didn't even look at me; her focus was on my cut knee.

"I know," I answered, surprised at the sadness in my voice. "Just this morning he was saying the necklace meant nothing, and he was just my friend. I don't know what's gotten into him."

"Him?" my mother asked. "There seemed to be a lot of you in that equation."

I sighed in response. I knew she was right. Whether he was the one to initiate something or not, I would not be the one to stop it. What had happened to us in the past few days? Couldn't we go back to playing Conquer the Castle and destroying monsters on his PlayStation?

"What's going on?" I threw my head into my hands.

"You love him," she replied.

"What?"

"Well, you do; you always have—both of you. Now, it's just grown into something a little bit more mature."

"But I still can't have him." It was a statement, not a question.

"No, honey, no matter how many amazing, rippling muscles he has," she laughed. "Your being with him is like a serving girl marrying a king; it's not going to happen. Life is not a fairy tale."

"What do I do?"

"Leave him alone, make new friends, and forget about him."

My heart plummeted at her words. I didn't want to do that. Forbidden romance or no, he was still my best friend. Not to mention that soon, he would be leaving me forever.

"I can't do that, Mom. He's leaving for Oxford in just a few months. Then... then, I'll never see him again."

My mom sighed at me. I could tell she didn't approve. She wanted me to walk away from him, but she couldn't stand to see me hurting either.

"Weren't you telling me just a few days ago how love changes you? How wonderful love is?" I couldn't keep the accusatory tone out of my voice, no matter how hard I tried.

"This is different."

"How is this different, Mom? It doesn't feel different."

"You will be able to tell the difference when you experience the real thing... when you experience something you can keep."

I looked at her for a long time. The way she had talked about Dad before, I could feel that same desperate longing in me now, and it kind of scared me.

"How many times have you been in love, Mom?" I asked her.

I saw her hesitate, her chest heave.

"You need to remember that he is your friend, Joclyn, not a boyfriend." She avoided my question, not even looking at me. "Give your heart to someone who can take it and not break it, honey; because in all honesty, I'm not sure what Edmund would do if he found out."

And that was the real reason anything between Ryland and me could never work.

Edmund would kill me.

CHAPTER 8
JOCLYN

I had been picking at the remains of my cafeteria pizza for about the last ten minutes, my eyes unfocused and looking off into space. I could hear the ebbing noise in the cafeteria, a sure sign that lunch was almost over, but I wasn't going to move until the bell rang. I sighed as another piece of pizza crust fell away from the whole and onto the plate.

I had been lost in thought for most of the day, my mind jumping back to my roller-coaster of a weekend. No matter how many times I revisited each event, I still couldn't make sense of it. Crazy father, awesome best friend who keeps trying to kiss me, and a mother who—although she is right—wants me to stay away from Ryland forever. I sighed again, in hopes that some of the stress would leave my tensed body.

"You must be new, too."

I looked up from my decimated pizza as a girl plopped down across the table from me.

She was small for a high school student, her frame appearing almost delicate and breakable. However, her large, brown eyes did not seem young; instead, she almost looked like she had seen and experienced too much of life. She had shoulder length, auburn hair that gently curled around her heart-shaped face. When she moved her hand onto the table, about thirty hard plastic bracelets clinked against the melamine surface. I had to smile at her choice of clothes; the "Styx" t-shirt was obviously vintage and looked like something my mom would have worn in high school.

"What makes you say that?" I asked, recovering from my shock.

"Well, you're sitting alone."

"Ha," I laughed humorlessly. "You are the new one. I always sit alone."

"I'm Wyn."

I took her extended hand and she shook it over-enthusiastically, plastic bangles clinking together. "Joclyn."

She grinned as if my name had made her happy.

"I just love your name!" she squealed, her joy was either infectious or nauseating—I couldn't decide. "It's like something out of 17th century literature. Who were you named after?"

"I don't think I was named after anyone." I lied. I was actually named after my dad's favorite aunt, but I wasn't about to share that with the obnoxious girl I just met.

"That's lucky. My full name is Wynifred, and my mother named me after some ancient relative who is supposed to be a queen," she chattered.

I began to wonder how I could get rid of this girl. At first, her over-exertive happiness was fun, but now she was starting to sound like a cheerleader. I looked around, wondering if I could find a quick escape away from her.

"I'm sorry," she said, her quiet voice losing its hyperactive quality. "I'm coming on too strong, aren't I?"

I just stared at her, unsure of what to say.

"Hi, my name is Wyn. I just moved here with my brother, Ilyan, who has taken care of me since my parents died," she said in a deeper, slower voice that seemed more natural for her. "I turned sixteen in January, but don't have a driver's license yet; I prefer to get around on my skateboard. My favorite band is Styx, which I know is way before my time; but I can't help it—I love them. I like rice pudding with raisins and think ice cream is too sophisticated for me. I like to read, but not so much that my brain turns to mush. Oh! And I love long walks on the beach with handsome men with rippling biceps."

We laughed together; it was the strangest introduction that I had ever witnessed.

"Well?" Wyn asked when the laughter had died down. She was staring at me, waiting for me to introduce myself in the same way.

"I'm Joclyn," I began, my nerves swimming in my legs. "I live with my mom; my dad took off when I was little. I turned seventeen last week, and I prefer a long board to a skateboard."

She grinned from ear to ear when I said that, glad for a connecting tie.

"Ummm... I love Fruit Loops and late-night British comedies. I don't have a favorite band, but I like to listen to music when I'm doing homework?" I ended lamely, as if asking her a question.

"And the guy?" Wyn prompted.

My insides turned to jelly as an image of Ryland flashed through my mind.

"Oh, you know: tall, dark and handsome. All that jazz," I answered, flipping my hand to the side.

"Well, I guess you'll do."

"Do?"

"Seeing as it's my first day, I need a friend, and I like you the best out of all the irritating cheerleaders and pompous nerds I have met today." She smiled, and I couldn't help but reciprocate.

I had always purposefully ostracized myself, but there was something about Wyn that made me want to know her better. Of course—in the back of my mind—I wondered how long it would take for her to figure out something was wrong with me. Everyone always did, even without seeing my mark. I had always been just a little bit 'off'.

"What class do you have next?" she asked, jumping to her feet when the bell rang.

"Advanced Drama."

"Oh, goodie! Me, too!" She grabbed my hand and towed me out of the now empty cafeteria, jabbering about how lucky she was to have found me on her first day. It wasn't until we had left the cafeteria that she realized she had no idea where she was going and opted to follow rather than lead.

I led her down the hall as she continued to ramble about how her first day had gone and all the irritating people she had met. I smiled at her description of our very eccentric American History teacher. 'Small, withering, Mardi Gras attendee' fit him.

I hesitated outside the door of the drama room. I had been placed in the advanced drama class by mistake this year, and as such, I was stuck with the notorious Cynthia McFadden. While it was unlikely that most people would mention anything about the cast list for Hamlet, I knew her kind. The probability that she would say something was high, and I preferred to steel myself against it.

The drama room was a large sunken performance space, surrounded by tiers of carpeted risers that rose up from the center. Ms. Flowers, the drama teacher, always kept the room dimmed during performance time with stage lights blaring; but during class time, we were treated to fluorescent lighting that made every soda stain on the carpet pop out. A large thrift-store couch sat right in the middle of the lowest tier, looking out on center stage. Most of the students lounged on the different levels as they prepared for class to start, leaving the couch for Ms. Flowers's use. Wyn ran off to find Ms. Flowers while I went to my usual alcove.

"Well, if it isn't Smelly MyHoodie," Cynthia McFadden's voice echoed around the room, causing several heads to turn. I crinkled my nose at her poor attempt at name-calling, waiting for the deeper onslaught.

"We missed you on Friday, at rehearsal... Oh, wait, I forgot. You didn't get a role." If anyone had read a book on how to be the quintessential high school diva, it was Cynthia. She had mastered this role better than she would any other. From perfectly plucked eyebrows and hair—hours of preparation—to overpriced shoes and backpack, she looked like a snob. It was more than her looks though. How she spoke, how she moved, it was all done to be anyone's high school nemesis or hero. If I had to pick, I would have to say she was my nemesis, although the term was a bit dramatic.

Cynthia had been one of the first in elementary school to realize there was something wrong with me. I hadn't always hidden behind hoodies, and in first grade, Cynthia had seen the same thing that had made my dad take off. Maybe it was the way I held myself, how I never talked too loudly, or the fact that I got suspended for climbing on the school roof. Something just bugged her, and she made it her business to get everyone else to see it, too.

I attempted to let her taunt roll off me, sealing my lips together to prevent a rebuttal. I attempted to walk past her; I wasn't one to create confrontation.

"Hey, I'm talking to you." She grabbed my arm hard, hindering my escape, and then jumped as if I had shocked her.

I turned toward her, keeping my jaw shut tight, ready to take whatever cruel punishment she had ready for me.

"You stupid, little girl. I'm so glad graduation is a month away. Then I won't have to smell you anymore. Too bad everyone else has to put up with you for another year." She looked at me, expecting a reply, but I couldn't think of what to say without my entire face turning red and a string of expletives pouring out.

"Why don't you just go hide up by the stage lights, pretend you're flying and casting magic, or whatever it is you do up there, you little freak." She flipped her long, bleached-blonde hair and turned away from me, only to come face-to-face with Wyn.

Tiny, little Wyn had her hands balled up in fists at her side, her face flushed red. Even though Wyn's full height only came to Cynthia's chest, the look on Wyn's face caused Cynthia to take a step back. Please don't let Wyn say something stupid that would cause criticism for the both of us.

"At least she can get up there *and* keep her clothes on," Wyn said smoothly, "or is that too much of a challenge for you?"

Laughter and whistling sounded throughout the large room; even my jaw fell in surprise at Wyn's forwardness. Cynthia stood still as Wyn pushed past her, grabbed my hand and pulled me to sit front and center in the room.

"Thanks," I whispered as we sat.

"No problem, anything for my friends." Wyn flashed me a wide grin before turning to face Ms. Flowers who was now beginning her lecture on the senior showcase, in which Hamlet would be featured.

I was not sure how much I heard of what she said; I kept looking at Cynthia who was still fuming. Ms. Flowers caught my attention as she began to prepare for the show by separating everyone into groups: the cast of the show, costumes, set and props. Each group sat together, the cast with their noses upturned. I rolled my eyes at them and moved to stand by Wyn in the "set" group.

We spent the rest of class reading through the script and making a list of set pieces. No one in our small group was excited about our task, and with five minutes to go, we had broken off into different conversations.

"Thank goodness school is almost over. I have about a season worth of Castle to catch up on," Wyn moaned as she threw herself back onto the rough carpet we sat on.

"Castle?" I asked.

She raised her eyebrow at me as if I had committed some form of heresy by not knowing what she was talking about.

"Yes, Castle. The TV show. Crime drama, starring Nathan Fillion, only the yummiest man to grace the screens of the television." She gasped at my obvious lack of understanding.

I had no idea what she was talking about.

"At least tell me you know what 'Firefly' is?" she pleaded.

"I don't watch TV, Wyn. I mean, I turn it on sometimes, but I never really watch it."

"I'm going to educate you. You need a good dose of several of life's necessities. Besides, Nathan Fillion is *really* nice to look at."

I laughed, the bell drowning out the sound of it.

We left the room and retrieved our boards from the office. By the time we got outside, word of Wyn's confrontation with Cynthia had spread, and students were giving her thumbs-ups and high-fives as they passed. All the attention went into Wyn like energy from a live wire, and soon she was bouncing up and down. I laughed as I watched her, her enthusiasm leaking over into me.

"I can't believe I did that," she repeated for the hundredth time.

"Well, it seems to have gone over well with the student body." I laughed as yet another student waved to her. Our school did not have a small campus, and word must have traveled faster than usual. I couldn't help but laugh as she bounced around yet again, adrenaline from her conflict with Cynthia coursing through her.

"Oh, yes, well done." I could recognize that sneer from a mile away. "So, you and your foul mouth seem to have made you a few admirers."

We both turned to face Cynthia McFadden, who was surrounded by half the football team once again. The moment Cynthia spoke, an eager group of onlookers materialized out of thin air, hoping for some action. I took a step behind Wyn out of habit.

Wyn opened her mouth to say something, but we never found out what. All the football players gathered behind Cynthia began to point away from us; several of them taking off in that direction. Cynthia looked like an angry kitten at her posse's departure. When she turned, though, her little fit stopped and she began to smooth her hair.

I turned my head toward what everyone was staring open-mouthed at and my heart plummeted to my toes.

A bright, yellow sports car I knew all too well had pulled into the teachers' parking lot. Ryland leapt out of the car, his dark, curly hair bouncing. He pulled off his Whittier Academy blazer and draped it over one shoulder, revealing a tight-fitting, white V-neck shirt which showcased his strong arms. He looked like an ad for cologne or men's underwear.

My heart kicked into overdrive; I couldn't move.

"Oh, no. Oh, no, no, no," I groaned, causing Wyn's head to whip in my direction. "He promised he wouldn't..."

"Do you *know* him?" she asked, her voice laced with a combination of entertainment and worry.

I couldn't bring myself to answer her, only nod numbly as Ryland scanned the crowd for me.

"Well, I will leave you to it then," she said. "See you tomorrow, Joclyn."

I didn't even register Wyn's departure; I was still staring at Ryland as he searched for me. He glossed over most of the student body, giving them all a chance to notice him and his expensive car. Finally, he found me and began moving in my direction. The second his eyes met mine my shock melted away, leaving me feeling blissfully numb. My heart called out in sheer joy to see him. It took a moment, but even that faded away as I registered everyone looking between us, and my joy deteriorated into a half-hearted anger.

He waved at me, and to my horror, Cynthia McFadden waved back, her blonde hair flipping in an obvious attempt at flirting. Ryland moved past her without seeing, pushing her to the side, and my anger morphed into laughter. He rushed to me then, sweeping me up in his arms and spinning me around as if this was some strange scene from a chick flick.

I couldn't help but laugh at his actions, the movement sending my stomach into cartwheels. He pressed his cheek against mine as we spun, his deep chuckle echoing in my ear.

"I'm in so much trouble, aren't I?" His warm breath tickled my ear as he whispered to me.

My heart sputtered. "You have no idea."

"Then, I might as well do the thing thoroughly." He set me down again and kissed my jaw line. His lips lingered for a second longer than they should have, freezing me into place. I just hoped I didn't look too much like a deer stuck in the headlights.

If my heart had been having troubles before, it was nothing to how I felt now. I couldn't move as my head began to swim around me, my legs feeling like Jell-O.

Ryland wrapped his arm around my waist and pulled me beside him, melding me into him as he led me forward, towing the longboard behind us. He kissed my temple before placing me in the passenger seat, his lips burning against my skin even after I lost contact.

Ryland walked around the Lotus much slower than he usually did, as if he were giving everyone one last chance to see me in the car and him with me. Most of the football team stood together, staring the car down. Cynthia McFadden stood in the middle of them, her face flushed red with anger, her arms folded across her midsection. It wasn't her face that caught my attention, though, it was Wyn's.

She stood behind the crowd, hiding behind a large conifer tree next to the red brick school. Her mouth moved as if she were talking to someone out of sight. Her face was screwed up with what could only be described as a furious worry. The combination of anger and concern did not sit well with her and only made her look like she was about to catch fire.

I looked toward Ryland as he hopped in, a huge smile on his face. By the time I looked back to Wyn, she had disappeared.

"Let's get out of here!" Ryland sang, kicking the car away from the curb and speeding down the street well above the speed limit.

CHAPTER 9
WYN

Joclyn was standing with Ryland LaRue.

She smiled at Ryland LaRue.

She calmed as Ryland LaRue kissed her cheek.

He knew about her.

They already fucking knew.

We were already too late.

I stared at them as I stepped back to where Ilyan was hiding just around the corner of the school, out of sight from Joclyn. He stood tall, with that long blonde hair of his hanging around his face, it was unbound as it always was. It just completed the 'ripped jeans cool' look he always had.

It was our first day here after Ilyan had dragged me out of bed three days ago. It had taken no time at all to find her thanks to Ilyan's mysterious source, and I had promised Ilyan I would bring her to the front of the school so he could see her.

So he could mark her as our target.

But I don't think either of us expected this turn of events, that much was clear with the fury on Ilyan's face. His magic seemed to vibrate in the air as he plastered himself against the wall, staring straight ahead in what I could only describe as horror.

For as long as I had known him I had never seen that look on his face before.

"Is she leaving with him?" Ilyan asked quietly in Czech, his voice strained. I turned back toward them, my heart dropping to my toes as Ryland helped Joclyn into his car.

"Yes, my Lord. And you are sure she is the right one, the Last Chosen?" I had to ask, he was one of only two who had seen her before. It was only Ilyan and the Drak who had given the prophecy that had seen this world, who had seen her.

"I have no doubt." The fear that was on his face ebbed briefly, replaced by the awe as though seeing her in the flesh had brought all of that back.

"You're not going to let her go with him, are you?" I looked up to him, I was a bit more upset than I should have been, but I had every reason to be. We had come here to 'save' this girl, this girl that everyone had spent centuries searching for, and now Ilyan was just going to let her leave with him.

Him.

Yet another of King's Edmunds bastard sons bred to hunt and kill the Chosen, and he was right there with her. He had been hunting her as long as we had.

If we didn't act soon they would take control of her, if they hadn't already, then all of this would be over.

"I don't have another choice, Wynifred," Ilyan's voice dripped with dejection, his jaw tight even though his voice was pained.

"He's going to take her right back to Edmund, Ilyan. Edmund gets her, we lose. We need to just go in and take her, like I said before we even got here. Let's end this."

Ilyan had always been understanding of my outbursts, but I knew I had stepped too far over the line that time. He turned from the retreating car, the students streaming around us as Ilyan leaned down to me, his tall frame folding so his eyes could bore into mine.

"Pochybuješ o mně?" *Do you doubt me?* Each word was slow, the command sparking in his eyes. I grit my teeth, all of that stubborn fight that made us butt heads so often over the last two centuries of working together boiling over.

"No, My Lord."

"Then tell me, Wynifred, what is my role, as laid down by those born from the mud?" He was using the voice, the 'King' voice. I recoiled from it and forced myself to look away, to look at the car that was now no more than a speck as it carried our prize away from us.

Before any of us were more than specks in the universe the four great branches of magic had been born from the wells deep inside Imdalind, the pool that was known only as 'the mud'. The four beings were birthed into being to set the world and all of magic as it should be. I had only met one of the immortal bastards and he was a piece of work, but it was those four that crowned Ilyan's grandmother and then his father as ruler, they were the ones that set all of the rules and laws of our world into play, and in some ways set the stage for the war that we had been trapped in since long before I was born.

"To protect those who hold magic, those who carry the gifts of the mud, those who look to you for guidance and are in need of your protection." I recited the words quickly in Czech, knowing I missed half of the official wording, but not really caring. I heard the words when Ilyan retook the oath at every council, neither of us really needed a refresher.

"Does that girl need my protection?"

"Joclyn." I corrected him without thinking, as was my usual. I would have regretted it but instead of hardening, Ilyan's face relaxed, his eyes closing as that tight line in his shoulders visibly relaxed.

"Her name is Joclyn?" He asked, his voice soft, the name sounding like lyrics to an opera with Ilyan's thick Slavic accent. I only nodded.

Ilyan closed his eyes and I could see the last of his anger melt away, his body relaxing as his eyes stayed focused in the direction Ryland had driven Joclyn away.

"My Lord?" I asked, careful to keep the formalities now. "Will she be all right?"

He said nothing for a long minute, he just stared ahead watching that spot that she had vanished into. He seemed content to just stare, I was still fighting with the need to just race after them, pull Jos out of the car, burn Ryland to a crisp and be done with the lot of them.

Say the word, Ilyan. I knew he wouldn't though, his nature would have us trying to save Ryland rather than punish him. It wouldn't be the first time he had tried, either.

"There is more at work here than even you and I are aware, Wynifred. The visions laid down by Sain are unfolding before my eyes and I have to trust that what was shown will lead us all to victory. It must be expected that the magic of the world is pulling the strings. We will wait until the time is right, until we know more. For now, we will protect her from afar."

I just stared at him. I couldn't expect to make sense of anything that Ilyan said half the time, and that was too confusing even on his usually poetic prose. Besides, I could tell by the look on Ilyan's face that I was missing something. This was more than just grab the girl, run, and defeat

Edmund. This was the future of everyone, and I was beginning to think it lay more with Ilyan than with Joclyn.

"Okay, so what do we do now?" Clearly burning people to a crisp was out of the question.

"We need to gain her trust. How do you feel about a girl's night?" He gave me the slightest smile before he shoved his hands in his pockets and led me toward the black sedan he had purchased for this expedition.

"A girls night?" Truth was, I was all for it, and Joclyn seemed like someone who would love a girls night. And we probably both needed a friend; there was just one problem. "How am I supposed to hold a girls night without giving us away?"

"Simple. We need to build ourselves a home. You invite her over, and then you can introduce her to me."

I stopped only steps from the car. The way he was straightening made me wonder exactly who he wanted me to introduce him. Saying this is 'Ilyan, strongest of the Skříteks and king of Imdalind, ruler of all magic' was not going to fly; especially since I had kinda already told her something else.

"About that... I might have told her you are my brother."

Ilyan froze, hand on the car door as he stared at me, eyes narrowing before he laughed.

"You know, Wynifred, I think I would like you as a sister. We may not always get along, but you sure know how to kick ass."

Of that, he wasn't wrong.

"Same to you, Ilyan." He looked for a moment as though he was going to correct me and the use of my title, but he just smiled and slid into the car, his eyes still focused on that spot down the road where Ryland's yellow lotus had vanished.

"Let's just pray that we can get out of this without having to resort to that."

He said the words, but we both knew just how impossible that might be. Now that Ryland was in the mix, it might be a good thing I was here.

If we were going to get out of here alive.

CHAPTER 10
WYN

It became even more apparent why I was the one to come on this mission with Ilyan minutes after we walked into the thrift store. Okay, it actually became more apparent when I was the one to not only suggest, but also find the thrift store. I had tracked it down like a hunting dog, head out the window as I told him which way to turn. He had wanted to go to some expensive strip mall we had passed to find clothes and furniture for the new make believe apartment that we needed to construct.

We were going to be here for more than a week, and he wanted a designer dresser. Sometimes he fit that King persona more than he wanted to admit.

Now, however, he didn't seem to know what to do with himself. He stood in the doorway, staring into the oppressive glow of too many fluorescent lights as they hummed and flickered. He looked around in confusion, his nose wrinkled at the smell of dust, borax, and sweat that always occupied these places. I just rolled my eyes at him.

"Come on," I grabbed him, hauling him after me as I made my way toward the guys t-shirts. Thrift shops were always a gold mine for 70's band shirts, and since we were here I was going to take the opportunity to add to my collection.

It may be my job to gain Joclyn's trust, but I wasn't pretending to be something I was not. 70's music would always be my favorite. I grabbed a Styx and an ELO shirt right off the bat and moved to my next target. I didn't haul Ilyan after me that time, thankfully he just followed. I was actually surprised he hadn't snapped at me grabbing him the first time. You would think that his first time in a thrift store had addled his brain somehow.

Humming along to the Fleetwood Mac song that played over the Muzak, I began to sift through the brightly colored plastic bracelets and necklaces that had been haphazardly thrown into a bin as though they were trash. Foolish mortals.

I would have to remember this store. It was a gold mine.

"We are supposed to be furnishing an apartment, Wynifred, not window shopping." I didn't even turn as Ilyan came up behind me, his eyes darting around as though everyone here was about to ambush him. He needed to calm down, I didn't feel anything out of the ordinary. Besides, with how much money Ryland and Edmund were kicking around these days, they weren't going to be seen within five miles of this store.

"I am. I need clothes to go in my drawers if I am going to invite her over." Or I was just in need of new clothes in general, but he didn't need to know that.

"And what *drawers* are you going to put those clothes in?"

I looked up at the furniture that was laid out on the other side of the store. All of it in nice rows, all of it nicked with peeling paint. It was all begging to be refinished and repainted, but for our purposes it would do just fine. Just from where I stood I could see a couch, love seat, TV stand, two dressers, two beds...

"Go buy all of that," I said, knocking my head toward the display. Ilyan wrinkled his nose. He had a certain aesthetic and that wasn't it.

"We aren't going to be here long enough for it to matter, Ilyan. Especially with Ryland involved, you know as well as I do that we need to get in and out even faster now. All of that will work for a girls night, then we can go back home."

I could hear Ilyan exhale, but I kept shifting through the jewelry before moving to the records. He followed.

"About that, I think we need to shift our priorities."

I froze, the Chicago vinyl slipping back into place on the rack as I turned, dropping my voice to a whisper as I looked from side to side. Now it was my turn to worry about being overheard.

"From what? We aren't going to give her to them?"

The idea was ridiculous, but I couldn't think of anything else he would be talking about.

"No. We need to find out what Ryland knows." Oh gods, that was somehow worse. It also wasn't happening.

I couldn't believe he would even suggest that. I gave him a look that breathed as much fire as I could feel boiling in my veins, he didn't even flinch even though I was sure he could feel the heat waving off me.

"I'm not going into that house." I was firm, if not a little panicked. "I don't want to call you stupid Ilyan, but that's a stupid idea, Ilyan. I mean, unless you want to blow our cover and start a war."

"I'm not saying you need to go into the house. Ryland doesn't know who you are, or what you look like. You do not resemble your brother, thank goodness, and I doubt they have mentioned you. It will allow us an in. You can get close to him. Get close to them both, find out what they know. Find out if they have enacted any of their plan."

I was still staring daggers at him. It wasn't as foolish of an idea when he put it that way. At least he wasn't trying to get me into that house.

"I doubt he knows she's the one," I hiss-whispered, going back to the vinyls. "She wouldn't be in a public high school if they knew. Hell, she might not be alive if they knew."

Seeing as Ryland had specifically been bred and trained to kill her, I highly doubted they knew. Which only gave more credit to the plan of grabbing her and leaving, which only meant Ilyan was planning one thing.

I would have crumpled the record I was holding if it wasn't a vintage Sonny and Cher, not my jam but still precious.

"I'm not going to help you try to save Ryland, too, Ilyan. We cannot save him," I said to the records and Ilyan exhaled loud enough it sent a plume of dust into my face. Well, at least I knew I was right with what he was planning. "The last time you tried to get him out of there you almost died. Besides, you don't even know if he wants to leave."

"He wants to leave, they always do. Ryland didn't kill me then, either, even though he was commanded too. That alone tells me he has good in him."

Gah, I hated that he was right about that. I gave him a look before turning back to the records, shifting my fingers over the old albums. I already owned most of these.

Even if he was right that didn't change one large part of saving Ryland.

"We don't have enough fire power to take them all on, Ilyan." I knew it wasn't wise to fight with the King, but he couldn't fight me either. He knew I was right. "I'll find out everything I can. But you can't push this, My Lord. Talon will be pissed if you don't get me back in one piece."

Our eyes locked, he knew I had won. He would never betray his best friend.

"I'll go buy that furniture."

With some careful negotiation and a little bit of bribery we were able to get the furniture loaded up in a few of the workers' cars. It was only then that we realized we didn't have a place to take it. We had been holed up in a hotel and had clearly missed a step. Two phone calls and an internet search later, Ilyan had secured us a tiny two bedroom apartment that was perfectly placed between the school and Edmund's compound.

With the old furniture in place and a few boxes stacked in random corners it actually looked like we had just moved in.

Best of all, it gave me my own room. Sure, the bed was small, lumpy, and smelled of fish and there was nothing on the walls besides grimy paint but at least I could close the damn door and not stare at the King of Imdalind as he stressed about the girl. Which was probably exactly what he was doing now.

Even with the door closed I could still hear the buzz of the news program that Ilyan was watching on a TV he had found by a dumpster. I was sure he could hear me, but I didn't care. My phone was out and I was pressing buttons before I had laid down on my fish mattress.

"Wynny?" Talon picked up the phone with a panicked gasp, he had clearly been waiting for my call. "How's everything going? You okay?"

"Yeah. We haven't bitten off each other's heads yet." Talon chuckled at that. He may be the only person who truly understood the extent of the tension between Ilyan and I. He had known each of us long enough. "But there's been some interesting developments." I hesitated, casting my eyes to the door and the buzz of the TV. Technically I shouldn't be telling Talon anything, this was a 'mission' after all.

"You mean like Ryland already knowing the girl." Of course, I hadn't taken into account that Talon was Ilyan's second in command and therefore privy to far more information than I was. As second in command he was bearer of the další v příkazu, the ribbon of high command. The crimson strand was usually woven through one's hair, as all Skříteks wore their hair long and usually braided. Well, all Skříteks but Talon.

Usually mated Skriteks would have their hair braided daily by their mate, the braid signifying that they were bonded. Those who weren't, like Ilyan, let their hair fall free and sometimes would cut it short. But Trpasliks held a promise with the earth in our mating ceremony, and wore their hair short. Talon and I compromised and he wore his hair short, although I did braid it from time to time.

Although that meant the crimson další v příkazu was usually around his wrist as he didn't have a braid. Not that it mattered, everyone knew who Talon was, and what his role was.

"Yeah," I chuckled, falling back on the bed that was even lumpier than I imagined. This was going to be a long couple of days. "I would say that means this will take less time, but you know Ilyan."

"He's going to try to save him again." Talon's voice was firm, he had clearly already talked to Ilyan and had also failed in trying to talk him out of it.

"Right now it's just information–" Talon exhaled, catching me in a very failed attempt of 'softening the blow'.

"True. You need to be careful, Wynny, and not just in keeping yourself hidden from them."

"What do you mean?" I sat up again, this seemed like more than just a 'don't let Edmund see you' pep talk.

"Now, you are dealing with not one, but two people that you know Ilyan will set down his life to save. He has spent centuries removing Edmunds children from his compounds, but he has devoted his entire life to looking for the Silnỳ. She is to save us all, and you know his commitment to that. But with Ryland..."

I sat right back up, the bed creaking underneath me. "Stupid Skříteks. Why are you all always such martyrs?"

"It's how we were raised, Wyn. To protect magic, to protect those in need. You know this," Talon's voice dropped an octave, his already low rumble vibrating the phone against my ear. I held it closer, as if we were both afraid that Ilyan would hear us. I focused on the door, on the strip of light right underneath it. "But as much as we need that girl, we need Ilyan more. If that girl is lost it will spell war. If Ilyan is lost..."

"It will spell the end," I finished for him, watching as feet moved over the light under the door. Ilyan paused there, his magic a warmth that pulsed through everything.

He was the most powerful of us all, and in a way, it was only through him that Edmund had been unsuccessful in driving Skříteks into extinction as he had the Víly's and the Drak's.

"So, I not only have to keep a bastard prince, and a chosen child alive, but a stubborn king as well?" I asked, raising my voice so that Ilyan heard. Talon laughed just as Ilyan moved away, swearing and grumbling in Czech.

"Yes, but you forgot the most important thing," Talon said, his voice dropping. "You need to keep yourself alive, too."

Somehow, that seemed like the least of my worries, even knowing who else was in that fortress looking for me. And knowing that the curse he had placed on my skin was that much more dangerous with him so close.

My brother, Cail.

CHAPTER 11
JOCLYN

If it weren't for the cat calls that echoed around the school halls the next Monday, I might have been punched.

"Get her!"

"Beat the weirdo!"

"Watch out, Joclyn!"

I swerved to the side at the noise and saw the angry, little fist whip through the air in front of my face. My quick movement upset my balance, and I tumbled to the ground, hood falling off my head as I landed hard on my tailbone.

One little punch and a crowd gathered around me, eager faces jostling over each other in their attempt to get a better view, many of them yelling 'catfight' over and over again. I looked away from them, unsurprised to see Cynthia pacing in front of me, her face screwed up in furious anger.

Seeing her fuming form made me cringe. Hell has no fury like a woman's scorn. Ryland's dismissal of her yesterday was going to cost me big.

"So, you thought you could show everyone how popular you are by paying some rich stripper to come pick you up?"

"He's not a stripper." The words escaped me without warning. While I should have been surprised that I had chosen to stand up for Ryland before myself, I was more surprised that I had responded to her taunts; I hadn't done that in years. That fact didn't escape Cynthia's notice either; her face lit up in joyous expectation for the coming fight.

"Prostitute, stripper; it's all the same." She walked up to me, her high-heeled foot swinging wide in a poor attempt at a kick.

I swung out of the way, sliding against the floor and into the crowd who stood me up and pushed me toward Cynthia. I rammed into her hard, the push from the crowd giving her the perfect opportunity to throw a tiny, angry fist into my stomach. I cringed, but it didn't hurt much. I had been sucker-punched harder by Ryland when I was eight and we were fighting over Ninja Turtles.

Without any warning, Cynthia began clawing and slapping at my face, the only exposed skin on my entire body. I yelped in a panic and tried to fight back as best I could, but it was no use. She was hell-bent on turning me into her scratching post. I pushed her away from me before her attack could get any worse, the palm of my hand slapping hard against her cheek.

"Leave me alone; at least I have friends who will stand up for me." It was a lame retort and I knew it, but I couldn't think beyond the burning in my face.

"Well, he sure isn't your boyfriend. After all, who could love an ugly, useless, insignificant, little nothing?" She hit me hard in the stomach, and this time, I doubled over, the wind knocked out of me. The crowd around us yelled as I fell to my knees, my eyes watering.

Cynthia walked up to me and lowered herself down to whisper in my ear. Her bottom stuck out precariously, causing several of the boys to whistle. "Your own father didn't love you, why would anyone else?"

My blood boiled under my skin. The truth of her words dug into me and fueled the intense pain and anger I always kept hidden. I could feel the necklace grow warm against my skin, the warmth fueling my intensity. Without thinking, I hurled my hand into her stomach in a pointless attempt to hurt her, to get her away from me, to humiliate her somehow. Instead of her scuttling across the floor on her ridiculous heels like I had hoped, she flew ten feet straight into the air. Her back slammed against the ceiling tiles before she fell like a rock to the ground.

The crowd went quiet.

What. The. Hell.

I stared in horror at Cynthia's motionless form. My heart thumped wildly as I desperately tried to make sense of what had just happened. I didn't know what had happened, but I did know I needed to get out of there.

I didn't even bother to meet any of the curious stares that were trained on me, and I didn't stop to check if Cynthia was all right. I just grabbed my bag, shoved the few things that had been scattered around the hall back into it and took off.

I held the bag against me as I power-walked away, my head down in my normal attempt to blend in. I hadn't lost control like that in a long time. Okay, I hadn't lost control like that ever.

Because I didn't think you could lose control like that.

Throwing someone ten feet in the air? That didn't just happen, right? I had heard of women lifting cars off injured people and defending themselves in times of danger; it didn't seem likely, but that must have been what had just happened to me.

An angry warmth leached out of me as I walked; my skin less persistent in its attempt to crawl away. The necklace that always seemed to echo my moods faded from a white, angry heat into a warm, calming sensation.

I turned into the hall that housed my locker, surprised to see Wyn leaning against the locker next to mine. Her eyebrows were about as far up as they could get. Had news of my superhuman feat spread that fast? I ignored her and caught my breath; I had no intention of discussing what had just happened.

"Tall, dark and handsome, eh?" Obviously, she hadn't heard yet.

"Don't start, Wyn," I snapped.

"Who is he? Why didn't you tell me you had a boyfriend?" She spouted out her questions, but even I, the new friend, could tell she was restraining herself; she was dying to ask a million more.

"His name is Ryland and he is my best friend, not my boyfriend."

"Didn't look like a *not* boyfriend to me," she said cryptically.

"He was trying to piss off Cynthia, just like you did." I snapped my locker door shut.

"Oooo, a kindred spirit." Wyn smiled as she fell into step beside me. "I like him more and more."

"Not my boyfriend," I reminded her.

"Yet," she said pointedly. "See you at lunch!" She waved at me before running down the math hallway, leaving me to walk alone to English.

I slid into my seat just as the bell rang, my heavy book slamming into the old wooden desk. Mr. Heart hadn't arrived yet, so I smoothed my hair and wiped my palm against my face to check for blood.

Even before Cynthia's little catfight, I had been the recipient of taunts and insults all morning; all ranging from asking how much he cost to wondering how I did it. I didn't give anyone answers and had kept my hood up more than usual. My carefully crafted 'disappear into the walls' routine had been broken wide open. I sighed and slammed my head onto the desk as Mr. Heart walked in, silencing the class immediately.

Mr. Heart got right to business, one of the few teachers to take the end of the school year seriously. A little more than half the class were seniors, and so, their minds had already moved to graduation. I, however, pulled out my notebook and began to take notes in preparation for the final exam in two weeks.

"Pssst."

I heard the noise, and I could already tell whoever had made it was trying to get my attention.

"Pssst."

Still going to ignore you.

"Pssst, Joclyn."

Great, now they want to get me in trouble.

"Joclyn."

I looked up to the whispered voice. One of the seniors on the football team had turned all the way around from two rows away to face me.

"You and that LaRue kid, eh? I always knew you was a gold digger." The hairs on the back of my neck bristled. I brushed my frustration aside and stuck my tongue out at him like a child.

"I bet he likes that, too, doesn't he? You dirty little minx." He licked his lips hungrily, and I ducked my head.

This is why I hadn't wanted Ryland to come and pick me up; I knew this would happen. I chewed on my tongue for a minute before returning to take notes.

That's when I saw him.

An unbelievably tall, lanky man stood with his back against the wall, not far from my desk. He stood tall, with long arms folded across his chest. A thick curtain of stark, straight blonde hair hung to his shoulders, framing his narrow face. His features were sharp and defined, but they suited him rather than making him look like a villain.

If I hadn't been so taken back by his piercing gaze, or even dared to get another look, I might have said he was handsome. I chanced a glance at him before looking away, he was staring at me. A blush rushed to my cheeks at the sight of his deep-blue gaze boring into me.

I wondered why no one else noticed him; he was so foreboding and his stare so piercing. I couldn't be the only one who felt uncomfortable with him being there. Then again, I was the only one that he was staring at.

I fidgeted and tried to focus, but it was no use. I looked straight forward, note-taking forgotten. Instead, I was trying not to continue to steal uncomfortable glances toward the figure who was now leaning toward me. I dropped my head, letting my long, black hair fall between us to take away the temptation to look back.

The minutes on the clock ticked by at a snail's pace, my whole body aware of the tall man's continued stare. My skin prickled with an uncomfortable energy that kept my nerves on high alert. I kept shifting my weight to see if he was still there, a chill going up my spine every time I caught a glimpse of his unmoving figure or ripped designer jeans in my peripheral vision.

I ran out of the room when the bell rang, desperate to get away from the penetrating stare, as well as from any new taunts from the football team. My next class was empty of tall, blonde men and open catcalls, giving me time to focus on the material and catch up on what I had missed last week. When the bell rang, I ran from that classroom, too, my nerves still on high alert from blonde men, and angry girls.

The news of my fight had now traveled through the school. As I made my way to the cafeteria, I was treated to the open catcalls as well as looks that ranged from curious to terrified. I can't say I blamed them; I was starting to get scared of myself.

I pulled my hood up over my head and attempted to disappear behind the long overhang of fabric. I let the catcalls wash over me and focused on the feet of the students. I walked down a tunnel of shame; everyone turning to look, everyone saying something. What I wouldn't give to have said something back, but the fear of a repeat performance plagued me. My progress was stopped by two large, worn, dress shoes.

Crap.

Everyone knew those shoes.

"Hood down, Ms. Despain."

I pulled down my hood and looked up to the old, withered face of Mr. Ray, our Assistant Principal.

"I hear you had an altercation earlier today. Do I need to remind you what our policy is, about fighting?"

I swallowed slowly and shook my head, waiting for the yelling or suspension or whatever usually came with these things. It did seem a little odd that we were doing this in the hall, however.

"You will be glad to know that Ms. McFadden is fine, but if you begin any more fights with any other students, we will be forced to place you under suspension."

"But, I didn't..." I opened my mouth to rebut—after all, I hadn't started the fight—but stopped dead in my tracks. His face had changed; his eyes were panicked and drifting, like he was afraid of me, too.

"Yes, sir." I said.

Mr. Ray didn't say anything else; he simply nodded his head and walked on.

I didn't wait long before I ran down the hall in an attempt to get away. Great. Everyone thinks I am crazy, or possessed, or something. I entered the cafeteria and headed for my usual place, not bothering to get any food. My stomach wanted to turn itself inside out already; I was afraid of what it would do if I put food inside of it.

I slammed my bag down on the table and pulled out my ancient phone, flipping it open to send Ryland a few choice words.

'You owe me. BIG!'

I snapped the phone shut and placed my head on the table, wishing more than anything that I could just disappear.

"You look terrible. I thought you would be happy after your PDA yesterday," Wyn giggled as she sat down.

"Not my boyfriend," I reminded her, not bothering to lift my head.

"Well, everyone else thinks so, so you might as well ride it for all it's worth."

I had to remind myself that Wyn didn't know me, no matter how much we hit it off. 'Going with the flow' was not my thing, neither were PDA's for that matter. My phone buzzed and I snatched it up.

'What happened? Do I need to come and set some minds straight? ;)'

I could feel the scowl creep into my forehead.

'No! Stay away from me! You're ruining my reputation!'

"So, what's wrong then?" Wyn asked.

"Just what happened earlier," I whispered, not wanting to elaborate.

"Why? What happened?"

I looked at her skeptically. How could she not have heard? My attention pulled from her as my phone buzzed again.

'No! People are talking to you! Acknowledging your existence! Scandal! I say, scandal!'

I was torn between laughing and scowling more, his jokes wriggled under my skin even over text, but it wasn't in a bad way.

"How's Ryland?" Wyn asked, looking up at me from over her soda straw.

"What?"

"Ryland," she continued, gesturing to my phone. "You're obviously texting him; you are grinning from ear to ear."

I shook my head, wiping the smile from my face. I hadn't even realized it, but I was. This whole thing had become a weird, tangled mess of trouble, irritation, and entertainment.

'Jos, I'm sorry. I thought it would help, and I was wrong. Tell me what I can do to make it up to you. Are you okay?' His text was followed by a picture he had taken of himself, his face twisted into a pleading puppy-dog face.

I laughed aloud, his face wiping away a bit of my stress.

'I think you owe me a movie.'

"He's fine," I answered her question a little late, snapping my phone shut.

I looked up to Wyn, grinning widely and then stopping short, the smile disappearing. Directly behind her, the blonde-haired man stood, leaning against the window-lined wall.

I must have jumped because Wyn shrieked and dropped her soda. The dark liquid began spreading across the table, threatening another one of Wyn's vintage band shirts. I grabbed a wad of napkins and began throwing them on the soda.

"What's up with that, Joclyn? You scared me to death; I thought you saw a ghost!"

I moved my head to look around her, but the man had disappeared.

"I don't know. I think maybe I'm being stalked."

"Stalked?" I could hear the disbelief in her voice.

"Yeah, there was this guy in my English class. He just stood there, staring at me. It's creeping me out." I knew I sounded crazy.

"First, you're dating the hottest guy I've seen in years, and now you're being stalked. You're one lucky girl."

"Not my boyfriend," I growled through gritted teeth.

Wyn just sat and smiled at me. Ryland always told me I was fun to tease; I guess he isn't the only one to think so.

"So you've said. Maybe your stalker was just a teacher's assistant, or even a janitor, who thinks you're cute," Wyn offered.

"I don't know. The way he was staring at me; it was creepy, like he was trying to see inside my soul."

Wyn raised her eyebrow at me. "See inside your soul?"

"Yeah, that sounded a bit crazy," I said.

"Ya think?"

My phone buzzed and I picked it up, ignoring Wyn's over-emphasized eye roll.

'How about hamburgers from Sonnies and a movie. My room, Saturday night. I found the perfect grade B movie – you're going to love it! The Evil Dead.'

I couldn't help the smile from creeping back onto my face.

'Sounds perfect, but you better throw in ice cream.'

"Well, if you see any more soul-eating monsters, let me know and I'll take care of them for you."

"Seeing, not eating, Wyn."

"Oh yeah, 'cause that makes more sense."

I knew it didn't, but I still couldn't help but laugh at myself.

"Darn it! We are going to be late!" Wyn jumped to her feet as the bell rang, throwing books and pencils into her bag. "Hey, do you want to come over tonight? I got a new movie in the mail, and my brother's going to be out. We can pretend to do homework, too." She looked at me so eagerly, I couldn't say no. Besides, spending time with someone other than Ryland might help my mom say yes to our new plans for Saturday.

"Sure."

"Great." The tension dropped from her shoulders as if she were worried I would say no.

My phone buzzed one more time as we ran out of the cafeteria, Ryland's message lighting up the screen.

'Anything for you, sweetheart. I'll even splurge and get Superman ice cream :)'

Sweetheart? When did things get so complicated?

CHAPTER 12
JOCLYN

I don't remember when I've laughed so much. That's not to say that I have never laughed with Ryland, I have. Somehow, though, playing and joking with a girl—a girl my own age—was different. We could joke about things I would never bring up with my mother and never even dreamed about sharing with Ry.

For the first time in my life, I regretted not seeking out a girlfriend. I had always felt complete with Ryland; but with Wyn, facing Ryland's departure in a few months seemed bearable.

We lay back on her bed, legs draped off the side, as we caught our breath from laughing, small chuckles still escaping. Just being here had made me forget all about the stress of the day, and we hadn't even gotten to the movie yet. *Night of the Living Vampire* was sure to suck as Wyn had said so poignantly.

"So, I know he's not your boyfriend," Wyn began, a smile on her face, "but how the heck did you become friends with the heir to Imdalind Forging?"

"What did you do, Google him?"

"Yeah."

I couldn't help but laugh, her voice sounded like a cornered child.

"My mom has been their in-house chef since I was five; I practically grew up in their kitchen."

"Really?"

"Yeah, Ry and I have been friends since day one. It drives his dad and

Timothy crazy; I am a little below their status." Saying it out loud made the whole 'falling for a prince' situation more real.

"Timothy?" Wyn asked with something akin to recognition.

"Yeah, he's kind of the head of the company and Ryland's wrangler. He *hates* me." As I did him.

"And they still let you two be friends?"

I was just as shocked as she was. "Not by choice. Ryland kind of makes them."

"And they don't just fire your mom?"

I almost laughed outright. "Oh, they threaten to, but I don't think they want to lose such a great cook. Besides, Ryland's leaving for school in a few months, so I guess they don't think it's worth the fight anymore. It's not like I can follow him to Oxford."

I hated talking about this stuff; my heart felt so heavy and broken, like part of me was leaving with him.

"You love him," she said.

"More than I should," I whispered. I knew I sounded ridiculous.

"It's okay to love."

"Not when they don't love you back." I sighed again; it felt like I was trying to get rid of all my stress through my lungs.

"Especially then. I think it makes you a better person. At least then you know what it feels like to love instead of living without ever knowing. I love a lot of people that I know will never love me back, but I am happier because of it." I could tell she believed what she said; her voice was so deep and heavy.

"You sound like my mom."

"I've never heard that one before!" she laughed.

"And who do you love?"

"Talon," she sighed.

The sound of desperate love made me giggle; I wondered if that's how I sounded when I talked about Ry.

"I'll introduce you to him when he comes to visit."

"He loves you back then?"

"Yeah..." Her voice was so airy I couldn't help but smile.

The song on the oldies station we were listening to changed and Wyn jumped up, squealing in delight. She leaped onto a pile of boxes that sat at the foot of her bed, pulling me up with her. She continued to jump and squeal as she danced around, the corners of the boxes heaving as she danced and moved.

Her hair swished around her face, heavy plastic bangles jangling and clanking. Her joy at the Styx song was infectious and I found myself singing and dancing along, even though I didn't know the words.

We sang the chorus together, our loud monotone voices clashing against each other.

Wyn jumped off the boxes, hair and arms flying, to land on the plush carpet in an air guitar solo. Her arms swung and wiggled in an attempt to play the nonexistent instrument she held in her hands. Her short, auburn hair flipped around her face as she swung her head in an attempt to 'rock out'.

The guitar solo ended and Wyn jumped up again, grabbing my hands to push me into her crazy dance. We jumped around the floor like clowns, pulling out dance moves that our parents must have done, in our rambunctious attempt at dancing.

"Please tell me you've been to a Styx concert," Wyn yelled between verses.

"Do they still have concerts?" I asked, jumping around alongside her.

"Yes!" Wyn grabbed my hands and began to spin me around as she continued to yell verses and choruses at full blast. And, quick as it had come, the song ended and we both collapsed on the floor, laughing at ourselves.

Why was something so simple, so wonderful?

"So," Wyn sighed after a moment. "You gonna show me your scar?"

Her question was so innocent, but my reaction was anything but. Time seemed to stop. My heart stopped. My breathing stopped. The only thing that didn't stop was my stomach, which flipped as my head screamed at me to run.

"What scar?" Maybe if I played dumb, I could deter her. I had already checked that my hair covered the right side of my head, and the dreaded mark. It didn't. I was always so careful; but I was having so much fun that I had gotten lazy.

Crap.

"Oh, come on," Wyn sighed as she sat up beside me, draping her arm over me and hindering my escape. "That one, right there below your ear. It almost looks like a dragon. That is *very* cool." She leaned forward and looked at it. "I'm kind of jealous."

"A dragon?"

"Yeah, here's his tail and his head." She traced a shape through the darker portions of the brand, her fingertip tickling the skin that never got touched.

I jumped up from under her arm and ran to the mirror that hung above her dresser. My hair naturally fell over the mark, so I pulled it back to get a better look. I had never really looked at it, but Wyn was right—the dark lines that moved through the raised skin did look like a dragon.

"How'd you get it?" Wyn asked, coming up behind me and leaning on the dresser. "Accidental maiming? Fall off a stage? Helicopter rescue gone wrong?"

I hesitated. I didn't know how much I trusted her. I just continued to stare at it in the mirror, part of me wanting to touch it; the other part continuing to scream at me to run.

"Nothing as cool as that," I managed, making it clear I wasn't going to elaborate.

"Have you shown it to Ryland? Boys love scars; I bet he would love this one." Her voice had taken on a strange quality that made me a bit uncomfortable.

I spun away from the mirror to face her. Her eyes were wide and eager.

"No! I would never show Ryland! You're the first person to see it, besides my mom." *And my dad*, but I wasn't going to get into that.

"Really? Wow. Now I feel special." She slugged me playfully in the shoulder. "That thing is awesome!" She bounced back over to the bed, landing in the center, springs creaking.

"Not to me," I mumbled.

Wyn looked at me as if she expected me to elaborate. I wasn't going to give her the benefit of an answer, not today anyway. Besides, what could I say that was believable? My life could be considered normal until it came to that mark and then it was full of mysterious illnesses and disappearing fathers.

The way this evening had turned out had become very confusing and complicated. Why did the past few days have to be so... weird? I just wanted to hide and forget that Wyn had ever caught a glimpse of the ugly thing, forget that odd men were watching me, forget that I could throw girls into ceilings, forget that Ry kept trying to kiss me.

"I gotta go." I was sure the disappointment in my voice was not missed. Before Wyn could fight me I grabbed my bag and started heading toward the door.

"Hey, Jos." Wyn caught up with me, catching me before I disappeared through the door. Her inadvertent use of Ryland's nickname for me sent a shiver up my spine. "I'm sorry I brought it up. I didn't know it was a taboo thing. I'll pretend I never saw it." She smiled at me, her voice sincere.

"Thanks, Wyn, it's just—" I hesitated; I had to tell her something. "It's just that, that... thing... has kind of ruined my life."

"Don't let it anymore, 'kay?"

I nodded and her face brightened.

"So, don't go. I won't mention it again, and we still have a stupid movie to watch."

"Thanks, Wyn, but I do have to go. I actually *do* have homework to do." I tried to sound indifferent, but I wasn't sure it worked.

"Oh, okay. I'll see you tomorrow then?"

I just nodded in agreement, shutting the door to her apartment behind me.

CHAPTER 13
JOCLYN

I stood outside Wyn's apartment complex for about ten minutes, trying to decide where to go. I needed to talk to my mom. I didn't know what I would say to her that wouldn't end in a fight, but I felt so naked and exposed after Wyn's innocent discovery of my mark.

I made sure my hair covered the right side of my face before I turned my longboard in the direction of the bus that would take me into the wealthy district of town. There were still about forty-five minutes until dinner would be served in the LaRue's dining hall, meaning my mom still had about two hours or more of work. Rather than wait at home, alone, for her to get there, I opted to face the hustle of the big kitchen at dinner time. Spending forty minutes alone on the bus was still better than waiting alone for two or more hours.

The bus stopped and I quickly boarded. The neon lights were already on, illuminating the plastic seats and metal floor with a strange, blue glow. I made my way to the middle and sat with my hood up, backpack sitting on my lap and my head leaning against the glass. As the blue sky deepened around me, it felt like everything inside loosened up, calming down and becoming brighter.

Wyn had said I had let the mark ruin my life. At first, I wasn't exactly sure what that meant. To me, my life seemed to be pretty okay. I had a great best friend, a mother who really cared, and I did well in school. On the other hand, I also hated school because it meant that I had to be around other kids—that I had to hide.

I didn't 'have to' do anything, though. I didn't 'have to' cover myself up. I didn't 'have to' pretend to be invisible. Maybe Cynthia only saw something off in me because I made her see me that way.

I had been hiding myself because of the mark, not letting anyone get too close. I wouldn't let myself make any friends. The only reason I let Ryland in is because he had been persistent. He had held my hand as I got over my insecurities and had promised, from a young age, to always be there. So, without Ry, I was friendless and alone.

My mother worked upwards of sixty hours a week, my best friend wasn't really allowed to be my friend, and I was picked on at school.

My life did suck, and all because I allowed a stupid mark to destroy me.

I laid my head against the back of the seat and watched as the city lights of old-fashioned neon and new-aged fluorescent blended together in a rainbow blur of colors until the city laid far behind and ever-expanding houses laid before me.

There had been a reason I let the mark control my life, and as much as I rationalized my behavior and my loneliness, the fact still remained that I was broken, that my dad didn't want me. Mark or no mark, the outcome would be the same.

Their last fight still haunted me. I would still revisit it in monthly nightmares; the screaming more intense, more audible, more of the blame placed on me. I would wake up covered in sweat, only to turn over and cry into my pillow in the desperate hope that my mom wouldn't hear. She never did.

I exited the bus, grateful for the evening air that swirled around me. My longboard clicked loudly as I traveled the last five minutes of alleys and side streets until I arrived at the door to the kitchen.

The click-click of the longboard ricocheted around my head as the fight replayed again. It still rattled me, it still hurt, but it wasn't as bad. And through it all, I realized something. My dad left me; he ran away from me. He ran away because of the mark, and I didn't want anyone else to run, too. So I hid. I just didn't want to get hurt anymore. All this time, and I hadn't realized how broken I was inside.

I arrived in the kitchen of the LaRue's just as dinner was being served to the family. As I had expected, the kitchen was in a frenzy of activity as the maids and wait-staff rushed around with trays of food and decanters of who knows what. My mom was busy rushing around and yelling different instructions to different staff members.

I dodged and weaved my way through the activity to find my usual barstool. It always surprised me that so many people were needed to serve only Ryland and his father. After a few minutes, the staff disappeared, leaving my mother and Mette to clean and prepare for the dessert course.

"How was your new friend's house?" Mom asked, setting a large bowl of leftover soup in front of me. She looked at me eagerly, excited I had taken her advice so seriously.

"Wyn," I provided. "It was fun. She likes Styx," I added, causing Mom's smile to widen.

"A girl after my own heart," she said.

"Yeah, I really like her."

Mom smiled and moved away from me, back to her cleaning. "And the movie?" she asked, spooning a strawberry puree into a crystal dish.

"We didn't get around to the movie; we mostly just talked."

"Girl talk? You?" she asked in disbelief.

"I know."

Mom wiped her soapy hands on her apron and came over, stealing a spoonful of chicken dumpling soup. "Mmmm, I do make a good soup." She licked her lips in enjoyment.

"The best," I agreed.

The platters began returning, most picked clean either by the family or by the staff on the way back to the kitchen. The trays and dishes clanged as they threw them, one after another, into the sink. My mom rushed back into action, directing the huge number of tasks with ease.

I remembered when she had first started. She had come home in tears after she had forgotten to prepare an appetizer course, and the roast beef had been served lukewarm. The next morning, we had arrived in the kitchen to a very uncomfortable Edmund who explained what had gone wrong, while also offering his compliments on her pear gelato. He had left after that, leaving behind a small, freckled boy with blazing, blue eyes and an absolute mop of dark, curly hair.

I had been hiding behind my mother's legs, and when I saw him staring at me, I buried my face into the back of my mom's thighs. He had come up to me, tugging on my arm in an attempt to get me to play with him.

"What's her name?" he asked my mom in his innocent voice.

"Joclyn."

"Hey, Joclyn." He tugged again. "Do you want to come play with me? I made a castle in my room; do you want to come see?"

I had turned my head to look at him. He smiled at me, and I felt more comfortable. I took his hand, my mom still prodding me along to go with him.

"You have very pretty eyes. They look like diamonds."

He was always charming, right from the start.

I smiled at the memory, the way I had when he had first said the words to me. Somehow, even all these years later, it still made me feel warm and fuzzy inside. I had been so uncomfortable about my newly-changed eye color, and he had taken all that fear away.

"You ready?"

I looked up. My mom was standing by the door of the now empty kitchen, hand perched on the light switch.

"Come on, honey; it's time to go home."

I stood slowly, my body stiff from sitting in my daydream for so long.

"Glad you're still with me," Mom said. "I thought I lost you for a little bit."

"Sorry. I was just thinking, I guess."

"Something good and not involving rippling muscles, I hope."

I ignored her obvious jab at Ryland before sliding into the old station wagon.

"No, Mom," I grumbled and closed the door behind me, shutting us into the small space. "Wyn saw my scar." Better get it over with right away; it was what I traveled out of my way to talk to her about, after all.

The mood in the car changed immediately; stressful energy dripping into the air. I wasn't sure who was more stressed about my statement, me or my mom.

"Mmmmhmmmm." My mom's noncommittal grunt prompted me to continue.

"And I think I know why I'm so scared to let people see it."

She didn't respond; she just drove, waiting for me to get all my thoughts out. She was always so good at that, just sitting and listening without interjecting.

"I'm afraid that people will think I am broken and leave me, just like Dad did." It felt good to say it aloud, to let my deep-rooted fear free for the first time. Somewhere between leaving Wyn's and entering the bright lights of the city, I had started to let that shy little monster of fear out from where he had been dwelling, hidden inside me for the past twelve years.

"I'm sorry, honey. I never... I didn't realize that everything had affected you so much."

"Neither did I. I figured it out on the way over," I sighed. "The way

Wyn talked about it, how she asked me not to let it ruin my life anymore... I don't think I realized that I was doing that until that moment."

We sat silently, street lights flashing in the dark, the sound of the overworked engine buzzing in my ears.

"Not everyone left you because of the mark, you know," my mom said, her hand patting my knee in a comforting way.

"Just Dad."

"Yes, just Dad. He left because he couldn't handle it."

"And because he was paranoid." I knew I was being a little too honest; I just hoped Mom didn't read too much into it.

"Maybe a little of that, too." She smiled, but it was a sad smile, as if she knew the truth, but didn't want to admit it.

"But not everyone left, Joclyn. I didn't leave; Grandma and Grandpa Despain didn't leave and Grandma Hillary didn't leave. Ryland didn't leave."

"That's not fair, Mom. Ryland doesn't even know about the mark."

"True, but if you were broken, he wouldn't have stuck around so long."

"I guess that's right." I knew it was; from the beginning it was. Even when he had found me crying in the bushes behind the kitchen when I was eight, he just smiled, handed me a rose and dragged me back to his room to play video games.

"Tell me..." Mom's voice cut through my memory. "Did Wyn run away?"

"No."

"Did she scream in fright?"

"No."

"What did she do then?" I had seen the trap from the beginning and had to smile at my mom's obvious attempt to make a point.

"She thought it was cool, and told me I shouldn't let it ruin my life anymore."

"I like this Wyn more and more. Maybe she will help me to get you out of those hoodies."

"Don't start, Mom," I pleaded.

"Well, I've got to try. We do have that shopping date on Saturday. You would look so nice in that brand new, red shirt."

"Okay, I'll make you a deal." An idea had come to me out of nowhere, although I knew it might not work, it was worth a try.

"Now, I am worried."

"I won't wear a hoodie all day on Saturday if you let me hang out with Ry that night and watch a movie."

"Joclyn, we talked about this." She was stern.

Stupid Ryland, having to take off his shirt! I don't think my mom would have ever started to take this stance if he had kept his shirt on. Oh, and if he hadn't tried to kiss me in the kitchen... I stifled a sigh at the memory before rebutting.

"I know we did, but I can't just walk away from him, Mom. He's my best friend, and he's leaving for Oxford in a few months and then he won't be my friend anymore, anyway. He will have other friends, and girlfriends, and a fiancée, and run a huge company. He won't just be Ry anymore. He will be Ryland LaRue, heir to a fortune." I spoke very fast. Even though it hurt to say it, I knew it was true. No matter how many fantasies had entered my mind, none of them could ever happen.

"He already is that."

"I know," I whispered. It took me a moment to find my voice again. My heart thudded around my chest in a desperate plea not to make this compromise with my mom. "Mom, can I just have him as a friend for a little while longer? Then I will leave him alone forever. I'll have no other choice."

"It's not just that, Joclyn." She sighed again, frustrated.

"Then, what is it?" I held my own though, my eyes digging into hers.

"Okay," she conceded, "you know how Timothy is always warning me to keep you two apart?"

"Yeah." I was hesitant; I didn't like where this was going.

"Well, it used to be a half-hearted warning. Now, it feels almost... dangerous." She looked away from me, the subject making her uncomfortable.

"Dangerous? Like 'Keep her away from him or else'?"

"It's more than that. Timothy made mention of your safety and how dangerous ovens are. I don't know. It just made me uncomfortable."

Edmund had said something similar in the hall a few days ago. Threatening my life was such an odd thing for him to say that I had dismissed it, but hearing it again from my mom was weird. Forget corporate drama, this bordered on super-villain.

"Anyway, I've started looking for a new job."

"What?" Panic, sheer panic, gripped me. I felt my chest get tight and uncomfortable. Not only was change not good for me, she was ripping my best friend away from me. "Mom! You can't."

"I have to, Joclyn. I have to keep you safe. You are my number one priority."

"Then, you have to let me go on Saturday, if you are going to take him away from me anyway," I pleaded with her, trying to ignore the earth-shattering pain that centralized in my chest.

"I don't know, Joclyn. A movie?"

"We've watched plenty of movies before." I was begging; I had to go now.

"Yeah, but alone, in his room."

"Done that, too." We had even watched a movie with the lights off, but it still wasn't as much of a scandal as my mom made it out to be.

"Yeah, but never with overactive, crazed, teenage hormones trying to stick you two together like magnets."

I paused. She had a point.

"Don't worry, Mom. Nothing will happen. I can't let it. I just want to enjoy the last little bit of time I have left with my friend."

"I'll think about it."

"Okay, but just remember, if I can't go to the movie, I am wearing the biggest hoodie I own. If you let me go, I will leave the hoodie at home, and I might even wear the skirt. Well, not the skirt; I'd look like a moron."

CHAPTER 14
JOCLYN

I tiptoed through the house on Wednesday morning, trying not to wake my mom. Wednesdays were the only day in the week my mom got to sleep in, having to go in for dinner service and the late-night weekly board meeting that night. Of course, letting her sleep in meant that I had to leave for school about twenty minutes before usual. That, coupled with the fact that I had slept in, meant that I was running far later than I was comfortable with. The problem with living in such a small apartment was that trying to be quiet was impossible when you were in a hurry.

I brushed my teeth in a rush, attempting to run a comb through my hair at the same time. The dark circles under my eyes had taken on a whole new shade of ugly, so I rubbed some of my seldom used concealer on them, vowing to eat a piece of fruit for breakfast. I brushed my hair, letting the sleek black strands hang low down my back.

I rushed out of the bathroom and into my small bedroom, throwing on one of my two, un-ripped, pairs of jeans and a fluorescent green tank top. Everything fit my small frame snuggly, something that would be hidden when I put on my hoodie. Of course, if my mom agreed to my compromise, I would have to spend all day Saturday like this. Not that that would be a bad thing, my arms and face could do with a little sun. I sighed, trying to figure out if I was ready to throw the hoodie aside, even for a day.

Although I could feel myself changing, I didn't think I was ready to change that much.

I grabbed a dark green hoodie as I walked out the door, locking it behind me. After my father had left, my mother had moved us as close to her new job as she could, which landed us in a tiny, overpriced apartment in a very upper-middle class neighborhood.

Most of our neighbors made six figures and tended to look down on those that lived in the complexes. Some of them were nice and tolerable, but every once in a while, you ran into someone who thought that we shouldn't be allowed to socialize with them.

It was amazing how much I dealt with financial stereotypes every day. My mom was a personal chef to a gazillionaire and I went to school with kids who got new Lexus's for their birthday.

I hopped on the school bus that stopped right outside my apartment complex with a few other kids and made my way to the middle, finding a bench to take up all on my own. We arrived at school about five minutes before the first bell, pulling up to the bus stop in front of the large, red brick building.

The school grounds were bathed in patches of sun from the rays that broke through the white, puffy clouds lining the sky. An unnaturally warm breeze wrapped itself around me as I stepped off the bus, the wind pulled my hair in odd directions. I pulled my hood up, the steady gusts causing me to hold it in place.

The large expanse of grass in front of the school filled up with last-minute stragglers as the morning bell prepared to ring. I walked toward the main entrance, wanting to get out of the wind as fast as possible. I had gotten about halfway when a tall figure distracted me, causing my feet to stop in shock.

The same, tall, blonde man stood just off to the side of the front entrance to the school. He leaned against the building with his arms folded across his chest. He wore a tight fitting, light blue, button-up shirt and another pair of strategically ripped designer jeans. Even with the wind whipping against his clothes, he stayed still. His head was bowed and I could just make out closed eyes amid the masses of his blonde hair blowing in the breeze. I knew he wasn't looking at me, but I couldn't shake that tormented feeling. Like I was being watched, or as I had put it earlier, stalked.

I looked away from him and picked up my pace, eager to get into the school. I had forgotten about him after everything else that had happened last night; however, seeing him there again brought all that anxiety back. I felt jumpy and nervous as I walked into my first class, French.

I looked over the room before sitting down, worried that the blonde man had followed me here. My irritation shivered up my spine, making me wonder if my paranoia level was becoming unhealthy. I settled in before Madame Armel could begin her instructions. I was only in this class for graduation credit, meaning the class was filled with a bunch of freshmen and sophomores, so I tended to sit at the back and blend in more than usual.

Madame Armel began her lesson on conjugation, while I opened my book in a futile attempt to follow along. My thoughts kept jumping from checking to see if the blonde man was around, to worrying about what I was going to say to Wyn when I saw her, and ultimately, to thinking about Ryland. My mind jumped from lip-locked fantasies that made my heart swim and pound, to the thought of his arms wrapped around mine in an intimate embrace, sending a pleasurable shiver up my spine. I couldn't think that way, though. I had promised myself that we would just be friends and that I would leave him alone. I was left with a hollow, empty feeling as I shooed the fantasies away.

The bell rang much sooner than I expected and I rushed out of class, my mind still overtaken by thoughts, worries and fantasies that didn't want to leave me alone.

Wyn sat down next to me, cafeteria tray and plastic bangles clanging. She didn't say anything at first. I didn't blame her; I didn't know what to say either. How could I start a conversation after what had happened last night?

"I'm sorry," I whispered, much softer than I had wanted to.

"I'm sorry, too," she responded, her bright voice sounding off against my strained whisper. "If I had known it was such a big deal, I wouldn't have brought it up." She paused and bit her lip, as if contemplating whether or not to say something else. I looked at her in expectation, but she had decided against it, looking back down to her food.

I was glad we had moved beyond it, but the awkwardness still wasn't over. I tried to think of something witty to say that would strike up a bright conversation, but nothing came to mind that I wanted to share. Every thought in my mind was an over-dramatic problem or involved too much kissing. Better to keep them all to myself.

I turned toward her just as the bell rang, surprised to see her already looking at me. Her dark eyes stared into me, pinning me in place with a look of mingled excitement and fear. She looked like she was expecting something from me. I opened my mouth to answer her unasked question, but closed it again, realizing I didn't know what she was going to say.

"I better get going to English," Wyn said without looking away from me.

I watched her as she turned to leave, a ratty shoulder bag draped across her back. I wanted to run after her, to explain why everything upset me and all about Ryland, and my dad, and everything. I just couldn't make myself move.

Wyn took a step to the side, leaving a break in the small group of students exiting the cafeteria. That small movement gave me a clear view of the door, and the blonde man standing next to it.

I looked away from Wyn's retreating back to meet the stare of bright, blue eyes. My stomach clenched in fear as his gaze bored into mine in a glance so intense, I felt the blood drain from my face. My frantic and panicked heart felt like it was going to beat right out of my chest.

There was no question now. He was following me.

In the back of my mind, I began to rolodex through every possible reason for being stalked. Everything from child predator to long-lost relative went through my mind in rapid succession. All the while, his eyes never left me; they kept me locked in place with their wide, eager expectation.

The man leaned forward, his back arching him toward me. A shiver wound its way up my spine, causing me to inhale for breath. At my sudden intake, a coy, little half smile spread across his face as if he enjoyed it. My stomach clenched in even further terror, my mind casting away any thoughts of what that smile could mean. I didn't want to know. He continued to stare into me before releasing me as he turned to walk out of the cafeteria.

I didn't dare move, even though class had already started. I was left alone with the janitorial staff and the smell of ammonia. I continued to stare at the vacant door as the edge of fear ebbed away and my spine started to relax. I shouldn't be so worked-up over one random man staring at me, even though he had been following me. It could be anything, right?

I shook my head in frustration as I gathered my belongings and headed out of the school. I knew I would get in trouble for skipping classes, but right then, I didn't care. I didn't want to be there, didn't want to risk being seen by either Wyn or the blonde man.

Turning around right outside the door, I placed my fingers in the grooves of the deep red brick that covered the school. I lifted myself up, worn sneakers gripping the brick as I began to scale my way toward the roof. My backpack bounced against my back as I climbed. With so little to cling onto, I was surprised I could do this at all, but something about heights and climbing had always drawn me in.

I smiled as the wind pulled my hair out of my hoodie and snaked it around my face. The feeling of the warm air made my skin tingle. With one more pull, I reached the top and sat on the edge of the building, my legs dangling over the side.

I sat, just looking at the tops of the houses and the small field where the freshmen were playing soccer. Before long, the fear of being stalked and the anger at the tension between Wyn and me came back and I sank down a bit.

I wanted someone to talk to. I needed to figure out what was going on, what I was supposed to do. I needed Ry. I needed his strong arms around me and his soothing voice telling me it was okay. I knew I shouldn't. I shouldn't indulge myself.

I reached into the pocket where I kept my phone, surprised when my fingertips brushed instead against something small and round.

I pulled it out, expecting to find a wrapper, but instead found the small purple marble. It rolled around my palm as the wind tugged at it. Watching it shine against the flickers of light clicked something together in my brain. The man, the bead, my dad.

My dad had referred me to a cult, and the cult had obviously found me.

CHAPTER 15
RYLAND

"Come on, Ryland! You can do better than that, stop dodging and actually try to kill me. Don't make me tell your father of yet another failure." Cail laughed with that dark sound that always preceded one of his kills, the snide taunt his usual for me. Cail was always taunting me, goading me into being something I was not. Into being something dark and dangerous and smothered with blood. Something like him.

His dark laugh deepened, echoing over the stone walls of the large underground training hall and rattling the rack of fighting staffs and ancient stones that lined the walls. I lifted my head, the guy was grinning, wiping my blood from his knuckles onto the dark denim of his jeans as he began to circle around me, the dark crackle of the magic that was unique to the Trpaslíks rippling from his fingers and up his forearms. I spit the rest of the blood in my mouth to the ground and grinned at him, blood-coated teeth sparking in warning.

As much as I didn't want to fight him, avoiding this would only make it worse for me. He had broken my arm last week, and I really didn't want a repeat of that. Bones were always tricky to heal with magic.

"Tell my father what? That you cheated..." I jumped up, letting my magic spark as I threw an attack at him. We weren't supposed to be using magic in this session, but he had already broken that rule.

Cail dodged the attack as though I had thrown a tissue at him and laughed louder, those impossibly dark eyes of his sparking dangerously.

"Come now, Ryland, we both know you are holding back." Cail stepped forward, grabbing two of the broadswords off the wall and throwing me one, it clattered against the floor and skidded over to me with an echoing grind worse than nails on a chalkboard. I grimaced but couldn't say anything. He had clearly won in fist fighting, even with the magic he shot into me after he sent me to the ground, the next weapon was his choice. "It's not like I can actually do anything to hurt that pretty little face of yours. That vile peasant girl you keep sneaking to your room will only swoon over a few bruises, anyway."

His dark eyes narrowed as he added that last part and I froze, back straightening as I stood. I wasn't supposed to have Jos in my room, I wasn't supposed to be associating with her at all. They had given me that threat enough, and I had ignored them enough. I thought I had done a good job keeping those particular escapades to myself as of late. I guess not. I took the sword and swung it once, the heavy steel cutting through the air.

"I'm sure I don't know what you are talking about." I forced a laugh even though I knew nothing about this was funny.

His smile didn't make me feel any better about the situation.

The guy was a brutal masochist. He tried very hard to make me the same. Just another malicious beast. Like his father, Timothy. Like my father, Edmund.

"You sure about that?" Cail flipped his sword before gripping it with both hands and pointing it directly at me. Broadswords. It was such an archaic way of fighting; the brutal slashing and weapons strong enough to both break skin and sever bone with one hit. It was no wonder that he preferred it.

"I'm sure." I let every bit of warning bleed through my eyes as I stared him down, sword held before me even as I sent sparks of light moving over my forearms like lightning. There was no missing the threat. I had never taken Cail before, but I would for Jos. I would do anything to keep her safe.

He stared at me for a moment before he shrugged, flipping the heavy sword around again.

"Not like I care, anyway. Do what you want with the girl, it's not like you will see her after we leave." The wicked gleam in his eyes grew with every word. I couldn't stop the absolute panic that bit at my heart at hearing that. I forced myself to keep my focus hard and not let the panic show. "I have bigger plans for you. Just a few more months at that pathetic academy, Ryland, and then you are all mine."

I avoided the shiver that wound up my spine. He didn't need to remind me. I had been dreading that right of passage since the day it had been made clear to me what my purpose was. All of my time at school, with Jos, it had all been part of the last gift my mother had left for me, the binding promise she had put on my father before she took her last breath. But the day I graduated high school that all ended. There was no fancy university, there was no inheriting of fortunes or crowns. It would just be Cail and I, off on the mission they had spent my entire life training me to complete. To find and kill the last Chosen Child, the one that had been prophesied. And then, once she was gone, find and kill Ilyan, the self-proclaimed king of Imdalind.

Death and destruction was all I was made for, it was all my father saw in me.

But I couldn't let that be it for me. I didn't want it to be.

"Is that why you covered for me after I disappeared in the aftermath of the Rugby match?" I circled him, our eyes locked as I watched his breathing, his footing, waiting for him to strike.

"Silly child, always thinking everything is about you..." He struck then; his motions quick as his sword swung around and came down like a club. I countered, barely lifting my broadsword in time. The metal clacked together loudly, metal grinding against metal in screech.

"Then why cover for me?"

"You really couldn't feel it? What have we been training you for, all this time we teach you to detect magic, to destroy magic, and you couldn't even feel it when it was right in front of you." Cail leaned in, his nose an inch from the cross of the swords before he pushed against it and sent me stumbling back.

Bastard! I shouldn't have fallen for that, but he had distracted me. Again.

You think I would be used to it by now, but my mind was preoccupied. I had been waiting days to ask why he hadn't outed me. I had gotten Joclyn away from my Father and Cail as quickly as I could, I didn't like her to be near them, and they had looked in her direction more than once. Perhaps that necklace was leading them down the wrong trail.

I had expected my father to be raging at my quick disappearance when I had returned and I had avoided him all day. But he didn't seem to care.

If anything, he seemed absolutely giddy.

"I am not weak, as you are aware." I said with a grunt, quick-stepping and swinging my sword high. Cail was too quick for me and blocked it easily.

"Am I? You haven't won a match tonight..."

I rose to Cail's prod, moving fast as I stepped left and right, swinging the heavy sword quicker than even the coils of my muscles should be able to handle.

Cail said nothing, he just moved to match me, grunts and taunts filtering through the air as we danced along with the clang of the metal. I faked a swing and sped to the right, placing the cold edge of the sword against his neck.

"Proud of yourself?" Cail hissed through gritted teeth.

"Yes, now tell me what I missed. What did you find?" The words were a snarl through the grit in my teeth, but he just continued to smile, even when I pressed the blade into his neck and the scent of his blood filled the air.

"Found what you failed to."

"Who–?" I began, but any further taunt was cut short by a slow clapping and a low voice that set my spine into attention.

"Good, son. I see you are finally improving. Perhaps soon you will be strong enough to do what I need of you." I stepped away from Cail, who neither hissed or reacted as the sharp end of the blade ground against his skin. He just stood, bowing slightly with blood dribbling down his neck as he faced Edmund. He stepped into the large training hall as though he was wearing a crown and cape and not the business suit that he usually wore. Timothy was right on his heels, the two men watching me as they approached in dark suits. It made them look ominous, as though they were leaders of some crime syndicate. The reality was so much worse than that. Neither man gave any mind to Cail who bowed before grabbing my sword and putting them both away, the collar of his shirt beginning to stain red. He could heal the cut with little thought from his magic, but instead he let it bleed.

"Thank you, Father." I straightened my back, my chin high as I met his gaze, his glee instantly faded to disappointment as he caught sight of the broken nose and swollen lip Cail had given me in our last match.

"Although not as much as I would have hoped." His fingers were ice against my chin, the pads pressing roughly as he forced my head around to inspect the damage from Cail's handiwork.

"That was easy," Cail yelled from the other side of the hall. "He's still weak."

"And whose fault would that be, Cail? You are the one training me," I snarled, trying to look towards the sniveling man, my father pulled my focus back to him, his fingers digging into my chin now.

"Cail can only do so much to mold weakness into strength. Work harder." He leaned in, his blue eyes narrowed as little sparks of heat and pain flew from his fingers only a second before his palm smacked into the side of my face. He held my chin still, his other hand slamming into me again and again.

"Work harder, boy!" He howled, hitting me one last time. His hand released my chin and as he hit hard against my jaw, this time with a fist. I went down to the ground, the pain that blossomed through my knees nothing to the agony that was swelling through my jaw and neck. My magic flooded to the pain, to the break in the bones in both jaw and cheek. Agony flared violently and I wanted to scream, I wanted to howl in rage and pain, but I locked it away. Crying would only lead to more pain, to more punishment.

It wasn't worth it. I had learned that lesson too many times.

"He shouldn't be weak," my father snarled as I forced myself to stand, keeping my magic locked away enough that it wouldn't heal me. That would have to wait until he left, if I healed myself too quickly he wouldn't be pleased.

"We've put too much work into this one." Timothy's voice was filled with the same level of hatred as his sons. "I would hate to have to dispose of another..."

"You won't have to dispose of me," I hissed, ignoring the agony that was everywhere, that was blacking out my visions in pops of jet black pain. I looked from Timothy to my father, careful to form each word even through the agony.

There was nothing more frightening than the pure vile that seeped from my father's eyes, but I had faced it enough. I had known what would come of me if I was to fail. I wouldn't be the first of his children he had killed because we weren't good enough. We weren't strong enough. We didn't have the right kind of magic.

"I was just distracted." At once I knew I had said the wrong thing; Cail laughed, Timothy made a sound that was near a choke, and my father stepped closer, the blue of his eyes darkening into a chill of ice.

Ice that was running over my skin.

I held my ground, chin high as I let just enough magic curl around the shattered remains of my bones so that I could see straight.

"Distracted? That girl..." The two words were a snarl, his focus drifting to Cail.

"No," I cut him off before he could say anything more. "I was not distracted by *that girl*," I tried to say the words with as much hatred as he had, I wasn't very successful. "I was distracted by what you had asked me to hunt down. Cail said something was at my Rugby match..."

Or rather he said I had missed something at the Rugby match. It probably wasn't the best choice to bring that up now seeing as I had clearly failed in what he had asked me to do, but anything that I could give him that would pull him away from Joclyn was worth it. I could fix my bones, hers were harder.

I never wanted her to get hurt.

"Ah yes, yet another of your failures." My father snarled, his lips pursing in the anger I had expected the other day. "Well, I'm sure you are aware that we found what we sought. No thanks to you. Cail secured my prize for me, all on his own."

"How...? Who...?" The words stuttered out and all the men laughed, my one joy was bubbling up, but not for why they thought.

If they had found it then that meant it wasn't the necklace. Something else had tripped my father's men. If the necklace was safe, then Joclyn was safe, and my way out of here was clear.

"How did Cail find him, or how did you fail me? The answer to either leads to the same." Edmund held out his hand, his palm up as the air heated and pulsed, waiting for me to place my hand against his.

Pain.

All this would lead to was pain.

"Of course, you would have known the answer to both if you had been doing your job as I had trained you to do. Now you may never know the prize I have in my possession again. Unless you prove your worth to me again," he stood there, his hand still outstretched as he waited for me to comply, waited for me to hurt. I doubted he would tell me what he had found regardless of what he did to me. He just liked to see me scream.

Before either of us could move, however, the door to the hall swung open and one of the men from my father's guard burst in.

"She's here!" He gasped and we all turned. "My Lord, you asked me to tell you when she is here, and she's here... and even better... he's awake."

All of the anger bled from my father's face.

"Perfect," my father grinned, still staring at me. "Perhaps I will find another way to discover your worth to me."

I had no idea what he was talking about, but at least I had avoided whatever torture he had planned for me.

"I'll go greet her, shall I?" Cail laughed before he ripped out of the room. He clearly knew who they were talking about, I was just left standing in confusion as Timothy and Cail left, leaving only my father and myself in the center of the massive training hall, his finger pointed in my face.

"I expect better, Ryland. I have not bred you, and trained you, for you to fail me. You already defied me last spring when you refused to kill that thief, and I will not allow that to pass again. Consider this your last pass. I would rather kill you than be ashamed by you again."

I didn't need the darkness and malice that covered his face to know just how truthful he was being, his history did that all on his own.

"Now, bow to your King, Ryland."

His eyes were a dark blue, his lips turned into a sneer as I felt the warmth of his magic spread over my spine. It seeped into my bones, forcing them to curl as I was forced to bow. My eyes never left his.

"What do you say, Ryland?" The painful heat of his magic was spreading, curling around every inch of me in warning as the pain in my bones grew, each one aching and screaming through my body as though he was cracking them.

Still, I did not look away. I did not howl in the pain that was cutting through me. I did not let one single tear pass. I grit my teeth, the still broken pieces of my jaw howling as I faced him.

"Yes, my King. Thank you, my King." The words ground out through the clamp in my jaw, but they still seemed to appease him.

"Good boy." He chastised me as he patted my cheek, the skin and bones he had already beaten screaming with the touch. The move could have been considered loving as he pat once, twice, before his fingers curled into a ball and slammed against my jaw. Sending me to the ground again. "Never forget that there are other ways I can hurt you, Ryland. That there are other people I can use to get what I want."

I didn't call out. I made no noise as I lay on the ground, blood dripping from my mouth. My father stepped forward slowly, standing over me as the same power twisted up my spine again, forcing me up.

Forcing me to stare at him.

My blood boiled, my power begging to retaliate, but I held it at bay, begging it to be still.

Not to rise.

Not to make this worse.

"This is your last chance, Ryland. Fail me again, and I will have no further use of you."

He laughed once as he sent me back to the ground, my body screaming as I knelt on the cold stone floor, watching him leave, the door slamming behind him.

CHAPTER 16
RYLAND

"She's still not here, Ryland," Angela called over to me the moment I walked into the kitchen. I glanced at the clock as I made my way over the long counter and the barstool that had been mine for the last few days. The same one I had sat in just that morning when I had hid in here to have coffee and a pastry before heading to training.

It felt like a lifetime ago to me, but only a few hours to her, which was probably why she was looking at me like I was a love sick dog who had lost his way.

Maybe I was.

"She won't be here today."

I nodded, I already knew that of course. Jos was on the west side of town at a new friend's house, as her mom had warned me about yesterday.

As I had felt all day by the warm pulses that the necklace sent my way. I knew she was safe; I also knew she was happy.

I should be glad for her, not just that she was happy, but that things were moving on in her life. That there were friends that could stay with her. I wasn't going to be here very much longer anyway. If she was going to be safe, she needed to move on with her life.

I was just being selfish, wanting as much of her to myself as I could possibly get before I was gone. Before I left.

Because I had to leave, the events of earlier had proven that. I could not stay here, and I most certainly could not leave with Cail to go hunt and murder as they always planned for me. I needed to find a way out.

I needed to escape.

"I know, I was just wondering if you had any leftover soup handy?" I worked hard to form each word. The bones in my jaw and cheek had thankfully healed, but I wasn't sure I could do too much chewing of the steaks and quail that I had seen leave in a line to the banquet hall not too long ago.

She nodded and bee-lined for the fridge but not before she gave me a look that I had been on the receiving end of more than a few times over the last few days.

"Are you sure that's the only reason you're here, Ry?"

"Yes and no," I mumbled, sliding onto the bar stool that had been mine and mine alone for the last few days. "I'm just worried about her. Ever since..." I paused, unsure if Joclyn had talked to her mom about the real reason for her mysterious illness. If she hadn't, I wasn't going to be the one to tell her.

Angela lifted a brow as she passed me a bowl of soup, the concoction already steaming from the few moments she had placed it in the microwave. Her motions were slow as she watched me with the same expression, the contemplation of conversation.

"You might as well spit it out, Mrs. D," I mumbled, before lifting a spoonful of soup to my lips. "I'm immune to mom glares. You're going to have to ask."

"I should say the same for you," she chuckled, thankfully dropping the x-ray vision. "Clearly you know something I don't."

I knew a lot of things she didn't, even about Joclyn, not that I was going to tell her any of it.

"Secrets, Mrs. D. Your daughter's secrets, which I will not be divulging. Role of the best friend." I lifted my spoon to her in salute before going back in to capture a carrot, it was near mush and required no chewing. It was bliss.

"I know I should be glad for that," she mumbled as she went back to work, spreading some sauce over some raw piece of meat. "But now you have me worried that I've missed something big."

"Nothing big, Jos is fine. Don't worry, I would tell you if it was something huge." Huge and wouldn't end in disaster. With my life there was no way of knowing if the two didn't go hand in hand. "I'll always protect her." I took another bite of the soup and Angela froze, sauce still dripping from her brush as she turned to face me, thankfully not with the mom expression. That time she just looked surprised. Awed? I couldn't place it, but it was almost worse than the mom look from before.

"You really care for her, don't you?" she asked, I nodded.

"She's my best friend. She's one of the best things in my life." Maybe the only good thing, but I wasn't going to share that. "I don't want to lose that."

I couldn't meet her eyes, so I just stared at the goo dripping from her brush, fully aware that she was tearing up.

Dang it. Now my eyes were burning, the truth of my words were stabbing me as deep as they were her. Time for a change of subject.

"That meat juice is getting all over." I nodded to the still dripping sauce and Angela jumped back to attention.

"Thank you, Ryland," she whispered. I wasn't sure if she was talking about the sauce or what I had said, so I nodded and mumbled some kind of acknowledgement, moving instead to loudly slurp at my soup in an attempt to cover it all up.

"And it's not meat juice," she said after a moment, her voice still choked a bit.

"What is it then?" I said through half-slurped carrots.

"It's sugar basting, for the breakfast ham." She waved to the meat that was in the baking dish, and I nodded. Meat sauce and meat mystery solved.

Well, kind of. Why she was putting it on, or how or any of that was lost on me. Although, if I had to guess, the sugar part was what made her ham so sweet.

Which, I suddenly realized, created a whole other problem I hadn't anticipated.

"I really know nothing about any of this stuff, cooking and cleaning... and all of it. That's going to be a problem when I go off to... Oxford in a few months." I had almost forgotten the name of the school I was supposed to be going to, although she didn't seem to notice. She was still doing her basting things.

"You'll still have chefs and dorms and maids there, I'm sure." She gave me a grin, still dunking and squirting and brushing brown sugar slop onto what was clearly a ham, now that I looked.

"Yeah..." If I was going to Oxford I would. But I wasn't going to Oxford.

Even if I was to go with Cail on his kamikaze mission to find the Chosen I was sure I would have maids and cooks and whatever join us. At least I would assume it would, with how prissy Cail was how could it not? But none of that really mattered. Because I would not have cooks where I was going, wherever I was going.

I still had some pieces of my escape plan to work through.

I would figure all of that out after I knew Joclyn would be safe after I left. Which, I suddenly realized, meant getting Angela out of this estate. Or, hell, out of this city. She couldn't stay here. If my father wanted me back enough, he would use both of them to make that happen.

"Maybe I'll just hire you to come along with me," I chuckled, knowing it was impossible even as I tried to figure out if I could make that happen.

Of course, it would probably require money, and even though I was the prince in a wealthy kingdom, or the son of a powerful businessman as it appeared to Jos and her mother, I had none.

"I'd go," she slid, placing the ham into the oven before turning back to me. "If it would get Timothy off my back."

I sat up a little straighter. Damn it, I didn't want to hear that, I had thought I had gotten him off her back again. Although given what Cail had said I really shouldn't be surprised.

"What is he saying now?" I tried to sound casual even as every muscle from nose to navel tightened, my magic flaring over the palms of my hands.

"Same as usual," she mumbled, grabbing my empty bowl and promptly filling it with more delicious soup.

"You know, with cooking like yours, you could get a job anywhere. Perhaps somewhere safer." Perhaps with me. Gods, if only I had the money. Perhaps I would take them with me regardless.

"Safer? Am I working for a mob boss?" She laughed uncomfortably, I shook my head perhaps a little too quickly. She had no idea.

"No, just bastards who don't appreciate you, and think that your daughter is a bad influence on me. Which couldn't be further than the truth, mind you," I shrugged, even though a pain in my chest was starting to form as I realized just how much danger that leaving them behind was going to put them in. "I'm sure there are better positions. I'll give you a good reference."

Angela kept glancing at me as she went around the kitchen in her usual hustle, her lips pressed together. I needed to protect both of them, and this was just the start of that.

If I couldn't take them with me perhaps all she needed was a nudge in the right direction.

"Or I could talk to Timothy." Not that I thought it would do any good.

She froze, slamming down the pan she was holding. "I don't want you to get involved, Ryland. You take on too much responsibility as it is. Go. Be a kid."

"I'm not a kid." I was too quick to answer and she turned, that mom glare already raging.

"You're not eighteen yet, so, still a kid."

"*Yet*. But I don't feel like a kid, well, unless I'm with Jos. She makes life feel normal. Like I can be myself." My chest tightened in that expectant pain of the day she was torn from me. Angela looked about ready to explode with tears again. I put my hands up, and backed away from the bar and the soup. As much as I wanted to devour the stuff, I really didn't want to cause any more problems for anyone.

"No need to gush, Mrs. D, you just raised an awesome daughter is all." Luckily, that seemed to calm her and I gave her my best grin before grabbing the soup bowl.

Screw it. I was leaving, but I was taking the soup with me.

"Tell her I said 'hi', kay?" I said, still grinning at the glossy-eyed cook.

As much as I would have loved to hide in the kitchen for the rest of the night, I knew Angela was off soon. Besides, if Timothy was threatening her then my being there was only going to make things worse.

Heck, Jos watching a movie in my room this weekend was going to make things a hell of a lot worse.

My father had already warned me that he could hurt me in other ways, and he had clearly already set that ball in motion.

Which meant there was only one thing to do. I had planned on our movie being so much more, but now there was only one clear path.

I needed to say goodbye.

I needed to leave.

CHAPTER 17
JOCLYN

For the second time in a week, I woke to the sound of Ryland's knock echoing through my tiny apartment. I fought the urge to yell when I looked at the clock, 5:15 a.m. My alarm wasn't set to go off for another forty-five minutes. I rolled out of bed and landed hard on the floor.

"I'm coming," I said loud enough for him to hear me.

"About time," I heard his happy voice yell back. Great, he's wide awake.

I crawled toward the door, grabbing a sweater I had discarded last night and threw it on to cover the light-weight cami I wore. I continued to crawl until I reached the front door where I pulled myself upright and threw the door open.

"It's five in the morning, Ry," I yawned, my hair falling around my face.

"Yeah, sorry about that." He ran his big hand through his dark curls, looking away from me. "I was just worried about you."

"You were worried about me?" My voice sounded more hostile than I had meant it to.

"Yes, Jos." He looked down, his eyes smoldering and I felt my heart sputter. "Why aren't you wearing my necklace?" He reached out and trailed the tip of his finger against my neck, his touch leaving a shivering trail behind it.

I grasped toward my collar bone, shocked to find the fine silver chain missing. "It must have fallen off while I slept." I looked back toward my room, as if just expecting to see it sitting on the fold of my comforter.

"Why don't you go get it? I'll get breakfast ready." He smiled and held up a bag full of greasy doughnuts. I couldn't help but smile at the look on his face; he was so adorable. I let him in before turning to retrieve the necklace from within the mass of pillows and blankets that was my bed. The necklace lay warm in my hand, as if I had been lying on it all night.

"See, not lost." I walked up behind Ryland as he searched for plates in the kitchen.

"Good." He took the necklace from my hands and went to put it around my neck again. I moved my hair for him, so as not to reveal my mark. For a split second, I almost didn't. I almost wanted him to see it, to see what he would do. That risk was too much for me, though, so I kept it hidden.

"Please don't take it off, okay?" he pleaded, his deep blue eyes boring into me.

"You act like I'm going to go hock it and buy a car." I laughed at the thought, but he didn't. My laughter died off as I sat the milk and some glasses on the table.

"Relax, Ryland, it's not like I could, even if I tried."

Ryland looked at me menacingly from beneath his long lashes.

"I couldn't, could I?"

He chuckled at me.

"I could?"

"More than likely, but please don't, Joclyn," he pleaded, coming to kneel in front of me and gathering my hands in his. His hands were warm and soft; the warmth radiated up my arms and through my body in a comforting wave that enveloped me.

"Please don't, Jos. Don't take it off, don't sell it, don't lose it, don't give it away. Think of it as a piece of me," he said and looked down at our interlocked hands. "You know I am leaving the country soon, and it may be a while until I see you again. I may... I may never see you again. Please keep it close. That way I will always know you are safe."

He lifted his head to look at me, and I was shocked to see his eyes brimming with threatening tears. He lifted our hands together and placed them over the necklace, right next to my heart.

"Promise me, Joclyn, please."

I didn't know how to react. Was this goodbye? I didn't think I could handle any more emotional daggers this week. It had been a week, one week since my birthday, and everything had flipped upside down. Ryland's thumb began to caress the back of my hand, waiting for an answer. The action sent my heart and stomach tangoing through my body in pure pleasure.

"I promise," I exhaled, hoping that this wasn't goodbye. Not already. It couldn't be; there were still four weeks until graduation.

Almost as soon as the words left my lips, my mom's bedroom door creaked open and Ryland left my side, sitting back in his own chair before my mom could even exit her room.

"Why, Ryland," her voice was laced with parental venom, "was that your knock I heard at such an ungodly hour this morning?" She wrapped her robe around her as she made her way to the kitchen in search of a coffee mug.

"Sorry, Mrs. D." Ryland slipped right into his normal voice, as if nothing had happened over the past few minutes. "I wanted to provide breakfast for my two favorite ladies." He winked at my mom as he shook the doughnut bag, causing me to almost choke on the maple bar I had just bit into. My mom looked between us in some sort of amused frustration. I wished she would just laugh; it would make everything go a lot smoother.

"Joclyn, I have given some thought to what we talked about in the car on Tuesday night."

I sat up straighter, swallowing my doughnut. I couldn't believe she was going to do this in front of Ryland, but, oh well. I chanced a glance at him to see that he was just as attentive as I was.

"I will let you two have your movie night on one condition."

I sat forward more; she had my full attention—this had to be good.

"No hoodies for the rest of the week."

Not good.

"What?" I shrieked. I looked over at Ryland. He was smiling ear to ear.

"Thursday, Friday, Saturday. No hoodie." She was firm.

I was doomed.

"Good one! I knew you'd get her out of those hoodies somehow!" He lifted his hand to my mom, ready for a high five. I rounded on Ryland; my face must have been terrifying because he turned that high five into a hair smooth real quick.

"Please tell me you had nothing to do with this, Ryland." My voice was a growl.

"Not a bit." He winked at me and I felt my resolve lessen. Stupid hormones!

"Mom!" I pleaded with her like a child. This was not a compromise; this was torture.

"Take it or leave it, Joclyn."

"Mom, this is so not fair! I can't go to school without a hoodie. Do you know what will happen?" Yes, I was begging. I didn't care. I couldn't lose Saturday night, but this was unacceptable.

"People will see what a beautiful young lady you are. Oooh! Maybe you'll get asked out on a date!" she said triumphantly.

I felt Ry tense behind me. I just wanted to melt into the kitchen floor.

"Whatever, Mom."

"Joclyn, if you want to go with Ryland Saturday night, you need to do this for me."

I felt the last of my resolve slip away. How many times was I going to get guilt-tripped this morning?

"Fine." I think I sounded like a beaten kitten. "I'll see you later, Ry." I waved to him as I tromped off to my room. If I had to put some thought into my clothes, this was going to take a while.

"Actually," Ryland began, stopping me in my tracks, "I am going to take you to school today. That's what I came over to tell you."

I swear my heart just shot right down to my toes. I was not sure if my mother laughed or gasped; either way, the sound that came from the kitchen was not very good.

Ryland looked at me with this heroic glee, like he had just won the best prize in the world.

"Fine!" I snapped and ran to my room, there was no way I could win against those two. I put some mindless music on a little louder than normal in an attempt to drown out the voices from the kitchen, and set to work.

I pulled out a pair of darker jeans that would fit snug, but still had enough room in them that I wouldn't look like I was trying too hard. That left shirts. Okay, so brand new red shirt was out—I had to save that for Saturday. That left a gray one with ruffles I never wore and a green one with fabric roses near the hem. Seeing as they would both get a turn, I grabbed blindly, draping the green shirt over the jeans. Grabbing the rest of the stuff I needed, I ran across the hall to the bathroom and took the world's quickest shower.

Without the hood to help keep my hair in place, I had to do something to guarantee that ugly mark didn't peek out. I brushed my hair before lifting the hair up above my right ear. There it was, the dragon, peeking out from beneath my ear to look at me. I covered it with a small bandage and then pulled my hair into a sleek side braid, guaranteeing that no one would see it.

I shoved my clothes on, not bothering to look at myself in the mirror. I didn't want to see myself and lose the forced confidence I had tried to rattle to the surface. I sprinted across the hall to my room, shutting my door behind me. Even my music couldn't drown out my mother's joyous laughter.

It was like my birthday all over again. I liked the way I looked; I just wished I felt more comfortable. I dabbed on some concealer and lip gloss before turning to the door, my hand freezing on the knob. It wasn't just my mom out there; it was Ryland, too. Beyond that, what was I going to do when I got to school? My false confidence morphed into a full-blown panic attack and I found myself hyperventilating behind the bedroom door. The skin on my chest grew hot, as if my panic had ignited the necklace that was hiding underneath my shirt.

The knob twisted under my fingers and was jerked out of my hand as the door flung open in front of me. Ryland grabbed me around the waist and pulled me to him, burying his face in my hair. He cradled me against his strong chest, his hand wrapped around my waist as the other smoothed my back. As his hand moved its way up and down my back, I found my breath slowing, the panic melting away.

"Shhhhh... it's okay, Jos. Just breathe. I'm here." I wrapped my arms around him as I came back to myself.

He moved me away from him; his hands never left my shoulders as his thumbs moved over the skin on my arms. I looked up at him in nervous anticipation, but his eyes didn't leave mine. He didn't look at what I wore. He didn't appraise my uncovered body. He just stared straight into my eyes with a passion I had never seen before.

"You're beautiful." His hands trailed down my arms, their warmth leaving a trail of goosebumps behind. He intertwined his fingers with mine for a brief second before leaning down, his lips brushing against the crown of my hair. "Your eyes, they are just like diamonds."

I shivered at his whisper, his voice lingering in my ear. He squeezed my hand before dragging me off to the kitchen where my mom sat, still in her robe. At the sight of me, she dropped her doughnut. Her face screamed pure joy; it almost felt like she was sending me off to my first day of kindergarten.

"Oh, Joclyn, you're beautiful." She cupped my face with her rough kitchen hands. She was crying, and I felt like crying, too. I had given her what she wanted, her dream. If only for three days, I was giving her that beautiful, little girl she had always wanted. Deep down inside, I knew I wanted to be that, too.

CHAPTER 18
JOCLYN

I didn't want to get out of the car. Who would? It was nice and warm, and the leather of the seats were soft and cozy. Ryland had turned the radio down low and he had his hand on my knee, thumb caressing me in a comfortable way. He was relaxed. I scowled at the large red school in front of us.

"Maybe I didn't think this through enough," I said.

"What do you think they will do; more than just notice you, I mean?"

I turned to glare at him. I wasn't in the mood to go over my fight with Cynthia just yet. His hand moved from my knee to trail up the pale skin of my arms, leaving another row of goosebumps behind.

"That would be enough to ruin my day." I tried to laugh, but it didn't come out right; my panic made it sound more maniacal than I had intended.

"Honestly, Jos, did you think I would feed you to the wolves?" His eyes sparkled as he reached behind my seat for a large wad of fabric.

I recognized it at once as a hoodie, and I couldn't help the smile that spread over my face. I untangled the mass of cloth to reveal a bright blue jacket with a small stamp of Whittier Prep's crest on the chest.

Ryland shifted in his seat and began to help me pull the sweatshirt over my head, careful not to let it run against my sleek braid. As it moved over me, I caught the strong, pleasurable smell that was so Ryland; grass from endless hours on the Rugby field and some sort of heavy smoke, not like the smoke of a drug user, but that heavy wooden smell like a million bonfires or fireworks.

"Thanks, Ry." I looked up at him and gave him my biggest, goofiest grin; all the while chanting in my head. *Only friends, only friends...*

"Anything for you, sweetheart."

Only friends, only friends...

His hand moved up to cup my face, his thumb trailing along my jaw and I froze. My mind went blank. It was only when he began to move closer that my brain went into overdrive.

"I've got to go." It took all my strength to pull my face away from his touch and move out of the warm comforting interior of his Lotus. My heart screamed at me as I pried myself away, desperate to get back to him. I closed the door behind me and leaned against it longer than would have been natural until I heard his dark chuckle from inside the car. I jumped at the sound and moved away, speed-walking toward the school.

"Hey, Jos."

I turned to his voice, he was leaning over the passenger seat and out the window so he could talk to me.

"Ryland." That came out a bit stiff.

"I'll be here to pick you up right after school."

I nodded at him and began walking. I only made it about two steps before he stopped me again.

"And, Joclyn, the sweater's a gift, another piece of me, okay?" He winked at me, his blue eyes flashing. My eyes were glued to his for a minute before he tore away, speeding off in his car.

I continued toward the school, my head buzzing in an odd swarm of happy mosquitoes. Nothing made sense; Ryland had sat at my kitchen table less than a week ago explaining that the necklace didn't mean anything, but since then, he has been trying to kiss me. Then there were all the gifts, like he was saying good-bye.

My heart thudded as I crossed the street, making a beeline to Wyn who was in a heated conversation with someone who stood with their back to me. I was determined to get over the weirdness so we could keep working on our friendship. After all, I would need her after Ryland left.

Wyn's voice rose a bit, the frantic tone increasing as I moved closer to her. She was so engrossed in her conversation that she didn't even see me step right up next to her.

"I'm not going to do that! Can you imagine how that would ruin everything? You would be making me start all over again." I ignored her comment and looked toward the man standing across from her.

My heart seized in an uncomfortable fear. The man who had been following me around campus stood right there, his bright blue eyes burning into mine. Now that I was close to him, I couldn't help but notice how familiar his eyes were, like I had seen them somewhere before. My mouth just hung open in a sterilized panic that I couldn't quite bat away.

"You know him?" I rounded on Wyn after my brain clicked back into place. She knew him. I mean, she stood here talking to him.

"Who?" Was she joking? He stood right here. She was talking to him.

"Him! My Stalker." I motioned toward him, my heart falling into my stomach to see him staring at me with an amused smile on his face.

"Hello, Joclyn." He spoke smoothly, his voice laced with some deep, throaty accent I couldn't place. His deep rumble vibrated through me, sending a shiver up my spine.

"Oh, great! You could have at least told me she saw you. I told her you were a janitor!" Wyn's voice sounded almost hysterical as she shrieked. The tall man turned toward Wyn, glaring down at her. Wyn bowed her head, her lips moving in some form of apology I couldn't understand before lowering in an unmistakable curtsy. That wasn't normal.

"Will someone please explain to me what's going on?"

"Joclyn, Ilyan. Ilyan, Joclyn," Wyn introduced. "Ilyan is my brother, Jos. And, apparently a big jerk. Sorry; if I knew it was him you kept seeing, I would have told you."

Ilyan turned on her again, but this time, Wyn stood her ground. They stared daggers at each other for a minute as if engaged in some form of silent conversation. Definitely brother and sister.

"I'm so sorry if I scared you," Ilyan began, his accent rolling his vowels in odd ways. "I am working on my thesis concerning high school peer groups and how they affect the grades and future outcomes of children and adolescents. I have been conducting my research here."

"Ummm." I didn't really understand all that just came out of his mouth. "So, not a member of a cult then?" I spoke my thoughts aloud without thinking, and my hand flew to my mouth in embarrassment.

Wyn and Ilyan only burst out laughing.

"No, no cult," he lilted with a curious half-smile.

I let out a big sigh of relief. Good, maybe my dad hadn't acted on his craziness yet. I couldn't stop looking at his eyes; they were just so familiar... Wyn cleared her throat. I guess I had been staring too long.

"So, what are you named after? Ilyan isn't a very common name." I spoke the first thing on my mind, hoping to end the rather awkward silence. "Are you named after a king or something; I know Wyn is named after a queen."

"I guess you could say that," Ilyan laughed with a rich, happy sound that seeped through me. Even Wyn joined in on the joke. I must be missing something.

"What?" I asked, looking between them. They shook their heads in unison; the joke, one they didn't want to share. I looked away in irritation to see the school grounds devoid of inhabitants.

"Oh, gosh! We are going to be late!" I whisked Wyn away from her brother without even bothering to say good-bye.

We parted ways at Wyn's locker and I kept running, thankful that it was an A-day and I had gym, instead of French with Madame Armel, who would notice my tardiness. Hopefully, I would have time to dress down before class began.

I ran into the locker room, my heart plunging to see it empty. Even if I dressed and went in, the teacher would make me run the mile. No, thank you. I sat down on one of the many metal benches. I was not having a very good track record—first, two classes yesterday and then, gym today. My mom was going to kill me.

I leaned against the locker, intending to sleep through the hour long block. For some reason, sitting still caused the smell from Ryland's hoodie to increase. I didn't move, letting the delicious scent waft around me. What was I going to do about him, or even about me, for that matter?

Without any warning, a vision of our bodies intertwined filled my mind. His heavy muscular form pushed against me as he wrapped his arms around me in a passionate... What was I doing? I shook my head in frustration, emptying the fantasy from my mind. It was obvious he wanted to kiss me, and I knew, beyond a shadow of a doubt, that I wanted to kiss him. My mom was right; we were both hormone-driven teenagers. What harm could one kiss do, though? He was leaving after all; I might as well make the most of it...

I slammed my head into a locker. Even with all my rationalization I still had made my mother a promise. As much as my heart broke, and as many times as I would have to repeatedly convince myself of it, I had to keep that promise. Until Heaven and Hell broke loose and we could somehow be together, I would keep the promise.

My mind jerked out of its heart-breaking reverie as my phone buzzed in my pocket.

How's the hoodie?

I couldn't help the smile that spread across my face.

Large, warm, and very hideable. Thanks.

I tucked the phone in the pocket of the hoodie and leaned my head back again. He must be ditching class, too, because the next message came right away.

Hideable?

It's a word! I knew it wasn't, but it should be.

Uh huh... I guess it's good you are a junior, because you obviously still have some leprosy to deal with. ;)

Leprosy? My loud laugh echoed around the walls of the locker room. I covered my mouth, scared I would get caught ditching gym.

Spell check! I meant learning.

Right; and I'm the one who needs extra 'learning'? It took a long time for him to reply, and by the time he did, students were already making their way back into the locker room, so I stood and made my way out of the room before I was discovered.

Be warned, we are doing pie tonight.

Pie.

We hadn't done pie for months. Although it wasn't as cool as it sounded, "pie" simply involved taking a chocolate crème pie—my favorite—up the canyon and hanging out at the fire pit. Normally I would be excited for pie, but right now, it just seemed like a bad situation that would end in forbidden kissing. My heart sputtered and my stomach swooped. I would keep my promise to my mom. I had to.

I can't, there is no way my mom will let me. I typed as I slid into my desk in my next class.

I'll take care of your mom. She will let you; don't worry.

It had taken quite a bit of compromise to get permission for the movie on Saturday; I doubted it would happen. Then again, she had already gotten me into a regular, old t-shirt.

I can't. I have lots of homework. I lied, knowing he would see right through it.

Why are you avoiding me, Jos?

I stared at the screen, knowing that class had already started and I wasn't paying even a scrap of attention. What could I say to him? It wasn't like I was doing it on purpose. There was just so much I couldn't tell him, no matter how much I wanted to. There were so many times I wanted to kiss him, to let him kiss me, but I couldn't. Just being his friend was going to be harder than I thought.

Fine. We'll do pie.

I put my phone away and attempted to focus on class, ignoring the continual buzzing from my pocket. My next classes passed in quick succession, and I worked hard to finish as much of my homework as possible.

My phone finally stopped buzzing as I slipped into my normal spot in the cafeteria, content to disappear for the rest of the day.

"I am so sorry about my brother," Wyn said as she dropped into the seat opposite mine, her tray laden with enough food to feed a group of girls. "He's an idiot," she continued without waiting for me to respond. "If I had known it was him you thought was following you, I would have told you. He's an idiot," she repeated and then bit into a French fry.

"Hey, I'm just glad to know I'm not going crazy anymore."

"Nope, not crazy. He is, though." She rolled her eyes. "Speaking of crazy, what's with that cult comment?" Wyn raised her eyebrows at me, but I just waved her off.

"Just something my dad said once." She kept waiting for me to elaborate, but I kept staring at my food, hoping she wouldn't pry.

"Well, anyway," Wyn began in an odd attempt to break the silence, "can you come over tonight? We never got to watch our movie from Monday, and Ilyan will be home so you can see how non-freaky he is."

"I can't. I'm doing pie with Ry," I said. I was sad I couldn't go. As much as I was looking forward to the evening with Ryland, I was still terrified at what might happen.

"Pie? Is that code for something dirty?"

My voice rang out in noxious laughter at Wyn's comment. I was so happy we were in the middle of the lunch room where no one would notice the high pitched noise I had just emitted.

"No!" I said through giggling. "It's just pie."

Wyn stared at me in confusion.

"You know," I prompted, "we get together, we eat pie, and we talk."

Wyn sighed as if that was the stupidest thing she had ever heard.

"We have done it for as long as I can remember. When we were little, it was just a way for him to get away from his dad, and we would hide in the bushes behind the pool."

"How romantic," she grumbled.

"Not my boyfriend," I reminded her.

"So, you hung out in the bushes with a boy who may or may not be your boyfriend?"

I decided to let that one slide.

"I was six and bushes were cool."

"Well, if I ever see a cool bush, I'll point it in your direction." Wyn gobbled up a handful of fries in an obvious attempt not to laugh at her bad joke.

"Gee, thanks. Anyway, once he figured out how to drive, we started going up the canyon, which is where I'll be going tonight." *Not to have a make-out session with my best friend,* I reminded myself.

"So, you're going up the canyon to have pie with your boyfriend..."

"Not my boyfriend," I grumbled.

"Whatever. You're going up the canyon with Ryland to eat pie. What a romantic date."

"It's not a date either, Wyn." She stared at me as if waiting for me to admit it.

I shook my head at her in frustration. No matter what she thought, this was not a date; it was only pie, which was still part of the problem.

"Well, how about tomorrow night then? We could even make it a sleepover!" I had never had a sleepover before, and the idea got me excited; but, I knew with all I had to barter for to get permission for Saturday, and now pie, a sleepover was out.

"I can't do a sleepover, but I can come over for a movie."

"And dinner," Wyn added.

"And dinner. We better get going," I said. "They are supposed to run through Act Two today with the set pieces."

"Do you think if we write 'Cynthia McFadden wears boys' underwear' on the side of the castle, she would get offended?"

"I doubt it, but all the boys might get in a fight trying to figure out whose underwear she's sporting."

"So, still worth a show then?" Wyn wagged her eyebrows at me in excitement. I knew she wouldn't, but part of me hoped she would. I could do with the laugh today.

It was the first time I would be seeing Cynthia since our bizarre altercation in the hall. After the first few days, the terrified stares and catcalls from the students had died down. I hadn't seen Mr. Ray since then either.

I opened the door, expecting the worst. Class had already begun. The actors were already in their costumes, so Wyn and I went right into action. Wyn, Jamison and I moved set pieces on and off the stage as the cast worked through their lines and blocking. At least once in every line, Cynthia would forget something, giggle like a maniac, and then proceed to mess up the rest of the line. It wasn't even worth it to mention that I knew the whole show by heart.

I had thought I was in the clear; the show was almost over and the last of the royals were dying rather poorly-acted deaths in the middle of the stage.

"I know what you did, you little freak." I spun around to face Cynthia, her face almost maniacal in frenzied excitement.

"I don't know what you're talking about," I said with as much confidence as I could muster.

"I think you do. You're a freak. I'm going to find out why, and make sure everyone knows."

I just froze, her acidic voice washing around the space.

"Knows what?" Wyn bounced into the conversation. I could have kissed her for arriving with such perfect timing.

Cynthia flinched a bit, her resolve lessening at my added support.

"Freak," she repeated before strolling off to join the cast for the curtain call.

"Ugh. She bugs me," Wyn spat. "It's like she thinks she owns the world."

"Yeah, well, maybe she does," I whispered to myself before going to remove a large wooden throne.

When the bell rang, the cast and the rest of the class stormed out of the room, leaving Wyn and me to finish putting the set pieces away. Even the teacher had disappeared.

"You were right, by the way," Wyn spoke out of nowhere. "Cynthia McFadden is an atrocious Ophelia. How do you think she got the part?"

"No one would pay the price of admission if there were a whole bunch of nobodies in the cast." It was honest, that's how all high school shows were cast.

"I bet you know every speech by heart, don't you?"

I paused, holding a large foam block in my hands and looked around me.

"Do you think everyone is gone?"

"Ooooo, yes!" Wyn's eyes glittered as she dropped what she carried and ran to the first tier of the audience space.

My confidence shuttered for just a moment before coming back tenfold. Wyn's excited face super-charged me. I moved to center stage and dropped my head. I ran through the entire piece in my mind before I began. I knew how I wanted to hold my hands, how I wanted my voice to sound. I just hoped it came out right.

"O, what a noble mind is here o'erthrown! The courtier's, scholar's, soldier's, eye, tongue, sword, Th' expectancy and rose of the fair state,

The glass of fashion and the mould of form." I recited each line with all the purpose and emotion I felt, my body and hands moving as I pleaded to myself and the invisible characters around me. Even though I was no good, my body still felt alive.

"That unmatch'd form and feature of blown youth Blasted with ecstasy. O, woe is me. T' have seen what I have seen, see what I see!"

I finished as I was taught, head down, arms to the side; but I was jolted out of my closed position by not one but two pairs of clapping hands. My head jerked up just as Wyn's hands stopped their furious applause to see Ryland. My heart calmed for just a moment, glad that it wasn't Cynthia or some other irritating senior, before going into turbo-drive at the sight of Ry standing in the doorway.

"See! I told you! You were amazing!" He rushed in and swept me up in a giant bear hug, his arms crushing me against his chest. "Wasn't she amazing?" He turned enthusiastically to Wyn who only nodded at him.

"You must be Wyn." He dropped me before rushing over to her, his big hands outstretched.

"How did you know about Wyn?" I asked, interrupting the enthusiastic handshake Wyn had been sucked into. I hadn't mentioned her to him at all.

"Well, see, someone has been avoiding me all week, and I have to hide from my father somewhere, which means that your mother and I have become the best of friends. And, I know where the cups are kept in the kitchen now."

"No!" I shrieked, my hand flying to my chest. Wyn stuffed her hand to her mouth in an attempt to stifle a laugh.

"Yes, it's true. I can now tell you where cups *and* plates are to be found in my own kitchen. I know it's a shock, but soon I may even be able to locate a bowl." Ryland spoke seriously, like he was announcing a death, his voice causing Wyn's laugh to come unplugged.

"It's a scandal," Wyn said between laughs.

"Not about that! Have you really been talking to my mom this whole week?"

A wide smile spread across his beautiful face, verifying the truth. My mom knew that Ryland had been calling me without even looking at my phone. She was up late this morning on purpose, knowing that Ryland was going to take me to school. I don't know why this bothered me so much, but it did.

"No," I whispered. "What did she tell you?"

"Absolutely everything! She even showed me your naked baby

pictures." I yelped in horror and did what any other logical girl with a crush would do; I slugged him in the shoulder. Unfortunately, my hand was weak and his shoulder was very strong. My hand exploded in pain as the muscles and bones separated from the rough impact.

"Ouch! Darn it, Ryland! Not fair." I shook my hand, waiting for the sting to go away, stomping my foot in the attempt to distract my mind from the centralized pain.

"Oh, you're such a baby. Come here." Ry grabbed my hand and placed it in between his big, warm ones. The warmth of his hands grew and moved into my hand as the pain melted away. It was comforting to have him hold my hand so tightly, his warmth moving through me like it was something tangible.

"Better?" he asked. I could only nod.

"So, Wyn," he didn't release my hand from his grasp as he turned to her, his wide goofy grin back in place, "are you coming with us? Pie in the mountains?"

"I take it my mom said yes?" I asked, perfectly aware that my hand was still clasped inside his.

"Of course, she did." He flashed me a wide, perfect smile before turning back to Wyn, waiting for an answer.

"I probably shouldn't." I could see the reluctance on her face, but I also saw a way out of being alone with Ryland.

"Please come, Wyn! It'll be fun!" I removed my hand from the warmth of Ryland's grasp to move toward her. I tried to make my eyes as pleading as possible, but having never done it before I wasn't sure the attempt worked. I stared her down for a few moments longer, pleading until she sighed in defeat. I jumped in the air in celebration as she nodded her head in agreement.

I led the way out of the drama room, now eager to get up the canyon and enjoy some time with both my friends. Wyn breezed past me, texting something on her phone to her brother, I was sure. I followed her until I felt Ryland's large hand on my back, his warmth spreading through me.

"Something tells me you're scared to be alone with me." His breath buzzed through my hair as he spoke; he was that close.

"It's not that," I began. "It's just..." He moved in front of me, placing his hands on my arms and stopping me in place.

"It's okay, Joclyn. I know. It took me a while to realize you were worth more than my father's commands. It took me a while to know what I want. It's okay to be scared. I'm patient." His face filled with a happy light that made my heart spin in pure joy. Ryland leaned down before I could stop him and placed his lips against my cheek.

I was overcome with his smell as his lips lingered there, the warmth of them spreading throughout me and making me dizzy. Far before I was ready, he ran away from me, running to catch up to Wyn and leaving me sputtering alone in the middle of the hall.

CHAPTER 19
JOCLYN

The fire pit was in a large clearing that you could only get to by parking off the side of the road and hiking for about twenty minutes through uncut forest. Some time ago, someone had dug a giant hole in the middle of the space, giving people a reason to call it the fire pit. I never knew how Ryland found this place, but I knew we weren't the only ones who came here. Every once in a while, we would come across crumpled chip wrappers or beer cans.

Ryland led us as we trudged our way through the undergrowth, pie in hand. I could smell the delicious chocolate fragrance drifting back to me, and it made my stomach jump in anticipation.

I stayed back by Wyn, thankful for her company. After what Ryland had said to me as we were leaving the drama room, I didn't need to be alone with him. I needed to think—and somehow prepare myself for Saturday night.

We entered the clearing and I went to go look for firewood. The cool mountain air was already starting to get a bite to it and being this far up the mountains, it was sure to get chilly quickly.

The clearing was surrounded by what appeared to be a perfect circle of giant oak trees. They all had to have been planted at the same time because each one was about the same height. They towered over us as we walked through them, much taller than the smaller beech and brush oak that lay behind them. I couldn't help but touch the trees as I passed; just being this close to them sent a live current through my veins. I loved the way they made me feel.

Ryland was already working on preparing the fire when I dumped all the dried kindling and twigs I could find into the make-shift hole. Ry smiled at me before turning back to the fire; he had always been amazing at getting the fire started. Even the first time we came up here, he had made a roaring blaze in minutes. He had tried to teach me once, but all I had managed to do was burn my fingers with his book of matches.

"1...2...3...4...5...6..."

"Why are you counting?" Wyn interrupted me.

"To see how long it takes Ryland to light the fire. Watch." We both turned toward him just as a blaze ignited in the pit.

Wyn's eyes widened in surprise and her mouth formed a giant O.

"How'd I do?" Ryland asked, wiping his hands on his expensive slacks.

"I don't know. I lost count," I admitted.

"Oh, great." His sarcastic voice echoed through the clearing. "Now how am I supposed to know if I beat my record?"

"What's the record?"

"Twelve seconds," I answered Wyn, causing her jaw to drop even further.

"Can you do magic or something, because that was wickedly fast."

Ryland balked at her question, his face falling pale to a ghostly shade of white like he had been caught at something.

"Ummm, no. I just like to light things on fire." He shook his curls, his uncomfortable face disappearing so fast I wasn't even sure if I had seen it.

"Too bad, that would be way cool if you could. You could pretend to fly and make things disappear!"

Ryland laughed at her. I guess magic wasn't cool to him. Then again, I couldn't see Ryland pulling rabbits out of hats with much flair.

"Well, for losing count, Jos, you owe me a race." Ryland leaned close to me, his face full of eager anticipation.

"You're on," I answered him, already standing tall; trying to meet him at his full height, which only brought me to his shoulders. I tried to look intimidating by squaring my shoulders, but it looked rather silly, and both Ryland and Wyn laughed at my poor attempt to psych him out.

"Oh, fine," I said, giving in and grabbing Wyn's hand to pull her over to the line of trees that surrounded the clearing. "You can play referee."

"You gonna cheat, Jos?" Ryland asked as he took his place at the tree next to mine, stretching his arms out in preparation.

"Nope, I am going to win." I gave him my biggest smile and then looked up to the tall branches above me. I knew I had a problem. Although I loved the feel and the smell of Ryland's sweater, it was way too big to be effective during a tree-climbing race.

"Oh, great," I mumbled.

"Losing confidence, Joclyn?" His taunts were pointless; he hadn't beaten me since the first time we had tried this.

"No, but I swear you're going to be in big trouble if I rip any of my clothes." I shed the large sweater and let it fall in a heap at my feet. I looked down to make sure my green shirt was lying flat before looking to Ryland who had fixed this strange look of happiness on his face.

"I like that shirt, Joclyn; it looks very pretty on you," Wyn said sincerely.

I turned to her and smiled in thanks. She gave me a big thumbs-up, which made me smile more.

"Don't worry, Jos. If you tear any clothes, I'll just buy you new stuff. I still owe you a pair of pants anyway; we'll have to go shopping."

"You wouldn't owe me anything if you would stop ripping my clothes off, Ryland."

Ryland's face blanched before spreading into a wide grin. Wyn laughed behind me. It took a moment for the reality of what I had just said to click into place.

"No! I didn't mean it like that." I rounded on Wyn, silently pleading, but she didn't even see me through the tears of laughter that rolled down her cheeks. "Ryland, tell her! Tell her you don't rip my clothes off!" All my pleading was for naught, even Ryland laughed gleefully.

"All right, Wyn," I yelled over their laughter, thankfully they stopped. "You tell us when to go. First feet to hit the ground again wins." She nodded in agreement, wiping the tears from her face.

I looked to Ryland, who winked at me before turning to his tree, still chuckling. My stomach twisted, whether with joy or nerves, I couldn't tell. I turned and faced my tree, nonetheless, stretching my fingers in excitement.

"On your mark," Wyn said. "Get set. Go!"

I lunged toward the tree, my hands pulling me up into the tangle of lower branches. The second my hands touched the bark, a fire ignited in my veins. A strange energy surged under my skin as I vaulted up the tree, propelling myself higher and higher. The familiar feeling of flying took over me as I moved up, my arms propelling me faster and faster.

I looked to the side to see Ryland keeping pace with me, although still behind. I grabbed the next branch and pulled myself up even higher, my legs kicking off to raise me up. I didn't look down. I wasn't afraid of heights, but I knew we were at least twenty feet up in the air now. I could see the deep notch we had placed in the tree all those years ago and knew it was almost time to make my descent.

"Goal!" I yelled as I pressed my palm to the large gash in the tree before twisting to speed my way down the tree.

"Goal!" Ryland yelled from above me.

If I was fast climbing up trees, it was nothing to how fast I was going down. I knew Ryland didn't have a prayer. There was a movie I had watched when I was a kid, that had a man and boy climbing out of a tree as a car fell down on top of them. They swung and jumped and leaped in their frantic attempt to beat the car out of the tree and not be crushed to death. It had scared me senseless at the time; but in all reality, that's how I felt when I climbed down trees.

I continued to drop, not bothering to look at where Ry was. Branches flew past me as I swung from one to another, dropping a few feet only to catch myself on a large outstretched branch at the last moment.

I released the branch that I had just grabbed, prepared to fall to another one a few feet below me. I realized moments after I let go that I was going to overshoot and miss the branch I was aiming for. I looked down; there was still another ten feet to the ground. Wyn cried out in fear, which broke my concentration.

Crap!

I pushed Wyn's panic from my mind as I twisted in the air to grab a branch that was next to me. I knew my timing was off and my leg slammed into the tree. A small branch poked into my skin through my pants, sending pain radiating over my skin. I ignored it and continued my descent, reaching for another branch below me, the twig ground against the skin on my calf as it ripped through my pants. Great.

I grabbed the last branch before swinging my legs down and let go of the tree, my burst of energy dissipating as I released the tree branch and dropped to the ground to pull my leg around to inspect the cut. My skin was slightly scraped, barely even bleeding. My pants, on the other hand, were a lost cause. The fabric was cut from my knee all the way down to the hem.

"Oh, my gosh! Joclyn, that was amazing!" Wyn came up right beside me, her voice bathed in awe.

"You think so?" It seemed so natural to me; to hear it described as amazing was kind of odd. I heard Ryland drop to the ground and make his way over to us.

"Yes!" Wyn squealed. "And, when you almost fell, I thought my heart was going to stop."

"You almost fell?" Ryland asked with something beyond alarm in his voice.

"Yes! She dropped from one branch to another, but missed the one she wanted, so she kind of twisted around to catch a different one. I was so scared." Wyn provided actions and everything like she was retelling the plot to an exciting action movie.

"Are you okay?" Ryland asked, looking me over.

I ignored his appraisal and pulled the hoodie back over my head. It was then he saw my ripped jeans and the long scratch, his sharp intake of breath was a little exaggerated for the situation.

"It's a scratch, Ry," I said as he once again swept me up in his arms and carried me to a rock in front of the fire. "You're being ridiculous."

"I guess I owe you a new pair of pants," he sighed as he inspected the rip and the cut.

"Two," I reminded him.

Wyn plopped down on the rock next to mine and mouthed the word "boyfriend" with heavy exaggeration.

I scowled at her before turning my attention back to Ryland.

"Does it hurt much? We can go if we need to." His concern was evident in his voice.

"I'm not a baby, Ry. I'm fine," I responded a little too loudly. I wasn't in the mood to be carried through the woods for twenty minutes. "I just need pie," I provided at Ryland's affronted look which turned into a wide grin.

"Boyfriend," Wyn whispered as Ryland went to the other side of the fire to grab the pie.

"Will you knock it off?" I hissed between my teeth as Ryland sat on the ground between us, opening the top of the box that held the delicious chocolate crème pie and about five plastic forks. This was one of those times when his 'grab a fistful' system worked to our benefit. I dove in, and smiled as the chocolate mousse hit my tongue. Mette made the best pies.

"So," Wyn began and I glared at her, terrified that she was going to start the boyfriend crap again with Ryland right in front of us. "How long have you guys been doing that tree-climbing thing? You both moved so fast; I couldn't believe it." I sighed in relief. At least this was something we could talk about.

"I think the first time we went up the trees was the first time we came up here. I was ten and you were twelve, right?" I asked Ryland who swallowed his bite of pie to answer.

"Yep. Two days after your tenth birthday. We stole Father's Vanquish and came up here. I don't think I'll ever forget that; it was the only time I have ever been able to beat you."

"You stole a car?" Wyn shrieked with her mouth full of pie.

I couldn't help but laugh.

"Yep." Ryland puffed his chest out proudly. "I had to sit on a phone book and could barely see out the window, so Joclyn had to steer most of the way."

I shook my head in irritation. I knew why Ryland was exaggerating. While I had driven most of the way—and been terrified, I might add—it wasn't because he couldn't see out the windshield; it was because he had been crying.

That day had been one of the first days that Edmund had ordered Ryland to leave me alone. They had gotten into a fight and his father had hit him. He had run into the kitchen and pulled me with him into the large garage. We had left before anyone had even realized we were both missing. I still remember the bright red handprint on his cheek.

Without thinking, I reached out and ran my fingers through his dark curls near the base of his neck, wanting to wipe the memory from both our minds. He turned toward me and smiled, his gaze piercing into me.

"And you didn't crash the car?" Wyn asked, oblivious to our exchange.

"Well, we did," I provided, "but not that time. They didn't know we were taking the car for about a year."

"Jake was very nice to keep that secret for us." Ryland forced a laugh.

"Jake?"

"The butler," I provided.

"So... when you crashed the car...?" Wyn prompted.

"We more like cruised into a field..."

"And hit a cow," Ryland finished for me. We both laughed at saying it out loud.

"And you didn't get in trouble?"

"Oh, we got in trouble," Ryland answered. "I was confined to my room for a week."

It probably wasn't even worth mentioning that I had been grounded to school, my house, or the kitchen for a month. Even after Ryland was 'released', I was still doomed to play fort under the staff table.

"Your father doesn't seem to be very hard on you; a week for crashing a car. I wish I was so lucky. My brother is ruthless."

"Oh, he punishes me, just not in the regular sense. He always expects me to be perfect, and accomplished, and make no mistakes." Ryland sounded so bitter and hurt. His father had always put him under so much pressure; I was constantly amazed he handled it so well.

"I guess it makes sense, seeing as he is raising you to run an empire." Wyn's logic made sense, but it was something we had talked through many times before. As much as Ryland wished to live up to his father's expectations, as much as he wished to meet his father's approval, Ryland still struggled.

"I don't want to run his company," Ryland said dejectedly.

"What?" I flipped around to look at him, but he took another bite of pie, keeping his gaze down. He had never made mention of this to me before; it was always how he looked forward to becoming like his father. I looked up at Wyn who had a strange look of shock and surprise plastered on her face.

"I don't want to run his empire. I don't want to go to Oxford. I don't want to take his lessons. I don't want to be anything like him." He had turned to me, speaking only to me. I am sure Wyn heard him, but he didn't seem to notice or care.

"Ryland?" I asked.

"But I don't have a choice; I have to be everything he wants, and nothing that I wish." He looked so sad, so dejected; my heart broke in half for him. "I want to be good."

"Oh, Ryland. Don't you realize you already are?"

I lunged into him, wrapping my arms around his neck, burying my face into the sweet smell of his skin. He held me against him, his large hands spreading their warmth throughout my back where they pressed against me. I tangled my hands through his curls as he held me tighter.

Right at that moment, I was grateful to have Wyn there, her eyes boring into us. Because, right then, I would have been the one to kiss him first.

CHAPTER 20
JOCLYN

I stood about fifteen feet away from the fire, trying to convince myself this wasn't the stupidest thing I had ever done.

Wyn had assured me that fifteen feet was enough space to give me a running start. That was part of the problem. After Wyn had displayed her running feat and heroic jump over the fire, she and Ryland had spent the next twenty minutes taking turns leaping over the flames with decreasing running distances. They now insisted it was my turn, but my stomach was flipping and my hands were sweating. I was not interested in this weird jump-to-my-death.

"You're making this out to be much more difficult than it is," Wyn whined. I had been stalling for the last few minutes, and although most of it had been spent giggling about my lack of nerves, Wyn had run out of patience.

"I've never done this before," I spouted back. "It's kind of scary."

Ryland gave me a small, sympathetic smile, but Wyn jumped off her rock and walked over to me, a mischievous grin on her face.

"Okay," she started, about eight feet from me. "You climb trees like you were born in one and fall thirty feet to your death without even—"

"It was about five feet, Wyn, and I didn't die. Stop exaggerating," I interrupted her.

"Fine. But, you still *could* have died," Wyn said.

Ryland chuckled behind her, which seemed to only fuel her fire.

"Either way, you're a tree-climbing genius! This should be a piece of cake."

"A tree can't burn me," I countered.

"But it can cut you and scrape you, and rip your clothes and break your bones," Wyn countered, motioning to the large rip in my jeans.

"But those heal." She had backed me into a hole and I didn't like it.

"Burns heal."

She was right, but it didn't mean that I wanted to jump over the fire anyway. I plunged my hands into the pockets of Ry's hoodie and hunched my shoulders.

"Not without scars," I added.

Wyn leaned in close and lowered her voice, "You don't want Ryland to think you're a chicken, do you?" she asked, her eyebrows wagging.

I just sighed at her. It almost wasn't even worth it to try to convince her I didn't care what Ry thought—because I did.

We both jumped when Ryland himself placed one of his large hands on Wyn's shoulder to get her attention.

"I think I can take it from here," Ryland said softly, dismissing Wyn with his sly smile.

Wyn seemed caught in headlights for a minute; I could tell when her brain clicked back into action and she slinked back to her rock without a word.

Ryland turned his gorgeous stare on me, and my blood melted into my toes. Shock must have shown on my face because he smiled at my reaction, his straight white teeth glimmering in the firelight.

Just a friend, just a friend...

"Do you want to do this?" Ryland asked me, his voice soft.

"No," I said, "but, Wyn will never let me live it down if I don't."

"You know we have done some crazy things, and you choose to get scared over jumping over a fire?"

"Yep."

"Breaking into an abandoned hospital?"

"Not terrifying," I said. We had done that last year; even got chased out of the building by a decrepit security officer.

"Cliff diving?"

"Not terrifying." It didn't miss my notice that he was moving closer with each question.

"Driving a car at ten?"

"Nope."

"But jumping over a fire?" He reached out and grabbed both my hands, intertwining our fingers. Even with the size difference in our hands, holding onto him like this was still comfortable. "Do you remember the first time we raced up the trees?" Ryland asked me, his thumb tracing comfortable circles onto the back of my hand.

"The time you beat me?"

"Yeah. You were so scared. I had to prompt you to climb all the way up and then coax you all the way down while you cried."

"I didn't cry," I said. Well, maybe one tear had leaked out at the time, but it still didn't count as crying.

"The point is, after you got your feet back down on the ground, you realized how much you loved it. I haven't been able to beat you since."

I looked into his face for much longer than necessary. The firelight flickered in his dark hair and against his tanned skin, casting the light into weird mesmerizing shadows. He reached up to trace his fingertip along the chain of his necklace that hung around my neck, sending a pleasant shiver over me that caused him to smile.

"I'll jump with you," he whispered down to me.

I turned from him to look at the fire and tried to convince myself I was being stupid. Ryland's thumb continued to caress wide circles on my hand. His hand began to radiate the gentle heat that I was so familiar with; it filled me, traveling up my arm and through my body until I was filled with warmth that made me feel both comfortable and confident. Ryland's smiling eyes met mine as I looked up at him.

"One," his silky voice smooth and even, "two, three."

Our feet took off running in succession, his pace slower so as not to surpass me. As we reached the fire pit, we both took off in a flying leap and I closed my eyes. My heart fluttered as the air moved past me. For a fleeting moment, I felt like I was flying. I wanted the feeling to last forever.

My feet made contact with the hard-packed dirt and I stumbled on the landing. Ryland righted me, placing his hands on my arms to steady me.

"You okay?"

"Yeah," I responded in a hyper voice.

"See? It's easier than you thought it was." He smiled at me before planting a swift kiss on my forehead and walking away toward Wyn. "And, that's how it's done."

I had a momentary flash of frustration at being used as a pawn between them, but the irritation dwindled as the warmth from Ryland's kiss spread over me.

We left soon after that, leaving large amounts of dirt on the fire to extinguish it. We tromped through the forest in anything but silence. Wyn and Ryland jumped and pranced through the forest, singing various Styx songs I had never heard before. Their loud, out-of-key voices echoed off the trees, making it sound like the forest was filled with a cheap Styx cover band. They kept rushing up to me at different times, grabbing my hands in a desperate attempt to get me to sing along. Their bad singing had me in stitches, and it was all I could do to tromp through the underbrush without falling on my face.

We broke through the tree line to the side of the highway where Ryland had parked his Lotus. The alarm twittered in welcome as Ry approached it and inspected every inch for scratches or a break-in. I smiled as he caressed the hood in grateful appreciation at finding nothing. His affection for his car was a fine, debatable line between uncomfortable obsession and a deep love. Ryland seemed to read my mind and glared at me, his falsely affronted look deepening my chuckle into a laugh.

We all piled in, Wyn stretching herself horizontally on the storage shelf that Ryland liked to pretend was a backseat. Ryland sped down the mountain doing at least ten over the speed limit. He put on an oldies station, in obvious tribute to their romp in the woods, and Wyn lay back to text on her cell phone again. I still wasn't sure what to say to Ryland yet, so I turned my head to look out the window, letting the song about some horse in the desert fill the air.

Ryland drummed his fingers to the music as he whispered the lyrics to the song. I fought the temptation to look at him; any conversation we could have would be forced with Wyn in the back seat anyway. Ryland had been acting out of the ordinary all night, and I don't think it was just because Wyn was here either.

He had always wanted to grow up and be just like his father; no matter how much the man had hurt him or dictated to him. It was always his greatest ambition to make his father proud. They butted heads and fought, but Ry had always sought his approval, except when it came to me. To have him say that he wanted no part of it made me wonder what had happened between them. I desperately hoped I didn't have anything to do with it; I didn't know if I wanted to be responsible for him throwing his life away, and severing his relationship with his father.

Of course, the first odd comment he had made had been back at the school. I still wasn't quite sure what he had meant, saying that I was more important than his father's rules. I could take a wild guess and make the assumption my heart wanted me to, but that was foolish. I had a sinking sensation that all of his revelations tonight were connected somehow. Part of me couldn't wait until Saturday night to find out what was going on with him. I needed to make sure everything was okay.

Before I knew it, we were winding down the canyon into the suburb where Wyn and I lived. I glanced up from the blackness of the window to look at the lights, their twinkling and shining dots looking like a million stars that had fallen from the sky.

Ryland reached out, grabbed my hand and squeezed, the action pulling me away from the lights. His eyes had a million questions behind them, a million thoughts, and a million words. I was lost in them, trying to figure out what he wanted to say to me.

He turned back to the road, his hand remaining around mine, keeping them both in my lap. Before I could stop myself, my fingertips had moved forward to trace the lines of our intertwined hands. My touch shocked him and he shivered, giving me a knowing glance. I looked away from him and down to continue running my fingertips over his skin.

"So, Wyn, where to?"

I looked up to Ryland as his loud voice boomed through the quiet car. My mind froze in place. I hadn't thought about the time between Wyn's house and my own. I was doomed. Luckily, Wyn came to my rescue.

"My brother is picking me up at Joclyn's place," she said, her eyes never leaving her phone.

I saw Ryland's shoulders drop, while my heart eased just a bit. I wasn't ready to talk yet.

Ryland squeezed my hand, conveying some form of sorrow that I wasn't sure I reciprocated. In just a few minutes, he pulled into one of the few empty stalls at my apartment building. I looked up to the third floor where the obvious flicker of a television lit up the windows to my apartment. Ryland reluctantly let go of my hand as I exited so Wyn could climb out behind me.

"I'll see you tomorrow?" Ryland asked. Suddenly, I was relieved I had already made plans.

"Actually, I'll be at Wyn's house all night." My heart almost broke as his face fell.

I took off his hoodie and handed it back to him.

"What's this for?" he asked.

"My mom won't let me come over Saturday night if I walk in wearing a hoodie."

Ryland smiled in understanding as he took the jacket from my hands.

"Then, I will see you tomorrow morning." He smiled before bidding Wyn goodbye and sped off, leaving us staring after him.

Moments after he drove away, Wyn's brother pulled up in a sleek black Mazda, his body stiff and tough, as if willing himself to only look straight ahead and not toward us.

"I changed my mind," Wyn said as she climbed into the car.

"What?" I asked.

"He's not your boyfriend; he's your true love." She smiled before Ilyan drove off, her door not even closed all the way.

All I could do was look after her, knowing full well my heart was beating erratically in my chest.

CHAPTER 21
WYN

"He's not her true love," Ilyan growled as he pulled away, his eyes focused forward, jaw tight. I could feel his anger twisting through the air and I sat back. I knew when it was dangerous to poke the bear. Half the time I still did, at least I had the good sense not to do so this time.

Although, I had no idea why this bear was getting poked in the first place. This entire mission had him on edge. Even from the moment he showed up at my rooms in the middle of the night, he was on edge. Nervous. Dare I say desperate.

The way he was reacting now, the weight of his magic so heavy in the car I was sure I could swim in it, it wasn't like him.

"I'm playing a role, My Lord," I said, making sure to use his title correctly as I watched him, his long fingers curling and flexing around the steering wheel.

"I understand that," he said, darkness clanging in his voice as he sped up, the headlights of the car flashing over dark streets and houses as he steered the car toward our make-believe house. "So, tell me what you saw."

"Ryland loves her," I admitted quietly, watching him closely for another volatile reaction. "And he said he doesn't want to be like his father. I think, with how he was acting, that is partially because of her." It was probably also because his father was a warmongering monster who engaged in genocide on more than one occasion, but if Jos had helped him see that I was going to take it.

"Can we get him out?" His voice relaxed slightly, even if nothing else in him did.

Luckily, this time I had good news.

"I think we can get them both out, if we are careful." Careful enough that my father and brother didn't find out I was here, or that Edmund didn't find out Ilyan was here. If they caught wind of him again that alone would take any chance of this working out the window. Edmund would send every last Trpaslíks to retrieve him. We would have no chance to retrieve any of them if that happened.

I didn't need to say any of that, however, he already knew.

"I've already made contact, so that part will be easy. How long will it take you to set up an escape route? I know Talon has already been working on one." It was true, if only because he did every time I was out on some errand. He didn't want me to get trapped again, and so he always built more than one escape route into any plan. I wouldn't be surprised if he wasn't already running the guard through more of their paces, just in case we needed a rescue. He should have already moved everyone to the safe house that was near here as a precaution.

"Not long, I'm not as familiar with this area as I once was--" He stopped talking abruptly, the car going from slowing down before turning into the parking garage before our apartment to speeding away down the pitch black street.

"What?" I asked, twisting in my seat to the entry to the underground garage. I half expected Cail to be standing there with his demonic smile of his. There was nothing but a flickering street light and a few parked cars.

I felt it before Ilyan could respond.

A dark web of magic hung through the air like invisible piano wire, a crisscrossed trap. I recognized the mutated force of it immediately, Trpaslík magic but straight from the depth of the underworld.

"Cail." Just saying his name brought as much panic as though I had seen him standing there.

"He's found us?" My heart was in my toes as I said it, my blood already flaring in preparation for a fight. Ilyan pressed his foot into the accelerator, forcing the car to dart one way, then another. The air was practically shimmering as the car flew through darkened streets, his magic flaring from him as he counteracted whatever magic Cail had left behind to track us.

"I don't think so," he said after a minute. "Every complex in the city has been trapped. He knows we are here, he just doesn't know where we are hiding."

"He was always a bastard. Should we weed him out?" That would mean the end of our mission, and we weren't ready yet, especially if there was a chance we could get Ryland out too.

"Not if we want to go home empty handed." Ilyan was firm, I nodded, already knowing what was coming. The fight wasn't here yet, but it would be. "I need you to shield us, Wynifred. We need to get home, and then I'll set some bait. But first, get him off our trail.

"What if he senses my magic?" I knew he would, even a shield would leave traces of the fire in my veins, and he would know exactly who was here as Ilyan's guard.

"Then he knows you are here. If we are lucky it will do little more than drive him wild."

I nodded in understanding, my body swaying as the car changed lanes at a speed that was clearly over the speed limit. Laying back against the chair, I stared at my reflection in the dark glass, the air shimmering as I released the hold my magic had on my skin, Ilyan's own magic that he had used to shield me and hide the curse I carried falling away. The magic that had been used to cover the black marks on my right side of my body slid away, revealing the twisted curls of the curse that Cail had branded into my skin when I had been exiled from the Trpaslíks and left for dead. The dratted things came into focus as I stared at myself, the long dark lines of black covered the entire right side of my body like a rotting tattoo.

Just as they had for the last hundred or so years.

Ilyan turned a corner, this street darker and thankfully void of cars. It was only us as we drove along, the sleek black vehicle reflected in the windows on the store fronts beside us.

My body grew warm as I focused, releasing all of the power that I had focused inside of me so intently for the last few days in an attempt to keep myself hidden. The flame of my magic flew out of me in a rush, the power strong that I was sure it would burn Cail's traps away before he would be able to track us. If he could see us.

One stretch of my magic, and our car had disappeared.

"Good girl," Ilyan said, still focused ahead as he began to weave the invisible car through the thankfully empty streets. "Now bind it."

He didn't need to tell me twice. I didn't want Cail finding us just as much as he did. With the traps that Cail had sent burned away I set my own, not just to stop him from setting any more, but to burn him in warning if he tried. Then, with a tug of the fire that burned against my soul I wrapped and bound it together in an attempt to keep the source of the magic hidden.

He would know who had set it, no matter how hard I tried to bind the magic, but at least the bind would slow him down.

As though he sensed my power twist through the streets in a web of shields that would take Cail more than his dark magic to break, Ilyan turned our car back toward the complex. The roads were as dark as the car as we drove underground and into one of the many open spots rather than to our assigned space. As much practice as I had, I knew how strong Cail was, he would break the bind and possibly find us sooner than we liked. The less links we left to our actual whereabouts the better.

Moving like silent assassins, Ilyan and I kept ourselves under my strong shield, our bodies invisible to view until we had closed the door to our apartment behind us. We didn't bother to lock the door, we both knew how useless it was. We just moved from corner to corner of each room. Checking the shields that we had put in place on our very first night here. Checking that the protective stones Ilyan had placed there were untouched.

We were safe. But one look at Ilyan and I knew how dire this was.

"We are out of time," I said, he nodded his head once. "Do you think they know you are here?"

"I don’t see why he would set such a wide trap if he didn’t. But if they do, and they realize you are here with me, they are going to put two and two together and realize that the Silnŷ is close."

If they hadn’t already it would be a miracle.

"We need to move this weekend," Ilyan said, moving to the door and running his hands over it, a glittering shield of white following the motion. “Can you get them both here?"

“Here to this apartment?” I asked, he nodded. I knew they had something planned tomorrow night, but if we planned for the next morning we could get everything in place and possibly get everyone out without Cail noticing.

I grit my teeth, it wasn’t an ideal plan, but it wasn't like we had another option.

“Just don’t try to help this time, okay? I’m still amazed she bought that story about you doing a dissertation.”

“If that is what amazed you, then you have underestimated her power, Wynifred.” Ilyan gave me a smile before he retreated to his room, whistling some song the whole way. At least the stress of our near discovery had dissipated.

Well, for him at least.

My skin still felt like it was crawling as I stared at him. He wasn't wrong. He had been shielded the entire time he had been following her around the school. She shouldn't have been able to see him at all.

CHAPTER 22
JOCLYN

N*ight of the Living Vampire* turned out to be just as horrible and sucky as promised. It was full of teenage humor that mocked the vampire craze with a nice splattering of cheesy gore thrown in. Wyn and I sat on the long couch in her living room with a bowl of popcorn in between us, while Ilyan occupied the overstuffed lounge chair. He was trying very hard not to laugh at the stupid jokes and dirty humor, but every once in a while a laugh escaped anyway, which sent my own hidden giggles into overdrive. Wyn chose to glare at both of us.

I pulled my hands into Ryland's bright blue hoodie that he had dropped off at school for me that morning and sank into the couch to watch the final fight scene of the movie. The lead vampire was running across a clearing after some girl he thought he was in love with; but instead, he decided she would make a better lunch. The whole thing was so over-the-top, it was ridiculous.

"Last minute, he decides not to eat her because he loves her, and they run away from the vampire horde together to live happily ever after." Ilyan's voice was flat, his accent rolling delightfully.

"Ilyan!" Wyn shrieked, her hands going in the air. "You're ruining it."

"How am I ruining it? These things are so predictable. Besides, don't you want them to end up together?"

"Well, yes. But, I wanted to discover that for myself!"

Ilyan just sighed at his little sister.

"Joclyn," Wyn whined at me, "don't you agree?"

"I'm sorry, Wyn, but Ilyan is right. It is pretty predictable."

Wyn huffed, folded her arms and faced the television just as the vampire took the human girl in his arms and proclaimed his love for her. Wyn just pouted and huffed again.

"This should be romantic, but you guys totally ruined it for me."

Ilyan and I laughed together, drowning out the vampire's declaration of love. Wyn huffed more and rewound it so we had to sit through the whole ending over again.

"I'm going to go order some Chinese food," Ilyan grumbled as he headed for the kitchen. Part of me was jealous he had an excuse to get away from the mush I had to endure.

Wyn had her hands clasped together as she leaned forward, her face glossed over. I sighed as the credits finally began to roll again, and Wyn leaned back with a tear-streaked face.

Oh, bother.

"Wasn't that so beautiful?"

"Not really."

She looked at me like I had skinned her cat.

"I don't get into this stuff, Wyn," I amended to make her feel a bit better.

"But it was funny, and scary and gory, and romantic. It had something for everyone!"

I chose not to reply to her; the whole movie was just silly.

"What kind of movies do you like then?" she asked in slight frustration.

"Sci-fi, super-hero, action and spy movies," I rattled off, knowing full well I had just listed all of Ryland's favorites. If she had asked me what my favorite video game was, however, I could have spouted off half-a-dozen racing games that I knew I enjoyed on my own. Ryland didn't like to lose.

"Super-heroes?" she said.

"Yes! They are brave and fight bad guys, and tend to look very nice," I said, fighting the blush that was rising to my cheeks.

"A woman after my own heart," Ilyan said as he fell back into his chair. "Which one is your favorite? I'm a Superman fan, personally."

"Iron Man."

"Really?" Ilyan asked, eyebrows lifting. "I wouldn't have pegged you for a Robert Downey, Junior fan, or is it the comic books you prefer."

"Ugh. You don't read comic books, do you?" Wyn grumbled at me in feigned horror, she sounded disgusted, but a smile still managed to creep onto her face.

"No," I said. Although Ryland had quite a collection, I had never touched them. "And, I don't think it's a Robert Downey, Junior thing. I think it's just the fact that he takes something difficult and something that could destroy him, and makes it into something amazing."

Ilyan looked at me with something akin to reverence, while Wyn stared me down with a knowing glance.

"It doesn't have to define you, you know."

I flushed at Wyn's comment, looking from brother to sister in panic. She had promised she wouldn't talk about the mark again. Luckily, Ilyan looked confused and had no idea what Wyn was referring to.

"Wyn," I begged, my heart thudding, "please don't."

Wyn huffed and sat back on the couch.

"Do I even want to ask?" Ilyan said.

"No." I buried my head in the sleeves of Ryland's sweater. Thankfully, the doorbell rang and Ilyan left to get the Chinese food.

"Wyn," I rounded on her the second Ilyan's footsteps left the room, "please don't bring this up. You promised."

"I don't know what you're talking about," she said stubbornly, spinning her plastic bracelets.

"Kung pow chicken, anyone?" Ilyan said, handing out white containers.

I opened my box of Mongolian Beef and dug in; it smelled and tasted so good.

Wyn kept switching from staring at me to eating her food. Ilyan looked between us before flipping on another movie. I laughed out loud when he turned on *Iron Man 2*. Ilyan winked at me before turning back to his food.

"Ugh, really, Ilyan? You're going to make me sit through this?" Wyn whined more around her brother than I had ever heard.

"Well, we could talk, but you seemed quite content to be angry and stare off into space."

Wyn glared at him and went back to her food.

"I apologize for my sister," Ilyan began with an oddly regal air. "She can be quite stubborn at times."

Wyn sighed deeper at him. I laughed at her; she seemed irritated by him, and that alone was quite entertaining.

"So, Ilyan. Where do you get your accent from?"

He raised an eyebrow at me in obvious confusion.

"Seeing as Wyn doesn't have one... It's just odd. That's all."

"Oh!" Ilyan chimed, realization dawning on his face. "I lived in Prague for quite a few years before our father died. I left so I could help raise my sister." While he didn't sound sad because of the situation, there was something else in his voice that made the entire thing sound practiced.

"Wow. Prague. That must have been amazing."

Ilyan opened his mouth to respond, but Wyn's sharp tongue cut him off. "Don't let him fool you. It was all party-party, very little work."

"Work?" I questioned. "You must be quite a bit older than Wyn to have lived and worked there." I thought I had stated something obvious, but Wyn giggled like I had given a lead-in to some inside joke.

"Not really," Wyn provided. "His mother still lives there. Our dad just got around a lot."

"I was born in Prague in the 80s."

"So, still too old for you," Wyn taunted.

My head snapped to Ilyan who winked at me again.

"Oh! I didn't mean it like that!" I said, embarrassment creeping into my face.

"Neither did I, Joclyn," Ilyan said. "Don't worry so much."

I ducked back down to my Mongolian beef and tried to focus on the movie. Even though I had seen it a million times, it was still one of my favorites.

"You need to be nice to her, Ilyan; she's my friend, and if you scare her away, I'll never forgive you."

"Fine, fine," he said "Ne že by na tom záleželo, stejně bude za chvíli bydlet s námi." The words fell off his tongue like diamonds and pearls. I looked over at him, taken by the beautiful sound. It seemed familiar, even though I had no idea what language it was.

"Ilyan," Wyn pleaded.

Ilyan gave her a grim smile and stood before walking down the hall to the bathroom.

"What language was that?"

"Czech; they speak it in Prague."

"It's beautiful," I sighed. "Do you understand it?"

"Enough to understand when he's being rude," Wyn said, still stabbing at her food.

I smiled and went back to the movie, sad that my food was almost gone. I would have to ask where they got this from; it was delicious.

Ilyan returned a moment later, and I excused myself to the bathroom.

The sun had gone down all the way now, and the first stars were beginning to twinkle from behind the frosted glass in the bathroom window. I sat down and grabbed the cell phone next to me without thinking. It wasn't until I opened it that I realized it wasn't mine.

The phone flicked open to a text conversation. The name "Wynifred" covered the top of the screen above the thought bubbles of the conversation.

'I think we are wrong about him'
'What do you mean?'
'Well, he says he wants nothing to do
with it, but it's more than that. He uses
kouzlo on her all the time to calm
her, help her, keep her safe. What
I thought was her is really him; it's
the residual that he leaves behind to
help her.'
'Are you sure?'
'100%'
'Hovno, tohle se Ovailia nebude líbit'
'Don't swear.'
'Respect, Wynifred'
'Sorry, My Lord.'

I looked at the last bit of conversation; it just didn't make sense. *My Lord*? And who were they talking about? The whole thing was too much like something out of a Bourne movie. Besides, they didn't seem like the types to be involved in some sort of role-playing game. I reluctantly looked away from the screen at a soft knock on the door.

"Joclyn," Ilyan spoke through the bathroom door, "I left my phone in there. Can you bring it out with you please?"

"Uh... yeah..." I answered, washing my hands before opening the door to see him standing against the door frame. His long, blonde hair hung straight and sleek around his face, his blue eyes sparkling, familiarly.

"Everything go okay in there?" he asked, hand outstretched.

"Gross, Ilyan," I chided and placed the phone in his hand.

"Thanks." He flipped the phone open to look at the screen before turning back to me with a smirk.

A smirk like that would usually excite me and send my stomach swooping, but then again, a smirk like that was usually accompanied by

Ryland. Coming from Ilyan, it made me curious; I felt like I needed to get to know him better. I shook the thought from my mind.

Ilyan crossed his arms over his chest as he continued to stare into me. I couldn't help but notice how nice his pastel dress shirt fit against him. He had a nice frame and the fabric clung to him in the right places. I could feel a blush rising to my cheeks, so I ducked my head to look at my shoes, unsurprised to see Ilyan sporting another pair of ripped, designer jeans. He must like the style.

"Do I need to leave you and your shoes alone?" Ilyan asked with a deep chuckle.

"No, I'm fine," I retorted, my head snapping up to meet his gaze.

"Well then, are you ready to go home? It's almost ten and I don't want you to get in trouble with your mom." He continued to lean against the door frame, trapping me in the bathroom.

"Yeah, I guess I better."

"Good, I'll go get my car," he said before jogging down the hall.

"Your brother is odd," I announced as I sat down on the couch beside Wyn.

"He's an idiot; don't let him fool you." She continued to bird peck at her food, not looking at me.

"Hey, Wyn," I ventured. I hoped this didn't give my spying away. "What does kouzlo mean?"

Her head snapped up in alarm, and her food almost slipped out of her hand. So much for being discreet.

"Where did you hear that word?"

I exhaled. Probably better to lie, even though Ilyan would give me away eventually.

"Just something Ilyan said to me in the hall."

She watched me, and I recognized the same look in her that I often had myself when I was talking about my dad. She was deciding how much of the truth to tell me.

"It's Czech," she said. "It means charm."

I guess that made sense. *He was using his charm on her all the time*; it fit anyway.

"Oh, that makes sense."

"What did he say to you?" Wyn asked, that same alarm lacing her voice.

"It's nothing. It was just an odd word, so I was wondering what it meant..." That seemed to pacify her, so I left it at that. Still. I knew that face; it gave me the nagging sensation that she wasn't being entirely truthful.

The sooner I got home and to a search engine, the better.

"Makes sense," she shrugged before rounding on me with a wide grin. "Hey, Ilyan is going to do some work thing this weekend, we should do this again. Maybe we can invite that hunk of a best friend of yours."

"Not my boyfriend, Wyn." She really wasn't going to drop it, which seemed fine with her with how she was grinning.

"Yeah, yeah. Just ask him, it'll be fun!" I knew she was right, besides, any excuse to see Ryland before I couldn't anymore was good to me.

I shook my head and Wyn got way too excited, if I didn't know she already had a boyfriend I would think she had a crush on Ryland.

I didn't like that one bit.

CHAPTER 23
JOCLYN

I had stayed up way too late last night trying to find the translation for "kouzlo" on the internet. The closest thing I found for a long time was "koza" which meant "goat". Why someone would give someone a goat to protect them, I didn't know. I finally found the translation I was looking for, and it did say that "kouzlo" meant "charm", but I still felt like Wyn was keeping something from me. After all, why would she have that reaction to the word charm?

Due to my prolonged internet searching, I was nowhere near ready when my mom burst into my bedroom the next morning, fully dressed, breakfast in hand, ready for our full day of shopping. She set the breakfast down and danced out of the room, saying she would wait for me in the living room.

I ate my breakfast—Fruit Loops and toast—as I tried to wake up. I had finally gotten to sleep at three a.m., and now my mom had me up at ten. Seven hours should have been enough, but I still felt like I was dragging.

I set my breakfast on the kitchen counter across from the bathroom and made my way to a nice, warm shower. The hot water did the trick, and after a few minutes my body felt alive and energetic.

I dressed in my red, birthday shirt and my only pair of jeans that weren't ripped before making my way to the mirror to figure out something to do with my hair. I slipped Ryland's necklace over my head and slid it into its normal place under my shirt.

I was reaching for my hairbrush when my eyes fell on the bright, purple bead. It looked so innocent just lying there on my dresser. I stared at it as something clicked in my mind. Kouzlo. Hadn't my father used that word in his letter?

I whipped around to look at the small wastebasket next to my dresser and cringed to see it empty, the letter long gone. My life was turning me into a lunatic. Crazy father, hopeless crushes, and bizarre foreign friends; no wonder I was losing it. I had made something out of nothing. I grabbed the bead and shoved it into my pocket before pulling my hair up in a half-ponytail, making sure to leave enough hair down to fall over my ears and cover the mark.

I blotted on some lip gloss, blush and a little bit too much eye shadow before leaving the bedroom and declaring myself ready. My mom turned off the TV and turned to face me. Cue the waterworks, she brought her hand to her mouth with a gasp, her eyes glossing over. Great, she was going to be crying all day.

"Mom," I said. I already felt out of place, and I didn't need to be cried over.

"Oh, honey," she said, "you are so pretty."

Her arms encompassed me in a big, motherly hug. I could feel her body shake as she leaked out tears of joy. I returned the hug, my arms hanging awkwardly on her back.

"Thank you," she whispered in my ear before pushing me away from her. "Forgive your blubbering mom, will you? I'm just a little bit excited to show off my beautiful daughter." She smiled before grabbing my hand and dragging me out the door.

We drove straight to the biggest mall in the city and wandered first into one of the few main department stores, much to my disappointment; I always enjoyed the smaller boutiques more. She led me straight to the misses department and began loading me up with graphic t-shirts and peasant tops. It was then that I realized what this trip was. I had been trapped in Dress-Up-Your-Daughter Day. I groaned, but hoped that I could finagle at least one pair of jeans out of her.

After I came out in my first shirt, I began to wonder if my mom was going to be able to turn off the waterworks at all today. She gushed at me in a bright, blue t-shirt emblazoned with Hello Kitty in camo gear on the front. Not the shirt that would be one to induce tears. I ran back into the dressing room and ripped the shirt off. It was cute, but I would never forget her crying over Hello Kitty-Goes-Army.

"Mom," I begged from behind the door, "you can't cry over everything I put on, please?"

"I know," her sniffles were breaking in her voice. "It's just... I have always waited for this day..."

"Mom..." I pleaded.

"I know. I'm sorry."

I tried to ignore her as I picked out my next shirt. I could hear her rummaging through her purse in the search for tissues.

"Oh! I almost forgot; Ryland sent this for you." Her hand appeared above the door, holding a small envelope.

I finished putting on an embellished tank top before reaching up to take the envelope from her. I ripped it open, trying to ignore the flip of my insides. A VISA gift card was inside, a small slip of heavy-weight paper resting against it. The paper that the card was attached to announced that there was an available balance of one thousand dollars. Leave it to Ry.

Please, ignore that this is a large amount of money.

I want to spoil you. Buy yourself a pair of pants (or two!) and at least one hoodie.

See you tonight ♥

I shouldn't have smiled, but I did; I couldn't help it. As a result, I exited the dressing room grinning like a madman. My mom took that to mean that I liked the shirt, and I just let her think that. It was a nice shirt, and I wasn't in the mood for a 'stay away from Ryland' lecture.

I was pushed from dressing room to dressing room as my mom shoved shirts, pants and even skirts and dresses in my direction. I took it all in stride; what else could I do? She was so happy, and seeing her smile was addicting. I paid for most of our purchases with Ryland's card, ignoring my mom's prying to find out how much he had given me; probably the equivalent of a week's salary, but I wasn't going to tell her that. She would freak out.

We came out of the last store before our lunch break, laden with bags of shirts, dresses, skirts, pants and jewelry. I had purchased more pants than I had ever owned before. Mom made out with more than enough to compliment her stingy wardrobe, and I had even convinced her to buy shoes that didn't have non-slip soles.

We sat down to food court pizza and soda, setting all the bags to the side of us.

"How's school?" Mom barraged into her monthly question-and-answer session. One of the *joys* of having a mother who worked so often that I never saw her was every once in a while she would start in on the standard twenty questions. It drove me crazy.

"Fine." I already knew my one word answer wouldn't do it.

"Did anyone say anything when you showed up without a sweater on?" She was eager, making me feel bad for deceiving her.

"Not really. I got looked at more than usual, but nothing big."

"Really?" she asked. "Any of them cute guys?"

"No, Mom. This isn't a good thing. I don't like being looked at; it makes me uncomfortable." I wanted to shiver at the thought.

"Well, one thing at a time, I suppose. At least we got you out of those hoodies." She smiled; I cringed at the thought of reminding her that the deal was up tonight. I let the thought fall.

"Sooo..."

Since this was going to keep going, I took another bite of pizza.

"Wyn's brother, he's quite the looker."

"Ew, Mom!" I cringed. "He's like ten years older than me or something."

"Really? He didn't look that old."

"Some people are blessed with good genes, I suppose."

"Hmmmm... Well, would it be considered cradle-robbing if I tried to hook up with him?" She grinned, so I knew she was kidding, but the thought still made me sick.

"Gross, Mom. I can't believe you even said that."

"Well, can you blame me? I am a tad bit lonely after all. I could use a—"

"Stop right there, Mom, please. Besides, I thought you were still in love with Dad."

Her face changed, her joyous smile slipping away to make room for an odd scowl. She looked almost, I don't know... mad.

"I am. And speaking of your father, why didn't you tell me that he sent you a letter?"

My face paled and my pizza crust dropped down to my plate. The empty trash can suddenly made sense; my mother never did household chores.

"I didn't want to upset you," I whispered.

"Well, at least I now know why you had such a hard time with it. Magic and cults... I wish your grandparents would have told me. I wish *you* would have told me. Maybe we could have gotten him some help."

"I know."

"I just don't know why you didn't tell me," she scolded again.

"I didn't want to hurt you," I explained.

"Ryland and I were so worried; I think we both could have helped you so much more if you had been honest."

I had been more honest with Ryland than with her, but I wasn't going to tell her that. I just nodded my head in agreement.

"That boy worries about you way too much. You should have heard him—"

"Mom," I cut her off, "why are you and Ry all of a sudden the best of friends?" She looked at me like I was being unreasonable. I didn't wait for her to reply; I just trudged on. "First, you tell me to stay away from him, and now you two are having heart-to-hearts in the kitchen."

"Well, we wouldn't be having heart-to-hearts in the kitchen if you hadn't been avoiding him all week." Her voice was calm and sweet, but her words still cut through me like a knife.

"You told me to!" I could feel myself getting hysterical. "You told me to go make other friends and start cutting Ryland."

"I was wrong." She spoke so softly I barely heard her.

"What?" I asked.

"I was wrong."

My head spun; my heart stopped beating. Was she saying what I thought she was saying? I didn't even dare to hope. My mind swirled in a steady beat of confusion.

"I don't understand," I admitted.

"It was something Ryland said the other day. I don't know; it just made sense." She paused and I held my breath, watching her in eager anticipation as she chewed her pizza.

"Oh, come on, Mom," I whined when I couldn't wait anymore. "Explain, please."

"Okay. He told me he has had to fight his father for everything he has ever wanted, and ever gotten. Nothing has ever been handed to him, with the exception of money, of course. But with all his fighting and bartering, he has never been happy. And he would give up everything just to be happy and live the way he wants to live. It made me realize how wrong I was to dictate your happiness. When I told you to stay away from Ryland, I had your best interest at heart, but I don't think that staying away from him can make you happy." She paused. "I was wrong for that; I apologize. Can you forgive me?"

I nodded.

"But what about Timothy and his threats?" I whispered.

"I just got spooked, Joclyn. He can't do anything to me," she said, leaning forward over the table like she was telling me a secret. "Besides, if he does fire me, I won't have any trouble finding a job. I've already received about four offers." She laughed and I joined in, although I wasn't laughing at her job hunting success; I laughed at my new opportunities.

I wasn't sure if this made everything easier or more complicated, but right at that moment, I didn't care. I could decide for myself. I could kiss Ryland, he could kiss me, or I could tell him to stay away from me forever. My heart soared away in endless joy. I wanted to run into his arms right at that moment. I wanted every single body-crushing fantasy to come true. At the moment, though, we still had manicures to complete.

I don't think I have talked to my mother so much in my whole life. I told her everything. With the odd permission I had just received, I didn't need to hold anything back. I told her how I felt about Ryland and how he made me feel when I was near him. I sighed as I explained the look he always got when he thought about something difficult. I cringed as I retold the story of the first time I came in contact with Timothy, a story she had never heard before.

I didn't have to lie. I didn't have to hide. My mom listened and laughed and sighed in all the right places. And when my toenails and fingernails were painted a shocking shade of pink and hers a bright yellow, we both began to cry as I thanked her for giving me such a wonderful, entertaining life and for letting me be who I wanted to be. It was a little bit of an odd thing to say, but it felt right, and so I didn't hold back.

Before I knew it, I had texted Ry to announce my arrival, and I sat in the car, waiting for him to make it out of the kitchen door in front of us. I couldn't back out now; the time with Ryland had come—the time I had been half-dreading and half-anticipating. Now, with my mother's blessing, I needed only anticipate. I didn't even care about Edmund and his opinion. There was only one thing for me to work out: was it worth risking a relationship in the possibility of finding true love? As he stepped out of the kitchen door, dark curls hanging low on his smiling face, my answer was clear. Yes. Yes, it was.

CHAPTER 24
JOCLYN

Ryland stepped right to the passenger side door. He opened it, letting the evening air and the fragrance of the rose bushes waft into the car. He leaned right in, his body hovering close to mine, so he could talk to my mom.

"Thanks for driving her here, Mrs. D."

"No problem, Ryland. Just make sure to have her home by midnight."

"You have my word. Home by midnight. Not harmed, scratched, or beaten. Perfect condition only." He held his hand up in the Boy Scout salute like he was making a vow to her then moved his head further in, stopping my progress out of the car.

"Oh, and, Mrs. Despain, thanks for everything." Ryland leaned even further into the car and pulled my mom to him, wrapping his arm around her shoulder. Her eyes grew wide before she registered what was happening and returned the hug.

This little moment brought a small, sad smile to my face. I had never met Ryland's mother, and we never talked about her. I had asked him about her once, a year or so after we had met. He had looked at me with this terrified face, threatening tears, so I had changed the subject. Even as we grew older it was something that we never discussed; so, to see him wrap his arms around a mother figure was heart-wrenching.

"Midnight," he repeated before moving out of the car and helping me out.

We both waved good-bye to my mom as she drove off, all of us with big, happy grins plastered to our faces. We watched the taillights disappear before Ryland grabbed my hand and intertwined our fingers and led me into the kitchen.

Dinner service had just gotten underway, so the kitchen was a crazed mess of activity. Even though Edmund would be dining alone tonight, he still demanded a full service be presented. Chantal, the cook who swung shifts with my mom, was calling out orders to the hassled staff who barely noticed our trek through the kitchen. We moved through the usual corridors and stairways, but when we were about to burst into the main hall that led to Ryland's room, Ryland stopped and pulled me behind him.

"I need you to do something for me," Ryland began, a mischievous smirk playing around the corners of his lips.

"Okay," I hesitated, curious.

"I need you to climb on my back."

"What?"

"Please, Jos. Timothy has been stalking this hall tonight, and I can move quicker if I carry you."

I nodded at him. Odd request, but, whatever. I moved behind him and placed my hands on his shoulders, unsure as to what to do next.

"Jump," Ryland prompted; so I did, my legs wrapping around his waist.

He moved my legs up a bit, wrapping my body even closer to his. His hands gripped my thighs as he ran down the hall. The door to his room opened the second we got there and closed behind us as Ryland shoved it shut with his foot. I moved to get down, but Ryland held my knees tighter.

"Wait."

I didn't move. My body stayed frozen on his back, waiting for something to happen, some sign that I could get down. His body tensed for just a moment before relaxing and releasing me. I found my feet, almost falling sideways into the large chaise lounge that sat by his door.

"You okay?" his voice strained as he fought a laugh.

"Yes. What was with that, Ry? You're acting like we're conducting espionage."

"Sometimes I feel like I am."

"Ryland LaRue, double O 4, Super-Secret Agent." I put my hands in a gun shape and aimed around his room until I landed my sights on him, only to find him smiling with that sexy smug grin of his.

I could see his intentions, and I was in trouble. I turned and ran as he did; him to the kitchen, me to the closet where the Nerf guns were hidden behind his shoes. I only hoped I was faster than he was. I took a flying leap, dive-bombing into the shopping mall of a closet and crawled on my belly to the Converse section. I threw the dozens of shoes to the side to find... nothing.

"What!" I yelled.

A monotonous chuckle sounded right behind me.

I flipped around, backing myself away from Ryland as he towered over me. It was no use; I had only moved three feet before his big hand wrapped around my ankle, pulling me out of the closet. The carpet rubbed against my back, grabbing my shirt and pulling it up to my bra-line. I tried to move it down, while desperately trying to keep my mark hidden. Why, of all days, did I not cover it with a Band-Aid?

Ryland had already dragged me back into the sitting area. His long legs straddled me as he looked down, his bright, blue eyes blazing.

"Thought you could get away from me, did you?"

"You stole my stock of guns, you menace! You wouldn't shoot a defenseless girl, would you?" I batted my eyelashes at him in a foolish and useless attempt to distract him.

"Your womanly wiles are no match for me," he laughed like a monotone villain as he pulled a bright, orange gun from behind his back. I cringed as he soaked me with stream after stream of freezing cold water. I sputtered and fought as he crouched closer to me, his body prohibiting mine from getting away.

"Mercy!" I screeched from behind a curtain of water. "Mercy!"

Ryland chuckled and wiped the water that was dripping from my face with the palm of his hand.

"That was mean, Ry. You moved my guns."

"Yeah, sorry about that." His voice seemed sincere, but he still hovered above me, biting his lip. He stayed there, above me, our eyes locking a bit too long. I felt my heart pulse.

"Can I get up now?" I asked, pulling my shirt back down to cover my exposed stomach.

"Yeah." Ryland moved away from me. A moment later, one of his white, fluffy towels landed on my face.

I sat up and began to wipe and blot at my face and clothes in an attempt to dry off. I moved my now damp hair around my ear, making sure everything that needed to be covered was.

"Where's the sweater I gave you?" he asked as he fiddled with the large entertainment center.

"I had to leave it in Ilyan's car last night, so my mom wouldn't flip."

Ryland froze, hand in the air as he began to shake. He looked as though he had seen a ghost when he turned around and took a frantic step toward me. The look on his face froze me in place on the floor.

"Who?" Why was he so angry?

"Ilyan. Wyn's brother," I said, my voice shaking. He was freaking me out.

Ryland relaxed a bit, but something still seemed off.

"He's a jerk, Ry. Like the epitome of a jerk older brother," I offered him the first explanation I could think of. Even though his reaction didn't fit with the protective crush theory I was going with.

Ryland studied me for a minute, his chest puffed and frozen in what...? Fear? Anger? I couldn't place it. Finally, he turned away from me, back to the entertainment center, and I made my way to the couch where a large chili cheeseburger sat waiting for me on the coffee table.

"Sorry, about that," Ryland said, his back still to me as he slid a DVD into the player. "I thought you were talking about someone else."

"It's okay, Ry. Don't worry about it." I looked at him, my heart still settling. Who in the world would incite that kind of reaction?

Ryland sat beside me as the movie started, already devouring his large burger. The title of the movie came up in bloody, red letters, right before scary music kicked in and the camera panned over a lake.

"*The Evil Dead*? How scary is this? You know I don't do scary, Ryland."

"I think it's more like over-the-top scary."

I still looked at him skeptically as some lady from the 70s began to sing a song.

"It's supposed to be funny."

"Okay, but if it gets too scary, we're turning it off."

Ryland nodded at me and went back to the movie.

It was scary. It was also just weird. I wasn't even sure what was going on. There was something about a book made out of human skin, and everyone kept turning into demons and trying to attack each other. And there was blood. Lots of fake, watery blood. By about halfway through, I ended up plastered next to Ryland, his arm wrapped around me as I kept hiding my face in the collar of his yellow polo shirt.

"It's over," Ryland crooned, his hand rubbing my back.

"That was cruel, Ry. You made me watch the entire thing." I didn't even want to move my head from his chest.

"Well, you didn't ask me to turn it off, either." My head vibrated as a deep chuckle moved through him.

I couldn't give a decent rebuttal. He was right; I hadn't asked him to turn it off. I just sighed and moved closer to him. In all honesty, I was comfortable, and I knew he had planned to watch that stupid movie for this exact reason. So what if he wasn't the only one who enjoyed it?

The minutes ticked by, but I didn't notice. Ryland's hand continued to trace the lines of my back, his heartbeat steady in my ear. The movie had returned to the menu, the light from the screen casting the room in a stagnant, blue glow.

"Can I ask you something?" I said, his hand still rubbing up and down my spine.

"Mmmhmmm?"

I heard his voice more as a vibration through his chest.

"Did you mean what you said?"

"I say a lot of things," he said, his voice almost a whisper.

"About not wanting to be like your father. About not wanting to run his company?"

He hesitated, and my body tensed. Was that not the right thing to ask him? I heard his heart rate accelerate and went to move away from him, but his strong arms held me in place.

"Yes, I meant it."

"But, you always wanted to be... I mean, you have always tried to be..." My words came out all jumbled. I paused; I wasn't sure how I wanted to say this.

"Growing up, yes, I always wanted to make him happy. I always wanted to become what he wanted me to be. In so many ways I didn't feel like I had a choice." His fingertips traced the skin at my neck before returning to my spine. My breath caught at the touch of his fingers against the nape of my neck; I could almost feel his smile at my reaction.

"What changed?" I asked.

"You have seen my father what... maybe a handful of times?"

I nodded in agreement.

"I see him every day of my life. He is a vicious, ruthless man, who uses people and throws them away, just to get what he wants. He used my mother to give him a son. He uses Timothy to make him powerful. He uses..." He stopped suddenly like he'd caught himself. "I don't want to be anything like him."

"Then what do you want to be?"

"I want to be good; I want to look back on my life and be proud of what I see and what I have done." His hand moved from my back to tangle through my hair, his fingers running down the long strands that fell down my back.

I felt my body tense for just a moment, but put it aside. I shouldn't be worried about a stupid mark right now.

"Well, that shouldn't be too hard. Just do it."

"I wish it was so easy."

"Why can't it be?" Our voices were whispers.

He paused. "I have to leave."

My hand tensed against his chest. *Leave?* What did he mean? Like leave the house, leave the state, leave the family? Where?

"Leave?" I asked in a panic, hoping for some clarification.

"Yes, leave. I don't know where to yet, but it has to be far away."

My heart felt like lead in my chest; a tense, un-beating mass, causing more pain than joy.

"I'm planning to tell him tomorrow. And, to be honest, I am terrified." He laughed to break the edge in his voice, but his heart rate still hadn't decelerated.

"Why are you so scared?" I reached my hand up and placed my palm on his chest, right over his heart. His heart rate increased again before dropping. Hearing the change made me smile.

"I am afraid of what he will do to me. He has... a temper." His last word ended as if it was not what he had meant to say. The idea of Ryland getting hurt by his father in some way made my skin crawl.

"Then, just stay, Ryland. Don't leave."

"I have to go; it would be worse if I stayed."

I didn't know what to say. His voice was so calm, but the terror behind it was so evident; it made my heart hurt. I wrapped my arms around his torso and pulled him toward me; he responded to my gentle tug, pulling me into him further.

"Will you wait for me?" His breath caught on my hair as he lowered his head to whisper in my ear.

"Wait for you? What do you mean?" I turned my head up to face him, surprised to see his face only millimeters away from mine. My words got caught in my throat.

"Oh, Joclyn," he sighed. "You are the reason I want to be good. The reason I have seen the evil in my father. You make me good. You make me whole." He paused, studying me as his fingers moved over the skin of my cheekbone. "I need to leave; for you, for me." He paused again, his eyes searching deep into mine.

I could have stared into the endless depths of those eyes forever. I could have asked a million questions to dissect the mysteries behind them. He stopped me with three words.

"I love you." He whispered it, his voice weighed down with the deep emotion of the million times he had tried to tell me.

I couldn't move. I couldn't breathe. My heart caught in my chest as his eyes continued to search mine. They were so full of passion, of conviction, of love. I felt tears build beneath my lids as I looked at him; overwhelmed at what he had just said.

"Oh, Jos. Don't cry, sweetheart." He reached up and wiped away a rogue tear that slowly trailed down my face. His finger trailed up the right side of my jaw, moving toward the mark. My body tensed for just a moment before I cast it away. He had told me he loved me; what did one little scar matter?

And then, his finger made contact with the raised mark.

It felt like a thousand volts shot through my body. I gasped in surprise at the sensation, shock whipping through me. My vision went white as the jolt encompassed me, my back arching in surprise or pain; I didn't know which. The electricity had gone as soon as it had come and my vision refocused on Ryland, but he didn't have the same look in his eyes as before.

There wasn't passion.

Only fear.

His body had tensed around me; his arms tightening as his eyes darted around the room. He stood up, taking my body with him, keeping me plastered against him.

"No," he moaned, and his voice sounded like an agonizing sob.

"No!" His yell of pain and fear echoed around the room as he tilted my head to the right side, his hands jerking my hair aside to reveal the mark that was so well hidden behind my ear.

"No," he repeated, but this time his voice strained into a sob.

He lowered his head to mine and pressed his lips to the brand, a smaller shock moving through me at his touch. He stayed like that, rigid arms surrounding me, his lips tender against my mark.

"I'm sorry." My voice was panicked. His reaction was so unexpected and fearful; I felt my body begin to shake.

"How long have you had the mark, Joclyn?" he demanded.

My body froze; my heart dropped. I wanted to kick and scream and hurt something. Why did this mark always have to ruin my life?

"Joclyn!" Ryland yelled in a panic. "How long?" He released my body and moved me away from him, his eyes meeting mine with the terrified look they held earlier.

"Since... since I was five," I whispered, my voice catching.

"You have hidden it all this time?" He didn't wait for an answer; he just crushed me to him again. "Oh, Joclyn, sweetheart."

Sweetheart? Wasn't he mad, angry? Wasn't he going to cast me away?

He crushed me to him even further before releasing me, placing me at arm's length. His hands held me in place, leaving me nowhere to look but right at him.

"You're the one. The one they have been looking for. And you were here... No! They have seen it by now."

"Seen it?" I asked, my confusion growing.

"The cameras, Joclyn; they watch me all the time. You have to get out of here."

And there it was. My heart sank to my knees and the tears started flowing.

"Leave? Ryland, why? It's just a mark—it's nothing. Please say it's nothing," I begged him, my hand clenching the front of his shirt in desperation.

"Oh, Joclyn, the mark means everything."

"Why? I don't want it. All it has done is ruin my life! I don't want to leave!" I screamed, my emotions and fear blending together in a boiling pot.

"If you don't go, they will kill you."

Wait. *Kill?* Was he serious? His terror started to seep into me, and as I watched his face, my anger melted into confusion.

"Kill? Ryland, what's going on? I don't understand."

Ryland pressed his forehead to mine, his eyes closed in agony.

"I don't know how to make you understand... There isn't enough time."

The blue of his eyes pierced right through me as he looked to something beyond me. His eyes darkened with a heavy determination I wasn't aware he possessed. "They are coming."

"Listen very carefully, Joclyn. My father is coming, and if he finds you, he will kill you. I will head them off as long as I can, but you must run." He kept his head pressed against mine as he spoke, his words tumbling over each other.

"Your father?"

"Take my car and go straight to your mother. Take her and go... go to Ilyan."

"Ilyan?" I asked. Why were we talking about Wyn's brother now? What did he have to do with any of this?

"He is tall, has blonde hair and speaks with an accent, correct?"

I could only nod in surprise; how did he know?

"Then it is him. Go to him, show him the mark; he will protect you. I have to... I have to keep you safe, Joclyn. I can't lose you."

"I can't leave you." I knew I couldn't; my body screamed at me not to go.

"If we go together, they will hunt us down like dogs. I need to fight them to give you time to escape."

"Fight?"

"I will find you, Joclyn. I promise. Just go to Ilyan; he will protect you." He moved his eyes away from mine to press his lips against my forehead, the connection spreading his familiar warmth through my body. It spread through me, stretching to my toes; it filled every part of me with a calm determination, my fear vanishing behind it.

He dragged me to the door, his back straight and his muscles flexing. His hand held mine, neither of us willing to let go.

"To my car, to your mom, to Ilyan," he repeated as he pressed a small key ring into my other hand. "Say it."

"To your car, to my mom, to Ilyan." My voice was small and shaky despite my new-found determination.

"Good. And, no matter what you do, do *not* take off the necklace."

The door opened before us, without anyone having touched it. I could hear running feet echo through the hallways like a stampede, the sound getting louder as they moved closer. My heart beat faster in its attempt to escape my chest.

"Run, Joclyn," Ryland pleaded. "Don't look back. Run!"

CHAPTER 25
JOCLYN

I ran down the hall, a man's voice yelling behind me. His angry shout ricocheted off the ivory colored walls, echoing in my ears. That one shout was followed by what sounded like a hundred others, but I knew that couldn't be right.

"Leave her alone!" Ryland's voice was like a magnet to my heart. It took all of my willpower to not turn around and to just keep running.

"What have you done, son?" Edmund's cold voice was a palpable thing; its angry mass hitting my back with a tangible force.

I ran to the door of the servants' corridors and swung it open, slamming it behind me. I didn't stop to see if it closed. I didn't stop for one last look at Ryland. I just ran. My feet moved forward of their own accord, taking the steps two or three at a time as I fled down a level toward the garage where Ryland's car was parked. I had moved about halfway down the staircase when the whole building rocked under my feet.

I was thrown into the metal hand-railing as an explosion shook the building, the loud booming of who-knows-what resounding around me. I stopped and looked back. My heart begged me to go to him, to save him; but what could I do against all those men? What could I do against explosions? I clenched my fist around the key in my hand, the plastic cover pressing into my skin.

I couldn't go back and help him. I couldn't. I had to do what he asked.

"To the car, to my mom, to Ilyan."

I burst through the final door into the large garage and looked among what appeared to be hundreds of cars for the yellow Lotus. I spotted it on the far side of the garage and began to move through the vehicles toward the expensive sports car ahead of me. I had only made it partway through the garage when another explosion rocked the ground. This one was bigger than the last one. I screamed out in fear as I slammed into a turn-of-the-century Ford; pieces of plaster falling from the ceiling.

I picked up my pace, trying to ignore the constant rumble on the floors above. I made it to the car and threw myself in, starting the engine. It roared to life and the garage door opened; the sound of the engine its cue to rise.

I gunned it.

Ryland had taught me to drive this car almost a year ago, but I hated to because I could never keep the speed reasonable; being behind the wheel felt like I was in the middle of a video game. My heart rate sped up even faster as adrenaline added itself to my fear. I tore out of the garage and down the street, the odometer reaching one hundred thirty miles per hour in just the first few seconds.

I caught a glance of Ryland's house as I drove in front of it. The third floor was in flames. I wanted to stare. I wanted to call the police. I wanted to do something. However, Ryland's instructions echoed through my ears; his warning of what his father would do to me. I strengthened my resolve and turned the corner. If I stayed at this speed, I could get home in five minutes. The challenge would be to avoid traffic and the cops.

I struggled to keep my speed high, but once I made it into the city I was faced with traffic lights and other cars. It was maddening to move so slowly. I hit the steering wheel in exasperation as I stopped at a traffic light, again. I screamed my frustrations and fear at the red light just as it turned green and then I zoomed between cars in my desperation to get home.

Moments later, I pulled up into the no parking zone in front of my apartment building. Out of habit, I looked up to my third floor window and my heart dropped. Even though it was night, my mom was sure to stay up to make sure I got home okay and share a play-by-play of the evening, but the window was dark.

I tore out of the car, leaving the engine on and the door open, to run up the stairs. With each step, the necklace bounced against my skin, its temperature steadily increasing. I reached the third-floor landing and froze; the door to our apartment was wide open. My breath caught as I stared at the dark expanse of space beyond my apartment door.

Mom.

Something in the back of my mind told me to turn around and leave, to just go to Ilyan, but I couldn't. The fluttering panic in my heart pulled me forward. I could taste the danger on my tongue. I could hear the voice of reason screaming at me to get away. At the moment though, I could only think of my mother.

I stepped into the apartment and waited for my eyes to adjust to the dark. Figures and shapes began to emerge from the black and I looked from one out-of-place object in the room to another until my eyes rested on an arm protruding from behind the half-wall that divided the living room from the kitchen. The fingers of the hand curled softly; the yellow fingernail polish was bright even in the dark.

I screamed out in fear and pain as I ran, my knees sliding against the linoleum as I dropped to her side. She lay on the floor of the kitchen, her body pressed against the painted wood cabinets. My hands floated above her, desperate to do something to help her. I could feel the racking sobs of my agony threatening to break through. I grasped for her wrist, trying to remember how to take a pulse. I thought I felt something, but could not be sure that, through my shaking hands and loud sobs, I had found her pulse at all.

"Mom!" I screamed. I could hear my own agony line my cries. "Mom! Answer me. Please be alive." I was still at her side when the door to our apartment slammed shut and two dark figures moved in front of it. I grasped my mother's hand as I turned toward the intruders, my wailing sobs dying down.

"Well, well, well," one of the two spoke with a light, mocking voice. "Is the little half-ling crying over her mortal mother? How disgusting."

"Don't give her any sympathy," the other said; a man whose deep voice made him seem much older than his body led me to believe. "After all, we were the ones who had to watch her in his room year after year."

"And all the while, she plotted to kill the prince."

"We would have done better to kill her as a child."

"If only we had known she hid the mark." The two chattered back and forth as if I wasn't there, their wicked voices making my skin crawl.

"Kill? Kill who? I wasn't going to kill anyone," I gasped, my voice breaking with tears. I clung to my mother's hand, desperate to feel her squeeze back. I needed her to sit up, to tell these wicked men to leave, and to just make everything better. In the deepest portion of my heart though—a part I was trying to ignore—I knew that it would never happen again.

"Oh, don't bother to lie," the man with the deep voice sneered. "We know all about the vile things inside your head." He took a step closer and I crept backward, my mother's fingers slipping from my grasp as my back pressed against the bathroom door.

"Cail," the first man spoke with a touch of boredom to his voice, "just get it over with and kill her. There's no use in playing with her."

"Kill me? I haven't done anything wrong! I don't know what you are talking about," I screamed at him in desperation as he continued to move forward.

In my heart, I knew it was too late. I had failed Ryland. I had told him I would run, and here I was, trapped and about to die anyway.

"Could it be?" Cail's voice was soft, but I could hear the amusement behind it. "Do you really not know?" He took a step forward, letting the light that filtered in through the window illuminate his face. Cail—I recognized him. He was the bodyguard from the Rugby game, the one who had accompanied Edmund, the boy who had constantly looked in my direction, the one who had seemed to sense I was there.

His lips twitched as he watched me place the connection. I shrank away from him, lost in the pitch-black hatred of his eyes.

"Recognize me, do you?" he said. "Yes, I could feel someone nearby at the Rugby game. I never would have guessed it was you, though."

"Didn't you say you saw Ilyan nearby? Perhaps she doesn't know anything."

"Yes, and now, he has waited too long to come and collect his precious 'Chosen Child', so I get to kill her." Cail raised his hand to me in what could have been perceived as a gesture of help, but I didn't wait to find out.

I jumped to the side as the door behind me exploded in a shower of splinters. I scrambled across the slick linoleum in an effort to find a hiding place and scooted behind the counters to slam against my mother's limp form. She still didn't move, even when the refrigerator slid across the floor toward us. I scuttled under the kitchen table just as the fridge launched into the counters, causing them to explode in a shower of sparks, pinning my mother's legs underneath it. She didn't even flinch.

I screamed and sputtered as my breath came in short spurts. I could feel a panic attack coming on as my chest seized. Nothing made sense. Things were exploding around me, my mom lay unconscious on the floor, and two men were trying to kill me by throwing refrigerators across the room and exploding doors.

Which wasn't even possible.

"The last of the 'Chosen Children', helpless and alone," the first man laughed from the other room.

I whimpered as I watched them step into my tiny kitchen, the first man still laughing. The table lifted itself away from me and slammed into the wall where the refrigerator had been only a moment ago. I wailed in terror and backed up, only to feel my feet come in contact with the wall. I was trapped. With nowhere else to go I stood, back dragging against the window frame behind me. If I was going to die, I would die standing, not cowering in fear.

"I'm sorry, Ryland; I failed. I didn't make it to Ilyan," I whispered to myself.

As I spoke, I felt a small tug in the pocket of my jeans. I looked down to see the small, purple bead wiggle its way free and fly up to hover in the air between me and my would-be assassins. I stared at it, confused, until a bright light filled the room like lightning. The flash blinded me, and when I moved my hand from over my face, the bead lay harmlessly on the ground.

"No!" the men yelled together.

"Ilyan," the first man spat angrily. "Kill her now; he will be here any second."

Cail raised his hand, and I sank against the window, cringing away from him.

I love you, Ryland. I bid him farewell, expecting the blow to come at any moment. Before anything could happen, a comforting warmth began to spread over my body. It felt so close to the warmth I felt when Ryland touched me that I focused on it, happy for the last connection between us. Tears streamed down my face as the man flexed his fingers, a bright light forming in the palm of his hand.

Just as the light in his hand became the size of a softball, a burning heat seared into me from the necklace that hung around my neck. I called out in pain as it burned me, but before I could even reach for it, a flame of blazing, white light shot out of it, intercepting the one that the man had just shot at me. They collided in the middle of the kitchen in an explosion that cracked through the walls and sent drywall over us like snow. The men were thrown back into the kitchen wall just as I was thrown backward out the window.

Glass window shattered around me, the sharp edges cutting into my skin as I plunged through it. Air swooped by me as I was thrown into the cool night air, knowing that below me laid three stories of nothing before the hard asphalt of the alley.

Time slowed down as I fell, tears flying away from my face and into the air. I could have counted each star, each cloud. I could have given them names and danced among them. I watched them as my mind caught up to what was happening.

The wind whipped around me, but it wasn't the welcoming sensation I had felt on the tops of buildings or up in the trees. This time, the wind moved through me as it bid me farewell. The night sky watched me as I fell, the twinkling eyes of each star shining, as if to say "I'm sorry." I reached for them in frantic desperation, wishing they could reach out and stop me from the impact that awaited me.

Far too soon, I collided with the asphalt. The alleyway filled with a resounding crack as my back snapped under the impact. As my body broke, a fire spread through me, burning me from the inside. It seeped and shuddered through me, consuming every inch of flesh and bone. I could feel its burning pain eat away at the nerves and muscles of my legs, igniting my hip bones. My body protested against the pain as my head added its own agony to the fold, the fire spreading into a resounding tension that shattered my skull into a million broken fragments, causing black spots to dominate my vision.

I opened my mouth to scream, but no sound came out. My mouth opened wider as it strained against the agony that consumed me. The rest of my body remained still, even though my insides felt like they were writhing, twitching and contorting with the pain. My mouth continued to open in a silent scream as my vision began to fade in and out of blackness.

I could feel my body giving out, and sadly, I didn't mind. The warmth I had felt before, the warmth that reminded me so much of Ryland, continued to move through me, the warm feeling intensifying into a numbing sensation that spread through my body like water. Although I could still feel the pain—the burning agony—I didn't care so much anymore.

Something around my neck pulled me, and I felt my body being dragged across the uneven gravel of the alley, my limp frame shaking and rattling against loose stones. My shirt ripped and tore against the rough stones, pieces falling away to reveal skin that I was sure was getting scratched and cut against the sharp gravel.

My vision faded in again as I was dragged into the shelter behind a large dumpster. Something heavy crashed against my feet, the weight twisting my body at an odd angle that I was happy I couldn't feel. I looked around, desperate to see who or what had pulled me into the shadows, but found nothing.

My vision kept threatening to fade out again, but I fought it, desperate to see what was going on. The sweet-and-sour smell of garbage filled my nostrils and gave me something else to focus on in the effort to stay conscious.

The steady sound of footsteps on crunching gravel filled the alley, the thudding of heavy feet running along the broken surface of the asphalt vibrating in my head. I listened as the steps grew louder, angry voices accompanying them. My head swam with sound and the vibration; the agony within my skull swelling with the new pain. My vision, and now my hearing, continued to fade as I fought against the blackness that was trying so hard to take me.

"He is going to pay for this!"

"...already is, mostly dead anyway..."

"If only... dead... get his car..."

Their voices faded in and out so fast, I could barely make out what the angry men were saying. I watched as two pairs of shoes ran past the dumpster, the vibrations beginning to lessen as they moved away from me.

They hadn't found me, but I was still dying behind a dumpster.

I lay amongst the garbage for who knows how long, my body unable to move, my vision and hearing blacking in and out frequently. I knew I only had a matter of minutes left; I could feel everything giving out in an undeniable finality.

Suddenly, the weight on my feet lifted and I heard a sigh of relief behind me. I couldn't turn to see who it was, but my muscles tightened in fear.

The dumpster that lay beside me moved to the other side of the alley, the heavy box making very little noise. The soft crunching of feet moved closer before carefully torn jeans kneeled down and a soft hand came to rest on my cheek. My vision gave way as I felt the person's warm hands move underneath my limp body and lift me to a hard chest.

"Don't worry, Silnỳ," a heavily accented voice said. "I've got you."

Ilyan had found me.

CHAPTER 26
RYLAND

"Leave her alone!" My voice rattled as it bounced off the paneling in the hallway, my magic trailing right behind as it sparked over the carpet. It was all a warning as she ran in the opposite direction away from me.

To safety.

To anywhere away from the three men that I faced, the wall of Trpaslíks that were already forming behind them, ready to take me on to reach her. But it was my father, Timothy, and Cail that I yelled at. It was to them that I sparked my magic in threatening waves.

It was them that I was willing to face, even though I knew there was no way I would survive it.

I had spent weeks wondering how to protect her and still save myself. Now, as I stood in the center of the hallway, facing the rage of my father so that Joclyn could get away; I knew where I had gone wrong.

She was the only one that mattered. And I would do anything to save her.

"What have you done?" My father's rage rattled the air, boiling through my blood as though just his rage was pulling my magic to the surface, readying every bit of it to fight.

"He has betrayed you," Timothy began, Cail standing beside him as the air around him rippled with darkness as he brought his own magic forward. "He is no better than Il--"

My magic rushed through my skin in a roar, the wave of power pulling into the palms of my hands as I grabbed at all the heat in the air and shot a fiery orb right at my father and his army.

The ball of flame barreled toward them in a roar before Cail stepped forward, swiping his hand to the side as he deflected my attack. Or rather, attempted to. My attack went wide as Cail directed it away, his eyes wide in shock at what he had intercepted. The burning ball of destruction slammed into the wall, sending bits of plaster and wood over everything as the fire erupted in an explosion similar to a bomb.

The ancient building creaked, glass shattering as the floor rocked and heaved. My father and his minions, however, barely flinched, their shields already tucked in tight around them.

I was going to have to give more if I was going to get out of this. The thought tensed through my gut; I didn't know if I had enough. But I would try.

"You dare attack me?" My father roared, clapping his hands as his own magic began to grow there, light and dark and fire swirling together in an ominous orb that I knew would intersect with me before I could dodge. I pulled my shield up protectively as the orb grew. The mass of it sucking the oxygen out of the air.

"I will do what I need to do to protect those I care about. That's better than you have ever done!!" My throat tore with my shout, muscles throbbing as I pulled at my magic, keeping the shield strong as I prepared for the battle that was coming. "I will not let you get past me. I will not let you reach her."

I slammed my hands together, pulling at air and earth as a lightning storm began to grow there. Again, not so much as a flinch from them men.

"You would protect her?" Cail laughed, stepping to me like a hunter to prey. "Use your brain, stupid child. We would never hurt her. We need her alive."

Alive was a sliding scale with him. Besides, even if they kept her alive, it would be as a prisoner as one of the men that my father kept chained and starved and screaming in the bowels of this place. I wasn't willing to risk it

"You can't have her." I slammed my hands together, sending sparks of lightning skittering down the walls and over the floor, a few of the Trpaslíks screamed as the magic hit them.

My father took a step forward, still holding his weapon before him. The mass of dark fire was a hole sucking away the hope in the world, even from here I knew it would devour what I had brought forward.

I had only seen my father fight once or twice; which meant I had only seen his magic a handful of times. Seeing it now, it made it hard to breathe. I was nothing before it, and with how he was smiling he knew it.

"She's the piece we've been looking for, Ryland. Did you really think you could stop us?" A greasy smile smeared over my father's face as he stretched his hand, the wicked, vile magic growing before he smashed his hands together and sent that giant ball of destruction right at me.

I had been trained to restrain. To control. To be the perfect son. The perfect warrior. The perfect weapon.

I would need to be all of that now.

But not for him.

As long as I could keep my father, Timothy, and Cail busy; Joclyn would have time to reach her mother, to find Ilyan. If she could reach him she would be safe, he would keep her safe, just as he kept them all safe. I knew that much. He had been my people's enemy for centuries, but I would trust him now. I had to.

For her.

I would do all of it for her.

Anything for her.

Pain blossomed across my chest, something inside of me cracking as I dodged my father's attack, my body shuffling to the side as I pulled that lightning forward, twisting it with threads of air and forming the mass into a spear that I sent into the wall just beside my father's head. The spear of storms impacted with an explosion that sent glass over everything, each of those shards their own weapon that I guided toward the three men.

They clearly hadn't expected that, and that time they weren't quick enough to stop them.

The shards of wood slammed into them, cutting over Cail's cheek and across Timothy's hands and arms. Edmund grimaced as something slammed into his side, although I couldn't see what or where as the Trpaslíks jumped forward, ready to protect their king.

He shoved them away before they could do anything, his nostrils flaring as he glared me down.

"No. But I will do everything I can to stop you." I heaved as I brought my magic back to my hands, ready for what would come next. Some attack of dark magic or twisted flames...

Instead, Edmund's smile stretched, Cail's growing right alongside.

"You seem to have forgotten something," Cail taunted, his smile pulling his face into that twisted grimace that had haunted my dreams for far too many years.

"What?" I asked the question through gritted teeth as I prepared my next attack, well aware it was nothing but sparks of light.

"We are not restrained by walls." It was my father who answered, his victorious smile a wicked match to Cail's as they all stood there, smiling at a victory I knew would come. I needed to stop them, to distract them.

I sent another attack, but Timothy waved it lazily to the side, sending it into a wall where it might as well have slid down the surface like sludge.

No.

"Cail. Find her. Kill anyone who gets in your way. That girl... The Chosen is mine."

"Yes, master."

"No!" I screamed as I attacked, again and again. Power ripped from me as I raced right to Cail who smiled before he turned and jumped through the broken window to his right. I caught a glance of him soaring through the air toward Joclyn's side of town, right to where I knew she was heading.

There hadn't been enough time.

There had never been enough time.

I raced forward, ready to take off after him. I only made it a few steps before a blast of heat hit me right in the gut. It slammed into me with a noise like wet against stone and I stumbled back, already sending my counter attack towards my father who laughed and deflected before easily attacking me again. This time heat wrapped around my arm, crushing the bones in a vice that I had felt many times before. This trick was a familiar one of his, something he loved to dole out when I failed, when I wasn't fast enough, wasn't good enough. It cut through me just as violently that time, yet somehow it was worse. So much worse.

I clenched my teeth, refusing to scream, as bones and tendons snapped. I only attacked again.

Again. Again. Back and forth we sent our magic as my father tried to kill me, tried to keep me from flying out the window after Cail. Fire ripped over carpet, glass lifted from the ground only to fly right at me like daggers. I waved my hand and turned them to dust with a shout, but it wasn't enough. A few of the shards snuck through, the sharp points embedding themselves in my neck and arms.

I swallowed the scream, I swallowed the pain as I turned to my father, tasting the blood in my mouth as I felt the hot streams of liquid drizzle from each and every one of those gashes.

"You can't have her." I snarled through clenched teeth, still facing him as I poured my magic over my skin, letting it crackle and glow in warning.

My father didn't so much as flinch, he laughed darkly as he stepped forward and snapped his fingers, the tiny action sending a wave of magic towards me so strong that I was thrown back, right into the far wall. The magic didn't fall away with the impact, it pressed against me as though it was a hand against my chest, my throat, my legs, it squeezed the air from my lungs and the life from my legs.

"Oh, Ryland, haven't you learned by now? I can have anything I want," he snapped again, my body flattening against the wall, pinned there by a magic stronger than my own. "Including you. You were never anything but disposable anyway. You will always bow to me."

He walked toward me slowly as I continued to fight the magical binding that only increased in pressure. Timothy turned to direct the rest of his minions into lines and formations, already sending them out of the windows to search out the Chosen. Others remained, the trained army lining the destroyed hallway as if they were all going to battle me.

Or capture me.

"I will never be your minion, not anymore," I gasped through the pressure on my body as it built, his magic flattening me.

"You are my son, my creation, you will be whatever I want you to, because you are just like me..."

"I will never be like you," I spat at him, snarling as I quietly let my magic build so I could face him one last time.

Maybe I could take him out. Maybe I could end him and save Joclyn that way.

I could escape him.

Escape this life.

"I am nothing like you. Never again." I was ready, one last attack and I would end everything, destroy him and this house and this terrible kingdom he had built.

I clung to the hope that she had made it to Ilyan. That she would be safe.

But then that spot on my chest where I always felt that connection with the necklace surged, her voice a hum in my ears as everything in the world shattered.

'I'm sorry, Ryland.' Joclyn. My magic flickered as her voice filled my mind.

"You are exactly like me." My father took a step forward, more of my air drained from my lungs and sent the burning hallway into a dark flicker.

'I failed.'

My magic sparked at her voice, shadows of a room I had been in a hundred times before filling my vision. Joclyn's kitchen, except it looked nothing like it. The tiny space was in ruins, appliances overturned, dishes shattered, a flickering light overhead and the person standing in the center of it shouldn't be there.

Cail.

"You will always be like me." My father slapped me, sparks of his magic flaring through my jaw as he once again splintered the bone.

'I didn't make it to Ilyan.'

Pain flared as he hit me again, more bones protesting under his attacks. I needed to fight his hold on me, fight back. I needed to get out of here. But as more of my air left, the shadows of the room became clearer, the image of Cail bright as he lifted his hand, his trademark attack glowing bright in his palm.

"No!" I screamed the word as my magic exploded. But, instead of exploding against my father's magic, instead of ripping through him and the hallway and ending him as I had planned, it traveled through the necklace. Through the line I had created to keep her safe.

With the last breath my father gave me, I sent an attack to Cail instead of my father and let myself fall into the svazovat, into the connection that I placed inside the necklace, my focus on protecting Joclyn, even as my father began to tear me apart.

CHAPTER 27
JOCLYN

I could have sworn I was flying. I could feel the wind whip through my hair, the calm sensation of rising and falling evident as we moved. I could very well have been running, although being held while someone else ran tended to be a jostling experience. What I felt now was smooth and calming, like a gentle rocking.

The wind in my hair ceased as the rocking motion stopped and I felt a subtle drop as Ilyan sat down, lowering me onto his lap, his folded legs were under my body as he laid me against them. It felt as if my body had been attached to someone else's, and I was only getting brief explanations of what I should be feeling.

"Come back to me now, Silnŷ," Ilyan crooned, his hand smoothing my hair. "I need you to see me."

Although I knew my eyes were open, I still wasn't seeing anything. My vision had blacked out shortly after Ilyan had found me.

Ilyan moved my head gently, placing it in a more comfortable position against his leg, so that I could see him, I assumed. Still, there was only black. My body continued its attempt to drag me into death, but I didn't take notice of its attempts, thanks to the overwhelming numbness that consumed me. Ilyan exhaled as he ran his fingers down my neck, tracing the silver chain of my necklace.

"Joclyn," Ilyan whispered reverently. "I need you to focus on my hand. Focus on my hand against your cheek. We have to do something, and it is really going to hurt."

Hurt? How could anything hurt? I felt so numb.

"Bratr," Ilyan said, and for one fleeting second I was terrified that someone else had found me, but Ilyan's voice was smooth and calm. Who else was here?

"Bratr," he repeated, "I have her now; I need you to release her." He paused as if waiting for a response, but none came.

"Listen to me, please," Ilyan pleaded. "I cannot save her if you don't let her go. I will protect her and keep her safe. But please, let her go. Let me save her life and give you the opportunity to save yours." Still, he waited, but nothing happened; no one responded to his pleas.

"She is dying, as are you. You must trust me."

I felt my heart go into overdrive. Dying? I knew it was true. In fact, I would have gladly chosen death not more than a few moments ago.

Ilyan waited before exhaling deeply, as if he had received a response.

"Focus on my hand, Joclyn." Ilyan had a panicked edge in his voice that jerked my mind right back to him. "I'm right here."

I couldn't understand why he was so panicked or what was so scary, until I began to feel it. First, Ilyan's concerned face swam into view as my vision returned, his hand plastered against my cheek. Soon after, the numbness began to dissipate. As it moved out of me, the intense pain of before began to come back. I felt it first in the tips of my fingers and toes then it moved up my arms and into my legs. A loud wailing filled my ears, the deep melancholy sound seeming to fully embody how I felt. It was filled with such sadness and heartbreak it rattled in my bones. My eyes darted around, desperate to find the owner, but instead only found Ilyan, his lips a hard line.

It was my own scream.

It took me a moment to realize what else was leaving my body; the warmth. The warmth which reminded me so much of Ryland was leaving right behind the numbness. It sucked itself away from me, until I felt nothing but pain and loneliness. My mouth opened further as my agonizing screams mixed with my tears. The pain, combined with the loss, created an emotional tidal wave that was too much for me to handle. I could feel my body begin to shut down.

My screams began to lessen as I let the endless nothingness that had stayed hidden off to the side of my consciousness cover me like a blanket. The blackness wasn't as nice as the numbness I had felt, but it still took the edge off the pain. It seemed to tell me to just give up, and I wanted to, so badly.

"Má ruka!" Ilyan practically yelled. "Focus on my hand!"

I forced my eyes back to his and tried to move my mind away from the comfortable blackness I had let take over and onto the hand I felt cupping my cheek. My screams decreased as I focused on him, finally coming out in panicked puffs.

A new warmth began to fill me; it radiated out from where Ilyan's hand rested on my cheek and filled my entire body. Although it felt the same as the warmth I always felt from Ryland, something was different and drastically wrong. My mind and body began to fight against it.

"Don't fight me, Joclyn," Ilyan pleaded. "You have to let me in."

I didn't know what he was talking about; my heart seized in panic as my cloudy brain tried to grasp hold of understanding.

"Let me in," he whispered.

Could he possibly mean that the warmth was him?

The warmth continued to spread throughout me, followed closely by the numbness I had only recently lost. I welcomed the numbing, glad that the pain was sweeping away into memory. I kept my eyes on Ilyan as the pain faded; desperately wishing I could clutch myself to him and demand answers. I wished I could yell and fight, or simply disappear. Nothing in my body worked properly; nothing moved and no words came.

Ilyan moved his hand away from my legs and produced a cell phone, leaving my limp body to fall like a ribbon over his folded legs. He dialed a number and placed the phone to his ear, all the while his hand never left my cheek.

"Get me Ovailia." There was a pause after he spoke as he waited for this 'Ovailia' to take the phone. When she did, his voice transferred into his native language. The words were full of consonants and deep sounds that rumbled in the night air.

My mind wandered off at the sounds, my fuzzy brain not able to understand anything that was being said. It was easier to not focus on anything and instead let myself drift off into the nothingness. I wasn't in pain now; it almost seemed like the blackness wanted me even more.

"Stay with me, Joclyn." Ilyan's voice broke off from his foreign chatter, the change in tongue bringing my mind back. "Focus on my hand. Focus on my voice." He stared at me intently while waiting for me to agree.

"Ovailia," he continued into his phone, "we will be returning home within the week. I need to get her body healed enough to travel." He paused as the person on the other side of the line spoke. I felt my heart soar at the talk of healing me. A hospital and a shot of morphine sounded just about right.

"Tell Talon I will keep her safe."

Talon? Wasn't that Wyn's boyfriend?

"No! Everyone needs to stay where they are. It is only going to cause problems if they empty the motel."

More mumbled chatter for the phone.

"Ovailia," Ilyan snapped, and his accent increased, making his voice difficult to understand. "I 'ave levt zoo in sharge, ind iv zoo canoot keep zings usser constrol for vun veek vifout my prezzanse ve vill haff to reffink zis arrangement. Iz zat clear?"

He snapped the phone shut and huffed angrily. Even through his angry rant, his hand had remained soft on my cheek.

"You're lucky you don't have a sister," he said, his accent lessened. I was confused. I thought Wyn was his sister; perhaps this Ovailia was their sister, too, and they just never mentioned her.

An uncomfortable pain seized through my spine, and my body moved involuntarily.

"We have to move." Ilyan stated, looking away from me in expectation. He flipped open his phone again and dialed a number.

"Wynifred?"

Wyn? My heart beat erratically at her name.

"We will be there in about an hour. We are in Sunnyvale."

Sunnyvale? But that was at least a two hour drive. How did we get here?

"I took us here to break the trail, but we cannot stay here long. She is very greatly injured. I need you to draw a bath."

A bath? Wasn't he taking me to the hospital?

He snapped the phone shut and placed it back into his pocket.

"Joclyn? We are going to have to move. I know you probably really want to go to sleep right now, but you can't. Try to focus, all right? Focus on me; focus on my voice. You need to stay awake, for Ryland."

"Ryland?" My voice came out like a sob; in fact, I was surprised I had even spoken at all.

"Yes, Joclyn, for Ryland. You need to stay awake for him. Can you do that?"

I stared at him intently, hoping my expression would display the 'yes' I felt in my heart.

"Good girl, Silnỳ."

Ilyan shifted his weight and moved my rag doll form into his arms, his hand never once leaving my skin. He moved smoothly, his body rocking and jostling me around with each step he took. This sensation was so much different than before; I could feel every step, every time his foot hit the ground.

The steps and swaying increased significantly before the wind returned and the rough movements stopped. I watched through open eyes as stars, street lights and buildings soared past us, faster than I thought possible, the shining orbs becoming blurs in my line of vision. The wind in my hair relaxed me even further and I felt myself move into the ever-present blackness once again.

No! I needed to stay awake for Ryland... and for me. I would never be sure, but I swear my arm jumped uncontrollably as I tried to force myself out of the comfortable warmth that the blackness provided.

"It's okay, Silnỳ," Ilyan said, his accent rolling out his vowels again.

I wanted to believe that it was okay, but everything was so confusing. Even in my foggy, hazy mind, I was having trouble understanding what was going on. I couldn't get the images of flying furniture, my aggressive attackers and my mother's body out of my mind. My heart shuddered at the thought of my mother's limp form. It sounded more like I called out to her. Ilyan looked down at me, shocked to see me looking at him.

"Your mother?"

My eyes grew wider.

"I'm sorry, Joclyn. I wish I would have gotten there earlier. I wish I could have saved her." He looked down at me again, and I saw the sympathy hidden in the chasm of his eyes.

My whole world had broken apart in one wild blow.

The truth of Ilyan's words was a wrecking ball against my soul. I saw her frozen body in my mind, and I knew he was telling the truth. She was gone. Even though my brain accepted it, my heart simply wouldn't. It fought and screamed inside my broken body. It begged me to hit and yell, and beg to know that Ilyan was lying. I could almost feel my body jolt as I attempted to act out what I needed to do.

"Calm, Joclyn. I need you to stay still. Try not to think about anything now. We will have time for questions and answers when your body is healed." Ilyan exhaled sharply. That wasn't going to be easy.

I wanted to yell, and cry, and demand answers all at the same time; but in the end, it was just another pain to add to all the others that encompassed me, and the numbness swept it away.

Ilyan's hand ran comfortingly against the bare skin of my back. The warmth inside me increased and my mind became fuzzy, Ilyan's touch taking everything away.

The wind across my face made me think of my many trips up the canyon with Ryland. I loved to roll the window down all the way and feel the air across my face, smell the scent of the trees, the water, the fresh mountain air; they all had a magic of their own. That's what this reminded me of—magic.

The wind decreased to nothing as Ilyan's feet hit against something hard and brought us to a stop. I recognized the balcony door of Wyn's apartment immediately. The large couch and overstuffed chair sat exactly where they had been only yesterday.

"It's probably best if you don't see Wyn right now." Ilyan's hand covered my face and lowered my eyelids. "It may only upset you more."

I felt him take a step forward and then heard the click of the patio door as it shut and locked us into the apartment. Wyn's frantic steps came up in front of us. I tried desperately to open my eyes, but the lids wouldn't budge.

"Oh! Goodness, please tell me she is alive, Ilyan?" Wyn's voice was panicked and deep, but something else had changed. I could almost detect a hint of an accent, an accent almost identical to Ilyan's. I almost didn't recognize her voice.

"She can hear you, Wynifred; please watch your tones."

"I don't see how that matters anymore, My Lord. Your little cover has been blown wide open."

Ilyan grunted angrily.

My Lord? My mind flashed to the text message. I knew I had missed something, but my fuzzy brain couldn't place anything together properly.

"The bath is drawn," the distorted voice of Wyn continued.

"Seal the door," Ilyan commanded before walking away, his arms holding me tightly to his chest.

"What happened, Ilyan?" I heard Wyn's strange voice come up from behind.

"I'm not exactly sure. All I know is that Cail and Drummond were trying to kill her." Ilyan's voice sounded like poison.

"Cail?" Wyn snapped, her voice full of malice.

I heard a door open and we moved into a humid room, the air strong with a deep smell of lavender, lilac, sandalwood and mint. Ilyan bent down and laid me on the bathroom floor, the tiles hard and cold against my bare skin and through my torn shirt. He shifted his hand from my back to my face, his hand never losing contact with my skin. Another set of feet entered the room, the impact vibrating the floor.

"Close and seal the door, Wynifred. I don't want anyone to hear her screams."

Screams? What was going on? I tried to pull understanding through my fuzzy mind, but nothing came.

"How did they find out about her mark?"

"I have no idea. But if it wasn't for Ryland saving her life and Jeffery finding us, she would be in much worse condition."

Jeffery? My father?

"It's a miracle she is still alive."

"Ryland? How did he...?" Wyn spluttered.

A strong hand gripped my shirt tightly and gave it one sharp tug. I felt the few strands of fabric that remained un-torn from the alley give way as my top was ripped from me and the shirt cast away.

"That's how," Ilyan sighed, his voice oddly reverent.

Wyn said something in Czech that I didn't understand.

"You need to be careful with the pants," Ilyan instructed her. "If you jostle her spine too much, it won't heal correctly."

I didn't even have time to think about lying in my underwear on the bathroom floor in front of Ilyan before he spoke.

"I'm sorry, Joclyn. I have to bring the pain back, but it's only for a moment. We will both be right here with you the entire time." Ilyan didn't even give me time to respond; he simply removed his hand from my face and the warmth and numbness disappeared instantly. It wasn't like before when the pain built into a rage; this pain flooded through me in an instant and I found myself screaming in agony, my immovable body desperately trying to escape the torture I was trapped in.

"Lift her!" Ilyan yelled over my screams.

I screamed louder as their strong hands moved me, sending another violent flame through my whole body. My screams bounced around the tile of the bathroom, trapping us all in the sound.

They lowered me into the tub, the hot water folding over me to envelop my body like a blanket, its touch relieving the pain. The mass of the water was heavier than what water normally felt like, but perhaps it was just my broken body that made it feel that way. My bottom hit the base of the tub with a thud, the impact sending an uncomfortable jolt up my back that made me call out in pain. The water smelled like an odd combination of burning wood and mint.

"I don't think this is moving fast enough, Ilyan; she is still weakening," Wyn whispered into the silence. "She is going to have to go under."

"I'll go get the Drevo," Ilyan said, the door opening and closing before leaving silence in the bathroom.

"Joclyn," Wyn's voice was hesitant; I couldn't help but notice that the accent had disappeared. "You'll need to go under the water. It is only for a minute, and Ilyan and I will be right here," she said, hesitating again. "We... we won't let anything happen to you."

The door opened and shut.

"Should we take the necklace off?" Wyn asked, her accent returning.

"No. Perhaps the kouzlo will transfer to him and we can save two lives tonight." Ilyan paused and I heard something heavy hit against the side of the tub. "Joclyn? Don't be scared, Silný." His voice was too distant; I focused on it as it echoed around my brain.

His hands pried my mouth open and something large and rough was placed inside. The large mass was coarse and uncomfortable against my tongue, the bitter dirt taste shocking me. I tried desperately to spit it out, but Ilyan's hand stayed tight around my jaw, not allowing it to open again.

"It's okay, Joclyn. It will help you."

My body twitched in panic as I continually tried to force the uncomfortable mass off my tongue. I fought against Ilyan's hand that was against my jaw, I fought against the invisible bonds that tied my body, but nothing responded.

What were they doing? Why wasn't I in the hospital? I tried desperately to piece together what I had been told, what had happened. I knew the answer was right in front of me, but I couldn't see it; I couldn't piece it together.

My eyes snapped open to see the two faces peering over the bath at me. Ilyan looked down with something akin to worry and fear, but it was Wyn who was shocking. At first, she looked the way she always did—chin-length auburn hair and dark eyes—but her features had changed so drastically, she almost didn't look like herself anymore.

Wyn's eyes were darker than normal, but not only in color, the whites of her eyes were almost nonexistent. Her eyes were not the most shocking change; against the side of her face was a dark tattoo that ran from her hair line and disappeared down the side of her neck and under her shirt. The deep black lines swooped and spiked over her skin with jagged edges that were sharp like the barbed tendrils of a wire. My stomach clenched tightly, afraid the wire was going to cut into her fine skin and rip her apart. The marks looked like the swirls and flowers and thorns of a tribal tattoo, but turned so much more sinister almost, as if it were an infection.

She didn't look ashamed or embarrassed as I looked at her, even though I was sure the surprise and confusion was clear on my face. She just looked at me sternly, her jaw set, before she reached forward and shoved me down, holding me under the water.

I panicked and fought against her, but my body couldn't obey my mind. I could only stare at them from under the water as I tried in pointless desperation to move. I opened my mouth to scream, but it wouldn't obey; instead it stayed clamped shut around the wad of dirt that still rested on my tongue. My chest began to burn for want of air. My vision began to darken again. Weight left my chest as Wyn removed her hand, but it was too late. I willingly drifted into the blackness.

CHAPTER 28
RYLAND

She was safe.

I knew that much. The connection in the necklace had blazed to life, my magic flooding to save her. Or I had hoped it had. I had felt her fall, felt every bone in her back break even as my own legs were being twisted and crushed by my father's magic. But still, I protected her. I kept my magic with her as I shielded her, as I took the pain away.

It was only when I heard his voice, when he told me to let her go that I did.

She was safe.

He would keep her safe.

Ilyan would keep her safe.

I had whispered a goodbye as I released my magic, as I faced my father who was speckled with the spray of my blood, his smile wide as he took a victory he didn't deserve. A victory he would never have. The Chosen, Joclyn, was with Ilyan.

Edmund would never have her now.

The knowledge was the small thread of hope I clung to as I hung against the cold stone wall, wrists and ankles bound by magic restricting irons that cut and pinched into my skin. Warm blood flowed from each pain point, the iron dampening my magic so that I couldn't even attempt to heal myself. I was left hanging and tortured in the bowels of my father's monstrous manor house.

The large manor house had been built sometime in the 1800's, when this part of America was still new and land was free for the taking. It had been built as a fortress for a war that had been going on since before the Crusades. These cells seemed to be pulled right from then, anyway. Stone floors, thick iron bars, a penetrating wet that dripped down that wall and pooled against the floor, seeping from who knows where.

I had been down here many times, helping Cail and my Father to torture, to maim, to pull information out from the Skříteks he captured. Now it was my turn. I think, deep down, I always knew I would end up here.

"You just going to leave me here to rot?" I yelled into the dark, my shout echoing over stone and iron to come back to me in a monstrous howl. My mouth filled with blood at the shout, all of my bones aching. Each one that my father had taken delight in cracking was still broken; with my magic restrained there was little I could do to heal myself.

"Did you get what you wanted from me?" I yelled again, iron chains rattling as I shook them as though to emphasize the point. Not that it mattered, there was only the rattling of chains in the dark.

I slunk against the iron restraints; their dull edges cutting into my wrists and ankles again, chains clanking loudly as I tried to find any sort of relief from the extended hang I had been trapped in. There was none. I tried to swallow the sob that built in my throat, the sound echoing over stone as a large shape moved off to my left and I turned, narrowing my eyes to see better. Without full access to my magic, my vision was nothing more than what a mortal would have, which turned the dungeon into nothing but a shadowed damp black hole. I swore I had seen movement, but I could see nothing more than a pile of rags now.

Great. I was weak. Drained. Beaten. And clearly hallucinating.

"Bastard." I tried to pull against the chains again, those dull edges cutting and butting. Digging deep, I attempted to find some flake of my magic that I could bring to the front, so that perhaps I could heal.

There was nothing.

I had ended up in the last place I wanted to be, and it was all my fault.

I should have left years ago. After what had happened to my mother. After what my father had wanted me to do in the forest. I should have left. I knew what he was. I knew what he wanted me to do.

But, I also knew what he *could* do. I knew what he *would* do and for some foolish reason I thought I could be the one to stop him. All this time, I thought I could do good.

So, I never left.

Although, the fact that I had nowhere to go may have fueled that as well. I had no guarantee that Ilyan would take me in, I was the youngest son of his sworn enemy after all. He had been my father's nemesis since this war began, and even though he had taken in so many of the siblings my father had tried and failed to end, I was still a risk. I could have been some kind of planted bomb, which ironically was exactly what my father had planned for me.

At least that future hadn't played out.

Besides, if Ilyan had Joclyn; if Joclyn was who everyone thought she was, then perhaps me staying could have led to the end of this war. I had gotten her out, and with Joclyn, Ilyan could end all of this and none of this would be in vain.

The creak of heavy iron doors ground through the dark cavern, a beam of light shining down stone stairs to illuminate the cluster of cells at the base. The pile of rags shifted again, shivering against the wall as heavy footfalls began their dissent. Okay, so I wasn't hallucinating. I also wasn't alone down here.

Still trying to pull at my magic, I watched as two pairs of shoes made their way down the stairs, a large mass of a body dragged behind them.

"No!" I screamed before I could see clearly, pushing against the chains to reach them.

It couldn't be Joclyn. She was with Ilyan. I knew she was. I had heard him promise to keep her safe. She was safe.

She had to be safe.

Please let her be safe.

"Oh no," a familiar voice whined as Cail came into view, one of his lackeys by his side. "Did the poor little prince lose again? Poor little prince proved he was useless all along?"

"What did you do?" Chains rattled as I fought, as I screamed at him. "What did you do!"

"What we could," Cail said darkly as he reached the bottom step and threw the body to the base of the cells.

My heart was on fire as I watched arms and legs flail as whoever it was rolled toward me, hair flailing, black kitchen shoes clunking the bars of the cell next to mine.

It wasn't her. Not that it was any better.

Angela Despain looked into the dark without seeing as she lay lifeless on the ground. I cringed, heart wrenching together painfully.

They hadn't gotten Joclyn, but somehow this hurt more than anything ever should.

Angela had cared about me. She was the closest thing I knew to a mother. She had mattered. She had meant something, and he had taken her away. Just like all the others. The bundle of rags made a sound that was close to a gasp and a sob as it shivered against the wall, Cail giving whoever it was a grin before his focus turned right back to me.

The door to the cell swung open without anyone touching it, Cail striding in as more quick steps began to descend the old stairs.

"How long did you know, Ryland?" Cail asked, stepping right up to me.

"Know what?" My words were broken as I stared at Angela, trying and failing to stop my heart from cracking. I didn't even try to stop the tears.

"This time you can't play dumb. Tell me!"

I pushed all that pain away as I looked from Angela to Cail, grinding my jaw as I stared him down. I was going to die anyway, so I wasn't going to make this easy for him.

"Know that I loved her? Since we were children." I was prodding him, but the truth still stung.

"Is that why you hid her?" I couldn't tell if he was angry or intrigued as his voice lifted in a taunt of his own. "Is that why you thought you could protect her?"

"I did protect her. I will protect her." I was confident, even though I didn't feel it. Cail didn't see through the facade however, the guy was posturing me as though I wasn't chained to the wall. His eyes were black pools as he stared at me, leaning into me so that he was mere inches away. I could smell his cologne, the aroma somehow complimenting the scent of death, sweat, and rot that was the dungeon.

"Then tell me where she is." He spoke slowly, and I was sure he thought I would simply crumble under the look of death he was giving me.

I couldn't help it, I smiled. I smiled, and then I laughed with a boom that sounded like a drum against the stone walls.

They hadn't found her.

"I think you already know. I think you were just too scared to finish the job. I think you were too scared to face *him*. You knew Ilyan was here. You knew he would find her. You just knew you couldn't win against him."

"I can rip that bastard to shreds!" Cail's rage grew, his breathing picking up as he roared and slammed his fist into the stone beside my head, his magic spider webbing over the rock in bright blue lines.

"Is that why he still lives to defy us?" I pressed against chains to grin at him, ignoring the pain as fletch and bones and metal all ground together.

"Do you dare--" He pulled his fist back, his fingers already glowing blue with that hot-ice power the Trpaslíks controlled. It would kill me.

I was ready.

Take care of her, Ilyan.

"Calm Cail." Edmund's voice was anything but soothing as it echoed from the base of the stairs. Cail stiffened, stepping back as though he was a mechanical wax works, his eyes glossing over as my father stepped into my cell after him. "You will get your chance."

"Yes, master." Cail's slimy smile drifted back into place as that glossed over look left his eyes.

"In fact, you might get it sooner than you think." Edmund turned to me and I fought the need to recoil, and instead leaned against my chains to face him. "Ryland will tell us all that we need to know."

"I already told you, Father." I couldn't help it; the moniker was acid. "I will never help you. I would rather die."

He stepped closer, his tight lipped smile widening to reveal unnaturally white teeth. "You say that as if you have a choice."

"I do. I will never help you. Besides, I don't know where she is anyway. Do what you will to me, Father, I will never help you."

I was firm, facing the man in a way that I never thought I would.

He had instilled my fear in him from a young age. Not just in the brutal way that he trained me, but in the things he had me do with that training.

I had been forced to kill the first time when I was only eight, I had been taken before my own mother, the woman chained and sobbing as my father sought to darken my soul. Instead, it contorted not into the monster my father hoped to create, but into something more. Something stronger.

I just didn't know it until now.

It took love, friendship, and companionship to build me into that, not the hatred and fear my father and his minions provided.

"I will always protect her." I felt the power in that vow, even as they all grinned with wicked malice that sought to tamper it.

"I know," he leaned in, Cail snickering behind him. "That's what makes this so perfect. You love her, and if I had to guess, she loves you. It's perfect."

"You have clearly underestimated love, Father." Because of course he did, how could he understand it if he had never felt it.

"Have I? Love is a weakness that I know exactly how to extort. How do you think I have gotten this far?"

"By brutally murdering everyone in your path."

He shrugged. "That too."

"That is what you will have to do then." My heart was breaking at the thought of never seeing her again. But I had no regrets. "Because I will not help you."

"Why do you still think you have a choice?" His breath fanned over my lips as he leaned in, his eyes bright even in the dark. "Years I have trained you. Molded you into what I want of you... and you are still--"

"Stupid," Cail finished for him. It was his favorite insult.

"Exactly. I'm tired of these games, Ryland. You will do what I say, now."

"I will not--"

I didn't get to say anything more before his fist intersected with my gut again, doubling me over as I pulled against the chains. I tried to right myself, to stare him down in defiance, but I couldn't move. His fist still pressed into me, holding me against the wall as though I was an insect pinned to a board. Worse, his magic was moving into me, flooding me.

The heat of his anger, of his power spread through every thread of muscle and every vein until it began to settle, right over my heart.

It burned and seared and I screamed, feeling the heat of it burn into me as though it was a brand. I knew at once what he was doing.

It was a Vymåzat. The twisted form of magic was a tether between two people, from a master to his puppet. The wicked mark would turn the person into something to control.

It was turning me into his.

The magic was forbidden. Not like that had ever stopped him before.

"No!" The word tore through my scream of pain as I felt his magic sear against my heart, my focus going from one monster to another as my father's magic began to feather from the brand against my heart. The ribbons of his power spread through me twisting out to lie against muscles and bones and claw through my mind as it took hold.

Infiltrating me.

Possessing me.

"I will not be your puppet! I will not help you!"

"You have no choice, Ryland, and trust me when I tell you that the more you fight me, the more of you I will take. Do what I say, or you will not be you anymore. Do you understand?"

There wasn't a hint of regret in his eyes as he stared at me. He didn't care how much he took, he didn't care how much was left. Because he didn't care about me.

"I will fight you, you bastard! You can't have her." His magic was so strong now that I could barely see straight, barely think. Even my thoughts were beginning to twist into the nefarious hatred that ruled him as he took control of every piece of me.

"But I can. You see, you gave her to me when you gave her your heart. I don't have to find her. You are going to bring her right to me, and bring that bastard king racing behind her. I'll take them both, and then I will end this war and control every last scrap of magic in this world."

"No!"

He punched me again, his second fist joining the first as his magic took over everything, smothering me.

I couldn't fight this, so I did the only thing I could, I pushed my magic into the thread that connected me to the necklace I had given Joclyn. I could feel her there, feel her heart, her fear.

So close.

So precious; and not just to me.

I pressed my soul against the line, pushing every bit of my magic that I could summon against it as I shielded the connection between us. As I held her precious warmth against me one last time.

As I shielded her from the monster that was heading her way.

Me.

CHAPTER 29
JOCLYN

The light was so bright I could see the veins in my eyelids. I opened my eyes, blinking furiously in an attempt to preempt a pain that never came. There was only a huge, white space with no doors, windows, or even walls that I could see—only an endless white.

I sat up from where I lay motionless in the middle of the expanse, searching all around me for something familiar. There was nothing but white, white and a small stretch of faded black that grew and throbbed off in the distance. Something about the black called to me, just like the blackness that haunted me in my pained body.

Pain.

I jumped up, surprised when my body obeyed my commands. I had been trapped in a pain-filled, motionless prison, but now I swung my legs around in front of me, my movement quick as I slipped on fleece pajama pants I had never seen before. I looked down at them curiously, trying to place them, but they weren't familiar at all. As I reached toward the pants, the long sleeve of Ryland's hoodie slipped over my hand. Unknown pajama pants and Ryland's hoodie; what odd things to be wearing in a dream.

Was this a dream?

I looked at my pants curiously, trying to think why my subconscious would place me in such odd clothing, and then I remembered Wyn holding me under the water. A flash of her tattooed face was all it took to incite panic in my chest. I gasped involuntarily, my chest heaving as though I still could not breathe.

At my terror, a large comforting hand rested on my back. I turned toward the touch, expecting tattoos or long blonde hair... but it was Ryland sitting next to me, his dark curls falling over his forehead, his bright, blue eyes seeking into mine. That wasn't right... How could Ryland be here? And, where was I?

My heart skipped a beat at seeing him there, right next to me. He wore torn and stained jeans, but his chest was bare, his muscles defined and glistening as if he had just run a mile or two. I thought carefully over what to say, worried my hundreds of questions would topple over themselves in a jumble.

"Am I dead?" I asked, my voice sounding perfectly fine despite the burn in my throat as I spoke.

"No." Ryland's voice was low and comforting.

"Are you dead?"

"Anything but."

"So, I am dreaming?"

"No." His answer was confident; it caught me off-guard as the question was mostly rhetorical.

"Then, where are we?" I could hear the desperate panic creeping into my voice.

Ryland leaned forward and moved my hair away from my face, letting his fingertips linger on the skin of my jaw.

"I think it's some form of shared consciousness," he whispered.

"I don't understand." This seemed more like a dream than anything else. It felt like a dream. It looked like a dream. Even through Ryland's confident answer, I still felt like I knew I was dreaming.

"That's all right. I wouldn't expect you to. Everything is so new to you. I wish I could be there to help you through it; you are probably very scared."

"Isn't it new to you?"

"No, Joclyn. I have known about this my entire life." His fingers continued to trail around my face, over the lines of my neck. The touch was warm and comforting; I was having trouble thinking straight.

"This?" I motioned to the white expanse around us.

"No, silly, not white spaces that lead into nothingness." His tone was exactly like Ryland; it was hard to believe that my dreams could be so accurate.

"Then what?"

Ryland exhaled deeply at my question and looked around him for something; or more like he was expecting someone.

"Tell me what happened to you." He moved closer to me, his voice soft. My previous question lay forgotten behind me as my memory of the evening began running through my mind in fast forward.

"I failed you, Ryland." I could feel the tears trying to burst out, my face growing warm as I attempted to restrain them.

Ryland leaned forward and pulled me into his lap, his arms winding their way around me.

"You didn't fail," he whispered into my ear, his lips rubbing against my mark. The touch of his lips against the mark sent a slight shock through me.

Same as it had in his bedroom.

"But I went to my house, and my mom was... she was..." My voice caught, unsure if I wanted to face it, unsure if I could accept it. "And things were flying and then there was an explosion and... and I fell out of the window..."

Ryland pulled me to him tighter, my tumble of words instantly ceasing.

"I'm sorry, Joclyn, for everything. I never wanted you to be dragged into any of this. If I had remembered there was a window there, I wouldn't have made the blast quite so strong."

He made the blast? I looked at him, confused, begging him to elaborate; but he only smiled at the look on my face.

"Your back seems to be healing nicely, though." He ran his fingertips up my spine, sending a warm shiver trailing behind.

"Healing? How?"

"The same way you are healing me, Jos." He ran his fingers up my back again, through my hair, over the soft skin of my face. His touch seemed so real, I found myself leaning into the bare skin of his chest, breathing in his smell.

"Everything is so confusing, Ryland," I said. "I don't know what's going on."

"It's all quite simple, isn't it, when you think about it?" The small smile evident in his quiet voice.

I shook my head against him. I didn't know what was simple about explosions and flying and... and... my mother.

"How is it simple, Ryland?"

"Oh, Joclyn, you are so special, and you don't even know it yet." His fingers trailed along my hairline comfortably. "Don't reject what's inside you, sweetheart."

"But—"

"You are powerful, and amazing, and confident. You may be the one..."

"The one to what?" I pulled away from him to look at him, but he only smiled sadly at me before pulling me back into his chest.

"It's nothing," he whispered against my hair, cradling me against him until my body melded into his lap comfortably.

I could hear Ryland's heart beat through his chest, feel his warm breath run along my hair. I wished I could stay there forever, but instead, Ryland's body stiffened underneath mine, his shoulder twitching.

"I have to go." It was almost a growl.

"No." I clung myself to him like a child, desperate for this small sense of normalcy to stay with me.

"I have to." He pulled my face up to look at him, his blue eyes deep and worried. "My father is trying to perform a Vymåzat."

"Veemayzit?"

"Yes, he is trying to get inside my brain, control me. I will protect you here..." He stopped, the pain dripping off his voice. He pulled me away from him, just far enough away to see his face as a whole.

"Stay with Ilyan, Joclyn. The time may soon come that my father breaks in all the way, and when he does, I won't remember you anymore. When that happens, I will only be a danger to you. But just remember that I love you; I will always love you. And locked inside me somewhere, I will always be waiting for you." He spoke in an urgent rush; I could only stare at him.

His head twitched to the side, his face screwing up into a pained expression, like someone was stabbing him. As soon as the pain had come, it went; he grabbed me roughly and held me in place, so I had nowhere to look but at him.

"Promise me, Joclyn!" He twitched again, but his eyes never left mine.

"Promise what?"

"Stay with Ilyan. Remember that I love you." He stood, his whole left side twitching now. He looked at me in agony. "I love you." He held my hand tightly, the last contact we had, but even I could feel that slip away.

"I love you, too," I said, the truth of my words surprising even me. Ryland's face broke into a wide smile that lit up his whole face.

He leaned down, his hand resting on the side of my face. He moved closer and my heart beat faster in anticipation of a kiss. Before he even made it halfway, his whole body twitched, sending him to the ground as he yelled out in pain.

"Ryland!" I moved to his body as he continued to twitch, my hands moving around him uselessly.

His body calmed quickly and without warning. He lay still, curled up on the floor. I tentatively went to place my hand on his shoulder, desperate to know he would be okay, even though it was a dream. My hand stopped halfway to him; it hung in the air as my fingers began to shake in fear. There, on his back, resting on the same shoulder he had wrapped during the Rugby game, was a mark; a small raised brand, almost identical to mine, even down to the dragon shaped squiggles.

"Ryland?" My voice was small. "What is this?" My fingertips touched the mark before pulling themselves away as a jolt spun through our bodies.

Ryland jumped up, his face coming only inches from mine.

"Still alive, are you?" His voice was a hiss and growl, the words dripping with venom and malice.

I jumped away from him. I knew it was Ryland, but nothing about him looked familiar. His eyes were wide and bloodshot, his face screwed up in a wicked grin. His eyes met mine, and I gasped. They were no longer the blue I loved so much, but a deep charcoal, almost a pure black. I stayed frozen to the ground, my mind sluggishly working through the shock to catch up to me.

"Not for long!" Fake Ryland lunged at me, and I leaped to the side, my fleece pants sliding me across the white space around us. My breath came in sharp bursts as my dream changed to a nightmare.

"Ryland?"

He only laughed at me, laughed at my panic. The sound was unlike anything Ryland had ever made before. It was deep and menacing; it ripped through me, sending a shiver of panic skipping through my heart.

Ryland began to twitch again, his body falling to the floor in yet another agonizing scream. He ran his fingers through his hair as he moaned, his white knuckles clawing through his curls. His hand jumped out, so fast I couldn't move my arm away before he grabbed me, holding on to me tightly, making my heart race. Ryland looked up at me. I breathed a little sigh of relief at his eyes, now back to their regular blue. Even through the relief, my heart still beat in fear.

"I have to go." His voice was strained between his deep breaths.

"Ryland?"

"I can't... my father..." He leaned forward, his shoulder and arm twitching more and more.

Ryland reached forward and ran his finger down the side of my face. His face twitched again before he pressed his lips against my forehead.

"Stay with Ilyan. I love you," he whispered against my skin, his lips brushing me softly as he spoke. He leaned into me again, his lips burning into my skin. I closed my eyes at his touch, and when I opened them again, he was gone.

I stared into the white space for a long while, trying to make sense of what was going on. Even though my mind was clear, I couldn't work through the pieces. Long before I was ready, before I had made any semblance of anything that had happened, the gray and black that had stayed at the edge of the white space rushed at me, sucking me into the darkness.

CHAPTER 30
JOCLYN

I could hear the TV.

The voices from some cheesy commercial chattered around me, almost like I was in the studio. I lay still, letting the sound wash over me as I replayed the dream in my mind, my face cringing at the lingering picture of Ryland's contorted face. I shifted my weight out of habit, surprised when my body obeyed my command. Unlike the dream however, the movement triggered a hundred aches and pains that prickled over everything. While it didn't feel as bad as the last pain I remembered, it still was far from comfortable.

"Yes, Ovailia, I have felt them a few times, but nothing close as of yet."

At Ilyan's voice I opened my eyes, this time to a dark room. I lay in a curled position on the long couch, a huge pile of blankets set on top of me. It made my body seem overly large and lumpy.

Ilyan sat on the floor, his back resting against the couch by my knees, looking unfocused at the television directly across from me, the screen dim with some show about crab fishing. I watched it for a minute before Ilyan spoke again, pulling my mind away from the flickering box.

"Her spine hasn't quite fused yet, but it is close. Once that has finished, we will be leaving. You need to keep him there; I will reunite them soon. Besides, I am not in the mood to babysit."

I looked away from Ilyan, feeling awkward for eavesdropping on his phone call.

"Manners, Ovailia, mràvy." Ilyan's voice was so stern it made my hair stand on end. The raised inflection must have awoken someone else in the room, and I heard someone gasp for air near my head. I rotated toward the noise, the movement sending an even sharper jolt of pain through my spine.

Wyn was curled up in the big overstuffed chair, sleeping with a blanket over her legs. Part of me wished that the Wyn I had seen before—the Wyn who had pushed me under the water—was just a figment of my imagination. But there she sat, dark tattoos running down the side of her face and arm. Looking at them now, they didn't seem quite as sinister as they had before. Their presence still sent an unpleasant clench through my body.

"Finish setting your trails, and wait for my signal." Ilyan clicked his phone shut and shifted his weight.

I couldn't look away from Wyn. I didn't want to try anyway; my body had begun to hurt and I wasn't sure I could move.

"The marks were a gift from her father and brother when they kicked her out of her home. I believe they had hoped the marks would kill her, but instead, they just linger."

I turned to the voice, shocked to see Ilyan sitting right by my head, his back arched so he could meet me at eye level.

"Broth... er?" I was surprised when my voice cooperated, even though it was almost agony to get that one word out.

"Yes, her brother. Not me, thankfully, but I might as well have been responsible; she was spying for me at the time, after all." His voice sounded so angry and upset, the blame he felt still ravishing through him.

"Broth... brother?" I tried again, desperately hoping Ilyan would understand my meaning and explain more.

"No, Joclyn, I am not her brother, but I am a friend."

I arched my back to get a closer look at Wyn again, the movement sending a violent spasm through my spine. I groaned in pain as it shot through me.

"Why... spy?" My voice strained, the words leaving me gasping, and my throat burning.

"Why was she spying for me?" Ilyan reworded my question, and I nodded my head, letting my back slide back into a more comfortable position.

"It's complicated," he said simply. "Wyn was spying on her father, her brother and their boss for me quite some time ago. She inadvertently saved me from a sticky situation and so I asked her to do me a favor."

"How... marks?" My words crept out, each one hurting.

"Wyn's kind—the Trpaslík—are a vicious race who punish traitors cruelly."

I opened my mouth to question further, but he cut me off.

"I would really prefer that you not worry about all this right now. You need to heal, and the faster the better." He must be irritated again; his accent was getting stronger and causing his consonants to turn into Zs and Vs.

"Please?" I wasn't begging. The words were coming a bit easier now, my voice stronger and laced with irritation.

"You're going to want to keep your back straight if you want it to heal properly." He spoke simply as he smoothly changed the subject, like healing on a couch was the obvious thing to do.

"Hos... hospital," I whispered, the rough movements sending sharp pains through me.

"I can't take you to a hospital, Joclyn," Ilyan answered my mostly unasked question softly. "They will be searching for you at hospitals."

His hands wound under the pile of blankets I had been placed under, pushing and pulling my body to straighten my back and bringing my head back to look at him. I called out as he moved me, each shift in weight sending pain shooting through my body.

"Besides," he continued, "I can heal you much quicker." He winked at me mischievously as he finished aligning my back, causing the pain to stop. He kept his palms flat against the skin on my back, sending that familiar warmth through me.

"What...?" I tried again, frustrated when I could still only manage one agonizing word at a time.

"What am I doing?"

I nodded my head, pain shooting down my back.

"Healing you."

My eyes must have bugged out of my head. That one statement had opened up a floodgate, and every unanswered question and unexplainable occurrence over the past few days begged to be expanded upon. Everything flashed before my mind in quick succession as they tried to fit themselves together; my mind flashing like a badly animated short.

"How?" I breathed out, not sure if I was asking Ilyan or my mind the question. Luckily, Ilyan answered.

"Your father insisted that he told you."

My head snapped to him, another jolt running down my spine; I ignored it.

"He promised me he would find a way to explain it all when he gave you the birthstone. I assumed he did, but he seems to have disappeared since then."

I should have cared more that my father was missing, and I probably would have if we had had any sort of relationship. However, my mind couldn't see beyond that one piece of information that fit everything together: the objects flying around my kitchen, the sensation of flying, surviving a broken back and who knew what else, even Ilyan healing me with his hands. My father wasn't crazy. He wasn't deranged. He had told the truth.

"Magic," I said, more to myself than anyone else.

Ilyan nodded solemnly before replying. "I am sorry to have to tell you this way. I had hoped we would be able to gain your trust a bit more before telling you all that was going on."

"Magic," I repeated strongly. My teeth clenched in surprise and anger as my stomach spun in a threatening manner. The warmth of Ilyan's hands grew and the wave of nausea subsided.

"Yes, Joclyn. Magic."

I didn't know how to react. Should I be relieved, excited, frightened? Instead, everything combined and my breath picked up in short, staccato puffs as I tried to cope with the onslaught.

"I wish I could make this easier on you. You are probably very scared."

Ryland had said that in my dream, but he also said he knew. I felt my panic surge as my need for answers grew.

"Calm, please, Silnỳ," Ilyan whispered. The warmth increased again and I found myself falling asleep, whether I wanted to or not. "If you can stay calm, I will explain some things to you right now. Can you do that?"

I wasn't sure, but I wanted to try. As the tired feeling in my body began to subside, I tried to keep myself calm, and my breathing even. Ilyan watched me, his hands still resting on my skin.

"The mark on your skin," he began, his voice calm and even, "is called a kiss. Although it really isn't a kiss at all, it's more like a poisonous bite. When the kiss—or bite—was given, a strong poison entered your bloodstream and changed you. It took the latent powers that you already had and enhanced them. We call those who receive this kiss, a Chosen.

"Now, not everyone has to go through this change. I, for example, was born with my magic. It is as natural to me as breathing. You, however, as with all humans who are lucky enough to receive a kiss, have to endure the change to bring the magic into your body."

"Not human?"

"No, Joclyn, I am not human. Although I do not differ much from your kind, I am part of a race known as the Skřítek. We are an ancient people who were once very plentiful; now there are only a handful of us left, only about a thousand."

"Scree..." I tried to say the word, but my tongue knotted around it. I needed to know more; my mind couldn't stop placing him inside a spaceship, but that didn't seem right. After all, he had told me he had been born in Prague, but now I was wondering if he had told the truth at all.

"Yes, Joclyn. Skřítek. Think of me as the gatekeeper for the birthplace of magic—the well in the earth where the powers within you originated."

I wanted to nod, but couldn't. Instead, I just looked at him, wide-eyed.

"As you know, the change a human must endure as they become one of the Chosen is very painful. The longer the pain, the longer the recovery, the more powerful is the magic." He paused and I could tell he was gauging how I was handling everything he was telling me. I tried to keep a straight face, even though I was still panicking a bit.

Part of me still didn't want to believe him. If I had been able to string more than a few words together, I would have been rebutting him at every turn. As much as I wanted to argue, as much as I didn't want to believe him, I still couldn't get the images of the balls of light colliding in my kitchen, the flying refrigerator, or the sensation of flying out of my mind.

"How long?" My throat burned again as I spoke, my vocal chords cutting off before I could complete my question.

"Your father says you were in the hospital for about six months, which is one of the longest I have heard of."

My heart beat uncontrollably. The longest? What was I, some ultra-powerful freak? Ilyan shushed me quietly as his thumb traced circles in the skin on my back. I wished I could shy away from the touch. It was something Ryland would do.

"Now, this could mean nothing. Most children focus and begin to use their powers days after awakening. It has been a bit longer than that for you," he said darkly. I just stared at him.

"How... Kiss."

"A kiss," Ilyan continued, "is given by a Víly to human children who already have a natural ability. A Víly closely resembles a small, winged dinosaur; although their faces are more human. They are brightly colored and almost seem to glow, making them easy to find."

The flash of blue, the glitter of wings; I remembered seeing both before the pain had hit. I had seen the little creature right before he bit me. I hadn't been paying close enough attention; I didn't know what I was seeing. If I had known what it was, would I have recognized it? Would it have made anything easier? I doubt it.

"Víly's have not been seen in more than two hundred years, which is why, when your father found me in Prague, we came right to you. We would have taken you with us right then, grabbed your mother and ran, but there was a complication."

My forehead furled; I hoped that my silent question was obvious for him. He only stared at me though, his blue eyes deep and troubled.

"What... complication?" I tried to keep my face calm; I wanted to know more, but was afraid he would stop.

"In all things in life, there is a good and a bad, a light and a dark." He paused and I couldn't help but realize that his voice had deepened. The change scared me. "Your kiss is one of those things that possess a dual nature as well. My life has been consumed by this purpose; in many ways it is the sole reason I stay on this earth. Myself, and all those within my family, have spent our entire lives seeking out and protecting the Chosen who have been kissed by the Víly's. For centuries, I have sought them out and protected them..."

"Centuries?" I cut him off, although my voice was a squeak, but he still sputtered to a stop at my words.

"Yes, Joclyn, centuries. I am very old, much older than I appear." His lips turned up in a curious half-smile. "I wasn't lying to you when I told you I was born in the 80s. It just wasn't the 1980s."

"When?"

"It was in the tenth century, Joclyn." His voice was ashamed, like he was worried about my reaction. He had every right to be, too.

I struggled to keep my head, but after everything he had told me, what was one more impossible thing? I held my breath in an attempt to keep myself under control, unsure if I would be able to accomplish it. Thankfully, he continued anyway.

"The kiss on your skin is unique. There has not been a child who has been given this mark in more than three centuries. And the ones who had received their kiss before then have all but disappeared. This is why we had to come right to you. This is why we lied and hid; you are that important. You are the last of the Chosen."

He spoke as if he were done and had told me everything, but he hadn't. What about the bad side he had spoken of, what about the complications? I looked at him skeptically as I gathered strength to speak again.

"Bad side?" I said. Ilyan just looked at me before looking down at the couch. I waited for clarification, but none came. My heart skipped a beat in fear; was the bad side really all that scary?

"Complication?" I tried again, the longer word feeling like acid in my throat.

Ilyan looked away from me to focus on a spot on the blankets that covered me.

"There are those among my kind, and among the Trpaslík, who believe that the kiss is a gift, a sign of royalty. For four hundred years, they have systematically exterminated, not only the children who bare the kiss, but also the Víly's who are the sole reason the marks exist in the first place."

"Extermin..." My voice caught; I couldn't even bring myself to say the word.

"Yes, Silný, they kill them. The men who attacked you in your apartment were there for that reason."

I knew the men were trying to kill me—they had made that blatantly clear—but that wasn't why I found myself hyperventilating again; it wasn't why I found my vision fading in and out so fast my eyesight was almost a flicker. There were others who had wanted to kill me beside those men, and if it wasn't for Ryland, they would have. If it wasn't for Ryland knowing about the mark, and what it meant, they all would have succeeded.

"Ryland," I gasped, my weak voice shaking even more.

"I am not sure we should go over this right now," Ilyan said.

"Ryland!" My strong voice bounced angrily around the room. Wyn said something, but I didn't bother to look to see if she had woken this time. I didn't dare let my eyes leave Ilyan. Ilyan sighed and looked hard at me as my breathing and heart rate continued to increase in tempo.

"Wyn's brother is Cail. Wyn's father is Timothy. They both follow the man who gave the extermination order for the children who bear a kiss on their skin; the man who bears the first kiss ever given—Ryland's father, Edmund LaRue."

Somehow, I knew; I had known from the beginning. I knew from the moment Ryland saw the mark on my skin. I knew when I saw his own mark, standing out so vividly on his back. I knew, but I simply didn't want to see it. I didn't want to accept it.

My breathing reached a rate that couldn't possibly keep me conscious. I looked into Ilyan's pained face for only a moment more before my vision went black. The warmth from Ilyan's hands filled me at an alarming rate, his magic seeping into me and allowing me to slip into sleep.

CHAPTER 31
JOCLYN

The sunlight streamed in innocently through the open window, saturating the faded carpet and white walls with the golden light of morning. A light breeze blew through the open patio door, bringing a sweet smell of flowers and grass into Wyn's living room. My face was warm and felt swollen, as if I had been crying the entire time I had been asleep, which I wouldn't doubt, given the reason I was sleeping in the first place. I shifted my weight under the heavy blankets that covered me, surprised to feel only a slight ache in my joints.

My rested body and serene mood lasted only until I realized the reason I had woken up in the first place. I could hear frantic yelling from the other room, the voices raised and lowered dramatically as they yelled at each other in Czech. Wyn and Ilyan were not angry though; they were panicked. The sound increased as a door opened and I watched Wyn walk out of the hall, a large bag draped over her back, an even bigger suitcase clenched in her other hand. The bags were so large in proportion to her body it looked like she would topple over at any moment. She caught sight of me staring at her and both parcels came crashing to the ground.

"Oh, thank all!" she sighed, her accented voice still odd in my ears. She rushed over to me, placing her hand right against my cheek. I looked at her in confusion, still unable to take my eyes off her dark tattoos.

"Ilyan! She's awake." She looked at me sadly, realizing that I was looking more at the dark marks on her face than at her. "I would hide them, Jos, but it hurts too much and I need to be able to focus right now."

"Good," Ilyan's voice carried from the other room. "Is it hotter than before?"

Wyn removed her hand from my cheek and moved the heavy pile of blankets from off my torso. The removal of the weight increased the soreness I felt.

"Sorry," she cringed.

She placed her hand against my chest, pressing Ryland's necklace against my skin. My jaw tightened as the hot stone made firm contact. How could I not have felt that before? The ruby burned against me, making my whole chest feel as if it was on fire. The second Wyn released the pressure of her hand, the heat lessened, but I could still feel the necklace's intense warmth from within Ryland's sweater that they had placed me in.

"It's hotter," Wyn called back down the hall where Ilyan was.

Ilyan swore in English before he appeared at the end of the hall, his hair pulled back into a ponytail and the knees of his torn jeans caked with what looked like dirt and blood.

"We are out of time. Get that stuff to the car; I'll be down with her in a minute."

Wyn obeyed with a nod, grabbing the large bags as if they weighed nothing and disappearing out the door.

Ilyan rushed over to me and stripped the top most blanket off the pile that covered me and laid it on the floor. When he removed the blanket, the aches increased just as they had when Wyn removed half of them before.

"I'm sorry, Joclyn, but they have found us; we have to move now."

My heart plunged. I knew beyond a doubt who "they" were: Cail, Timothy, Edmund... Ryland. I kept my head about me this time, the magic-induced sleep seeming to have helped me cope with the reality of Ryland's association with the man who would stop at nothing to kill me.

"Ryland?"

"I don't know, Joclyn. He could be with them. He could be... I just don't know." Ilyan stripped the remaining blankets from over me, causing my body to tense with deep aches.

"I am sorry, Joclyn. I would do this gently, but we really do not have the time. I had hoped to have your spine healed before we moved you, but Edmund has other plans." He kneeled down beside me and ran his hand down the right side of my face, his thumb resting on my mark. I expected a jolt or a pain like that which had accompanied Ryland's touch, but I felt nothing.

"I need you to be as quiet as you can. I can't take the pain away right now; you need to be strong." He slid his arms underneath my body and I knew what he meant. My body wasn't as close to being healed as I had thought. With the heavy blankets gone, the aches and pains covered every inch of me. I felt like I had been thrown out of a third story window, which I had been.

I tried desperately to keep the majority of the sound in my throat as Ilyan lifted me and placed me on top of the blanket he had laid on the floor. I lay like a rag doll, my body unwilling to move.

As Ilyan straightened me out, I caught a glimpse of fleece pajama bottoms—the same ones I had been wearing in my dream with Ryland. My heart caught, instantly aware that Ryland was right; it wasn't a dream. But if it wasn't a dream, then what had happened to Ryland?

Ilyan wrapped the blanket around me tightly, like one does an infant, and then prepared to lift me. My body tensed as his hands began to slide underneath me.

"Ilyan," I pleaded, "I can't"

"You can, Joclyn. You have to. If we don't leave now, they will kill you. There are too many of them for me to fight on my own. You are the last of the Chosen; the last one between Edmund and his "perfect" world." He slid his hands under me and lifted me to his chest in one quick movement. I groaned as we moved, allowing too much sound to escape my lips.

"Do it for Ryland, Joclyn. He may need you soon."

I clenched my teeth. I thought of Ryland, the way he twitched and writhed as his father fought his way into his brain. Ilyan was right; someone had to save Ryland, too.

I turned my body into Ilyan as he ran out the door of the apartment and down the stairs toward the small parking garage that sat below the complex. I kept my teeth clenched as my body jostled around, my hands wrapped around the blanket. I focused on my tensed muscles in an attempt to ignore the sharp pains.

I could tell when we entered the garage; Ilyan's footsteps changed to a flat gait that echoed around concrete walls. He walked straight to the black Mazda he always drove, the rear driver's side door opening on its own before we even reached it. He leaned over and placed me in the center of the back seat.

"How many," he asked Wyn, who sat in the passenger seat looking stressed.

"At least a hundred, but they are spread out."

Ilyan reached around me and firmly placed the seatbelt over my shoulder and waist, placing large bags and suitcases around me in an obvious effort to stabilize me.

"You still need to be strong, Joclyn." He placed his hand against the right side of my face, his thumb resting on my mark. I twitched away from the foreign, uncomfortable touch again. "It's more important to get us out of here alive than in comfort."

"For Ryland," I sighed, trying desperately to keep my mind focused.

"For Ryland." Ilyan slid into the front seat, and turned the key in the ignition, revving the car to life.

"Where is the strongest?" he asked Wyn as he backed the car out of the parking stall.

The force of the car's movement slammed me into the large bag on my left. I cringed at the pain of the impact.

"There are more bodies to the east, but the strongest power is coming from the north. That would be my guess as to where they are."

"To the north then." Ilyan's jaw clenched as he hit the accelerator and gunned us out of the dark parking garage.

The warm summer sun poured through the back window, and I leaned my head against the seat, letting the sunlight hit my skin a bit. It felt nice; if only this warmth wouldn't go away, I might be able to endure the pain.

"To the north?" Wyn asked. "You can't be serious, My Lord. We would be walking into their trap."

There it was again, *My Lord.*

"We are already in their trap," Ilyan reminded her with a growl. He flipped his phone open and pressed it against his ear. "Ovailia," he spoke the second someone answered the phone, "set a trail to the east; we are going to go to the north. Meet us at the second safe house."

Ilyan did not wait for a response; he simply threw the phone to the side and turned the car around a sharp left-hand corner, followed by a quick right. My body flung around in the back seat like a rag doll, each impact sending more pain through me.

"What do you suggest we do when we come face-to-face with Edmund?" Wyn asked in a panic.

"We run." Ilyan pressed the accelerator down all the way as we turned onto the large highway that cut its way through the city.

"Run?"

"Yes, Wynifred, we run. We fly. We save our lives. I can save the battle for later. There are more important things to face tonight." They turned toward each other as a silent agreement passed between them. Ilyan turned back to the road again and increased our speed. I sat in silence, listening to their quick conversation, their infectious panic creeping into me.

"How far?"

"About two miles."

"Find all the usable cars, trees, buildings; I need to know what I have to... dammit!" he swore, causing both me and Wyn to jump. The car decelerated, making my body lean forward.

"What?"

"They have a barrier up. They can track us. Switch me places."

Wyn didn't say a word; she simply moved over to the driver's side as Ilyan moved to the passenger's side, the car never deviating a millimeter from the road.

"Pace yourself with as many cars as you can, and keep your speed steady," he instructed, his accented voice filled with insane determination.

"Are you going to try to break through it?"

"No, I am going to demolish it." Ilyan looked toward Wyn, his face filled with enjoyment or madness, I wasn't sure which.

Wyn nodded to him once before accelerating, the force sending me against the back of the seat, Ryland's necklace pressing against my chest.

The necklace was a white hot brand, flaming through me, the warmth pulsing hotter and hotter like the beat of a heart. It was more than just heat though; it was pain beyond my own: hate, love, fear, and excruciating heartbreak. None of the emotions were mine, but with that one touch, they filled me; they destroyed me. I couldn't help it, the second it burned into me, my mouth opened in an agonizing scream. My voice ricocheted around the car, growing louder in the cramped space.

I heard Ilyan yell along with me as a bright light moved away from him through the window, only to explode against an invisible barrier that broke into a million pieces. As the wall broke, my scream continued, only silencing when Ilyan turned to clamp his hand over my mouth.

"You need to drive as fast as you can, Wynifred; they know exactly where we are." He removed his hand from my mouth, and I instantly clamped my mouth shut.

"I'm sorry," I said quietly, "The necklace... it's in pain." I didn't know why I had said that, but the phrasing was right. The emotions that the necklace filled me with felt as if it was in severe pain.

Ilyan's eyes grew wide, his jaw clenching. He looked over my head sharply as he looked for something. I could see his clenched jaw pulse angrily.

"Fast, Wynifred; they are both here."

Wyn hit the gas, and we sped away from the cars we had been pacing with. All the cars became blurs as we soared by them, the black Mazda swerving in and out between the others on the highway.

"What do you think of your brilliant plan now?" Wyn grumbled as she cut in front of a yellow Hummer.

"Faster Wyn!" Ilyan screamed.

The words had no sooner left his mouth than Wyn swerved to the left, barely missing another car. Only a second after she had moved the car, an explosion filled the space we had just left. I turned my head to the side, the red and white of the fire filling the air.

The explosion sent a panic through the cars and drivers on the highway. Half the cars pulled to the side of the road in confusion or curiosity as to what had happened, while the remaining cars sped ahead in a desperate attempt to outrun the fiery blast. All the cars began to drive erratically; they paced and swerved, several cars ramming into each other in violent collisions that filled the road with the sounds of grinding metal, and shattering glass, and the smell of smoke that masked the magical onslaught around us.

The car swerved around each accident as we weaved our way through the masses. I could see the fear on the other drivers' faces; almost *feel* the palpable energy of the screaming men and crying women. I wanted to scream at them to run, beg them to find a way to get far away; they were all getting hurt, many of them dying, because of me.

My mother had died because of me, too. Her life had been stolen, just like all the others.

Wyn swerved again, this time sending me into the corner of the suitcase. I yelped out in pain as my breath was knocked out of me from the impact. Wyn moved the car and another explosion hit the road, sending bits of asphalt against the side of the car. The residue of the blast pelted us, a large piece slamming into the side window near my head with a resounding crack as the glass shattered.

"Ilyan, do something!" Wyn screamed as she swerved once again to escape another explosion.

Ilyan hesitated before raising his hands above his head in silence and then placing his palms flat against the top of the car. His hands glowed bright blue as the roof of the car ripped apart in a loud explosion that ricocheted through the enclosed space. I screamed as the pieces of metal ripped and curled away from the car and flew into the remaining highway traffic. The hot wind of summer flew into the now topless car, whipping my hair haphazardly around my face.

Ilyan turned and placed his feet firmly in the soft seat of the car. He stood, his torso extending out of the top of the car as he faced what I could only assume were our pursuers. The wind caught his hair and whipped it around his face. The violent nature of the flying strands matched his face perfectly; his eyes were set in a dark, stoic blue, his jaw set in an oddly patronizing smile. There was so much power and determination that I couldn't look away from him.

"Hold on tight, Jos," Wyn screamed from the driver's seat. "All hell's going to break loose now that they know he is here."

Sure enough, three simultaneous explosions ripped through the asphalt around us, Wyn said something Czech and the one right before extinguished enough that we could drive through it. Smoke filled the car, Wyn's driving becoming more erratic as more explosions were hurled our way.

I looked up at Ilyan whose smile had increased tremendously as he raised his hand to the side and sliced it through the air.

The car vibrated as a large, abandoned dump truck skidded across the road, rumbling violently in the opposite direction. The truck followed the span of Ilyan's hand as it swept behind us before a large pulse of light left Ilyan's palm. The light must have collided with the truck, as only moments later, our car rocked to the side, an explosion violently pushing it around.

Wyn swerved the car to the left, cutting over two lanes. Ilyan swayed, but stayed atop the seat, shifting his feet to compensate for the dramatic movement. He raised his hands above his head again; his palms open to the sky, his face toward whoever followed us. At first, I thought nothing had happened, but then I saw the flock of birds, their path changing to reflect the movement of Ilyan's hands. The stoic V of the birds was thrown apart as he moved his hands. A rush of wind sped above the car as they made their way toward our attackers, whipping through my hair on its way. It tugged at the bag I sat against, the destructive force shredding the plastic.

Ilyan moved his hands again, this time to the side. I felt the wind rush past us before it picked up a small sedan that had been abandoned at some point in time. The car lifted easily into the air, the large metal frame spinning like a leaf in the wind. It hovered there until it zoomed away to crash into something or someone behind us. I jumped as the noise of the collision hit us, the sound echoing around the speedily emptying highway.

Ilyan smiled at the impact, his face alight with enjoyment. "There he is," he growled, and he lowered his torso for only a moment to speak quietly to Wyn. "You'll need to be on your toes. You know your father's temperament better than I do; Timothy is going to play dirty."

"You just keep yours under control, and we may escape this mess we are in," Wyn responded forcefully.

Ilyan laughed wildly at her before standing again, facing our attackers.

Wyn slowed the car briefly before accelerating again, her driving sending us barreling through empty lanes and around frantically driven cars. Ilyan only laughed at the movement of the car, his body swaying gracefully as we swerved.

He waved his hands above him, his face going from glee to panic as he turned. I watched his actions in confusion until a large van came into view, maneuvering through the air above us. My heart jumped at the sight of the family still trapped inside. Ilyan had only been using empty vehicles as ammo, but someone else had thrown more than a vehicle at us. Someone else had thrown people. My anxiety lessened as Ilyan set the van down at the side of the road, and hopefully, into safety. He didn't waste another moment before sending a massive explosion toward our attackers.

Ilyan lifted his hand again, his eyes taunting the enemy as he sent long strands of violent color from his fingertips, like electricity. The sound of explosions and grinding metal penetrated the air so completely; I could not tell what was going on.

Wyn swerved out of the way to avoid yet another explosion, but the tires still strayed into the broken road. Bits of asphalt flew into the empty cavity that was once the roof, littering me with small burning rocks.

I could hear Wyn's quick erratic breathing from where I sat, and I could hear her whispers as she spoke to the empty air around her. She spoke to Talon; she moaned his name as tears streaked down her face. She was trying to be brave, but her heart betrayed her. She knew there was no hope; she knew we were going to die.

Part of me knew she was right, and sadly, I was okay with it. I wanted to see my mother again; I wanted to apologize. As much as my heart ached and screamed for my mother though, a much bigger part knew I could not leave Ryland. I needed him, just as much as he needed me.

Ilyan sent another round of ammunition flying past in a steady stream of large rocks, small cars, and everyday mundane objects. Ilyan had grabbed everything he could with his mind and launched it away from us like weapons.

He lifted his hands again as a large, brilliantly-red, ball grew from his hands, shooting away from his palms like a bullet and pushing him back inside the car. The sound of the explosion rolled through me, the power loud and angry. My body called out in pain; my voice moaning and gasping with each movement. I remembered what Ilyan had told me; we had to escape alive and not in comfort. He had also said there were too many for him to fight alone.

His face no longer held the joy, the solid determination, that it had held a moment before. Ilyan's face was screwed up with panic, a bead of sweat dripping down his forehead. Wyn swerved blindly to the side in an attempt to escape another explosion, the front of the car nicking another of the escaping vehicles.

"Take Joclyn and run, Wyn. Get back to Talon. I will hold them off to give you time." Ilyan gripped Wyn roughly, his voice a panicked command that made my stomach flip.

"You'll never make it out! I can't... can't let you."

I could tell how much it cost Wyn to say the words, to actually be willing to not make it back to Talon.

"Don't worry about me, Wynifred; I can do a lot more when I don't have to worry about keeping others safe."

I twisted myself in the seat, my body screaming out in agony as I moved. Behind our speeding Mazda, a line of black SUVs followed, each one large and foreboding. Their gauntlet herded everyone down the highway, moving us into certain death. In the center of the line, speeding in front of all the others, was a bright yellow Lotus.

My heart stopped beating, my breath caught, and I felt the tears of panic splash down my face out of nowhere.

"Ryland." Had I meant to say it out loud, or simply speak to him in my mind? My voice caught in my throat, but the reply was right in my ear.

"Run, Joclyn. Stay with Ilyan." Ryland's voice was a whisper, but clear as day. I whipped my head to the side, devastation filling me to see nothing but the gray bag. I looked back to the Lotus, desperately searching for his dark curls.

"Ryland." I lifted my hand and placed it on the glass of the back window. The firm, smooth surface of the glass was hot under my touch. It felt like the burn of the necklace that still pressed against my skin.

I focused on the warmth, on the heat, the image of his face floating into my line of sight. The warmth grew, both in the necklace and in my hand. It moved into me, the heat seeping into every part of my soul. I pressed my hand harder into the glass in my desperation to see Ryland. The glass shattered under my hand.

A million pieces scattered across the trunk of the car, over the road. I didn't have time to look at it; I couldn't be surprised. Only a moment after the glass shattered, the road behind us shifted. I screamed as the asphalt heaved itself into a giant pile, the earth moving to lift it upwards toward the sky, building itself into a mound. The sleek SUVs moved up the increasing mountain for only a moment before they were hidden behind the large pile of asphalt, stones and earth that spanned the freeway.

I spun around, my body aching, to face Ilyan. I expected to see him standing with his hands extending out, but instead, he remained inside the car where he had fallen, his eyes wide and staring.

"Drive, Wyn." His voice was calm and awed.

I flipped my head back to the mound of earth and back to Ilyan, wincing at the pained movements.

"What happened, Ilyan?" I asked quietly.

He just looked at me. The answer was clear on his face—he didn't know.

I turned my body around, looking toward the distancing earth pile. Behind that pile, somewhere, was Ryland. I lifted my hand to my necklace, the warmth receding. The heartbeat of scorching heat left it, leaving only a slow throbbing. I held it tightly again, still staring back out the window.

"Did I do that?"

"I'm not sure."

"You're not sure?" I rounded on him; how could he not know? I stared into him in a panic, my throat burning, my body aching.

"I will know soon, Silnŷ."

"When?"

"Soon." He reached forward and placed his hand against my cheek. "We will be home soon and then I will know everything. And, I will tell you. I promise."

"Home?"

"Joclyn, I'm sorry, but I can't let you know where we are going quite yet."

I felt the warmth of Ilyan's magic flood through me, the numbness moving through my body and into my brain. I turned to see the last of the city flash past me before my vision blacked out and Ilyan's magic put me to sleep again.

CHAPTER 32
JOCLYN

"Just wait. You will see what I mean."

"I don't have time for this; can't it wait until later?"

"No, Ovailia, it can't. If he—"

"Fine."

The bed depressed as someone sat down near my feet. A bed. The more I woke up, the more I could tell it was a bed. I could feel the soft and hard combination of a spring mattress made far too long ago, and smell the musty stench of blankets left too long in storage. I opened my eyes, trying not to move.

It looked like I was in an old hotel room; the décor was something out of the sixties. The wallpaper was faded and peeling in places, but still had the obvious brown-on-orange striped pattern that was popular then. An orange, angular lamp sat on a darkly varnished table, a hard plastic chair pulled up to the side. The look of the room explained the musty smell of the bed and the blankets; they all must have been here since the day the hotel first opened for business.

Although the shade to the window near the table was open, the light filtering into the room was dim and filled with the blue light of dusk. Even with what came in through the window, there wasn't much light, which was further diminished by the dark color scheme.

"Ugh. More commercials. I don't know if I can wait any longer." It was the same woman's voice I had heard before. It was deep and nasally. She was irritated, and by the sound of it, she was irritated all the time.

Her voice held only a subtle hint of an accent, as if she had been trying to get rid of it for far too long and had only partially succeeded.

"Ovailia..." Wyn pleaded. I could pick Wyn's voice out now, accented or not.

"You have one more minute, Wynifred; that is all. I hate human news; it's so boring," Ovailia's voice drawled out angrily.

The bed moved as someone shifted their weight. I held still. I wasn't sure I wanted to let them know I was awake just yet. Ovailia did not sound like someone I wanted to meet right now anyway.

"Here it is!" The sound on a television they had been watching was turned up, and someone shifted their weight again.

"We have a further development on the kidnapping of seventeen-year-old Joclyn Despain, who has been missing for twelve days. And in the murder of her mother, fifty-three-year-old Angela Despain."

Murder.

I thought of her still body spread over the kitchen floor, her beautiful, yellow nails. Ilyan had said it before, and I felt the same destructive force move through me now as it had then. The dilapidated house that contained my soul ripped apart with a violent explosion that rushed over me in a torrent of depression so deep, I was drowning in it.

I was barely able to stabilize myself amongst the flow that swirled around me. I did though; I caught my breath and found a hand-hold somewhere deep inside. I was stable, but empty. I could tell automatically that this pain, this emptiness, would never leave me.

"Ryland LaRue, who was last seen with the young girl, and continues to claim his innocence in her disappearance, has stepped forward in a press conference this afternoon, offering a reward for information leading to her safe return." The sound cut out as a video clip was loaded.

"Good afternoon, ladies, gentlemen, and members of the press."

I sat up the second I heard his voice.

Ryland.

His voice felt like an electrical current that shot through me. The blankets tumbled down around me as I sat, my body surprisingly not protesting the quick movements. The two women at the foot of the bed did not register my actions; they, too, were focused on the TV screen. I was vaguely aware of them; Wyn with her short, auburn hair, and Ovailia with an absolute sheet of sleek, honey blonde that fell well past her hips and cascaded over the grungy brown bedspread.

"I would like to address you today..." My ears did not hear another word. The sound of his voice faded away into the air around me.

At first glance, he looked like the Ryland I had always known, the Ryland I had always loved; dark curls falling over his face, strong jaw, strong body, bright blue eyes. However, once my heart stopped seeing and my mind was left to linger, I instantly felt the tears come.

He had been beaten.

His left eye was swollen and tinged with an ugly purple, a large gash ran from his cheek and down across his neck before disappearing underneath his shirt. A few more deep purple bruises were just visible from underneath his hair and around the collar of his shirt. Although he gestured with his left hand, his right and dominant arm hung loosely at his side. I could almost see the pain in his eyes, the strain in his face. I recognized the same pain in me, the same entrapment I had felt over the last few days as my body ached and tried to heal. He was in agony.

Then, he flinched. It was so subtle I almost didn't catch it. His left arm moved toward his chest and then out again. I reached toward the image on the screen, my heart calling out to him. The bed lifted as Ovailia stood and took a step closer to the screen.

"You see it, too?" Wyn whispered.

I tried to focus on what Ryland was saying, but I couldn't; my heart beat too hard in my chest. He seemed fine, until another twitch, this one bigger, caused him to stop. He paused and lowered his head, his chest heaving as he breathed. The clip played for only a second more before cutting back to the announcer and then the TV shut off.

"How much time does he have left?" Wyn asked.

I saw Ovailia's mane of hair shake, her shoulders sagging.

"A week, maybe two, if we are lucky."

I didn't flinch at Ilyan's voice, even though it was so close to me. He stood to my side, beyond my line of sight. I stayed still, my arm still extending toward the television screen.

"Why would he do something like that?" Ovailia snapped. "And to his own *precious* son, too." The words dripped off her tongue like poison.

"It wouldn't be the first time he has hurt his own children, Ovailia. You should know that better than anyone."

I turned toward Ilyan at that, my arm finally dropping down to the bed. He stood at the side of the bed, his back leaning against the ugly brown and orange papered wall.

"But if he only has a few weeks before his mind is lost..." Wyn began, her unfinished thought fading into the steadily darkening room.

"It's true then, everything he told me in the dream." My voice was so quiet, my throat burning as I spoke. I looked to Ilyan who raised an eyebrow at my question. In my peripheral vision I could see both Wyn and Ovailia whip around to me in surprise.

"What dream, Joclyn?"

I looked at him skeptically, second guessing myself.

"He came to me... I thought it was a dream..."

"What dream?" Ilyan repeated.

I felt a heavy panic creeping through me, the reality of what was happening hitting me hard.

"When you held me under the water, Ryland was there..." My voice gained in intensity as the panic continued to grow.

"What did he say to you?"

My fear rose, knowing exactly what was going on. I knew why he was twitching, what was happening, because Ryland had told me.

"His father... he is deleting his mind. Edmund's killing him, isn't he?" I looked hard at Ilyan, my panic demanding the answers I desperately needed.

"He's not going to kill him."

My heart swelled in relief, until Ilyan's tone, his desperation, sank in.

"A Vymåzat is when someone uses their magic destructively on another person. In essence, they delete, or partially delete, that person's mind. They remove all memories and personality. A Vymåzat creates a shell of a person that can be molded to become what the one who uses the magic wishes them to become. In Ryland's case, Edmund will not kill him; instead, he will delete all of him and turn his body and magic into a weapon." Ilyan's voice was so deep, it almost didn't sound like him.

"No! We need to save him." I went to remove the covers from me, fully intent on running to his aide; but my head swam so uncomfortably, I was sure I wouldn't be moving anywhere soon.

"I don't know if that's possible, Joclyn. There is no known way to reverse it," Wyn said.

"What else did he say in your dream?" Ilyan asked gently, pulling my attention from the other two.

"Only that..." I paused as I replayed the dream in my head, trying to pick out important pieces of information. I stopped as I recalled him writhing on the ground, my memory vividly showing me the small mark on his back. The mark he had kept hidden from me. My breathing picked up again.

"He had a mark like mine on his back."

Ilyan only nodded in acknowledgment at me.

"Why did he have a mark?" I said to Ilyan in a panic when it became obvious he knew and wasn't going to provide me with an explanation.

"Do you remember when I told you that Edmund and his servants have been hunting the Víly, and that it is the Víly that gives a kiss?"

I nodded, waiting for him to continue.

"Well, Edmund captures them and siphons off their poison. He's been doing it for years, so that when his next child was born, he could create a child with such a large amount of magic that no one could defeat him."

"Ryland?" It was obvious who he was talking about, my stomach turned in worry or excitement at just saying his name.

"Yes, Ryland. He injected him with the poison when he was two. He didn't awake from the injection for eighteen months... it's a miracle he survived."

"How do you know this?" I asked, trying to ignore the bile churning its way up my throat.

"It doesn't matter how he knows, little girl." Ovailia's voice was ice against my back.

"But you said I was unconscious for—"

"And yours remains the longest *natural* awakening. Ryland's mark was forced, and therefore, an unnatural anomaly," Ilyan cut me off.

"Where were you in this dream?" Ilyan changed the subject as he came to sit next to me on the bed. I shifted away from him a bit, feeling uncomfortable with how close he was.

"I don't know. It was all white. Ryland said it was some sort of shared consciousness."

Ilyan smiled almost knowingly at my words, while Ovailia and Wyn gasped in unison.

"A Tȍuha?" Ovailia exclaimed. "How is that possible?"

"What is that?" I asked "A Tȍuha?"

"It is exactly what Ryland told you it was," Ilyan commented quietly. "A Tȍuha is a place where your minds can go and be together, no matter how far apart you are in distance. It is normally only reserved for those who have gone through the Zêlství, which is why it is so surprising that you shared one with Ryland."

"Zêlství?"

"He means bonded," Wyn translated the word from Czech for me. "You would refer to it as a marriage."

My jaw dropped.

"Marriage?"

"I had a feeling your connection with Ryland was stronger than any of us thought after you raised the highway into a mound when we escaped." Ilyan's eyes dug into mine sharply.

"I did that?" I asked.

"Yes, but not on your own," Ilyan continued. "Ryland helped, too."

A pin could have dropped and it would have sounded like a herd of elephants. I could only stare at him, my jaw dropped in awe.

"You don't mean... the necklace?" Wyn asked, her voice almost a squeak of nerves.

Ilyan nodded in response to her question, his focus still on me.

"What necklace?" Ovailia scowled. "What have you been keeping from me, Ilyan?"

Ilyan finally released me from his gaze to stare down Ovailia with hard eyes.

"I keep from you whatever I deem, Ovailia."

Ovailia wilted under his sharp gaze.

"You will have to excuse my sister," Ilyan's voice was impregnated with something akin to diplomatic anger. "She forgets her manners from time to time."

"Or on a daily basis," Wyn grumbled under her breath.

Ilyan chuckled at her comment while Ovailia only growled.

"Yes, because I am the one that behaves like a--"

"Ladies." Ilyan's one word was enough for the two of them to stand down.

I probably should have been more shocked, given how fuzzy my mind was when Ilyan told me that Wyn was not his sister. Looking between Ilyan and Ovailia right then, I felt supremely stupid for ever believing that Wyn and Ilyan were siblings in the first place. Wyn was so short and darkly colored; she looked out of place between Ilyan and Ovailia with their tall, fair beauty. So much was alike between them; their high cheekbones, the shade of their eyes, and the golden color of their long hair. Ovailia's features were refined, her high cheek bones and cat-like eyes giving her the look of aristocratic beauty. Still, somehow, her attitude ruined it and turned some of her striking elegance into rubbish.

"Since you have chosen to keep things from me, do you wish to enlighten me now?" Ovailia waved one of her hands impatiently to the side, her long fingers extending like a dancers.

"Show her your necklace, Joclyn."

"What does any of this have to do with my necklace?" I asked, clutching the ruby tightly through Ryland's sweater.

"You are going to have to tell her, My Lord," Wyn spoke, her weight shifting on the bed to face me.

He stood and began to pace, only moving a few steps in either direction as he ran his hands through his hair in agitation.

"Ilyan?" I asked after I could take no more of his uptight movements. He stopped at my voice and came to lean against the bed, his face only millimeters away from my own. I flinched back out of habit.

"The necklace is more than just a gift; Ryland has infused it with his own magic as a way to keep an eye on you, to protect you. Every time you have ever felt it grow warm, it signals to him that you are in danger."

I nodded, remembering his sudden appearance at the Rugby field, and his apparent knowledge of my fight with Cynthia.

"But I am afraid it inadvertently became more than that. You see, the entire time you two have known each other, Ryland has been infusing you with his magic—to calm you, to heal you, to protect you, to comfort you."

I nodded before looking down at my lap. "The warmth," I sighed. "I pushed you out the first time you tried to heal me because Ryland's m... magic..." I struggled to get the word out. "It had just left me and I was scared."

"The day we went to the fire pit," Wyn interrupted, her voice low, "he healed your hand after you hit him, he used his magic to calm you when you were jumping over the fire, and you... you used his magic to help you climb the tree."

"What?"

"When you climbed the tree," Wyn continued, "you drew his magic off him and used it to sharpen your senses. It's why you are so fast. It's why it feels so natural."

"Ryland did it all without knowing that you possessed your own unharnessed power," Ilyan continued. "The more your magic mingled, the more they became dependent on each other, the more they became one. When Ryland gave you the necklace, he made it so that his magic would always be close to yours, and with that, he inadvertently sealed your fate. He permanently fused the magic, and in turn, your lives together."

"What are you saying? That Edmund could infiltrate my mind as well?" I couldn't keep the panic from seeping into my voice. I needed to save Ryland, but now it wasn't just him—it was me as well.

"I do not think it will come to that," Ilyan said. "Mostly what this means is that you can draw off each other. In essence, your magic cannot survive without his and vice-versa."

"In the apartment," Ilyan spoke solemnly, "it was Ryland controlling his magic through the necklace that saved you. In the alley, it was his magic that was taking the pain away. He consciously saved and protected you, even though his father was torturing him at the very same time."

"Torturing him? But in the dream he looked okay... Why does he look like he has been beaten, Ilyan? What's happened to him?" My thoughts strung together before settling on the brutal image of him that still flooded me.

"He *has* been beaten, Joclyn; possibly more than the television images show us. They can cast a spell on him, make it appear that he is not as injured as he is," Wyn spoke plainly, the truth cutting me.

"What worries me the most," Ilyan added, "is that Edmund is not allowing Ryland to be healed, or even allowing him to heal himself. He is kept in pain to weaken him, so that he doesn't fight back."

"Pain?" I asked, remembering my first assumption that he looked like I had felt the last few days.

"Yes, Joclyn, agonizing pain. Almost the same type of pain you felt when you first received your kiss. He feels that every second of every day and must live with it."

"But he didn't look like that... in the dream, I mean."

"That's because you were seeing with your heart." I turned to Ovailia's acidic voice. "If you had taken the time to see with your mind, you would have seen the true extent of his injuries. Then perhaps we could know with more certainty how much time he has left."

"Enough, Ovailia," Ilyan commanded, but I couldn't take my eyes away from her.

"Ryland is dying inside. His father is trying to *delete* his mind. When you say he has maybe two weeks—"

"I mean in a week, maybe two," Ilyan whispered, "Ryland will be no more. He will only be a shell to be manipulated by his father."

I clutched my necklace, pressing the cold stone against my chest. I felt my heart beat wildly against my fingers. Once again, the mark had destroyed everything, everything I needed and wanted within my life. However, this time I knew the truth; the mark had truly given me the power to get everything back, the power to fix it.

"I will save him." My voice was quiet, but still confident. I knew I would do whatever it would take to save Ryland, to honor my mother, to change my life.

"I know," Ilyan whispered.

I turned to him, unsurprised to see that wild anticipation and crazy confidence he had had in the car. It wasn't the joy I had originally mistaken it to be, though.

It was power.

CHAPTER 33
RYLAND

Everything felt cold. The air, my clothes. Everything was shivering and frozen, right down to my bones. It was as though I had turned into my own personal freezer. My joints shook with it, my muscles tensed with it; the chill making each motion stiff and frozen.

Possibly because each of the motions that I was trapped in were not my own.

'Block, attack with iron.'

My father's voice filled my mind, the dark hiss acting like a tether as my magic flared and followed his command; blocking Cail's attack and sending another one his way.

Cail grinned and countered, sending my attack uselessly to the side.

'Block on left. Attack with right. Kill him.'

My muscles pulled, my mind screaming as Cail sent one attack and then another after me. My body, my magic, did exactly as Edmund commanded it to. I attempted to fight it, my body twitching as I did.

It was pointless. My magic fired anyway, the attack a violent stream of smoke and flames that darted right toward Cail. He darted to the side, the attack streaming passed him to slam into the wall behind.

A boom rang in my ears as the attack hit with an explosion greater than I had ever created as the true strength of my magic was made clear to my father for the first time. I had been holding back, and now he knew. My muscles sagged as I reverted to some kind of puppet on strings, forced to watch Cail, Timothy, and my father surround the aftermath with a differing array of surprise and eagerness of their faces.

"I must admit, I am impressed." Cail kicked a bit of the still smoldering rubble, sparks of flame following it as it bounced along the marble floor like a tail. "We should have done this years ago."

"Just think of all we can do now that we have harnessed all of that power you spent so long cultivating for our use? I agree, it's a brilliant plan, sir." Timothy said as they all turned to me. They were all grinning with malice now, each of those wicked eyes staring right at me as though I was their new favorite toy.

A pet.

Something that they had full control over.

They were getting ahead of themselves. Hadn't he realized yet that I wasn't going to go down so easily? That I wasn't simply letting him win?

My mind was screaming against the iron bars that surrounded it, pounding and raging as they pointed at the attack, at me, and made their terrible plans.

"I don't see why we just can't send him to finish it all off now. Screw the girl, Ryland can take down Ilyan for us, and when he is done with that, he can mangle the gi–"

"I will never do that!" The words burst out as I exploded out of my cage, my feet taking one staggered step forward as my control exploded out of the iron cage inside my mind. "I will never hurt her!"

"That is why," Edmund grumbled with a sigh, his lip twitching. "The bastard has not been tamed. Yet."

'Stand down, son.' His voice roared and creamed in my head and I flinched in my attempt to keep it at bay, to keep him from forcing me back into that cage again.

"No!" I screamed in response to the voice and forced another step. "I will never obey you."

'You are worthless, Ryland. You will never be anything other. Give up, now.' The taunt sliced and cut over me, the brand of the Vymåzat burning hot as he engaged that connection. I winced, the burning rumbling through me as I tried again to take another step.

This time I was forced back, no matter how hard I fought that magic pushed through.

"Do you really think you can fight me?" My father continued, his words echoing both in the cave and in my head.

No! I couldn't let this happen. I wouldn't. The burn of his magic was everywhere, but I pushed it back, away from when I could feel Joclyn inside of me, away from all of those precious parts of me I would never let him have. I took another step forward, the panic in his eyes growing.

"I will. You..." My words were coming slower now, as though they couldn't press themselves out all the way. "Will never..."

My tongue froze, just like the rest of me. They all smiled as my father's voice, his commands, grew louder in my head.

'You will do as I say, Ryland...' He was near screaming now, his voice everywhere.

His power wound through me as though it was my own, it twisted up my spine and I stood up straighter, my arm jerking violently as I continued to fight him off.

"I will always fight you."

"If that's what you want," Edmund seethed, my arm twitching again. "By all means, keep fighting. The more you fight, the more of *you* I will take. The less of you that is left, the more I control. You know you can't fight this, Ryland. You were never strong enough. Never good enough. No matter how much work and power I put into you, you were always a disappointment."

Each of his words sliced the way they always did, the barbs and prods moving fast and deep into me. That time they did what I was sure he had meant all along and my magic slipped, letting him take even more control.

"Maybe we should let him keep fighting then," Timothy said with a drawl as he leaned against the wall. The guy actually sounded bored. "Destroy him completely and we won't have to deal with his pathetic outbursts and then we can finish this."

"Agreed. He whines about as much as Wynifred does. *'Please don't hurt me. Why are you trying to kill me?'*" Cail said as he flailed his arms in the air, mimicking someone. Wynifred. I had heard that name before, hadn't I? "Pathetic. Let me just beat him, master, weaken him so you can finish it. So you can control him."

"No. This shouldn't take long." Edmund didn't pull his gaze from mine as he stepped closer, his voice still screaming in my head as that burn continued to flare and slice.

"I won't--" I tried to scream the words over the pain, but they came out as little more than a whisper.

"You won't *what*?" My father interrupted my stuttered words, the three of them stepping closer. "You won't bow? Fine, but you also won't remember who you are when I am done with you. Keep fighting. I'll just take more of you faster. Give in and perhaps I will let you keep a memory or two."

His eyes were pools of hatred as he reached me, his hand on my forearm as his magic spread through me deeper than it had before. My heart beat rattled in my ears as his magic moved into my mind like slimy fingers. I could feel it penetrating, all of the puppet strings moving to attention as images flashed before me.

My mother's smiling face.

The first time I drove my Lotus.

The smell of the pines when Jos and I drove up the Canyons.

Jos...

At the thought of her, my mind snapped together, pushing him away and sending those fingers curling back into him. He may be deleting me. Stealing me. He couldn't have that. I would never give him that.

"Do you really want to fight me, son?" He didn't seem to be enjoying it as much that time.

'Not that you can, you're pathetic. A fool. Just bow, Ryland.'

I wanted to snap. I wanted to tell him how ridiculous he was, how I would never bow to him. But just watching the three of them stand there, murder and hunger in their eyes, I knew I would just be wasting my energy. If I was going to find a way out of this and protect Joclyn, I needed to conserve every inch of energy and magic I could.

I knew I could.

But for now, I needed to let him think he was winning.

So, I stood like my father's puppet, my arms and magic jumping as he pulled the strings and my magic came right back into his control, the sparks jumping between my fingertips.

"Good. Good." Edmund looked absolutely overjoyed with himself. "You see, Cail. Never doubt me."

Before any of them could react, my magic was pulled from me, soaring right towards Cail. This time he couldn't dodge in time and the attack my father had pulled from me rammed right into Cail's chest, sending him backwards, right into the still burning stone behind him.

I couldn't even be happy that I had hit him.

"If you can't dodge Ryland, no wonder you couldn't take down your sister," Edmund said to Cail as he turned to leave, Timothy behind him like the shadow he always was.

Sister? Cail had a sister?

"Yes, master," Cail said as he stood, facing me as I stared at him, wishing I could look anywhere else. But I was still stuck in broken marionette form.

"Now, I will leave the rest of this lesson to you. Remind him what happens when he fights me."

"Gladly."

My father and Timothy left, leaving Cail before me with magic growing on the tips of his fingers, and me with absolutely no way to defend myself.

With what little control I could muster, I forced my eyes closed and pulled at the bit of warmth that remained in my soul, the line of the necklace that was the only safe place.

The only place I could hide.

I sunk myself into it, just as the first attack of Cail's magic slammed into my chest and I felt my ribs crack.

CHAPTER 34
RYLAND

"Here you are, little Prince. Your suite."

Cail didn't even chain me up anymore. He simply placed the heavy metal shackles on my wrists and threw me onto the wet stone, locking the heavy, barred door to my cell with a clang.

"Another day like this, Ryland, and I doubt you will even remember your own name, let alone hers."

I groaned and attempted to shift my weight into something more comfortable, but I only managed to fall back down to the stone with a grunt.

"Normally, I would have killed you by now," Cail taunted, the sound of his retreating feet echoing up the stairs. "Too bad your father still needs you. I'll just have to enjoy my time with you in the meantime."

'Unless you just give in and give me the control I need. You can't fight me, Ryland.' Even here there was no escape from my father's control.

The door at the top of the stairs slammed shut, shutting out the sound of his laugh and plunging the lines of cells into darkness.

I tried to shift my weight again, but my body wasn't having it, so I just lay there on the cold stone in the position I had landed in, water dripping over me as I let my mind wander.

Every night I lay here, what little of my magic that I still had control of trying to heal my body as I pulled through my memories and took an account of how much I had lost. It was an impossible task, how would I know what I had lost if I couldn't remember it? But it didn't matter, I still tried, I tried to remember, tried to cling to what I knew.

'There is no point, you are weak. Pathetic.'

It was getting harder and harder to pull things to the surface, luckily, I had felt like this before.

Felt this muscle ache after a day of fighting, the bruises and broken bones after my father's ministrations.

It was a start, an open door into my memories, I just had to follow it down that path. Muscle aches, broken bones, hard work...

"I play rugby," I whispered into the dark. "I was the captain at... uh... Whitmer Preparatory Academy. We won the championship. At the last game, Cail was there. She fell and I helped her. I protected her. She... Jos. Joclyn."

I knew I had protected her. I had felt the line of the necklace burn hot and I had rushed to her so that my father or Cail wouldn't see her. I could remember healing her cut with my magic, and taking her to her car... and the kitchen... Someone was there.

Who was there?

Who was always there?

"No... I can't have forgotten."

With a grunt I stretched my hand forward as if I could see her there, lying on the ground before me. I stared into the dark as I tried to find something more recent. Who was in the kitchen?

'You belong to me.'

The shadow of the memory bled down the stairs as I remembered Cail dragging her body down the stone.

"Angela Despain." Joclyn's mother.

The pile of rags in the cell next to mine shivered as I said the name, a small noise seeped from it as though it was crying.

"You okay in there?" I asked, my spine screaming as I tried to move closer to the bars that separated us.

I had tried a few times before to speak to the pile of rags, and it hadn't answered. I still hadn't completely ruled out the possibility that I was hallucinating.

No movement, no noise.

I shifted back to the patch of stone and wet, groaning in my attempt to find someplace comfortable to sneak in some sleep before Cail came back for me in the morning.

"Did you know her?" I jumped at the scratchy male voice that rustled over from the rags like sandpaper.

It is a person, and even better, they can talk.

"So, you are alive."

"Did you know her?" he repeated, a hand appearing from the rags to wrap around the bars between us. "Angela Despain?"

"Yes. She is... was my father's cook. She's dead." Saying it aloud brought the memory back with a scream, and with it the pain.

"Yes, I know. And you are who they say? Ryland LaRue?"

I looked around, suddenly wondering if this was just another part of Cail's torture.

"I am." I stared at the rag, waiting for more movement, for a face to emerge. It was still just darkness and that one grimy hand.

"I should have never come back," he said after a moment.

"Come back?" I shifted my weight, moving forward as I continued to search the rags for something more human than an arm.

"What... who... are you?"

'You are mine.'

"Your father's other prized possession." The pile of rags shifted as they sat, blankets and towels and everything else he had been using to keep himself warm down here falling away to reveal a man with feet of dark knotted hair and a beard that was just as long and just as matted. I could barely make out wrinkled green eyes through the hair and grime that covered him.

He looked as though he had been down here for years. Knowing my father, I wouldn't be surprised if he had been.

If he had gone through what I had.

'I saved my worst for you, son.'

"Is he deleting your mind too?" I asked as I twitched, as though the motion would somehow banish my father's voice from my mind.

"Is that what he is doing to you?" Filthy hands wrapped around the bars of the cell, the man leaning in. His eyes were so dark that they looked like pools of ink. Odd, I had sworn they were green. "A Vymȁzat?"

"Yes. He always wanted me to be his greatest weapon..." He had done everything he could to create it, and I had done everything to fight him.

"You're not going to let him, are you?"

"I am fighting him, but I am starting to forget." I sagged against the bars again, hand fluttering over my heart. Over where the necklace I gave Joclyn hung on her neck. Over the place where I had given her part of me to protect her, the svazovat.

"Forget people like Angela Despain? She wasn't that important." For being so worried about her before he suddenly seemed disgusted and upset at just saying her name.

"Even cooks can be important." She was important.

I really didn't want to get into it with this guy. I didn't know him, I didn't trust him. The way his dark eyes were pouring into me was making me uncomfortable, anyway. Especially because he wouldn't look away.

"I lost my memory, too," he continued and I sat up straighter. "Not by your father. From someone else. But I am starting to remember. I can help you remember too."

"Can you help me stop this? I need to stop this. I need to get out of here." I turned to face him again, his dark eyes trying to swallow me.

"I can, but on one condition." I was sure he was smiling under the rats nest of a beard.

I wasn't in the mood to barter, but seeing as we were both prisoners in my father's dungeon, I didn't see any other option.

"What's the condition?" I asked, a dark panic lashing through me as though I wouldn't like the answer.

"When the time comes, you are getting me out of here. You don't leave me behind."

I nearly jerked back in surprise. That wasn't necessarily the hardest thing, except that the idea that we could get out of here was nearly laughable. Looking into his eyes I could tell that he wanted it as bad as I did. If he had recovered his memory, and could help me do the same and regain control of my magic, then maybe we could stand a chance.

Maybe I could get back to her.

Of course, that would rely on a dozen other things, like trusting a prisoner of my fathers that he had locked in a dungeon. The last time I had done that it hadn't ended well. Of course, last time I hadn't been locked in the dungeon too.

Trust was going to be hard, but I had to try.

"Who are you," I asked carefully, leaning forward so that I did not miss the answer. "Besides my father's prized possession, I mean?"

He smiled, dark eyes squishing together like beetles as he blinked. When he looked back at me the green in his eyes was back, the darkness of the dungeon having swallowed it whole. He stuck his hand between the bars toward me.

"I'm Sain." He said it as though I should know who he was, or why my father had him here. I didn't. I stared at him, waiting for more. When he gave none, I shook his hand once, his brow furrowing in confusion.

He was odd, and I wasn't sure I could trust him. But it wasn't like I had many options.

"Ryland," I said and that time he smiled.

CHAPTER 35
JOCLYN

We watched the news conference all day, everyone ripping it apart until Ilyan had suddenly excused himself, saying that there would be a council in an hour and he needed to prepare. Ovailia had followed close behind him, her nasally voice whining about something I didn't understand. The second the door had closed, Wyn rushed to me, flinging her arms around me in a tight bear hug.

"I am so sorry, Jos, so sorry. If we could have gotten you out earlier, this never would have happened. If we..." Her voice caught and I could tell she was trying not to cry. I returned the hug, my arms hesitantly wrapping around her.

"I wanted so badly to just run away with you the night we watched the movie at the apartment, but someone had caught sight of Ilyan that morning, and he didn't want to risk being followed or trapped. If only we had..." She jabbered on and on, and even through the accent, I could tell she was the same old Wyn. Hearing this bit of normalcy made me smile. It took the edge off the desperate panic I felt with Ryland's situation, and the crushing depression over my mother. I sighed deeply and leaned into her, grateful for the emotional support.

"Can you forgive me?" she pleaded, pulling me away from her to look at me. Her eyes were so off putting; the all-encompassing blackness of them, combined with the dark tattoos, made her look ominous. I moved my hand up a fraction of an inch, as if to touch her skin, but put it down again. The movement didn't go unnoticed.

"I know I look a little… odd. You'll get used to it. It took me a hundred years to come to terms with my new face, so take all the time you need." She smiled widely at me, but my jaw had dropped.

"A hundred years?"

"Yeah, I am a ripe old lady. I was born in about 1795 and received the marks on July tenth of 1867."

"1795?"

"Yeah, and exiled before my hundredth birthday. That's why Ryland didn't recognize me; we've never met, and I highly doubt Timothy ever spoke of me after he marked me. In a century or so you can tell me if you think they suit me or not."

"Wait, what? A century? I can't possibly live that long."

"All magical beings possess some realm of immortality, Joclyn. But it's kind of contingent; if you don't use it, you die. So, I guess, no, you won't gain your immortality unless you actually start to use that magic of yours."

I had accepted the fact, almost without question, that Ryland and Ilyan, and even Wyn, had used magic. In the back of my mind, the idea that *I* possessed a magic of my own still felt like some kind of joke.

"But you won't be living until the world ends unless your back is healed. I apologize in advance."

Wyn lifted my sweater and placed her hand firmly on my bare back and instantly began to spread her magic into me as she checked my spine. I shuddered involuntarily. Her magic felt like ice inside my veins; it was the polar opposite of the relaxing warmth I got from Ilyan and Ryland.

Ryland.

"Will Ryland be alright?" My question was that of a child, and I knew it. I needed answers; I needed to know exactly what was going on so that I knew how to save him.

"He will if we get to him in time."

I shivered, my shoulders jerking uncomfortably. I wasn't sure if my jolt was due to Ryland's fate or to the icy magic that was moving through me.

"Sorry," she whispered. "The magic of a Trpaslík tends to be very cold. Of course, most of my kind use their magic to kill rather than to heal, so that may be why."

I could almost hear the sarcasm in her voice.

"A Trpaslík?"

"Yes. Once, a very long time ago, my kind were the keepers of the fire magic."

Ironically, I shivered as the icy cold of her magic continued to move into me, chilling every part of me.

"Sorry, I'm almost done."

"Why is your magic so cold if you used to keep the fire magic?"

"I was told as a child it was taken from us by the Skříteks, and in the absence of heat, we froze. But I don't believe that anymore. Everyone here is a Skřítek; I am just the odd man out."

"A Trpaslík."

"Yep."

"Why have different names at all, if you all look so much like humans?" I asked.

"It relates to our magic. Skříteks are the keepers—or the warriors—of all magic. They were once a powerful army that kept balance over the rest of us, but have since been almost driven to extinction. The Trpaslík are destructive by nature; our magic relates more to earth elements, and we can control them at will. We were the builders. Draks were the keepers of foresight and worked as some kind of government. Víly's were the givers of emotions, and kept the humans from their vices. The names relate to what we do, not who we are."

"Then why do you still call yourself a Trpaslík if you no longer live with them?"

"Because I am destructive above all else." She grinned menacingly. "Trpasliks are very good at making things explode. I'll show you sometime."

I couldn't help the shiver that spread up my spine. She enjoyed that reaction and smiled even more.

"Well, your back feels fine." Wyn jumped off the bed and flung the covers off me. I still wore the mysterious fleece pants and Ryland's sweater. I sat and picked at the soft fabric. Thinking of Ryland had made me edgy, like I needed to go run a marathon. My soul called for him, begging him to be okay, to wait for me.

"Broken back, huh?" I asked quietly.

"I know, hard to believe, isn't it? It actually broke in two places. Right here," she placed her hand at a spot right between my shoulder blades, "and here." Her hand slid down to rest a bit above the small of my back. "If it wasn't for Ilyan, you would have died."

I only nodded. Ryland had saved me, too. The images of Ryland's beaten face and my mother's broken body filled me. I felt my heart constrict again in its futile attempt to control the waves of emotion behind the dam I had built. I tried to push the heartbreak away; I needed her to be proud of me, wherever she was.

"Are you okay?"

I could only nod, my emotions moving far too slowly back behind their fortification.

"Where are we anyway?" My voice broke uncomfortably at the attempted subject change. I obviously couldn't handle thinking much about my mother just yet.

"This is one of our safe houses; it's an old motel that Ilyan bought and remodeled in 1968, hence the décor. We call it 'The Motel' strangely enough. Most everyone has updated their rooms, but this one and a few others have kind of been left alone."

Wyn helped me to swing my legs over the side of the bed, her hands assisting me to stand. My spine creaked, and I inhaled sharply as pressure was placed on it. Although the sensation was uncomfortable, it didn't hurt. It felt like I had never stood on my legs before.

"Come on," Wyn coaxed. "I want to show you something."

Even though stiffness had replaced the pain, I still needed help to walk; my legs needed to be reminded how to do it. Wyn helped me, step by step, as we moved slowly forward, stopping after a few steps when Wyn turned me to face the window.

The window opened to a beautiful courtyard that was surrounded on all sides by other rooms. It was full of flowers and vines that covered stone paths and beautiful wrought-iron patio furniture. And in the middle of it all, stood a giant tree. I had never seen one so large. It wasn't a pine tree, like the massive redwoods; it almost looked like an oak. Its broad leaves stretched up and out, covering the courtyard in a relaxing canopy of quivering leaves.

"It's beautiful."

"I know. The view in Prague is just as nice, too. You will see it when we get there."

"Get there?" I couldn't help the panicked edge that crept into my voice. I couldn't go anywhere without Ryland.

"Prague is the city where all magic originates; it's where we live. I am sure we will go home after we get Ryland out." She smiled sadly as she answered my unasked question. I couldn't help but feel the waves of uncertainty she was broadcasting, like she didn't think rescuing him was a possibility.

"When do we go get him?" I could feel the jittery feeling coming back.

"That's what Ilyan is in council right now to decide, Jos." She moved some of my hair behind my ear, and I fought the urge to yell at her, not because she had touched me, but because I felt the need to leave to save Ryland right then. It bothered me that this need to rescue him had come on so strong, so fast.

"Can we go for a walk?" I asked the first thing that had come to my mind, hopeful that my anxiety would dissipate with the movement.

"Ummm, yeah. You are not allowed in council, and everyone else will be there. So, we can both go sit in the courtyard and wait for Council to be released, or we can go get some food in my room."

It didn't take much thought to decide which I wanted. I would probably never be in the mood to meet new people. The thought gave me an overwhelming urge to pull the hood of the sweater up over me and hide, but I fought it.

"Food sounds great."

Thankfully, the hall outside the room did not stink so much of the sixties. It had been covered in wood paneling, but painted a nice cream color and carpeted in a plush Berber that helped it to look much more modern.

As we reached the end of the cream-colored hallway, I noticed that only this hallway was covered in the lightly colored paint and carpeting. The new hall we approached was a deep green and had hardwood floors. Right at the transition, Wyn stopped and turned to a man I hadn't noticed. He stood tall and still, right at the entrance to the hall, his focus down the hall ahead of us. At Wyn's approach, he turned to her, but said nothing.

"Tell his lordship we have gone to my chamber. The Chosen has requested a meal and he is welcome to join us when Council concludes."

The man clicked his heels together, and Wyn bowed before turning and guiding me down the green hallway in the opposite direction. I looked back at the man to see him still against the door frame.

"What was all that about?"

"I hate talking like that," Wyn said. "I am so much younger than everyone else, and they all get stuck up on rules, regulations and traditions. I'm lucky I have you; now we can be the irritating rule breakers together." I looked at her sharply; she hadn't answered my question. She sensed my gaze boring into her and stoically kept her vision forward.

"Wyn," I pleaded.

"Okay, they get stuck up on tradition, right? You have to address Ilyan in a certain way, bow to Ovailia in a certain way. You have to use the right verbiage in order to be properly understood," she sighed.

"Address Ilyan in a certain way," I repeated in a whisper. My Lord. His Lordship. "So, Ilyan is like your ruler."

"King," Wyn corrected. "King of only about a thousand people, yes, but still king."

My chest seized at the new information. Of course it made sense, but now I couldn't stop worrying about how I had acted around him, and if I would get in trouble for it.

"Considering they are the last of their kind, they take it very seriously. Well, everyone except Ilyan anyway," Wyn said.

"Does Ilyan not take his role seriously?"

"Not really. You'll see what I mean soon enough, though. Here we are." Wyn turned me toward a door that had been painted a green so dark it was almost black. In the middle of the door were two handprints, one small and bright purple, and the other large and dark red. She smiled before pulling me into the brightly decorated apartment.

I couldn't help but smile, too; the room was so Wyn, it was infectious. The bright bubbly colors made the last of my anxiety evaporate. A large king bed covered with a squishy leopard-print comforter occupied most of the space. The bed had an intricately carved footboard, but instead of a headboard, a gigantic Styx poster covered the light, yellow wall. Wyn guided me to an oversized, upholstered, purple chair that sat in front of the window that overlooked the courtyard.

"Food," she chanted and bounced away to a half-sized refrigerator that sat next to the bathroom door.

"I like your room,"

She turned and smiled at me.

"It's so bright and fun," I said.

"Thanks! It's probably a little too much, but out of all the time periods I have seen, I could live in the 70s and 80s forever." She sighed as if caught in a silly memory and then turned back to the fridge.

I couldn't help but laugh. I wasn't even alive in the 80s; but from what I had seen, it probably wasn't a time that I would have wanted to have participated in anyway.

"I probably don't have much that's edible for you." Wyn had buried her head in the fridge, her voice coming back to me muffled. "Talon doesn't keep this thing very well stocked when I am gone." Her head emerged from within the tiny fridge, her arms laden with a few things.

"Talon? Do you share a room or something?" I had almost forgotten about Wyn's boyfriend.

"Uhhh... yeah... I'm over two hundred years old, remember? I like to sleep with my husband as much as anyone."

My jaw dropped just as Wyn giggled and looked down. She was so much like a bubbly teenager, it was hard to think of her as quite literally old and, I guess, married.

"So," she placed the containers on the table next to me, "we have Maso, which is kind of a casserole made with berries, and lentils. This is Listy, which is a leaf stew made with root vegetables. Or, I found some cheese that I think Delia made a few months ago."

"Leaf stew?" I asked, poking at the containers. My stomach flipped. I hoped better food appeared soon; I didn't think I could live on leaf stew and lentils for very long.

"I made the same face about the food you eat, too," she said. "We are all vegetarians and most of our recipes dates back from before Ilyan was born, when all the earth were hunter-gatherers." She shoved one of the smaller containers at me with a grimace. "Try the Listy; it's closer to what you would normally eat, so you might like it."

I looked down at the contents of what Wyn had just handed me, and bile rose in my throat. It looked like someone had shredded the branch of a tree and boiled it with leaves, carrots, potatoes and tomatoes. Wyn was already chowing down on some purple goo. I could already tell this would take some getting used to.

CHAPTER 36
JOCLYN

The Listy didn't taste as bad as it looked. As long as I didn't look at what I put in my mouth, I could almost imagine it as a really thick meat stew. I didn't know how long I could last eating leaves and carrots, though. As much as I loved a good vegetable, I missed meat already and I was only one meal in.

Wyn finished two containers of food in the time it took me to finish my one. The entire time, she talked about how much she had missed normal food. I let her babble; the majority of what she said washed over me as noise.

My anxiety had not left yet; I was still far too restless for Ilyan's return. I needed to know when we were leaving.

I ate another spoonful and forced down the gritty leaves again. I was surprised that I wasn't starving. I was hungry, but not ravenous like I should have been. According to the news, everything had happened almost two weeks ago; meaning the half of a chili-cheese burger I had at Ryland's house was the only thing that had sustained me for so long. I asked Wyn and she waved it away, saying it was all part of the healing process.

I had just set down my empty container when the door swung open and a very tall, very muscular man burst into the small space. Wyn squealed and jumped up, practically throwing herself at him. The man grabbed her as she wrapped her legs around him, his face moving to nuzzle her neck. I couldn't help the stab of jealousy that rushed into my stomach at seeing such raw, heartfelt emotion.

Talon was large, so large that seeing the two of them together looked uncomfortable. He had slick, light-brown hair that was cut a bit shaggy and the same refined features that I had grown used to seeing on Ilyan. Beyond the straight lines of his face, there was little resemblance between the two. Talon almost looked like a barrel-chested football player, grown and stretched too tall. His arms were large and cylindrical, his legs long and slender. It was disproportionate, but looked good on him.

He finally pulled away from her, the surprise obvious on his face at seeing me sitting there. It took a moment for recognition to set in.

"Sorry about this," Talon said in an airy voice that didn't really match his size. "Wynifred has spent most of her time with you, so I haven't seen her much." He tried to remove her again, but she clung on tight. Finally, he accepted defeat and went to sit on the bed and allowed her to stay positioned on his lap.

"I'm Talon, by the way," he said

"Joclyn." My voice was barely above a whisper.

"So, Joclyn, you seem to be all that anyone is talking about now."

I could tell Talon meant his comment to be just a conversation starter, but the way he looked at me made me uncomfortable.

"Why?" I asked, alarmed.

"Well, last of the Chosen, and all that." He flung his hand mindlessly to the side.

"Oh." My shoulders slunk and I looked down to my lap.

Talon laughed, with a big booming sound that fit his body better than his voice did. My head snapped up to see Talon and Wyn, who had finally emerged from her hiding spot, both looking at me.

"Jos prefers to hide, Talon. She doesn't like to be noticed."

"Well, she will just have to get used to it then," Talon said. "She's the talk of the town! Finally, someone who can beat the socks off old Edmund!" He gave the air two rough punches with his hands, jostling Wyn around.

I felt the color leave my face.

"Talon, you can't say that," Wyn scolded as she detangled herself from her husband to sit next to him.

Talon opened his mouth to argue, but I cut him off.

"It's all right, he's probably right anyway," I sighed. "After all; if I'm going to save Ryland, I might as well knock the socks off somebody." I felt my shy resolve melt away at the thought of saving Ryland. As much as I wanted to stay hidden, I wanted to save Ryland more.

As if on cue, a loud knock sounded on the door, followed by a deep voice announcing Ilyan's arrival. Wyn rolled her eyes, but Talon only laughed again, nudging Wyn as if preparing for some great joke. He got up from the bed and moved to the door in two strides, throwing it open and instantly going down on one knee, his head bowed in reverence. Even in this extreme position, I could still see the wide smile on his face.

"My liege, I bid you welcome to my humble home. It is an honor to welcome you into my presence."

Ilyan walked in, looking thoroughly un-amused, and shut the door behind him.

"Get up, Talon. You look ridiculous," Ilyan scolded. Talon jumped up and clasped Ilyan's arm tightly, his white teeth flashing.

"Sorry, Ilyan, I just didn't want our guest to get the wrong idea."

Ilyan turned away from Talon to face me, his smile widening just as he passed Talon to kneel before me, taking my hands in his. I wanted to pull away from the close contact, but held still. I didn't know much about Kings, but I was sure pulling away would not end well.

"Are you alright? Are you in any pain?"

"I'm fine. A little stiff when I move, but nothing hurts like it did."

"Good, I'm glad to hear it. I had hoped to keep you in bed for longer, but it seems I need to make things like that an order." He smiled before turning to Wyn who wilted a bit under his gaze.

"I am sorry, Ilyan. I couldn't stay in that room another moment. It's so dark and musty. Besides, I hated the 60s," Wyn grumbled and folded her arms.

"Yes, but my mother loved them."

"Your mother?" I asked, my voice catching on the word. Odd, since I wasn't even talking about my own mother.

"It's okay," Ilyan said. He had caught the heartbreak in my voice and brought his hand up to rest against my cheek. "You will get used to the pain you feel now. It will become part of you, eventually. I promise. But in the meantime, it's okay to cry." His voice became so low, I was sure that Wyn and Talon couldn't hear him. I nodded numbly at him, and he smiled, finally letting his hand drop from my face. My body loosened gratefully at the end of the contact.

"Now!" Ilyan announced, jumping up and clapping his hands together. "The Council has decided that it is worth the risk to go and remove Ryland from within Edmund's grasp."

"What are you saying?" I asked, not daring to hope.

"That, on the night of his graduation party, we will be going into the mansion and bringing Ryland back with us. We have to get to him before the Vymåzat completes itself. I know how to stop it, but only before it completes, so that's the key." My heart swelled at the renewed hope, my body's restless energy seeping into me again.

"But his party is more than three weeks away," I said in a panic.

"You are forgetting that you have been healing and unconscious for the past twelve days. We have eight to prepare."

"Eight days?" Wyn asked.

"Yes, which means we have eight days to get Joclyn ready to go and to be able to marginally defend herself. A Vymåzat is powerful magic, so I need someone who can keep him in his right mind for as long as possible. The strength of Joclyn's connection with him is unparalleled; meaning, you, Joclyn, are more likely to be able to do that than anyone else."

"Me...? Go into the mansion...?"

"Yes, Joclyn. You must be willing to do anything it takes to save him. How far are you willing to go, Silnŷ?"

I looked up to meet his piercing blue eyes, so full of confidence.

"I would do anything to save him." I was shocked at the confidence I suddenly felt. I had never been one to hold my own, to stand up to someone. I had practically hidden from Cynthia McFadden for years. Now, knowing I had a chance to save the one person who was the most important thing to me, my confidence felt more secure.

"Good," Ilyan said.

Eight days. Eight days and I would be back in the mansion I had practically grown up in. A shiver ran up my spine, but not in a good way.

"But... the mansion... it burned down," I said, suddenly panicked that we wouldn't be able to save him after all. "I saw it; the whole third floor was in flames."

"I can only assume that much of the damage was repaired or contained magically. Either way, the party will be held in a different part of the estate."

"Wait," Wyn's voice was loud and panicked from behind Ilyan. "You say you need her to defend herself; you can't possibly mean you are planning to center her, are you?"

"That would be the natural choice, yes," Ilyan responded as he stood.

"Now?" Wyn said.

"Yes."

"You can't, Ilyan."

"Don't worry so much, Wynifred. Joclyn is a very strong girl, I think she can handle a little bit of centering," Talon said.

"It's not Jos I'm worried about," Wyn grumbled behind clenched teeth.

"What exactly are we talking about?" I interrupted, becoming more and more confused by the minute.

"He just wants to center her, Wynny."

"What's centering?" I tried again, hoping this time to get an answer.

"Right now, your magic is spread all over your body," Ilyan provided. "It's hiding in your muscle tissue and in your bloodstream. When we center magic, we collect it all and bring it to one central place, making it usable. Right now, you can't use your magic because it's spread out. It's been spread out for so long, it doesn't really know where it's supposed to be; so for you, it will probably hurt much more than it's supposed to."

"Great, more pain," I moaned.

"Not that much pain," Talon provided with a smile. "No reason to worry, right, Wynifred?"

"I told you, I am not worried about her. I am worried about Ryland."

"Ryland?"

"Ryland?" Talon echoed me. "What does he have to do with any of this?"

"Joclyn and Ryland have undergone the beginnings of a Zêlství, Talon." Wyn provided gravely. Talon's jaw dropped. "If he is as weak as I am thinking, then centering her might well kill him."

"No!" I stood in alarm, but my legs almost instantly gave out and I tumbled back down to the chair. Ilyan was at my side in a moment, his warm magic plunging into me.

"It's all right, Joclyn. We are not going to hurt Ryland."

"But, Wyn said—"

"I think I have found a way around that," Ilyan interrupted me.

"How?" Wyn demanded angrily.

"We will use the Drevo."

"Again?" Wyn exclaimed. "So soon? What if the magic rejects her?"

"I don't think it will."

"But what if it does?"

"Wynifred." Ilyan ended their conversation with one word. "Please go draw a bath."

"I can't use the tub in her room, Ilyan; it hasn't been cleaned. I—"

"You can use mine, Wynifred."

"Yes, My Lord." Wyn curtseyed and exited. Talon followed her, but not without clapping Ilyan hard on the back. Ilyan flinched before turning back to me.

"A bath? The same as before?" I asked once the door closed behind them.

"Yes, so please, try not to fight us this time."

Ilyan helped me to stand and guided me out the door and down the hall, one arm wrapped around my waist, the other holding tightly to my hand. I was grateful for the extra help, no matter how uncomfortable his proximity made me. The small amount of walking to and from Wyn's room had winded me, and I wasn't sure I could walk without his help.

We turned into the cream-colored hallway, Ilyan nodding to what I now assumed to be a guard.

"You will be staying with me in my corridor for the time being. I would like to have you close, just in case anything happens." He smiled at me. I tried to return it, but couldn't. Being so close, and having someone want me so close, was weird.

"This room is yours." He nodded solemnly to the door to the left. "And don't worry; we will strip it of brown and orange by morning. This room here," he nodded to the door directly across the hall, "is Ovailia's. I would say to stay out of her way, but you will find that to be an impossibility soon enough." I got the distinct impression that his sister was more of a bother than I had originally thought. We came to the end of the hall, which housed three different doors; one directly in front of us and two at either side.

"These doors here all belong to me, irritatingly enough, and you are welcome any time." His hand fanned across my back as he led me through the door directly in front of us. I drew into myself at his touch; I don't know why it made me so uncomfortable. Ilyan had found me, saved my life; but in some weird way, it felt disrespectful to Ryland to even let him touch me.

The room had been decorated in much the same way as the hall, with cream walls and cream carpet. Tucked into the corner, next to a window, was a giant bed with a white bedstead and white comforters, a large squishy divan nestled up against it. The room was so white and airy that even with the dark light of evening, it still felt comforting.

I could hear the sound of water running from one of the side rooms, the burning wood and mint smell stronger than I remembered. My body tensed-up, the memory of being held underwater still strong and terrifying.

Ilyan rubbed my back comfortingly as he led me to the bathroom, which was only just smaller than the entire brown and orange room. The walls and floor were covered in a white tile that brilliantly reflected the light from a large crystal chandelier that hung from the center of the ceiling.

Wyn was swirling dark blue water around in a huge, claw-footed tub, the color fading the more she moved the water. A small hand-carved wooden box sat open on a marble sink top, revealing the contents of what looked like chunks of dirt, weeds and bark.

"What is that?" I asked, my mouth going dry.

"It is the Drevo. It is a mixture of bark of the Pristÿat tree, dirt that comes from the standing stones in Scotland, and the leaves of a Vzkrí," Ilyan explained.

I nodded. "I am just going to pretend I understood what you just said."

"The combination, along with the water, creates an amazing healing property. It can heal and repair anything."

"Even broken backs?" I asked with a smile.

"Even broken backs. But, it does more than that; it also cleanses your soul."

"Why…?" I tried again, "How is this going to work?"

"The hope," Ilyan began, "is that the healing magic, the Drevo, will bypass you and pass directly to Ryland so that we can center your magic without harming him. And, if we are extraordinarily lucky, it will heal him as well; which may make the difference in how strong we find him to be in a week."

I nodded and stared between the now crystal-clear water and the box of mud. I had to do this; it would be gross, but I had to—for Ryland. It was becoming my mantra.

Ilyan left and allowed me some time to undress and wrap up in a towel. I felt odd standing in the middle of this gorgeous bathroom in only a towel. I took a deep breath and moved my head forward, allowing my hair to fall around my face.

"I can do this," I sighed to myself.

"Yes, Jos, you can. You ready?" Wyn said.

She stood by the tub, offering me a hand. I took it shakily and stepped into the incredibly warm water. The towel glued itself to me as I sank down into the warmth, thankfully giving me some semblance of modesty.

The water felt just as thick as I vaguely remembered, like stepping into a vat of warm hair gel, but without the stick. I sighed and closed my eyes as I leaned against the side of the tub, feeling the warmth move into me. A moment later, Ilyan returned.

"How is it going?"

"The water seems to have accepted her; so far, so good."

"Joclyn." I opened my eyes to look at him. "I don't know how this is going to work, but if it opens up another connection, another Tȍuha, between you and Ryland, you can't let him touch you, okay?"

"Why not?" I asked, suddenly worried.

"If his father breaks in when you are in contact during a shared consciousness, he could use your magical connection to track you down. He could follow the pull of your newly-awakened powers to find you. A connection like that could put everything in danger. Do you understand?"

I nodded my head before leaning against the tub and closing my eyes.

"Open your mouth."

I obeyed, but didn't look as Wyn placed the bitter, gritty Drevo on my tongue again. I closed my jaw around it tightly, fighting against the reflex to spit it out.

"Ready?"

"MmmmHmmm."

Ilyan's wide hand lay flat against my collar bone, the warmth of his magic swimming into me. The heat stretched to every corner of my body. It stayed there comfortably before his hand moved me under the water. I fought the temptation to gulp in air as he pushed me under. The warmth of his magic gained in intensity as I lay there, under the water, my lungs beginning to protest the lack of oxygen.

Ilyan's magic continued to increase until it grew into a pain, my lungs adding their own throbbing in their panic for air. My eyes snapped open again, just as I was about to pass out. I didn't see Ilyan and Wyn.

I saw Ryland's bedroom, I saw Edmund sharpening a knife, and I saw a lot of blood.

CHAPTER 37
JOCLYN

I saw only a flash of the bedroom before I was dragged into the white space again. I stood frozen, in the middle of the large room, not daring to move. My hands flexed at my sides, every part of me on high alert. I heard a scuffle and a whimper, followed by a pained sob. I spun around at the sound, my heart plunging to see Ryland curled up in a ball on the floor, his body naked except for a pair of boxer shorts. His hands gripped his curly hair tightly, his knees pulled up to his chest. He sobbed as his body writhed.

I ran to him, but as I got closer I couldn't help but think that something was off about him. Just seeing him curled in a ball on the ground, he looked smaller, leaner and less muscular. I had almost reached him when I stopped short, remembering that I couldn't touch him. He cried out in agony again before reverting to his tortured ball.

"Ryland!" I called out, lifting my voice above his screams.

"Stay away!" he yelled, his voice panicked and high pitched. "Don't hurt me! I can't take any more."

I gaped at him; his body looked completely fine. Everything was smooth and perfect. Except for his boxers. I looked at what were obviously blood stains, some of the pools of red still wet and glistening.

Edmund, sharpening a knife.

My heart caught and sputtered, my stomach threatening to turn out its contents. What had Edmund done to his son? Ovailia had said I could see how he really looked by seeing with my mind and not my heart, but when looking at the wet pools of blood, I wasn't sure I wanted to see.

"Ryland," I kept my voice even.

"Don't hurt me!" He curled himself into an even tighter ball, his joints turning white from the tension.

"I am not going to hurt you, I promise."

"You will hurt me! Everyone always hurts me!"

"I won't hurt you. I want to keep you safe."

His whimpering and terror lessened, but his body remained wrapped in a ball.

"Everyone hurts me," he repeated, but his voice wasn't as terrified.

"I won't; I promise."

His body unwound from within itself, and he moved his hands from in front of his face to peek out at me. His blue eyes pierced me from behind dark lashes as he removed his hands all the way, looking at me from the ground where he lay.

I tried my best to stifle a sob. The boy that lay on the ground was definitely Ryland, but not the Ryland I had shared a cheeseburger with just days before, not the Ryland I had almost kissed. I looked into the face of a much younger Ryland; a Ryland who I stole cars with and snuck into his parent's pool in the middle of the night. He couldn't have been older than sixteen. He looked at me in confusion, the lack of recognition evident on his face. My heart plummeted.

"Who are you?" he asked, his voice catching in between tears.

"Joclyn," I answered honestly. "Don't you remember me?"

"Joclyn?" His face screwed up in fear. "You're too old to be Joclyn."

I guess he was right; if he was sixteen, he'd remember me at about fifteen. Fourteen maybe.

"It's me, Ryland. I promise. I just look a little different." I gave him a little smile and his body relaxed a little more.

"How do I know it's you?"

"Do you remember when I was ten and we stole the car? Or when I was eleven and we snuck into the swimming pool, and you tried to do a flip and split your head open on the diving board?" His body began to relax with each memory I shared, so I kept going. "Or how about when we first met and you said that my eyes—"

"Looked like diamonds," he finished for me.

"Yeah."

"So, it's really you?"

"Yes."

"And you're not going to hurt me?"

"Never."

He unwound himself from off the white floor and sat up, looking around with wide eyes.

"Where are we?"

I followed his gaze, wondering how to answer him; I wasn't sure what to say or how to handle this. Ilyan hadn't mentioned anything about lost age to me.

"A special place only we can be—"

"Where no one can hurt me?"

"You're safe with me." I sat down near him, but far enough away I wouldn't be tempted to touch him. He looked at me skeptically for a minute before sliding his legs around and bringing his knees to his chest; the movement left a giant smear of blood behind on the ground. I couldn't take my eyes from it.

"Why do you look so old?"

I forced myself to look away from the blood and focus on his face.

"Magic," I stated simply. I felt like I was walking on eggshells, trying to figure out what to say. Although, at sixteen he would know everything, so much more than I even knew now.

"Magic? What magic?" His voice gave him away. I knew him far too well to know when he was covering something up.

"You told me about the magic, Ryland. You told me about your kiss." I had apparently chosen to say the wrong thing because he instantly began to panic, his arm flinging around to cover the mark on his shoulder.

"What kiss? I have no kiss; he took it away from me!" His voice was high and screechy again, the panic ricocheted off the white walls.

"The kiss, Ryland. The mark on your shoulder. You showed it to me..." I tried in vain to keep my voice even, but I knew it didn't work.

"He took it away from me!" Ryland screamed again like he hadn't even heard me. "He called me unworthy! I'm unworthy to bare the kiss. See. See! It's gone. All Gone!"

Ryland removed his hand from his back and shoved it toward me, the fingers stretched out in manic desperation. I looked at the hand, at first seeing nothing but white calloused skin, until it began to fade and change. I felt the change in me as my heart rate increased, and my vision shifted. The fingers were no longer white and beautiful; they were covered in blood. My mouth dropped in a panic as I looked at the smears of dark red.

I couldn't stop the part of me that wanted to see the real Ryland. I couldn't stop the desperate need to see him as he really was, and so my eyes lifted to his face.

Ryland sat on the floor in front of me, his dripping hand still extended toward me. The bruises from the press conference were darker and stood out vividly on his face and neck, many appearing where there were none before. The gash that ran down his face was wider and swollen in an angry red. Blood and sweat had matted his hair, causing the curls I loved so much to droop. Bruises and cuts covered his torso and chest, some oozing green fluid, and even more of them, a deep shade of blue. His right arm hung lifelessly to his side, trails of red flowing freely down the limb, over his fingers, and onto the floor.

I screamed and scrambled away from him. My hand flew to my mouth in an effort to cover the sound, but it was too late; the damage had already been done. Ryland screamed at the same time, and flung his younger body down to the ground, back into his ball. The action revealed his back to me, and I futilely fought the scream that rose in my throat. The shoulder where his kiss once lay faced me, revealing an ugly red hole where Edmund had dug the mark out.

Ryland's cries filled my ears and pierced my soul in a way I couldn't ignore. Through my tears, through my shaking body, I crawled across the white space to him. My hands hovered uselessly over his body as Ilyan's words echoed in my ears. At that moment though, I didn't care. I wrapped my arms around him as he had me so many times before, and I gathered him onto my lap. His frame was so small; it only caused my tears to flow more. It took a moment for his body to relax and his arms to wrap around me. I slid my arms over his back, the warm wetness of his blood spreading over my skin.

I just sat there, holding him and shushing him. We sat like that, the smell of blood and tears swirling around us. Eventually, he untwined his body from mine and moved away, lifting his red hands to cup my face. I looked into his young eyes, my heart breaking with the reality of what was happening to him.

"I love you, Joclyn."

I balked. His face was young, but his voice was mature. My tears turned to sobs as I lifted my hand to his face, his own blood leaving my handprint against his cheek.

"Ryland?"

"I love you, Joclyn, but I can't stay here. I have to protect you." His hand slid over my skin to cover my eyes, and I knew when I opened my eyes again he would be gone. So I didn't open them.

"I love you, Ryland." I spoke the words to no one. My voice caught and I repeated it to myself over and over as I sank to the ground and savored the memory of his touch, his voice, no matter how brief the contact had been. I sobbed and moaned until the blackness took me and the connection gratefully ended.

CHAPTER 38
WYN

Joclyn's eyes went white as she screamed, the sound dampened by the water that we held her under.

"Do you have her?" I asked Ilyan, his brows pulling together as he watched her scream, his hands still on her collarbone as he held her down.

"I do." His voice was calm, even though no other part of him appeared to be.

"How close are you?" Centering magic always took time, centering magic while using a Drevo to heal someone that is somehow connected to the other... more time.

"This is going to take some time, her magic is everywhere. It's strong." There was something in his voice that I couldn't quite place. Almost like, awe, which coming from him was saying something.

Ilyan was the King of his people. It was also widely known that he had more magic than anyone of his kind. So much that he had killed people attempting to heal them just by the strength of it. If Ilyan thought she was strong, well, maybe I could use that while we finished the healing roulette.

"Perfect. You'll have to be stuck there regardless, but maybe we can still time this right."

"Do what you need, Wynifred," Ilyan whispered, his hands caressing Joclyn's skin as her screaming began to lessen. "As long as this works."

"Well, that I can't promise you," I said, pulling my hands from the thick water as I left ribbons of the dark earth magic trailing around her, each strand pulling at the magic in the Drevo as it began to work. I tapped the surface with my fingers before any of the magic could escape. A blue flame smothered the surface with the spark of my magic, hardening the water as though it was glass; trapping Joclyn and the magic underneath, and Ilyan's arms inside.

"We will know if it works when the water breaks. Well, and if Ryland is still alive after this." I still had a bad feeling about this, but I knew better than to argue with Ilyan. I knew how Trpaslík magic worked. He knew how Skřítek magic worked, I just hoped he was right in how they would work together.

"He will be alive." He was much more confident than I felt.

The intensity of his magic surged in the air as he closed his eyes. Focusing on the girl below the water and leaving me in silence to clean up the mess of the Drevo and the water and everything else.

Drevos were rare, and now we had used two of them on the same girl in a matter of days. I would be happy if we had some way to help her, but the herbal magic was an ancient Trpaslík skill. It was hard enough for me to get the ingredients for it, and now that we had Joclyn... Let's just hope we didn't need to do any more quick healing anytime soon, the chance of me getting into Trpaslík territory to collect the ingredients to make another was slim to none.

"How is it going?" I jumped at Talon's booming voice. I had been so focused on cleaning up that I hadn't noticed him come in, his massive frame blocking the door as he stared at us as though we were doing the most normal things in the world. To anyone else it would probably look like Ilyan was trying to drown Joclyn.

"Better than expected," Ilyan said, his voice soft as he kneeled by the tub, his hands still stuck in the solid water. "Her magic is very responsive. She is so strong... so powerful... so..."

He somehow sounded even more awed than the last time.

"I never thought I would find her," he finally finished. I had never heard him choked up before.

"We only searched for centuries." Talon chuckled like that was nothing more than a few weeks and Ilyan was being unreasonable. Weird ancient men. "And here she is."

"She's just as I expected. Just as I saw her."

I turned from my cleaning; it wasn't often that Ilyan spoke of what that Drak had shown him regarding her. Everything I heard came second or third hand; at this point, she was more fable than anything.

"So, the Drak were right?" I asked, something in that question was twisting my gut like the worst kind of guilt.

"The Drak were always right, they are seers after all." Ilyan spoke as though there were any left, but they had been extinct for centuries; the last ones hunted down by Edmund's men in a massacre that was still talked about.

"True. But if they were right, that would mean that she is--"

"Going to save us all," Ilyan finished for me, just as the water cracked and Joclyn floated to the surface, her dark hair floating around her like she was some kind of angel you see in those old cathedrals in Europe.

I rushed forward, plunging my hand into the cool water to grip her wrist. I could still feel Ilyan's magic there, the last of the centering magic fading away and leaving hers behind. For the first time, I could feel her magic.

Waves and waves of powerful magic that almost pushed me back. "Man, she's strong."

Ilyan nodded as he twisted his fingers over the surface of the water, moving her hair off her face.

"I don't think I've ever felt anything like it." I was supposed to be checking the Drevo, but feeling her power was distracting. "Like heat and chill and... ash..."

That part didn't make any sense to me, I'd never felt ash-like magic before. Neither had Talon with the weird look he was giving Ilyan.

I had a feeling I was missing something, probably some boring discussion from their last high council meeting. Sometimes I was glad I missed those; sometimes I hated being in the dark. This time would be the latter.

This time I gave Talon a look in question, but he just shook me off with a nod of his head. If he thought he was getting away with not telling me anything he had clearly forgotten who he was married to.

"Did the Drevo work?" Ilyan asked and I forced my focus away from her magic and to her heart, my free hand clutching the necklace. Still warm. Still beating.

"I have no way of knowing if it helped him, or just kept him alive, but the necklace is still warm."

"I will take that as a good sign." Ilyan sounded as though a weight had lifted from him. "I just wish I knew more about what that necklace was doing."

"Or how he made it." Talon had come up behind us, all of us staring at the necklace. “The only magic I know of that would keep a connection over such a long distance is a death promise.”

I shivered. The result of that magic lived up to its name. It could do pretty much anything, but would kill one if the other died.

“You really don’t think that Ryland would bind his life to hers like that, do you?” I asked, thinking about the violent fiery way in which a death promise took its victims. Extreme pain, basically being burned from the inside out. There was no stopping it either, there was no promise in the world that was worth that. “He had to know what his father was planning for him after all.”

“That’s why it doesn’t make any sense.” Talon gave a shrug.

“Your guess is as good as mine, my friends.” Ilyan tapped the necklace with his finger, pressing the same pad against the mark behind her ear before he began to dry his hands. “We know that they are sharing a Tȍuha, but I am beginning to question if that’s from a Zȇlství or if it is from the connection in the necklace.”

“True. They haven’t completed a Zȇlství, so it can’t be that. But a death promise could prompt a Tȍuha. Or a soul bind,” I shrugged like it was nothing, but both men stood as though they had been zapped, their faces blank as they stared at me.

“A svazovat. Why didn’t I think of it before?” Ilyan said in quick Czech before he began to rattle off something about protecting but never having. “You’re right, Wyn. It’s a soul bind. He’s put a piece of him in there. That would connect them. That would also create something like a Tȍuha.”

“You are forgetting one thing, Ilyan. It would also give Edmund a direct connection to her.” The words booming from Talon’s voice made them much more ominous than they should be.

Except that they were just that ominous. If Edmund had Ryland under a Vymȃzat, then he could track her down through that connection. He could track us all down.

“What was Ryland thinking?” Only a child would do something so desperate, which was exactly what Ryland was when it came down to it. Because, in a weird way, it was romantic.

Or it was if you were a twenty year old magic user who was lonely and heart sick.

“He was thinking he needed to protect the one thing he valued.” Ilyan sighed, back on his knees as he leaned over the tub. “He didn’t know who she really was.”

"Okay, so do we take it from her?" I was ready to huck the thing into outer space if he asked.

"No," Ilyan whispered, his fingers moving from her mark to the necklace again. "We teach her to bind it. We teach her to fight him. And when we get Ryland back, we return whatever he used to make it to him."

CHAPTER 39
WYN

"Use these for now," Ilyan emerged from the mess of his closet with two articles of clothing and threw them on the bed with a flourish.

I took one look at them and burst out laughing.

"You want me to put her in your underwear?"

Ilyan looked at me curiously, dragging his hand through his long hair as he looked at the button up shirt and plaid boxers.

"Those are not my underwear." He pointed to them as though I was the one talking nonsense.

"Those are boxers."

"Yes, and I have never worn them as underwear. I have, in fact, never worn them." That didn't make it better.

I raised an eyebrow at him, everyone knew Ilyan had far too many clothes for his own good. But never worn boxers? The corner of his mouth quirked up as he leaned in, his blue eyes flashing with a brightness I had never seen before.

"I am a boxer-brief kind of guy."

"Ew." Kill me now. "Do I need to put that in next months 'get to know your king' newsletter?"

"Only if you value your head on your neck." I just rolled my eyes at him. Ilyan was deadly, yes, but he wasn't an insane murderer. Not like Edmund.

"Ilyan! Leave my wife alone!" Talon's voice boomed from the bathroom I had charged the men with finishing to clean. Ilyan just laughed and turned away.

"Those will work for tonight, tomorrow we will collect clothes for her to wear," he said as he shut the door to the bathroom behind him. We really should have done that tonight, especially considering that I didn't usually wear pajamas and anyone else we could borrow from was asleep. So, here we were; with Ilyan's underwear.

"I'm really sorry about this," I mumbled, turning to the bed and the soaked girl that lay there. Ilyan and I had mostly dried her, but she was still wrapped in a wet towel, completely unconscious thanks to the Drevo.

Dressing an unconscious woman was much harder the second time. Possibly because I hadn't slept much in the last few days and was even more exhausted from using the Drevo. Even worse, she seemed even more rag dollish, if possible. With the way her head and joints were moving I was starting to wonder if she was just made of hinges.

"You know, it's a good thing I've never had kids. Because I suck at this," I grumbled as she flopped back to the bed and I was secretly praising Ilyan for bringing me a button-up shirt and insisting that her hoodie needed a wash. Which it did. Getting her into that was impossible the first time, I couldn't imagine trying it now that she was all bendy and far too slippery.

"Okay, step two," I mumbled, hands on hips as I caught my breath before deciding to wrestle her into the boxers.

Luckily, that was easier.

"She looks just like him." Talon's deep boom seeped from underneath the closed door. He was clearly attempting to whisper, I only heard him because it was so quiet.

"I know," Ilyan returned, just as quietly, this time in Czech. "When I saw her in that classroom, I was transported back to that first time. I was surprised I didn't see it before."

"I wonder if he did."

"Well, if he did, he's better at concealing things than he should be." There was something dark in how Ilyan spoke, that tiny bit of King coming out. It made the hairs on the back of my neck stand on end.

"Of course he is, Ilyan, he's a dr--" Whatever Talon was half whispering was drowned out by the sound of running water, the voices mumbled beneath it. I stepped closer to the door.

Should I be listening in? No. But was I going to anyway? Yes.

"Has there been any sign of him?" Talon asked as the water cut off and I stepped back to Joclyn as quietly as I could, already grabbing the mostly done buttons in case they came back in.

"No. I sent him with a small guard." Ilyan said something else that was drowned out by more water and then, "I have sent a few teams out to look, but there are signs that Edmund got to him first. Perhaps to use as another trap to get her back."

What in the world were they talking about? Usually, I could decipher the things I overheard just based on what Talon told me about council and working with Ilyan; but they might as well have been talking gibberish that time.

"Well, then we should be happy that Ryland helped to get her out," Talon countered. I was moving so slow on these buttons that they would take me hours to fasten all the way. "Could you imagine if Edmund had them both?"

"There wouldn't be any war left to fight."

I froze, buttons forgotten as I stared at the door. What in the world were they talking about? And who in the world would create an end game scenario besides Joclyn? I had always been told the Silný was the endgame.

Gah! Stupid me being the lone Trpaslík and not getting to go to councils and other Skřítek-ey things. Sometimes Talon would let me in on small secrets, clearly this wasn't one of those times.

"All the more reason to get Ryland out now," Ilyan said, their footsteps moving toward the door. I moved back to the buttons so fast I might have pulled a muscle.

"Do you think she will be up for it?"

"With what I saw," Ilyan said, opening the door and busting his way out. "She will be."

"And what did you see?" I asked, turning to the two men who froze in their tracks. Talon looked to Ilyan for whatever answer they were allowed to give, but he was staring at Joclyn.

I probably should have smoothed out her hair, with the way it was fanned out she looked like she had stepped out of a hurricane. Any sign on the floating angel had been lost in the tangle of hurricane curls.

"The sight, Wynny," Talon finally answered. "Where she was prophesied."

I nodded and fiddled with buttons and hair. I knew that of course, everyone did, I was just hoping for a bit more.

I would have to bug Talon later, not that I was going to get my hopes up.

"Too bad we can't find ourselves a Drak to know for sure," I mumbled. It wasn't the first time I realized that the fate of the world rested on the word of an extinct magic. "If only they weren't all dead."

We all stood in silence, the air heavy with the truth of it.

"She appears to be fine," I said after a minute, setting my fingers on her collarbone again. Everything was still buzzing along nicely. "Talon, why don't you carry her back to her--"

"No," Ilyan interrupted. "I want her here for the night. If anything happens to her, I would like to be nearby."

"You are only one door down," I began, forehead wrinkling together before Talon shook his head, cutting off what I had been about to say.

"I will sleep at the foot of the bed. It will not be the first time, will not be the last." He was still staring at her, his jaw tight, his long hair falling around his face. He seemed to have forgotten that we were here at all.

"Good night, Ilyan," Talon said, clapping him on the back before he dragged me out.

I gave him one last look and bit my tongue. I knew I didn't need to worry. Ilyan was as honorable a man as they came. Plus, the guy pretty much lived like a monk.

The second the door closed behind us, however, I rounded on Talon.

"I need answers," I hissed, knowing that Ilyan could still hear us, even if Talon was dragging me down the hall.

"Answers about what?" He was really bad at pretending to be innocent. Even his voice dripped with guilt.

"Who she is or who you two were talking about in the bathroom." I hissed as low as I could, I really didn't need Ilyan overhearing that part.

"You heard that, huh?" He didn't look a bit guilty as he opened the door to our room for me. Clearly, he had planned for that.

"Who is missing?" He gave me a look. Okay, strike one. "Fine. What is so important about the sight? Who is she?"

He gave me a look before he sped up, "She's the Silnỳ."

"I know that." I slugged him on the arm before I collapsed onto our bed. "But what exactly did Ilyan see, besides her saving us all?"

"A future he can never have. A future he is trying to save for us all."

I opened my mouth to counter, but Talon was dead serious. He clearly thought what he was saying made sense.

"Why hiss whisper so I could hear you if you won't tell me anything?"

He just smiled. Loyal to their king to a fault.

"Darn Skříteks!"

I clearly wasn't going to get any information out of him.

CHAPTER 40
JOCLYN

I woke up screaming, my hair still damp from the Drevo.

I sat up, kicking the covers off me aggressively as I looked at my hands and arms, in search of the blood I knew to be there. I panted and scrubbed and screamed. I barely registered that someone was there with me until a warmth began to spread through me, the panic receding. I let the warmth take over me, let it calm me down. Although it wasn't the warmth I really wanted, it would do for now.

My mind became clear as I continued to stare uselessly at my hands, part of me still wondering where the blood had gone. I was like Lady Macbeth, scrubbing and clawing madly at nothing. *Out Damn Spot. Out, I say!* Except this wasn't a play, the blood was real; it just wasn't on my hands anymore.

"Calm... Joclyn... calm." Ilyan's arms wrapped around me as his magic left my body. He pulled me to his chest, his hand running down my hair. "I'm here; it's okay."

I wanted to pull away from him; I wanted to run to Ryland. I grasped for the necklace, desperate to bring back the connection, desperate to see him again. Ilyan grabbed my hands and steadied them, his warmth moving into me again, the force of it weaker this time.

My screaming subsided into a low sob that racked through my chest. I forced my gaze away from my hands, surprised to see Ilyan's bedroom and not the brown and orange of the room I had been given. Ilyan clutched me to him as I continued to cry, grateful that my tears were finally leaving.

"What happened, Joclyn?" he asked when my crying had passed enough I could finally talk.

"Ry... Ryland... he is in pain... so much pain."

"Another Tȍuha? What happened, Silnŷ?"

"I saw him; the bruises, the cuts... the blood. Ed... Edmund cut out his mark." Ilyan's arms tensed around me, his breathing increasing in what I could only assume to be anger. "He was young... he didn't recognize me. Why didn't he recognize me, Ilyan?" The panic came back, that desperate edge creeping into my voice.

"Oh, Silnŷ, his mind is being deleted. He remembers less and less each day. Did he remember you eventually?"

"Yes, and before he left, I could have sworn it was him, that he wasn't sixteen-year-old Ryland anymore; that it was really him." I felt Ilyan's body relax a bit. "Is that good?"

"It means that all of him is still there, that he is still fighting."

"Why did he look so young then?"

"Because as much as he fights, he is still losing the battle. The longer he fights it, the younger he will look in your Tȍuhas. But when he forgets you completely, when he is only a child, then it will be too late."

Ilyan's words had a sharp edge that cut through me; it broke the dam I had made deep inside and let every single pent-up emotion and fear out in a tidal wave. I began crying uncontrollably again, but I didn't want Ilyan to take the pain away and put me to sleep with his magic. I needed to feel it. I cried and clung to him as I let everything out.

I howled over the death of my mother, the image of her lifeless body, vivid and vibrant. I cried at the memory of our lunch, the last time we were together, and how I had given her everything that she wanted; the daughter she had always wanted me to be.

I sobbed over the loss of my normalcy. I balled up against Ilyan as I thought about the changes in my life, the drastic differences that had occurred within such a small amount of time.

I mourned with the agonizing pain of a broken heart; my heart broke into a million pieces as everything hit me simultaneously, for the last time. Every memory of Ryland flashed by, and although I wanted to smile and laugh, the memories only hurt. Hurt that I could not have him; hurt at how much everything had changed.

Through it all, Ilyan just held me, his wide hands rubbing my back.

He shushed and cooed and sang to me as I cried, and all of it made me want to cry more, because his weren't the arms I craved.

When it was done, I knew it was done. I knew I was stronger than the pain now.

"Why would he do that, Ilyan? Why would he cut the mark out?" Ilyan moved my hair away from my face, his finger lingering on my own mark. I jerked my head away, not wanting such an intimate touch from him.

"Do you remember when I told you the kiss is more like a poisonous bite? Well, the kiss itself is caused by a pool of poison. If it's cut out, you release the poison into the person who bears the kiss."

I gasped and the tears came back again.

"Will it kill him?"

"It can, but I think Edmund only hopes to weaken him further, and gain control over his magic that much faster."

"Why? Why is he doing this?"

"A punishment probably, but also to increase his control. Edmund has always viewed Ryland as a weapon, and now he sees the best opportunity to use him as such."

"We will be too late, won't we?"

Ilyan's face made it clear that he didn't know. Our eyes locked together in some silent agreement that we would try, but I couldn't shake the feeling that trying wouldn't be enough anymore.

Ilyan would say no more; he simply laid me back down in his bed and put me to sleep with his magic. I was probably more grateful than I should have been, considering all I dreamed about was chasing a bloody trail through the golden hallways of the LaRue mansion.

CHAPTER 41
JOCLYN

The following morning, I realized the downside of the white-on-white scheme of Ilyan's room. The moment the sun began to creep over the horizon and the gray light of dawn had begun to fade away, the room became supercharged with light. The beams of golden sun shone through the window that Ilyan had pushed his bed up against. They bounced around and increased in brightness as the white walls and carpet reflected them back. Once the light had infiltrated my troubled sleep, I sat upright, sleep leaving me much quicker than I would have liked.

I was still in Ilyan's bed, still in Ilyan's rooms. I shouldn't be here.

I sat there trying to plan some form of escape. Even if I made it out the door, I wasn't sure I could remember which door led to the brown and orange room. I was having trouble focusing; a subtle buzzing was taking over my body, causing my mind to bounce around. It felt like the warm heat I had always felt from Ryland and Ilyan, but more alive, more electric. More mine. I brushed off the feeling, trying to focus on my escape again. The buzzing under my skin grew steadily, making me feel jittery and anxious.

I threw the blankets away from me, intent on just storming down the hall in the hopes of at least finding Wyn, when a loud grunt issued from the foot of the bed, followed by a large thump that shook the room. I looked toward the noise, terrified in my jittery state, that some explosion had gone off. Instead, I was treated to Ilyan yelling, or perhaps swearing, in Czech before he crawled on hands and knees into the bathroom, slamming the door behind him.

I stared at the door in bewilderment; I wasn't sure whether I should laugh hysterically or not. I could hear him thump around in the bathroom, random foreign words filtering through the ivory-colored doors. I sat up, fully intent on making my escape when Ilyan's thumping and yelling was joined by another voice, from someone running rapidly down the hall toward me. My heart sputtered as the door flung open and a very agitated, while still perfectly poised, Ovailia burst through the door.

"What in heaven's name..." She froze at the sight of me, her eyes bugging out of her head as her jaw worked mechanically in place.

Seeing Ovailia there with such a terrifying look on her face sent the energy into overdrive as it buzzed and vibrated through me. I grabbed the covers and pulled them up to my chin, realizing too late that that was probably not the best action to take. Ovailia's jaw only dropped more. I looked down; I was wearing one of Ilyan's light colored, button-up shirts... great.

"This isn't what it looks like," I said, desperately hoping she would believe me and not question any more. After all, I had absolutely no idea what I would say.

The energy under my skin increased, and I felt a desperate need to get rid of it.

"What are you doing here?"

"Sleeping?"

She didn't buy it, even if it was the truth. I could feel my cheeks turning a deep shade of crimson. Ovailia glared at me before rushing to the bathroom door without saying another word, her eyes never leaving my blush stained face.

The door to the bathroom slammed behind her and my head dropped into the white cotton blankets. Great. This was not the way I wanted to start my day. The yelling in the bathroom increased as Ovailia joined in the fray. I could make out the two voices distinctly, even though I couldn't understand the words they were yelling at each other. I was secretly glad I didn't understand Czech. I wasn't sure I really wanted to know what they were saying.

I jumped off the bed, heading toward Ryland's sweater that lay across the foot. I grabbed it and went to tug off the yellow shirt that Ilyan had dressed me in. My blush deepened and melted into an embarrassed anger at the thought of what state I had been in after the bath and exactly what I was wearing now. I froze for only a moment before removing the shirt and tugging on one of Wyn's band shirts that had been laid out next to Ryland's sweater. I pulled the shirt and sweater on, keeping a close ear on the argument going on in the bathroom, just in case someone walked in on me. I glanced around for my pants, my heart dropping at finding nothing, not even the pajama pants I had worn last night. I guess I would have to stay in the plaid shorts I had been dressed in a bit longer.

I tugged the sweater down in hopes of hiding what I could only assume were Ilyan's boxers. I pushed down my anger at being left to sleep here and thrown into such a situation; after all, how hard would it have been to just walk me down the hall?

I turned to make my escape just as Ovailia burst through the bathroom door, still yelling something angrily in Czech. She was followed close behind by Ilyan who was soaking wet with soap in his hair and a white towel wrapped haphazardly around his waist. The sight of him supercharged my agitation, bringing the level of buzzing on my skin to new heights. I looked back and forth from him to Ovailia, who yelled angrily. Ilyan rebutted something before Ovailia stormed out, slamming the door behind her. Ilyan exhaled angrily before turning to me.

"Pants are in 'ze clozet." His accent was thick, and it took me a moment to register exactly what he had said. He waved his hand toward a door on the opposite end of the room before turning back to the bathroom. I immediately decided to forgo the pants and continue with my original plan to track down Wyn.

"Oh, and Joclyn," his head poked out from behind the bathroom door, "don't go anywhere. I'll be right out..."

Normally I would hightail my way out of here anyway, but I wasn't sure disobeying a king would go over very well.

I fumed angrily at him before he closed the door to go back to his shower. I rubbed my arms abrasively in the hopes of lessening the buzzing. It seemed to be working, the motion also calming my heart rate. I breathed deeply as I made my way toward the closet, the buzzing now only a hum. My anger and frustration had never reacted this way, but then, I wasn't sure I had ever been so emotionally charged before.

Ilyan's closet was a strange place. It was as large as the bathroom, with clothes stacked floor to ceiling. There was little rhyme or reason to it, and it took me a bit to locate pants among the heaps of clothes. I dug through the stacks of designer jeans, grateful that none of these would fit me. I chose one of the only pairs that didn't have the perfectly placed tears that Ilyan favored, pulling them on over the shorts.

Finding a belt in the mess was surprisingly more difficult than locating pants. I held the pants around me as I searched through drawers and boxes that were littered around the large space. I carefully lifted a sheet that covered one section of the wall and stopped short.

Behind the curtain was a perfectly organized wall of clothes. Each piece of clothing hung on its own hanger, covered with a clear protective bag. On its own, it would have been surprising, given the lack of organization among the rest of the clothes.

It wasn't just that though; at first, I thought they were costumes. Each shirt was longer and would probably fall to the knee on an average-sized man. Given the lengths and the style, I would almost call them tunics. The light colored garments were cut from fabrics that I could automatically tell were expensive. I fought the urge to remove the bags and run my hands over the soft silks, touch the fine jewels and golden ropes that adorned each one.

I hungrily ran my eyes over the glittering stones, the deep colored embroidery. The sleeves on each piece were exaggerated, but I couldn't tell by how much, given how loosely they hung on the hangers. Claudius, Macbeth, Lear, Romeo. I could see these on-stage in a million different plays, but they weren't fake, like costumes; they were shockingly real.

"Pretty, aren't they?" I jumped at Ilyan's voice, my hand clutching my chest.

"You scared me!" I spun to him and balked. While now soap-free, he was still only dressed in a towel. I inhaled sharply and stepped away, hoping he hadn't noticed my reaction. His chest was strong and thick with sinewy muscles, but that wasn't why I had reacted. The skin across his chest was crisscrossed with hundreds of raised scars, all of them red and angry as though he had been whipped and they hadn't healed properly.

I shook my head and looked away. My skin buzzed as my agitation returned, coming in full force again. I wasn't as mad as I should have been to see him dressed in only a towel.

"Sorry, but you were looking at my private collection; you kind of deserved it," he chuckled.

"Private collection?" I let the sheet fall over the clothes again. "Now, I'm really sorry."

"Don't be. They are not a secret after all. I wear them to council." He handed me a belt he had removed from under a pile of undershirts; I would have never found it.

"Council? You mean the meeting you had yesterday?"

"Yes, it is an official meeting, so I have to look the part." He grinned, but it looked more like a grimace.

"You mean, like King?"

His face fell. He turned from me and grabbed a few items of clothing off the many disorganized piles.

"Not 'like', Joclyn, just King." He gave me a sad, little smile and disappeared behind a partition I hadn't noticed due to the large amount of clothes draped over it.

"So, do I need to call you 'My Lord' now?"

He flung the towel over the side to join the clothes already there, and I instantly looked down at my feet, turning my back to him in embarrassment and frustration.

"That depends on a few things."

"Like what?" I asked as he came out from behind the partition, still pulling his shirt over his head.

"Well, for starters, when we are together like this." I blushed, which only caused him to smile. "Just the two of us, I mean. Or with Wynifred and Talon, then, no. But around anyone else, then, yes."

I nodded my head in understanding, knowing I would mess it up.

"Why not Wyn and Talon?"

"Wynifred was not raised with us, so she forgets from time to time. Most of the time, I let it slide as she and Talon have undergone the Zêlství, but there are times when she probably needs to remember her place a bit more."

"And Talon?"

"Talon and I grew up together; it would just be weird if he started calling me 'My Lord' and bowing all the time."

"Were you not always king?"

"No, Silný." His answer was definite, and strangely final.

I shut my mouth, sure he didn't want me to ask any more questions about his royal status.

"What does that mean?" I asked, hoping my change in subject was easy to follow.

"What?"

"*Silný*?" The word sounded odd on my tongue.

He looked at me quietly, his eyes narrowed suspiciously.

"It means, 'little one'."

I only nodded at him. What an odd nickname.

"Now, what do you say to a little bit of training for that newly awakened kouzlo of yours?"

"Training?"

"Yes, that buzz in your fingertips? I think it's dying to get out."

I looked at my fingers; it seemed silly that I hadn't realized exactly what it was before.

"It's..." I stopped mid-sentence, the proper words not finding the right place.

"It's your magic, Joclyn. Perfectly centered and dying for you to learn to control it."

I looked up at him, stunned; the buzzing grew a bit at Ilyan's sly half-smile.

"I think it's waited long enough, don't you?" He left the closet quickly; I padded after him in bare feet, so that I could keep up. He nodded to the guard and kept moving. I finally caught up to him as he opened a large door that led outside.

"Now," he announced, "the real fun begins. What do you say to growing a tree?"

"Growing a tree?" I asked, confused. "How is that going to help me save Ryland?" The buzzing grew as worry joined my confusion.

"It will help because then you will be able to use your magic," he chuckled.

"Ummm... so how is that going to help me? Grow a tree and then go hide in it? That doesn't help anyone. Well, unless you are a monkey and I'm not a monkey."

"I have noticed that. But starting with something simple will help you understand your magic. It is better if you know even a little bit of what you are doing than nothing at all." Ilyan was an endless calm, even if I was a bundle of snappy nerves.

"When will I learn magic that can help me save Ryland?" The buzzing grew more with the fuel from my stress. I felt like I was going to explode. I breathed deeply, trying to gain control.

"We have eight days, Joclyn. I can't possibly teach you everything in eight days. So we will be learning the basics." His calm voice was a whisper compared to mine. "We will begin with plant growth so that you can gain control of your power. I will then teach you how to control wind, and if you are very lucky, we may touch on energy fields."

"That's it?" I couldn't help but be disappointed.

"Yes, Silnỳ. I will teach you enough so you can go in, defend yourself if you must, and so you can run away when necessary."

"Run away?" My heart plunged into my toes, my voice dropping in tone as my heart rate increased in timber. "I thought we were going to save him."

"We are." He left it at that and strolled away from me.

"Then why do I need to know how to run away?"

"Because you will not be strong enough to fight any of them. You are going with the sole purpose of getting Ryland out, and that task requires you to run away. You must know how to run away from Edmund, from Timothy, and maybe even from Ryland."

I hated to admit that it made sense, so I just nodded and followed him to the courtyard Wyn had shown me last night. I didn't know what to say; my anger had lessened, but now I felt somewhat worthless. All my life, Ryland had protected and supported me, and now it was my turn to protect him, and I couldn't do it. Even with all the power that I now had buzzing under my skin, I couldn't. There wasn't enough time to learn how to do that.

The courtyard in the middle of the motel was the type of place I would gladly waste days in. The large branches of the tree that stood in the center of the space reached far over us, shading most of the courtyard throughout the day. What light seeped through the canopy speckled the stone paths and grassy patches with pools of warm sunlight and golden color.

I sat in one of the sun bathed pools of light, Ilyan by my side as he gently taught me to stretch and bend my magic. At first, all the pent-up energy came out in a rush and I covered us with dirt as a small area of ground exploded rather than causing the flower to grow, as I was supposed to do. I was elated; if it was really that easy, then perhaps I had a chance to actually help Ryland after all.

After the initial use however, getting the magic out was a different story altogether. I could still feel it tingle and move under my skin, but I could no longer get it to move beyond my veins and into my control. The buzzing grew and swirled around inside as my frustration twisted into anxiety. Perhaps this was all just a pointless exercise; my magic had been hidden too long. My magic simply didn't know what to do and was just as stubborn as I was. It made me feel dead inside.

By the time the sun had cleared the roof of the old motel, Wyn and Talon had joined our group. They sat off to the side, a sleepy Wyn curled up against Talon. I was happy they were there, but grateful that they weren't offering their own advice. I didn't know how much more failure I could take anyway. After about three hours of trying, I slunk away and leaned against the giant tree that was shading us.

"I give up," I moaned as Ilyan came over and joined me.

"Don't be ridiculous. You give up and Ryland dies, simple as that."

I flinched at his brutal honesty, his stern voice cutting through me.

"Are you still going to give up?"

"No."

"Good. Now, I have an idea, but it involves breaking a rule. Are you okay with that?"

"What rule?" I wanted to agree, but I was apprehensive about what he was going to ask.

"Just answer the question, Joclyn."

"Let's break the rule." I was still apprehensive and Talon laughed at me from across the clearing.

I followed Ilyan back to the space where we had been working, he invited Wyn and Talon over to join us. Wyn bounded over with a wide smile on her face as she barreled into me with a bear hug before settling in next to Talon.

"All right," Ilyan began, "I need you to take off the necklace."

"What?" I clutched it in a desperate panic; I couldn't take it off—I had promised Ryland.

"Don't worry; you can put it on the second we are done."

"Why? Why do I need to take it off in the first place? It's just my magic, right? You said it probably just doesn't know what to do."

"While that may be the problem, I think it is something else. I think Edmund's magic, that is repressing Ryland, is repressing you as well."

I heard Wyn breathe behind me, but I could only stare.

"But I thought you told me... you told me Edmund couldn't affect me."

"I thought he couldn't, but it looks like he might be able to. If that's the case, we need to get you using your magic so we can train you to block Edmund's barrier. Do you understand?"

I nodded solemnly before moving to take off the necklace. My stomach flipped around inside of me. Not only was Edmund hurting Ryland, but he was hindering me as well. I sincerely hoped Ilyan's guess would be wrong. I handed the necklace to Ilyan, who wrapped it up in a cloth.

"Now," Ilyan looked at me eagerly, "make the seed grow."

I exhaled deeply, flexing my fingers as the buzzing shifted into the tips of them. I closed my eyes and focused. I could feel the energy; I could feel what it wanted to do. I placed my hand onto the ground and felt my magic move out of me and into the ground. Everything shifted under my fingers and a loud popping noise filled my ears. Talon and Ilyan yelled out in irritation while Wyn laughed hysterically.

My eyes popped open. Instead of being surrounded by large craters or flames, I sat in the middle of long grasses and prairie flowers up to my head. I hadn't conjured all of these, had I?

I looked around in a panic before jumping to my feet. Ilyan, Talon and Wyn all sat in the same places they had a moment ago, except that now they were all covered in dirt and sticks. Wyn continued to laugh hysterically as Ilyan spat and wiped dirt out of his mouth and ears.

"Well, I don't think we have to worry about how strong your magic is, just how to control it," Ilyan said between dirt clumps.

CHAPTER 42
JOCLYN

I was devastated that Ilyan was right, that Edmund's restraints had moved through the necklace into me. I didn't want to think about what Edmund could do to me if he knew about the necklace, about the connection. What worried me so much more was the thought that if Edmund's magic was restricting me that much, what was he doing to Ryland? I couldn't get the image of Ryland's blood-covered bedroom out of my mind; it added to my tortures.

"I can't believe it was that easy. Especially after all the trouble I had before," I spoke quietly to myself as I stared at my hands. I almost expected them to catch on fire.

"Evil overlords can do that to you," Talon said as he handed the wrapped necklace back to me.

I took the necklace and looked at it solemnly. I desperately wanted to put it on, but wasn't sure if I could, or even if I should. The thought of how much it hindered me, of what it was now beginning to mean, was a heavy, choking weight.

"Go ahead," Ilyan urged as he sat beside me again. "Put it on."

"What if it keeps restricting me?" I carefully peeled away the folds of fabric to look at the jewel nestled there, the fine silver chain circling around like a snake.

"It will. Which is why I want you to try something," Ilyan replied. "Put it on, tell me what you feel."

I removed the necklace from the cloth and carefully placed it around my neck. At almost the exact moment that the ruby touched my skin, I felt my magic slow down, the energy losing some of the wriggling nature that I was becoming used to.

"How bad is it?" Ilyan asked, and I knew what he was referring to.

"Everything slowed down; it almost feels like my body has become sludge."

Ilyan nodded his head in understanding.

"Your magic is very strong, Joclyn. I think you can fight through this. In fact, if you can master it, it might help everyone in the future, especially Ryland."

My head perked up. I leaned closer to him, even though my instinct was to move away. My dark hair fell around my face as I bent toward him.

"How, Ilyan? How do I do it?" I asked.

"I don't know. You will have to figure it out yourself." He smiled, and I had the distinct impression he did actually know what I was supposed to do.

"Can't you just tell me?"

"I would, but I have never actually witnessed something like this. I have ideas, but they will probably not work for you."

"Why not?"

"Well, Joclyn, because your magic is still underdeveloped. For example..." His voice had taken on that deep, commanding tone that I had heard in him the first moment I had met him, in front of the school.

I flinched away.

"...if I told you to try to perform a double barrier and reverse it, would you be able to do it?"

I just stared.

"Or, how about an extended growth spell? No. You would not know what to do. I could teach you all that in a month, maybe two, but not today, not when your knowledge of magic is so limited. You have to figure it out for yourself because you don't know all of the basics yet." He looked away from me with superiority.

Wyn rubbed my back sympathetically, whether because Ilyan had just put me in my place or because I looked absolutely forlorn, I had no idea.

I lay back in the grass, dejectedly. Of course, it couldn't be quite so simple. I looked through the grass to the dirt, my mind spinning as I tried to figure out what to do. I could feel the low buzz of my magic. I still felt the desperate need for it to get out, but no matter how hard I tried, it wouldn't come.

I flexed my fingers and placed the very tips in the dirt, digging them in a bit. The warm earth and the electric hum from within me combined aggressively, but the magic would not move. I had the foolish thought to cut my skin to simply let it out. While probably a very natural progression, the image of cutting my own skin brought visions of Ryland being tortured to the forefront of my memory.

I flinched at the image, wiping it from my mind. Then I paused; the image had instigated something. I could still feel the super-charged buzz as the magic released into the ground where my fingers touched it. I knew what I needed to do, and although I sincerely didn't want to, I brought a vision of Ryland to my mind.

This time, I chose the gentle image of him placing the necklace around my neck. The beautiful memory caused my heart to swell, and with it, a tiny bit of energy expelled itself. It wasn't enough to do anything, but it was something. I felt the warmth of it leaving my fingertips before it subsided.

I tried again, this time remembering the first time we had climbed the trees and how he had gently coaxed me down and hugged me tightly. My soul flew at the imagery, the magic surging momentarily and shooting out of me, causing the grass to grow about an inch.

I sat up, staring at my dirty fingers in amazement. I had felt it; felt the change. I could have sworn I could almost feel the restrictive cover that the necklace placed over me shift. If only I could shift it enough to overcome it.

"What is it, Joclyn?"

My head snapped up to see all three of them looking at me, confused. I could tell they had just been laughing about something; Wyn's shoulders still shook as if trying to restrain a latent laugh.

"It's... I thought..." I paused. No matter how much I was learning to trust Wyn and was growing to like Talon and Ilyan, I still wasn't sure I was ready to go into everything quite yet. "It's nothing," I finished lamely.

Talon turned away from me, returning easily to whatever conversation they had been having a moment before. Wyn stared at me a moment longer before shrugging and returning to jabber along with Talon. Ilyan, however, continued to look at me curiously. The intensity of his gaze locked me in place, the familiar blue shooting into me, sending shivers up my spine.

I didn't like the sensation that his gaze gave me. My stomach glittered with the attention, while simultaneously shying away from him. I was thankful when he looked away, releasing me from my inner turmoil.

I threw myself back into the grass and focused on what should be my only thought: getting my magic under control so I could help save Ryland.

Last year, when the spring flowers had begun to bloom, Ryland had taken me up the mountain to have pie. We had arrived right at dusk, and Ryland had been quieter than usual during our trek through the forest. When we had gotten there, he had produced not only the pie, but a chicken dinner he had obviously bribed my mother to make; he knew it was one of my favorites. I could still see his broad grin as he produced the food, the memory surging my magic. I plunged my fingers into the dirt again as a small amount escaped. I pulled my attention back to the memory, desperate for more magic to find its way out.

I think it was that night in the mountains that I had started to fall in love with Ryland. After we had eaten and laughed and joked as we always did, we had chased each other through the forest with the water guns that Ry had brought along. I had snaked through the trees, unable to keep my giggling contained, giving Ryland more than one opportunity to soak me. My sneakers had squished as I walked, another sure give-away. I had caught sight of Ryland ahead of me and prepared to make my attack when a perfect circle of flowers caught my attention.

Purple pansies grew among the pine needles and forest decay in a dainty, four foot wide ring. It was such an odd flower to find in the forest, and the circle so perfectly round. I had walked around it slowly, something pulling me to stand in the middle of it, even though I was sure it was taboo.

"Go ahead," Ryland had said. Now, even a year later, his voice remained crystal clear in my mind.

My magic surged again, but none escaped.

I had stepped over the border of flowers slowly, laughing at the intent of this new game. Ryland had walked around me, hailing the king of the fairies and urging him to accept me as a gift and to treat me well, his voice barely able to contain his laughter. Ry had leaned down slowly and plucked one of the beautiful flowers, presenting it to me with smoldering eyes...

"How did you do that?" Wyn said.

I shot up, surprised at the garden of pansies that had grown around me. Ilyan and Talon had disappeared, leaving only Wyn to witness my amazing breakthrough. I reached out and touched the soft petals; they were almost identical to the ones from my memory.

"Ryland. Our memories together," I whispered, fighting the tears that still fought their way out from my extended visit with such beautiful memories.

"Really?"

I didn't dare look at her; I only nodded.

"You think of Ryland, and your magic can move? What do you think of? Kissing him, his rippling muscles...? What?"

My heart thudded as I looked up to her: I didn't know what to say. "No, nothing like that. Just him. Memories of him."

Wyn's shoulders slunk sadly. "Like kissing him?"

"No, Wyn," I whispered. "I have never kissed him."

She stared at me in shock; she almost looked scared. "Never?"

"No, never. I mean, we got close," I added, just in case she got the wrong idea, "but we never actually made the connection."

Wyn continued to stare at me with that strange look on her face. I ran my finger through the flowers again in an attempt not to look at her.

"Is that bad?" I asked when the silence had become too much.

"No, no, no." Wyn reassured me. "It's just that... normally to have a connection as strong as yours, you would have at least kissed."

I began to feel even more uncomfortable. I looked down into the carpet of flowers as the blush crept up my cheeks.

"Your souls are connected." I couldn't help but hear that teenage longing in her voice. "It's like you are meant to be."

I rolled my eyes at her, but secretly, I hoped she was right. At least then I would be able to save him.

CHAPTER 43
JOCLYN

Ilyan had knocked loudly on my door at daybreak to command me to meet him in the courtyard in ten minutes. Even without being awakened by the bright sunlight in his room, I still wasn't allowed to sleep in, this close to going and saving Ryland I was surprised we had time to sleep at all.

Train and sleep. Train and sleep.

I rolled out of bed, thankful for the disappearance of the ancient décor. The brown and orange paper had been replaced by white walls with a deep green stripe circling the ceiling. The lumpy bed with the ancient bedspread was also gone; a small, squishy, pure-white day bed in its place. The dark table and orange lamp were still there, but they didn't look as old as they had before; they looked almost chic. It wasn't really my style, but I liked it anyway.

I had opted to shower first, deciding that since I hadn't actually taken a real bath in a while and knowing that I could be in and out in five minutes, it wouldn't be a problem. When I stepped into the hot water though, I knew I was in trouble. The jets of steaming water hit my skin, and every muscle in my body relaxed into a comfortable jelly. I let the water flow over me in long rivers as it wiped away the grit and grime of everything that had happened to me in the last two weeks. Granted, the water was clear and I actually had no real dirt or grime, it still felt wonderfully cleansing and invigorating.

I stood there for longer than necessary, feeling the now-constant buzzing. After my success with the circle of pansies, I hadn't been able to accomplish anything else without removing the necklace, despite trying late into the night. Standing here without the necklace, I felt my magic surge again. I didn't dare attempt anything for fear that it would hinder any success later. I turned off the water and stepped out, knowing Ilyan would be upset with my tardiness.

Sure enough, without the sound of the water, I could hear Ilyan and Ovailia shouting at each other in Czech again, their voices carrying through my door. I was beginning to wonder if this was a daily occurrence.

I dressed quickly as the angry yelling continued, trying to pick out clothes from among the mismatched array of what had been brought over for me. I could tell that most of these clothes had belonged to several different people. I opted for a band shirt I was sure was Wyn's and a pair of baggy, gray pants. Thankfully, a pair of flip-flops near my size had been left for me, so I slid them on as I pulled Ryland's sweater over my head, his lingering smell still clinging to the fabric. I flung the door open, and the yelling stopped.

"Look who it is," Ovailia sneered in a sugary sweet voice. "Finally decide to grace us with your presence, did you?"

I looked from Ilyan to Ovailia in confusion. Ovailia kept her eyes glued on me, her lips pursed, while Ilyan had his jaw clenched and eyes narrowed toward no one in particular.

"Here I am." I sang the words in a mockery that only pissed her off more.

"Wonderful." Ovailia walked away, her hair swaying ominously behind her. Ilyan followed her, beckoning me to follow.

My guard went up instantly. I wasn't sure I wanted to spend an hour, let alone a day, with the two of them together. My experiences with them had so far been less than stellar. Ilyan led us, once again, into the courtyard, but my heart plunged at seeing the thirty or so people who were milling around the large space. My hands moved to pull my hood up, but stopped half-way; I needed to be brave.

"Sorry," Ilyan said sheepishly. "I had hoped to prepare you for this, but I didn't count on your needing a shower." He grabbed my hand and placed it gently in the crook of his arm. It didn't escape my notice that his posture improved almost instantly. "'My Lord', remember." He smiled bashfully at me before leading me into the large courtyard.

Everyone stood and faced him. I couldn't help but feel that my baggy pants and sweater left me terribly underdressed for this. Even though

Ilyan wore his trademark torn jeans and button-up shirt and no one else was wearing anything out of the ordinary, the air of the situation demanded something better. As we walked past each person, they would bow their head and lower slightly. Ilyan would return the bow with a slight head nod and sometimes say a name. Thankfully, by the time we made it to the tree, most everyone had returned to what they were doing previously.

"Is it always like this?" I asked quietly, noticing that several of the people continually looked over toward us.

"My Lord," Ilyan reminded me under his breath.

"Is it always like this, My Lord?" I asked stiffly.

"Unfortunately," he mumbled.

"It should be like this more often and handled with much more dignity, but my brother seems to think otherwise." Ovailia said, glaring me down, "Now that you are here, should we continue?"

"Ummm... sure," I answered, unsure if I should be adding some form of a title to Ovailia's name. She acted like she was entitled to one, so I wasn't sure.

"Good. Now, Ilyan tells me you have mastered plant growth easily enough. Let us hope the same rings true for your command of the wind." She held out a heavy muslin cloth. I hesitantly removed the necklace and placed it in the folds. Ovailia wrapped it up tightly and placed it near some bushes on the ground. I looked at it, longing to put it back on, but knew it would only hinder me, and I needed to get control of my magic fast.

"Now," Ovailia continued, "the concept of manipulating wind is much the same as plant life. You must infuse the wind with your magic until you receive the ability to control it. It is through this control that you will be able to manipulate yourself and objects around you."

I just nodded my head numbly. I knew that should make sense, but I couldn't seem to wrap my mind around it.

"Think about how you move your magic into the plants and tell them what to do," Ilyan said. "It's much the same concept, except with wind, you can do more; move cars or buildings, fly."

"We *were* flying that night you saved me!"

"Yes, we were," Ilyan said happily. Ovailia however, cleared her throat.

"Sorry... My Lord," I added hastily.

"I want you to learn this skill, so in case anything happens this week, you will be able to get away and save yourself."

I nodded. I wanted to be able to save Ryland, and if that meant running away, it meant running away.

"All right," Ilyan said, "bring your magic to the front and release it into the air around you. I want to see if you can summon wind from nothing."

I focused intently on the air and felt my magic seep out of me like a slow leak, pleased when I felt the air softly move itself into a subtle breeze. I pushed more magic out, excited at the quick success. The more I released into the air, the bigger the breeze became, until it swirled swiftly through the courtyard, pushing into those who remained watching us and eventually knocking me into Ilyan.

"Sorry, My Lord," I whimpered as he set me straight again.

"Don't be. That was wonderful!" Ilyan was pleased. Ovailia looked anything but.

Ilyan grabbed my shoulders and steered me to stand right in front of the large tree.

"Okay, now, climb the tree," Ovailia snapped impatiently, ignoring my quick success. "Show me how you accomplish these tree races that Wynifred has told me *so* much about." Why did she always sound so irritated?

I felt excited for a whole moment, until I looked up into the tree branches. The tangled knot of the tree extended high above me; no matter how hard I looked, I couldn't see a way through. It was more than the impossibility of the branches though, it was the fact that I could fall. That fear was new... and I hated it.

My hands moved to wrap around my back without my even knowing. My fingers spanned flat against, the fingers touching the places where broken bones and nerves had been only a week before. Great, my broken back had given me a fear of falling.

"You won't fall," Ilyan whispered in my ear.

"How do you know I won't?"

"I won't let you." His finger moved up to trace a circle around my kiss.

I tore my eyes away from the tangled branches to look at him, stepping away from his touch.

"But there is no way up, Ilyan—My Lord."

Ilyan smiled at me before turning to Ovailia. "If you will excuse us, sister, I believe this lesson will not require your assistance today."

Before Ovailia could open her mouth to rebut, Ilyan had opened his hand, the necklace flying into his open palm from within the bush. Ilyan then took my hand and began to lead me out of the courtyard. Everyone looked surprised that we were leaving so soon, but they stood and paid their respects to him as we walked by, nonetheless.

Once we had made it through the door from the courtyard, Ilyan's pace increased until we had emerged on the other side through yet another door, this one leading to a wide expanse of untamed forest. I couldn't see a city or town; we were surrounded by hills of forest, misty mountains just visible in the distance.

This was the weirdest location for a hotel I had ever seen.

"Do you trust me, Silnỳ?"

The answer to the question was obvious. He had saved my life. I nodded once.

"Good. Now, do you trust me to not let you fall?"

It took a moment for me to get my wits about me. As much as I was scared of falling, scared of breaking my body again, I knew that I trusted Ilyan. He would not let anything happen to me; of that, I was sure. I nodded once in agreement, and a wide smile spread over his face.

"Good. I am going to teach you to fly the way my father taught me. I want you to use the wind to launch yourself into the air, straight up. Can you do that?"

"No," I said, panic seizing me.

"I won't let you fall, Joclyn. I promise you this above all else, I will never let anything hurt you. I am only here to protect you."

He was dead serious, his voice reverent, like he was giving me some kind of vow. My heart jump started.

"Okay."

"Now get down and prepare to jump."

I gave him one more look before I crouched down to the ground as Ilyan had instructed, my palms lying flat against the ground.

"Now call the wind to you," he whispered behind me.

I closed my eyes tightly, attempting to forget that anyone was there, forgetting my previous failures. I breathed out, letting my magic come to a boiling point under my skin. My magic moved away from me easily, stretching away and bringing the wind back with it. The warm tongues licked at my feet and the tips of my fingers. I moved it around, amazed at the control I had over it. It obeyed my every thought.

"Now, jump."

With one swift movement, I kicked off from the ground, the wind propelling me upward, my arms extending out, warm air whipping past my fingers. The sensation was amazing; I could have never guessed that so much freedom lay in this, in flight. My face rose to the sun, enjoying the warm rays and the breeze that moved across my skin. The feeling of the wind's soft touch brought back memories of a million car rides up the canyon and a million tree races. Even through the bitter-sweet memories, I smiled. Then the wind began to change.

The air zoomed past me as I began to fall. I looked around desperately for a branch large enough to land on, my instinct from the tree races kicking in. There was nothing, not even a stem big enough to support my weight.

I had flown too high.

I had been here before. I had fallen. I had almost died. I screamed in fear and agony as gravity pulled me toward the earth again. My body tensed, preparing for the awful impact that waited for me below. Instead of hard dirt though, I felt strong arms. My body clenched further as I looked into Ilyan's face, his arms cradled around me as he propelled us upward. His wind moved around us as we flew toward a tree, a large branch stretching out before him as if welcoming us. Ilyan landed on the branch safely, his arms still wrapped around me.

"I told you I wouldn't let you fall."

"Thank you, My Lord." I moved away from him, careful to keep myself standing on the tree branch.

"I am just Ilyan now, Joclyn."

"Thank you, Ilyan."

"You are very welcome." He smiled softly. "Now, we are going to do it again, but this time I want you to focus on the wind. Set your mind on what it is doing and how I am controlling it. Do not let fear enter your mind. I will be here, always."

I nodded and closed my eyes, calling the wind again. The warm breeze came almost instantly, but it wasn't just my magic controlling the movements of the wind. Ilyan's magic intertwined with mine as the wind swirled around us. It was not my magic that eventually forced the wind to push us off the tree branch. Ilyan's magic surged, sending us flying into the air. My body tensed in panic as my feet lost contact with the branch.

"Relax your body; do not think of the movement you are about to accomplish." Ilyan's voice was soft in my ear as his hands moved to grip my waist. "Focus only on the wind. Focus on its movement, on its warmth. Focus on how your magic will bring it to you. And do not worry, Joclyn; I will never let you fall." With that, he threw my body into the air, the wind he controlled pushing me up and away from the tree.

I screamed as my body left the security of his arms, terror grabbing hold of me. Before I could act on the fear, Ilyan was there again, his arms wrapped around me as he held me against him, our bodies floating through nothing. He stayed there for just seconds before throwing me in a different direction, spinning me through the air away from him.

As I twirled through the air, my magic moved away from me, my calm body giving it leave from its prison underneath my skin. My magic mingled with Ilyan's as he controlled the wind that supported me, our combined magic flowing and dancing. I continued to fly forward as our magic worked together to guide me. Ilyan grabbed me gently and continued moving us through the open air.

As Ilyan threw me away from him again, wind and magic swirling in a perfect dance, I understood; all trace of fear was gone. I knew exactly what to do. I grabbed the wind that Ilyan had surrounded me with and pushed it another way, my body moving alongside it as I controlled it.

This was familiar.

This was the feeling I got when I climbed the trees with Ryland; this supreme happiness and freedom. It was just as Wyn had said; I had used Ryland's magic to climb the trees, except now, it was my magic giving me those same feelings. Even though I missed Ryland's comforting warmth, there was something empowering behind doing it myself.

"Now catch me," Ilyan's voice called after me. I turned my head to see him speeding away through the trees in the opposite direction from where I was headed, dodging in and out of the high branches. I laughed happily before easily changing my course to fly after him. Ilyan moved swiftly, his powerful arms propelling him further, his wind racing him ahead of me. He moved with an ever-increasing speed as he changed his course several times. His smiling face continued to look back at me as I desperately tried to catch up to him. I followed behind, not making much headway before he changed his course yet again.

As he moved, I saw a path that would give me a straight shot right to him. I smiled at the idea of winning the game before plunging myself down into the lower branches of the tree. It was harder to move here with the branches growing smaller and closer together, but being out of sight gave me the opportunity to cut across a corner that led straight to him. I broke out of the lower branches, a rush of wind pushing me up to where Ilyan flew. I wrapped my arms around his neck, pushing him off his course, and slamming us into a large branch of a tree.

"Got you," I said.

I rolled onto the branch as my body began to register the effort that was involved in not only flying, but also propelling through branches. I leaned up against the trunk of the tree and looked at where we had ended up, my breathing ragged and forced as I attempted to catch my breath.

"Very good," Ilyan said. He leaned forward and placed his hand gently against my face. I stiffened as his warmth moved into me, moving right to my back. It spread comfortably down my spine, wiping away the small aches that had popped up from our impact.

"I didn't break my back again, if that's what you're checking."

"I know, but it's always best to double check." He smiled before removing his hand, letting his fingers trace the kiss again.

"Why do you do that?" I said, moving swiftly away from his touch.

"Do what?"

"Touch my kiss. It seems you take every opportunity to touch it."

He withdrew his hand. "I'm sorry. Does it bother you?"

"Not as much as it should, I suppose." I hated how true that was. "When Ryland touched it, I kind of blacked out. Why doesn't it do that with you?"

"Because you are not bonded to me, Joclyn. I am not your mate and so our bodies don't react."

"Mate?" I exclaimed, terrified.

"Yes, Joclyn. The Zêlství, remember? Everything just has a different name."

I nodded my head like I understood, but my stomach still spun. *Mate*? I was seventeen, barely.

"Why do you keep touching it?" I asked, freaking out a little bit. "You don't expect the same thing to happen, do you?"

Ilyan laughed, which I should have been happy about, but instead it only made me feel really embarrassed.

"No, Joclyn, you don't have to worry about that. I am only here to protect you. It's just..."

"What?"

"It's just been so long since I have seen one, since my father... My father had a kiss just as you do, did you know that?"

"Your father? But I thought you were a... a... Skry..." Darn it, I had forgotten the word.

"A Skřítek, Joclyn."

"I thought you were a Skřítek?"

"My mother was. My father was a Chosen, just as you. I suppose I am kind of a half-breed," he said.

"A half-breed... who is king of the Skříteks?"

Ilyan nodded at my connection. "My father ruled over all magical beings for a time, many years ago. So, I guess you could say that I inherited the title."

"Your father was king? Of the Skříteks?"

"More along the lines of king over everyone. In that time, there was no true segregation."

"What happened to him? Did Edmund kill him, too?"

Ilyan hesitated, looking away and running his hands through his straight hair.

I instantly regretted asking the question.

"My father was the first person that Edmund destroyed," he clarified.

CHAPTER 44
RYLAND

The giant gash in my back was never going to heal properly. Partly in thanks to my father still restraining my magic, but mostly from the poison that cutting out my kiss had unleashed on me.

Which was the whole point.

The weaker I was, the more control he had.

I sat in the corner of the underground prison, shivering from the cold and pain. Trying to find any scrap of my magic to help me heal, or even just any shred of strength to keep going. That last part was getting harder to do.

"What else do you remember?" Sain whispered from the darkness of his own cell. I pulled one of the blankets he had given me up a bit higher in an attempt to trap any warmth against my chest and stop the burning ache in my chest from turning into a cold.

"I remember the way her hair smells. The way it always fell in long tangles of curls. I remember the way her brow pulled together when she thought I was being ridiculous but was too scared to say anything." My heart tightened and my magic zinged again.

"How about her mother?" Sain sounded half asleep from where he sat, staring straight ahead as he went through his usual line of questions.

"She was the first person to ask me what was wrong, and that actually wanted to help. She made a delicious beef stew." She made everything delicious, and while the memory of her made me feel warm and safe in different ways, it was nothing compared to how the thought of Joclyn buzzed through me. "I don't know if anyone can be an anchor for me as much as Jos can."

"Then she is your ticket out of this." Sain turned his head to me, his green eyes sparking in the dark. "Not that I am surprised."

I had meant to chuckle, but that burning flared to life and what came out was half a whimper, half a cough, and only sounded as though I was in pain. Pressing my head back against the stone wall I breathed deep, as if the damp air would help my lungs. They only burned more.

"We will focus on Joclyn," Sain said as though I hadn't just wheezed in a sound like death.

With how much I had talked Sain's ear off about Joclyn, I think we both would have been surprised if it hadn't been her.

"What do I do now?" We had spent the last few days going over memories, but they were still leaving at an astonishing rate. I needed Sain to deliver on his promise.

I couldn't forget any more of her.

"We need to preserve your memories," he began, still leaning against the bars. "I want you to think about building a box someplace in your mind, or in your heart. A strong box that your father can't reach."

"Okay." I lifted an eyebrow at him, waiting for something more. That couldn't be it, could it?

"And I want you to fill it with every memory you have of Joclyn. Even if it means you forget them for a little while, I want you to put them in the box to keep them safe."

Now I was raising two eyebrows. Sain just chuckled at me and went back to staring off into the dark.

"You want me to build an invisible box in my mind and hide my memories in it?" I really hoped I had missed some vital piece of this that made any type of sense.

"Yes." He chuckled deeper, the sound twisting into a cough that echoed through our prison. "I know it sounds crazy, but it will work. Even if you don't remember her anymore, as long as the strongest parts of your memory still exist, your father can never have full control over you. Which means that there is still a chance for escape."

"I thought you were going to teach me how to get my memories back? Tell me how to fight this," I snarled, my chest burning again. I tried to control the anger, but it was suddenly boiling. I had trusted him, and he had lied.

"I am." He grinned at me as though he was proud of himself and I fought the urge to hit him.

'Why don't you. You like hurting people now, remember?'

"This will work, Ryland."

I wanted desperately to believe him. In a way, I was already doing what he asked. I had been holding my most precious memories safe inside of me, locking them away from my father. It just so happened that all of those memories revolved around Joclyn. No wonder I was so disappointed. I had expected a miracle cure, some grand reveal. Some way to get us both out of here. I got none of that.

I got lies!

'Nothing but lies! How does that make you feel?'

"Lies!" I yelled, the word, shock rippling through me that something had broken through, that his voice had rampaged into me.

Sain was looking at me in shock, his eyes wide as I shrunk away from him and the voice that was now laughing in my head.

"This can help, Ryland. I promise it will help."

I could only nod. I wasn't sure anything could, but at this point I had to try.

Pushing that still boiling anger away, I sagged against the bars and pulled my tattered blanket up to my chin. The cold darkness fell into silence, my mind drifting back into memories of Joclyn. Each one a precious gift that I slowly began to lock away, placing inside the svazovat that connected me to her. Well, connected me as long as she wore the necklace. It was the safest place.

I didn't know if I was asleep or just locked inside my memories, but I jumped when the door at the top of the stone staircase opened, all of my muscles and nerves going into high alert at what was coming.

I had never truly trusted my father. I always feared him, but this fear was something I had never experienced before. I recoiled, shivering in panic, eyes focused on the stairwell as my father and his cronies began to descend.

"I am tired of waiting," Edmund was saying, leading the charge down the stairs. "This may be our easiest opportunity to capture them all. We could retrieve her and end him, end it all. I could finally take control."

"They will come." Timothy was clearly cowering. "They will have seen him on the news by now. You know, Ilyan. He will not be able to resist saving him. Ryland is the trap we have been waiting for."

"No," Edmund snapped as they all came into view; Edmund, Timothy, and Cail all clustered together. "Ryland is the bait. I need to know how to set the trap." They all turned, and the muscles in my spine knit together. But they weren't looking at me. They were looking at Sain. "I need to know when and where."

Sain shivered, pushing himself into the wall as he tried to disappear beneath the grungy rags.

"I can't." The confident man of a moment ago was suddenly replaced by a whimper.

"Sain," my father began. I looked between them in confusion. "Are you hungry?"

"No." For the first time, the old man sounded scared.

"You must be starving." I was sure I could hear Sain whimper at his taunt. "Would you like something to eat? To drink?"

My father sounded like he was talking to a dog, and Sain responded in kind. Then my father reached behind him, holding his hand out to Cail who handed him a simple brown clay mug.

It looked like a poorly done pottery project done by a child.

With how Sain reacted, you would think it was plated in gold. I stared between them in confusion, but it was as though they had forgotten I was there. They were all staring at that stupid mug.

Sain scuttled forward, still whimpering, before cowering back, his fingers still twitching.

"What do you want, Edmund?" He asked, and my father pulled back the mug. Another whimper. "What do you want, my Lord?"

"I want to know when they are coming. I want to know how to beat him." My father had barely extended his hand before Sain grabbed the mug, placed his hand over the rim and then drank from it as though it contained a never ending supply of liquid.

Odd. I could have sworn it was empty.

Sain drank greedily, water that almost appeared to be the color of gold flowing over the side and down his cheeks. His entire body sagged as he drained the mug, everything relaxing as though he had been drugged. He leaned back against the wall, his focus going right back to the spot on the wall before my cell. Except, it didn't look like Sain at all. His eyes were nothing but black; a swatch of ebony fully encompassed them as his mouth sagged and a voice that was not his hissed to life.

"The night is long in celebration of a date long sought," Sain began, his voice changed to a heavy dead tone. Almost as if he was being controlled by someone else. "In the high halls of coronation a blast will begin the battle that will sing of your victory. Gain control and you will win. Lose your spoils and the end will be near. Only a child that was once lost will tip the scales."

Words spoken, Sain sagged back, mug all but forgotten as his eyes faded back to green.

I couldn't even move. I was frozen as I watched the man, my father turning to me with a wide grin on his face. "Looks like you are going to get a graduation party after all."

I barely heard him, I didn't even care.

Sain had told me he was my father's other prized possession, but I had no idea what that had meant. Until now.

Sain was a Drak.

CHAPTER 45
RYLAND

The familiar sounds of the hallway rattled in my head as an echo. Shouts, the sound of feet, a dozen lockers all slamming at once; they all buzzed in my head as though they were a million miles away and not just a few feet.

I stood, blinking, as I tried to focus on the cool touch of the locker as if that would help to pull my mind out of this prison.

"Damn, Ry. You look like shit."

I turned at the voice, the sounds and faces becoming clearer as I stared at the guy who had spoken. He leaned against the locker next to mine, uniform jacket over his shoulder, hair a coiffed mess.

I knew him.

I blinked, trying to pull his name out of the muddled mess of my mind.

'Yeah, I got into a fight.'

"Yeah, I got into a fight." My own words echoed those of my father in my mind, a smile that I didn't want following. "Don't worry, I won."

"You sure? It doesn't look like it."

'I'm sure.'

"I'm sure. He deserved it."

"Like Marcus, last term?" The kid added, nudging me with his elbow as I slammed my locker shut and we made our way through the crowded hall.

Even in the fog that I was trapped in I noticed that every single head turned to stare at me. My father had forced most of my injuries to heal, although he left me with a few as reminders. Yes, I looked like I was in a fight, but that wasn't the reason they were staring at me.

This was my first time back in school since everything had happened. Since the explosion, since the news conferences, since everything important had vanished.

'They all think you killed her. Maybe you did.'

No. It's not my fault. She's alive.

'Not yet. Her death will be your fault, after all.'

I twitched at the voice, not that the guy next to me noticed. He was blabbering on about some fight that I didn't remember.

Just like his name.

"Hey, Ryland! How does it feel to kill a girl? Did she tell you no and you just... lost control?"

I stopped at the voice, both of us turning to the group that were staring at us with a mix of horror and intrigue.

"Tyler, how can you stand next to him?" They all turned to the guy at my right.

Tyler. That was his name.

We had been friends for about six years. And I had forgotten his name. No, it had been taken from me.

Like everything.

'Tell them how wrong they are.'

"She's not dead. She's missing. Men attacked our home." The story my father had concocted came out as though I was a robot. They clearly weren't buying it.

"Is that why the police have searched your home multiple times?"

'It was the last place--'

"Of course they've searched my house. It was the last place she was seen. It's a crime scene. They are looking for clues." I was firm, or rather my father was firm. I just stood, letting him control me.

I had more important things on my mind.

Just talking about Joclyn was sending my magic into a surge. It rumbled through me like little sparks of electricity. It was just like Sain had said.

The anchor.

Focusing on her, the magic buzzed louder, swelling from that line of magic where I had hidden it. The one that connected me to the necklace, to her. I wanted to follow it, I wanted to check on her, but I used the time to keep that damn I had built against it strong, and her hidden.

"Have you ever seen a crime scene?" My father continued through me.

"Of course not," one of the boys countered, all of them laughing nervously. "Because we haven't committed a crime."

"Would you like to see a crime scene?" That statement pulled me right back, my heart fluttering at what Sain had said. At what was about to happen. "No, they don't."

I snapped those last words on my own, my arm twitching as I broke through.

My father's magic zinged through me at that, snapping my spine to attention and sending what little magic had escaped back into its hiding place.

'Do not play this game, Ryland, or Joclyn will not be the only one that is hurt.'

He didn't need to say more for me to know what he was talking about. I looked from the foggy shape of Tyler to the others. I may not remember their names, but I wasn't going to turn them into casualties.

'You are weak. Your mercy makes you weak. Pathetic.'

No, it doesn't.

'Invite them.'

There was no chance of fighting him now, my response came almost without prompting, my voice sounding as boisterous and happy as it always did. "I'm having an early graduation party. Next weekend."

"You gonna kill us too?"

"No, but you can check out the 'crime scene'." They actually looked interested in that. "Or work your way through my father's wine cellar."

"Now that we can get behind." They laughed and pounded fists, already turning to spread the word of the party.

"You really going to invite the whole school to your house?" Tyler asked, catching up to me as my feet trudged me toward my first class. "I mean, I haven't even been past the pool house."

"Then this is the perfect time to check out my digs." Digs?

My father may be controlling me, but if he kept that up it was only a matter of time before someone caught on.

'You are a fool. No one will, because no one cares enough to see you. Pathetic.'

Jos does. Again, my magic reacted.

'No one who will be alive much longer.'

My heart tightened, arm twitching. Tyler turned to me in confusion, that time he had noticed. But, he didn't say anything. I could see the same look in his eyes as the others. Fear, maybe.

He thought I had killed her too.

“See you later, Ry.” He went to clap me on the shoulder, but stopped short, as though skin contact would kill him instantly.

He walked away without another look, his feet moving faster with each step until he was running. It only confirmed my father’s taunt. His laugh echoed in my head as I watched him go.

‘No one cares about you.’

He was wrong though, because someone did care. Someone who mattered.

My magic attempted to break free at the thought of her, of her smile, but I held it at bay. I may not be able to stop what was coming, but I might be able to use the trap my father had set to get Sain and I out, and that would take more than a weak strain of magic.

CHAPTER 46
JOCLYN

After my flying lesson, I spent the next two days in the air, although it wasn't exactly by choice. Ilyan had insisted that once I had grasped the concept, I perfect it. I knew it was all with the pretense of my need to escape, and it made me mad. I had perfected moving wind, even under the barrier the necklace gave me, for short distances. It wasn't enough for Ilyan; he insisted I do better. He demonstrated ways I could use the wind defensively, and I learned them easily, my skills improving swiftly now. Moving around pebbles and benches wasn't enough for me, I needed to be stronger. Be better. I needed to do my part in rescuing Ryland.

Which is why I had worked through dinner, attempting to throw anything I could against the lines of targets Ilyan had built me. Rocks. Tree trunks. I had even accidentally grabbed a rabbit. Luckily, I noticed before I had hurled the terrified thing through the air. I only came back to my room when it was too dark to see and my stomach was trying to eat itself for want of food.

I sat on the windowsill that overlooked the courtyard with my head against my knees. I looked out into the yard, seeing nothing except a green haze as the light of the moon streamed through the green leaves of the massive tree.

I had been throwing a button back and forth across the room for the last thirty minutes, only stopping when the news had come on a few minutes ago, my ears perking up at the sound of my name. It seemed I was still big news, and what was more, Ryland was giving another press conference—live this time.

I tried to keep my focus off the screen, terrified of the condition I would see him in, but my ears were tuned to it intently, my heart thumping in anticipation. The possibility of hearing his voice had electrified my senses. I grabbed the necklace from its resting place on the table, desperate to be close to him in any way possible.

"And now we go live to the LaRue estate where Ryland LaRue will be addressing the press."

I reluctantly turned my head to the screen, my heart beating in eager, terrified, fear. The "Live" icon lit up the bottom corner of the screen and I couldn't help but think of how he was right there, standing on the steps of that massive house. My heart longed to be next to him. I clenched the necklace tighter as Ryland walked out of the door to the small podium that stood at the bottom of the front steps where the press had gathered.

I would like to say he looked like he had healed a bit, but I knew better. His right arm still hung lifelessly beside him, his right shoulder larger than the left one thanks to some bulky bandages. His bruises appeared to be better, and the cut was almost gone, but he was twitching more than he had been the last time. Each jerk was so subtle that most people wouldn't have noticed it, they shot through me like I was being punched.

Ryland paused and shifted the papers in his left hand before looking at everyone in front of him. His bright blue eyes met the camera, and everything stopped. Ryland was terrified; I had never seen him look so scared. Seeing him on the screen shoved Edmund's magic-enshrouding blanket completely off me. My uncovered magic surged, the energy prickling my skin like a thousand needles. I expelled it from me, surprised to find it willingly going into the necklace that I still held in my hands. I looked at the ruby, reluctant to take my eyes from Ryland for too long. My magic flowing into the ruby had increased its warmth, the heat comforting against my skin.

"It's okay, Ryland. You can do it," I spoke softly to myself, wishing I could help him.

On the screen, Ryland shifted, but it wasn't the twitch of the Vymàzat; that was something different. His eyes met the camera again, and his mouth turned up in that coy, little smile that always caused my heart to skip a beat.

"Ladies and gentlemen, I have asked you to gather together today with the intent of addressing an assumption that has been prevalent among the press. This assumption concerns the disappearance of Joclyn Despain."

A twitch.

"Fight him, Ryland, please. Fight him for me."

He smiled again. "I know it has been inferred that I may have been involved in her disappearance." A bigger twitch. "And I would like to state, again, that I was not involved with this tragedy in any way. I am proud to say that I love Joclyn Despain with all my heart, and her disappearance has taken an even bigger impact on me than she may ever know."

He looked right at the camera, his eyes shining with tears. "I love you, sweetheart."

"I love you, too." The necklace dug into my hand as my magic continued to surge into it.

"I know you do. And that's why I need you to listen very carefully."

I froze, focused on the necklace, on the warm heat that I instantly recognized as not being my own.

"You need to..." He paused when a twitch so large came over him that he had to hold onto the podium tightly, his knuckles turning white before he could raise his head.

"Fight him, Ry."

"I'm... trying... Jos... Stay... where you are... Don't come... Stay where you are..." He twitched so intensely that his head slammed into the podium. I could hear the press yell and call out in alarm in the background. He rose slowly, and I could tell he had lost. The blue from his eyes was gone, the pitch-black filling them once again.

I yelled in fear, the necklace falling to the floor.

"Ryland!"

"I'm coming to get you," Ryland's voice hissed angrily.

I screamed out just as the door to my bedroom burst open and Talon rushed in. He caught me right before I fell to the ground. I fought against his hold as I yelled, reaching toward the screen in vain, my voice echoing around the room. Wyn had followed Talon in and grabbed a pillow from the bed, she covered the necklace with it, her hands pushing it hard into the floor.

"What's going on?" Ovailia yelled angrily, her agitation at being interrupted apparent.

"Get Ilyan!" Talon yelled, his arms wrapping around me protectively.

"Don't you dare talk to me that way," Ovailia scolded, affronted.

"Get Ilyan, now!" he amended, his voice loud enough to reach over my screams.

Wyn came up beside us, her arms wrapping around me tightly, her head resting against my back. Her cold magic flowed into me, the iciness shocking me, my panic stopping immediately. She withdrew her magic, leaving my own residual warmth to boil through me angrily at the absence of the necklace around my neck.

"Thanks, Wyn," I whispered.

"It's okay. He's okay." Wyn's soft voice vibrated through me.

"Did... did you see?"

"Yes, we saw."

"Saw what?" Ilyan's voice was laced with worry.

I heard the door close and footsteps approach as Ilyan rushed over and pried me away from my friend's strong arms. He pushed his magic into me, concerned that I was injured in some way.

"I'm fine, Ilyan," I sighed as I shifted, breaking the contact with his hands. "It's just... I mean..." I stopped. I didn't quite know how to explain what had happened.

"Ryland spoke to you through the television, didn't he?" Talon said.

Ilyan's head whipped around to stare at me as I nodded. He exclaimed something in Czech before turning to face me head on.

"I need you to tell me exactly what happened, Joclyn. Everything. Don't hold back, not now." Ilyan grasped my hands tightly in his.

I jerked my hands away from him. I didn't want him; I only wanted Ryland.

"I saw him on the TV; it was a live press conference. Seeing him there... I could feel everything. I pulsed my magic into the necklace and then Ryland started talking to me... and then... he changed... and..."

"Ovailia!" Ilyan yelled when I was done. She opened the door, obviously having listened from the hallway the entire time. "Get me a copy of the press conference, as quickly as you can."

Ovailia walked away, leaving the door to my room wide open.

Ilyan began to pace as Talon filled him in on what they had seen in the press conference and how Ryland had begun to talk directly to me. I filled in the gaps on my end when needed, glad I didn't have to say much.

I couldn't take my eyes off the pillow that Wyn had used to smother the necklace. It called to me, my heart thumping at my need for it. Before I knew what I was doing, my hands were hovering over the pillow, desperate to remove it.

"Joclyn, don't." Talon's voice was stern, and I froze.

"Why not? I just... Can I put it back on?"

"No," Ilyan said simply. "He may be possessing the necklace."

"He?"

"Edmund." Ilyan's voice was like ice.

"He knows now?"

"I'll have to see the video to know for sure."

I nodded, my eyes rolling back over to the pillow involuntarily.

"If he has, I need you to teach me how to block him from the necklace, from controlling me?"

"I can try. As I said before, Joclyn; it involves magic you don't understand yet."

I sat up straighter, still staring at the pillow.

"None of that matters, I'm going to try." I had mastered flying and throwing more than he expected me to. This should be easy.

"If anyone can figure out how to do it, I am sure it will be you." He seemed way too confident in me, but I used it like a fuel.

"It's queued up in your room, Ilyan." Ovailia spoke from the doorway, making it obvious she did not want him to stay in here. Ilyan stood and dismissed her before walking over to stand next to me.

"May I borrow your necklace, Joclyn?"

I nodded and let him take it, although I did not move from where I sat on the floor.

I just sat in silence, staring at the carpet where the impression in the plush pile still marked the place the necklace had landed. I could hear Wyn and Talon shift and whisper behind me, but I ignored them stubbornly.

So, I could speak to Ryland through the necklace; I could connect directly with him. While the possibilities were exciting, Ilyan was right, the bigger problem was what Edmund could do to me.

I was only vaguely aware of the whispered conversation occurring between Wyn and Talon. Their voices were like chicken scratches in my head, blocking most of my thoughts. The buzzing under my skin had reached an all-time high, I was sure I could throw more than just a tree. Maybe I could make something explode.

Just as I was about to give it a try, the door opened and Ilyan charged in, necklace swinging before him.

"I can wear it?"

"Yes. I think Edmund went on a whim with his comment. I can't sense any connection with Edmund; it's all residual through your bond with Ryland."

I took the necklace from him greedily, eager to put it back on.

"Just don't purposefully push any more of your magic into it, all right?"

"Why not?" I spoke in a panic; not allowing me to push magic into it was hindering any exploration, any contact with Ryland. My heart froze uncomfortably in my chest.

"I just don't want you to get hurt."

"How could I...?" I began to ask the question but Ilyan shook his head, unwilling to give me an answer.

"I'm leaving," he announced instead.

"What?" Talon and Wyn asked together.

"I will be back on Thursday, so everyone needs to keep preparing for Friday night."

"Is everything okay?" Wyn asked quietly.

"I am not sure; I need to check on a few things. But don't worry; I'll be back soon." He smiled sadly at us, his eyes lingering on me before turning to go out the door.

"Oh," Ilyan added, his head peeking around the doorframe, "I'm terribly sorry, but Ovailia's in charge." He winked before disappearing and I felt my insides plummet. I wasn't the only one.

"Great," Wyn groaned, flinging herself back on my bed. "There goes my week."

CHAPTER 47
JOCLYN

"Again."

I flinched at Ovailia's voice. I had never really liked her, but now, I felt something akin to pure hatred toward her. I grumbled and flexed my fingers, hoping desperately that the magic I knew was hiding inside me would finally come out. It was no use, my body was already exhausted.

Ovailia had awakened me early yesterday morning, pleased at her chance to train me since Ilyan had left the night before. She dragged me unceremoniously out to the courtyard and demanded I begin producing the energy orbs that I had seen Ilyan and Cail create. At first, I was ecstatic for the opportunity to learn something useful, but it quickly became apparent that she was going to be a relentless teacher. Ilyan had been kind and patient, even going so far as to make the lessons into games so that I could learn more quickly. Ovailia demanded instant satisfaction and results without even bothering to explain what she wanted me to do first.

To make matters worse, she insisted I keep the necklace on and work through the barrier before even learning the new tasks. I had worked hard all day yesterday to break through the blanket the necklace put over my magic with no results. I was exhausted. I had struggled for hours without meals, only eating a small amount of stew before crashing into bed and falling asleep.

I had planned to wake up early and practice without the necklace on, so that, if anything, I would be able to at least know what I was doing before I had to try to break through the barrier again. My plan was foiled by a loud knock on the door before the skies had even begun to turn gray.

I had answered the door reluctantly, my whole body hurting from yesterday. Ovailia had demanded I follow her right then, not even letting me get dressed. I had been trying to create an energy orb ever since, with no luck. I had watched the sun rise, the birds wake for the day; but nothing had happened yet.

I stifled a yawn before focusing again. I let visions and memories of Ryland be my guide, but the barrier didn't shift. The blanket that Edmund had placed over my magic was as strong as ever.

"You're not trying hard enough," Ovailia scolded from across the courtyard. She sat stoically in one of the many wrought-iron benches, a pile of small pancakes sitting next to her. I looked at them longingly before turning away. My hunger was not helping me focus.

I bit my tongue to keep from responding to her and flexed my fingers again. Closing my eyes, I thought deeply about the first time I had met Ryland in his kitchen. The memory made me smile, and the barrier shifted just enough to let all the pent-up energy out of me in a rush. My focus had been solely on producing the energy, so when my body finally complied, it didn't have any direction or purpose. The magic shot out in a rush, flying out of both my hands and knocking me to the ground.

"You finally shift the barrier and you can't even control your power. Pathetic," Ovailia's voice sneered wickedly across the courtyard; my smile of accomplishment vanished.

"Hey, I'm trying, okay?" I snapped as I jumped to my feet, rubbing my hip.

"You are not trying hard enough."

"I'm exhausted, Ovailia. You haven't allowed me to get enough food or sleep for the past few days! I can't even think straight!"

She stood with her eyes narrowed at me angrily.

I shrank back a bit before planting my feet defiantly. I didn't want her to think she was getting the better of me.

"And how do you think it will be in two days when you enter the LaRue estate to save the 'love of your life'?" she sneered, lip curling. "Are you going to have your wits about you? Are you going to be able to think straight?"

Ice snaked down my spine at the reminder of how little time was left.

"Yes!" I yelled. "I know what I am doing! I have been in that house more times than you could ever manage."

Ovailia stared at me, and for a wild moment, I was sure that I had won, that she understood that I knew what I was doing. Then, she began to laugh. The tinkling sound could very well have been beautiful, but it was so full of mocking malice that it only made me angry.

"I know what I am doing," I repeated defiantly.

"No," she continued. "You have no idea what you are doing. And when we get there, it is going to be worse. You are going to be terrified; you are going to be a hindrance to us all. I'm just trying to make it so that you don't accidentally kill anyone."

I squared my jaw and lifted my head. I was beginning to wonder if hate was a strong enough word for how I felt about her right now.

"I am not going to kill anyone." I was confident.

"Oh yeah? What about your beloved Ryland? What if, when he holds you, the barrier shifts just enough that your magic surges? What if you can't control it? What if you kill *him*?"

The mention of Ryland's name, combined with my anger and frustration, was a tidal wave. The barrier shifted aggressively off me. My pent-up magic surged under my skin, rippling over my body like the prickling fur of a wild animal. That's how it felt within me—wild. I clenched my hands in an effort to keep it inside. No matter how much I hated Ovailia right now, I knew she was right.

She sensed what I was going through, and her smile widened broadly.

"You can't even control it right now, can you? I don't know what Ilyan sees in you. There is no way you are the Silnỳ."

"What?" I whispered. She had used my nickname like a title.

Ovailia smiled at my lack of knowledge. "Ilyan hasn't even told you. He must not trust you with such valuable information, just like he doesn't trust you to save Ryland." Her voice was snide, condescending; it only increased my power more.

I aimed my hands at her just as the magical energy reached a breaking point. A stream of light and flame burst out of me, hitting Ovailia in the dead center of her chest. She flew through the air before landing and skidding against the long grasses of the courtyard, leaving a long trail behind her.

Part of me was worried for her, while another only cared if I was going to get in trouble or not. My magic continued to stretch as I brought the wind up and lifted myself into the air, only to land next to her a moment later.

I was about to ask if she was all right when she slammed her hand across my face. The slap, combined with the angry magical pulse she had filled it with, sent me spinning through the air to land hard against a small bush.

"You stupid, little girl!" Ovailia spat as she flew at me. "You know absolutely nothing. You think you can just waltz in and steal your boyfriend and everything is going to be fine! You'll be lucky if you leave alive." She raised her hand again, a large crack sounding through the clearing as the earth next to my head exploded.

"I can do this!" I detangled myself from the bush, desperate to move in case she aimed for my head next time.

"No, I don't think you can!" Her hand rose toward me again.

I dodged out of the way, the smell of burning wood filling my nostrils. The smell was so similar to Ryland; it filled my head and mind with him. The smell that I always dismissed as campfire was really the smell of magic; the smell of a million spells, a million burning targets, the smell of each nightly practice he had with his father. It was him.

I turned around to face Ovailia again. The images of Ryland causing my magic to crackle on my fingertips, the electric energy determined to escape any way it could.

"You are going to kill us all!" she growled, her hands rising toward me.

I swung my hands forward; the powerful electricity that shot out of my fingers combined with the wind I had already conjured and collided aggressively with Ovailia. The energy pushed her across the courtyard, slamming her body into the wall of the building.

I looked after her, watching her crumbled body slide down to the ground. She yelled angrily at me in Czech, the furious anger dripping from her voice. I didn't wait for her to regroup. I took advantage of the temporarily-shifted barrier and launched myself off the ground.

I took off into the sky, my body flying away as fast as I could manage, terrified she would follow me. I made a beeline to the forest where Ilyan had taught me to fly and glided into the leafy canopy.

I shot through branches and flung myself around trunks and over small meadows before coming to a stop on a large branch of an old willow tree. I clung to the tree as I caught my breath, air pumping out of me in energized spurts. My breath was coming way too fast; my face stung with my over-emotional heat.

It wasn't fair. I was stuck training with Ovailia who had run me ragged, belittled me, and was determined that I was too dangerous to help. Then, in the end, I only proved her right.

I slunk down on the bough of the tree, my legs dangling over the sides as I waited for my heart rate to slow down; but it wasn't my heartbeat I was feeling.

I pulled the necklace out from underneath my sweater, letting the ruby sit on the palm of my hand. It had the normal warmth from its constant contact with my skin, but I could have sworn the ruby was beating. I wrapped my hand around the gem, surprised to feel the throb of a heartbeat, the quick tempo not matching my own. The beat was panicked. Desperate.

Ilyan had asked me not to push anymore of my magic into the necklace, but I didn't care. I didn't even hesitate; I let my magic surge out and fill the ruby. I felt the beat of the necklace fill my mind, the rhythm echoing around my skull like a drum. I let it consume me as Ryland's warmth followed steadily behind it.

My magic surged again, this time pushing the magnetic energy out of me. It collided with the necklace, and my body grew heavy, like my bones had turned to lead. I closed my eyes, calling out when the white room that Ryland and I shared came into view.

I spun around, scanning the white space for Ryland. Finally, I saw him, a boy sitting on the floor only a few feet away from me. I could tell he was younger, and my heart sank to my toes. He wore clothes that were ripped and stained, each article sagging off his body, many sizes too big. He sat quite still, humming a song that I was sure I had heard him sing before. His hands moved as if he were playing with something, but as I walked around to see what it was, nothing was there.

He jumped back, clutching the invisible toy to his chest as my feet came into view.

"Who are you?" The bright blue eyes of a thirteen-year-old looked up at me; the blue, deep and heavy, like he had already seen too much of the world. "Are you my new nanny?"

"Yes," I answered hesitantly before moving to sit next to him. "My name is Joclyn."

"Joclyn?"

I nodded my head.

"I like that name. My very favorite friend's name is Joclyn. I call her my diamond girl." He froze. "But you must never tell her I call her that! Can you promise?"

"I promise," I said sadly.

"Good."

"Why do you call her that?" I asked, though I already knew the answer.

"Her eyes... they are beautiful." He smiled widely for a second before the grin faded to nothing. "They are gray like yours, but much more beautiful. They are almost silver, like diamonds." He looked at me intently before returning to play with what I could only assume to be a car. The toy and his actions were out of place for how old he appeared, he was acting like he was about ten. But something else was off. I couldn't quite place it. He moved his hand around the invisible object, back and forth, back and forth, as he continued to hum.

"Do you know why I need a new nanny?" he asked, his focus not leaving the car.

"No, why?"

"I scared the other one too much."

I didn't miss the strong mocking in his voice.

"Oh, really?" I smiled. "And how did you scare her?"

"I told her what my father did."

"What did he do?"

He looked up from his toy to look at me

"Not going to tell you. You remind me too much of Jos. Besides, I like you."

"I like you, too," I conceded, "but you won't scare me."

"Yes, I would."

"Try me."

He sat back and looked at me closely, his nose scrunching up a bit. The look made me smile; he had stopped making that face when he was about thirteen.

"He made me kill my mother." His voice was calm and plain, but I didn't miss the pain behind it.

I controlled my reaction carefully, knowing he was watching me, even though I wanted to panic. "I am sure he didn't..." I stated what was in my heart, willing what Ryland had said to be false.

"Yes, he did," Ryland snapped, his voice hitting a higher octave. "He kept her locked up until I could control myself and then he made me kill her." He started to cry, and I instantly regretted making him tell me.

"Why... why... would he..." I couldn't finish. I wanted to run away; I didn't really want to hear the answer.

"I let out his Víly when I was seven, so he locked her up. He doesn't want anyone else to be like us." He dried his tears and went back to playing with his car, his humming loud and broken as he cried.

"You're not going to leave me, are you?" He didn't look up, but I could hear the longing in his voice.

"No." I reached forward and ran my finger through his curls, the soft hair moving through my fingers. "I'll never leave you."

"What if I asked you to?" My hand froze. His voice had deepened into that of an adult, his head still hanging down.

"Ryland?"

"What if I asked you to leave, Joclyn?" He looked up at me, his thirteen-year-old face looking strikingly like my Ryland, the Ryland of today.

"I can't leave, Ry."

"I'm sorry, Joclyn. But it's too dangerous now. Stay where you are. Leave me." His hands reached up and grasped my shoulders tightly, his small fingers digging into my skin through the sweater. With one mighty jolt, he pushed me backwards. The white room disappeared as it faded into trees and sky. Ryland's face continued to look down at me as I fell, fell away from him, fell out of the tree.

Wind I didn't control came out of nowhere and caught me, just as my hand hit the ground in a precursor to the impact. The wind ceased as I dropped the last foot, landing hard on my back.

I grunted as I sat up, rubbing the now sore spots that had been so recently broken. "Ow."

"Yeah, I'd say so," Ilyan spoke from behind me. "You're just lucky I was looking for you or that would have been much worse." He was smiling broadly, but his smile faded away as he looked at me. It was like he could see right into me and knew what I had just seen.

CHAPTER 48
JOCLYN

"What did you do, Joclyn?" Ilyan asked, his voice sounded like my mother's.

I flinched. "Oh, you know; the usual. Got mad at your sister, threw her into a wall, and flew away."

"You're not the first to do that," he smiled, "but that's not what I am asking."

"What are you asking?" The cornered teenager reflex was coming on strong.

"What did you do, Joclyn?"

I backed away from him as he continually stepped closer to me.

"Pushed my magic into the necklace, even though you told me not to; shared a Tȍuha with Ryland, who was younger, by the way, and told me all about how Edmund made him kill his mother."

Ilyan's face went from angry, to concerned, to furious as I spoke.

"Is it true?" I asked softly, hoping to deflect his anger away from me.

"Is what true?" he snapped.

"That Edmund made him kill his mother."

"Yes."

"Why?"

Ilyan pinched the bridge of his nose in frustration, his eyes screwed up tightly. "Edmund tortures his children, Joclyn." He dropped his hand to look at me. "He uses them to increase his power, to bend their will so that they only answer to him. He trains them to be destructive weapons and pawns in his little game. He holds no love for Ryland; he probably made him torture his mother as a way to break him, to teach him a lesson."

"Them?"

"Yes, Joclyn. Them. All ten of them."

I stared at him, my hands opening in a question.

"What do you want me to tell you? It's nothing good."

I could tell how uncomfortable the subject was making him; he was very edgy.

"I think I have handled quite enough to prove I can handle a bit of bad news." My voice was firm.

He sighed exasperatedly at me before turning away, his hand running through his long blonde hair.

"Ilyan." I wasn't sure if I was angry or worried. The way Ilyan was reacting, it was so unlike him. I could almost feel the waves of negative energy flowing off him. He spun around to face me, his eyes damp.

"He tortures them, Joclyn. He tortures them until he breaks them and then he uses them or he kills them. It's not a monarchy he is running here. There is no next-in-command. It is only Edmund and the children he gobbles up and spits out. He did it to Zetta; he did it to Markus, Thom, Drayven, Ovailia, Sylas..."

"Wait," I interrupted him, my heart clenching in my chest, "Ovailia?'

Ilyan breathed out deeply, his face looking like a cornered dog. He looked away from me, his hand dragging through his blonde locks again.

"Ilyan?"

"Yes. Ovailia. He tortured my sister by making her watch as he killed her mate. He forced her to track down and kill her friends. She bears a scar from her neck to her tailbone where he cut away, bit by bit, until she agreed to do it." His voice was so bitter, so pained.

I reached out to him, desperate to comfort him, to make it go away. Then, my hand dropped; the awful truth of what he was saying hitting me hard.

"Your sister." My voice was a whisper.

"Yes."

"No!" I took a step back in horror.

Ilyan looked into me, that unyielding defiance I was used to, coming on strong. His eyes, so familiar, so much like Ryland's. I had been too focused on Ryland to put the obvious puzzle pieces together. I felt ridiculously stupid.

"No!" I repeated, but my voice had lost its shock.

We just stared at each other. I had no idea what to say. All my life I had hidden. I had moaned and groaned and whined about some stupid mark. I had let it ruin my life, and all the while, my best friend, the one person who meant the most to me, was being tortured every day of his life. And it wasn't just him; it was the man who had saved me, it was his sister, it was seven others who had lost their lives. I could have cried; my body almost begged me to. Instead, I squared my shoulders and held it in.

"We need to save him." My magic surged beyond the barrier as I spoke.

Ilyan looked at me for only a moment before striding away from me. I ran up beside him, his pace winding me.

"We are going to save him, Ilyan, aren't we? He's your... your brother."

"We are going to try."

"Try? I thought this was a sure thing!"

Ilyan looked at me, his pace quickening even more. I wanted to ask him to slow down, but didn't dare.

"Edmund has increased the security around the estate. We will have to get through a lot more of his 'henchmen' than I had originally hoped. What I could glimpse of Ryland did not paint a pretty picture; he can barely move at times, and when he does, he twitches so badly that he can't accomplish much. However, the party seems to still be ready to go on as planned, which can only mean that we are walking into a trap."

I stopped in my tracks, remembering all of Ryland's warnings to stay away from him, to leave him alone. He was still trying to protect me, and here I was, preparing to stroll into the lion's den to save him. It was ridiculous.

Worth it. But ridiculous.

Ilyan noticed I was no longer walking beside him and trotted back to get me, now dragging me by the shoulder beside him. My feet stumbled before I caught up to his pace again.

"Don't sulk like a child; we are still going in to get him."

"We are?" My spirits soared.

"Yes, I need you two together."

"Why?" I knew I needed him with me, but it seemed odd that Ilyan felt the same way.

Ilyan grunted and stopped walking right at the edge of the forest. I could see the door to the motel through the break in the trees. He pulled me around to face him.

"I saw the video, Silný. He risked everything to talk to you, to tell you how much he loved you. And I know you love him, no matter how hard you try to keep it hidden." He smiled sadly, his hand reaching up to cup the side of my face.

"Your bond is strong and I am becoming worried that if he dies, you may not be far behind. And I can't let that happen. Because I need you, too."

"*You* need me? Why?"

"I just do." Ilyan leaned forward and kissed my forehead softly. We both stepped back far too quickly.

"Wynifred is waiting for you in your room. We leave in the morning." He left me standing in the trees. I stared after him for a minute before I wiped my forehead off and stormed toward my room.

CHAPTER 49
JOCLYN

It was official; I hated the smell of hair dye. It burned my eyes and nose, the ammonia smell making me sick. I shook my head to get the smell out of my nose, but it was no use. It was burning off my nostril hair, which wasn't necessarily a bad thing.

"Hold still or I am going to dye your face pretty colors, too."

I said nothing, but let her move my head to where she wanted it. When Ilyan had told me Wyn was going to help me get ready, this was not what I had in mind.

I had arrived in my room to a very excited Wyn who was armed with a pair of scissors and a bottle of hair dye. Even though they could alter my appearance magically, it would be easily seen through by Edmund and his men, which meant they had to alter my appearance physically. I had tried to convince Wyn to do something simple, but she wouldn't hear of it. She said that I needed to stand out enough that no one would guess it was me. It didn't make much sense, but I didn't want to argue.

I had been sitting dutifully in the chair since Wyn placed me here, my eyes closed as I refused to see what she was doing. I bit my lip until it bled when she cut off all my hair. My head felt instantly lighter. I only felt a bit of it fall around my face and on my neck before she began to coat it with the thick, sticky stuff I was now being tortured with.

I huffed angrily in the hopes of showing my frustration, but regretted it instantly; my throat was now coated with the burn of the fumes.

"Oh, calm down, Jos. I am almost done."

"You better not have made me look terrible."

"No one will recognize you. That's for sure," she laughed.

"What does that mean?" Now I was worried.

"Nothing. Stop freaking out. You can open your eyes now. You have to wait twenty minutes for it to develop and you're going to look like a loon sitting still with your eyes closed for that long."

I opened them, letting my eyes get used to the sharp chemical burn. Wyn stood in the middle of my bathroom with a huge grin on her face as she began to remove her gloves that were covered with cherry-red hair dye. She had told me she was dying my hair red, but for some reason, I had pictured an auburn color like hers.

"Red? Wyn! That's red!" Wyn grinned at me evilly, flexing her one hand of still gloved fingers at me.

"And black," she provided happily. "It's kind of all blended and fun! You're going to love it!"

"Wyn! My hair was already black! Why did you dye it *more* black?"

"Really, Jos. Calm down. You're going to look *so* good," she squealed and went back to cleaning up, dancing to the Styx music she had playing on the stereo.

"I don't feel like I am going to look *so* good."

Wyn just sighed at me and cranked up the radio in an effort to tune out my complaints.

"Wyn!" I attempted to yell above the music.

She turned down the radio and looked at me skeptically. "You're not going to keep complaining, are you?"

"No," I said. "I was just wondering what you could tell me about Edmund's other children."

She stopped dead in her attempts at cleaning up, her arms falling to her sides. "I am not sure I am supposed to tell you about that."

"It's okay, Wyn. Ilyan told me."

"What did he tell you?" Her eyes narrowed dangerously.

"What Edmund makes his children do. He let it slip that Ovailia was one of them."

She waited before nodding and leaned against the sink to face me.

"Edmund wasn't always like that, you know. Ilyan's father and mother were bonded about twelve hundred years before Ilyan was born; Ovailia was born about thirty years after that. About two hundred years after that, Edmund began to change. They have legends and songs and beautiful paintings of the love shared by Edmund—the bearer of the first mark—and Filare—the Skřítek he shared his life with."

"What happened? I mean, if he loved her so much, why did he leave her?" The eager light that had filled Wyn's dark eyes vanished at my question.

"Edmund saw a woman in a town called Farcina. He lusted after her. Timothy..." she spat the word with venom, "my father convinced Edmund to take her, convinced him that he should be the only one to bear the mark. He left everyone. Broke all magical beings apart. Edmund planted the seeds of distrust and started a civil war that almost killed all of the magic. And while everyone fought among themselves, Edmund massacred the Drak in secret."

"The Drak?" I swear I had heard that name before.

"The Drak were a people who were bred from the mud to be the Keepers of the Waters of Foresight. They were the only ones who could look into the black waters and see the past, present and future. There were stories that they saw a Chosen who would destroy Edmund, and stop the madness that he had created. I think that's why he killed them."

"You mean, like a prophecy?" I tried to keep the disbelief out of my voice.

"I guess you could say that, but they were really anything but. Ilyan was there to witness it. He told Ovailia, not knowing that she was being used as a spy. Because of what Ovailia told Edmund, he ordered the extermination of the Chosen."

"And Ilyan still trusts her?" I was appalled. The bubbling turmoil in my stomach at what I was hearing was making me sick.

"Yes. It's been several hundred years, so he must have a reason. After all, Edmund did almost destroy Ovailia."

"Does Edmund... Does he really make all his children do... terrible things... or he..."

"Kills them, yeah." Wyn moved over and sat down next to me softly.

"After Ilyan and Ovailia, there were Markus, Zetta, Drayven, Sylas, Gielle, Mym, Thom and then Ryland. After Ovailia, each one had a different mother, each one forced to do different things. Markus was murdered in 1480, Zetta has been missing since she was a hundred and thirty, Drayven and Mym fought with Ilyan for a while, but you can't always escape the shadows of your past. They eventually turned against Ilyan, and he had to fight against his own siblings. He won.

"Edmund found and probably killed Thom, about thirty years ago. He was hiding as a college student somewhere in the US. One day, his letters stopped coming. We all ran out to find him, but we never did. Not even a body. That was when Ilyan commanded that everyone stay together at all times. I never met him, but the way Ilyan talks about him, he was very brave. They all are, or were."

My stomach clenched.

"He made Ryland kill his mother."

Wyn turned to me with her mouth open in shock. It took her a second to recover.

"I am not surprised," she said darkly. "Edmund made Ryland torture Ilyan, too."

"What?" I asked, the memory of Ilyan's scarred chest filling my mind.

Wyn looked at me guiltily for a minute, thinking she may have said something she shouldn't have.

"About three years ago, Ilyan was captured in Greece. Edmund could have killed him then, but he made Ryland do it instead, or rather try to; Ilyan is exceptionally powerful..." she faded out and I looked away, not really wanting to hear anymore.

Ryland was about thirteen in the Tӧuha. Only years before that, he had been forced to kill his mother. About the same time, the bright red hand print had appeared on his face and we had fled to the mountain for the first time. Three years ago would have made him about fifteen, about the time we started breaking into hospitals and defying his father even more. Ryland had gone through all that, and through it all, he had smiled and never said a word. I felt the bile rise in my throat.

"I need a shower."

"You still have five minutes," Wyn protested, but I just waved her off. I doubted five minutes would make that much difference.

I was grateful it took so long to get all of the hair dye out. The bright red and dark black streams of color swirled around each other as they slid across the floor of the tub on their way down the drain. I watched the water as I thought about all the people Edmund had hurt, all the people he was still hurting. Strangely, I didn't feel like I wanted to cry; I just felt sick and angry. I fought the anger; I didn't like the way it consumed me.

The swirls of red against the tub began to fade as I thought of my mother, even though the pain of her loss was still an open wound. I thought of how Ryland had hugged her the last time I had seen her alive. I thought of our happy smiles and of painting our fingernails ridiculous colors. I thought of Ryland when we got lost in the cemetery, when we played in the fountain at the park near his house. Also, strangely enough, I thought of my father.

He had, in his own way, tried to save me, too. I thought of the good memories from my childhood, part of me wondering where he had disappeared to since giving me the stone. Even Ilyan had said he didn't know where he was. Before long, I was smiling. While the anger at what Edmund had done was still there, it no longer dominated me.

As I continued to rinse the dye out of my hair, it became apparent exactly how much Wyn had cut off. I wasn't even sure I had any hair left. The hair on the back of my head was all but gone; only short hairs, about an inch long, were left. The front half was longer, one side more than the other. I guess I needed some hair to cover the kiss.

I stepped out of the shower reluctantly, not really wanting to look in the mirror yet. I threw on my pajamas and went to find Wyn, a towel wrapped around my head, even though there was no point. I walked into the bedroom to find not only Wyn, but Talon, Ovailia, Ilyan and about seven other Skříteks as well. I wished I could run back into the bathroom, but the sight of Ilyan made me stop short.

He was dressed in one of the many perfectly-laundered tunics I had seen in his closet that first day. The shirt was long and white, with simple trim in deep gold and purple. A large gold medallion hung around his neck, reaching down his chest halfway. The shirt was cinched to him with a dark leather belt that matched the boots that came to his knees. The worst part was the intricate, jewel-encrusted gold crown he wore on his head. He looked like he was going to a masquerade party. I fought the urge to laugh, instead opting to stare at him, open-mouthed.

"Manners, Joclyn, mråvy," Ilyan scolded roughly.

I looked around me confused and then did the only thing that made sense, given the situation; I curtseyed.

"My Lord."

"Let me see it, Joclyn," Ilyan commanded sternly, his eyes glancing toward my hair line. I removed the towel obediently, feeling uncomfortable. I felt the two remaining clumps of hair swing forward, a chilled breeze tickling my neck.

Ilyan came forward and ran his fingers through my wet hair as he dutifully inspected Wyn's work. My hair was now so short, I could feel his fingers rub against my scalp. The touch sent a shiver down my spine, and my shoulders jerked up toward my ears. Ilyan just smiled at me.

"Good, Wyn. The darker, the better on the face, I think." He moved away from me, his small entourage following him to the door.

"We leave tomorrow at nine. Sleep well, Joclyn." His voice softened just enough to take away the tension that had formed in my neck. He motioned the others out and closed the door behind him, leaving Wyn and me alone.

"Tomorrow," I repeated.

My nerves and butterflies came back instantly; twenty-four hours and Ryland would be here. Safe.

I could do this.

CHAPTER 50
WYN

"Do you think she's ready?" I stifled a yawn as I threw myself back on our squishy purple bed. Even the sexy smiles of Styx that I had taped to the ceiling couldn't calm me tonight.

"Ready for what?" Talon asked, no sign of his usual chuckle in his voice. "To fight?"

I shook my head. "To not get her or anyone else killed."

I loved Jos. She was sweet and bubbly and she hadn't backed down when faced with everything that had been thrown at her. Was it a lot, yeah, but she kept fighting. I had seen a whole different side of her the past few days. But I also knew how volatile her magic, and how strong her magic was. We hadn't even scratched the surface of what she was capable of, and the chance of that going off when she was faced with an army of Trpaslíks trying to catch and kill her was just too high.

Normally I would guard her, protect her, but the moment Cail and Timothy saw me they would be after me. I was the bait to keep them away from Joclyn, I couldn't be near her.

Ilyan was the only one who could really protect her, and hopefully together they could get Ryland out.

Of course, Ilyan was being reckless just going in there in the first place, and the side eye Talon was giving me said that he knew it too.

"Ilyan seems to think so," he mumbled, confirming the glance he gave me. "Ovailia on the other hand." He signed and shook his head, the usual sign that drama had gone down between those two at the council meeting he had just returned from. It usually did, it just tended to be worse in council meetings.

That was when all the drama happened.

I sat straight up. "What happened in council?"

I had been busy dying Jos' hair and keeping her company while everyone else was in the meeting. Usually, I would at least try to eavesdrop, but tonight I was at Talon's mercy.

"The same thing that usually happens in council," Talon sighed, stripping off his shirt and replacing it with the white tank he usually wore to bed.

"You mean Ovailia interrupting and trying to undermine Ilyan?" And I was back to laying on the bed, my excitement fading at the lack of good drama. "Or were they full out yelling this time?"

I always loved it when they yelled, that was when I got to know exactly what was going on in there.

"I would say it is somewhere in the middle. Ovailia still doubts she's the one." He shook his head, that same look he had when I had overheard him and Ilyan talking the other day returning.

He really did know something, and I really did need to find out what.

I turned on the bed to face Talon, both of us wiggling ourselves under the covers. I gave him a look of question, but his brow just furrowed. Guy was dead serious tonight.

"How can she doubt? Didn't Ilyan see her in the sight that Sain gave?" I had lowered my voice, this part of the whole 'vision of the girl who would save us' legend wasn't exactly public information.

"He did. But he can't admit that he saw her. Not yet."

I knew what that meant. "You mean, not until he tells Joclyn what she really is." We'd had this conversation before. "And he won't do that until after we get Ryland."

"He doesn't want her to lose focus."

I knew he was quoting his best friend, and I knew Ilyan had a point. But something was gnawing at me about the whole thing. If Ilyan didn't tell her what she really was, and what she was meant to do, then sending her in against Edmund and his men was even more risky. She needed to know exactly why she was so desirable if she wanted to protect herself. Granted, I didn't know everything, but I knew more than she did.

"Which brings us back to the question at hand," I said through another yawn, curling into Talon as his large arms wrapped around me, pulling me into him. "Is she ready?"

"You've been with her more, Wynny." He yawned himself and kissed my hairline. "You tell me."

"I think she can escape well, but she wants to do more. She's a wild card, and you know how I feel about wild cards." Dangerous. Deadly. And they reminded me way too much of myself.

He just chuckled and kissed me again.

"Pretty sure you are going to make an exception for this one." Another kiss. "If only because you like her."

"Well, yes, there is that." This time I kissed him.

"Besides, if you kill her, Ilyan would never forgive you." No, he wouldn't probably kill me, especially after how long he had spent looking for her.

I pulled back, giving him a smirk. "He forgave me for marrying you."

"Are you equating marrying me to killing someone?" He couldn't quite restrain his laugh.

"Not entirely... maybe..."

We both knew that wasn't one-hundred percent accurate. I was always testing Ilyan's patience, but we had always gotten along fine. He was the one to save me from Cail and Timothy's attempt to kill me after all. Talon had been the one to nurse me back to health.

Ilyan had always felt responsible for what had happened to me, seeing as I was spying for him at the time. But I didn't remember much of what happened before the marks were on my body. Another side effect of the curse. Loss of memory.

"Ilyan was more surprised that we did. You use to hate me--"

"I know." I rolled my eyes and kissed him again, if only to shut him up. He had told me the story for years.

Enemies to lovers and blah blah blah.

As much as he wanted me to be shocked about it, I was more just entertained. Silly guy, he just didn't see how romantic it was. He also didn't read enough smutty romance novels.

"But I love you now," I finished in a whisper against his jaw, kissing him deeper and letting my tongue slide over his bottom lip. I would never get tired of the way he tasted.

"As I love you."

His hand was firm against my lower back as he pressed me into him, his lips peppering mine again and again. I could feel his heartbeat, feel the pulse of longing between us.

"Meet me in our Tȍuha?" I asked breathlessly, not even pulling away to look at him.

"Please." I could already feel the tug of his magic against mine, feel him pull me into our own sanctuary.

The place that would always be ours.

The place where all of those kisses would turn into fireworks.

CHAPTER 51
JOCLYN

After Wyn had finished with my makeup the next morning, I didn't even recognize myself. My eyes looked like pools of black on a pale face. Every time I opened them, the glittering silver of my irises flashed menacingly, the shimmering color surprisingly bright against the black. My lips were dark, too; the dark burgundy setting off the vibrant red that saturated the front of my hair. The severe cut was nothing near what I would have chosen for myself. It was almost like a reverse mullet; a short, boy-cut in the back and stark, straight, longer lengths plastered to my head near my face. The back was dark black that faded into the bright red that framed my face.

Wyn had gone one step further by giving my body the persona to match my hair. She had insisted I place a small magnet in my nose that resembled a nose ring and had taken about an hour to draw on a tattoo with a ballpoint pen. The constant pressure of the tiny pen-tip against my skin had hurt, although not as much as I assumed a real tattoo would. After an hour of being drawn on, my skin had thankfully gone numb, and she had left me with an intricate spider web that stretched all the way down my left arm and across my back.

I wore what could only be described as "club clothes": tight black pants that Wyn had to magically get me into, matched with what my mom would deem stripper heels, and a lime green, loose-fitting, backless shirt. Combine the face and hair with the tight-fitting, revealing clothes, and I felt a desperate need to appear more confident than I really was.

I still felt like the insecure, scared girl I had always been. I looked at myself in the mirror and tugged at my clothes to find some sort of comfort. Standing there alone reminded me so much of my first day without my hoodie. I clutched my necklace, remembering how Ryland had been right there to support me that day, how he had only looked into me and told me how beautiful I was. I exhaled deeply, the memory heaving through me like caffeine.

After Wyn had placed the finishing touches on my disguise, about twenty of us met in the middle of the courtyard in preparation for leaving. I wasn't the only one who had changed my appearance. Ilyan had cut his hair short and dyed it brown. Talon had kept his hair long, but had bleached it white; from the back he almost looked like Ilyan. I got the distinct impression that was the idea.

I pulled and tugged at my clothes as I walked toward the group, not wanting so much of my body to be visible. We all gathered together and took off into the sky, following Ilyan to a small run-down conference center in a city I didn't recognize. He herded us into a small room, with the sole intent of holding a planning meeting.

Ilyan had been speaking nonstop since the meeting began; he wrote on an old chalkboard, separated us into groups, and spoke to each member of each group individually. I didn't understand a word; everyone was speaking only in Czech. I shifted my weight again, my body sore and stiff against the folding metal chair I sat in.

I looked around; luckily, I wasn't the only one who was uncomfortable. Wyn sat in the back next to Ovailia whose icy stare was penetrating Ilyan as he continued to lay out what I could only assume was the plan of attack. Ovailia had spoken up several times during the meeting, and although I had no idea what she was saying, her voice was still venomous.

Suddenly, everyone stood in succession, the quick movement startling me. I stood with them, but immediately regretted it as they all began to pull chairs together and sit down in smaller groups. I sat back down, hoping no one had seen my blunder, and focused on my strappy four-inch heels as I once again adjusted my clothes.

"So, did you enjoy the meeting?" I looked up just as Ilyan pulled up a chair directly in front of me. His hair was too off-putting; I couldn't seem to stop looking at it. It just made him look too much like Ryland would look without his curls.

"I suppose it would have been great if I had understood anything."

"Sorry about that. But don't worry, I'm here to give you the Cliff

Notes." He leaned forward and my eyes drifted to his short brown hair again in an effort to avoid eye contact.

"Gee, thanks."

"We discussed our attack plan."

I looked up expectantly, but he just sat there staring at me.

"And?"

"That's it."

Two hours of sitting in a hard chair and they had discussed the 'attack plan'. Great.

"What are they doing now? Planning the after-party?" I spat bitterly, but instead of laughing, Ilyan's face fell instantly.

"They are saying goodbye to their loved ones, Silnӯ."

I peeked around him to see Wyn and Talon with their arms wrapped around each other, a few other pairs coupled off around them. Most of the others were quietly talking on cell phones. I sat back in my chair, my nerves jumping angrily.

"Are you saying goodbye to your loved ones, too?" My eyes floated to Ovailia who stood against the wall, her head bowed.

"Of course."

My stomach jumped at his response. I opened my mouth to say something, but closed it as my confidence wavered. Ilyan chuckled at my indecision and leaned back against his chair with his arms folded as if he was getting ready for a show. I determinedly looked away from him, but my eyes were automatically drawn to his hair again.

"Are you going to be looking at my hair all night, Joclyn?"

"No!" I responded, a blush at being caught rushing to my cheeks. "It just looks so weird on you."

"You don't look too bad yourself," Ilyan said, pulling on one of the long, red strands that hung down at the sides of my face.

"Don't remind me. My hair grows slowly, too; I am going to be stuck with this hairdo forever."

To my embarrassment, Ilyan laughed, causing several people to turn.

"What?"

"You can grow it back with your magic, Joclyn." Ilyan chuckled deeply, causing a furious blush to deepen against my cheeks.

"What?"

"Didn't Wyn tell you?"

"No!" My mouth hung open in frustration.

Ilyan only continued to smile. "No wonder you looked so depressed when I saw you last night."

Truthfully, I hadn't been depressed because of my hair; I had been more concerned about his wicked father, but I wasn't going to get into that right before we left to rescue his youngest brother.

I shook my head and slammed my bare back against the cold, metal chair. I tried to shift my clothes again, I really needed to give up trying.

"So... are you going to tell me what this attack plan is?"

He sighed before nodding once and then angled his chair so we could both see the group that was still shuffling around the conference room.

"Wyn, Talon, Evert and Glenna will be clearing the roof. Ovailia, Ferne and Nyse will be clearing the upper hallways. Adyl, Benton and Eber will already be stationed at the party. Delia, Iolo, Jevon and Evadne will be clearing the exterior; and Tace and Zilla will be our forward guard. You will be with me." He pointed each of them out as he spoke; my mind unable to connect faces with their unusual names.

"And what do we do?"

"Rescue Ryland," he stated quietly. "I need you to get him to leave with you. We will all serve as some form of a distraction and guard while you get him out. Once you leave, we all leave. The longer you wait, the more dangerous this mission is for everyone."

"Get him out, sounds easy enough," I sighed sarcastically, thinking my task sounded anything but easy. "As long as he is still Ryland."

If he wasn't Ryland, I wasn't sure what he would do. He had attacked me in the Tȍuha when he had changed. If he did attack me tonight, I was not sure I was powerful enough yet to fight him off. Worse yet, what if I got him out as Ryland, and he changed once we left.

I sighed and sank into my chair a bit, feeling completely useless.

"Then let's hope he will be." Ilyan's hands writhed; he seemed to be thinking along the same lines I was. "We will go in under Zmizêt and make our way into the main hall; that is where Ryland will be."

"Zmizêt?"

"Yes, it's a shield that can cause you to be invisible. Of course, if it works in the LaRue estate with the same effectiveness it did on you, then we are all in trouble."

"What are you talking about?" I asked, my face squished together in confusion.

"All those times you saw me in your school, I was shielding myself with Zmizêt. But it didn't work so well on you." He narrowed his eyes at me curiously. "I wonder why that is?"

I shrank away from him as his blue eyes flashed dangerously. Was I broken or something? I couldn't get my magic beyond my necklace, but I could see people who were supposed to be invisible? Definitely broken.

"You're the king; you tell me." I wished I could move away from him a bit.

"Manners, Joclyn." Ilyan didn't even flinch as Ovailia came up beside him. I, however, got the full extent of her glare and had to fight the urge to run away. "I hate to interrupt, but it is time to go."

"So it is." Ilyan stood and moved away, leaving Ovailia alone with me. I had hoped she would follow him, but instead, she stepped closer.

"I would like you to know, Joclyn; I am only doing this to save my brother. I have no intention of saving you. If you get cornered, you're on your own." She smiled acidly at me, waiting for me to respond. Her look reminded me of the way Cynthia McFadden would egg me on. I shrank away from her instinctively. She glared toward me for only a moment longer before striding out of the room. I slumped back down in my chair.

I had the excited nerves of an audition, mixed with the raw, icy fear of going into the unknown. I shook my head, emptying the thought of Ovailia's comment from the nervous strangulation that was taking hold of me. The room had emptied of everyone but me and Ilyan before he turned and gestured toward me.

"I am going to have to carry you to Ryland's house, if you don't mind?" he said as we walked outside to where the others had gathered.

"What?" I was suddenly appalled.

"It's a risk for everyone if you have liquid memories of how to get back to the motel."

"What do you mean? I'm not a risk," I retorted, remembering all too vividly Ovailia's words in the courtyard.

"If you are captured, I don't need your memories to guide them to the motel. Since I don't have time to teach you to perform a Zmizêt, I need to be in contact with your skin."

"And you have to carry me? Why can't we just hold hands or something?" I suggested, irritated by the idea.

"If you won't let me carry you, Joclyn, I will just put you to sleep."

I grumbled in acceptance before allowing him to cradle me in his arms. I wrapped my arms around his neck, worried that he would drop me. He laughed at me softly; I knew full well how ridiculous I was acting, especially considering that the last time he had carried me like this, I hadn't been able to move.

We all swept into the air in unison, Ilyan leading us to what I was sure was certain doom.

This whole week, I had been confident that this was a sure thing, that everything would go perfectly. Then, last night, Ilyan had shattered my little delusional fantasy. This was not going to be easy; it would be dangerous. What was worse—we might fail.

"You need to close your eyes, Silnỳ."

I obeyed him.

"What happens if we can't get him out, Ilyan?" I asked into the darkness.

"We will get him out." His voice was so determined, I could almost detect that maniacal power in him already.

"But what if..."

Ilyan's arms tightened around me, pushing my torso into him.

"We will get him; do not worry."

I didn't dare say anymore. I didn't really want to think about it, anyway; thinking of failure almost seemed like a curse on this whole venture.

We landed among the lilac bushes, azaleas and roses behind the kitchen door to the large estate. Ilyan put me down, and I opened my eyes apprehensively, surprised to see only Ilyan and the two he had pointed out as our "forward guard". The others must have already taken their positions.

I looked up at the building curiously, surprised to see nothing but pale white stone. I knew the fire and explosions must have spread to this part of the mansion, yet there was nothing damaged. Ilyan must have been right; they must have repaired the building magically.

Being so close to entering the mansion made me edgy and I found myself shifting my weight and exhaling more than I should. This gained me quite a few dirty looks from Tace and Zilla, but I didn't care. I doubted anyone could hear me over the noise, anyway.

Happy screams and catcalls filled the air from the pool beyond the bushes; the heavy beat of the music inside pulsed through the air and shook the ground. Ryland's graduation from high school should have been a happy occasion, not the site for a rescue mission.

I could feel the tension; the pulsing, magical energy flowing from each of us as we sat ready, waiting to pounce. The magic seemed to beat in time with the music that surrounded us; the longer we waited, the louder it grew. Ryland's necklace sat hot on my skin under my lime green shirt, the intense heat warning me that danger was nearby. I pulsed my magic reflexively, hoping that being this close to Ryland, to Edmund, would provide me with additional control. Nothing happened; Edmund's restrictive blanket remained a suffocating force over my ability. I swallowed hard, hoping that when the blanket slipped off me, I could control the pent-up energy it would surely release.

The four of us looked up in unison as a large, red firework lit up the sky above the manor. The excited squeals from the pool echoed the deep boom of the explosion. It was our cue to go. Tace and Zilla bolted out in front of us, their bodies breaking through the bushes toward the door I had entered a million times. I screamed out in surprise as Ilyan grabbed me and flung me onto his back before he followed their lead.

The door to the kitchen flung open in a burst of wind that carried all of us into the hustle and bustle of the elaborate space. The wind pushed over trays of food and plates, and sent napkins flying through the air. The resulting mess sent the kitchen staff into a panicked frenzy. We took advantage of the disarray as we sped through the kitchen without having to worry about the Zmizêt being ineffective. Even without the diversion and the cloaking spell, our speed would have made us invisible. I just caught a glance of Mette's frazzled face before we took off down the staff hallway that led from the kitchen.

Tace and Zilla continued in front of us, our pace quick and fleeting. We moved through two corridors before Zilla's pace reduced to a casual saunter. Ilyan and Tace followed suit, Ilyan moving us right up against the wall.

Only a moment after the change in pace, two small men I had never seen before came around the corner to face us. At first, it was obvious they couldn't see us, but realization dawned on them as the Zmizêt seemed to fall away from our bodies.

Tace and Zilla did not wait; they moved so fast their bodies blurred. One moment they stood in front of us, and the next, they were directly before and behind the two Trpaslíks. Two dim flashes of light lit up the hallway before their bodies fell to the ground.

Ilyan rushed to their side, his face falling in alarm and frustration.

"Well, so much for stealth," he sighed. He turned to Tace and Zilla and spoke to them in Czech before the two went into action, moving and hiding the bodies in the many servants' quarters surrounding us.

"I need you to stay right beside me, Joclyn." He didn't look at me; he continued looking straight ahead as he spoke.

Tace emerged from the rooms first, followed by Zilla who shook her long, blonde hair as she spoke to Ilyan. He didn't wait to translate; he simply grabbed my hand and towed me behind him as we ran from hallway to hallway.

The music increased in volume as we raced forward. We had abandoned any attempts at stealth, although it probably wouldn't have mattered since the music became so loud that any noise we made was drowned out.

We almost made it to the connecting servants' hall when Tace and Zilla plastered themselves into the alcoves of the doorways; Ilyan towed me after him into another doorway. He kept me hidden safely behind him, his hand holding me against the door as he looked at what was going on in the hall. I heard a small yelp, shuffling feet, and two dull thuds before Ilyan released me from the small space behind him. By the time I made it to the hall, the two Skříteks were already hiding the bodies in a storage closet.

Ilyan held me back as we reached the door that would open up into the hallway that connected to the main hall before turning and speaking to the others. His lips moved as he spoke, but I could barely hear him, the overwhelming music drowning him out. Before he even finished speaking, Tace and Zilla exited from our hallway into another. My body tensed; I felt strangely unprotected without them.

"They are going in first," Ilyan yelled into my ear. "They will be watching you in the hall. Are you ready?"

I couldn't respond, my body tense.

Ilyan plunged us through the door and didn't slow down as we approached the ballroom that housed the party. The hall light dimmed as we got closer until we were moving through a faintly lit hallway, the flashing lights of the party reflecting out of the open door and onto the wall in front of us. I kept my gaze on the dancing lights, trying desperately to keep my head on straight while still focusing on the dynamic energy that was building under my skin.

Ilyan stopped abruptly before we made it to the main hall and threw me roughly against the wall. I tensed; this wasn't part of the plan, and the look on Ilyan's face suggested trouble. He pressed his body against mine, every inch of him, from his shoulders to his toes, pressed against me. His hand grabbed one of mine and restrained it above my head.

My body froze; his proximity sending angry surges of magic vibrating over my skin. I tried to pull away from him, but he held me roughly in place, his grip increasing. I looked up to him in a panic, just as he leaned forward to place his cheek against mine. My heart thudded uncomfortably.

"Close your eyes and pretend that this is natural for us." His voice was rough in my ear as he nuzzled his face into my neck, his warm breath running across my skin. I let my lids drop over my eyes and raised my hand to cup his neck. My heart beat erratically as I felt the negative energy pulse toward us, heavy footsteps announcing the arrival of someone unwelcome.

"Keep them closed," Ilyan instructed as he moved his head, hoping to mimic the look of an intimate kiss against my neck. I screwed my face up into what I hoped was a pleasurable expression as the negative power hit its peak. Ilyan intertwined his fingers with mine and pushed against me harder, the ridge of the wall pushing into my bare back.

Ilyan didn't wait for whoever had passed us to get very far before pulling me beside him and leading me into the large hall.

I had barely caught my breath before I stopped in place. The main ballroom had been transformed into a night club. I no longer felt out of place with my hair and clothing. Flashing lights flickered and vibrated to the beat of the music, lighting the mosh pit as everyone moved together in some odd semblance of a dance.

I didn't have time to linger as Ilyan pulled me into the crowd, a hundred other bodies instantly pushing against us. He moved us deep into the writhing mass, enclosing us within it. The lights flashed and pulsed as the crowd danced and moved against everyone around them.

Ilyan pulled me into him, his hands fanning out on the bare skin of my back as he moved me against him in a seductive dance. I fought the urge to shy away from him. I cursed my clothes; he wasn't the only person who would be acquainting themselves with my body tonight. I felt sick.

"Remember to play the part, Silnỳ. Rich, powerful. And don't touch him unless you know it's him. I don't need Edmund to be able to trace you." I nodded as he whispered in my ear, his hand moving up to cup my cheek for just a moment. "I'll be close by." He looked into my eyes, his finger running the length of my jaw bone.

I looked up and screwed my jaw in defiance, my eyes opening in a seductive powerful way that I hoped fit the look Wyn had given me. I popped my hip and squared my chest, trying desperately to mimic the ridiculous movements I had seen Cynthia McFadden do every day of my life. Ilyan nodded once in approval before turning from me, leaving me alone in the crowd.

I couldn't let my nerves get to me. I kept my jaw tight, my other facial features soft and wide as I was passed from person to person as I made my way through the throng of tightly packed people. I mimicked the sensual dances as I moved against the bodies that pressed against mine in ways that made me blush. I never wanted to be in a place like this again. I was here for Ryland, and that was enough.

A hundred faces blurred together as they danced, each one with hooded lids and open mouths in some drugged-out ecstasy. I danced through bodies so carefully entangled I could never be sure exactly what they were doing. I skirted around couples who had fallen to the floor in a blissful madness that I never wanted to see again. I moved through them, hoping my alert face and body didn't give me away.

I had almost reached the edge of the wall of people when someone grabbed me around the waist and pulled me into them. My face fell out of place in fear as I whipped around, expecting some attacker. Instead, I looked into the face of Ryland's friend, Tyler. He held me tightly to him as he looked down in pompous ignorance. His face looked like all the others: glossed over and void of all normal expression. I moved with him for a minute, trying to plan my escape when he leaned down to nibble on my ear. I jumped back in repulsion, remembering all too well what Ryland had told me about private school boys.

"What?" Tyler yelled over the crowd. "Too dirty for you?" He placed his hands on my hips and moved me back to him. I screwed my face back into position and pulled his shirt to bring him to eye level.

"You have no idea." I let one eyebrow rise in what I hoped was an alluring way. "Get me a drink?" I asked and wound my arm through his, letting him lead me the rest of the way through the crowd.

I didn't feel comfortable attaching myself to one person, but if I was lucky, he would lead me right to Ryland. I tried desperately to focus on my character and not let my nerves sneak through to give me away.

I gave him a small smile as he thrust a drink into my hands. I could smell the alcohol before it even made it to my lips. Of course there would be heavy drinking; it made sense given the state that everyone was in. I lowered the glass and set it on the table next to us, I didn't need any distractions.

The raw magical energy that had been boiling under my skin shifted. I checked to see if the barrier was still firmly in place. Being this close to the energies that controlled me was sure doing weird things to my body.

"You okay, little bunny?" Tyler asked in my ear. My irregular magic had caused my cover to slip. I put the face back on as I leaned into Tyler in a poor imitation of what Ilyan had done to me, but I failed miserably.

"You wanna get out of here?" he asked. I cringed—wrong direction.

"Let's dance," I yelled and dragged him back toward the mosh pit.

Luckily, Tyler didn't seem to object to my mixed signals; he must have been beyond drunk.

I led him deeper into the horde of people again, my body dancing to the thumping music. He danced behind me blindly, his free hand trailing over the bare skin on my back as we walked; I fought the urge to cringe against his touch.

We weren't going the direction I needed to go, but now I was faced with the bigger problem of getting rid of him. My big idea had backfired.

I had only moved a few steps when my magic shifted again, this time taking the constrictive blanket with it. My magic reacted hastily to the unexpected freedom, and it took all my strength to keep it inside. Ovailia was right. I was in trouble. I was running out of time. My magic lurched again, still shifting in the same direction. I took a chance and followed the pull. The music continued to thump through me as I danced with Tyler, moving us through the crowd, grateful he was drunk enough to be led along on my little game.

My magic surged even stronger as we reached the edge of the crowd, this time near the DJ table. Tyler grabbed me and pulled me toward him into a position I was not comfortable with. I pushed him away and began to dance on my own, hoping that the alcohol surging through his system wouldn't make him too possessive.

It did.

He came up behind me, grabbing me roughly as his hands snaked around my waist, lifting the front of my shirt. I jerked away from him, only to be pulled back against him aggressively. I could feel his fingers like claws against my back. Tyler attempted to get me to dance with him for a minute, but his fingers were starting to hurt me, and I fought him, pushing him away from me.

"Come on, baby!" he yelled, coming up to me again. "Don't fight the power." He smiled greasily and grabbed my forearm tightly.

I cried out in pain as I tried to fight him, but his hold on me only increased. "Let me go!"

"No, baby, not until you give me what I came for."

I gasped as he yanked my arm, pain shooting through my shoulder.

"You're hurting me!" I pleaded as I looked around me in a panic now, desperately searching for Ilyan or someone willing to help me.

"Come on, I know you like it like that."

"Not with you. Now, let me go!" I yelled as I caught sight of Ilyan breaking his way through the crowd, his jaw tight in anger.

"What? You here to catch a little rich boy? He'll just murder you like he did his other little bunny." His fingers dug into me as he shook me, his words cutting deeply. I looked toward Ilyan; my heart plummeted to see him dancing again, staring dangerously at something behind me.

I turned myself roughly against Tyler's grip to see what Ilyan was staring daggers at. I guess my plight hadn't gone completely unnoticed. Ryland was striding toward me, his face screwed up in a more furious anger than I had ever seen.

Even with the anger in his beautiful blue eyes, his look made me feel like I was coming home again. My body grew extraordinarily warm. I felt like I could fly away right then. I kept my energy and my desperate need to be with him under control, but just barely. My heart beat even faster as his blue eyes met mine. I could have run to him, if it hadn't been for the vice grip around my arm.

"You can have him," Tyler spat, his free hand punching me aggressively across the face.

I fell to the ground just as Edmund's restraints flew off me in a torrent. I screamed out against the pain, clutching my head in an attempt to keep the overwhelming power of my magic restrained under my skin. The pain in my cheek, the rumbling headache from the impact with Tyler's fist, were all but forgotten as I screamed out, my voice ricocheting off the smooth floor.

It was too much to focus on, restraining the magic and managing the pain. My chest was heaving with the power of my magic, my fingers flexing against my head. I focused on the floor as I yelled out deafeningly, the power moving deeper into me.

"Breathe deeply and push it into your stomach." Ryland's voice was like honey in my ear as he lifted me off the floor to hold me against him, his hands resting on my lower back as he moved me to dance along with him.

I followed his directions, not willing to look up at him quite yet, just in case I lost control again. I pressed my face into his neck, almost losing my focus at the intensity of the memories, the joy that his scent caused me. I refocused and pushed it all back into my stomach, focusing on the space behind my belly button.

"Thanks," I mumbled as the energy was contained. I looked up at him, focusing with all my might on the surplus power I now kept locked in place.

"I told you not to come." He looked around nervously, and I knew Ilyan was right. We had walked right into a trap.

I followed Ryland's line of sight, my stomach clenching as ten

Trpaslíks came barreling into the large room. They stopped momentarily before the man in the lead directed them out like a fan. We were trapped. Ryland moved us into the crowd, lifting me off the ground to plunge us into the gyrating mass quickly.

"Ilyan said you wouldn't leave if it was only him."

"I wouldn't. But I can't leave because you are here, either," Ryland said.

"I can't just let Edmund take you away from me," I stated emphatically.

"Stubborn to the end." He looked down at me, his bright blue eyes sending a shock through my system. He reached over and placed his hand softly against my face, covering my aching jaw where Tyler had just punched me. I leaned into his touch, needing him to be close to me.

"Are you okay?" he asked softly, his hand growing warm as his magic filled me.

I could only nod as my magic lurched again; I jerked with the energy.

"Focus, Jos," Ryland whispered, bringing me to rest right against him. "Jeez, how long have you been awake?"

"A week," I whispered. It was becoming harder to keep the energy restrained.

"Ilyan's an idiot." He pulled me against him, his cheek against mine. My heart sputtered and I heard Ryland laugh deeply. I suddenly felt very uncomfortable, not being able to see him properly.

"I need to see your eyes." I pulled away from him, trying to keep my body moving in the odd dance.

"You don't have to worry about that, Jos; you've already walked right into his trap. You saw all the men that swarmed in here, and there are only about ten times more surrounding us." He smiled, trying to break the fear that gripped me, but it only grew.

"He's already so far in that it's a miracle I can remember you at all. I'll just let this moment be one last anchor." He smiled, but it was so sad, so heartbroken.

"You need to come with me," I begged. "We need to get out of here right now." I pleaded my case to him, but he said nothing. He only smiled sadly at me and pulled my body to press against his.

I should have fought him, begged him further, but my heart was lost in his touch, his smell. I leaned into him, my soul swelling with joy. He pressed his cheek against mine as we moved. He held me so tightly that it felt as if we simply could not get close enough. I welcomed the contact; it felt so right. I felt so whole in that moment; my magic so close to its other half, my heart beating right next to his. We slow danced among the manically dancing pairs, lost in our own little world.

"I'd sacrifice anything," he sang softly in my ear, the Frank Sinatra song blending with the loud club music. His voice broke; I could tell he was crying. "Come what might..." I pulled my head away to look at him. The glistening tears streaked down his cheeks. "I will not let anything take away what's standing right in front of me."

I reached up, my fingertips softly wiping away the wet tears from his face. As my fingers traced the lines of his cheek, the bruises and cuts swam into view. I gasped as I saw him up close; his face, his agony, making everything that much more real. My hand flew to my mouth, my own tears falling down my cheeks.

"Don't cry," he whispered. "Please, don't cry."

"But, Ryland," I spoke through my tears, "what has he done to you?" The tears came fast and hard as I placed my hand against his face, the ridges of his swollen jawline hard against my skin.

"It's okay. You're here now. Don't cry." His voice was soft. He held me tightly and I felt the warmth of his magic surge into my back. As he had for almost every day of my life, he comforted me, even though he could barely move. Even through his pain, his agony, he helped me.

I let the magic in, pulling it into me. It filled me in a way it had never done before, as his warm tendrils blended and moved with my own, intermingling in a familiar way that I never wanted to lose. The energy inside me continued to build uncontrollably, my skin prickling as the surges fought their way out. I knew he felt it, too; his smile was so triumphant, so happy.

"Now, I can never leave you. No matter what happens, no matter where I go. You will always be mine."

"Forever," I whispered through the tears.

Ryland leaned toward me, his eyes boring into mine, searching me. In that moment, I didn't care about the hordes of people surrounding us. I didn't care about Ilyan frantically yelling at us to stop. I needed him like I needed oxygen. I closed the gap between us and pressed my lips firmly to his.

That's all it took for my magic to explode.

CHAPTER 52
JOCLYN

I had been waiting for this kiss for months, dreaming of the way it would feel to have his lips against mine, our bodies pressed together. My fantasies weren't even close to the reality I was now experiencing.

A warm tingling began in my toes and spread rapidly at his silky touch. His hand trailed up my spine to get lost in my hair. My magic expanded; his, still intertwined with mine. Our magic bubbled together like a pot overflowing. The two separate powers became so infused that I couldn't tell where mine ended and his began.

He pressed me to him roughly, a deep groan issuing from the back of his throat. I sighed at the sound, the touch, the pressure. My hands wrapped around him, clutching at his hips and elbows in a desperate effort to be closer to him. He answered my call. I gasped as our magic became a white hot heat that rocked inside our bodies with a violent force. The white heat grew, his touch tingled, the kiss deepened. My body became limp in his arms as the magic within me reached a point I could no longer control.

Our combined energies exploded out of us in a blinding, white light. It was the same light as when Ryland had touched my kiss for the first time, but now, it had more force and energy. It whooshed out of us as the ground shook violently in an explosion of energy, fire and wind. Flimsy human bodies were flung away from us as a result of the blast, slamming them into tables and walls with such force that I couldn't imagine many of them surviving.

Ryland held on to me tightly as screams filled the room. Teenagers ran for the exits in a wall of people that clogged the doorways, which resulted in yelling and fighting as the drunken crowd attempted to escape. I didn't dare move from Ryland's embrace; he held me in place, his arms shielding me protectively.

"You couldn't wait to seal her to you until we had gotten you out of here?" Ilyan yelled as he ran through the crowd, his hair long and blonde again, his skin glowing with energy.

"You knew you weren't getting me out of here in the first place, Ilyan!" Ryland yelled back.

"Ha!" Ilyan laughed without any humor. "You always did underestimate everyone, Ryland."

"You walked right into his trap and you accuse me of underestimating! You..." He stopped abruptly, his body twitching violently.

"No!" I yelled, clinging to him; he twitched again, his arm flying away from me.

"He's close." I heard Ilyan mumble from somewhere behind me.

The Trpaslíks who had walked into the room before had begun disentangling themselves from the wreckage around us. I looked around in a panic as more of them began to appear; from beneath the rubble on the main floor, on the balcony that surrounded the large room, in front of every doorway. Tace, Zilla and the other guards appeared out of nowhere to encompass the three of us in a wide circle, each of them with their hands palm side up, prepared for an attack.

The Trpaslíks began to approach us, their steps slow and measured. They kept looking from one to the other, gloating as if they were overjoyed with the prospect of battle.

Ryland twitched again, the violent motion sending him flying to the ground. I sank down with him, my hands hovering uselessly above him; it was like the first dream all over again.

"Fight it, Ryland," I pleaded.

"Get him out of here, Joclyn," Ilyan said as sparks flew from his fingertips.

I grabbed Ryland and hung on to him, a gust of wind swirling around us as I prepared to take flight. My wind vanished in fear as an explosion rocked the room. The main doors flew off their hinges, the large slabs of wood flying right toward us. Ilyan raised his hand and stopped them in mid-air before shoving them in another direction, both doors now flying toward the Trpaslíks who were approaching us. The screams of the teenagers who were still in the large hall increased as they watched what was going on.

"Well, well, well." I jerked away from Ryland at hearing that detestable voice, my eyes searching for him in the mass of people standing in the doorway. Edmund stood in the middle of them, his tall frame and shortly-cropped hair giving him an almost militant look. Next to him stood Timothy and Cail, both of whom looked pleased, anticipating the events about to take place.

Ryland flinched again and I threw my body over him, foolishly thinking I could protect him.

"My prodigal son has returned!" Edmund clapped his hands together in joy, an ominously pleased smile lighting up his face.

"No," Ilyan interjected powerfully, "I just came to save my little brother."

"Ryland!" I yelled out as Ryland flinched in my arms again, the reality of it all jerking at my magic again.

"Oh, look!" Edmund called out joyously. "Little Joclyn came, too! What fun! You sure have grown up since the last time I saw you. So beautiful. Such a pity to destroy you, but then I destroy things all the time." He smiled cruelly at Ryland who jerked again, his voice calling out in an agonizing scream.

"No! Leave him alone," I pleaded with Edmund, but he only smiled at me like I was the most pathetic thing he had ever seen. Ryland jumped again.

"Fight it, Ryland, please," I begged him, my hands pressing against his back. I desperately tried to push my magic into him, not sure if I was succeeding. Ryland lifted his head to mine, resting his hand against my face.

"You're so beautiful. I always thought so... with those eyes... They are just like diamonds." Ryland's body jerked again, and he screamed out in pain, his body tensing and convulsing as he fought his father.

"Fight it, Ryland!" I barely got the words out before Ryland's hand shot out to wrap itself around my throat. He lifted me up in one swift movement, my feet leaving the ground as he stood.

His black eyes looked into me with a look of evil pleasure that did not match his face. He smiled his beautiful half-smile, but this time, it held no pleasure for me. I clawed at his hand as my lungs called out for air, my chest heaving as it attempted to inhale.

A ball of light hit Ryland's side, shooting him across the large room.

His hand lost its grip on my throat, and I went flying, Ilyan's wind bringing me right to him before I had a chance to hit the floor. He wrapped his arm around me securely, his eyes never leaving his father's.

"Well, that was fun." Wyn came up to stand next to me, wiping her hands against her jeans.

"Wynifred!" Timothy's deep voice had taken on a panicked quality I wouldn't have thought to ever hear from him. I jerked my head around to see the panic evident not only on Timothy's face, but on Cail's as well.

"Isn't this a veritable family reunion," Edmund commented in a bored voice. "Didn't want to bring Ovailia, I see; didn't think she could handle being near me again?"

Ilyan smiled, that look of power covered his face as a visible wall of energy moved away from us, shooting across the ballroom and ramming into Edmund and his men. They all stumbled back a step; many fell clear to the ground.

"Oh, I'm here, Father. I just prefer not to get my hands dirty." Ovailia's voice echoed around the room from somewhere behind us.

"I'm tired of this," Wyn said, stepping forward before she jumped in place. With the impact of her feet against the floor the whole room shook and shifted; pieces of the ceiling and balcony broke apart and tumbled down around us. Her action opened up a floodgate, and the ballroom began to explode in a torrent of energy. Wyn laughed happily as she continued to jump; no wonder she had said her magic was destructive.

I covered my head and dropped to the ground as chunks of marble and wood came crashing down, leaving a giant hole gaping in the ceiling. I dodged and weaved away from the falling debris until I slid under a large table, finding two trapped party-goers who were screaming frantically.

I looked up as Wyn clapped her hands; the wall behind Edmund and his men exploded, sending them all running in a panic. The room groaned at the loss of a supporting wall, the structure heaving as it was torn apart from the inside out. Wyn's explosion separated the Trpaslíks from each other. Edmund seemed to have completely disappeared, leaving his minions to do his dirty work. With the Trpaslíks separated, Ilyan and his guard were free to pick them off, one by one. Wyn laughed before heading straight for her brother, Cail, her look of determination was terrifying.

She met up with him as he broke out from behind the rubble. She pushed her hands toward him, a magical pulse pushing him back down into the rubble he had just escaped from. Cail recovered quickly, jumping to his feet as he shot a fiery orb of energy her way. Wyn dodged it, but lost her footing. Without thinking, I sent wind to her and righted her before her brother could attack her again.

My actions caught the attention of three Trpaslíks who flung away the table I was hiding under, slamming it into an opposing wall. My head jerked up to see the three small men approaching me excitedly. I jumped to my feet, shooting three waves of fire toward my attackers, or at least I think it was fire. I had never really mastered that skill. The tiny burning orbs collided with them, the impact thankfully enough to send them skidding against the floor. The fire burned their clothes and singed their flesh, but the weak, unfocused energy wasn't able to do much more than that. They were already back on their feet, heading right towards me. I didn't wait for their attack; I exploded into the air and away from them, only to land clumsily in the middle of the floor, not having planned where I was going. I spun around wildly, hoping to get my bearings.

The whole ballroom was now madness and chaos. Explosions rocked the air. Wind and magic flew between fighting pairs, leaving paths of fire and destruction behind them. I watched as Talon swung his arms wide, a trail of fire spitting from his fingertips. Zilla wrapped electrical ropes around her opponents, causing them to fall to the ground. Ilyan disappeared from one spot, only to appear across the room a moment later, hovering behind one of Edmund's retreating allies. He placed his hand lightly on the Trpaslíks head, causing him to yell out in pain before dropping to the ground.

Another explosion rocked the building, sending more debris crashing down from overhead. Talon appeared behind me, grabbing me around the waist and sliding me across the floor just as a boulder-sized piece of the balcony crashed down where I had been standing. He shoved me behind him as he shot light and wind away from us.

"Get Ryland and get out of here!" Talon yelled as he sent a table skidding across the ground, the hard edge slamming into the back of one of Edmund's men.

I took off toward where Ryland's body still lay, crumpled from the impact.

"Ryland!" My voice broke as I reached out, grabbing his hand and pulling it up to my face. His touch triggered my magic and I felt it surge into him, instantly moving to intertwine with his power. His head turned toward me, the knot in my stomach releasing at the sight of his blue eyes.

"Jos," he whispered my name, a smile trying desperately to form on his lips, "you came."

"Yeah, Ry. I did. Now we have to get out of here. Come on, let's go, just you and me." I tugged on his arm, but he didn't budge.

"What did you do to your hair, Jos? I always loved your hair." His eyes were fading out on me, focusing on something far behind me.

"Ryland! Come on. Focus! We have to leave now!" I clutched onto him and brought a powerful gust of wind around us; I felt my magic fade as we lifted off the ground a few feet, only to crash back down to the floor. I tried again with the same result.

"Ryland, I need your help." I was becoming desperate; he still didn't respond to me. "Ryland! Please."

"Do you want to go steal the car, Jos?" His voice slurred as it faded away, his eyes gently closing.

"Ryland, no, no. Ryland!" He didn't move, and he didn't react, he just lay there.

The prospect of losing him clicked something together in my brain. I was instantly consumed with panic-stricken desperation. I called his name over and over as I pushed him, prodded him and even slapped him across the face. He didn't react to any of it. My movements became more desperate as the seconds clicked by in my mind.

I could hear the yells and screams of the fight that surrounded us, feel the rattle of the building as it was rent with explosion after explosion. I stopped hitting him, stopped screaming at him; I just sat there, staring at him.

He could have been sleeping. The way his hair fell across his face, the way his arms lay lifelessly at his side. I watched him, expecting him to grumble something in his sleep and roll over the way he always did; my heart almost willed it to happen. I traced the dark purple circles of his bruise, let my fingertips run the length of the healing scar across his face. He was in pain.

My voice howled in agony as I fell onto him. My arms wrapped around him and my magic rushed into him, glad to be home. I felt it swirling within him, mingling with the flaring embers he had kept hidden inside himself. I cried into his chest, feeling the connection grow within our bodies. His arms reached around me, his strong arms clenching me against him.

"Ryland?" I pulled myself away from him, my magic pulling back into me as I moved. I looked up into his face expectantly; my hope shattered at the black eyes smiling back.

"You are exquisite, aren't you? No wonder this body seems to want you so badly."

My heart screamed inside my chest at the deep voice that came out of him. I wrenched out of his arms and scurried away, my feet slipping against loose rocks that littered the slick marble floor.

"What? Don't you want this body, too? You seemed to be desperate to have it just a second ago." His body uncoiled toward me dangerously, the shoulders squared and back straighter than Ryland ever held himself. He towered over me as I continued to slip in the rubble. The building rocked with another explosion and I lost my balance, landing on my stomach.

Ryland reached down as I slid around in a desperate attempt to find my balance, and his large hand wrapped around my neck as he lifted me up. I was being choked at the pressure, my lungs unable to take in breath.

"Hello, pretty girl," he sneered as he brought me up to face him, the depths of his black eyes staring back at me acidly.

I didn't have time to react before he shot a flame against my abdomen. The powerful surge collided against my stomach, burning away the lower half of my shirt. The strength of the pulse shot me away from him, flinging me through the air to land hard on the marble floor twenty feet away, the impact sending a painful jolt rippling through me. I sighed as I rolled over onto my back, my body protesting the movement.

I should be hurt. I felt a powerful warmth, smelt the burnt fabric, but there was no pain. I looked at my stomach in confusion. The bottom of my shirt had been destroyed; the skin below it was blackened like charcoal, but nothing more. I wiped away the black residue, surprised to see my stomach was intact, the skin pale and smooth beneath the ash.

A white orb collided angrily against my chest, sliding my body across the floor with the impact. My attention was pulled from my stomach as Ryland's new attack sent me slamming into the wall. I looked up just in time to see him land in front of me, another pulse already prepared to fling my way.

I knew I should fight him, I knew I should attack him as he was attacking me, but I couldn't bring myself to do it. I couldn't bring my magic to me with enough strength to defend myself. The thought of purposely harming him set my heart into a flutter of pain.

I scuttled to the side, the attack shattering the wall behind me instead. Without thinking, I grabbed a table next to me and flung it at him. My heart sank as I watched it fly, terror gripping me at the impending impact. It had almost reached him before he swayed to the side, the table flying uselessly away.

He walked toward me, smiling wickedly as I continued to shoot objects in his direction. All my attempts were useless; the small pieces of what my wind could grab and carry were either dodged, deflected, or they bounced uselessly off his chest. I knew I needed to fight back more intently, I knew I needed to try, but my heart wouldn't let me.

"Throwing things with wind; is that the extent of your power?" Ryland raised both of his hands toward me; I could feel his wind build around me as he shot all the useless objects I had sent toward him right back at me, but with a much greater force and in a quicker succession. I shielded my head as the wall on either side of me was pelted with the arsenal. Plaster and small rocks flew into my hair and bounced painfully against my bare skin.

The onslaught ended, and I looked up to Ryland, hoping to see his blue eyes staring back at me. Instead, I saw a table. The table I had thrown at him was coming back to me at full speed. My mind went blank as I watched it barrel toward me, its four legs spinning in my direction. I wrapped myself into a ball just a moment before it hit. The legs had sunk deep into the wall around me, the tabletop stopping right before it came in contact with my body, pinning me in place instead of crushing me.

Ryland took the last few steps toward me, stopping right in front of me. I shrank away from his acidic gaze, terrified to find that there really was nowhere for me to go.

He reached down to cup my face, his hand cold and unfamiliar against my skin.

"You know, if I could break you, I would keep you." He smiled as he leaned down, his eyes level with mine. "My own pretty, little pet. Maybe I will. After all, I know of someone who is dying to meet you."

He dragged his icy fingers against my lower lip, the weight of his touch pushing my lip roughly to the side. I couldn't rip my focus from him. His face looked the same, but he wasn't Ryland anymore. He wasn't the boy I had grown up with, the one I loved so deeply. My heart whipped back and forth as I fought my feelings. I had to get out of here before the monster in front of me did something that Ryland would regret. I knew I needed to fight—actually fight him. I just hoped that I wouldn't hurt him.

I placed my hands against the table that entrapped me, surging my magic aggressively into it, hoping that it would have the desired effect. While not the explosion I had hoped for, the table did fly away from me, taking Ryland with it. He flew helplessly through the air, only to land twenty feet away, the heavy table landing on top of him.

CHAPTER 53
JOCLYN

I jumped up, desperate to escape from the monster that had possessed Ryland's body. I ran only a few steps, my body preparing to launch into the air before a dead weight hit against my back, pushing me back down onto the floor. I tried to fight it, but couldn't budge against the power that held me in place. I looked toward where Ryland had landed; fear now gripping me as I saw him approaching, his hand rising to aim in my direction.

An energy stream of blue waves shot over me, ramming into Ryland's chest and stopping his progress. He only sneered at its sudden appearance, as if the powerful magic was no match for him. The magical barrier lifted off me and I rolled onto my knees, surprised to see Ovailia standing with her hands extended before her. My mouth dropped in shock at her perfectly poised figure, her cold-set eyes. She didn't even acknowledge my existence; she simply stepped over me as she approached Ryland.

I didn't dare look back before turning to run. The ground around me exploded and shook. I bobbed around, desperately attempting to avoid the fights and explosions around me before jumping into the sky. I sped through the air up onto the balcony that encircled the large room. I landed swiftly and continued moving, looking for a doorway or an alcove where I could hide.

The balcony below my feet shook, and I dropped to the dust-covered carpet with a thud. I cautiously moved myself toward the edge to look below me. The floor of the ballroom was chaos. Colored explosions shook the air as unguided objects flew around and collided. Tracks of color and power flew from hands as the two sides fought relentlessly against each other.

Snakes of red surged from one Trpaslík, only to collide with one of our group whose name I couldn't remember. The red tendrils wrapped around her as she was slammed aggressively into the floor, her screams only barely audible over the sound of battle. I scanned the crowd, looking for anyone I knew. Ovailia was running, her direction taking her right out the door in pursuit of someone. I kept looking, happy to find Wyn still alive, battling back-to-back with Talon against her own brother. I reluctantly looked away from her in an attempt to find the person who was responsible for this whole charade, but Edmund had vanished.

Ryland was walking determinedly toward Ilyan who had caught sight of him, but was still engaged in another fight. I watched as Ilyan dashed from one place to another, lightning shooting toward the small Trpaslík he was dutifully fighting. The Trpaslík was no match for Ilyan, who swiped his hand before him and sent his enemy flying right into a group of trapped teenagers who had taken refuge under the stairs.

Ilyan turned and faced his brother, his hands moving roughly to either side, sending every bit of rubble that lay uselessly on the floor up into the air and toward Ryland's advancing form. Ryland yelled and called out in pain as he was pelted by the array of ammo, the force of the attack causing him to slide away against the floor. Ilyan did not wait for him to recover; his hands moved again, producing what could only be explained as a chain of magical energy.

The links of power crackled and sizzled in front of Ilyan, the bright white light, shining throughout the room. Ilyan pushed the chain toward Ryland; it wrapped around him, restraining his movements. It was only just visible before his body seemed to absorb it. Ryland moved his hands up in a counterattack toward his brother, but I didn't see anything further. A large crack sounded in my ears as a heavy body landed directly to my left.

I spun around with a small scream. A well-dressed man with a neatly-trimmed beard was hovering near me, his sneer barely visible through the brown hair.

Timothy.

"Thought you could hide up here? You are just as weak as he is." I backed away from him, careful to keep my body from falling off the unstable edge of the balcony.

Timothy laughed as he raised his fingers and snapped repeatedly. At each snap, small explosions shook and shredded the ground around me. I squealed and screamed in panic as I was littered with sparks and debris from the explosions. The Trpaslík took another step forward, his hands still raised menacingly.

I flung my hands toward him, his body flying away from me as my attack hit him square in the chest. Timothy hit the floor, came to a standing position, and began to advance, more explosions rocking the floor with each step he took toward me. I raised my hand again, sending a weaker wave toward him. He stepped back as it collided with him, but recovered quickly.

I needed to get out of here. I couldn't fight Ryland, I *really* couldn't fight Timothy. I rolled off the balcony, sending my body flailing into the fight below. I had only fallen a few feet when I caught myself, my strong wind catching my spinning body as I moved myself toward yet another portion of the steadily deteriorating balcony.

I only made it halfway across the large space before a large mass landed on my back, dropping me down to the floor of the ballroom like a boulder. I crashed hard into the marble floor, my back instantly clenching in pain. I screamed out as I fought to get away from whatever had landed on me, surprised when hands shot out and enclosed my wrists.

"Thought you could run from The Master did you? Stupid, little half-breeds." Another Trpaslík pushed me down onto the floor, his legs straddling me as he restricted my movements.

I clawed and fought and threw any little rocks I could at him, but it was no use. He batted away my pathetic arsenal before clasping his hands on either side of my face as I had seen Ilyan do to someone else only a moment before. I screamed out as I felt the heat growing in his hands. It continued to build until it felt like a fire was burning inside my skull, its raging power boiling inside of my head. My vision blacked out as the pain grew, as my screams increased. Then it was gone.

The Trpasliks weight left my hips as he fell to the side, his lifeless body slumping onto the cold floor. I sat up, my vision returning. I didn't wait to find out who my savior was; I simply turned and jumped, taking off into the air again. My fear had supercharged my magic, and I slammed into the balcony on the opposite wall, unable to stop myself in time.

I panted as I stood, my back seizing in pain. I ran forward, toward a door that would lead me out, my left leg dragging a bit. If I could just get to the door, I could make it to the large, second-floor balcony and escape as Ilyan had wanted me to. I didn't make it far before another body landed in front of me, the body unfolding to face me.

"Cail," I gasped. First the father, now the son.

"Awww, you remember me. How sweet. Probably not as well as I remember you." He raised his hand to me and a bright red light flew toward me. He didn't let it build as he had before; I had no warning this time. I leapt to the side, my back flattening against the hard wall. The red ball erupted right where I had been standing, sending out the wood and stone of the wall in a splintering explosion. Cail looked at me and smiled.

I raised my hand and released the prickling energy in a rush. It slammed into him, but the energy wasn't strong enough to do any damage. He laughed as he straightened out to face me, while I turned and went to launch myself off the balcony again.

My feet had just left the ground when Cail's wind intercepted me and slammed me back, hard against the wall of the balcony I had just left. The wind continued to move around me and hold me in place, the remains of my shirt whipping around.

"You and your mother," he mocked as he walked toward me, his steps faltering as an explosion from below shook the room. "You are both such fighters. Why can't you die easily? You know it's going to end the same way, don't you?" He came to stand right next to me and I cringed against him, my body unable to resist the pull of his magic.

"You both end up dead." He placed his hand against my stomach, his palm against my skin. I grew cold as his magic entered me before beginning to warm as he generated a ball of energy. He formed it inside of me, the weapon building underneath my skin. I screamed out as the warmth turned into a burning heat.

"Let her go." Ryland's powerful voice filled the air as he landed roughly on the balcony beside us. He leaned against a large pillar, his body obviously weakened as he continued to fight his father's invasion of his mind. His body twitched uncomfortably, but his eyes were back to a bright shade of blue.

"Really?" Cail mocked, the heat continuing to move and grow inside of me. "You think you have enough energy to fight me?"

"I don't..." Ryland panted, "but she does."

The ball of fire within me grew to a tumult as my energy drained away, filtering out of my body. I could feel my magic move into Ryland, the power increasing as our magics intertwined with one another, growing stronger with their union. My magic drained as Ryland shot a ball of intense golden light toward Cail. The impact sent him flying, his body tumbling off the balcony into the fight below. Ryland collapsed to the floor, his body twitching as he sank.

With no wind to hold me up, I fell roughly to the ground as well, the heat from Cail leaving a terrible pain in my stomach. I crawled to Ryland, placing my arms around his neck when I reached him. He twitched again, and I forced his face up to look at me, thankful for his beautiful blue eyes.

"How did you do that?" I panted, the pain still lingering in my belly.

"I can do anything with you." He tried to smile, but it was only a grimace.

Ryland reached forward and placed his hand on the skin of my stomach exactly where Cail's hand had lain. I felt my magic swell and grow as Ryland pulled it toward him, stopping it right before it left me to join him. The warmth stayed there and took the pain away almost instantly.

"How...?"

"Anything... with... you..." He twitched again, his whole body was shaking, but he refused to take his eyes off me.

I reached my hand forward; he grabbed it, pressing my fingertips to his lips.

"Love... you... always..." His shaking became uncontrollable as his eye color began to fade. I watched in agony as Edmund took over.

"No!" I clutched his hands desperately. "Don't leave me!"

"Always." His voice was broken and wispy in my ear as he pulled my hand against the side of his face. He pressed my fingers roughly to him, his grip tightening in his fear of losing me.

"No!"

Before the change could complete, the balcony shifted and collapsed. I held tightly to Ryland's hand as we were thrown over the edge, our bodies tumbling toward the fire-filled conflict that raged below. I swept wind to us, hoping the weak energy would catch us before we landed hard against the floor; instead, the wind flung us into a heap in the corner.

My body was entangled with Ryland's as we collided with the wall, but I wasn't there for long before Ryland grabbed me and shot me away from him in a surge of wind and energy. My body slammed into another wall, and I felt my back pop. There was no agony with it, so I stood, thankful that it had not broken again. I steadied myself just as Ryland landed in front of me, a wave of energy slamming into my stomach. I felt no pain; only pressure as the energy surge pushed me back, trapping me in place.

"Hello again, little pet," Ryland sneered as he walked toward me, his black eyes shimmering wickedly as he laughed. I cringed away from his advance, but my body was restrained again by his magic.

"Not going to try to attack me again?" Ryland was right in front of me now. He leaned intimately close to me, one hand resting on the wall beside my head. I could feel his breath against my face; feel his hip as he pushed it against me. He smiled wickedly, and I felt the bile rise dangerously in my throat.

"That's okay; I have another idea." His voice was a sickening purr.

His hand moved into my line of vision, his fingers twiddling together, small sparks flashing from the surge in his magic. The sparks he produced continued to grow as his fingers rubbed together wildly. In only a moment, a small dagger appeared in his hand, the small silver blade glinting wickedly in the magical light that flashed and pulsed around us.

"You love this body, don't you, little girl?" He smiled wickedly. I couldn't look away from the dagger that spun between his fingers. "You love the way it looks, the way it makes you feel." He pushed his hip further into me; I gasped in pain at the pressure.

"Well, this body, it loves you, too."

The dagger stopped spinning and my eyes flew to his with a glimmer of hope. It was pointless.

"But I don't," he said.

I didn't even see the movement; I was too consumed with looking at his face. One minute there was no pain, and the next, the pain had moved beyond me. I screamed as the tiny dagger began to dig its way into the skin that covered my heart. I felt the warmth of my own blood drizzling down my chest as the dagger slowly worked its way into my chest, deeper and deeper, toward my beating heart.

"That doesn't hurt, does it?" Ryland's voice was so joyous; he enjoyed watching my agony as he tortured me.

"Ryland!" I screamed his name, my voice finding form as the pain grew. "Fight him, Ryland!" The evil imposter who restrained me only laughed as he dug the knife deeper into my skin.

"Sad. I don't think he can hear you."

"Ryland! It's me. It's Joclyn. Snap out of it, please!"

He only laughed with increased malice. I screamed again, feeling the blood pool around the waistline of my tight pants.

"Ryland!" I panted between screams, calling to him, desperate for him to make a connection. "Remember the tree... the old guard... at the hospital... Remember when we... ran away..." I screamed and panicked as the pain increased. He only laughed as he looked at me through the depthless pit of his black eyes.

"Remember when you kissed me..." I tried one last time before my voice broke; my mind too dizzy and confused to focus properly. My head slumped down; I focused on my own heartbeat, hoping that Ilyan would find me, that someone would see me, before it was too late.

"Joclyn."

My head rose slowly to see him—Ryland, blue eyes and all—looking at me. I couldn't bring myself to say anything; I just looked at him. His eyes looked me over, stopping in a panic when he saw the dagger that still remained in my chest, his hand and my skin covered with wet, sticky blood.

"Oh, God, what have I done?" he asked as he released his magical hold on me and I fell into his arms. He held onto me tightly as his magic surged into me; warmth filled me as the dizziness retreated and the flow of my blood seemed to stop. I looked up at him carefully, the obvious request lining my face.

"We have to get out of here," he whispered, not waiting for me to respond before he exploded into the air, my body still pressed tightly against his.

We didn't even make it past the hole in the ceiling before the entire process was reversed. A gust of wind I knew neither of us controlled pushed against us in the opposite direction, dragging us back down to the destroyed floor below.

Ryland's arms went limp and I tumbled out of them, heading down toward the ground, fast. My fear of falling only lasted a moment before Ilyan's wind grabbed me and pulled me, soaring across the room, straight into his arms.

"It's time to go," he hissed in my ear.

I turned from Ilyan, searching for Ryland. He stood across the room from us, his body tall and still as he looked intently in our direction, his eyes back to the colorless cast. He didn't move; he didn't flinch; he stayed still, just as his father commanded him to do.

Edmund's hand was placed on Ryland's shoulder, the fingers curved aggressively as they dug into Ryland's skin. Edmund seemed to taunt us from across the room, his stance just willing us to come and attack him. I knew we would lose if we tried, but I did not want to accept it.

"Ryland!"

"We can't take him, Silný," Ilyan said. He wrapped his arms around me as he pulled me away from them.

"No!" I yelled out in a panic, reaching for Ryland.

"I can't get him away from Edmund and get you out of here safely, Joclyn. You are my number one priority now. We have to go." Ilyan grabbed me tightly around the waist, and jumped us back. Edmund had just released Ryland's shoulder and Ryland was now advancing toward us surprisingly fast.

"No! I can do it! I can save him!" I don't know what made me say that; I knew I couldn't. My heart beat wildly as I fought against Ilyan's arm; my body, my heart, desperate to get back to Ryland.

"I can do it! Let me go!" Ilyan held me tighter as I fought against him, my hands clawing uselessly at his strong arm.

Ryland kept advancing as Ilyan restrained me, the members of the guard surrounding us again in an attempt to escape together.

"Ryland. Ryland!" I screamed until my voice broke, my mouth filling with the taste of blood. "Let me go! Ryland!"

Ilyan tightened his grip and I felt us take off into the air, the wind blowing against my skin as Ilyan took me away from the one person I wanted, the one person I needed.

"Ryland." I continued to fight, not caring if I fell. I needed him.

I fought Ilyan, calling Ryland's name in a desperate hope that he would change back, that he would see me and follow. Our eyes locked as Ilyan flew me through a wide hole in the roof, the night sky swallowing us up and taking me away from him.

Now, I knew it was too late. His eyes faded to blue just as we passed beyond the roof of the building, but Ryland only looked at me in confusion, no trace of recognition on his face.

No matter if I came back, no matter how hard I would try, it was too late now. Edmund had erased every part of him.

CHAPTER 54
JOCLYN

I watched the fire that had embraced the building; I watched the purple and green flames lick the roof and reach their slinky arms up to the sky. I saw the red and blue flashing lights of the emergency vehicles that surrounded the mansion, the hordes of people who came, either to watch or to huddle around the ambulances in panic. I watched as the bodies became indiscriminate specks and the flames became tiny orbs of colored light. I watched as the building became nothing more than a colorless speck in the midst of the city lights. I watched as it all disappeared into the blackness of a starless, moonless, hopeless night.

Through it all, I cried; my heart calling to Ryland as he disappeared from my life forever. I clung to Ilyan as my chest was wracked with sobs, my breathing ragged and broken. I drenched his shirt with my tears and any other gross secretions that joined my broken heart. He didn't seem to care.

Ilyan held me close to him as he flew us through the air, his arms holding me securely. In the back of my mind, I knew that he was singing to me. I could feel the rumble of his chest; hear his deep, comforting voice in my ear. I didn't know what was being said, though; I didn't understand what the words meant.

"Teď tiše, moje malá. Upokoj se, buď klidná. S novým úsvitem se svět změní. A když se změní, uvidíš, jaký bychom měli být, ty a já." He sang it to me slowly, over and over.

My tears slowed, but the pain didn't go away. I had lost everything.

My father had left me, only to disappear shortly after renewing contact. My beautiful mother had been murdered; a casualty of the war I had been thrust into. My best friend, the new love who was so ruthlessly torn away from me—his mind had been erased and all memory of me had been stolen from him.

I was only vaguely aware when Ilyan landed. His arms loosened as he attempted to lower me down, but I held onto him tightly, my heart terrified of losing one of the last things I had. I clung to him like a terrified child, locking my fingers together in a panic.

"It's okay, Silnỳ." He tried to release my arms again, but I only held on tighter.

"No!" I wailed into him, clinging to him. "Don't leave me."

"I am not going anywhere. I will be right back."

His magic surged through my bloodstream, and my body instantly relaxed. I sank to the ground, eyes only barely registering Ilyan's retreating footsteps. I looked around myself, not really taking in the dirt, dried leaves and pine needles.

I had barely registered where I was—the fire pit—before Wyn kneeled before me. Her pants were torn and covered in dirt, the brightly-colored 'Queen' t-shirt burned and ripped at the hem.

"He's gone." My voice broke with my tears.

"I know." Wyn's voice wasn't condescending, or comforting, but my heart still ripped open to hear it from someone else.

"I failed him, Wyn." I sank down further, my body falling forward into Wyn's lap. She wrapped her arms around me, her head resting on my back. I felt her warm breath against my skin, her tears falling like dripping ice against me.

"It's all right, Joclyn. We will get him back."

I sat up, throwing Wyn off me, my blood heating to a sudden boil.

"Get who back, Wyn? He's gone! There is no more Ryland! He's gone!" I screamed as loud as my sore and broken voice would let me. It was probably a good thing Wyn's battle-worn face already looked like someone had punched her or I probably would have.

"I was supposed to save him, and I failed. I was supposed to protect him from his father, and I couldn't. He's not there anymore!"

"He has to be there, Jos. He loves you so much, he—"

"Loved me. The Ryland who *loved* me doesn't exist anymore. I lost my father because of a stupid mark! My mother was murdered because you people cursed me! And now I have lost Ryland, the one person who meant the most to me!" I felt that uncontrollable anger seeping into my soul again; the desire to fight and yell and scream hit much stronger than it should have been.

"Enough, Joclyn." I heard Ilyan's commanding voice flow over me; Ilyan's magical barrier freezing my emotions in place.

I felt the anger vanish, leaving me with the soul-crushing sadness of my heartbreak. I sank into the ground, my body curling in on itself. I ran my fingers over the dirt as I looked to the tops of the trees I had climbed so many times.

"It's okay, Ilyan; she's just hurt. She doesn't mean what she's saying." Wyn's voice was tiny; I could barely feel her hand against my shoulder.

"I know, Wyn." There was a pause and I heard Ilyan exhale deeply, his magical restraints peeling off me a bit. "It's time to go. You and Talon are going to carry the tail of the western evacuation and go home through Los Angeles."

"And Joclyn?" Wyn's voice was hesitant.

"Joclyn will be going into hiding with me. Ryland marked her, the Zêlství is complete. I am not sure if Edmund is going to use their connection to track her down or not. Until I know for sure, she is staying with me."

"Then I am staying with you, too." Wyn's voice was forceful, but sad; I couldn't imagine what it had cost her to say that, to commit to leaving Talon again. I unwound myself from my cocoon of pity to look at her, my heart melting.

"You can't leave Talon, Wyn." My voice was soft and broken. "I left Ryland, and now he is gone. Please, for me, stay with Talon."

Our eyes locked as she reached forward to take my hands. A million thank yous, a million emotions passed between us before she stood, our hands extended between us in a last goodbye.

"I'll see you soon," I whispered. She could only nod. The phrase 'going into hiding' did not bode well for quick reunions.

She squeezed my hands before turning away from me and then she and Talon took off into the inky night sky.

"It's time to go, Silný." I looked up at Ilyan, surprised to see tears falling down his own cheeks.

Ilyan didn't expect me to stand; he leaned down and lifted me securely into his arms. He didn't cradle me as he had before, but held me against him in a bone-crushing hug that took my breath away.

"It's okay to be angry, Joclyn. It's okay to mourn. Feel. Sit with those emotions. Just don't let them rule you. Soon, we will let them fuel you." He pressed me against him as we soared into the air, the wind whipping his hair and what was left of mine around us. My emotionally drained body sank into him, a few soothing lines of his calming melody sinking into me before I fell fast asleep.

I woke up the next morning in a gray apartment. The walls were gray, the curtains were gray. It was an ugly gray palette that I had no interest in seeing. I rolled over and pulled the covers over my head, trying to block out the light. I breathed deeply, but it came out ragged and torn. I had cried all through the night.

"Did you get everyone out?" Ilyan's voice was calm and even. I could tell he was on the phone by the way he switched back and forth between Czech and English.

"We made it to the third safe house. I made everyone go before us, so they all should be safe."

I rolled over to lie on my back, throwing the blanket away from me. As I moved, the necklace shifted onto my skin; I had almost forgotten about it.

"Yes, get everyone to Prague. I will start the evacuation on my end. The more of a trickle we can form, the safer everyone will be." He came around the corner, surprised to see me awake.

"I am still keeping her with me, Ovailia; we have a lot of work to do and she is safer with me." He snapped his phone shut and leaned against the wall.

"How are you doing?" he asked, his voice tentative and quiet.

I looked at him before turning away, fixing my eyes on the ceiling.

"I'm sorry, Joclyn." His voice was deep and soothing, but I brushed his condolences away. I just wanted to be mad. "Everything will be alright, Silnỳ."

I just nodded at him; I didn't trust myself to say anything polite.

"We are going to be staying here for a week, maybe two, so make yourself comfortable. But please, stay inside. It's not safe to go out right now."

I nodded again, my head falling to the side, looking blankly at nothing. Ilyan smiled sadly at me before leaving, calling behind him his plans to take a shower. I heard the door click and desperately hoped there was another bathroom I could hide in; somewhere I could lock the door. Judging by the fact that I could see the kitchen from the bed I lay in, I wasn't holding out much hope.

"I'm sorry, Ryland. I failed you."

My head was throbbing. I focused on the pain until a new throbbing interrupted me.

The necklace was beating.

I sat up in one movement, desperately clawing at the fine chain around my neck. I didn't care about what Ilyan had told me; I didn't care about the danger. I just needed to see him, to know he was okay. I plunged my magic into the necklace, the efforts draining me. I closed my eyes as I fell back against the bed, the white room appearing before me.

"Ryland! Ryland!" I called out the second I entered the open space.

"Yes?" I spun around, eager to face him, and saw nothing.

"Who are you?" a little voice asked.

I gasped, falling to my knees as my eyes came level with his. My heart broke as I looked at him. He was only a child, younger even than when I had first met him. My hand flew to my mouth as I sobbed, his blue eyes growing wide at my reaction.

"It's okay," his little voice was soft as he placed his small hand on my shoulder. "Are you hurt? I can make it all better; my mommy says I am very good at making things all better." He smiled widely, his mop of curls bouncing.

I just shook my head no.

"Are you scared then? I get scared sometimes. The cook, Marie, taught me a song about whistling that takes the scares away. Do you want to hear it?"

I shook my head no; there were fewer tears, now. I was gaining control, trying desperately to ignore the heartbreak.

"I'm... just... sad..." I choked out.

"Why?"

"I lost someone very important to me, someone I love."

"Who?"

"My very best friend."

"Oh." He paused and dug his toe into the ground. "I don't have any friends. You can be my friend if you would like." He was so eager, so much like he had been that first day when we had met.

"I would like that very much."

"I'm Ryland." He stuck out his hand; I took it eagerly, expecting something to happen, my heart breaking when nothing did.

"Joclyn."

"Joss-Lyn. What a pretty name," he giggled, his body shaking.

I couldn't even bring myself to smile.

Ryland looked at me with all the innocence, all the sparkly-eyed, new-world wonderment a young child has—a child who has known no pain and felt no heartbreak.

"You have very pretty eyes," he said softly. "They look like diamonds."

Hearing those words steeled something through me. Ilyan was right, all of the pain and agony of before buzzed through me, becoming a fuel for the determination that set my jaw and spine into firm lines.

Edmund had done this.

Edmund was going to pay.

And I was going to be the one to do it.

EXTENDED RUBY EDITION

EYES of EMBER

IMDALIND SERIES BOOK TWO

REBECCA ETHINGTON

PROLOGUE

The stone cavern they called home was colder than usual, which could only mean one thing, the door was open.

The man swore as he jumped from his bunk, darted around the hanging blanket he used to give himself some privacy and bee-lined to the 'door'. In reality the door was nothing more than a large rock that they moved over the only entrance to their cave, but it was the only protection they had from the murderous winter winds that dwelled this high up in the mountain.

The man looked to the line of bunks behind him, all empty, and then to the line of winter wear to his left. All there.

Great. So, the old man went outside without even bothering to put on a coat.

"I'm not your nursemaid!" The younger man swore again and slid his feet into his boots, grabbing both coats as he raced into the swirling snow of the mountain side.

He didn't even bother yelling, the wind would have carried it away anyway. Hand over his eyes, he trudged through the snow that was already past his ankles, secretly praying he wouldn't have to journey too far up the side of the mountain.

He had to do that last time, and the old man had nearly lost a toe from frostbite.

"Old fool!" The man turned, looking through the endless white to a spot of red not too far away. At least he had the good sense to wear his shawl.

"What are you doing?" The man hissed as he approached the withered old man. The old man didn't turn, he stood still, staring blankly into the swirling white of snow and nothing.

His eyes were an endless sheet of black.

His mouth moved as some sight plagued him, most of the words carried away with the wind.

"She comes... the end... for in his sight... the lie was laid..."

The young man didn't even bother to retain the words, he had heard them all before, a hundred times. Over and over.

"Come on! Move!" The young man heaved his shoulder into the old man, but he didn't move the magic of the sight he was trapped in had frozen him in place.

As always.

Putting on his coat and wrapping the other around the man who still stared blankly forward, the young man shivered as he let his magic spark into a shield. The Zmizêt glittered as it grew into a globe around the two, keeping all of the worsening blizzard on the other side. It was a reverse snow globe, snow and cold on the outside, warm and mostly dry on the inside. In another time, with another person, it would have been romantic.

There was another time that it was. But the person was long gone. A hundred years gone. He would never get her back.

So he was stuck with the old man. Why he couldn't have these sights inside where it was slightly warmer and far less blizzardy the young man hardly knew. They were definitely becoming more frequent.

"You're here!" The young man jumped at the voice, the old man's eyes fading back to green as he stared at him.

"Of course I am here. Where else would I be when you wake up in the middle of the night and wander into the middle of nowhere? You're worse than a toddler." He didn't even try to hide his grumble. "Let's get you back inside."

The old man reluctantly followed him back to the cave, the snow still swirling around him.

"Yes, yes," the old man said, his voice oddly chipper. "We need to prepare."

"Prepare what?" The young man asked as he let his magic swell and move the massive boulder over the opening, locking them back into the cave. "Is Ilyan coming back?"

"Yes, and he is bringing someone with him."

No wonder the old man was excited. No one visited them besides Ilyan. No one besides Ilyan knew that they were even there. Ilyan was the one that had hidden them away, and for good reason.

"Who?"

"The Silnỳ." He almost looked to be crying, even the young man felt the burn of tears as something large lodged itself in his throat.

"They found her? But it's been a thousand years..."

"Yes." The old man seemed torn between joy and panic. "And she will be here in days. As long as he doesn't kill her." Something in the old man's voice made the cave seem even colder. The young man shivered.

"Edmund? Has he already found her?" The young man snarled as the old man turned to him, the blackness of sight had left him, leaving his eyes their usual dark green as he looked at the young man, both of their magic flaring.

"Yes. And he is going to use your brother to end her before she can even begin."

CHAPTER 1
JOCLYN

'I *am going to kill Edmund LaRue.'*

The words rang like a battle call in my head, the conviction growing stronger by the minute.

The thought had started as a mere ember of possibility when I had seen Edmund wipe the last of my best friend Ryland's memories two nights ago, and Ilyan had grabbed me and dragged me away.

Being forced to leave the one person in the world that I loved had snapped something deep inside of me, which caused the thought to grow; the ember growing into a spark.

That spark promised me that I would be the one to kill Edmund. He had destroyed my best friend, the one person left for me to love. He had destroyed his own son. I would make him pay for that.

The spark became a flame when I went back and visited Ryland in our space between dream and reality last night. Inside of our Tòuha I had seen him as a little boy who looked at me and told me my eyes looked like diamonds. I could feel the flame in me then; an inferno of hatred, desire and power.

My chosen path was clear, I would be the one to end him.

Which was why it was so irritating that I couldn't seem to pull myself out of this bed. It was like I had been drained, or caught a bad flu. Maybe it was a normal reaction after using so much of my magic. The fact that I was heartbroken and had gotten hardly any sleep wasn't helping either.

"Silnỳ, it's time to wake up." Ilyan's voice was soft in my ear, his hand soft against the side of my face as his fore finger pressed softly against the mark behind my ear. There was no zing like when Ryland touched me, just warm skin. I pushed his hand away and covered my head with the thick comforter in an attempt to ignore him.

I couldn't believe he was so chipper. Not only had we lost in our attempt to rescue his brother, he hadn't slept. All night long Ilyan had moved around the tiny studio apartment like he was a trapped animal. He made soup, he sat at the table cutting some kind of fabric, at one point he had even made a nest of blankets on the small stretch of floor near the bed. He had laid there, on the phone with Ovailia every hour on the hour, getting updates of who had arrived in Prague. Part of me wanted to be there with Wyn and all the others like me, but the other part reminded me how much danger I was in and how important it was that I stay hidden.

"Joclyn." The pressure of Ilyan's hand increased as he moved it around to rub my back.

I pulled down the blanket enough to look out at him. His scraggly blonde hair was longer than usual, hanging down to his shoulder blades, his face was full of worry.

"Ahoj," he whispered as I emerged from underneath the blankets. "How are you feeling?"

I closed my eyes, unsure of how to answer him. I was angry, desperate, lost, determined, broken, in pain, furiously plotting murder, and I was sad. It shouldn't be possible for one person to feel so many emotions at the same time.

"I hurt," I said, my voice cracking with uncertainty.

"Where?" he asked, alarmed.

"In my heart." It was the best response I could come up with. While my heart did hurt, it was more than that. Everything inside me was shattered. Rather than a broken heart, this felt more like I had broken everything. My heart was constricted, but around it, my whole body felt tight and as though it was bound together with hot wire.

"I feel the need for lethargic revenge."

It shouldn't be a thing, yet here we were.

"I know how you feel."

"You know how lethargic revenge feels?" I gave him a look, and Ilyan chuckled with a light sound that could have been magic all on its own. He continued rubbing his hand against my spine, the pressure somewhat dulled through the blankets.

"Edmund has taken something away from me, too, Silný. Ryland was my brother as much as he was your friend; your mate. I can't help but feel that I failed you as much as I failed him."

"I failed him, too. I failed you. I failed everyone." I pushed the blanket away from myself as the frustration of what I was saying hit me. "All you asked me to do was get him out, and I couldn't even do that."

I cringed at how bitter my voice sounded, how angry each syllable tasted against my tongue. I had mulled over the 'what-ifs' from the second we left him behind. What if I knew more magic, did more? It was pointless.

I shifted my weight as I repositioned myself to sit, the pressure in my unwilling joints building as I moved. Ilyan reached out to help me as my back seized and I swayed, my body torn between crying, yelling, and falling over.

"You didn't fail, Silnỳ," Ilyan's hand moved from mine to rest against the skin of my cheek. His touch was hot with the warmth of the powerful magic that pulsed underneath his skin. Ilyan kept his ability restrained inside of him, just the opposite of Ryland who had comforted and healed me with every touch.

Ilyan caressed my cheek, letting his fingers trail behind my ear to rest on my mark. He kept his hand there, his eyes wide as he looked into mine. "Everything happens for a reason, Silnỳ. Perhaps we must move through this trial to meet our true purpose." His voice had taken on the regal air that was so fitting for him as the ruler of the protectors of magic, the Skřítek. I cringed against his tone.

"True purpose," I repeated, shocked to feel the flame within me grow stronger.

"What do you want to do, Joclyn? What is your true purpose?" Ilyan asked softly.

His words were like gasoline on an open flame. They burned and smoldered inside of me, igniting the need for revenge, making it stronger. The web of heartbreak and confusion shattered, the remaining fragments swallowed up by my growing determination. I already knew the answer to this one.

"I want to avenge Ryland. I want to be the one to destroy Edmund LaRue." My voice rang clear through the apartment, the power behind it causing Ilyan's eyes to widen in shock.

"You want to fight?" Ilyan asked.

"Yes. And none of this flying away stuff. I want you to teach me to fight back."

"I promise, I will teach you everything you need to know," Ilyan replied as my nerves jumped in anticipation. I could feel my soul piecing itself back together with the thought.

"Everything?" I was skeptical.

"Yes, Silný. You need to know everything. Before, I had wanted to keep you safe, and I foolishly hoped that by bringing you and Ryland together that I would be able to unlock your true ability away from Edmund. It was very foolish of me. But now, Ryland has lost his memories of you and become his father's puppet. He is now only a weapon at Edmund's disposal. Ryland, as he is now, will stop at nothing to hunt you down and kill you Joclyn. If you wish to be the one to avenge him, you must prepare."

"I'm ready. Let's do this." I nodded once and moved to jump up. I nearly laid back down with how everything spun. Ilyan squared his jaw and stood to face me, his hand extended toward me.

"Come, Silný. Let's begin." Ilyan pulled me to standing, my joints swelling in subtle pain as I moved. I stood facing him, defying the agony of my long-inactive body. I had only been standing for a moment before I knew something was wrong. My head swam and my body felt like it was turning on the spot, even though I knew I wasn't moving. My balance left from the crazy motion, and I fell sideways. Ilyan's arms reached out to catch me just in time.

"Are you all right?" Ilyan asked. The alarm in his voice surprised me. I nodded my head, the room spinning less and less.

"Yeah, just tired." Not that I was going to let that stop me.

"Hmm. Well, perhaps we should do this in the correct order. You look a mess." His voice was low, as if even he didn't believe his words. His grip on my elbow tightened as we began to move, obviously worried I would fall again.

When he looked at me, his forehead crinkled before grabbing one of the half-filled glasses of water that he had been forcing me to drink from for days.

After I drank, Ilyan walked me toward the small bathroom. I looked behind me reluctantly to where the small double bed was pushed into a corner. A sliding glass door was at the foot of the bed and the tiny kitchen was on the other wall. The only floor space to speak of was between the bed and kitchen, but most of that had been taken up by Ilyan's makeshift bed.

It was a tissue box that someone had mistaken for a studio apartment. The idea of spending any amount of time in this claustrophobic space was nauseating; sharing it with another person was terrifying.

"I want you to take a shower. There are clothes in the bathroom for you."

Sure enough, sitting on the counter in the bathroom was a small pile of clothes, including a black hoodie I had never seen before.

"Where is Ryland's hoodie?" I asked, unsurprised by my alarm.

"It's gone, Joclyn. When we failed, many of our number fled to the Motel. They were followed. Anything that was left there was destroyed out of necessity."

My heart sunk and my head swam, Ilyan's hold on my elbow increased as I swayed again.

"Maybe now is not the time for a shower," he said.

I looked down. My shirt consisted of merely scraps of fabric and my stomach was covered by dried blood and ash. My mind flashed back to memories of the other night; to Ryland digging a tiny blade into my chest. I swallowed hard, willing the tears to stay away.

"Now is fine." I needed to wash more than the blood away.

"Good, but first..."

Ilyan placed his hand against my face, his eyes boring into mine as he pushed his magic into me. I wondered what he was doing, but he only smiled at me, his blue eyes twinkling. My head began to prickle as his magic congregated there, causing my hair to grow back to how it had been before.

Ilyan removed his hand. I turned to look at myself in the mirror. Dark black make-up was still smeared all over my face, my bright silver eyes twinkling among the smudges, but my hair was black, straight, and long again—maybe even a bit longer than it had been originally.

"Thank you."

"Of course," he said as he turned on the steaming water before moving toward the door. "Enjoy your shower. I'll have a surprise waiting for you when you get out."

The door clicked shut behind him and I spun around to the sink. My reflection was staring at me through the mirror, my mouth opening in shock at the haggard face that looked back. All my battle wounds were still visible and much of my body was covered with dried blood. I ripped off what was left of my shirt and followed the trail of dried blood up to a small scar that now lay over my heart.

A small line of raised skin stood out where Ryland had stabbed me, in his attempt to kill me. The scar was rough from the quick healing Ryland had done in the brief time that he had regained control of his body. That had been the last time he was himself, before his mind had been erased forever.

I ripped my eyes away from the scar to the ruby necklace that hung around my neck; another gift from him. I reached up and grabbed it, removing the chain from around my neck, and scraped off the blood that had dried onto the beautiful ruby.

I hadn't touched the stone since I had used it to enter the Tòuha last night. It had been the final proof that Ryland, as I knew him, was gone.

I threw the necklace into the sink, the stone clinking loudly against the porcelain. I didn't want to enter the Tòuha ever again, yet seeing it there in the sink made me want to snatch it back up and keep it safe.

The bathroom had filled with the steam from the shower and I was surrounded by the sweet smelling fog. It smelled vaguely of plant life, making me wonder what Ilyan had placed in here. Something to help settle my nerves, I was sure. The hot mist filled my head and I swayed as I slunk out of my pants and stumbled into the shower.

Hot water scalded my skin, but I didn't care. I let the water run over me as it burned the heavy makeup off of my face, washed the ash and blood from my body, and scrubbed away the dirt and rubble from what had been Ryland's home. The heat moved into me as if it was trying to thaw the emotion out.

I leaned against the side of the shower, breathing deeply in an effort to regain some stability.

It wasn't working.

The spinning was only increasing as I looked at the faucet of the shower, trying to focus on it to steady myself. The silver fixture moved, spun, and duplicated itself, even though I was certain I was holding still.

My eyes closed as I breathed in the steam, hoping that somehow the dizziness would leave. It got worse. I was forced to stumble out of the shower, hair unwashed, only to have my foot catch on the shower curtain and send me slamming into the ground.

My shoulder impacted hard on the tiles while a jolt of pain seared down my spine. I yelled out on impact and frantically tried to right myself, however the dizziness expanded, and I collapsed back onto the floor. The cool tiles under my skin seemed to clear my mind a bit, so I focused on them.

"Joclyn!" Ilyan yelled through the door, his voice panicked. "Are you okay?"

"Yes." My voice was muffled by the tile. I wasn't sure Ilyan had heard me seeing as he continued to pound on the door. I tried again, but his panicked yelling drowned out my voice. Great, he was going to barge in and I was lying naked in the middle of the bathroom floor.

I forced myself up and grabbed the hoodie and pajama pants from the counter, pulling them on over my damp body. Right at the moment that I pulled the hoodie down, my body collapsed again as the door was flung open, allowing Ilyan to tumble into the room, blonde hair swinging.

"Joclyn!" he yelled.

"I'm here."

I was surprised by how weak my voice was. I knew I wasn't feeling well, but I didn't think it was that bad. I shook my head hoping that the dizziness would leave, but it only got worse.

Ilyan kneeled down next to me. His hands flew to my cheeks, his magic plunging into me as he checked for any injuries.

"I'm fine, Ilyan." I batted his hand away from me, breaking the connection.

"Are you sure?" His accent was so thick, I barely understood him.

I nodded, but I was starting to wonder if I really was. This was beginning to feel more like I was being drained than a dehydrated dizziness. It was as if someone was reaching inside me and scrambling everything together.

Ilyan wrapped his arm around my waist and pulled me to standing, his body supporting me as my head continued to spin. I didn't dare say anything, so I let him lead me out of the bathroom.

"Bacon?" I asked, surprised at the smell of bacon and eggs that had filled the small living space. Ilyan was a vegan and had eaten no more than fruit or vegetables for the last few centuries. The fact that he would even attempt to make bacon and eggs was humorous as well as heartening.

"Yes," he grimaced. "I just hope I did it right. I think the influx of protein might help you."

Ilyan placed me on one of the chairs at the tiny table where what was surely a full pack of perfectly crisp, browned bacon sat in all its greasy goodness before me. I hadn't eaten meat in what felt like months and just the smell was making my mouth water.

"Thank you, Ilyan." I smiled brightly at him, ignoring the swelling and swimming that was going on inside my brain.

His eyes were shining joyfully, but it wasn't only happiness I saw behind his eyes, there was something there I couldn't quite place. I was trying to figure out what it might be when the swelling in my head grew into something more painful and I called out, clutching my hands to my head.

I could barely make out Ilyan rushing towards me from the kitchenette; calling to me, yelling for me. The pain continued to grow as my vision blacked out, and the air swirled past me as I fell from the chair.

I never felt the impact, but on my way down I could have sworn I heard someone laughing.

CHAPTER 2
JOCLYN

"Sakra, Ovailia! I don't know how it happened!"

Ilyan's voice woke me up from a deep sleep, and I immediately regretted it. My body hurt and my bones creaked and ached as if they were swelling. My chest fought with every breath, a heavy weight restricting my movements.

Ilyan yelled something in Czech and I reluctantly opened my eyes. Even my eyelids hurt.

It was night. The only light in the room came from a small lamp near the balcony that lit up the room eerily with a heavy, yellow glow. The bacon still sat on the table, and the chair I had been sitting in was knocked over. A large, dark stain spread over the carpet nearby. I moved to try and get a better look, but a pressurized pain spread over my skull. I closed my eyes tightly against the threatening migraine.

"That's just it, Ovailia, it's as if her magic has been drained. Normally it's a suffocating torrent when I try to heal her, but now there is nothing there. Nothing is fighting me."

My magic was gone? I reached inside of me and pulled it up as I had been taught to do, but it didn't respond as usual. It was slow and heavy, like when you move your hand through sludge. Even the attempt to work it up and push it outside of me caused pain.

"That is why I am calling you. I need you to tell me what to do," Ilyan spoke harshly before transitioning into Czech again. I shifted my weight again and my back seized up in the exact places I had broken it a few weeks before.

"Ilyan!" I called out to him. My spine curled, arching itself out in a fan before freezing me in place.

"I have to go." I heard the phone click shut, and a moment later Ilyan's hands pressed against my skin. His magic filled me instantly. It raced through my skin faster than lightning and with more strength than I had ever experienced.

My eyes opened wide in surprise at his power filling me so aggressively. If the way Ilyan's magic burned into my body at that moment was any indication as to how powerful he was, I was beginning to understand why he was revered.

Moments after his hands had touched my skin, my back relaxed and straightened. Some of the bone pain had also left, and I was feeling blissfully relaxed.

"Are you alright?" he asked, his voice strained.

"I think so." I shifted a bit, but decided against any larger movements as my body protested again.

"What happened, Joclyn? Do you remember anything?"

"Not really. I remember my head swelling, and then I was falling, and someone was laughing..." I looked to Ilyan, concerned that I sounded like a mad man. He moved aside the thick braid he had obviously placed in my hair and pushed his hand against my neck. My nerves jumped a bit in confusion about what had happened.

"Someone was laughing? Do you know who?"

"No," I whispered.

Ilyan's hand still rested against my neck, his magic reaching into every part of me. It was warm and comforting, like a blanket you want to curl into.

"What's going on, Ilyan?"

"I'm trying to figure that out, Silnỳ." My eyes grew wide and my heart raced until his magic surged again and my nerves calmed.

"Trying?" I repeated, my eyes falling to the dark spot on the carpet.

Ilyan's line of sight traced mine, and I saw him stiffen at the sight of the large, dark splotch. "You fell, and then you began to bleed a dark fluid. It wasn't blood, but it was foul. Your whole body was shaking. I thought..." He lowered his head, hiding his glistening eyes. "I thought I had lost you."

"I was leaking car oil?" I asked, confused.

"No. But, I suppose that is one way to explain it. Something formed on your skin then poured out of your eyes and ears." Ilyan looked away and closed his eyes. I could feel the stress rolling off of his body in waves. It added to my fear and I grabbed his wrist, needing some form of connection.

"It's okay, Joclyn. You're going to be okay." His voice was strong, but I could hear the lie. He didn't really know if I would be alright, and it scared me.

"I guess you never should have forced me to get out of bed," I joked, trying to lighten the mood. Ilyan's head snapped up to look deeply into me, the intensity of his gaze like a pressure against my soul.

"I guess not," he said with half a smile, his hand moving to trace the lines of the braid.

"I heard what you said to Ovailia." Ilyan's body stiffened as if I had caught him saying something he shouldn't. "About how my magic isn't fighting you anymore," I clarified. He relaxed a bit, surging his powerful tendrils through me again.

"You are the only one I have ever met who actively fights me, or is strong enough to do so."

"What do you mean?"

"My magic is stronger than most, Joclyn. Most of the time it floods into another person. There was a time I had trouble controlling my own strength so as not to hurt others. It took me centuries to master the skill. But you have always fought me. You are as powerful as I am, it seems."

My eyes opened wide as I tried to process what he had said. I wasn't sure if he was kidding or not, his tone could go either way. Regardless of whether I was normally powerful or not, I still couldn't reach my magic right then.

"I tried... I tried to use my magic, but it didn't respond." Ilyan's eyes grew wide and my heart thumped again in fear. "What's happening to me, Ilyan?"

"I don't know," he said. "But I have ideas."

"What?"

"Do you remember at the party?" he asked, and my body stiffened automatically. "When Ryland sealed himself to you, completing the Zêlství?"

I didn't respond. I only stared at him, waiting for him to continue.

"When magic is sealed together it is a permanent union. If Edmund has made Ryland break the connection between the two of you, your magic would be separated from half of itself. When one of our kind who has mated dies, they take half of their partner's magic but leave half of their own behind. Yet, if Ryland has broken that connection..." Ilyan paused and dragged his hand heavily through his hair while his eyes darted away from me.

"He's broken..." My voice caught as the air sucked itself out of my lungs. The Ryland I had known was gone, but breaking our bond would mean there was no hope of getting him back. The thought terrified me.

"So, what makes you think that this could be caused by a broken bond?"

Ilyan looked away, making me nervous about what he was about to say.

"Ilyan?"

"I have seen it before. When my father broke the bond with my mother, he severed her power. With half of her own magic gone and none of my father's to replace it, her body began to shut down. It would be akin to what happens to humans when an organ in their body does not work. They fade and suffer until they die."

"So I am dying," I cut him off.

"Not necessarily. There have been other times that this happened, and both parties survived."

"Okay, so let's do what those guys did." Panic clenched my stomach, spreading pain deep into my legs. I ignored it. "What do I do, Ilyan?"

"That's what I am trying to figure out." His eyes were shining with tears, boring into me with that same pained look he had before. He moved his hand from my head to rest his fingers against my mark. "I can't let you die, Silnỳ. I will do everything in my power to stop it."

"Well, at least that makes two of us," I rolled away from him, calling out as the pain engulfed my body again.

"I need to call Ovailia back," Ilyan whispered as he covered me with the heavy blanket. "But get some sleep, Joclyn. You need your strength."

What was I, an invalid?

"Like hell if I'm going to sleep. I'm going to kill Edmund if it's the last thing I do," I hissed, throwing the covers off me to sit up. Ilyan had offered to teach me how to fight, and like hell if I was going to let this get in my way.

It was too much, though. My head spun and I sagged back onto the comforter.

"I know you will, Silnỳ," Ilyan said, the screen of the phone in his hand going white without him even touching it. "Of that I can promise you. But for now, lay there, perhaps see if you can get your magic to cooperate so that I *can* teach you."

I nodded as he turned away, phone to his ear in quick Czech. Lifting my hand above my lap, I focused on my power, the usual buzz of energy sluggish and slow. Almost as if something was weighing it down.

It took focus, but as Ilyan's voice shifted to that commanding tone of his, I felt it react. I watched my fingers, waiting for the spark of light to appear. Instead, it was a drop of black, a liquid ooze that looked a bit too much like car oil.

Like rot.

CHAPTER 3
RYLAND

I wasn't sure I would ever feel warmth again. The cold of this cell had permeated so deep that my joints were frozen, my bones splinters of ice. They creaked as I shifted my weight, as though they would crack inside of me. Sain and I sat back to back against the bars of our cells as if we could trap all of the heat between us. If there was any heat to trap.

"Tell me again what happened," Sain's teeth chattered as he pulled me out of my doze, causing me to jump and hit my head against the bars. I barely winced, it was just another ache to add to the dozens that rumbled over every inch of my flesh.

"Ilyan took the girl. We beat them." I said the words that my mind commanded me too. "We killed two. We were... we won..."

A pressure was building in my chest, as though something was there that was trying to get out. Trying to tell me that I was wrong. What I was missing.

"I know the information is in you somewhere, Ryland," Sain hissed, the bars creaking as he turned to look at the back of my head. "Tell me what happened with the girl?"

That pressure grew at his question.

"The girl?"

"The one with dark hair. The one your father sent you to hunt."

Cail and I had followed the pack of Ilyan and his men as they had fled my home. We had tracked them as far as an old motel in the middle of nowhere. But the girl was not with them. Ilyan was not with them.

We had set fire to the place anyway.

That memory was new, fresh, and it sent a zipline of terror through me, my heart constricting to an ache of loss that I didn't understand.

'You will find and kill the girl. You will do it for me.' The voice of my father, Edmund, echoed in my head as he took control. The slimy words weaseling into my mind, into my soul, as he manipulated me.

"Tell me about Joclyn," Sain continued, his voice hissing in my ear. He would have sounded like a villain, the low rumble of his voice a twisted growl, except for what he said.

That one word that sent fireworks exploding inside of me.

"Joclyn." I repeated her name, all of those electric sparks moving through me. I didn't know who she was, or why she mattered, but she did.

'Joclyn will die.' My father's voice repeated in my head, but I roared against it, my scream lifting from my throat as my magic continued to buzz, feeling like something I could control.

"She is the girl." I lifted from the bars, feeling the warmth of hope for the first time.

That was until the heavy metal door at the top of the old stone steps opened.

"Sain! What are you doing to my son?" Edmund roared as his and two other sets of footsteps began to race down to the dungeon after us.

All of the joyful energy that hearing that name had given me flatlined at the sound of his voice, the rage of his yell echoing both against the cold stone and in my head. Sain whimpered and scuttled back to the dark corner of his cell, leaving me to face my father alone.

'Do you really think you can face me? Do you really think you can survive it?'

"Yes." The word in response was really more of a whimper, and my father chuckled with that deep mockery of his.

"Do you even know why you continue to fight me?" he asked, the words both in and out of my mind as he paced on the other side of the bars, like he was the trapped animal, just waiting to rip me to shreds.

"Yes." I was even less confident that time, and Cail and Timothy laughed alongside my father, the two of them are never far behind him.

"Tell me, Ryland, who do you fight for?" He stopped pacing, Sain's whimpers were the only sounds in the underground prison as my father's ice blue eyes dug into me. Waiting.

I gave him the only name that came to mind, the buzz in my soul increasing as I said it again.

"Joclyn. I will fight for her. I will save her." Saying that cracked something inside of me, some forgotten hiding space, opening to give me one shy smile and a sparkle of silver eyes. I didn't know that it was her, and yet, there was no one else it could be.

All of that burning energy grew and I lifted my hand, sparks of my own making dancing between my fingertips.

"Always for her."

I lifted my eyes to my fathers, determination buzzing through me as the magic grew. I only caught a glimpse of Edmunds furious horror before Cail stepped between us and sent a strip of black and red right into my gut. The power impacted against my stomach like a razor's edge. It felt as though I had been cut in two as I was thrown back, my body slamming into the wall only to slide down it. I couldn't move.

I lay there like a rag doll as the iron door to the cell swung open soundlessly and the three of them entered.

"We need to dispose of him, sir," Timothy snarled, nothing but hatred in his voice. "We have been trying to tame him for weeks. He will never bow and the longer we let this go on the more dangerous he is."

Dangerous. They think I'm dangerous. Dangerous because I am fighting them. I must keep fighting.

'He will bow.' I couldn't be sure if the voice was in my head or out loud with how he was looking at me.

"I will never bow." My voice was as weak as my body felt. "I will always fight for her."

"He is too much of a liability. If he had fought when he was out with Cail... I will end him. Let me do it," Timothy continued; his eyes eager at the possibility of killing me. The guy was even rubbing his hands together and licking his lips. He almost looked more sadistic than his son. I couldn't help it, I shirked back, wincing in fear of that look. Of the memory of what Cail did to me when he forced me into submission.

"I have trained him too long, too hard. He is worth the risk." My father reached out to me, his eyes glazing over as he stared at me like the prized possession he saw me as. Not as his son.

I turned from Timothy to my father as he spoke, as those eyes boring into me as all of that wicked defiance came back.

'Bow to me, Ryland.'

"No. Never." The two words were near agony to escape. It was as though the torturous weight of Cail's attack was growing, the edges of his power still slicing away. He stared at me with those dark eyes of his, his focus narrowed as though he was controlling it. As though he was searching for something.

Because he was.

In my defiance, in my fight, I hadn't even noticed where his magic had localized. Right on that spot near my heart, that spot I had taken to protect her, the spot that still connected me to her, even when I had trouble remembering who she was.

"No!" I yelled, trying to move against the weight. Trying to fight against his prying eyes. "You can't have her!"

My father raised his hand, ready to strike. I lifted my chin, ready to take it. Ready for pain. It never came.

"I found it. The connection is there, master. As you assumed." The dark slices of Cail's magic froze against the last bit of warmth and hope that I possessed, his smile stretching as he turned to my father. All three of them grinning again.

"So, it was a Zêlství." Edmund said, even Sain shifted at that, a weird noise coming from him. They all looked at him before turning back to me, their smiles spreading.

"Wonderful, Cail. I want you to use it, find the line to her. Follow it and take her. I think it's time we take control of the situation." Edmund squatted before me, his finger cold against my already icy skin as he traced a line over my jaw.

"You can't... I won't let you." The words were harder to say with him this close, when the Vymåzat he used to control me was ripping through my body, taking away my control. Taking away my mind.

"That's where you are wrong, son. You will. Sain has already seen it. And, seeing as you won't bow willingly, I will just have Cail control you. Perhaps we should have done this from the beginning."

I tried to turn my head to Sain, to ask what he had seen. Ask how he had betrayed me, but the guy was nothing but an inky smudge in a dark prison as I felt Cail's magic swell inside me.

"You thought you could keep her all to yourself, but now even she will belong to me."

'She will be your biggest enemy.'

"I think I may have found that connection. The girl is here," Cail said through the ever darkening world. Now it wasn't just my fathers magic that was smudging me out, it was Cail's. Cail's dark sticky magic that was spreading through his attack to leach into me.

His magic felt different than when my father used me as a puppet, when I was still aware of what was going on. It was as though I was being pulled away from my own consciousness, and someone else was taking control.

"Good. Let's turn him off, Cail. Let's see what else we can find."

I could have sworn I heard Sain gasp as the world faded to nothing, and the prison faded away to darkness.

Nothing but black.

My father was gone. Cail was gone. The jail was gone.

It was only me, standing before a girl with long dark curls and silver eyes. My mind pulled her name to life as though I had known it all along.

"Joclyn." She smiled at the gasp in my voice, and I ran to her, ready to wrap my arms around her and pull her to me as I had a million times before. As I wanted to for the rest of my life.

Before I even reached her, however, that smile turned into something dark, the corner pulling up as Cail's always did.

I stopped in place.

"Joclyn?" She just chuckled in response, but the voice was not hers, it was Cail's. It was his voice, his smile, plastered on the girl that I had tried so hard to protect. But the more I looked, the more I wasn't sure if that was right. It was just Joclyn there. Just the girls that I loved. Cail was nowhere to be found. It was just Jos and I.

"Joclyn?" I could only stare as she smiled in a twisted glee and let her magic twist around me.

Attacking me.

CHAPTER 4
RYLAND

"How could you ever think I wanted you?" The words were accompanied by a laugh that moved from high and rancid to low and demented.

I knew that laugh.

"Turn him off Cail," Edmund's voice echoed in my head as the world faded into the gray stone of the prison. My legs twitched, a gasp of a scream escaping as I writhed in an attempt to move away from Joclyn as she attacked me.

Over and Over.

But Joclyn was gone. The black nothing was gone.

It was just my father and Cail standing over me. Even Timothy had gone, probably off on some errand for my father.

"Good. Perfect," my father said through a greasy smile. "This will work."

"Yes, master." Cail actually sounded winded. "The connection of their Zêlství is strong. I can feel the tie, although it is well protected, I still think I can sever it. Or, rather, I can make him do it."

No, I couldn't have heard that right. I would never let that happen.

'You think you can still protect her? Fool.'

"Wonderful." Edmund stood quickly, his hands flying to his hips as he moved. The motion was so quick that it triggered something inside of me and I flinched, which only caused the depraved man to smile more. "Do it."

Edmund looked giddy, Cail eager for what was about to happen. But all I could think was that I didn't want this, that I didn't want to lose her.

'Lose someone who hurt you?'

She didn't hurt me... that was... that was...

My mind struggled to find the correct answer as the two men stepped forward and Cail placed his hand on my shoulder. His magic shot through me, buzzing through everything and right into that line in my heart that I had protected. The line that connected me to her.

"No!" I yelled, attempting to push his magic away. He just smiled and pushed harder, his magic feeling like a branding iron inside of me.

"No!" I yelled again, and screamed, lunging for him as though I could fight him physically, but I was trapped. My body ached from beatings, broken bones not yet healed. I was fatigued from lack of sleep and food. No matter how hard I tried I could not not reach him, I could not banish his magic from boring deeper and deeper.

Burning lines of iron lashed through me, slicing at that line that connected me to her. At her. I heaved, refusing to scream as I continued to fight him. He just kept slicing deeper.

"Stop! Stop Edmund!" The shout did not come from me, but from Sain, who was now pressed against the bars behind me, his face squished awkwardly. "You don't want to do this!"

"Do you want to be next, Sain? Do you want to lose all control?" I could hear the threat in his voice, but Sain did not move.

"I don't but neither will you." Sain was strangely calm given what he was facing. "You know what I saw. The Zêlství--"

"You saw me taking my true throne! I will not lose this." Edmund rushed forward, facing Sain within inches. Cail's magic retreated at the outburst, giving me a moment to breathe. "Unless you have been hiding something, Sain. Have you been hiding something?"

"N...no...no... you know everything. It's just..." Sain hesitated and I turned, my father so close I could see the red veins of fury in his eyes. But it was Sain who was looking at me, his green eyes pleading. "If you sever the connection. They both die. She will die."

She will die.

'She will die anyway, and there is nothing you can do to stop it.'

Something in me said I didn't want that. I would be glad to die, but I needed to protect her. Cail's magic stalled out, all of the knives of his magic slowing and leaving me feeling raw and open inside.

I sat, heaving, little pieces of a life I didn't remember bleeding through the sawed off edges of my heart. The sound of a laugh. The touch of a hand. The glimmer of a laugh in a silver eye.

Joclyn.

I needed to protect her. I gathered up those shards of memory and shoved them deeper, locking them not in the box that I had built but in that warm spot in my heart that was just for her.

"I don't care," Edmund said with a snarl. "If they both die, then I still win. Besides if all of your sights have been correct, then killing her will end Ilyan as well. I can't lose."

'And you can never win.'

"I can protect her, I will." I was firm and Cail and Edmund turned to me, my father's laugh rumbling in my head as Cail's magic lashed again, driving me to hide her faster. To protect that line that connected us. To keep the connection strong.

"Ilyan is not connected to her. Not yet," Sain hissed, face against the bars. "Your pride is blinding you. This path will lead to your end."

"Master," Cail interrupted and everyone turned. I froze, my heart rate rattling in my chest as Cail's magic's bored deeper until pressed right against that that warm spot, right against where my magic had pooled.

Blocking him.

"What is it? Why have you stopped?" Edmund looked at me, clearly not understanding why I wasn't screaming. Cail was just smiling.

"This isn't simply a Zêlství--"

'You bastard! Fool! You will pay!'

"What?" My father was furious, but Cail was still smiling.

"Do not worry, master. This is something more. Something better." Cail's smile spread and I still tried to fight him, to push his magic and his hands away and slam him into the wall. I could barely do more than lay there and whimper, something warm and wet dripping from my eyes.

"A connection better than a Zêlství?" Even Edmund didn't believe it, but I already knew it was true. Because I knew what Cail had found.

I had thought he had found it before, but he hadn't seen the true depth of it. In my haste to protect those few memories, however, I had led him right to it.

"No. No." The sound was more of a moan, it was answered by nothing more than an echo of a laugh.

"Yes. It's a svazovat."

"A soul bind." Edmund almost sounded hungry, but I clenched my chest, clenched that part of me that I had given her so I could protect her, so I could keep her safe. The part that would now betray us both.

"We might be able to pull her magic through to us," Cail continued, his magic still prodding against me, against that precious piece of me that connected me right to Joclyn. "We might be able to control her as well."

"A svazovat! How could he be so stupid!" Edmund asked as they all turned to me. "Show me."

"No!" I screamed, attempting to fight against them. But my body was still too weak, too tired. "You can't have her! I will always fight you! I will never let you win!"

'You will always fail. You are nothing.'

"Turn him off, Cail," Edmund demanded as I screamed, as I fought. But it was useless, the world plunged back to black before I could blink.

I was left staring at nothing, Edmund's laugh echoing in my mind as I heard her scream.

CHAPTER 5
JOCLYN

I had been here before. But not in this dream. I had *been* here.

I had stood in the center of this clearing a hundred times and eaten pie, shared secrets. I had looked up into these trees and watched their long arms stretch to the sky, begging me to climb them. I watched them now, and although they were the same, something was terrifyingly different. Perhaps it was the color, or the way the branches cut a jagged edge into the night sky. A night sky that only existed in nightmares.

A thick mist swirled around my legs, picking up the light-weight cotton of my pajama pants. It crept over the forest floor in a dense cloud that wet my bare feet and made the forest floor look like a living thing with its rise and flow.

A deep growl echoed behind me and my body tensed, although I didn't dare to turn. There was a pause as the mist continued to roll and swell before the growl returned accompanied by a warm, putrid breath against my ear. The deep sound rumbled through me as the fog swelled at the same time that the owner's hard chest rippled against my back.

"Hello, Joclyn."

Cail.

The fog took on substance, the sound of his breathing freezing me for a second. I could almost feel his warmth, his excitement, rippling off of him and increasing my fear. I felt his magic pulse, one influx of energy reverberating through the heavy sludge of magic inside of me. It was enough to serve as a warning. So I ran.

My feet carried me out of the clearing, plunging me into the pitch dark of the forest. I ran as my eyes adjusted to the black and starless night. The trees flew by me as I picked up speed, what was left of my own magic attempting to carry me faster. I could still hear his foot falls behind me from the crunch of the dying plant life as he passed, marking his progress.

He was getting closer, his breathing louder; he was almost right behind me.

"Run Joclyn, run to my master!" he yelled from behind me, but I barely heard him. I picked up my pace and ran faster, only to sense the world around me shift and change. I slowed as carpet emerged under my dirty feet, the air no longer smelling so crisp and vibrant. Everything here was dying.

I looked down the hall. Once again I was in a place I knew, but nothing about it was quite right. The cream colored walls were dirty and covered with black spider webs of soot and flame. The carpet had been burned away in giant patches and part of the wall to my right had been blown away, leaving a gaping hole straight into the night sky.

I walked along the burnt fragments of carpet toward the door, a door I had entered almost every day of my life—Ryland's. My heart thudded angrily in my chest as I moved closer, the slab of wood dangling by one hinge.

I ducked underneath it into his room, a room that was gutted by flame. Embers still glowed in the corner where fragments of his bed were scattered. I stepped cautiously around the partition to where his big, squishy couch sat. The sofa had been torn into pieces that lay haphazardly around the space, exposed stuffing melted into the carpet and walls.

"Jos," Ryland's tender voice spoke from behind the battered couch. "You came."

I stepped around the couch, my feet guiding me to where he was burrowed into his collapsed closet. Embers of a still burning fire glowed near him, the light shimmering in his hair.

"Ryland!" I almost threw myself into him. He was broken and bruised, the way I had last seen him. His body was crumpled in on itself as he fought for control over his mind.

"What did you do to your hair, Jos? I always loved your hair."

"My hair is long again, Ryland. See." I pulled the braid Ilyan had given me around so he could see, but his eyes were focused somewhere off in the distance, his arms lifted slightly as if he was reaching for something.

"...Steal the car..." His voice faded in and out before he slumped even further. His body gave out as his arms fell.

"Ryland! Come on! We need to go." I grabbed at him, summoning the sludge inside of me, determined to find some way to escape. My hands shook as I looked around, my heart pulsing frantically. There was nowhere to go.

"What? Not going to save your love?" I froze at Edmund's voice, my body tensing.

"Edmund," I gasped, moving closer to Ryland in fear.

"Go on," he taunted, his voice deep and menacing. "Save him. Let me see how powerful you are."

I placed myself between Ryland and Edmund, glaring at the old monster. He was right there; right in front of me. My magic may have been thick and stagnant inside of me, but that didn't mean I couldn't fight him. I could try, anyway. I grabbed a small, burning stick and hurled it at him. It was a start, even if it did fling itself uselessly to the side.

"Now, now," Edmund said, "none of that. After all, what's the point of your pathetic weapons when I possess the most powerful weapon of all?"

"Miss me beautiful?" Ryland's twisted voice whispered beside me and I spun to face him. My stomach plummeted as I came face to face with the pitch black eyes of a new Ryland. The Ryland who had lost his fight with his father, whose memory had been erased.

"No!" True terror filled me at seeing him.

"I believe you have something that belongs to me." Ryland's hands pulled me to him and lifted the back of my sweater, letting his hand come in contact with my skin. I began to scream in fear as his magic rushed into me the second I felt his cold touch. It flowed in an angry wave that spread to the very tips of my toes and lasted a moment before it began to sweep out again. As the heat left, so did my magic.

The thick, useless, almost dead bits of magic that had hidden inside of me seeped away and into Ryland. My screams died down as the pain left and I slipped out of Ryland's arms and onto the ash covered floor.

"Dispose of it," I heard Edmund say.

Ryland's hands surrounded my head, placing pressure against my skull. His hands grew hot as the pressure grew. As I could have sworn the bones began to crack.

My own scream jostled me awake, my eyes adjusting to the dark studio apartment. My legs fought against the heavy comforters Ilyan had covered me with. I kicked and screamed to get away from them, to make it back to Ryland.

"Ryland!" I yelled out loudly. I was sure he was right there; sure he was going to answer me.

Strong arms encircled me, and for one fleeting moment I was certain it was Ryland. But the arms were wrong. They were leaner, stronger.

"Joclyn! What's wrong?" Ilyan stammered, his eyes as wide as mine in his panic at being awoken.

"Ryland!" I yelled out again, not giving Ilyan an answer. I scrambled across the floor, my legs giving out a few steps in. I tumbled down to the ground as another wave of pain shot through my spine, crippling me.

"Joclyn!" Ilyan was at my side immediately, his hands moving to press against me.

"Don't!" I yelled, pushing him away. I didn't need his magic to calm or heal me. I didn't need him. I needed Ryland. "I have to find Ryland!"

I clawed my way toward the window, desperate to get out, to see if I could sense him. To see if I could save him. He had been in my dream; he remembered me in the dream. No, it hadn't been a dream, it was a Tȍuha. A shared consciousness. I still had a chance at saving him.

"You saw Ryland?" Ilyan said.

"Yes!" I yelled, continuing to claw my way toward the glass. "He was there. In the Tȍuha. I saw him, he... he remembered me... I can save him..." I reached the glass as my spine clenched again. I screamed as my body threw me to the ground, the pain incapacitating me.

Ilyan was there a moment later, his magic rushing into me in a wave of power. My body relaxed as the pain seeped away despite its attempt to possess me.

"He's gone, Silnỳ. He's gone," Ilyan said.

"No! I saw him, in the Tȍuha. He remembered me. He..."

"It wasn't a Tȍuha, Silnỳ..." Ilyan moved me toward him, my pain-filled body unable to resist the unwanted contact.

"It was... I saw him." I was becoming desperate. I needed him to understand. I was running out of time.

"No. Your necklace still lies in the bathroom and your magic... Silnỳ, the bond is not strong enough to connect with him without it." I tried to push away from him, but it was useless. My body was too weak.

"I saw him, Ilyan... I saw him." I needed to get to him; I needed to open the window and find him.

"It was a dream, Silnỳ. He's gone."

"No!" I sobbed, attempting to move away from Ilyan again, yet he held me in place. "No, I saw him."

"He's gone."

Slowly I gave in, the tears of my pain and my broken heart too much for me to fight. I cried into Ilyan's bare chest, his hair falling around both of us as he cradled me and began to sing. I leaned into him as he sang the same song he had comforted me with the night he had flown me away from Ryland.

The rough Czech words surrounded me as he sang over and over, soothing me back to sleep.

CHAPTER 6
JOCLYN

"Jos! Jos! Did you fall asleep again?" Wyn's voice was loud over the speaker phone. I startled awake from my doze, my head swimming with the pain.

"Sorry," I looked toward Ilyan who had obviously begun standing in alarm at Wyn's exclamation. Seeing me awake, he settled back into his seat, returning to the leatherwork he had been working on since we had first gotten here.

"What were you saying?" I prompted. I heard her exhale on the other end of the line. I knew it was irritating talking to me like this, but I was finding it hard to stay awake for long.

I had been haunted by the same dream every night since it had first awakened me in a panic five days ago. While I had given up on my foolish attempt to track Ryland down, the lack of sleep mixed with the screaming panic I awoke in had made me exceptionally weak. I wasn't awake for much of the day anymore. If it wasn't for Ilyan—calming me, protecting me, and healing me several times throughout the day—who knew what shape I would be in.

I looked up to Ilyan again, unsurprised to find him watching me, his eyes lifted from his work.

"I was saying," Wyn replied and I was sure she was rolling her eyes, "I have finished your room in Prague for whenever Ilyan lets you out of that jail he's trying to pass off as a living space. Nice white bed, a huge loft you can fly up and down from all day long. Talon insisted that I make it brown, though."

"No I didn't!" Talon's voice broke through the speaker phone, the man having obviously grabbed the phone from Wyn. "Don't you dare listen to her, little girl. She wouldn't even give me a say in the matter." I heard Ilyan laugh from across our small living space. I couldn't help laughing along with them, but the action sent a sharp pain through my chest and I winced.

Ilyan set down his work and moved over to me, his hand pressing against the skin on my hands the second he was within distance.

"We don't need your lungs to collapse today, do we?" he said low enough that the phone couldn't pick it up. He smiled sadly, and I twisted my lips up in frustration.

I reached out and grabbed Ilyan's hand, and held on. I needed contact, and I was learning to accept Ilyan.

"Not ever," I hissed back. Stubborn to the end.

"Anyway, as I was saying," Wyn continued after having wrestled the phone away from Talon. "It is brown, but there is no orange. It looks nice. You're going to love it."

I smiled and turned to Ilyan who shook his head. We hadn't told Wyn what was going on, mostly because we didn't want her to worry or run back to the United States. She was safe in Prague. She needed to stay there.

"I bet I will," I agreed. "Unless it's too brown, then I may never talk to you again."

Wyn laughed and I tried to follow along, but my chest hurt too much even with the magical crutch that Ilyan's magic had given me. He let go of my hand and reached up to touch my cheek.

"Wynifred," Ilyan interrupted, his eyes focused on mine while his hand remained resting against my face.

"Yes, My Lord." I smiled at how her demeanor changed at Ilyan's one word.

"Joclyn needs to work on her magic now. We are going to have to continue this conversation at another time."

"Goodbye, Wyn," I said softly, cringing as my chest pulsed with pain.

"Later, Jos. My Lord." Ilyan didn't give me a chance to respond. He simply pressed the button to end the call and let his magic surge a bit more.

"They do seem to come in waves don't they?" Ilyan said. I nodded in agreement, my head spinning as I did so.

"Is that what we are calling them now? I thought we had settled on crippling destruction pulses."

"So, tell me." Ilyan swiftly changed the subject and I knew what was coming. I shifted my weight, I was ready.

At my insistence, Ilyan had begun mentally training me the morning after my first nightmare. He recited different ways to use defensive magic, the process of building shields, and every other bit of magic he hoped could help me defeat Edmund. Once he recited it, I would recite it back. I'm not sure who held out more hope for my survival, me or Ilyan, but I couldn't deny the burning desire to defeat Edmund that still glowed brightly inside of me. I was determined to beat this and I needed to be ready. Either way it was still a good way to get my mind off of what was happening.

"What happens when two fire-based, water-bound orbs collide?"

"A fire wall." I said, giving him the simplest answer as I felt his magic wrap around my lungs, fixing who knows what.

"Good. And redirection of objects without the use of wind?"

I cringed as I felt his magic snake its way up my spine, the warmth wrapping around my bones like a blanket.

"Is based in the thoughts of the mind and the second tier of energy storage. Both must work in succession for the task to be successful."

"Good," he said with a smile. "And the magic of the Vilỳ?"

"It awakens that hidden magic that humans possess. They can manipulate that magic for the human's benefit. Magic is only awoken in mortals by the bite of a Vilỳ or from bonding with a magical being." My voice caught as something shifted inside of me. Ilyan froze for a moment before asking another question, his deflection barely covered up his worry.

"What else is based in the mind?" He didn't look at me, and my fear increased.

"Internal sight, movement of thoughts and images from one person to another..." I stopped at the look on his face. He wasn't overly concerned or angry, he simply looked heartbroken. The misery in his eyes took my breath away.

"Ilyan?" I whispered, and his head turned toward me. "What's the damage?"

When Ilyan hesitated, I squeezed his hand, hoping to prompt him to tell me. He returned the gesture, looking away from me.

"Your kidneys have failed; your lungs attempt to collapse every time you are pained there. You also have what I can only relate to a tumor snaking its way up your spine. I'm trying to stop them..." I cringed and clung to his hand tightly. Hearing him actually say what was going on inside my body made it more real.

"I can survive a broken back, but being separated from my mate is what kills me." I tried to smile. "Go figure."

"Go figure," Ilyan repeated, the American saying sounding awkward with his accent. He smiled slightly and reached out, running his fingers along the mark below my ear.

"I had an idea on how to repair the bond," he said. "But first, I think you need to see Ryland. It might be the last time you can."

"I can't, Ilyan. I can't control my magic enough to visit him."

Ilyan moved his fingers away from my neck then opened the palm of his hand as the ruby necklace flew through the air to land gracefully in his outstretched fingers.

"You can." He let the necklace fall so he was only holding it by the chain. The ruby sparkled, taunting me. "I will help you."

I hesitated, my eyes unwilling to leave the glistening surface of the ruby. I did want to see Ryland again, but not the little boy in the Tȍuha. I wanted *my* Ryland. I suppose, given the chance to say goodbye to either, though, I would take it.

"Okay, I'll go see him."

"Good, and when you come back, I want to talk to you about one last thing. I may have a way to save you; it's a long shot, but it might work."

"What is it?" I asked.

"We will talk after you return. Are you ready?"

I wasn't, but what else could I say. I didn't have the time to prepare myself, and I was aware that I would talk myself out of it if I waited too long. I nodded again before I lost my confidence.

"Good." Ilyan's magic bubbled and boiled inside of me as it worked to move the dying sludge that was poisoning my body. He pushed, pulled, and prodded it until it reached the surface. I could feel the thick acid burning underneath the skin of my hand, the rancid magic eating me away.

Ilyan dropped the necklace into my hand and began to work again as he pushed my magic out of me.

My hand began to fill with a fluid that seeped out of my skin as Ilyan pushed. Thick like mud, but smooth and the color of congealed blood, it bubbled out of my skin slow and hot.

I had done this multiple times, and it never ceased to gross me out.

"Do you know what's wrong with it?" I couldn't tear my eyes away from the warm goo that was now seeping around the necklace.

"The best explanation I have is that it has rotted and died within you and in turn is poisoning you." His magic continued to push mine through my skin, the color becoming almost purple as more moved to join the growing mass.

"Can't we remove it, then?"

"I've tried, but it did not work."

"You've tried?" I asked, affronted.

"Yes," he spoke simply, as though this odd invasion of privacy was nothing more than a handshake. "I tried it after you had the first nightmare while you slept. I hoped that draining what was inside of you would heal you. Unfortunately, it keeps coming back."

"You've done it more than once?"

"Every night. I will try everything to save you, to protect you, Joclyn. Until the day you die. I promise you all that and more."

Ilyan looked at me for a moment, but all I could do was smile. Ilyan had saved me so many times, and he expected nothing in return. For someone with such a rough exterior, he could easily melt someone to goo if he tried.

"Thank you."

He nodded.

"Are you ready?" His question tore my mind back to the dying magic in my hand. He had stopped forcing the rancid power out of me, leaving the necklace in a small pool of the stuff in my hand.

"I will be with you the entire time, Joclyn. Don't worry. And when you come back, we will talk." His eyes lit up for a moment before his determination took over, his jaw set.

I grit my teeth and nodded once before I closed my eyes and let myself step into the white space that I shared with Ryland. Except now it was full of color.

I gasped and spun around. I was surrounded by thousands of crude drawings that covered the walls and floor in a rainbow of color. What once had been an undefined space was now enclosed by four walls. There were no windows or doors, so someone had taken the liberty to draw them in.

"Joclyn?" I spun around at the small voice to see Ryland standing in the middle of the room. His petite, five year old frame seemed to be glowing as I faced him, his blue eyes shining at seeing me there. Ryland as I had known him, as I was bound to him, was not this boy. He was not this age. This boy was only a subconscious projection, the last of the memories that his father had left him with.

"You came back!" He squealed and barreled into my legs, almost knocking me over onto the hard ground. He hugged me tightly, chalk and crayon dust wiping off onto my pants. I leaned down and ruffled his shaggy black curls.

"I take it you missed me then?" I asked softly.

"Of course I did! You were gone so long that I thought I would be alone forever."

"You haven't left?" I asked as Ryland enthusiastically shook his head in answer. I arched my brow in confusion; that didn't make sense. Ryland had always been able to leave before. He had left me alone in our space a number of times, and yet this time he was trapped.

"Nope, so I drew you a gift!" He motioned around him, his wide smile returning. "Do you like it?" He spun his fingers, and a bright red crayon appeared in-between them.

"You drew all this for me?" Ryland's face lit up at my response.

"I even drew a really, really special one for you. Do you want to see?"

"Umm... yeah." I smiled at him and he skipped away, excited to be showing me one of his many masterpieces.

I followed him until he stopped near a wide expanse of blue that I assumed to be a swimming pool.

"What is it, Ry?" I asked, coming to stand next to him and still not quite sure which of the surrounding images I should be looking at.

"It's you," he said quietly.

I followed his line of sight to a crayon drawing that was obviously meant to be life size. The portrait Ryland had drawn was of me with long, dark hair, big eyes that were actually crude sketches of diamonds, and stick hands and legs.

The figure wore a purple robe and had a pink crown on her head. I wanted to laugh, but instead I smiled, feeling exceptionally happy.

I kneeled down next to him, wrapping my arms around his tiny shoulders.

"You drew this for me?"

"Yeah," he said.

"It's beautiful, Ry. Thank you."

"You like it?" he asked, his little voice bursting with pride. I squeezed him against me, his frame so small against mine. I was overcome by a memory of Ryland, the way he should be; large, older than me, muscles, and scars.

"I love it." I said.

"Good! Now, you can draw one of me." He pushed a blue crayon into my hand and struck a pose in expectation.

"Actually," I said, feeling guilty as Ryland's face fell. "I came to say goodbye."

"Goodbye?" he asked, and my face fell more.

"Yeah, I may not come back. I'm not sure. I'm... I'm very sick. My friend is trying to help me, but I am not sure it is going to work... I wanted to say goodbye, in case." I felt the tears come and I cursed silently. I didn't want to cry. I didn't want to be weak anymore.

"You don't look sick," Ryland said.

"Not here, but where I come from I am very sick."

Ryland screwed up his face like he didn't believe me, but then seemed to think better of it. His face brightened a bit, but I could tell his smile was forced. I felt bad leaving him here alone. I didn't have a choice, though. I was quite literally lying in Ilyan's arms as he kept me alive long enough to say goodbye.

"You'll be back," Ryland said. "I know you will."

"I hope you're right, Ry." I ran my fingers through his curls, the way I always used to, and he smiled a bit.

I couldn't bring myself to say any more. I turned away from him and walked determinedly to a black door that was set into the endless space. I wasn't sure if it was the right way to exit because I had always been forced out before, but the door seemed right, so I grabbed the knob.

"Goodbye, Jossy," Ryland whispered, using a nickname I hadn't heard since I was six.

"Goodbye, Ry," I whispered softly to myself, not daring to turn back to face him again. I bit my lip and turned the knob, grateful when my eyes opened to Ilyan's worried face leaning over me.

I could tell right away that something was off; Ilyan's face was relieved but also... disappointed. Then I felt it; the strong buzzing under my skin. I could feel my perfectly healed body, the energy, the power. I hadn't felt this strong since I had flown into the LaRue mansion.

I sat up, sending blankets tumbling around me. Nothing hurt. My magic had restored itself, and in turn, healed my body. I stared at my hand numbly; I was going to be okay. I could have danced and sang, but everything in me was frozen in shocked relief. I stood and spun to face Ilyan, his face as stunned as I felt.

"It healed me." I wasn't sure if it was a statement or a question. I was awed. I still couldn't believe it. Relief washed down my spine and I exhaled shakily.

I fought the urge to call Wyn and scream into the telephone receiver about what had happened, or storm out the door right now to track down Edmund. Instead I stared at my hand in disbelief, the tingling warmth that occupied me taking over. I looked at my hand that had held my liquid magic not long before; the slime had dried into a film that coated my palm, but otherwise, nothing remained.

"Did you know it would do that?"

"I can honestly say I had no idea. I had assumed the bond was broken, but to have a connection strong enough for it to repair the bond within a Tõuha... I didn't think that was possible."

My skin prickled and pulsed as I flexed my fingers and toes. I had been lying down for the last few days like a slug at a beer festival. I had almost given up hope of seeking my revenge on Edmund. I had tried to find comfort in the possibility of seeing Ryland in whatever life was after this. After that, however, I could find him, fight him. Now Ryland's sacrifice could be worth something. I smiled brighter and threw myself at Ilyan, wrapping my hands around his neck only to get a face full of hair.

"Thank you," I whispered. Slowly, his arms came around to encompass me.

"Of course, this means Ryland can track you easily now." Ilyan had spoken offhand, though the few words had been enough to shatter my celebration.

"What do you mean?" I untangled myself from Ilyan to stand in front of him.

"If your bond is strong enough to reseal your magic during a Tõuha, then it is strong enough to track you over large distances. If he can do that, I do not know where—if any place—you would be safe. I can shield you as long as we stay together and in one location, but for now, it limits you to the interior of this apartment."

My jaw dropped, all my hopes at a celebration of good health dashed. Part of me wanted to yell at Ilyan for spoiling my joy, but he still had that devastated look on his face.

"So, are we trapped here?" I asked, finally able to process all that Ilyan was saying.

"Until I know how far he can track you, and until you are strong enough to fight him if he does." I couldn't help noticing that Ilyan's jaw was set into a hard line. He didn't seem to be celebrating my miraculous recovery at all. It worried me.

"Which will be how long?" I asked, my frustration rising.

"I do not know, Joclyn. Perhaps a year, maybe more."

CHAPTER 7
WYN

"Thank God! Everyone's finally home!" Talon's voice boomed over the large stone hall that served as the entrance to the underground caves of Imdalind. His joy echoed the way it always did, rattling the large decorative chandeliers of mirrors and glass that we used to get adequate light down there.

Imdalind was our home, and had been for centuries. The whole thing was a large, intricately carved, circuit of tunnels hidden in eastern Europe, just outside of Prague. It was, at its core, the center of all magic. Just being here made my skin all fluttery. As though it could feel all of that magic that had been here for centuries and could somehow harness it. It was a ridiculous thought, but it certainly felt like all of that ancient magic knew me.

Maybe it did.

Or maybe I was going bonkers.

"It only took us three months," Ovailia spat with a hint of disdain. Okay, not a hint, her voice was dripping with it.

She hadn't exactly been quiet about her distaste for how long all of this had taken. She wanted us all to just come running home like lost dogs with our tails between our legs.

"Yeah, I don't know if you remember, but Ilyan asked everyone to go slow, and you know... not get caught. Didn't he put you in charge?" I didn't hold back as I looked up from the book I had been occupying myself with while Talon and Ovailia had checked in and questioned the last of the Skříteks to make it back home to Imdalind.

Ovailia turned toward the carved alcove I was camped in, her blue eyes sparking dangerously. Her look of warning was only matched by Talon's. Talon might be Ilyan's second, and held the crimson ribbon of the další v příkazu that denoted that title, but when he was away from home the ruling title passed to the 'next in line to the throne'. Which technically, and to everyone's distaste, meant Ovailia was in charge.

Which meant I was essentially goading the Queen. Which was fine because I was loving every minute of it.

She was such a piece of work when she was snarling. And so easy to prod. Who could resist?

"This used to be done in weeks, Wynifred. Or don't you remember?" She grinned at me, her smile stretching as she goaded me. As she always did.

"Ovailia," Talon's joy was gone and replaced with a snarl of warning, something we both ignored.

One of Ovailia's favorite games was 'prod the Trpaslík who can't remember her childhood thanks to the stupid curse that still covers her skin.' I could already feel my anger rise, my magic boiling in waves of hot and cold. It wouldn't take much to explode the ground underneath her and send her tumbling through the air.

I smiled at the thought of her ankles going over her head as she shrieked. Something for later, maybe.

"I remember how to respect the king's orders." My fingers tightened around the book and she took a step forward.

"Do you?"

"Ovailia!" Talon's commanding tone just made her fume more, but I waved him off. I could take her.

"What are you even doing here, Wynifred? You are not part of Ilyan's command."

"I am, even if you keep forgetting." I shrugged and went back to my book, turning a page with a bit too much flourish, "Besides, I live here. Oh, and I'm bonded to the King's second."

I could hear Ovailia's jaw pop in frustration, Talon not too gracefully restraining a chuckle as he tucked the binder under his arm.

"Do you really dare to speak to me that way?" Ovailia was practically shrieking as she rushed me.

"Oh, I dare."

Talon wasn't even trying to hide his laugh now. "I think we are done here, Ovailia."

I turned another page with an unnecessary amount of theatrics. Ovailia opened her mouth as though she was going to retort before looking between us. She had lost, and she knew it. She gave one of her trademark shrieks and stomped away, mumbling something about having better things to do anyway.

"I win."

"You really should stop pestering her." Talon loomed over me, casting a shadow over my book. I looked up and gave him a grin.

"And miss out on all the fun?"

"I'd rather you not end up as a smudge on the stone floors." He was serious. I closed my book and stood, standing on my tiptoes to kiss him.

"That's half the fun. You know how much I would enjoy sparring with her. I would win, and she knows it. Which is probably why she always storms away rather than letting me egg her on that much." It was true. Years of trying, and I had never faced Ovailia in a fight. It would be a good fight, I liked to think that we were pretty fairly matched magically. At least she wouldn't defeat me in one blow like Ilyan did.

"I'm pretty sure she is under strict orders *not* to fight you, on account that you would both end up a bloodied mess." Poor Talon, he almost sounded worried about that.

"That's half the fun, Talon. And don't worry, I'd beat her." I gave him a grin as we turned out of the large entrance hall and into one of the smaller tunnels. This one led past most of the working rooms; the orchard, kitchens, gardens and what not. There were also a few annex rooms for meeting spaces. Those were my favorite; they were close enough to the kitchens that they always smelled like whatever was for dinner that night, and hadn't been used in years so they were mostly forgotten. I could practice my magic and bask in the smell of roast carrots to my heart's content..

"I know you would." He stopped, pulling me around to face him just as a gaggle of Skříteks moved passed us, nodding to Talon as they always did. "I just don't want you to get hurt, Wynny."

For that, I slugged him in the shoulder.

"Ow!"

"You deserved it. You know I can take care of myself, Talon. Even against Ovailia, no matter how much she pesters me about my 'oh so mysterious past'." I couldn't help but moan and wave my hands through the air in false mockery.

Talon sighed. "I'm going to have to talk to Ilyan about her. Again."

"Please don't. I keep hoping she will slip and tell me something I don't know." I gave him a look. He knew that look and exhaled with as much frustration as I had come to expect from him. "You made Ilyan bind our tongues, Wynny. You locked your past. I can't tell you what I don't know."

I knew that, but it was still frustrating. "Okay, then make it up to me. Tell me what Ilyan isn't telling us." He gave me a look, but I plowed on. It was time I knew something. "What's going on with Joclyn?"

She was my friend, practically my best friend and I was tired of being in the dark.

"You know I can't tell you everything Ilyan tells me. Besides, I don't know what is going on with Joclyn."

"Really?" I didn't believe him, and I made that clear in my voice.

I had not been oblivious to how weird the phone calls with Jos had been lately. Ilyan was even more protective than he was usually, which I didn't think was possible. Something was going on.

"Joclyn is--" His voice dropped as another group of Skříteks came around the corner, following the scent of Mernine Stew that was quickly filling the halls. Talon grabbed me by the arm and dragged me into the orchard, letting the fruit trees surround us as though they could mask our conversation.

"Is that why we are hiding in the orchard now? Because you don't know?" I was teasing him, and he knew it.

"I will say this. He was asking Ovailia about Sain."

"Sain? The Drak that gave the sight that prophesied the Silný?" The word was a shriek and he shushed me, dragging me deeper into the trees. "But all the Draks are dead."

"I only heard part of the conversation. I'm not sure what they were talking about, but it wasn't about the sight--"

"Don't touch me! Leave me alone!" We both turned at the shout.

Anything he had been about to say faded away as a shriek-like cry echoed through the large orchard, the feminine shout high pitched and in English. That alone was weird, we usually spoke Czech when we were at home.

"Did you hear that?" I took a step closer as an indistinguishable scream that drifted through the trees. This one softer, as though they were being dragged away.

"I did."

"You can't have her! I won't tell you anything!" The woman was frantic, hysterical.

"That's not normal," I mumbled, sending my magic away as I tried to search for whoever was making the noise. But the orchard was too big, and my magic was not skilled in scans.

My blood had turned to ice. Imdalind was a place of safety. Calm. Screams like that didn't happen here, not unless...

"Something is wrong..."

We exchanged a look before we took off, darting into the orchard in search of the voice.

In search of whatever might have followed us home.

CHAPTER 8
WYN

After five hours of searching the orchard we had found nothing and no one.

No source of the screaming. There wasn't even a sign of a fight.

We had even called everyone to the meeting hall to do a roll call. But no one was missing. No one had seen anything.

It was as though there was a ghost.

I would think I was going mad if Talon hadn't heard the voice too.

It didn't make it any less frustrating, though. Someone was hurt, and we couldn't find them.

My frustration was bordering on fury, which is why I had dragged Talon to the large caverns that were used for magical training.

And sparring.

I let all the frustration out in a blast of magic that soared across the large stone hall, bee-lining to Talon, who had graciously agreed to be my partner for this unleashing of the fury titans.

The look that he gave me as he dodged the attack made me wonder if he was regretting the decision.

"Do I need to go easy on you, old man?" I yelled across the cave to him, the Styx that I had playing in the background echoing around us. He rolled his eyes at me. He might be a few hundred years older than me, but we both knew that that didn't mean jack.

"Hell no!" He yelled over to me and set his feet in a fighting stance.

"Okay, if you say so." I gave him a second to rethink before I let all of that icy magic boil inside me, the waves of my power moving over my skin like a winter wind. I sent it toward him, intent on destroying the wall just to his left and showering him with rock.

It was one of my favorite things to do, make things explode. Normally, I would send the attack to the stone right before him, but I liked Talon and I did actually want to take him home in one piece.

He, however, knew what I was doing and threw up a Zmizêt, casually stepping to the side as he sent his own strings of magic to me. I threw up my own shield, although my Zmizêt was made of stone which shattered under the impact of his attack and showered me with shards of rock.

It was made even better by the song in the background. I was sure we looked like we were in some 70s sci-fi battle royale.

I nearly fell to the ground laughing. "Figures I would do what I was trying to do to you, to myself."

Talon's answering chuckle wasn't nearly as confident as mine. I popped my head above the rubble and gave him a smile and a wave. He visibly relaxed, until I sent another attack right at him. This time I didn't hold back.

I went for the stone under his feet, making it spread and crack in an attempt to trap him.

This was where the differences in the magic of a Trpaslík and a Skřítek became really noticeable. Skříteks manipulate things like air and fire to an amazing ability, whereas Trpaslíks harness the power of the earth like it's an obedient house dog.

We both can use the other, but never as well. I could never throw a fire spear like Talon could, for instance. Which is why I jumped to the side when he did just that, cursing at myself that I had missed him building that. My attack fizzed uselessly against the stone, while Talon's singed the shoulder of the shirt I was wearing, my skin burning hot as the attack made contact.

Crap! I was going down.

"Wynny!"

I landed on the stone, hard. My bare arm smashed against the stone with an impact that sent the ground vibrating underneath me as though I was a hundred ton boulder and not a tiny one-hundred-ten pound, five foot nothing, female.

Talon also collapsed to the ground as the ripples of my impact hit him, sending him to his knees. His eyes were wider than I had ever seen them, the grey-green orbs shaking as he froze, staring at the ground.

"What was that?" My voice was shaking as I sat up, watching the stone floor ripple as though I was a stone in a pond. "What in the world?"

"Wynifred! Are you okay?" Talon pushed himself up, practically sprinting the distance between us. Talon was clearly panicked, not only did he call me Wynifred, something he never did, but he looked like he had seen a ghost.

"Yeah," I shook my head and looked at my hands, wondering if I was covered with blood or something with the way he was looking at me. Nothing was there but a few scrapes from where I had tried to catch myself as I fell and failed. Well, that and the black tattoos from the curse I carried.

Those covered the entire right side of my body, and always would. They were still there, and regrettably intact.

"Yeah," I repeated, "I just lost track of my magic. I think."

We both knew that was a giant lie. I never lost track of my magic. I went to push myself up, but the second my hands made contact with the ground the same thing happened. The ground shook, ripples of earth moving away as though I had somehow turned it to water.

"What the hell?" I stared at my hands, trying to figure out what was going on. I had felt my magic flare that time. Except it hadn't felt like my magic at all. It had felt warm. Almost hot. Like it was flames inside of me.

As I looked at my hands, however, the heat vanished, leaving me with just the icy cold waves of the Trpaslík magic I was used to.

"Wynifred," Talon's voice was right in my ear, both of us kneeling on the stone as he held his hands out to me. "Let me see."

I gave him my hands, but instead of looking at the cuts on my palms, or feeling my magic, he turned my right hand over, his eyes glancing over the marks on my arm. As though they were responsible for whatever had just happened.

"Are you okay? How do you feel?"

"I'm fine. Although I would like to know what the hell just happened." I snatched my hand back and Talon straightened.

"It's just like the tourney in Milan, with Philip," he chuckled, eyeing me nervously as he spoke what might have been gibberish. I wasn't even sure he was talking to me, nothing about what he said made sense.

"Milan? Tourney?" I pushed myself to stand, carefully placing my hands on the stone. Thankfully nothing happened. "Tourneys are like a medieval thing, with knights and stuff, right? I'm not that old." I laughed, but somehow the sound was forced. "What are you talking about?"

"Nothing," he laughed, helping me to stand. "That's just a lyric from one of your bands, right? Electric Who Styx."

Now I couldn't help but laugh, "No, it's not, and that's not a band."

He shrugged, swiping his hand over the arena to clean it up. "It was a valid attempt. Do you want to..."

He let the question linger, looking between the sparring hall and the door back to our rooms.

"I think I would rather not turn any more stone into water," I swallowed, blinking a few times as I stared at the now perfectly normal sparring hall. "That did happen, didn't it?"

He nodded, pulling me closer to him as he practically pulled me out of the sparring hall and toward our rooms. Great, he was going into full body guard mode. Always the worry wort that one.

This whole thing was getting weird. I was the composed one. The powerful one. The one that liked to explode things while REO Speedwagon blasted on my Ghetto Blaster. But right then I was really, really freaked out. The way Talon was suddenly hovering over me like a worried guard dog was not helping.

"I'm fine, Talon." I tried to push him away so I could at least breathe, he was not having it. "Although I would like to know what that was all about. I could have sworn my magic felt hot for a second."

Talon pulled me to a stop and I almost tripped over his big feet.

"Talon?"

"You said it felt hot?" he asked, still stopping in the middle of the hall as he stared straight forward. I nodded in agreement. "Like boiling or like fire?"

"Fire." Okay, this was really starting to freak me out. That look was back on his face, the split second worry heightened before it was gone again.

This level of reaction for a little bit of weird magic, albeit creepy, was getting out of hand. I grabbed his hands, pulling him around to look at me. He would not escape my scowl.

"What is it Talon? What is going on with my magic?" *What are you not telling me?* I didn't ask that last one, even though the question rattled around in my head. Talon told me everything.

Well, everything except what I had Ilyan bind. Everything about my past.

He shook his head, "I don't know enough about Trpaslík magic to know. Maybe that happens when you exert yourself too much, or when a fire attack hits you."

I looked at him for a second. He wasn't wrong. We didn't know enough about my magic, and it wasn't like there were any more Trpaslíks here that we could ask. For all I knew it was normal. Even if it felt very, very wrong.

But I think we both knew that wasn't what I was asking. Not that he was going to tell me. Besides, if it was something to do with my past he couldn't.

"I've never been hit by fire before," I said, feeling like I was picking at straws. "If that's what it does, though, bring it on. Imagine how cool that could be in battle."

Talon only nodded numbly. He didn't seem nearly as excited as I was.

Poor thing. I really needed him to enjoy exploding things as much as I did.

CHAPTER 9
JOCLYN

The steady thrum of feet followed right behind me. I didn't have to turn to know who it was. It was the same man who always stalked my nightmares.

Edmund.

I turned a corner in the dilapidated house and squished myself against the burnt wainscoting, knowing full well it would not hide me. It didn't matter. The sooner they found me, the sooner I found them, and the sooner I could be released from the nightmares that had haunted me every night for months.

The nightmares were always different, although the general theme of them stayed the same. Cail would chase me from the forest to the house where I would die at the hands of Edmund, Ryland, Timothy, or Cail.

I felt a heavy thud in my chest as the sound of the shoes grew louder, Edmund's gait easily decipherable to me now.

Thump, whack, thump.

I pushed myself into the wall, my magic flaring in preparation as he came around the corner, Cail following him like an injured dog.

Tap, tap, *thwick!*

I pushed my hands toward him, sending a stream of light, but the attack bounced off of him, causing him to smile more. I pressed myself against the wall, eyes wide as I sought escape, knowing it was useless.

"Ah! There you are!" Edmund said joyfully, like an old grandfather welcoming home a prodigal child. Well, a prodigal child that he enjoyed torturing. My spine froze in terror and I hesitated a moment too long, allowing Cail to come up beside me and pin me to the wall.

I cringed away from the contact, away from what was coming, but it was no use. I could already hear the second set of footsteps approaching.

A soft step on the left, a slight drag on the right. My mind must have been paying much more attention than I gave it credit for to have pulled this little detail of Ryland into my nightly terrors.

"We were worried you didn't want to play," Edmund continued lightly, as if I wasn't being restrained. "We were worried we would have to chase you down all night."

"Chase me? Naw, I'm attacking you." I tried to flare my power toward him again, but he twisted his own magic in my gut and I felt my own retreat.

Edmund smiled and leaned toward me. I recoiled away from him, turning my head against the wall. A large lump blocked my throat at seeing Ryland slinking toward me, his eyes black, his beautiful face covered in a sheen of sweat.

"We didn't want to chase you down, did we Cail?" I couldn't pull my eyes away from Ryland as Edmund spoke. I stared at him as I tried to control the beating of my heart, the frantic mixture of panic and need making me dizzy.

"No, Master," Cail's voice was right in my ear, the putrid smell of his breath washing over me.

I was surrounded.

"Let me go, you bastards!" I tried to fight against Edmund, attack them all with my magic, but nothing was coming.

"You really are a silly little girl, aren't you?" Edmund laughed, Cail's laugh echoing it.

I had yet to understand the relationship my subconscious had created between Edmund and Cail. Edmund used him as a puppet, and every time Cail would obey without question. Sometimes his face would be screwed up in maniacal joy at what he was asked to do, and other times I could have sworn he was disgusted by it. It was as if my mind didn't know what to do with him.

I gasped at the pressure Cail put me under as I turned toward Edmund. Ryland now stood in between us, Edmund's hand resting lightly on his son's shoulder. It was the same image that had been burned into my head right before Ilyan had flown me away from them.

Edmund smiled at the panic on my face; his joy at my torture evident.

Cail laughed in my ear as he prepared for his part in this twisted performance.

"Look at you, thinking you can escape us," Ryland's light voice was laced with a venom I had grown used to hearing in these dreams.

"I can escape you," I snarled, my hands growing warm against him. It was no use, he ignored the attack and his hold only grew.

"What should I do with her, Father?"

Ryland's eyes never left mine as he smiled, Edmund's wicked grin joining his sons in perfect synchronization.

This was the only part of the dream I couldn't bat away, the only part I couldn't blame on my subconscious. I couldn't ignore it because the pain was real. It never followed me as I woke, but I couldn't shake all the pain that Ryland caused me. I couldn't wipe it from my mind.

"Pull her through."

It was a command I had never heard before and so I cried out in anticipation of the unknown. Seconds later, I felt Ryland's hand make contact with my stomach for a moment before the pain hit and the contact changed to something deeper. My stomach burned as his hand began to move through me, pulling my insides apart. I screamed louder.

I was still screaming as the dream faded away and the grey room that had been my prison for the last three months drifted into view. The comforter shifted as Ilyan came to my rescue. He moved to lay behind me and pulled me against his bare chest, his magic flowing into me and calming my frayed nerves. His arms were tight, pulling me against him before they caressed the skin on my arms. My screaming died down, but the tears remained. They flowed freely down my cheeks and onto the pillowcase, wetting a spot so soaked every night that it had been stained with the salt water from my tears. It was the only time I cried anymore; the only time my emotions were raw enough to let the dratted things escape.

"Shhh... Silný, it's okay. To je v pořádku."

I leaned into Ilyan as he began to sing his song, the words whispered gently in my ear. As Ilyan sang, I sang with him, my voice shaky against my tears, the Czech words flowing roughly off of my tongue.

"Hush now, child. Be still, be calm. The world will change at the new dawn, and when it does, you will see how you and I were meant to be."

I sang it over and over again, long after Ilyan had fallen asleep, his arms still wrapped around me.

I wasn't going to get any more sleep tonight. And not just because

Ilyan's arm around me had become a deadweight over my side. Those dreams were a little too real, and the fear of another one kept me awake.

I lifted his arm off me and slid from the bed and onto the floor, my knees coming up to press against my chest. I pulled my black hoodie over my knees, trapping the warmth against my body. I sat like that with my fuzzy pink socks poking out, my eyes focused on the carpet that once had held the dark stain of my rotten magic.

We had been confined to the claustrophobic depths of the studio apartment ever since I had survived the attack of my own magic on my body three months ago. I knew that hiding away was the only way to keep my magic hidden from Ryland and his father, but that didn't help the 'prisoner for life' vibe it gave me. I was restrained inside of this space with Ilyan's strong, immovable shield around me at all times.

Which left me with nothing to do other than perfect, expand, and stretch my magic. I had thrown myself into preparing to fight; to keep myself alive for when I came face to face with the real Edmund.

The real bastard, not his dream version.

It was going to happen. I had to leave eventually.

Until then, though, I practiced and I visited Ryland in our Tòuha.

That was just as much of a requirement as preparing to end Edmund. If I went too long between Tòuhas my body began to ache, my energy exhausted.

Even though I loved the sensation Ryland's magic gave me, even though I longed to see him, I still dreaded going into the Tòuha. Every time I saw Ryland inside, it was the equivalent of seeing someone through glass, never being able to truly touch them. Never knowing if you would ever be able to break the glass and get them back. It was painful, but I had to go. If I didn't my body would waste away to nothing again.

Pulling out the ruby necklace, my finger rubbed against the scar that rested over my heart, the skin raised and jagged.

I hated that scar as much as I hated the mark below my ear, each one a painful reminder of what I had lost, but sadly, I could handle my mark better. The mark had just appeared there, it hadn't been carved into my skin by someone I loved. Whether or not he was in his right mind at the time, it was still Ryland's body, his face, that had hurt me.

I pushed the thought away and filled the necklace—my only connection to Ryland—with my magic. My body grew warm and filled me with the heat of Ryland's power as his latent magic that lived inside of me awakened. It was the same comforting warmth I had grown up with, the same feeling my body constantly craved.

My eyes closed and I wandered into the colorful world that lived beyond my eyelids. I had spent every morning of the last few months coming in here and coloring with Ryland, sharing our dreams, talking about stories and making up our own.

It was a place where we created new memories while our old ones lay forgotten.

Well, at least his did.

"Jossy!" Ry bolted toward me, running headlong into me so that we both fell backwards onto the hard floor. Ryland sat up from where we landed, his pointy elbows digging into my stomach. He smiled his large grin that I loved so much, his blue eyes twinkling.

"Hey Ry, did you miss me?" I asked, pushing his long, black curls out of his eyes.

"You know I did, Jossy, you're so funny."

"You sure about that?" I asked, poking him in the ribs.

He could hear the mischief in my voice so he jumped up and away from me before I could grab and tickle him.

"Don't, Jossy," Ryland squealed.

"Why not?" I asked, moving up on all fours in an attempt to look like I was going to lunge at him.

"Because, if you do, I can't show you my new drawing,"

"A new one?"

Without being able to leave, Ryland had continued to spend all of his time coloring new masterpieces to fill the white void. Every time I came he had a new drawing to share or a new story that he wanted to tell me.

He grabbed my hand and towed me behind him toward a divot in the floor we had lovingly named 'the swimming pool'. I willingly followed; his joy at sharing his new creation infectious.

"Just wait until you see it," he called back to me, "I want to play 'Princess and the Dragon of Delagn' after you see it, 'kay? It looks just like a dragon."

"Okay, but can I be the dragon this time? I'm tired of being the... princess," I stammered to a stop as Ryland signaled toward the wall where he had drawn his masterpiece.

A giant cage stood as tall as I did, the huge drawing made with heavy black lines. Inside the cage unintelligible figures had been drawn in hundreds of colors. The door to the cage stood open, Ryland standing next to it, and on his finger perched Ryland's 'dragon'. It was small and scaled like a dragon or a dinosaur, but it wasn't a dragon at all. Its scales were a bright jewel blue and on his back were large, feathered wings. The face of the creature was somewhat feminine yet distorted somehow. Its cheek bones were high, eyes large and wide, and its nose was almost nonexistent. Even though I had only fleetingly seen one before, I knew what it was immediately.

Ryland had drawn a Vilỳ.

The little creature that had given me my mark, his poisonous bite awakening my magic. My hand moved to cover the mark underneath my ear.

"Do you like him?" Ryland asked, "I am going to name him Opal because he kind of looks like a woman, but I really think it's a man."

I only half heard what Ryland had said. I couldn't rip my eyes from the intricate drawing. This picture was much more detailed than Ryland had drawn before, more than a child his age should be able to.

"When did you draw this, Ryland?"

"Last night, it took some time, but it was worth it. See, this is me, holding Opal. I am about to let him loose and he's going to grow big and strong and destroy an evil wizard. You can be Opal, and I'll be myself and the wizard, cuz I always wanted to be a wizard..."

"Did you see this somewhere before?" I interrupted him, panicking a bit. "Why did you draw this?"

Ryland screwed up his face and squared his shoulders, upset I wasn't going to play his game. "I just drew it, Jossy. It didn't come from anywhere. I thought it would be a fun game."

"A game." I ran my fingers over the delicate chalk of the Vilỳ's face, careful not to smudge the marks. "Do you know what this means?"

"If you want to be the wizard that's fine, I just thought it would be cool if..."

"You remember me," I spun to him and grabbed his tiny little shoulders.

I looked deep into his eyes, expecting him to smile and be his old self right away, but nothing happened. He gazed at me like I had gone mad.

"Of course I remember you, you're right here."

I stood and wheeled away from him, back to the black door that served as my exit.

"I have to go."

"You have to go?" he called after me, his little voice upset. "But, you just got here! We have to play the game. Don't you want to be Opal?"

I turned back to him when I had reached the door we had created in exit, my gut wrenching to see tears in his eyes. "I'll be back, Ry. Okay? I need to go tell Ilyan something and then I'll be right back."

"You promise you'll come back today?"

"Of course I do." I ruffled his hair before turning the knob of my door, my eyes opening instantaneously to the brightening apartment.

"Ilyan!" I noticed the empty mass of blankets on the floor and turned to the bed to find it empty as well. I hadn't been gone long—less than twenty minutes in the Tŏuha, meaning it would only have been a matter of minutes in the real world. I stood up and ran to the bathroom door, hearing water running behind it. Steam seeped underneath the door, filling the room with a warm, musty smell.

"Ilyan!" I called through the door, knowing he would ignore me the first few times. Ilyan needed his morning showers to wake him up or he was grumpy all day.

"Ilyan!" I called again, this time letting my magic flow through the door to turn off the water. I heard Ilyan swear loudly in Czech before turning it back on. I knew I shouldn't bug him, doing this would only make him more upset, but I didn't care. My heart beat uncomfortably, the drawing still visible in my mind's eye. I knew I shouldn't dare to hope—dare to dream—but I couldn't stop myself.

"Ilyan, it's important!" I tried again.

"Is someone dying?" he yelled back. "Are *you* dying? Because I think I have reached my quota for saving your life this year!" Yep. Definitely surly.

I kicked my toe against the door and offered up my own brand of cussing. Fine. If he wasn't going to come out, then I would send the drawing to him. I pressed my palm against the door and let my magic flare, sending the image right into Ilyan's mind. I waited a moment, and then I heard it, a sharp intake of breath. The water shut off and a moment later the door opened to reveal Ilyan; wet, soapy, and only covered by a towel from the waist down. His wet hair fell over his shoulders, dripping down the skin of his scarred chest. I gulped and looked away. This wasn't the first time I had seen him like this, but it always made me uncomfortable.

"Where did you get that?" he said, ignoring my reaction to him.

"Ryland. He drew it," I said, my face breaking out into a wide smile.

"He drew it?" His eyes narrowed as though he didn't believe me. I folded my arms and stared him down.

"Yes, he drew it. He wanted to play a game about it. He didn't understand what it was."

"Show me." Ilyan grabbed my hand and placed it against his forehead. I sighed as his magic pulsed and flowed into me, pulling the memory out of my head.

I watched the Tồuha replay; the speed picked up, slowed down, and repeated itself as Ilyan gleaned the information he wanted. The second he was done, I pulled my hand away. Ilyan had done that to me once before, when he was trying to teach me how to do it myself, and it had given me a headache then, too. He could only perform that particular magic with certain people, and seeing as I was one of them, I guess he figured he had permission to do it whenever he wanted to without asking.

"See?" I asked, still bouncing on my toes in excitement. "He remembers, doesn't he?"

"I am not sure. He could, or it could simply be a desire he had at that age."

I stopped bouncing immediately, my hope falling to my toes. "What do you mean, a 'desire'?"

Ilyan shifted his towel and ran his fingers through his wet hair, his tell for when he didn't want to share something with me. I folded my arms over my chest, refusing to look away from him.

"Ilyan," I said, "tell me." He hesitated a moment longer.

"Edmund kept Vilỳ in that cage for hundreds of years. Ryland must have known about their existence from the day he was born. He is not without a heart; he can't look at a trapped creature and not wish to release them. The drawing could very easily be a projection of his desire to let them go at the time. I didn't even know it was Ryland who had let the Vilỳ out until you told me last spring, and besides that, who knows how he let them out, or how many, or even what color." He finished, his eyes never leaving mine.

"But the Vilỳ was blue, just like the Vilỳ who bit me." I said, my resolve weakening as I clung to my last bit of hope. Even though Ilyan's irritating logic was drowning it far too fast.

"It could be a coincidence."

"So, you are saying he doesn't remember me at all?"

"You know where I stand on this, Joclyn." Ilyan reached out to put a wet hand on my shoulder, but I moved away from him.

"But, I saw it. He can't... He has to..." I stumbled around, my chest heaving angrily.

"I am sorry, Silnỳ. I didn't know you were still holding out hope." I snapped my head up to him, the magic in my fingers prickling angrily.

"You should be holding out hope, too, Ilyan. Even if you don't think it could ever happen, you should still believe there is a chance. He's your brother. You can't turn your back on that."

Ilyan opened his mouth to rebut, but said nothing. His lack of response made me more upset.

"Enjoy your shower," I spat, and with one thought, I sent him flying away from me. He hit the shower curtain and crumpled into the shower as I turned the hot water on over him. I looked at his startled face for a moment before slamming the door between us, my hands still in balls by my sides.

CHAPTER 10
JOCLYN

I sat with my back against the sliding glass door that led out to the tiny balcony. The balcony I wasn't allowed to enter, that was filled with fresh air I wasn't allowed to breathe. I sat this way so I didn't have to look out onto the city of Santa Fe and be taunted with the possibility of leaving my prison.

My head leaned against the cool glass, my eyes closed in concentration. I leaned my head against the glass, hands on my folded knees, fingers extended as I allowed my magic to pulse and flow into the air and used my mind to control the objects that littered the ground in front of me.

A top spun gracefully on its point, a block changed color in a rainbow of hues, the carpet they sat on grew in length while flexing and bending around the other two objects. All the while, a flurry of conjured snowflakes danced and spun around me as I sat cross-legged against the glass.

It was probably a little excessive, but I needed to keep my mind off of my fight with Ilyan.

Ryland's drawing had dug up my passionate hope that he was trapped instead of erased. Then Ilyan's offhand comments had just as quickly dashed them. I was trying so hard not be mad at him, but I was fighting a losing battle.

I closed my eyes tighter as the water from Ilyan's shower stopped. My anxiety increased the speed of the top, the influxes of color, and the movement of the carpet. Without opening my eyes I could still see the objects moving in front of me. It was just as Ilyan had taught me, my magic served as my second eye, the whole room visible within my mind.

The door to the bathroom creaked open and my mind glanced away from its work to see Ilyan exit. His blonde hair was wet and hanging down to his shoulder blades, soaking the top of his yellow, button up shirt. I returned my sight back to the objects in front of me, increasing my workload to include the carpet in the color changing cacophony. I accelerated the snowflakes that danced around my head until they were a white blur.

The distorted mass of white and color all became too much and I shut off my internal sight to sit in the blackness, the cool glass pressing against the back of my head, until Ilyan's soft hands wrapped around my fingers, distracting the flow of my magic.

His touch was gentle against my skin, his hands holding tightly to mine. I felt the top fall to the side and the snowflakes melted back into the air as my magic disconnected from them.

I looked up at him, ready to bicker or battle or whatever he had in mind after I had thrown him into the shower, but instead his eyes were closed. His face was calm as he sat before me, his tall frame folded gently.

"I was thirty-two when Ovailia was born, an old man by human standards at the time. I remember running to Prague to see my parents, leaving the monastery I lived at in the middle of the night. There had been some complications with the birth, but I was told my mother was healing fine. I was still worried, which is why I didn't wait to go to them. I ran into her room expecting healers and burning oils, but my mother was alone. She looked so fragile in her giant bed, her small frame swallowed up by blankets. She placed this tiny baby in my arms; a girl with hair that looked like sunlight. That's what Ovailia means, 'light of the sun'."

Ilyan looked at me, his face blotchy enough that I knew he had been crying in the shower. His grip tightened on my hands, keeping me close to him. He knew me well enough now that he could tell when I began to shy away from contact, but this time even I was fighting that impulse. I had never heard Ilyan open up before, and I desperately wanted to know more. His voice was so soft that I leaned in to hear him better.

"She had blue eyes, like me, like my father. He was so proud." It was weird to hear such a normal memory of Edmund; my brain almost fought the image of him as a normal, loving father to Ilyan.

"He clapped me on the back and said soon it would be my turn." Ilyan smiled, but it was a sad smile. For the first time I wondered why he wasn't married, why he had never bonded. I opened my mouth to ask, yet thought better of it. It wasn't my place, and besides, I really wanted to hear what he had to say.

"I held this little baby in my arms and promised to protect her. To keep her safe. I guarded her as she grew, taught her, and played with her. She could beat me in a flying race before she was ten... and then my father turned. Ovailia had always been closer to him than I was. They had gone everywhere together; had secrets I would never understand. I didn't know what had happened until it was too late. Until I couldn't protect her anymore. She had seen one hundred and twenty years when she came to the small chapel in France where I lived, covered in blood and begging for help. I wasn't even sure then that I could trust her. I am still not sure."

I squeezed his hands, not knowing any other way to comfort him. Without thinking, I reached up to touch his face, but my hand stopped halfway there and fell to my lap. Ilyan dropped my other hand and stood, turning his back to me as he dragged his fingers through his hair in frustration.

"He has done it to all my siblings, Joclyn. Destroyed them. Hurt them. Ovailia was the first of many. He's destroyed all of them, leaving me only one shattered sister that's willing to side with me. That's why I don't hold out hope. Because I know what he is capable of. But, please, I don't want to dash your hope. It was never my intention to hurt you; I never wanted to break your heart. If you believe, then I will believe, too. Can you forgive me for dashing your hope before? For being so rude?"

I stared at him for much longer than necessary, my brain still processing this little bit of his past. For the past few months I had gotten to know Ilyan better than I had anyone else. Anyone other than Ryland. I had thought I understood Ilyan, but hearing this part of his history made me realize how little I knew. There were a thousand years of him I did not know.

Even with all of that, I knew the face he had when he was truly sorry. I knew of his goodness. And I saw both of those now.

"Yes, Ilyan, of course." His face lit up at my words.

"Thank you," he replied softly before he stood, his eyes gleaming with the maniacal energy I had seen too many times before. I cringed at what I already knew was coming. For the last few months that look had usually accompanied our training sessions. "I have a little proposition for you."

"Do I need to be worried?" I asked, sliding my hand through the air in front of me to send the block and the top back to their places on the table.

"Perhaps." Ilyan grinned and lifted his hands. The table and the nightstand moved themselves into the kitchen at the same time that the bed stood on end in order to give us the most space possible. I groaned and leaned my head back against the glass.

"Sparring... really? This is how you make it up to me?" I hated sparring. I hated holding weapons that were hundreds of years old. I hated hitting Ilyan with power and magical attacks, but most of all I hated being hit with them. "This is punishment, not a reward."

Ilyan seemed to find my response humorous; he laughed and slid his hands down in front of him, a large sword appearing from nothing.

"Swords? You are so archaic."

"I'm a thousand years old, Joclyn. So, yes, I am."

I screwed up my face to keep from laughing. He was right, of course, when battling ancients I guess the use of broadswords was a necessary skill to learn.

"I still think this is a punishment." Magic alone was more effective to use fatally against another magic user and guns were of no use because bullets would be easily disintegrated by a simple shield. He was just being mean.

"Oh, trust me, this is half reward and half punishment for throwing me into the shower." His eyes twinkled as I moved to stand. I could stubbornly sit on the floor and refuse to participate, but he would attack anyway. I had tried it before and the results were not positive.

"I am sorry about that," I pleaded, I even jutted out my lower lip comically, even though I knew it was no good. "Can you at least tell me the reward portion of this?"

I slid my hand through the air to produce my own sword for the battle I was about to endure. My weapon was nowhere near the caliber of Ilyan's. His was engraved with jewels, the metal twisting beautifully. Mine was a boring, solid metal t-shape; the kind they used in theatre class. I needed to work on creating something better, but I wasn't sure I cared enough. I groaned and swung the sword, the metal feeling awkward in my hands.

"Well, since you have decided that Ryland's mind might still be intact..."

"We," I corrected him, rolling my eyes.

"Yes, well if he is in fact 'there' I know someone who can help us, but he is a bit too far away at the moment. Which means, we will have to go to him." Ilyan began swinging his sword around in preparation while mine clattered to the floor.

"We're leaving the apartment?" I said.

"Yes, but...."

I didn't let him finish, I squealed and ran to him, wrapping my arms around his neck tightly.

"Thank you, thank you, thank you," I sang as I danced around on his toes.

"You are welcome, but you do need to let me finish." He pried me away from him and I stepped away, still dancing.

"We will leave the apartment once you can beat me in a sparring match." Ilyan concluded and my shoulders dropped, my jaw falling open.

"Really? I'm never getting out of this hell hole." I kicked my sword in frustration, the heavy metal popping my toe out of joint. My magic quickly repaired it and I stomped around a bit, cursing the tiny apartment and its lack of space. I gave up after a minute and pulled my hood down lower over my head.

"I'll make you a deal," Ilyan said from behind me, and I turned.

"Weren't we already making a deal?"

"This is a new one."

"If it's anything like your last deal, I don't think I am interested." I folded my arms and glared at him. Ilyan took two steps forward and tugged on some of my hair that stuck out of my hood.

"If you can mark me once, right now, I will take you out on a date tonight."

"A date?" I scoffed, confused.

"Alright, well not a date. A non-committal dinner and movie outing with a friend." He winked and I felt my insides shift. "It gets you out of here..."

"I just have to mark you once?" I was very skeptical. Marking Ilyan once was usually still the equivalent of winning a match against him, only slightly more attainable.

"Just once," he assured me. I nodded and reached my hand out, the sword flying into my grasp.

"Just once," I repeated. "Consider it done."

I moved my sword in front of me as Ilyan had taught, the point looking him right in the eye. Ilyan did the same, but his face held a curious little smirk, not the terrified expression I was sure I displayed. I held still, clenching my jaw and waiting for him to make the first move. When it became obvious he wouldn't, I lunged at him. He smoothly moved from one position to another, his sword clanging loudly as it hit mine. The impact sent me off balance and I stumbled to the side, ramming my shoulder into the wall.

"My point." Ilyan announced. I scowled and turned around to see him shifting his sword from side to side, spinning the blade. I didn't wait this time, I lunged. Ilyan moved quickly and the clashing of our blades reverberated through the small space as we fought.

I continued to try to mark him, to hit him, or throw him off balance with no success.

"Ugh!" I yelled. I had to be able to do something. Ilyan merely smiled at me in response and continued his attacks.

While I wasn't bad at this by any means, Ilyan was just that much better. I swung wide and aimed for his blind side only to be pushed away by his swift movements. Then, as he arced wide for another attack, I stumbled again and flailed around in an attempt to block him, my sword barely meeting his.

"Come on, Silnỳ!" he yelled, his accent deep and rumbling. "Play hard, fight hard."

"Maybe if you'd stop moving so fast..." I growled under my breath.

"I heard that." He smiled.

I shook my head and came at him again, this time trying for his legs. Ilyan saw my move and jumped away, his sword sweeping out to tap against my shoulder.

"My point," he announced, his cocky undertone grinding on me.

I jumped up, instantly going for another attack. I almost had him when an invisible barrier blocked my path. I always forgot how quick he was until he used his magic against me.

"Not fair! Foul Play!"

Ilyan smiled at my outburst.

"I didn't say magic was off limits, Silnỳ. In fact, I ask that you use your power. In battle you will not be constrained to weapons, if you use them at all." He bowed deeply to me, his sword disappearing back into the air it had come from. I swallowed and let my sword fall to the floor, clanging loudly. Now I was in trouble, our sparring matches always led to this, and I always failed miserably.

'Attack me with magic.' he would say.

'Why don't I stand still so you can land all your attacks on me without hassle?' I would rebut.

Well, not really. I wouldn't dare say that to him. That was how it always went, though. There was no glory in this for me, only pain and more broken toes.

Ilyan spread his hands once in a high arch and the walls shimmered as he trapped us in another protective shield. This one guaranteed that we wouldn't destroy the tiny prison.

But it wouldn't be a prison for long. I just had to mark him once and I could leave for the night. Win the match, and I could leave forever. I jumped to my feet, I could do this.

I didn't hesitate this time. I needed the upper hand if I was going to have any chance of marking him. I sliced my hand through the air, sending a long chain of magical energy soaring to him like a javelin with the intent to wrap him in it like a vice. Ilyan jumped back as he diminished the flow of my attack, but not before the end of the chain sliced through his shirt.

"Very nice, Silnŷ. But not good enough." I saw his motion a moment too late and dove to the side as a ripple of energy impacted with the shield that surrounded us, sending a wave of colors vibrating through the protective layer.

"Try harder," he yelled as he sent a line of freezing water above my head. I winced when it hit the shield above me, showering me with droplets of ice.

I threw my hand out, shooting a pulse of light and fire toward him, which breezed through the bright colors that fluxed around us. I didn't stop to see if it made contact, instead I scrambled to my feet hoping to gain my bearings. I faced him and instantly threw a handful of conjured metal beads in his direction. The pellets disintegrated against Ilyan's personal shield as he streamed electricity toward me. I threw a shield up just in time, the powerful magic crashing into my barrier instead.

"Fight back, Joclyn. You would have won in the bathroom. You had it all, emotional force, surprise..."

"The fact that you were only wearing a towel didn't hurt, either," I countered, throwing another attack in his direction only to have him dodge it. Ilyan laughed boisterously at me.

"Yes, but how often are you going to be fighting someone in a towel?" He shot another surge in my direction, which I countered, and the two streams collided in the center surrounding us with brightly colored sparks.

"Not often enough," I said under my breath.

"That is why Ryland will always defeat you. He can play on your emotions, and he knows it."

"Don't remind me." I shoved wind in his direction, smiling when he skidded away from me again.

Ilyan brought this up every day. This time, however, I realized that he had given me a weapon, too. I could play on Ilyan's emotions.

I waited for his next attack only to dodge it. I embraced my speed, moving as quickly as I could to sidle right up to him. I grabbed his shirt and pulled his tall body into me, his face millimeters away from mine.

"Don't hurt me." I said softly as I placed my hand gently against the skin of his neck. I let my hand grow warm with power for a moment to signal to him that I had won. His eyes changed from soft and concerned to a smoldering pride so fast I might have missed the change had I not been looking directly at him.

"I win."

"Now, *that* is dirty, Joclyn." I stepped away from him, laughing victoriously. "I am not sure if I can accept that as a win."

"You better!" I snapped, "It had all the elements of a successful attack plus surprise and a play on emotions, just like you said. Although why it worked on you, I will never know."

"I'm your protector, Silný. I am hard-wired not to hurt you." He released the barrier and put the room back together with one swipe of his hand, but I stayed still, my brain clicking together.

"My protector?" I asked. "What do you mean, *my* protector?"

Ilyan stopped and turned to face me, his hand dragging heavily through his hair again. "I protect everyone, Joclyn. You included."

I just stared at him in disbelief. He had said that before and I had taken it to mean just that, but this time his inflection had been different. Something had been off in the way he said it, as though it was a job he took pride in. It didn't just mean wandering around and saving people to him. He was still dragging his hand through his hair, making it obvious he was keeping something from me.

"Get a better poker face, Ilyan. What aren't you telling me?" Ilyan smiled at me before returning from the kitchen, a small box in his hands.

"Až jednou pochopíš všechno a přijmeš, kdo jsi, poté, a teprve poté, ti povím všechno, má lásko. Ale ani o vteřinu dřívě." I glared at him. He knew my Czech consisted of 'pass the leaves' and 'where is the bathroom'.

"Understand? Accept what? Love what? What did you say, Ilyan? You know I don't understand most of what you said. My Czech is not very good." He smiled at me and placed the small box in my hands.

"Exactly."

I jerked the box away from him. I hated cryptic answers, and Ilyan was full of them.

"I made those for you, for Prague, but wear them tonight. They will look nice in the city. I am going to go get you something besides pajama pants to wear. Stay inside." He smiled at me once before leaving, the door locking behind him.

I looked down to the box, a small pink ribbon tied around the top. It never ended well when a man made anything for a woman to wear, and the thought of what could be inside this package worried me.

I slipped the bow from the box and tipped it, letting the contents fall out into my hands.

The most intricate red leather shoes rolled onto my palms. I could tell right away they would fit perfectly. The toes of the shoes were folded into a fan shape that gave the impression of a blossoming rose. A tiny pearl was nestled in the middle of each one. Surrounding the sole of the shoe was a five part leather braid that circled seamlessly around. I couldn't find the beginning or the end. The stitching around the sole and around the top was small and intricate, each one done with precision. I stared at the shoes in awe. That these could be made by a person, let alone Ilyan, was impossible. I lay the sturdy shoes on the floor and slipped my bare feet into them. They were beautiful.

Of course, I recognized them as what he had been working on while I had lain dying months before. While he had been nursing me, healing me, he had also been working on these shoes. Even then, he hadn't thought I was going to die.

I hadn't considered it in three months, but now I couldn't help wondering what Ilyan's backup plan could have been. I had known he had something else in mind if joining Ryland in the Tȍuha hadn't cured me. Something deep inside told me these shoes were meant for that, not for a night on the town.

CHAPTER 11
ILYAN

I was torturing myself.

Talon had warned me of this for years, and now it was here.

She was here.

All of her stubborn, fiery, beautiful self.

As much as I tried to distance myself, to create a firm line between us, I was failing. I would fail every time she woke up afraid. I would fail anytime that she was in danger.

I would fail again and again.

No where was that more evident than this morning. I was so used to my father destroying my siblings, so ready to take my place by her side, that I had already assumed Ryland to be a lost cause.

But he wasn't. To her he would never be. So, to me he would never be. And not just because he was my brother.

But because of the role he was playing in all of this.

I would never cross that line. I knew what she was to me, and what she would always be.

I just hadn't expected the heartache that came along with it.

Torture. Talon had warned me and Talon was right.

"A non-committal night out to dinner," I grumbled the words to myself in Czech and opened the door to the apartment complex with a bang, scaring the old lady who had been on the other side.

"My apologies," I bowed and opened the door for her before stalking away, hair swinging around my face as I raced across the street to the lines of stores there.

I needed to get her clothes and get back. I hated being away for too long.

Thankfully, most of the stores featured mannequins covered in preconceived outfits for women of nearly Joclyn's height and build. It was perfect. One store in and I already had an outfit for her, perfectly selected from the mannequins and the magazine they had thankfully been selling at the checkout. The bright colors of the top would stand out nicely against her hair, blend with those eyes that were always so full of determination.

I hoped she liked it.

Of course, I knew her well enough now to know that wearing such small amounts of fabric was not something she took pleasure in. She needed a hoodie. Santa Fe was too hot to wear one outside, but I wanted to do something nice.

I had only taken one step into the store when my phone buzzed, 'Hall of the Mountain King' playing loud enough that a few heads turned.

"Ahoj, Talon," I said, slipping right into Czech. There were already too many people staring at me and I didn't want to be overheard.

"Wyn's magic slipped."

I froze. My fingers curling around the flimsy plastic hanger I had just picked up. It snapped in two.

"No. That's not possible," I said as I put the now broken hanger back on the rack. "That bind hasn't shifted, I would know. I would have felt something."

"I know, Ilyan, but there is no mistaking it." His voice was low, strained. I hadn't heard Talon so worried. Not since the day we had all gone after Edmund and we had lost track of Wyn in the fight.

The day Cail put that damn curse on her.

I stood up straighter, my magic pulsing. "What did she do?"

"You know that trick she used to love? The one with the waving rocks?"

A smile twitched on the corner of my mouth. Yes, I knew that one. Anyone who had been around Wyn before the mid 1800s knew that one. "Did she do it on purpose?"

"No. Just when her hand made contact with the ground. She didn't know what happened."

So, the bind hadn't slipped completely. Not that it made the situation any better. If the bind slipped and Wyn's magic was freed, there was no way she could control it without her memories. Which would mean I would have to unbind those too. It had taken her hundreds of years to master it the first time around and we didn't need to turn all of Imdalind to rubble.

"Did you tell her?" My voice was a rumble as I moved to another rack, this one full of sweaters emblazoned with different logos referring to Santa Fe. As I moved, a group of women in the back watched me. Eyes wide. Smiles a little too plastered on.

My magic flared. I couldn't feel anything from them, but that didn't mean they weren't connected to Edmund in some way.

Edmund couldn't be here already could he?

"How can I? You bound me against it."

"*She* bound you, Talon. I just completed the magic." I moved to another rack, two of the girls full on following me now. Giggling, daring each other to ask me out.

So, not Edmund's men, but perhaps just as bad.

"I know."

"So chances are the bind is still there. But something is releasing--"

"Could it be the curse?" Talon interrupted me, and I put down the sweater I was holding, my heart rate picking back up again.

"That is bound to Cail," I held the phone closer, watching the still prowling girls out of the corner of my eye. "If it's that, then Edmund has done something to him. Or is doing something to him powerful enough that it weakens him so he can't control it like he has been." Like controlling Ryland. Like weaponizing the boy. Neither of those were wanted. "How are her marks?"

"Strong. Still dark."

"That's good. Watch her Talon, if it happens again, or the marks start to fade, let me know."

"And what if they do?" That question was not the question he was truly asking. He knew what Wyn had demanded as much as we did. No memory or a swift death. She didn't want to live with what she had done, or what she had lost.

Unfortunately for her, I was the King, and I got to choose what sacrifices to make.

"I don't care what promises I made her in the past, keeping her alive now is vital. I care for her too, Talon. If it happens again, I will break the bind, and I will tell her everything."

"She asked us--"

"A woman from over a hundred years ago asked us to bind her memories, Talon. The woman of today has asked to know." I knew I was grasping at straws. He knew it too.

"She won't like what she finds."

"I know." There was a reason she had made the demands she had. "Just watch her, Talon."

"I will. How is everything going with Joclyn?"

I had been busying myself with digging through a bin of clearance t-shirts in an attempt to avoid the still prowling women, but at Talon's question I stood up. Heart going into overdrive.

"Torture." I repeated his word choice back to him and he chuckled.

"I told you it would be."

"You warned me for a thousand years, and I walked into the trap anyway." We both laughed at that, the sound pulling every head back over to me again. It was only then I noticed I had at least three women skirting the edges of my vision.

"*Yours to protect but never to hold.*" I mumbled the line of the sight to myself, accidentally snapping a hanger in two in the process.

I needed to get out of here.

And not just the store. Here. I needed answers, and there was only one Drak left that could give those to me.

"We are moving tonight. There is someone I need to see. Someone I need Joclyn to meet," I said as I paid for the hoodie, a green one with Santa Fe written in orange and green. It seemed warm, she would need warm for where we were going. I had also gotten a size bigger than I knew she needed.

"Do you need an escort?"

"No," I shook my head and took my bag with a nod to the cashier who was also batting her eyes at me. I was beginning to wonder if this part of Santa Fe was somehow devoid of men. "But keep your phone on."

"I will, My Lord."

"And Talon." I stopped, letting my magic flare outside of the building. If I was about to be attacked, I would like to know. Thankfully, I couldn't sense anything from here to Joclyn. It was safe. She was safe. "Go easy on my sister. I've gotten five calls from her today."

"That is not me. That would be Wyn."

I sighed, of course it was.

"Perhaps we should unbind Wyn's memories; if only so those two can finally have it out with each other." I had said it as a joke, but Talon was dead serious.

"If you want a home to come home to, I would highly suggest against that."

I laughed as I hung up the phone, the girl that had been eyeing me through the whole conversation stepping ever closer.

She was pretty, a slight little thing with a nice smile.

I knew what she wanted.

She couldn't have it. I would always be someone else's, even if she could never be mine.

I gave her a curt nod and turned, striding out of the store and back home. Toward the girl that would always be out of reach.

CHAPTER 12
JOCLYN

It took a minute after Ilyan had left our tiny apartment for reality to click in. Ilyan was getting me clothes, and I was going to leave. Of course, this would mean being around people again—something I really wasn't fond of—but I would be outside my current prison and that was all that mattered.

I bounced on my toes and took the few steps to retrieve the cell phone Ilyan left for me from the kitchen counter. I flipped the phone open and speed dialed to call Wyn. As the phone rang, I paced the floor in anticipation. It was surprising how soft the shoes were. The leather clung to my feet with the few steps I took. I could tell I was going to love them.

"Hello?" She sounded groggy. Odd, it was only nine at night in Prague right now.

"Wyn!" I almost screamed, my excitement exploding out of me. "I get to leave!"

It didn't even take her a moment for what I had said to sink in. She squealed and repeated it, presumably to Talon who was always nearby.

"When are you leaving? Are you coming home? Please tell me you are coming right home," she rattled on, Talon chuckling in the background.

"I'm not sure yet. Ilyan is taking me out for dinner tonight. Then we get to leave soon."

"But you don't know where to yet?" Her voice had dropped, and my heart sunk with it. I was so excited to be leaving the apartment, I hadn't thought about where we would end up, yet the thought of not getting to see Wyn again soon was depressing. As much as I was getting used to Ilyan's company and beginning to enjoy being around him, I would like to see Wyn too.

"Don't rain on my parade, Wyn." I grumbled.

"I'm sorry," she said. "It's just that I miss you. It's been months, and with everything that's happening, I worry."

"What do you mean with everything that's happening?" I asked.

I plopped down on the bed, curling my toes in the beautiful shoes, and waited. There was a much longer pause than I was used to as Talon whispered something in the background. It wasn't like Wyn to hesitate. She usually said what was on her mind whether it would offend someone or not.

"Wyn," I prompted. "What's going on?" My stomach tightened a bit in anticipation.

"Just with everyone looking for you, people being able to track your magic, and all that."

I knew Ryland could track my magic, and would presumably be looking for me, however Wyn made it sound like something more active.

"*Everyone's* looking for me?" I said quietly. "Everyone like Ryland everyone, or everyone-everyone? I don't suppose you and Talon were planning a rescue mission to get me out of my studio-sized prison?"

"Ryland everyone, Jos." She paused, and my shoulders knit together in frustration.

Twice in one day I wasn't being told exactly what was going on. Worst of all, people were keeping things from me that directly pertained *to* me. 'People' being Wyn and Ilyan, even though I knew Wyn was probably just following orders. I knew that Ilyan had a right not to tell me everything, it was still frustrating. I trusted him with my life, my secrets. He had become more than a friend. Hearing that he was keeping something from me for the second time in under an hour made my head hurt.

"He can't track my magic behind Ilyan's shield, Wyn," I said, a little perturbed that my good news had been smashed.

"I think it's a little bit more than that. I think it's more of an active searching." Active searching? Wyn made it sound like someone was hovering on the balcony waiting for me to absent-mindedly walk out.

"Why wouldn't Ilyan tell me?"

"I am not sure Ilyan knows, Jos." Her voice was quiet.

"What?" I asked, my back straightening in alarm. "What do you mean he doesn't know?"

There was a scuffling and more whispering on the other end of the line. I held the phone to my ear tightly, desperate to hear anything.

Ilyan always knew what was going on. He had spies and contacts everywhere who reported back to him. His phone rang off the hook most of the day with reports on Edmund and Ryland, Prague, and who knew what else. The fact that he could possibly not be aware of something was worrisome.

"Wyn?" I asked when I couldn't wait anymore. There was a bit more of a whispered fight and then Talon took the line, his deep voice booming through the long distance connection.

"Hey, Jos. It's Talon, how're you doin', little girl?"

"I'm fine, Talon. Can you please tell me what's going on?" I was practically begging, but I needed someone to pull me back from the edge of my growing fear.

"Sure kid," he exhaled deeply, and for a moment I was worried he was going to lead me on, too. "Last week I was harvesting in the orchard when I overheard someone crying and whimpering, though I'm not sure who. They were begging for help and pleading with someone. We've heard your name mentioned a few times. I ran to find out what was going on, but nothing was there. No one was in the trees."

"A few other people have heard it, too," Wyn broke in, having obviously put me on speaker phone, "someone whimpering and crying. But no one can figure out who."

"What are you saying; that there is a spy in our midst?" I said, purposefully making my words sound like a spy movie in an attempt to break the tension. It didn't work.

"That's exactly what we are saying, Jos," Talon said.

I threw myself back on my bed. I should be happy. I was finally getting out of the house, we had decided Ryland might still be able to be saved, and soon I was going to leave this prison forever, yet at that moment, I was stressed and uncomfortable.

"And Ilyan doesn't know?"

"Ovailia is looking into it, but I don't know if she has told him yet. I would assume not if he is planning on taking you out to dinner tonight," Wyn replied. Afterward, I could hear Talon whisper something behind her again.

"Why didn't you call and tell me or Ilyan?"

More whispering, I waited for a minute, my impatience growing.

"Jos," Wyn sighed, "Ovailia is looking into it. If she had found something, she would have told him, right?"

Ovailia should have told him even if she didn't think she had 'found something.' Something wasn't right. My heart ached and beat uncomfortably. I didn't like things being kept from me, and these were the worst types of things; things that affected me. To make it worse, not only were things being kept from me, but from Ilyan as well. I needed answers, and being stuck in this apartment was limiting my resources.

"Can I..." I was going to regret this. "Can I speak to Ovailia?"

"Why?" Wyn asked, worried. I didn't blame her, being around Ovailia was uncomfortable enough, asking about something like this was sure to be an unpleasant experience.

"Because I need to hear it from her, and I have something else to ask her anyway." I said, quickly stringing together one worry with another.

"Ilyan will be very upset if you go behind his back," Talon warned, his voice deeper than usual.

"Nah, if he is, he'll just torture me by making me spar with him again."

Talon chuckled softly, his voice making the phone's microphone vibrate. Talon and Wyn had warned me about Ilyan's temper, but I had never seen it. Maybe it had something to do with this protector nonsense he had been throwing around, which was the other thing I wanted to ask Ovailia about. My stomach tightened as I began to second guess myself. Ovailia on the phone. What was I thinking?

"Alright, but it's your funeral."

I heard a knock on a heavy door and then Talon said something, his voice muffled. Ovailia snapped something back. I instantly regretted this decision and she wasn't even on the phone yet.

"Hello, Joclyn, what a pleasant surprise." Ovailia's voice was as sweet as acid, as usual. It didn't sound like she was pleasantly surprised, it sounded like I was asking her to pluck all her hair out strand by strand.

"Hello, Ovailia." I tried to sound chipper.

"What can I do for you?" I almost lost my nerve, but decided to plow through. If for nothing more than to be off the phone with her. Trying to explain why I wanted to talk to her without asking my questions would have been worse.

"Wyn tells me there is a spy in Prague, and I know Ilyan doesn't know." It wasn't a question, it was a statement. I hoped my bluntness would prompt her to tell me what I needed.

"How could you possibly know if I have told Ilyan or not?" I could almost see her eyebrows arch and rise delicately on her perfect face.

"Because, if he knew, he wouldn't be taking me out to dinner tonight." There was a pause, but it wasn't the pause of someone who was contemplating how much information to tell you. This was Ovailia, and her pauses ended with her decision of how much to scold you.

"He's taking you out? Out of the apartment?" I was surprised by the alarm in her voice.

"Yes, and I am concerned that as 'My Protector' he doesn't know that Edmund might already know where I am hiding." I placed it well, hoping the words were heavy enough that she would either give away what Ilyan had meant or verify that the words meant nothing.

There was a pause, and I waited. I didn't dare say anything, worried I wouldn't get any of the answers I needed, however instead of answers, Ovailia began to laugh.

"Your protector?" she said through her wicked laugh. "Your *protector*. Oh, you stupid little girl, don't make me laugh. If he had told you that, you wouldn't be saying the words with such pride. You would be terrified." She laughed harder and my stomach dropped. "I will tell Ilyan when I have information that this is not all just a prank. Don't you ever come prying for information from me again, or I can assure you, you will get more than you bargained for."

The phone went dead, and I dropped it to the floor like it was poison.

That hadn't gone at all as I had planned. Not only did Wyn dash my joy at getting to leave the apartment, but my impromptu espionage for answers had blown up in my face. The only positive information that I had gleaned was that it was obvious that the news of the spy was being kept from Ilyan, and that Ilyan was in fact 'my protector'—which sounded much worse than I thought.

Secrets, lies, spies. I didn't like it at all.

I stood and stumbled around the apartment for a minute, waiting for my brain to tell me what I should do next. Ilyan wouldn't be home for an hour at least, and who knew how much trouble I had just gotten Talon and Wyn into—I cringed at the thought.

I needed to talk to someone, and there was only ever one person I could really talk to.

Without thinking, I grabbed my necklace and pushed my magic into it. This Ryland wouldn't hold my hand and talk me through my problems like he used to, but I could at least talk without him judging me.

I opened my eyes to the Tòuha and gasped. Everything had been destroyed in the few short hours since I had left him. Every single drawing, every one of Ryland's masterpieces, they were all smudged and smeared, some erased completely. I looked around me in shock, my mouth hanging wide open in horror. Could this day get any worse?

"Ryland?" I asked softly. Normally he was right here waiting for me. But no one was here. No running feet. No happy, smiling face; just months of masterpieces, destroyed.

"Ry?"

I ran through the room filled with smudged and destroyed dreams until I heard him. His little whimper was soft and broken. I ran toward the sound until I found him hunched against the wall, crying into what had once been the drawing of him holding the Vilỳ. He rubbed his fist into the face of the creature, his body shaking with sobs.

"Ryland?" He spun at my question, his face screwed up in anger.

"Go away!" He yelled, throwing broken bits of chalk and crayon at me. "I don't need you anymore!"

"Ryland? Wha... what happened?"

"Go away!" he yelled again, his words cutting through me.

"You don't mean that, Ry."

"Go Away!" He turned away from me, rubbing harder into the blue smudge and turning it into a blur.

I rushed to him, wrapping my arms around his tiny frame. He fought me off, but I fought back harder while he cried and continued to push away from me. I held on as he battled, his cry getting louder rather than softer as I had been hoping for. His pushing turned to punching and finally I was forced to let him go. He skidded away from me, both of us panting hard. I couldn't stop looking at him. I didn't know what had happened; where this had come from.

"Ryland?"

"Leave me alone! Go back to wherever you come from and never come back here again!" he screamed at the top of his lungs and backed himself into the wall. I wanted to reach for him, but was scared as to how he would react.

"I can't do that, Ryland, you know I can't do that. I'll die." I spoke softly, partly in the hope of calming him down, but mostly because I was scared. I didn't know how to react or what to say.

"Then die!"

"Ryland!" His words cut through me; he couldn't possibly mean that.

"You don't care what happens to me, you don't care that I am here alone, and you don't care about me. You just want that other guy!"

"What other guy?" I asked, confused.

"The one you are waiting for, the one you lost. You think I'm him, but I'm not. I am just me, and you don't care!"

"Ryland, I do care... I—" I pleaded with him as I tried to piece together the puzzle of his outburst. He interrupted me, his next words like lemon against an open wound.

"No, you don't! I hate you!"

"You don't mean that." My voice was almost a whisper.

"Yes, yes I do," Ryland was losing momentum as his tears took over. "I have to."

"You have to? Ry, you don't have to do anything. I know you don't hate me, so please don't say that." I moved closer to him, watching his movements to see how far I could get. He stayed against the wall, crying and eyeing me as I got closer.

"You don't hate me," I said as I carefully placed my hand on his knee to comfort him.

"I have to, Jossy. He said... you don't..." He stuttered until his voice disappeared.

"He?"

"You don't love me anymore, you love the other guy." His shoulders shook, and my heart shattered.

"Of course I love you, Ry. You are my *everything*."

He stared at me, I could see something click together in his mind, and a weak light began to return to his eyes. I took the opportunity and moved closer to him.

"Really?" His face brightened with hope. I returned the smile and wrapped my arms around him, pulling him to me.

"Yes, really. I couldn't live without you, and I never want to hear you say you hate me because I know it's not true."

He nodded against me and I squeezed him tighter, grateful when he returned the hug. I held him for much longer than necessary, but I wanted him to calm down; to know the truth of what I had said. I wasn't sure how to communicate that to a child. A hug seemed the simplest way.

"Now, about this 'other guy' I don't think you are the other guy. I think you are you. I loved your drawing, and I am sorry I didn't say so. I shouldn't have said those things before, and I am sorry I did."

"Thanks, Jossy."

"No problem, little man. Now, I did come bearing good news."

"You did?"

"I did. I get to go to the city tonight." I smiled brightly, hoping at least one person would be excited for me. Instead, his face fell a little bit.

"But I'm still stuck here."

I sighed. Obviously this was not the best timing to have told him, given the outburst he just had.

"How about tomorrow, after I get back, we get rid of our white room and make the city. Then we can have our own adventures; pretend to be superheroes and magicians and anything you want. I'll spend all day with you"

"Really?"

"I would love to."

Ryland's face lit up like a million fireworks and he crashed against me in a big hug. Giggling like crazy, I reached for him as he jumped up, his face serious again.

"You've gotta go! That way you can bring the city back with you." He grabbed my hand and heaved until he pulled me to a stand, dragging me toward the door. "I'll make superhero capes, and villains, and all sorts of stuff." He jumped up and down a bit before running away, presumably back to where his chalk lay scattered.

"Bye, Jossy!" he yelled behind him, his focus on his new tasks.

"Bye, Ry," I said softly before turning the knob on my exit door, my eyes opening to Ilyan staring right at me.

CHAPTER 13
JOCLYN

"Been busy have we?" Ilyan said, his lips pulled up in a half smile.

"I wouldn't call it busy." I grumbled as I stood, stretching my joints out a bit. My body was supercharged after the Tȍuha, though strangely stiff from sitting. I glanced toward the digital clock on the floor. I had been sitting for twenty minutes which meant I had been with Ryland for a little over two hours. We had done the math when I first started having to visit the Tȍuha every day. Two hours in the Tȍuha was equal to about twenty minutes of real time, and it was a good thing it wasn't the other way around because I needed about forty minutes of real time in the Tȍuha for my body to stay perfectly strong.

"More like stressful and confusing."

"Hmmmm, yes," Ilyan said, moving away from me. "Ovailia called me."

"Great," I grumbled, dreading his response to my foolish phone call, however instead of yelling, Ilyan only smiled.

"Don't worry, Silnỳ, despite Ovailia's best efforts, I am not upset with you. I have decided that the one who kept things from me in the first place should be the one to gain the punishments."

"So Ovailia's in trouble?" I said.

"I don't know what *you* qualify as being 'in trouble', but she is no longer acting in my stead, that role has been taken over by Talon."

"Talon?" While he seemed the obvious choice, something about changing leadership in Prague made me worried.

"Yes, Silnỳ. This would not be the first time he acted in my name. Many years ago, before Ovailia returned to us, it was expected that Talon would take my place if I was to pass. He is my second. He wears the další v příkazu."

"The další v příkazu?" I asked, I had heard Wyn say that before, but still had no idea what it meant.

"Yes, the další v příkazu is a crimson ribbon that is normally wound into the hair of the second in command. It denotes power and place in the ruling family."

"Like a crown?"

"Something like that." He smiled faintly, pushing some of his long hair out of his face. "But Talon will display it now as my další v příkazu."

Ovailia being stripped of her power did not sound like a party I wanted to be invited to. Knowing how much Ovailia felt she was entitled to, taking away the power she had scraped into her possession would mean trouble.

"I'm glad I'm not in Prague. I don't know what would be worse, Ovailia in charge, or Ovailia mad because she is not in charge."

"Ovailia not in charge is worse. She tends to snap and act out when she doesn't feel respected."

"As opposed to...?" I opened my hands in question. Ovailia was always snapping and acting out.

"My point exactly."

I grimaced, suddenly glad I was safe and hidden in our little apartment since I was the one responsible for her dethroning.

"Poor Wyn." I said

"Poor Talon." Ilyan agreed. "I wouldn't worry. If anyone can rein in Ovailia's temperament when I am not there, it's Talon. Although, he may be calling a bit more than Ovailia does."

"Let's just hope that doesn't backfire."

Ilyan cocked his head to the side and looked at me heavily, his eyes digging into my soul.

"Why are you worried?" he asked.

I sighed and joined Ilyan in the kitchen. "I don't know. Something feels off, like a snake has wound itself up my spine." Ilyan raised an eyebrow at me, or perhaps at my odd description.

"Shouldn't we be running back to Prague right about now? I mean someone is 'crying' information about us all over the city."

"You mean the caves?" he asked, his eyebrow still raised.

"Excuse me?"

Ilyan narrowed his eyes and pulled out our two juice glasses. "Everyone is confined underground, in the side of a mountain near the city of Prague. When we say Prague we mean our caves. So someone is going around our underground caves—not the city—crying and doing who knows what."

Everyone had made Prague sound like this wonderful place, but if it was really just hiding under a mountain, it sounded just as terrible as the tiny room I had been trapped in.

"Shouldn't we go back, though? Make sure everything is okay?"

When Ilyan came over to stand next to me, I craned my head to look up at him, his face soft and concerned. He reached out and placed his hand against the side of my face, his fingertips tracing the rough lines of my mark as always. I didn't move away from him; I didn't flinch. I only stood there, my heart thumping at the contact.

"I would if I thought something was wrong, but I am not sure if I do, yet. Talon will be looking into it for me. I will keep you safe, Silnỳ, that I promise you."

"My Protector." I had barely spoken above a whisper, but he still heard me, making me regret my words. His face darkened as his hand dropped from my face to a tight hold against my elbow.

"Ah, yes." He said softly before moving away from me. "That is another thing, please don't go to Ovailia for answers. I keep things from you because you are not ready to hear them. You will not receive the truths you are looking for from Ovailia. She will only paint a canvas with lies to manipulate you."

"If she is going to manipulate me, then why do you trust her?" I had expected him to be angry at my impolite question, instead he only spoke quietly to me.

"I trust her because of what she has done to redeem herself. I trust her because, out of all of my siblings, she has stood by me. She may not be the best in character, but she is the best on word. Although, she might be a little bit jealous. So, for now, I will trust her."

Ilyan's voice had strengthened into that commanding tone I had grown so used to. I fought the urge to sink into my sweater and hide from him. Instead, I took a deep breath and looked at him firmly.

"So you will trust her with every bit of information about me, but you will not give me the same information?" I tried to keep my voice level, yet I wasn't sure it had worked. I was starting to get a little upset. The darkness in Ilyan's face faded away, but I barely noticed.

"I have not told her everything about you, only enough so that she understands my position."

"Which is...?" I prompted, but Ilyan only raised an eyebrow at me.

"I will tell you when you are ready, Silnỳ." Ilyan said simply, which only added to my frustration.

"Why can't I be ready now?"

"Because I am not the one to tell you."

"Then who is?" I begged, leaning over the countertop to him.

"You will know him when you meet him." Ilyan turned, his voice playful even if his face was stern.

I hated that he was keeping something from me. I hated that he treated me like an all-important piece of his life but wouldn't tell me why. I hated that he didn't trust me. I threw my hands in the air in exasperation before I sunk into one of the chairs at the table.

I would have gone to the other room, if we had another room to go to.

"Silnỳ, do not be upset with me." His hand rested on the back of my head, his fingers moving through my hair. "You will know all soon enough, and then the weight of the world will be on your shoulders."

When I turned my head to look at him, his tall frame crumpled a bit so he could meet me at eye level.

"Is that why you are keeping things from me, Ilyan, because of 'the weight of the world?'"

"You already have so much pain in your heart, Silnỳ. I do not want to add to that. I only wish to see happiness in your soul, and when the time comes for your knowledge to change, I will be there to help you carry it." I didn't know whether to be grateful or scared, but I smiled all the same. Ilyan's hand moved from my hair to trace my mark, his sad smile melting me.

"I would say thank you, but everything you said sounded way too ominous and dramatic. Even for me."

Ilyan smiled as he poured me a glass of fresh squeezed orange juice from a jug. Ilyan never ate anything processed, which meant I never ate anything processed, which meant pulp-free orange juice and fruit loops were a casualty of my predicament. I sighed at the memory.

It only got worse when Ilyan set three bowls on the table, each filled with honey covered strawberries, boiled greens, and berries wrapped in dandelion leaves. When I grabbed a blackberry and began to untangle it from the leaf it had been wrapped in, Ilyan looked at me as though I had brought Fruit Loops into the house. I ignored him. I could eat the leaf separately, however with the berry it made my stomach spin.

"You're never going to gain enough strength to defeat Edmund if you don't eat the food I give you."

"You sound like my mother." I said without thinking. My heart thumped uncontrollably when a flash of her crumpled body on the kitchen floor raced to the forefront of my memory. Ilyan didn't seem to notice the pain in my face, which was probably for the better.

"Well someone has to look out for your well-being." He was dead serious and pushed the sickly looking bowl of boiled greens in my direction. I always steered clear of his boiled greens. They looked like cat vomit.

"Might as well be 'My Protector' then," I said a bit acidly, sliding the bowl back to him.

Ilyan froze and leaned over the table toward me. I didn't raise my head to acknowledge him. I just shrunk into my oversized hoodie.

"Don't," I said, "I'm sorry I said anything." I didn't like the feeling his stare was giving me. I looked up, unsurprised to see his gaze still boring into me.

He paused, contemplating what to say while his penetrating stare froze me in place. His eyes never left mine as he grabbed the bowl of strawberries and placed it in front of me. Ilyan reached for my hands and wrapped them around the cold bowl. I could feel the warmth of his magic pulsing and flowing under his skin.

"I will always protect you, Joclyn." My breath caught and I pulled my hands away from his, the bowl dragging along the table with them. Ilyan only smiled.

"Go get ready, Silný. There are clothes for you in the bathroom. I want to leave in about an hour, so we can get some sight-seeing in before dinner."

"Leave?" I was confused. He couldn't possibly mean we were still going to go out. Especially with some super spy giving away information about us to who knows who in some bunker in Prague. It sounded like the plot to a B-grade movie. "We aren't still going into town. You can't be serious?"

"You marked me. A bit dishonestly, but you marked me," he said with a smile. "A deal is a deal."

"But what if they find us?" I could hear the panic in my own voice; obviously I was more freaked out about this than I had been admitting to myself.

"Then they find us, Silný. It has always been a risk."

"But..." Ilyan stood up so fast my words fell from my mind in shock.

In one swift movement he had come around the counter and was kneeling down before me, his hands wrapped around mine, his skin warm.

"Vždycky budu tě chránit, drahá moje." I froze at the words, my heart thumping uncontrollably.

"Protect." I said softly, repeating the only word I recognized.

"Yes, protect." He smiled brightly and pulled me to standing. "Now, go get ready, please."

Without another word, Ilyan placed the bowl of strawberries in my hands and shooed me off to the bathroom.

I shut the door behind me, my stomach swimming with eager anticipation. One hour. In one hour I would be escorted from my prison and into the world outside. Even though I was nervous about leaving given the current state of things, my excitement was stronger. I grinned at myself in the mirror and plopped a strawberry into my mouth, my face twisting a bit at the raw honey flavor.

I wrapped my hair up in a high bun on top of my head and jumped in the shower. My mind buzzed in expectation of getting out of the apartment, and I spent the majority of the time dreaming of what I would see and how I would recreate the city for Ryland. His little heart had seemed so broken by what had happened before that I needed to do something to help him cheer him up. He needed to know how much I cared for him. If I had learned one thing, it was to never bring up who he used to be.

What if he never remembered? What if I was doomed to visit the Tȍuha every day for the rest of my life? Or worse yet, what if the possessed form of Ryland died, taking my Ryland and the Tȍuha with him. If that happened, I knew I would die, too. Maybe then Ilyan could save me with whatever mystery procedure he had planned to try before.

I shook the thought from my head and stepped out of the shower, thinking again of magical cities and already planning games we could play in a newly built realm within the Tȍuha.

I had dressed without thinking and now that I was looking at myself in the mirror, I wanted to scream. What had Ilyan been thinking? Tight, bright turquoise jeans, and a bright multicolored t-shirt? I gaped at myself in the mirror, horrified. Colors? Tight fitting clothes? I wanted to throw up. I grabbed for the hoodie, desperate for something to cover up with. It was bright red, to match my shoes I guessed, and fit as tight as everything else while the fabric was so thin it was almost non-existent. I yelled out in a panic, and stormed from the bathroom, determined to make Ilyan go out and purchase something more reasonable.

I had made it a few steps out of the bathroom when I froze. Ilyan was leaning against the kitchen counter speaking in Czech, his focus on the phone he had pressed against his ear. My jaw dropped; he looked so different. I had never seen his hair braided before. The long, blonde strands were perfectly woven together in a golden weave that trailed down the back of his head to fall halfway down his back. The absence of sheets of hair framing his face defined his facial features. He looked more distinct, stronger somehow, and his light hair contrasted starkly with his tight black polo shirt. For the first time he wasn't wearing torn jeans, either, instead he had opted for dark-washed skinny jeans. I cursed his style sense. He looked good.

Ilyan looked up at my entrance, and his line of sight trailed to the precarious bun on top of my head before he laughed. I pulled the hair tie out, having forgotten the silly thing was still up there. When he clicked his phone shut and moved toward me, I finally closed my mouth after realizing it was still hanging open.

"What?" he asked, his accent rolling around the word.

"You look..." I paused, unsure of what to say or even how to phrase it. The only word that came to mind was sexy, and saying that aloud to Ilyan was wrong on every level.

"Did I do it wrong?" Ilyan asked, alarmed. He jumped away from me and ran to the nightstand where a magazine was folded. He unrolled it and flipped through it looking for a specific page. Having found what he was looking for, he rushed back over, shoving a picture right under my nose.

The magazine picture was a Louis Vuitton ad featuring a man dressed in exactly what Ilyan was wearing. I looked from the ad to Ilyan a few times in shock before I began to laugh. So much for style sense, Ilyan had just been copying ads he had found in fashion magazines. My laugh continued to grow as I snatched the magazine from him, flipping the pages until I found a similar ad, this time with a girl wearing what Ilyan had provided for me.

"Vut?" Ilyan asked, his agitation accentuating his accent. He shifted his shirt, obviously worried he had done something wrong.

"Nothing," I managed through my laughter. "It's nothing, I thought..."

"What?" Ilyan asked again, his face screwed up in alarmed confusion. I dampened my laughter and placed my hand on his arm.

"Have you really been taking style hints from magazines all this time?" Okay it was more than hints, it was downright plagiarism, but I wasn't going to call it that.

"Yes! How else do you expect me to fit in? Your clothing styles make no sense to me." He shook his head and walked away from me, ignoring my returning laughter.

"Well, I am going to need new clothes; I can't go outside in this."

"Why not?" Ilyan rushed back to look at the magazine, obviously not understanding.

"Well they are tight, and have colors, and... and..." Ilyan hiked an eyebrow at me like I was crazy. "This hoodie has no fabric what-so-ever."

I threw both the magazine and the offending hoodie at him. He caught the sweater and the magazine floated before him for a minute before settling itself on the counter. His face broke into a wide smile, happy his clothes weren't really the issue.

"Pants I will replace, I have purchased you another hoodie for later. One, I think you will find more appealing. But this one," he handed it back to me, "this one you are going to want to keep."

"I can't wear this out, Ilyan. There isn't anything to it."

"It's one hundred and ten degrees out there today, Silnỳ. If you wear any other hoodie, you will pass out from heat stroke."

"One hundred and ten degrees?" It never got that hot back home, ever. I would be surprised if it had even gotten to ninety in the summer. I cringed. That extra twenty degrees sounded miserable. I couldn't go out without a hoodie, I couldn't. I grumbled and grabbed the hoodie back from him, trying to ignore the way his face lit up as well as the joy behind his eyes.

"Fine, you win."

He just smiled more.

CHAPTER 14
WYN

I loved Prague right before sunset, when the golden rays of twilight streamed through the high spires and glass windows of ancient architecture. It was its own kind of magic with the sun dancing through history like it was.

I breathed in the air, and quickly stepped toward the market. My magic was stretched from covering the marks on my face and arm, but I could still hear every sound and a dozen different languages all at once.

"Let's visit the bridge next." In Dutch.

"I really need to get you new shoes." In Czech.

"What do you mean you didn't make a reservation?" In French.

"The train leaves in an hour, I'll be home soon." In Spanish.

"This city is magic!" That one was in English, and I turned, already smiling. The bottle blonde woman was grinning up to where the sun had caught the high spire of the Cathedral and was sending rays through a partially clouded sky.

If she thought that was magic then she would be slapped silly by what this city was really hiding.

"What'll it be today, miss?" I turned at the gruff voice of the vegetable seller, his rainbow trays of every vegetable that could be grown in the region spread out between us.

I began pointing out things, placing an order I didn't really need. While I loved to be in the city, this trip to the market was out of work, not necessity.

Truth was, I was trying to get information.

It had been weeks of phantom crying appearing and then vanishing all over Imdalind and no one had found anything. No one had fessed up to what was becoming the most horrific prank of all time.

Then last week, on a routine scout, one of the Skříteks had sworn they had seen a Trpaslík in the city. She had said they had felt their cold magic from a mile away.

So, here I was, in the city. Buying vegetables for the third day in a row. Watching. Waiting.

"Děkuji," I said to the seller, exchanging money for my now filled bag and turned, my eyes still darting everywhere.

Silently, I slid into one of the many tight alleys that peppered this part of Prague and let my magic flare, a Zmizêt sliding over me and erasing me from view. One glance behind me to make sure no one saw and I took off into the air, loose trash and bins rattling from the force of the wind that propelled me up to the roof.

This building was one of the tallest in old town, and while I couldn't see every person milling about from up here, I could sure feel them. It was the magic I was looking for, after all, not some update of when someone was going to be catching a train home after visiting their mistress for a week.

Or, at least, that's what I would assume that was with the way that woman was clinging and kissing on him.

I released my magic from the marks on my skin and sat under my shield, legs swinging off the side of the building, eating a tomato. Listening.

To nothing.

No magic. No secret spies.

I was moments away from falling asleep when the phone in my pocket sprang to life. I half expected it to be Joclyn. She had caused a bit of drama with that phone call the other day. Hell, half the reason I was out here was to be as far away from Ovailia screaming into the phone at Ilyan as I could. My magic had been a bit weird since the incident with the fire spear, and as much as I wanted to spar Ovailia, now was not the time.

It wasn't Joclyn, however, Talon's goofy face was looking up at me from the screen.

"Hey, hot stuff," I answered with a mouth full of tomato, phone against my ear. "Tell me something sexy."

“The screaming woman was in the lower hall, just now. It sounds like she is being tortured, someone is trying to get information from them.”

I nearly choked on the tomato, what was left in my hand falling the sixty or so feet to the ground. I didn’t care. I didn’t even laugh when someone screamed from having been hit in the head by a half-eaten tomato.

“That’s not sexy, Talon.”

“I know. I need you to come back. I’ve told Ilyan, and he wants us to do a full search again. Someone is in Imdalind, and we need to find them.”

“But we’ve done that before--” I was standing, looking toward the entrance to the caves of Imdalind when I felt it. Ice cold magic just like my own, rushing right toward me.

“Wynny?” Talon’s voice shook, I hadn’t even realized that I had stopped talking.

“I feel them. The Trpaslík. I’ve got to go.”

I snapped the phone shut and threw it in my pocket before I took off, shield still firm around me as I soared through the air right to where I could have sworn I felt the magic. It was zigzagging, not through the air like I had expected. But through the streets.

I landed in the closest alley I could find, the narrow streets leading to a cathedral that was as packed as they always were at this time of night. Letting the shield drop from me, I darted through the crowd, looking for the source of the magic. Trpaslíks were always shorter than Skříteks, but Skříteks were taller than humans, which meant that this person was blending in perfectly.

It didn’t matter.

I found him anyway.

I would find him anywhere.

Timothy.

My father was in Prague.

And worse, if he was in Prague was he the one that had been hurting someone in Imdalind? It was impossible, there was no way for him to get past the Zmizêts that Ilyan had set to protect against Edmund and his army.

Yet, here he was, darting through the crowds, clearly racing away from the main entrance into the caves of Imdalind. He didn’t even turn. I wasn’t even sure he knew I was there.

My magic flared angrily. I had only faced Timothy a handful of times since he had tried to kill me. And every time he had been behind an army. But this time he was alone.

I couldn't even stop the blood lust that completely took over me, not that I tried.

I could take him. I could make him pay.

If only I could get him away from all of these people. Committing murder, especially magical murder, in front of a gaggle of humans would not end well.

I grabbed a stone from a flower pot as I darted through a clump of backpackers, my magic still flooding my senses. It wouldn't take much to just send this rock into the back of his neck. Finish him and no one would know who or what.

It wasn't the long torturous death that I had spent so many years imagining for him, but it would work. I balanced the rock on my palm, my magic surging in preparation.

Instead of sending the rock hurtling through the air toward him, my magic screamed inside of me in the same way it had the last few days, all hot and angry and I jumped. The strength of it made me feel like I was going to explode or catch fire.

"What the hell?" I mumbled to myself, clenching my fists together in an effort to control the heat of my magic. I meant to grip the stone in a hope to center myself, but the stone was gone.

I froze in place, opening my hand in confusion. The stone was still there, but it just wasn't a stone anymore. A pool of liquid rock sat in my palm; the heat level nearly identical to what was raging over my skin.

"What the hell?" I nearly shrieked that time, dropping the puddle of rock to the ground as it started to burn me. It had turned into a slither of stone by the time it hit the ground.

Tourists turned at my shout, and I looked up, expecting Timothy to be charging my way.

There was nothing but hundreds of heads, eager happy people that streamed through the streets, parting around me as I stood in the center of them staring at my hand.

Timothy had gone, but somehow that hardly seemed to matter anymore.

CHAPTER 15
WYN

"It was Timothy." I slammed my hands on the surface of her stupid desk. Ovailia didn't even jump, she just crossed her legs on top of her desk, red heels clicking together. Knowing her, it was some kind of show of seniority. I was just happy in my chucks and band shirts thank you very much.

Not like now was the time for either of that.

"I saw Timothy in Prague." I was leaning over the desk now, she just smiled.

"How do you know you saw Timothy in Prague? Could it have just been some other fat man in a suit?"

"He's my father." It was getting harder and harder to control that boiling rage. "I know it was him. I know what he looks like."

"Yes, so you've said. But how do you *know?* I mean, it's not like you have very many memories of him..."

I launched myself across the table just as Talon barged his way in. Ovailia stood, hands out in preparation to grab me. We both froze.

"Sorry it took me a few minutes to get away I was--" Any excuse he had been about to give faded to nothing as saw us, both leaning over the table in an attack that clearly wouldn't have ended well. Neither of us turned, we were both too busy staring daggers at each other as we both recoiled back to our seats. "What is going on?"

"Wynifred here claims that she saw her dear old daddy in Prague." Could she sound more like a raging hornets' nest?

It made me want to kick her.

"Not claims. I did," I snarled.

"So why is he not here with us now?" Ovailia stood, waving her hand over her room like a game show host. She looked the part with her hair and frilly shirt. "I know you are powerful enough to take him down on your own. So why not grab him and bring him here for questioning?"

"He's... I mean..." I looked at my hand, well aware that Ovailia was smiling victoriously. "I lost him in the crowd. It's tourist season, Ovailia. You don't expect me to magic my way over to him and blow up half a block just to capture him, do you? "

She shrugged. "I would. Especially if he was the one running away from Imdalind."

"Wait." Talon snapped and that time we both turned. "You saw Timothy in the city, running away from Imdalind?"

I nodded, "I first felt his magic near the entrance. I tracked it, found him. He's the one that's been in Imdalind."

"You expect us to believe that Timothy, Edmund's right hand man, has somehow broken into Imdalind and is torturing women?"

"Yes, Ovailia," I made sure to snarl her name. "Your daddy sent my daddy into Prague. Stop trying to pretend your blood is innocent in all of this." I let the snide flow, but Ovailia just laughed, her eyes harsh before she turned to Talon.

"I knew you said she was slipping, but I didn't expect it to be this bad."

Talon sputtered at that, a weird clicking noise coming from the back of his throat as he looked between me and Ovailia. He looked as bewildered as I felt.

Except that my bewilderment was quickly turning to fury. Ovailia had been prodding at me and past for decades, but something about what she was saying felt much more recent.

And much more dangerous.

"What is she talking about, Talon?" My voice was a squeak, a weird pain in my chest growing as I looked at Talon's growing fury, and Ovailia's growing victory. That string of anger and frustration continued to grow, little pops of that heat traveling right alongside.

"What hasn't he told you?" Ovailia mocked, her words were like an iron poker, boiling all of that anger to the surface.

"Ovailia, I think we have had quite enough from you!" Talon roared, rushing the desk and sending Ovailia sinking back into her chair, not that she seemed scared at all.

"Fine, then you can leave, this is my office after all. But I suggest you not tell Ilyan of Wyn's delusions. Unless you want him to take action."

"They aren't delusions!" I snapped, ready to lunge across the desk and send all of that heat that was now roaring through my veins right into her ugly, smug face. I didn't get more of a step before Talon wrapped his hand around my bicep, practically dragging me out and away from Ovailia's prodding.

He didn't make it very far before I yanked my arm free and turned on him.

"What was she talking about, Talon?" I was trying so hard not to yell that my voice came out in more of a hiss.

"She is trying to goad you, as she always does." He was talking through his teeth as he did his best to avoid eye contact. Yeah, there was no chance I was going to believe that.

"No. That was not just her goading me, and you know it. Unless you were horrified over the stabbing possibilities in her ridiculous shoes, which I doubt." I jabbed my finger in his chest, pressing into him until he shifted back. "Talk."

"I'm telling you, Wynny, she is just pestering you." His voice was soft, that low rumble calming me like it always did.

"Fine. But I am about ready to demand Ilyan remove the block on my memory. I'm so tired of this. There can't have been anything so bad that I would want to forget thirty years of my life."

He pressed his lips together and shook his head.

"I wouldn't know, I can't remember either." I don't know why, but that time I didn't quite believe him. I opened my mouth to say so, but he plowed on before I could make more than a sound.

"Sometimes things are better left in the past. Don't let Ovailia get in your head." His eyes were soft as he reached up and grabbed my hand off his chest. He tried to weave his fingers with mine, but found that there was a rock in the way.

A twisted, tangle of rock that was form fitted to the palm of my hand.

"What's this?"

"I guess whatever is going on with my magic also means I can melt rocks now. That's why I lost Timothy. I should have just attacked him... Wait." I paused, all of that anger and horror growing with the way Talon was looking at the rock. Eyes so wide I could have sworn that they were shaking. "This is what she was talking about, isn't it?"

I kept my voice low, not that it mattered. No one ever came over here.

This hallway was for the royal family, and seeing as Ovailia was the only one here at the moment, everyone avoided it at all costs.

"Yes." At least he didn't fight me, not that his reaction made me any calmer.

"What? Why? Talk." I poked his chest, my panic was quickly growing and I needed answers.

I knew it would be impossible to get them out of Talon but he just sighed and closed his eyes for a second before responding.

"Ilyan thinks it's a Trpaslík thing. But he doesn't know why, and he doesn't think it's anything to worry about. You know, as do I, that if your power gets stronger it just makes you more of a bad ass."

I narrowed my eyes at him. I knew it would be impossible to get answers from him with all the blocks that Ilyan has on my past and royal secrets and all that, but that answer came just a little bit too quickly.

"He's not worried that I can suddenly melt rock and turn it to water?" I lifted an eyebrow at him, even saying it out loud was a little freaky. Talon seemed way too calm and confident; all things considered.

"No." Talon leaned closer, his breath filtering over my lips. "Because we both know that you will harness it. Besides, what's wrong with a little strength?"

It was something I had said before, and I nodded. I had no problem with strength and power. Accidentally burning rocks and collapsing caves on the other hand...

Something about this didn't seem to be about just strength. Not with the way Talon was looking at me.

You would think I had died, or that I was about to.

CHAPTER 16
RYLAND

"This still isn't working." The voice was just an echo as the black hell that Cail trapped me in every night began to fade away and I was left in a heap on the cold floor. Gasping. Crying. Shivering.

The cold never left now. It just got worse.

"It's not my fault, master, he is still fighting me. He is blocking the way to the svazovat." Cail was actually heaving. I would have felt victorious for having accomplished something, if everything didn't ache.

'You have accomplished nothing.'

"Why do you still fight?" Edmunds voice was in my ear and I jerked, hands flying to my hair protectively as I looked up into the snarling face of my father. The rest of the world faded back into focus as my heart rate picked up.

"I'll always fight." I could barely get the words above the sound of a gasp.

"Foolish child!" My father's voice rattled the bars as he rose, his fist thundering down on me like a hundred pound weight. The world shook and buzzed as his fist made contact, shoving my head back into the bars. Everything was ringing.

"Cail. You should have weakened him. Destroyed him. Yet you continue to make excuses." The darkness still shook and rang and Edmund whirled on Cail, the masochistic demon standing tall.

"His magic is strong."

"I love you, Joclyn." I whimpered the word and they both laughed, the sound echoing painfully in my still ringing head.

'You really thought that love would be enough.'

"I have followed that connection master, he has fortified it. I cannot reach the svazovat."

"So you need something stronger to bypass it?" The slimy sounds of his supposed victory pulled even Sain's focus. I could hear him shift behind me, although I did not dare turn. "Something that can break love."

"No." I whimpered, the sound a sob as I pushed every scrap of strength against that spot on my heart. I didn't like the way he was looking at me.

"You can't Edmund," Sain's voice was a moan in my ear, his body pressed against the bars that divided us. He was so close I could feel the scraggly hairs of his beard on my arm. "It is too vile; you would only be feeding into the sight."

Edmund rushed forward, hands jutting towards the bars and I flinched, afraid he was going to hit me again, but he only grabbed the bars above our heads and shook. Unfortunately, my flinch did not go unnoticed by Cail who was smiling even wider now. I grabbed my hair again, tugging as though I could hide. As though I could transport myself back to when this all began and simply run with Joclyn and find Ilyan and be free from all of this.

"You said that last time, but if I hadn't listened to you and had just severed the bond all of this would be over." Edmunds' voice rattled above me and I flinched more. "Do not play me Sain. You know what I am capable of."

"I do. I do." Sain mumbled and I could hear him shift away.

"Good" My stomach was a tangle of nerves as Edmund stepped back, the fear of what was coming smothering my determination.

I looked up to the man, his face more victorious than I had ever seen. Cail's expression nearly matched, except that his eyes were focused on me. I jutted out my chin, attempting to sit taller and face him. No matter how useless it was.

'Useless. Just like you. Stop trying, Ryland, you are an embarrassment.'

"Cail," my father began, his focus darting back to me. "I want you to fetch the mug for the Drak. And then I want you to go fetch dear old Rosaline."

Even Cail seemed surprised at that, a shadow of something like pain or anger crossing his face before it faded back to his usual scorn.

"Yes, master." Cail nodded once before he stepped out of my cell, returning seconds later with the mug before he turned again and ran up the stairs. The sound of his retreating footsteps would have been a saving grace if we hadn't been left with Edmund and his demonic grin.

He squatted before us, his eyes like ice as he looked between us, fondling the mug in his hands.

"Do you want a drink, Sain?" Edmund whispered, holding the mug out to the old man. I shifted, trying to get as far away from my father and that mug as I could. All my life, I had been told that Draks were nasty liars, and the water they produce in those mugs little more than poison. I had no desire to get too close.

The little movement, however, sent pains through my body and I winced, sure one or two of my bones were still broken.

Neither man looked at me, Sain was too focused on the mug, his hands reaching forward greedily. Desperately.

"You can have it, if you can tell me where they are."

'Or you can tell me. Make all of this end, Ryland. Just give up.'

Sain's hand dropped, "You know it doesn't work that way, Edmund. Besides, isn't that where you sent Timothy?"

Edmunds smile faltered, I just watched, not daring to ask, not daring to pull focus.

"Then see the fight. Tell me the landscape. Tell me of our victory." He held the mug out, and Sain took it with a quick swipe over the rim, refilling it with some unknown magic before he drank. The sound of his swallows were the only sound in the underground prison.

He had barely finished before his eyes went black, his focus fading to nothing as he stared far into the distance. Not that I was entirely sure he could see with eyes swathed in black as they were.

"The night is warm when the magic swarms," he began in that same deep monotone and I shifted away, all of my nerves twisting into knots of fear and disgust. Perhaps it was because he was the first Drak I had ever come across, but nothing about this was natural. It made me uncomfortable. "The child will be guided like a puppet on a string, taking you into victory. The chance to win, will only be won, after the golden bird has sung. Make your way, and silently chase, there is only one way to win this race."

I had no idea what Sain was mumbling about, but he was back to drinking from the mug in the corner, sucking from it like a greedy toddler. Edmund's eyes however, were back on me.

He clearly understood every word.

'You can never escape me. I will always control you.'

"Seems I still have use for you. I hope you are ready to kill your little girlfriend for me."

"No!" I yelled, all of that rage and pain and fear exploding out of me with that one word. My head rattled with the sound, my bones aching as I tried to stand to face him, only to fall back down to my knees. "No, I won't."

"Oh Ryland," he soothed in false mockery, kneeling before me as he lifted my chin to look at me. His palms wrapped around my face. I could feel his magic through his skin, feel the danger.

It was the power of a thousand years of control, of training, of pushing his magic to be something unnatural. I could feel the power thrumming through me, a power that I could never find victory over.

"You say that like you have a choice."

CHAPTER 17
RYLAND

Rosaline was not a person.

When Cail returned, he held a square of crushed velvet fabric in his palms as though it was the royal jewels of some long forgotten reign. He actually looked scared for what he held, holding it away from him as though it was going to slither up his arms and infect him.

"Ah, finally," Edmund rushed toward him, his face beaming. He took the square of cloth from Cail greedily, Cail's face relaxing as Sain made one of his weird whimpering noises behind me.

Their reactions were making me scared. I pushed myself against the bars as my father turned to me, his hands and the package now stretched toward me as though I was supposed to take it.

"I don't want it," I hissed in half paranoia.

'You don't have a choice.' My father's voice echoed in my head as he kneeled before me, holding the velvet square out to me now.

"You don't even know what it is," he said aloud, balancing the package on one hand as he began to unwrap it. "Don't you want to meet her?"

"No." I gasped, unable to look away from the fabric as he lifted the scarlet material to reveal a twisted shard of what looked like stone.

It was dark red, the shade of blood. The crystallized shard was twisted and jagged with a bit of leather wrapped around one side so that it looked like a blade. The leather was old and worn, it was clearly hundreds of years old.

"Do you know what this is?" Edmunds voice was revered, I was still pressed against the bars trying to get away from it.

"No," I wheezed, still shifting away.

'It's for you.'

It wasn't just the look of the thing that was freaking me out, there was something about it that was pulling at my magic, at me. As though it was begging for help. As though it was trying to devour me. The longer I looked at it, the worse the feeling got.

"Get it away." He only moved it closer to me, taunting me.

"Now, now, you aren't scared of a little piece of stone are you?"

"It's not stone." I said the words without thinking, it may look like stone. But stone does not pull at you as though it was pulled out of hell itself.

'Don't you want to know what it is? What I am going to use against you?'

I didn't ask. I didn't rise to the voice. I just pressed myself against the bars, aware that both Sain and Cail had moved themselves as far away from it as they could.

"It's the soul's blade."

All of that fear turned to jagged edges that sliced against me and I was suddenly panicked, pressing against the bars in an attempt to get out. To escape.

A soul's blade was the most wicked of magic. A blade made of blood and soul. To make one, you had to torture a person until their soul released from the flesh. Until they were in so much pain that the release of a soul is the only option for peace. But not just any soul could create such a thing. It had to be a pure soul. An innocent soul.

If I had to guess, whoever this Rosaline was was whose soul was trapped in there.

I didn't have any siblings with the name Rosaline, so I had no idea who this could be. Somehow, that made it worse.

"No!" He just smiled at my outburst, reaching out to grip the leather hilt on the demonic thing.

"Oh yes, I made this beauty hundreds of years before you were born. Siphoned the soul off a creature who had been made and hidden from me only by the power of pure love. You are barricading your connection with Joclyn with love? I will break it with love. Rosaline will give me a direct line. And you will help me, won't you Rosaline?" He spoke to the knife as though it was a lover, bringing it close to his face as though he was going to kiss it.

I could have sworn I heard it scream.

Although, that might have been me as he raised the knife toward me, ready to sink the blade into me. Ready to connect it to my soul. Ready to slice it in two.

'I have warned you, Ryland. Now there is no escape.'

Sain yelled as he swung the blade down, Cail caught between horror and amusement as he watched and smiled. The blade never made contact.

"Master!" The voice echoed not from Cail, but from down the staircase. Edmund turned, quickly placing the cloth back over the blade as Timothy entered.

"What is it, you fool!" Edmund turned, but I couldn't relax. I couldn't look away from the blade.

"Master," Timothy finally emerged on the stairs, beaming and unaware of what he had just walked in on. "I have done it. I've found them."

Edmund stood, pocketing the blade as he faced Timothy. I still couldn't relax. I was too tightly wound, too aware of what had almost happened.

"It seems your sight will come to fruition quicker than you anticipated. Turn him off, Cail," Edmund gave Cail a nod before he turned to leave, Timothy following behind him. "We will continue this later... if we need to. I have a good feeling about this. It's time to end Ilyan's reign."

Cail approached me, his magic already winding his way through my mind as he took control. As he 'turned me off'.

"Everything is going to plan." The words were a hiss as the world faded away. The rough edge of the voice was unfamiliar. I had no way of knowing who spoke, but I didn't care, because Joclyn was already standing in front of me. The hate that always looked at me through those silver eyes now was cutting through my soul as much as the soul's blade would.

CHAPTER 18
JOCLYN

The city of Santa Fe was full of life. From what I had seen from the confines of my tiny prison, I never would have thought that city streets could have so much energy.

Ilyan had walked me out of the apartment and into the boiling heat of the city, his hand wrapped firmly around mine with his shield protecting me, keeping me hidden.

I had not been very happy with the idea of holding his hand, but the skin connection was needed to keep the shield in place. Besides, Ilyan had promised me it would only be for an hour, and then he would release me, taking the shield with him. I wasn't practiced enough to hold my own shield yet.

The idea of being unshielded in the middle of the city scared me. The thought of Ryland finding me—scratch that, hunting me—sent an uncomfortable mix of jitters and nerves through my already bristling stomach. I tried to settle it with the knowledge that Ilyan would be there. No matter how much this 'Protector' nonsense gave me the heebie-jeebies, I knew Ilyan would in fact protect me, and that made me feel more comfortable. I felt safe with him around.

Ilyan took me out of the apartment and onto the street where a green taxi was already waiting for us. He held my hand tightly as he helped me into the car then slid in to sit right up against me even though there was plenty of room in the backseat.

The car had barely begun to move before my nose was plastered against the window. I watched in wonder as the driver sped us downtown at Ilyan's instruction. It had been almost four months since I had been outside. Three months since I had been able to feel the wind or the sun. I felt it briefly before we got in the cab, but now it was right outside the vehicle, taunting me. Without permission, I rolled down the window and stretched away from Ilyan to get as close to the hot breeze as possible.

Warm air moved into the car where it swirled around and made the air conditioned space uncomfortable, but I didn't care. I could feel it. I could feel the energy in the wind and the pulse of the sun. My magic began to buzz at the sensation the wind gave me, the feeling of earth energy—or whatever it was—filling me up.

"Maybe sightseeing wasn't such a good idea," Ilyan laughed behind me. "Perhaps I should have taken you into the mountains and let you roam free for a few hours."

"You make it sound like I'm a caged animal, Ilyan." I didn't look away from the window. I leaned closer to the moving air, letting it pick up the strands of my black hair and move them around.

"If you get your head any further out that window, you are going to look like a dog. A caged dog."

I could hear the chuckle behind his voice, the happiness infectious. I looked back at him briefly before leaning away from him, pulling his arm and torso with me as I stuck my head and shoulders out the window. The driver began to yell as I stretched my face to the sky, the sun and the wind warming my face, but I didn't hear what he said, I didn't care. I smiled at the way the sun warmed my nose, the shiver of energy flowing down my spine, and the way my shoulders seized as if I had been tickled. Ilyan said something back to the driver a moment before his hand tugged me into the car, his arm wrapping me against him.

"You are going to upset our driver, Silný." Ilyan spoke against my temple, the latent smile evident in his voice.

"I didn't even get to stick out my tongue."

"Next time, little puppy, next time." Ilyan patted my head condescendingly and I laughed before moving away from him with a joking snarl.

"Caged animal, remember," I said. Ilyan smiled widely at me, his shoulders shaking as he held in a laugh.

"Yes, I remember." His smile broadened as the car pulled to a stop, the driver announcing our arrival and the charge, which Ilyan promptly paid. "How would you like to be free?"

"You gonna let me fly?" I asked, although I already knew the answer.

"Not today." Ilyan pulled me from the car, lifting our intertwined hands to eye level. He moved my hand close to him until his lips pressed against the back of it. His eyes met mine over the top of our hands, giving me that look I couldn't quite understand.

My stomach flipped and I stepped back, gasping. I didn't like the contact and I really did not like the way my body reacted because of it. I fought the need to pull my hand away, knowing I needed the connection, so instead I held on tighter and darted down the busy street without saying anything, towing Ilyan after me.

After a few steps, I slowed to a stop. This part of Santa Fe was nothing like I would have expected it to be. Instead of tall, glass skyscrapers, there were perfect rows of adobe buildings, each carefully built to replicate the old style of the Native Americans and Spanish Settlers. The burnt orange color of the buildings contrasted with the blue sky beautifully. At the head of the street there was a large, sandstone cathedral. It was a graceful box of ancient architecture with its elegant stone arches and circular stained glass windows. It was beautiful even though it didn't look complete without the tall stone towers that are common in cathedrals.

"Wow." I said, a bit more awed than I had intended, however the way the street was designed kind of deserved it.

"I take it you like it then?" Ilyan said and began leading me down the street, his hand tightly wound around mine.

"Honestly, I would like anything as long as it had moving air, but this has a unique charm. It's kind of... unexpected."

"Santa Fe has a long history. The buildings are designed this way as a reminder and a link to the past. It's one of the reasons they don't have a larger downtown."

"I don't think they need it," I countered. My eyes dragged over one of the buildings as we passed. Its interior was an upbeat teen clothing store which had a window filled with graphic t-shirts and feather accessories —clothing that Wyn would wear. The contrast between the old and the new was somewhat silly, but it didn't take away from the nostalgia of the architecture.

"Prague is mostly the same. There is the old town and the new town. The new never mixes with the old."

"And is there a cathedral there as well?"

"A few," Ilyan said. I could tell there was more to his answer, yet part of me didn't care at the moment. I wanted to focus on this city and my current freedom.

I let Ilyan take the lead, his embrace gently pulling me along as we walked by small boutiques and larger restaurants. I finally had to pull him to a stop when we came to a row of street vendors under the overhangs of the buildings. Each person had a blanket set in front of them with jewelry, watches, and other handmade objects laid out, each with a tiny paper price tag. I slowly walked by them, taking in the large amounts of turquoise and silver.

My feet stopped when I saw it. The simplicity of my need made my legs weak.

A long board.

It wasn't even for sale. It was simply someone's possession that was being used as a different way to showcase the intricate turquoise jewelry that lined its top. Still, I needed it.

Mine had been lost forever when Ilyan had picked up my broken body from behind that dumpster and brought me into this crazy world I now lived in. I missed it. I hadn't longed for it in that deep, pining way I had seen other teenagers do; I simply missed it. I missed what it represented; the part of me that had disappeared when it had. I missed being normal.

I kneeled down next to the street vendor's blanket without letting go of Ilyan's hand. When I looked up at the old wizened woman, her legs covered with a beautifully woven blanket, she looked down at me happily.

"Which one do you like?" Ilyan's voice was soft in my ear. It took me a second to grasp that he thought I was ogling the jewelry.

"I don't wear jewelry, Ilyan," I answered honestly, suddenly worried that he would buy me something.

"Which one?"

I scowled at him, unsurprised to find him smiling at me expectantly. I sighed before pointing absentmindedly at the board. Ilyan raised an eyebrow still trying to figure out which piece I was referring to.

"I like the longboard, Ilyan," I clarified, looking away uncomfortably. "It reminds me of mine."

"Sometimes I forget how much you have lost. People, loved ones, even objects. It's all part of you." Ilyan squeezed my hand, and I turned back to him as his fingers trailed over the jewelry lightly. They fluttered around the bracelets and necklaces before stopping on a small, turquoise bracelet with stones flat against one another; it wasn't jagged like the others.

Ilyan picked it up and held it in his hands, his eyes closed as if he was measuring something.

"Turquoise," Ilyan began, "can draw out negativity. Did you know that?"

"No." I was a little surly, I didn't like the idea of Ilyan buying me jewelry, and I had a bad feeling that was exactly what was going to happen.

"And this particular turquoise will help bring up feelings of love and of family." Ilyan looked up at the old woman who nodded her head in agreement, her beautiful face breaking into a smile.

"Your young man is right," she said, her voice shaky and warm. I almost wanted to laugh right out at her comment. Ilyan was neither young nor mine. "That is Navajo turquoise, it will bind you to your family and to the ones you love."

The old woman smiled knowingly at Ilyan, her face lighting up. I turned to bat her assumptions away but was stopped by Ilyan's smile. My eyes instantly widened in surprise; Ilyan rarely smiled like that. I must have looked ridiculous because Ilyan continued to grin happily at me.

"We will take it." Ilyan held the bracelet underneath my wrist, his magic unclasping it and snaking it around me. I looked away nervously from his obvious use of magic to the old woman who was busy counting the money Ilyan had paid her with.

"Ilyan... I..." Ilyan pulled me away from the seller before I could argue more.

"I think it will help you, Joclyn. Trapped in rooms, hunted, people trying to betray you, running for your life," he smiled, but it was sad, "I think you could use a little bit of a negativity release. With all that's going on, you could use a stronger connection with those who care about you. It's no longboard, but I will replace what you have lost—as much of it as I can—when all this is over." I could only nod at his words and the sincerity behind them.

I lifted my wrist up to look at the stones. They were pretty, though part of me wanted to take it off and give it back to the old woman. As much as I didn't like the message of the stones, I could already feel my magic collecting around my wrist, seeping through them and then back into me. It did it of its own accord, whether I wanted it to or not. I smiled before shrugging my sleeve over the bracelet, letting it disappear from view.

Ilyan continued to move down the street at a slow pace, but somehow it was more focused than it had been before.

When we reached the end of the street with the large cathedral now towering over us, Ilyan dragged me over to where another street vendor was selling empanadas, but my eyes never left where the large church rose up above the street level. Smoothly cut stone formed delicate arches that surrounded the beautiful stained glass window that sat directly above the door. It was breathtaking.

"The Cathedral Basilica of St. Francis of Assisi," Ilyan said as he placed a hot pastry in my free hand.

"It was built in the late 1860s. Back then, this city was made up of the Palace of the Governors and a handful of adobe homes. Seeing it like this makes me long for the old."

I knew I shouldn't be surprised, but I still was. Ilyan was being more open about his past than usual and it was weird to be reminded of how old he was.

"So you lived here then?" I tried to keep my voice level.

"No, not here. But I did live in the church that was here before they built the cathedral. La Parroquia. It resembled a fortress more than a church, but I still loved it."

I turned and looked at him, his gaze never deviating from the large building in front of us. The picture of him in some religious get up did not fit in my eyes, but he had now mentioned living in a monastery when Ovailia was born, a church in France, and a cathedral in New Mexico.

"You and churches. I am beginning to see a theme. I wouldn't have pegged you for the religious type." I had seen the look in his eyes when he had faced a fight; I doubted he could live without that for long.

"I'm not." His answer was firm as he turned his head a bit to look at me.

"Then why all the churches?"

Ilyan looked away. He wasn't happy or sad, simply distant.

"Have you ever been around very pious people, Joclyn?" I almost laughed at the thought, but kept it inside. The tone of his voice was far too serious for laughter.

"We stopped going to church after my dad left. He always insisted we go together. After he was gone, my mom didn't want to go anymore, so we didn't."

Ilyan turned back to face me and smiled; his expression was almost understanding.

"I don't remember a lot," I finished, wishing he would look away from me.

"Pious people, those who are truly spiritual, are amazing creatures. I am almost convinced they are humans at their best. Now, mind you, I have seen some terrible things happen in the name of a God—wars, conquests, sacrifices—but on the whole—at its very base—religion can make people better. That is not to say that without religion people can not do good. As time has passed I have seen more good in the world among those that hold no faith in a higher power. But to be among the calm tranquility of a pious people, there is something there that soothes my soul."

"So, you believe in God then?" I asked.

"I believe in something. I am not sure if it's God, though. The stories of where I come from differ from yours. There is no Adam and Eve in my past."

I turned toward Ilyan, taking a bite of the pastry he had given me. I hadn't heard this story before and I was content to hear him tell it from the beginning. I gestured my pastry hand toward him, prompting him to continue.

"My kind, the Skřítek, guard the wells of magic. There is a place deep inside the earth, under Prague where magic bubbles up in what can only be described as mud. We call these the wells of Imdalind."

"Wait, what?" I asked, interrupting him. "That's the name of Ryland's family's company."

"Now you know where Edmund got the name. We call our cave 'Imdalind' as well."

"So does that make you 'The King of Imdalind'?"

"It does," he smiled. "And its protector. It is Edmunds greatest desire to take control of the wells of Imdalind again."

"Why? What would he do with them?" I asked, although I already knew it would be nothing good.

"Create a new race, destroy the world, or stop the existence of magic. The possibilities within Imdalind are endless, which is why those that are left of my kind are sworn to protect the wells of mud with our lives."

"What has the mud done before? Besides hold magic I mean?"

"It was through this mud that the first of every kind was bred. We do not know where they came from, only that they woke with their legs in the mud, their lungs stinging with their first breath. They walked out of the mountain, and as each bonded with a mortal it awoke something inside of the mortals, their own magic. It is from the wells of Imdalind that all magic begins and where it will all end."

"How do you know that that's what really happened?" I asked, holding in a laugh. The story sounded more like a legend than a history.

"Because we know who was there. The first of each of the holders of magic. The first of the Drak, the first of the Vilŷs, the first of the Trpaslíks and the first of the Skříteks—my grandmother, Frain."

"Your grandmother?" Would there ever be anything about Ilyan that wouldn't surprise me?

"Yes, I have heard this story since the day I was born. My mother and grandmother would tell it to me at nights when our home was lit by candlelight. My mother also told me as she lay dying from the loss of my father's magic."

Ilyan turned away from me, looking toward the church, but I could tell he wasn't seeing anything. I knew that look. I had been trapped in that look for months. It was the look of one trapped in their memories. I reached up and placed my hand on his shoulder. At my touch, he turned to face me.

"Which is how you knew what was happening to me all those months ago?"

He nodded once.

"But you would let me help you while my mother let herself waste away." He sighed heavily and my heart tensed. I knew exactly how he felt.

"I'm sorry." I let my hand fall from his shoulder, not knowing what else to do.

"It was a very long time ago, Silnŷ."

"I am still sorry."

The silence between us stretched uncomfortably. I willed myself to look away from him, to ignore his warm hand wrapped around mine. I finished my food, shoving the wrapper in my pocket, and turned to him, unsurprised to see his unfocused gaze on something beyond me.

"So," I began, desperate to end the silence and break Ilyan's intense gaze. "If you believe that your kind came from this mud, do you believe there is a God, too?"

"Not particularly," he said, coming back to himself.

"If you don't believe in a God, then why do you spend so much time in churches?"

"Because of how humans act when their souls are so close to God. They care for one another beyond how they would normally. They help, and support, and love one another. It's amazing to watch."

"You must think me an uncaring, hateful person then." I shifted my weight, wishing I could remove my hand from his. He must have sensed my discomfort because the heat from his hand around mine increased as his magic pulsed.

"Not in the least. As I said, as years have passed I have seen more goodness outside of church walls than within. You are one of the most caring, brave people I have met in quite some time. You willingly risked everything to save Ryland, handled ultimate losses with grace, and—"

I snorted and Ilyan stopped to look at me, his forehead furled in confusion.

"I wasn't graceful, Ilyan. I refused to move and then practically let my body kill me."

"But you didn't," Ilyan said.

"Because you're stubborn," I said, shoving our entwined hands into his chest. When Ilyan smiled, I glowed assuming I had won.

"Not as stubborn as you." My mouth dropped, odd clicking noises coming from my throat. Ilyan laughed deeply, the happy sound ricocheting off the people around us. Several people looked toward us, smiling at the exchange. I could only guess what was on their minds. First date, young love, newly married, and it got worse from there. I instinctively sunk into my thin sweater, pulling the hood up around my face with my free hand. Ilyan's laugh stopped, but his smile remained.

"When are you going to stop hiding?"

"As soon as people stop looking at me," I said, affronted. Ilyan raised an eyebrow at me and I crinkled my nose at him in frustration.

"I don't see that happening any time soon, Silný."

"Then don't count on me coming out of hiding anytime soon," I spat, grumbling a bit.

"And you say you are not stubborn." Ilyan grinned, his eyes shining before he dropped my hand then, his warm magic and the protective shield leaving my body. Now it wasn't a question of *if* Ryland would find me but how fast. Suddenly I felt unprepared to be attacked, to fight; unsure if I could come out of a fight still standing.

I stiffened in fear, my eyes darting around the street as if Ryland was simply going to step out from behind a garbage can. My panic softened when Ilyan placed his hands on either side of my face, forcing me to look at him.

"You're brave, Joclyn."

"What if they find me, Ilyan?"

"Then they find you. You are strong enough to fight them now. You are strong enough to face him." He didn't need to elaborate. I knew who he was talking about.

"Ilyan, I—"

"I know you are," he cut me off, not letting me give voice to my fears.

His words were so soft—his eyes so gentle—that against my better judgment I felt my anxiety dissipate, replaced by a heavy confidence I wasn't used to.

Ilyan moved his hands from my face to move the hood down from around my head, releasing my hair to fall down my back. "And then we will know if they can track you and how fast."

I cringed. Being unshielded made me uncomfortable. This was worse than having people looking at me. I couldn't hide under a hoodie to escape. I wasn't even sure what would happen if they did find me, or if I really wanted to know if they could. Having that knowledge didn't seem like something desirable to me.

"I need to know so that I can keep you safe, and if they do come, I will be here to protect you."

"My Protector?" I said.

"Yes," he spoke softly, his hands trailing around my neck to rest on my shoulders, the soft touch of his forefinger grazing my mark. "Now, let's go have some fun."

CHAPTER 19
JOCLYN

I sat underneath the twinkling lights that had been draped around the large outdoor patio of the cantina, listening to the fast paced salsa music that filled the air. Couples danced and swirled on the floor in front of me with their bodies meshed together in a seamless blur of color.

I sat back in my wicker chair, pressing my strawberry lemonade to my lips. The sun was setting behind the mountains that surrounded the city, giving a soft yellow glow to the sky. It touched the facades of the buildings and kissed them into a honey color that glowed from the inside out. I had never seen a city that was so unique and beautiful; I was in love.

Even though the sun was setting, the temperature hadn't dropped. My hoodie felt heavy and hot against my skin while a thin layer of sweat had built up on my neck. I was contemplating taking it off, but didn't want to be the recipient of the told-you-so look from Ilyan, though the thought of dying from heat stroke due to my own stubbornness was just as uncomfortable. I took another sip of lemonade; at least I could keep myself hydrated.

I shifted my hoodie a bit to help the airflow, but I was still uncomfortable. I glanced to Ilyan hoping he hadn't seen me fidget. Luckily he was still intently watching the dancers.

He looked completely out of place in this melee of noise and color. The rugged lines of his face caught in the lights, giving him an ethereal hue almost as if he himself was glowing while he sat in his chair, smiling serenely. It was a stark contrast to the drunken, boisterous group we were surrounded by.

He turned and caught me staring at him, so I smiled brightly and turned back to the dancers, feeling strangely odd about being caught. I heard him chuckle and he returned to his glass of wine.

The waitress had looked at him like he had lost it when we ordered and he requested wine instead of the obligatory tequila. Ilyan had only raised an eyebrow, sending the girl to retrieve wine I was sure hadn't been in their stock before then.

"Come on, Silnỳ." Ilyan's hand jutted into the space in front of me. "Let's dance."

"Oh, no," I said, sinking into the chair. "I don't dance."

Ilyan bent down slightly, bringing his eyes closer to my eye level. "Don't dance, or don't know how?"

"Both, considering the last time I was on a dance floor didn't end so well." My insides scrambled together at the thought of Ryland's graduation party, my first and only kiss, and then the disastrous failed rescue mission that had followed.

"Yes, I know. I was there."

"Then you know why I don't want to participate," I said smugly, hoping he would walk away.

He didn't.

His lips pulled up into a half smile, his eyes twinkling.

"Would it help if I told you I invented the Salsa?"

"You did not," I said, trying to restrain a smile. His eyes lit up as he laughed, his hand still jutting toward me unwavering.

"Well, no, but I have been dancing it since it was invented. Come, let me show you." Ilyan wrapped his hand under my arm and pulled me up.

"I'd rather not." I stepped away from him, but he mirrored my movements.

"I won't hurt you, Joclyn," he promised. "And if you don't dance with me, I'll be forced to take away your win and we will have to stay in the apartment for an additional week."

My jaw dropped a bit at that, but Ilyan only smiled more. Although I would normally have guessed it to be an empty threat, I didn't want to take the chance. I plopped my hand down in his and rolled my eyes, trying to ignore the grin that lit up his face.

Ilyan led me onto the dance floor, the swirling and moving couples making way for us as we weaved through them until Ilyan had placed us directly in the middle where the cobweb of lights zigzagged over our heads.

Ilyan took my hand in his and brought our joined hands up to eye level. His other hand brought mine up to his arm before moving to rest lightly on my back. He looked at me intently as the music flowed around us. I could have sworn he was waiting for me to move first, but there was no way that was going to happen. I rolled my eyes at him and went to drop my hands, but he held onto me tighter.

"Follow the way my feet move," he began. "Mine move forward. Yours move back. Watch."

I looked down, nerves rising as I watched his feet move smoothly across the floor. I tried to follow, but it was harder than I thought it would be. Ilyan made it look easy.

I missed my longboard. I could control that perfectly, and I was sure Ilyan would fall off after about ten feet. I smiled at the thought and missed a beat. My supporting foot rolled and my other one kicked him in the ankle. I was no good at this. I swore loudly and tried to pull away, but Ilyan increased his grip and pulled me back, crashing my body into his.

"Don't think so much, Silnỳ," he whispered in my ear. "Feel the music and move with the beat."

I could feel Ilyan's hand grow warm against mine, his magic bubbling right under the surface, but it never crossed the barrier of our skin. I groaned and pushed my lacking self-confidence to the side in an attempt to move with him in the right way. Ilyan's hand increased pressure on my back, pulling me against him as he began to push and pull me in the right direction. While still not perfect, at least I wasn't stepping into anyone anymore.

"Now, you move your hips a bit more..."

"Did you say 'move your hips' to me?" I interrupted trying to keep the laugh out of my voice. "That's not going to happen."

"It is part of the Salsa, Joclyn, you must try it." At that, Ilyan began to move his hips in the way that all the other men on the floor were. It looked absolutely ridiculous.

I laughed loudly at him, but he didn't stop the movement. He continued stepping and swaying and shaking as he took my giggling, stumbling form along with him. He spun me once, and I over spun, crashing into him. I felt a laugh build in his chest as he continued to move. I had never heard him laugh like this before. This was natural and carefree; Ilyan was having fun. His emotion enraptured me and I began to awkwardly sway my hips along with him. Ilyan's laughter increased as I moved ineptly around his perfected movements.

We moved as the band played. Ilyan's movements were flawless while I stumbled along with him as we both laughed aloud. Ilyan smiled at me with the same confusing look in his eyes before spinning me under his arm. I turned around awkwardly in front of him, my eyes tracking the crowd as I became dizzier and dizzier.

That was when I noticed that others were watching. For one fleeting moment I hadn't noticed, I hadn't cared. Not until I saw a beautiful Hispanic woman looking at me. She was laughing, possibly finding joy in the happiness that Ilyan and I shared, but even her notice cut into me. I stopped spinning and sunk into myself. Moving instinctively, Ilyan's arms came up to wrap around me, pulling me into his chest. I wished he wouldn't, right now I wanted to run from the dance floor. Coming out here had been a mistake.

"Others will notice you, Joclyn," Ilyan whispered in my ear, his chin resting on my shoulder. "But you cannot let it change who you are deep inside. Have fun for you, not for the people around you."

He spun me away from him, my eyes scanning the crowd. Everyone was laughing, joking, and playing; all of them were happy, and none of them were looking at me.

Ilyan came up behind me, his arm wrapping around my waist as he returned me to the dance with my back against his chest.

"See, no one else is even noticing you. No one else matters. Only you. Only me. Only the Salsa!" I could hear his smile as he pushed me away from him causing me to spin around to face him again. His feet continued to move and his hips to sway as I poorly mimicked his movements.

I couldn't say I got better, but I did actually begin to enjoy myself again. Before long Ilyan was laughing just as loud as I was while we danced our way through the endless Salsa music.

Ilyan had pulled me out of another turn when his face fell. He never missed a beat, but his eyes had turned from joyous to serious far faster than I had thought possible.

"Well, that was fast," he said, his voice hard.

"What was fast?" I asked, trying to follow his line of sight, but he had returned to staring back at me.

"Go for a walk with me?" he asked.

"Umm... okay."

Ilyan had barely waited for a response before winding his fingers through mine and taking me with him as he turned and began to swerve through the crowded cantina. We passed by our table and Ilyan held out his hand, letting his drink fly into his open palm. He drained the glass before lowering it to another table on our way out.

"Ilyan?" I whispered, sure I wasn't going to get a response.

Ilyan was about to plow us into a large group of people when my body grew warm with his magic. It didn't flood me as fast as it had when my magic was killing me, but the speed was still startling. Something was obviously wrong.

The warmth filled me just as a large breeze came and lifted us off of the ground. Ilyan held onto my hand tightly as he flew us out of the crowded restaurant and onto the golden tin roof of the building. I looked down at the confused people below who all seemed to be commenting on the wind, but no one had noticed our odd departure.

"Ilyan, what—" Ilyan clapped his hand over my mouth as he held me still, his eyes focused on the lively party below us. My body felt stifled as his magic pulsed stronger within me before turning into a low, simmering heat that siphoned away to form a shield around me again.

"Two hours, Joclyn. That's all it took for them to track your magic." His face lit up in a wicked grin that I knew a bit too well, and my heart beat erratically. I looked down to the dance floor as a short man with broad shoulders and dark red hair walked into the space followed by a hulking mass in black leather. Cail and what I could easily recognize as Edmund had found me. Their movements were slow and focused. Their static figures standing out in the torrent of activity.

"He's come himself, I see," Ilyan smiled with a wicked joy. "Well, I suppose he needs a challenge every once in a while."

Only one person could track my magic. I swung my head toward Ilyan, my eyes wide. Finally he removed his hand from over my mouth.

"Is *he* here?" I whispered. Ilyan's fingers moved up to touch my mark, his touch light on my neck.

"Yes, but don't go looking for him." My heart fell at his words.

"I need you to stay here. If anyone approaches you, fly right to me. Don't hesitate. Don't try to fight them."

He looked away from me, his eyes scanning the party below us.

"I can fight, Ilyan," I said the words confidently, even if I wasn't so sure. I had been training in a hotel room against someone who wouldn't hurt me. I had pushed myself to be ready for this day. But now that it was here, I was scared.

One look at Edmund scanning the crowd for me, however, and all of that fear faded away.

He had hurt Ryland. He would pay.

"Not well enough, Silnŷ. Not well enough to face Edmund, not yet." He turned toward me and wrapped his hands around my forearms. "Not. Yet."

"But you said earlier..." I began, remembering the softness of his voice, the strength of his earlier confidence in me. I felt like he was suddenly taking it all back. I didn't disagree with him, yet the seemingly abrupt change of his mind still stung.

"I know, I—"

"I can do this, Ilyan! I am not a child!" I pulled my arms away from his touch and tried to move away from him. I regretted it instantly. The simmering heat of the shield left, and within moments, Cail's face turned up to the roof of the cantina where Ilyan and I stood.

Ilyan grabbed my hand and took off into the air, dragging me behind him. His magic swelled inside me as he shielded me again, flying us down the street to land near a large white statue that adorned the façade of the main cathedral.

"I'm not treating you like a child, Joclyn," he hissed icily.

"Then why won't you let me fight, Ilyan?" I wasn't sure why I was fighting this. I didn't even think I was ready to face Ryland. I certainly didn't know if I would be able to fight him.

"I need to protect you, Joclyn. I have to keep you safe and this is the only way I can do that."

"By hiding me?" Ilyan stopped me with one look, the desperation in his eyes deepening the blue hue.

"Yes, until you are strong enough to fight."

"I am--"

"And now is not the time to test that."

I didn't respond. I knew Ilyan was right. I couldn't seek Ryland out. He would kill me. Even though I wanted to believe I was ready to fight, I was not sure I could, or if I was strong enough.

"Stay here. Don't do anything stupid, Silnŷ."

"Why would I do anything...?"

"*Please*." Ilyan removed his hands and waved both over me once like he was framing my body. The heat of the shield stayed with me even without his contact. I stared at him wide eyed.

"I thought you had to be touching me to shield me."

"This shield is unmovable, Joclyn. If you move even a step out of the way, it will shatter. It is as strong as the one I placed around the apartment, but it is fickle. I can control it when I am away from you, but it is around you, not inside you. It cannot move like you can." His eyes were a combination of fear and excitement as he kept glancing behind him, an eagerness to fight battling with his need to stay with me.

"So, if Ryland finds me?"

"It should hold, but if you move..."

"Then it's gone," I finished for him, my heart beating wildly.

"And you fly right to me."

I nodded once in understanding and Ilyan took a step away from me before moving back, his internal conflict still raging.

"Stay," he commanded me like a dog and I fumed a bit, but pushed it away to nod at him.

Ilyan looked at me one last time, his fingers flicking as though he was going to reach out to me. There was pain in his eyes I didn't understand, but before I could ask he flew away, directly toward his father who stood in the middle of the busy street.

CHAPTER 20
JOCLYN

Ilyan shot through the air like a bullet to land gracefully a few steps away from Cail, who stood protectively around Edmund in the middle of the main road.

As the three faced each other in anticipation, I could feel the pressure of the situation even from a distance. While I watched, their words flowed up to me much louder than I would have expected.

"Hello, son," Edmund crooned, and I cringed at how happy and normal he sounded. The impending battle didn't seem to bother him at all.

"Father." Ilyan's voice was tense and I could tell he was gauging what he should do.

Cail silently paced in front of Edmund, his body tense and ready as his eyes moved from Ilyan to the street around him as he searched for me. I instinctively held my breath and controlled my jitters.

"I hear you stole something that belongs to your brother," Edmund continued as if Ilyan's tense voice had been nothing other than a casual greeting.

"I stole nothing. I am simply holding it for safe keeping." Ilyan ground his foot into the road, and for one ridiculous moment, I was reminded of an old-time gun fight. Except, you know, with magic instead of bullets.

This was going to be bad.

I was suddenly wondering if we should have just run away.

"Hmmm, that is not what I hear," I saw Ilyan flinch a bit at Edmund's words, his back tensing. "Stop that, Cail, you're going to wear me out."

Edmund gave one casual swipe of his hand and Cail stopped pacing immediately. Moving himself to stand in front of Edmund, he never let his dark eyes leave Ilyan.

"Yes, Master."

This time I flinched.

At the Rugby game, and even in the ballroom of the mansion, I had never seen Cail respond that way to Edmund. It might have been that I hadn't been paying close enough attention, but he had never struck me as the subservient type. I had only seen Cail act that way around Edmund in my dreams, and the fact that my subconscious rendering of him could have been that precise made me uncomfortable.

"Don't move," I said to myself, as if my own voice would be able to help me keep still.

"Well, job well done I'd say. She's safe. You're safe. Everyone's happy, and we are here to collect." Even though his words were still upbeat, Edmund's voice had begun to darken.

"I don't think so," Ilyan said just as monotonously, as if Edmund's words had been some great joke. The sound reverberated up to me, making the whole street sound as if it was haunted.

"I was afraid of that," Edmund sighed, his feet stepping back as he moved himself out of the way.

"Cail." Cail stepped forward at Edmund's words. His anticipation was palpable as his eyes never left Ilyan's. "Restrain him."

"With pleasure."

Ilyan bowed his back slightly in preparation for Cail's assault.

Cail turned to face Ilyan with a stream of power and light shooting out of his fingers. Ilyan didn't dodge. He simply stepped gracefully out of the way. The energy, however, continued on and slammed into a supporting beam of the cantina's outdoor overhang.

The Salsa music was replaced by screams as the roof to the patio collapsed. Without hesitation, Ilyan lifted his hand and detached the entire roof, sending it flying toward Cail. The screams from the people in the cantina increased as the air seemed to explode around them.

The roof made contact, sending Cail to the ground. The pile of wood, fabric, and fairy lights sat in a crumpled heap in the middle of the street.

Edmund clapped his hands as if he was enjoying the show, and I knew why the second I looked down to the street.

With the roof to the cantina gone, a stationary dark figure stood alone in the center of the once crowded restaurant.

My heart beat was disconnected at seeing Ryland there. As Ilyan turned to face him, I took a step forward without thinking, the shield wavering at my movement. I hesitated. I didn't know what I wanted. Did I want to be near him? Did I want to fight him? Or did I want to save him? What did I actually think I could do?

My whole body shook as I struggled through my options. My mind called for one action and my heart for another.

"Ryland." I stepped back, hoping my movement hadn't broken Ilyan's shield. My magic pulsed and flowed with more heat and power than I had ever felt, but still I knew it wasn't enough. I couldn't even mark Ilyan without playing dirty, and tricks like that with the possessed Ryland would get me killed. I clenched my fists and focused on Ilyan's slow movements toward Ryland, trying to keep my thoughts off of my inability to help.

Before Ilyan could move too far toward Ryland, the shattered remains of the cantina roof exploded into fragmented bits, leaving Cail standing in the rubble. Distracted by the commotion, my eyes flew back to where the now empty dining area was devoid of any dark-haired men.

Raw fear rippled through me, taking my breath and logic away. Ryland was coming to find me. I stood still, listening to the beat of my heart, expecting Ryland to come around a corner at any moment.

Ilyan must have jumped to the same conclusion because he began to battle Cail, his eyes scanning around for Ryland while also keeping tabs on his father, who seemed content to let Cail do his dirty work.

"Hello, little pony, have you come to be broken?" I froze at the words, my whole body going rigid as my pulse skyrocketed. Ryland's hand trailed down my scalp, his fingers running through my hair. I didn't dare turn. I didn't know if I could manage it.

"I like your hair better this way; it's beautiful. I think—seeing you like this—I *would* like to keep you as a pet." As Ryland came around to face me, his black eyes were the only things I could look at. Not for the first time, I had to remind myself that his mind was gone.

He wasn't there.

It isn't him.

It isn't him. I reminded myself over and over, trying to ignore the heavy thump of my heart against my chest.

Then Ryland reached up and placed a cold hand against my skin. I felt the warm buzzing of Ilyan's shield evaporate. Ilyan must have felt his magic surge as his power returned, but I couldn't look away from the black depths of Ryland's eyes to see if Ilyan had noticed.

"What? Not going to say hello?" My eyes ran down his face to his lips to the lips I had only gotten to kiss once. Even though my face burned with happiness, I had to tell myself again that it wasn't him.

It isn't him.

My head was buzzing with internal yells, many prompting me to run.

It isn't him

"Goodbye, Ry." I whispered the words before slamming my hand into his stomach. I filled my palm with all the abnormal buzzing I felt and lunged it at him, sending him spinning through the air to land on the street twenty feet away.

I didn't dare look. I took off into the air, needing to get to Ilyan.

At some point in my brief contact with Ryland, Ilyan had begun fighting with Edmund, leaving Cail to take a supporting role; the scene before me was terrifying. I landed further away from Ilyan than I wanted to, scared to get too close.

Ilyan's and Edmund's hands moved seamlessly as they fought. Tables, daggers, swords—objects both real and conjured—everything flew across the space between them. Physical weapons and magical attacks blended into one another. The energy fields and magic that they fought with sent flashes of color through the darkened street.

I watched for a moment, stunned into a stupor. I needed to get to Ilyan, but more importantly, I needed to help him.

My hand flexed in preparation for an attack when I was struck across my back by a long strand of white-hot heat. I fell to the ground as the burning pain seeped into me before dissipating. I scrambled to flip around on the asphalt only to get tangled up in the remains of my hoodie, which had been shredded by the whip-like attack. I yelled as I pulled at it, frantic to remove it. My efforts were halted by Ryland's legs straddling me and holding me in place.

"Now, where were you going?" he sneered. "I told you that I need to break you."

He sat down on my legs, the pressure inverting my knees painfully. I moved to place my hands against his skin, ready to attack him, but Ryland grabbed my wrists before I could make contact. He transferred both of them into one hand and leaned towards me, pushing my arms above my head. His searing magic moved into me and blended with my own, his negative energy stopping the flow of magic and blood to my arms. I attempted to pull my hands away—to kick him off of my legs—

but he was too strong and his weight too much for me. I could feel my body weakening the more I fought him.

"Do you know how they break a horse?" He increased the weight on my legs and against my wrists as I fought him. "You have to whip it."

Ryland sliced his free hand through the air in front of me sending the same burning sensation against my skin, this time through my chest. I screamed out at the centralized pain. He swiped his magic across me again and again, the pain surging with each new impact. I continued to fight him as I screamed and writhed, my hands still bound as he pinned me down.

I was desperate to escape the agony, but I also knew I should be hurting more. With each painful swipe of his hand the pain grew only to be swallowed up by my body as I absorbed his energy, the Zêlství forming a loop between us.

I waited until his next strike and grabbed the burning energy before my body dissipated it within me then combined it with my own magic and shot it back at him through my hands, directly into his face.

Ryland yelled in pain as he fell off me, freeing my legs. I scrambled up, the now shredded fabric of my hoodie falling to the ground. I didn't wait to see if Ryland was still down. I did the only logical thing that I could think of, I ran.

I bolted into a dark alley, the large adobe buildings towering over me and enclosing me in the dark space. A few steps in and the darkness engulfed me, leaving me alone with my pounding heart as I felt my way along the rough wall, waiting until I was far enough into the alley not to be seen, then I jumped into the air. The wind caught me and hoisted me onto the nearest roof.

I knew it was pointless to run. I could already feel my own magic pulse toward Ryland; the heavy weight of the pull increasing the closer he got. It was part of the magic of the Zêlství, the bonding. The connection that was supposed to have been such a joyous occasion had turned into my own personal hell. I was, at that moment, being hunted by my mate.

I darted behind a large air conditioning unit, throwing up a shield so weak that the magic simply flickered and died. I needed to fight him; but how was that possible if our magic just loops around? It would be an endless battle, constantly hurting the one person that I didn't want to hurt.

I didn't have a choice.

The pulse of my magic continued to grow as he moved closer while the sounds of Ilyan's battle with Edmund and Cail from the street below echoed in my ears. The air was becoming thick with the smell of dust and burning wood. I had only vaguely begun wondering what had caught fire when Ryland suddenly pulled me up by my hair.

I controlled my breathing, squaring my jaw to face him. His gaze was so full of hatred that my stomach tightened and churned in warning. I fought against his hold, my arms swinging wildly at him when it became obvious he wasn't going to let me go.

"If whipping doesn't work, make the horse submit." he stated blandly, as if reciting the words from a book just before his hand flew through the air and made contact with my stomach. I gasped as the air left my lungs and was replaced with the pain of the impact.

I reached up and cupped my hands around his face, letting my magic flow into him in a boiling heat. He should have screamed in pain, but instead he smiled before slapping me hard across the face. Ryland released the hold on my hair, sending me tumbling to the roof's surface. I reached up and touched my swelling face, unsurprised by the trickle of blood flowing from my nose.

"Stop this, Ryland! Stop! It's me!" I knew it was pointless, but I had to try. I gasped the words as I moved onto my hands and knees, fighting the pain so I could face him again. On my hands and knees, I spit blood just as his leg swung forward, his heavy shoe making contact with my stomach. Pain jolted up my spine and stayed there, centering in the tender bones and tissues of my back.

I fell to the ground, my stomach landing hard on the gravel of the roof. I tried to sit up, but was stopped as Ryland once again came to sit on my legs. I cringed in pain as he leaned over me, the weight of his body adding to my agony.

"Stupid girl," he said, pushing me further into the gravel; the large ruby of his necklace pushing hard and cold into my skin. "Haven't you noticed? Our magic doesn't have any effect on each other. If I wish to break you, I'll have to do so literally. One. Bone. At. A. Time." With each word he ground my wrist into the gravel, pressing the delicate bones into a dangerously compacted state. I felt the snap as my bones broke, the turquoise bracelet Ilyan had given me shattering under the pressure. I screamed at the pain that shot up my arms as each bone cracked.

My magic pulsed, attempting to heal me even as he broke me, and then I realized, magic didn't work on him, but it could still work against him. I pressed my hand into the gravel beneath me and pulsed the panicked flow of my magic into it, sending thousands of pieces of gravel off the roof and into Ryland's face. He jumped away from me, unable to breathe or see through the arsenal that I had propelled at him. I spun around, ignoring the pain that still shot through my body to send my magic to the air conditioning unit. My power surged as I ripped it off the roof and right into Ryland.

The large metal box smashed into him and sent him flying onto the street below. I crawled to the edge of the roof and peeked over. Ryland had landed with the air conditioner on top of him, right in the middle of the brutal battle that Ilyan had been fighting.

At first all I saw was his hand sticking out from underneath the large unit. It was like the Wizard of Oz. I expected the fingers to curl away into a lifeless form, but instead they flexed and moved with strength. We didn't have much time.

The whole area lay in ruins. Most of the cantina was on fire, the street had been ripped apart and was full of giant pot holes, and pieces of asphalt were littered around like odd pieces of modern art. In the middle of it all, Ilyan stood straight and tall with his braid remaining sleek as it fell down his back. Cail was gasping and clutching his side while Edmund stood next to him laughing. When the air conditioning unit had hit the ground, the fighting had stopped and Cail had fallen to his knees. Edmund, however, seemed uninterested in the interruption and had squared his shoulders, his hands moving swiftly through the air, a wave of energy falling behind. Color and energy built as he gathered his magic together. It was obviously meant to be a death blow.

Ilyan seemed to sense that as well, and without even a word, he took off into the air. Edmund's explosion lit up the air behind us as Ilyan scooped me up and continued his flight. His magic grew fast and strong inside of me as the shield returned thanks to our physical contact.

Almost immediately, the glow of Edmund's useless attack faded, and I could hear him yelling angrily.

"Run boy! We both know that's all you can do!"

Ilyan didn't turn, he soared through the night sky, the hot wind whipping at our clothes while I looked back to the destroyed city street, relieved to see Ryland standing. My heart began thumping all the more at the possibility of being followed, though. They had proven once already how quickly they could find me.

"Are you alright?" Ilyan's panicked voice broke through my thoughts and I turned to face him.

"A little beat up, but what's new?" I tried to laugh, but my lungs ached from the large bruises I was sure I had.

"I'm sorry," he said, his lips pulled together in a tight line.

"For what? You protected me, and I got to show that I at least learned something from your lessons."

"For that, you should be proud."

"Oh, I am." I grinned at him, and he smiled back although the look was clouded by the concern in his eyes. I didn't blame him. I was sure we both looked a mess.

Ilyan's magic flowed stronger through me as he checked over my injuries, his face growing hard at what he found. Part of me wanted to push him away, yet I was grateful for the comfort his warmth provided me. His arms around me were a reminder that at least there I was safe.

I leaned into him as he held me, healed me, and flew us away from the man I loved.

The man who hunted me.

CHAPTER 21
ILYAN

I needed the cold air to calm me down.

I was furious.

My magic was pumping through me so rampantly that it was taking far more of my self-control to keep it from flooding the girl in my arms. I had hurt too many people with the strength of my magic, she would not be one of them.

But it didn't help my anger as I found more bruises, more burns, more broken bones.

My father had done this to her. He had used Ryland against her.

It was enough to send me soaring back to him. To end him. If he hadn't been surrounded by so much of his guard I would have, but I would not risk her life.

So, I continued flying endlessly north, letting the chill night air take the edge off my anger. Not that I was about to let my guards, or my shields, down.

I still did not understand why they hadn't followed us. All the more reason to hurry.

"How much farther?" Joclyn asked in a whisper, her teeth chattering.

"We are almost there, Silnỳ." It was a lie, but I needed her to relax.

Carefully, I pulsed more of my magic into her, binding the broken bones of her wrist together and warming her until she relaxed in my arms.

I held her closer. Part of me knew I shouldn't. Part of me didn't care.

With a sigh, she laid her head against my chest, the smell of her filling me. It took self-control not to fly back to Edmund, but keeping my heart calm, my wits stable, with her so close was *torture*.

Her breathing softened, her body pressing against mine comfortably.

"I'm sorry, Ilyan." I nearly jumped; I could have sworn she was asleep.

"For what?" I asked, glancing down at her, she stared straight ahead, her brow furrowed in over-worry. Something that I was realizing was far too common for her.

"For ruining our noncommittal night out to dinner."

I couldn't help but laugh, the phrase had been so perfect before. Now it was a brilliant mockery of what had happened.

"I wish Ryland couldn't track me so easily. I wish he..." I looked at her and she stopped. She was doing it again. I resisted the urge to smooth the wrinkle between her eyes and instead ran my palm over her arm in an effort to warm her.

"At least we know how fast he can track you now." I spoke the truth to calm her, she only seemed to grow more concerned.

"Which is?"

"Too fast for me to be comfortable." Her brow furrowed more. I exhaled, my eyes flitting to faded lights in the distance that marked our destination. "I am sorry you got hurt, Silnŷ. I should be there to protect you at all times."

I was firm, determined. My heart beat faster with the truth of my words. I had made that promise to her centuries ago. I couldn't help but wonder when she would remember.

I pushed the thought away and ran my fingertips over the skin of her wrist, my magic flowing through her skin to the healing bones.

Ryland had broken at least four of them.

"Does it hurt much?"

"No." That time the crease in her brow furrowed for a different reason.

She was stubborn.

"Why did he do this to you anyway?"

"His magic didn't work against me," she said in confusion. I almost dropped her. "I only absorbed it. He never actually did any damage."

"Vut?" My words slurred with my accent in my rage.

"I felt the pain initially, but it would disappear. The same thing happened at the... the... party." Her voice caught. I was sure all of those emotions were too raw, especially after seeing just what Edmund had managed to do to my youngest brother. After seeing him, I didn't blame her. It only made my rage fire more. My father was ruthless, and while he had done worse things, this was yet another thing I would never forgive him for. I would make him pay.

"Every time he attacked me, nothing happened."

"And what about him, does the same thing happen to him?" I asked, my voice hard and controlled.

"Yes. In the end he didn't even react, that's why I pushed him off the roof."

"This is bad." I held her tighter, as though Ryland would just zoom through the air and grab her from me. I checked to make sure the shield was tight around us, just in case.

"What? Why?"

I hesitated. I knew Joclyn was powerful, and she was right in what she had said before. She was not a child. I could protect her, but not baby her. This balancing act was tougher than even Talon had warned me about.

In the end, I knew she needed the truth. Even when I knew what that led to.

"First and foremost, it is limiting you. Ryland will always go after you. He will never choose to fight me. He will seek you out until he kills you, and if your magic will not work against each other, you are even more limited in your ability to fight him. Ryland would gladly enclose you in a fiery building or drop a semi-truck on your head, but would you do the same to him?"

"I threw an air conditioner at him. Isn't that enough?" She probably would have put her hands on her hips if she had been standing. We both laughed at that, the sound cutting through the still air of middle of nowhere Montana.

"Yes, and I believe that may go down in history as the best counter attack I have seen." The sound of our laughter quickly faded. "But the moment you did, you worried for him. I can guarantee you, he did not do the same for you. If I had not taken you away, he would have crumbled the building underneath you, hurled a fiery car toward you, or flung your body into a telephone pole. What would you have done in return?"

Silence stretched, and she looked away, jaw tight.

"You're right. But how do I overcome that? Why I... when I did... I can't hurt him."

"I know. That is part of what makes you good. Never lose that." I held her closer, the pain in her voice echoing the tension that filled my own.

"Never lose that, but also kill my boyfriend?"

"We will find a way, Joclyn." My heart ached, my magic firing in lines of white hot heat as I touched the mark behind her ear, hoping for the millionth time that I would feel the buzz of connection. I dropped my hand quickly, silently cursing Talon for what would be the hundredth time.

Torture.

CHAPTER 22
JOCLYN

"Are we going to be farmers, Ilyan?" I asked, my voice stretched out as I yawned again, my focus on the large farmhouse that Ilyan was slowly descending towards. The place was in the middle of nowhere.

"No, I have had more than enough of that to last me a lifetime," he chuckled, his voice full of a million stories.

I couldn't think of why Ilyan would choose to be a farmer. The work seemed far too slow and monotonous for a guy who ruled a people, led armies, and was far too skilled at kicking trash in battle. But then again, he had also lived in at least three churches that I knew of. They were both mysterious choices for him.

Or what I knew of him.

The guy was an enigma.

Ilyan veered course, taking us toward a town that was a bit farther off from the farmhouse. Well, by town, I meant one street of buildings that weren't acres away from each other.

"Do you see that house in the middle of the main street, the one with a green roof?"

I looked eagerly toward the center of the town, easily picking out the green roof amongst the brightening buildings. The house was huge. Daydreams of my own bed and bathroom filled my mind. I had lived in close proximity to Ilyan for far too long.

"It's not much," Ilyan said, but I scoffed at him.

"As long as there is a giant bed in my own bedroom that I can sleep in for the next two days, I will be happy." I grinned and bobbed happily, Ilyan let out a noise that wasn't quite a laugh.

"There is a bed, of that much you can be sure."

"A bed?" I asked, terrified. "What do you mean *a* bed?" I craned my neck to look at him.

Ilyan looked down on me for a minute, his lips turned up at the corners, before looking away.

"I mean, there is one bed where we are going." I didn't miss the hint of sarcasm in his voice.

"Not two?"

"Not two." He didn't seem too torn up about this.

"But the house is huge..." I looked toward it aimlessly, my excitement dashed.

"We call it the haunted house. We haven't used this safe house for decades, so I am hoping that if there is a spy they won't be able to find us here."

"The haunted house? Why would you call it a haunted...?" We were close enough to the house now that I could see large portrait windows and the family inside having breakfast.

"Someone lives here?" I yelled in a panic.

Ilyan clasped his hand over my mouth as we landed on the roof right against a window that obviously led to the attic. The glass was so old and grungy I couldn't see inside. Ilyan's hand moved down my arm to wrap tightly around my unbroken hand, keeping contact with my skin. Keeping me shielded. Safe. Protected.

I had a feeling he wasn't going to let go anytime soon.

"Someone lives here?" I asked in a whisper the second Ilyan had removed his hand from my mouth.

He looked to me with an exasperated face that I knew all too well, our feet securing us precariously on the steep roof.

"Yes, Silnỳ, someone lives here. The safe house is in the attic. We will be confined to a very small space for a week, and only a week," he added hastily as my mouth fell open in panic. "We call it the haunted house because while they can't see us, they will be able to hear us moving around and talking."

"So we are like ghosts?" I couldn't keep the amusement out of my voice. Despite my horror, this could actually be very entertaining.

"Ano, and thanks to your nightmares, we are going to be very loud, scary ghosts."

I swallowed, my amusement turning to something closer to dread.

My nightmares. I still needed Ilyan every night when I woke up from my tormented dreams. No wonder he hadn't been worried by the one bed thing. He was turning into an overprotective older brother. I shook my head and turned to Ilyan who had opened the window to pull me inside.

'We stay in the attic' had been an exaggeration. Ilyan pulled me into a tiny alcove that was partitioned off from the attic by wood paneled walls. Each wall had a window that looked into the family's cluttered attic. I could see the windows having been installed for security purposes, but my guess would be that they were actually to prevent someone from going crazy in the eight by eight box I had been led into. The windows mirrored the one we had come from, magic shimmering over the glass to keep the family from knowing we were here.

Clever.

"Okay." I was trying to be positive. "At least there's a bed."

I plopped down onto the bed that took up the whole room, and a plume of dust filled the air. I forced a laugh, which turned into a maniacal crazy sound. I had gone from a studio apartment with a kitchen and a bathroom to a room with a bed in the attic of someone else's house.

"It's only for a week, Silný." He squeezed my hand and gave me a sympathetic smile. At least he didn't think I was going absolutely mad considering the sound I was making.

"Okay, but if the next place isn't a Murphy bed in a bowling alley I'm going to be disappointed. We have degrading standards to keep up." I let my snark fly, both of us laughing, and then hacking on the dust that filled the air. "I would throw myself back on this bed if I didn't think I would die of dust inhalation."

I did anyway, thankfully not as much dust exploded out of the mattress that time.

"Don't worry, Silný, our next stop is somewhere much better than this. I promise you."

"Where?" I asked, sitting back up again.

"I have a little house in the south of France. It's right on the beach and has a few bedrooms and bathrooms. It is mine. It is not a safe house. No one except Ovailia and Talon know it's there. After a week here I am going to take you there until we figure out who has betrayed us and you are ready to kill Edmund with your own hands."

"A beach house?" My spirits were soaring already. I had never been to a beach in my life, let alone one in France.

"Yes." Ilyan said. "With your own bed."

I bounced a bit, sending more dust in the air, as I wrapped my free arm around his neck, bringing his tall torso down to my level.

"Thank you, Ilyan," I said. "That sounds perfect."

"I am proud to do it, Joclyn." Ilyan returned the hug, his hand strong against my back, I leaned heavily into him. His arms were so comforting and the wildflower smell of his hair was so relaxing that I found myself slipping into sleep right then. He must have known it, too. I felt his magic pulse against my hand, the heat of his energy growing strong for a moment before receding.

"Don't fall asleep yet, Joclyn. I have a surprise for you." I pulled away, his smiling face greeting me. I stifled a yawn, but he only smiled more.

"Look, Silnỳ." I looked away from his intense glance and into the rest of the tiny room.

In that one pulse of energy Ilyan had completely changed the place. The bed was clean and covered with a new comforter. The carpet on the floor was new, and the walls were white instead of the gross brown wood paneling. There was even a dark blue, black-out curtain over the window. My mouth dropped as I looked at it. It would have taken me hours to create such a change, but Ilyan had done it in less time than it took to inhale, and while shielding me too.

"I take it you like it then?" Ilyan smiled from beside me. I quickly snapped my jaw shut.

"I can't believe you did this..." I let the sentence trail away, unsure of what else to say. He was far more powerful than I gave him credit for.

"I can take it back if you prefer to sleep on dust..." I only laughed at him and swatted his hands down, as if that would stop him.

"No, no. This is fine. Thank you, Ilyan."

"Anything. Now, unless you want to hold my hand for the next week..." Ilyan held our hands up to eye level and squeezed. I didn't feel awkward holding his hand or being near him anymore, yet being obligated to have him touch my skin for the next week sounded miserable.

"Uh, no. Shield me please." I sat down on the new squishy bed, expecting Ilyan to place an immovable shield around the house. It would mean I was trapped again, but I knew there was no other option. I braced for my new prison and closed my eyes to dream about being in a beach house in a week.

Instead of shielding us, however, Ilyan froze for a minute before coming to kneel in front of me.

"I want to try something new if you don't mind." His voice was soft,

soft and mysterious. That tone never led to something normal with him. My guard went up immediately, warning lights firing.

"What? I will not spar with you here, if that's what it is. I'm bound to catch the bedspread on fire."

He chuckled and shook his head. "I want to create a Štít inside of you that will hold some of my magic. It will never infiltrate your body, and I will always have control over it, but this way I can keep a stronger barrier around you as well as be able to track you if we ever get separated."

Ilyan had spoken very fast, his voice strained like he was having a hard time breathing. I raised an eyebrow at him in confusion.

"A Štít?" I repeated. Just when I thought I was getting a decent hold on our abilities, he threw something else at me that I had never heard of.

"Yes. Think of it like a bubble inside of you that holds my magic. It will help me to keep you safe as well as allow you to leave this tiny room from time to time." I jumped in excitement, and Ilyan smiled broadly at my response.

"I can leave?"

"If you let me do this." He wasn't as excited as I was. More warning lights went off and my hope deflated like a punctured balloon.

"What's the downside?" I lifted my brow at him, lips twisting. I didn't want to hear it, but if I was going to do this I needed to know what I was getting myself into. He sighed and looked away, his classic hesitation. I reached out with my free hand and pulled his chin back to face me.

"Ilyan. What's the downside?" He sighed again and I ran my finger along his hairline out of habit; it was something I would do to Ryland. I regretted it instantly. His face went blank as he stared at me. I pulled my hand away, screwing up my face like I had eaten moldy cheese, which was actually how I felt inside.

Thankfully, Ilyan shook it off.

"I have only done this to someone who has undergone the Zêlství a few times before. I am not sure how it will work. It could upset the balance between you and Ryland in some way, or it could upset your magic and you could fight against me even more when I try to heal or calm you. It's a risk."

My heart plunged down like a lead weight. Hearing him talk about the connection between Ryland and I breaking made me uncomfortable. Silly, considering that the connection was the reason I was being tracked, the reason I was bound to enter the Tȍuha on a daily basis, a probable cause of my nightmares, oh and also why any fight I would get in with Ry would be utterly pointless. I still wasn't convinced that one was a bad thing.

I wouldn't have to have a Štít if it hadn't been for my bond with Ry. The only good part about my bond with Ryland *was* Ryland, and he didn't even remember me anymore.

"What if it does break the connection between us? Will my body turn against me like before?"

"It's a risk," Ilyan said, his other hand joining mine. I could still feel his magic surging through me, his shield keeping me hidden from Ryland.

"And if it does? Do you still have your mysterious back-up plan?" Ilyan smiled at my question, that odd look back in his eyes.

"Yes."

"And what is this mysterious back-up plan?" I asked, hoping to get some more information out of him.

"Something a good friend told me about eight centuries ago." He smiled coyly and I could tell that was all I was going to get out of him.

"I hate cryptic answers, Ilyan! Why do you always have to be so mysterious? It doesn't add to the good-guy persona very well." I gave him a look and threw myself back on the bed in an overly dramatic fashion, pulling Ilyan with me.

"Strangely, I am only cryptic with you," he said as he pulled me back to sitting. "And I only do it to protect you."

"My Protector." Saying that this time was like a lead weight in my chest. I was starting to understand just what that meant. Just how much danger I was in, and why I would need a protector in the first place.

"Yes, Silný, and as your Protector, I need to be able to keep you safe." He paused and looked away from me, the pained look back in his eyes. "Will you let me place the Štít?"

I understood Ilyan's warnings, but part of me—a very selfish part—desired the freedom that a Štít might give me. Ilyan ran his free hand over my back, his other still attached to my palm. I wished I had the strength and the ability to cast my own shield—to keep myself safe—but I wasn't there yet. And even if I was, I knew I didn't have the focus to keep it up 24 hours a day. I needed to get better at that, at all of it. And if neither of us had to worry about shielding me, then I could train harder.

I could prepare to kill Edmund.

With that in mind I didn't have to think about my answer at all. "Let's do it."

"Lie down, Joclyn." Ilyan whispered, suddenly tense. This wasn't boding well for his previous warning.

I swallowed and laid down slowly, Ilyan's hand slid up my arm to rest on my shoulder, his fingers never losing contact with my skin. His other hand moved to my other shoulder, leaving his head to hang over me.

We looked at each other, nerves and a heavy sense of personal-space-invasion creeping through me.

"Try to push your magic into one place, Joclyn. Move it all to your toes, or your stomach. Focus it somewhere. I am going to have to battle through the barrier you have against me. It may hurt, but the less you fight me, the less it will."

"You didn't say anything about pain, Ilyan." I choked out, second guessing myself.

"It may not hurt at all, Joclyn. I have never known anyone to be able to fight my magic before, so I don't know what's going to happen." I could feel the warmth in his hands build as his magic congregated right under his skin.

"But you have done this before?"

"Many times, Silnỳ. You have nothing to fear."

I nodded and pushed my magic down to my toes as he had asked, nodding my head once it was done.

"Brace yourself."

"What?"

Any protest was lost as Ilyan's magic flooded me. At first it felt as it always did—warm tendrils circling through my body—but then they began to grow. It reminded me of when I had been sick; when Ilyan's magic had whooshed into me with a speed I had never expected. It was so strong I couldn't breathe. This time I could feel not only his power, but also a wall inside of me; the force of his magic building against a barrier that I hadn't noticed until now.

"Ilyan," I gasped when the pressure built into a pain.

"Let me in, Joclyn. You have to break your barrier down."

I focused through the pain—tried to find a way to break the barrier I wasn't even sure I controlled. The pressure grew, Ilyan's intent to break the barrier obvious. That was when I felt it; what could only be described as a tear inside of me. I focused on it, trying to force it to get bigger. The pressure within me grew and I did the only thing that made sense to me; I relaxed my body, starting at the tiny tear in my barrier.

As soon as I did, the wall fell away and the pressure of Ilyan's magic flooded into me stronger than anything I had ever felt. It was pain. It was pressure. I felt as though I was going to explode.

Screaming, I arched my back in an attempt to escape the pressure and heat which leapt into me. I howled as it continued to build, Ilyan yelling and swearing in a panic as he sat over me.

Before it became too much, before I felt I would be torn apart by the intensity, it slowed. The heat swelled in a spot inside of my left shoulder and seeped away from the rest of me—the pressure leaving—and my body relaxed.

I wasn't sore. I wasn't hurt. My body merely felt heavy and tired, my lack of sleep from the night before and the exertion of the last few minutes draining me. I sunk into the blankets, letting my body fall like a dead weight.

"Joclyn." Ilyan shook my shoulders, but my body didn't want to respond. I could hear him. I could feel the desire to answer or reach out and touch him, but I couldn't make myself do it.

"Joclyn! Please answer me! You must be alright!"

Heat from the spot in my shoulder seeped into me, magic that was unmistakably Ilyan's crawled through me. It was like lightning and my energy returned, well enough that I opened my eyes to his face, lined with worry.

"Oh, God! Thank you!" He grabbed my shoulders and lifted me into him, my body collapsing against him. "Are you alright?" He pulled me away, eyes dragging over me. I could still feel his magic seeping through me. "Did I hurt you at all?"

"I'm fine, Ilyan." The words were more like a gasp.

His face lit up at my words, relief washing over him. The tendrils of his magic returned to my shoulder, but the all-encompassing warmth remained, his shield around me already in place.

"I'm so glad. You have no idea..." Ilyan shook his head, abruptly ending his thought.

I leaned forward into his chest; my body too tired to support my weight. "Was that supposed to make me so tired?"

"No, but I may have exhausted your body a bit more than usual. Having to break down your barrier caused an added toll. I can't normally push that much magic into a person."

"Why not?"

He hesitated, his body tensing underneath mine. I pulled away to look at him.

"Because I kill them, Silnỳ." He was serious and I tensed, Ilyan's magic instantly moved into me, relaxing me. It was odd to have him so willing to calm me; he had never used his magic on me so freely before.

"Kill them? I thought you said that the Štít was safe?"

"It is Joclyn. I could never hurt you. I was just scared," he pulled me to him, his arms wrapping heavily around me. "So scared."

He sounded it too, his voice was so accented that I was sure if I hadn't lived with him for the past few months I wouldn't have understood him at all.

"How do you know you couldn't have hurt me, Ilyan?"

"The same source as my mysterious back-up plan." He winked at me and forced a smile, but it didn't quite cover up his pain.

I swallowed, hesitating. I knew I shouldn't ask, but like the fool that I was, I couldn't help myself.

"You said you killed someone?"

"I was very young at the time. You asked me why I was in the monastery, and that is why. Repentance for my sins I guess you could say. It was an accident and I have since learned to control it."

"An accident?" Despite being so tired, my mind was now wide awake. Fear at what had almost happened, along with curiosity at a piece of Ilyan's past, woke me right up. I felt Ilyan's arms stiffen around me, his unwillingness to let me go evident.

"I was fifteen. I went hiking with my two best friends, Talon who was only eight, and Sarin who was eighteen at the time. We were trying to scale a cliff when Sarin was bitten by a snake. A combination of fear and the snake's venom froze his magic and he fell about fifty feet."

I listened to his voice through his chest. He was speaking so quietly that he was barely audible, just a low rumble of sadness, pain, and regret that rumbled in his chest. So much regret, for something that had happened more than a thousand years ago.

"Talon went for help, but I knew I could heal him. My father had taught me how, and besides, I was the King's son. I could do anything... or so I thought."

He paused, and I couldn't help smiling since thinking of him as cocky was quite humorous. Ilyan didn't like it when people used his formal titles even now. I had done it once in the last month when I had been mad at him, and the glare he had given me would forever be forged into my memory.

"I pushed my magic into him as I had been taught, looking for his injury. I kept pushing as I continued looking, and the more I pushed, the more his body began to shake, the wider his eyes grew, the less he could breathe..."

"And you killed him?" I wrapped my arms tightly around him, keeping my head firmly against his chest. His heart was beating erratically now, the panicked beats echoing through my skull. I wished I knew how to calm him or help him to feel better, however I wasn't sure I knew how, so I moved closer, holding him.

"Yes."

"But it was an accident. It didn't mean you had to hide in monasteries for hundreds of years."

"I know. But when my father found out what had happened, he wasn't mad. He was overjoyed to think that his son possessed so much magic that he could kill a man with one thought. I could see then that he wanted my power for his own use, but I only thought it was for a simpler cause. I was so young, so naive."

"Everyone makes mistakes, Ilyan." I pulled away from him, and wrapped my hand firmly around his, wishing I could comfort him more.

"I make more than my fair share," he said stiffly "But no more. I have been careful with my magic ever since, Joclyn. I am very sorry if I hurt you."

"I'm fine, Ilyan," I said, shaking him off. "Does everyone hurt when too much magic is used? Could I have..." I had fruitlessly attempted to push my magic into others before—into Ryland. What if I had hurt him?

"No, Silnŷ, this curse is my weight to bear on my own," Ilyan said, his eyes digging into mine. "Since then, I have perfected my control over it in the last eight hundred years. I will never hurt you, and now, I can always keep you safe."

I felt the pulse of his magic in my shoulder and my heart dropped right to my toes. Ilyan's words reminded me so much of Ryland's promise right before he had been erased. There was a chance that Ryland could still be there, though, and the Štít with Ilyan could hinder my connection with him.

"What happens if it breaks my connection with Ryland, Ilyan? Besides my not being hunted as easily, I mean." Ilyan laughed at my question and I pulled away from him, already scowling. He just chuckled deeper. The rich, deep, sound so close to his brothers.

"What?"

"You can't feel it can you?"

"Feel what?" I couldn't help it, my frustration was seeping through.

"You let your barrier down long enough to let me break in, but now it is as strong as it was before. The Štít may be here," he said, placing his hand on my left shoulder, right above my heart, "but I still have to fight your barrier to go anywhere else. Your connection with Ryland, and you, should be fine."

I couldn't help the smile that spread over my face. I probably shouldn't have been so happy considering all that the connection between Ryland and myself meant, but I couldn't lose Ryland. Not yet.

My heart relaxed at that and my eyelids sagged closed a bit longer than usual. Ilyan chuckled before lifting and moving my body gently to the inside of the bed against the wall.

My head sunk into the pillow and my body was swallowed by the soft comforter he covered me with. I missed the fabric of a hoodie against my skin, however I was exhausted enough not to let it bother me too much. Ilyan tucked me in, his hands sliding over the blankets and flattening the fabric against me.

"Sleep, Joclyn. I will be here when you wake to take all the bad dreams away." I smiled up at him—my eyes hooded and groggy—he ran his finger along my jaw line, but my eyes had closed before his finger made contact with my mark.

CHAPTER 23
JOCLYN

The dreams never came, yet I still awoke that evening to Ilyan's arms wrapped around me, his deep breathing in my ear. While I had become comfortable with Ilyan in a lot of ways, that wasn't one of them. I don't know what made it okay with the dreams as opposed to without them, but there was a line there. I moved as far away from him as possible—which, unfortunately, wasn't very far—while shrugging off his proximity as being an effect of the cramped quarters. After all, where else was he going to sleep?

I pressed my back against the wall to gaze at the dim light of dusk seeping in through the heavy blackout curtains. We had slept all day, and thanks to the absence of the dreams, I felt more refreshed than I had in months. Of course, I still didn't feel perfect. It had been over twenty four hours since I had last visited Ryland in the Tõuha, and I was already beginning to feel the effects of that.

Rested in one way, exhausted in another. I yawned widely and pulled the necklace out from underneath my dirty white shirt. I sincerely hoped a shower would be in my future today.

I looked at Ilyan, sleeping with his mouth slightly agape, and silently thanked him for not being a snorer before I turned away and plunged my magic into the necklace. I smiled in excitement, looking forward to building a city with Ryland this morning, before closing my eyes and opening them on a disaster zone.

I didn't know how else to explain it. Ryland had destroyed all of his masterpieces before the last Tǒuha I had shared with him, but now our white space held even more destruction. What had once been perfectly smooth, white walls were crumbling and cracking to reveal dark grey veining and what I could only describe as slime. The entire place looked like it was rotting.

I turned on the spot, but the space was empty as far as I could see. I couldn't even hear any crying. This time, everything was filled with silence.

I began to walk, making sure not to step on any of the dangerous looking fissures that were lining the floor, my footsteps echoing around me ominously. I couldn't help the fear that crept up my spine. The air was filled with tension, and my heart was screaming at me in warning.

This deterioration didn't make sense. Ryland's behavior in our last visit might suggest a connection to my dreams, but I didn't know something like this was possible. Everything here reminded me of the nightmares I had been plagued with, not the sweet moments I had shared with Ryland.

"Ryland?" I didn't dare talk too loud, scared I would find him in the same disgruntled state I had before.

"Ryland?" No answer. I continued walking, my panic growing as the destruction increased.

I had made it about halfway across the silent space when a smell of intense rotting reached my nose. It was sweet and pungent like rotting fruit yet with the terrible undertone of death. It reminded me of the dumpster in the alley behind our apartment complex; the dumpster I had almost died behind. The smell continued to grow as I moved until I could go no further.

I pressed my hand against my face trying to disrupt the smell, but it kept coming in waves of nauseating intensity. My vision began to blur as my brain was deprived of oxygen, so I moved back, still scanning the space where the smell was emanating from. The veins of deterioration increased the further you moved in that direction until the floor became a black mass. Not the gentle black of velvet, but a deep, pulsing mass of oil and dirt.

I felt a pull toward the darkest area. I didn't need to be told what was over there, I knew it had to be Ryland. The thought of my little friend trapped in that mess made my heart clench. I took a few steps forward only to be pushed back again by the smell.

"What are you doing here?" I spun at Ryland's small voice, his tiny frame standing behind me.

I looked down on him, surprised to see his face twisted in fear and anger. I had seen that look on him once before, but he had been much older then. Seeing it on the little boy made my stomach flip.

"I came to see you, Ryland," I tried to speak as normally as I could. "What happened here?"

"You shouldn't have come," he replied, ignoring my question.

He wasn't even looking at me, he was looking behind me at the black mass as if he expected something to jump out at him. I followed his gaze, freezing when I saw that it had moved closer.

"What is it, Ryland?"

He didn't answer, he simply grabbed my hand and began dragging me away, his little body putting as much of his strength into it as he could. Even with that, he barely moved me. I could still feel the pull toward the darkness, something calling me toward it, however my feet stayed planted as he pulled.

"You have to get out of here, Jossy," he pleaded, his fear growing even more.

"Ryland? What's going on?"

He shifted his feet at the question, his eyes still not meeting mine. I could tell he was crying. I kneeled down to him, gently placing my hands on his shoulders.

"You have to go," he looked at me with pain and fear and anger—everything meshed together in a face that only said heartbreak to me—and then, he firmly placed his palm against my forehead and pushed me away from him.

My eyes opened to the tiny room where Ilyan slept next to me, his mouth still sagging open. I looked around wildly, trying to place what had happened or how much time had passed. The light had almost fully left the sky and the first few stars were now visible from the gap in the curtain. I hadn't been gone for too long, maybe only ten minutes. An hour in the Tǒuha wasn't long enough for me to fully recover.

I blinked furiously before dropping the necklace; the cold, lifeless stone becoming more of a dead weight than ever. I wasn't exactly sure what had happened.

"Ilyan?" I spoke his name far too softly. I knew I wouldn't be able to wake him that way. But, I didn't want to. I could still feel my heart call to the black pit of rot in the Tǒuha, still screaming that that was where Ryland was stuck. I knew it was foolish, but I also knew that his memories weren't completely gone. I needed to get him out.

I grabbed the necklace again and pushed my magic into it, the moldy room flying into view the moment I closed my eyes. I got a glimpse of the black wall, my feet turning toward it when I felt a heavy weight against my back.

"Get out!" The words ricocheted around my head and followed me back to the small attic room, my breathing becoming a frantic pant.

I dropped the necklace again and leaned forward, shaking Ilyan's shoulder roughly. I hoped he woke up in a good mood. I wasn't sure how prevalent showers were going to be, and we still had a whole week until we went to France.

"Ilyan?" I spoke louder this time. I needed him to wake up. I was scared and confused about what had just happened.

He inhaled sharply as my voice startled him awake, his body jolting upright. Ilyan grumbled and yelled something in Czech before his brain caught up to his body. His hair waved down his back as he shook his head.

"Ilyan?" I whispered, not wanting to disrupt his waking routine and make him even surlier.

"Joclyn?" He turned slowly, his eyes widening to see me sitting there, awake and not screaming.

"You didn't have any nightmares?" I shook my head in confirmation. Ilyan's magic flared in my shoulder, his excitement surging his energy.

"Do you think it has anything to do with..." he stopped himself abruptly, shaking his head.

"With what?" I asked, leaning away from the wall.

Ilyan mumbled something in Czech, his eyes looking anywhere except at me. His lack of response brought back the real reason why I had woken him in the first place.

"Can a Tȍuha rot?" I asked before he had a chance to answer.

"What do you mean?" Ilyan's nervous mannerisms stopped and he swung his legs around to sit cross legged in front of me. "Did something happen?"

"I'm not sure." Now I hesitated. I didn't know how to explain it and I didn't want Ilyan to do his crazy, headache inducing, mind reading thing on me again. My head was already pounding enough from trying to figure out what was going on.

"I went to see Ryland, and everything had been destroyed more. It looked like it was dying, and then there was this smell..." I cringed at the memory of the stench, my face wrinkling.

I shook it off only to see Ilyan staring at me, his eyebrow raised in confusion.

"When you say 'destroyed more' what exactly do you mean? Was it destroyed prior to this?"

I sunk into myself. Crap. I had forgotten that I hadn't told him about Ryland's destroyed artwork, about his outburst or anything that had happened in the last Tȍuha. I had been too wound up in all that had happened with Ovailia that I hadn't even mentioned it.

I pulled the blanket up around me in a desperate attempt to hide in any way possible as I told him about what had happened the last time. His face grew more and more concerned.

"But this time it wasn't something that he had caused, Ilyan. It was almost like everything was rotting."

"What do you mean *rotting*?" He seemed as panicked as I felt.

"I don't know," I sunk back against the wall and closed my eyes, the memory of the place popped right back up. "It almost looked like everything was crumbling away, as though it were a piece of molding bread."

Ilyan looked at me; his magic pulsed and swelled in my shoulder. The feeling was comfortable and yet...

"It's the Štít, isn't it?" My voice was soft.

"I don't think so," Ilyan replied hesitantly, but I could hear the strained undertones that had weeded their way through his voice.

"Then what?"

Ilyan stood, his motions making it clear he was going to pace. The small amount of space hindered him, though, so he stood still, fidgeting uncomfortably.

"Ryland reacted negatively in the last Tȍuha before the Štít was placed, so it can't be that. It has to be something else."

"What?" I repeated, but Ilyan only went back to mumbling in Czech.

"If I knew, I would tell you, Joclyn." I could tell he was trying to make his voice soft, but he was irritated. Whether that was because he had just woken up or because of what was happening, I wasn't sure. But I was irritated, too.

"Just when we solve one problem, here comes another mess." I held up my hand, ticking off every irritating problem as I went. "Ryland can track me faster than either of us thought possible. He is pushing me out of the Tȍuha, but if I don't go, I'll die."

"You still sound like a surly teenager," Ilyan said, his usual morning grumble mixing with his laugh.

"I am a surly teenager." I made a face at him. He didn't laugh. "We just need to work harder. I need you to train me more. Train me faster. You said I'm supposed to save everyone. So, let's do it."

I leaned into him, and Ilyan didn't lean away. He froze, our eyes locked as his fingers intertwined through mine, his magic swelling through me from the Štít.

"We will," his words were as determined as his magic. "But first, we need to do something. Come on, Joclyn."

"Come where?"

Ilyan smiled and pulled me up, the door leading into the attic and the house creaked as his magic opened it.

"I know you said it was the haunted house, but sparring in the attic does not seem like a good idea." I chucked nervously. I didn't feel comfortable going into someone else's house, although it did feel an awful lot like the crazy adventures I used to go on with Ryland. My heart thumped, more out of excitement than nerves.

Ilyan didn't respond. He simply smiled at me and dragged me out of the little room, weaving us through cluttered walkways lined with boxes before stopping in front of the hatch and fold out ladder that led below.

"Ilyan," I tried again, "what are we doing?"

"You're hungry, aren't you?" he asked as he rolled his eyes. "Well, they have food and bathrooms down there and I don't feel comfortable leaving the house yet, so..." He turned toward the hatch as it opened to the dark house below.

"What if they see us?" I asked, but Ilyan only smirked and pulled me down the ladder.

Ilyan hit the bottom and turned, grabbing me around the waist and helping me down.

"Don't worry, Joclyn, everyone is asleep, and even if they were awake, I'd make sure they couldn't see you." Ilyan smiled as his magic flared in my shoulder to send warm ripples through my body.

He then took off down the hall, his feet silent as he moved. Okay, time to be a ghost. I quick-stepped after him, but I felt like every step I took caused louder and louder squeaks around the quiet space. Finally I gave up trying to be quiet and took off down the hall to catch up with Ilyan.

He led us to the kitchen, stopping at a large, ornate bathroom on the way. It wasn't as nice as Ilyan's bathroom at the motel, but it was five star after the tiny bathroom at the apartment.

"I want to take a shower later," I said as we entered the dark granite kitchen.

"Later," Ilyan whispered back before placing his finger to his lips in a reminder to be quiet.

I rolled my eyes at him then turned to rummage through the cabinets. I could tell after looking through the first cabinet that we had walked into Ilyan's own personal hell. I carefully picked up a box of 'Chicken and Dumpling' dinner, displaying it for him like a game show host. Ilyan stuck out his tongue in disgust before he moved to the cabinet next to me. I leaned around to peek over his shoulder before having to press my hand against my mouth to stop laughing. The cabinet was absolutely stuffed with mac and cheese, ramen noodles, and Vienna sausages.

Ilyan made another disgusted sound and moved away with a look on his face of what I would have expected if he had unwillingly walked into a butcher's shop. I grabbed a box of mac and a small can of Vienna sausages and shoved them in his face.

"They go good together," I said, unable to keep the smile off my face.

"If you're human," he countered. I rolled my eyes at his not-so-subtle reminder of his differing species.

"You're half-human. You could at least try." I shoved the box into his hands, and he held onto them like they were poison.

"No, I am half-Chosen." He tried to place them back in my hands, but I side-stepped him, failing to restrain a laugh.

"I'm all Chosen and I love them. Besides, the mac and cheese has milk in it." Ilyan's scowl deepened further, making my laugh grow more.

He attempted to get me to take the box back, but I side-stepped him again only to run into the counter. I spun around and grabbed a container of flour off the counter, ripping the top off in a threatening manner. Ilyan rolled his eyes at me.

"Come one step closer and I'll get you," I said as menacingly as I could.

Ilyan placed the mac and cheese on the counter before over-dramatically stepping toward me. I froze, the look in his eyes stopping all thought. I let one nervous chuckle escape me as he continued to come closer.

"I'm sorry," he said, his voice laced with honey, "you will do what, now?"

I opened my mouth to retort, my rebuttal paused when the light to the kitchen flashed on.

"What's going on in here?" The old man's voice was loud and stern, shaking just enough to show that he was scared.

His yell combined with the sudden appearance of the light startled me. My magic surged through my hands and into the flour, causing the whole thing to explode in my face. The old man took one look in my direction, froze, and turned down the hall screaming and swearing as he went.

"He could see me, couldn't he?" I asked.

"Well, not you," Ilyan said through a smile as he moved to wipe the flour from my face with the palm of his hand. "But he could see the flour. So you were essentially a floating face."

I stared at Ilyan for a minute before joining in with his laughter, the ridiculousness of what had happened hitting me.

"So much for getting a shower tonight," I said through my giggles.

"True, but you do make one great ghost," Ilyan said lightly before pressing his lips against my forehead.

My laughter stopped. I hadn't been prepared for the gentle swoop my stomach experienced at his touch.

CHAPTER 24
WYN

Ever since the incident with Talon's attack and the moving ground I had been plagued with dreams.

The dream usually featured a beautiful little girl dancing in a meadow. She danced through the tall grasses with flowers in her blonde hair. At first, I wondered if it was some repressed memory of me dancing as a child. But I didn't have blonde hair. My hair was dark; it always had been.

After a while it was obvious that I was sitting in the grass, watching her with some guy beside me.

I would like to say the guy was handsome, but he was not Talon. No one could hold a candle to Talon. Talon was tall and built like a football player. This man was sinewy, his skin a burnt brown. Besides, the mystery guy from my dreams was dressed like Henry the Eighth and there was nothing attractive about that.

He looked like a peacock.

It didn't look good then, and it wouldn't look good now. Not like anyone would dress like that now.

It didn't take me long to realize what it was. A memory.

I had been wanting information from what had happened before for years, but now that it was here, I was not sure I did.

A child. A man. Clothes from a time that I wasn't supposed to be alive.

The dream had always started the same; I sat next to the man in my dreams as he talked, his lips moving, no sound coming out. Then the dream would morph. The girl, the man, and I would move from the meadow to a village, then to a marble lined room, and then to the darkness. It was in the darkness that the sound would begin. The only sound the dream ever had was in that room; when the little girl screamed as Edmund tortured her.

The dream only grew worse as whoever was screaming around Imdalind grew louder. The more the mysterious woman in Imdalind yelled, begged and screamed, the more my dream changed. Now, I was forced to watch the little girl succumb, her screams dwindling to nothing until I would wake up and scowl at the high ceiling of our room.

Except for this morning. This morning, I was awoken by the blasting of Ilyan's phone playing 'In the Hall of the Mountain King'.

Wait.

Ilyan's phone.

His direct line.

I rolled over and kicked Talon, my magic surging through him. He jerked as I zapped him, my not-so-nice way of waking him up shooting him out of bed. He tried to crawl back in, grumbling at me before he jumped when the sound of the music hit his ears.

Talon's fingers reached toward the phone as he sat down on his side of the bed, already mumbling. I just curled up under the blankets in the spot Talon had just vacated. It was so warm. I probably looked like a cocoon, a pile of blankets and wide eyes as I stared at Talon's tense back.

"Ilyan?" Even Talon's voice was tense.

Yes, it was the middle of the day where Ilyan was. Yes, he was free to call whenever he wanted. But, the fact that he would have known it was the middle of the night here, and he was calling the white phone that was a direct connection to Talon, was not a good sign.

If someone had hurt Jos I was going to go bat-shit on them. My magic was already flaring in preparation.

Nothing positive was going to come out of this call.

"Princess Mudgy." Talon's voice was low, the statement making no sense to me. For all I knew it was a code word, and if it was a code word...

And I was sitting up, watching Talon as he listened to Ilyan talk, his shoulders knitting together more and more. His body language spelled danger to me. Ilyan's voice was a mellow buzz that slipped through the air until the line went dead and Talon dropped the phone to his lap. Talon hadn't said anything more after the code words.

"What is it?" I didn't dare move.

Talon sat with the phone in his hands, his knuckles white from clenching the small, white box.

The silence was painful. I wanted to hear. I wanted to pry, but I knew I wouldn't get answers anyway.

"Talon?"

"Meet you in my dreams," Talon said tersely. Not once did he look at me as he lay down and opened his arms for me.

Okay, I was seriously on edge now. Whatever had happened was monumental enough that neither he nor Ilyan wanted anyone else to know what had happened. I lay down next to Talon and closed my eyes, letting the magic of the Tõuha take me away to meet with him.

My mind pulled right into his, the large expanse of the Münzenberg Castle courtyard surrounding us. Wispy projections of people walked around us as Talon's memories fueled the Tõuha. The castle was as whole and intact as it had been centuries ago, when Talon remembered it. I was never alive in this castle's time, but this was Talon's mind, what he envisioned our Tõuha to be.

"Okay Talon, you've got to talk to me or I'm going to go crazy. What happened?" I pulled away from him and put my hands on my hips.

"They were attacked."

The tension that now flowed between both of us was too much to contain, and the people around us zapped into vapor, colors floating through the air as they disappeared.

"I knew I should have gone with them! I knew this was going to happen!"

"Calm down, Wynny." I took a breath, knowing he was right. We were both too tense. Me for Jos, Talon for Ilyan.

Talon had been raised to guard Ilyan. It was his job, but Ilyan had dismissed him when he took me as his mate. No matter how much he tried, Talon could never move past what had been his entire life up until a hundred years ago. He still felt responsible for Ilyan, and blamed himself if anything went wrong. Like now, judging by the look on his face.

"We should have gone with them," I amended my last statement and Talon nodded once. "Are they okay?"

"He claims they are." He clearly didn't believe him, neither did I. I could see the sparkling sheen in his brown eyes, the tears threatening to escape from him.

"It's not your fault," I said before he had a chance to let the words he was painting himself with become more of a weight against him.

He nodded once and swept me up against him, his hold tight as his breathing slowed. He finally lowered me back down to the ground, the wetness was gone from his eyes. He did not show emotions like that very often, but when he did, it was my job to build him up and always love him. I would always do that.

"Does he know who betrayed him?" I asked as Talon moved away from me and toward the large, carved stone bench we always sat on. I followed him, my bare feet slipping against the slickness of the cobbles before sinking into the hard, unrelenting seat next to his.

"No," Talon answered simply. His hands brought my feet onto his lap and he began to trace the dark marks that graced my left foot, the jagged swirls matching the ones that ran along the entire left side of my body. "He wants me to watch for signs that someone might know what happened before we announce it. It is probably our best chance at tracking whoever it is down."

"You mean, like a certain screaming woman."

He said nothing, not that he needed too. Everything Talon had said only reaffirmed that someone was inside of Imdalind, someone who should not have been able to get past Ilyan's protective shield. You had to have Ilyan's blessing in order to get past the gate to the caves, you couldn't even use a stutter to get inside. Somehow, though, someone had managed it.

All it would take was one.

We still hadn't seen any more signs of Timothy in Prague, and while we had told Ilyan, he needed more proof. I was already certain. I already wanted to act.

Get one of Edmund's men inside and then, like ants, the rest would follow. They would place themselves in dark corners and hide where no one else would go, waiting until the time was right. Then they would jump out and attack, and within moments, the last of the Skříteks would be gone. I had seen it happen before. There was a reason there were so few of the Skříteks left. It was probably the sole reason I still was not fully accepted in these halls—I had marched against them once upon a time.

Well, my kind had. I was more like the kid with the magnifying glass, burning all the ants away.

"Okay, so we need to find the screaming woman. Because we've been so great at that up to this point." I couldn't help my snark. Not that I was trying to squash it.

"I'm going to order extra patrols. Maybe even a curfew."

I screwed up my face uncomfortably. I guess it had really come to that if Ilyan was being tracked.

I didn't know how to phrase what I was feeling. I wished we could find the traitor, and fast. I wished I could tear their arms from their sockets and torture any of my kind they had let into the halls of Prague. Okay, so maybe that was a little dark, but Imdalind was my sanctuary now, too.

My magic increased beneath my skin, my heart thumping erratically in either excitement or fear; I wasn't quite sure which.

"I will keep you safe, Wynny."

"Oh no! Not this again!" I was up, swinging onto my knees to face him, my finger in his face. "I can take care of myself."

"I know you can," he said, his voice soft as he grabbed my hand and kissed the tips of my fingers. "But I will still honor my promise to you, Wynifred. All of them."

He knew I could take care of myself, I didn't need him to protect me. I heard what he said between the lines, though; I heard how much he cared, and so, my frantic heartbeat continued. I listened to the sound of my full name on his lips, the promise of my safety heavy on the air.

"You promise?" I asked as he kissed my fingers again, my stomach giving a gentle swoop.

"I will protect you above all else."

"Even Ilyan?" I asked, unable to help the question and the accompanying laugh from seeping out of my lips.

"Even Ilyan. I took a vow to protect him the day he was born, but that vow was broken the day I sealed myself to you. It is the vow I made with you that is the most important bond to me. I will honor and protect that before all else." His voice was serious, his tone so true and honest. I felt it melt into me, and our magic surged together.

As our magic intertwined everything inside of me caught fire. I felt a dulled version of this connection outside the Tŏuha, but here, inside the Tŏuha, everything was heightened. Like our magic, our connection, was fire itself.

I was not sure how long we spent in the shadow of the castle, but before either of us were ready, we were pulled away, only to find ourselves in each other's arms in the flesh, the door already being banged off its hinges.

I sighed as Talon left me, his další v příkazu responsibilities already in full force, just as I assumed they would be. Of course, because he always wore his hair short in honor of my people, he had the crimson ribbon that denoted that role wrapped around his wrist, much the same way Ilyan did with the golden ribbon that denoted his crown.

He was gone most of the day, leaving me alone to attempt to clean the huge mess I had made when I had attempted to make dinner the night before, something I never do.

Talk about a nightmare. I had cut my finger off when trying to chop carrots. Yes, *off*. Luckily, I was magical, or I would have forever been walking around reverse flipping people off. As it was, I just reattached it. Though, after the soup became inedible and more solid than it should have been, and I had burned the Galder, I remembered why I never heated food. It was better cold anyway.

The whole experience was a great reminder as to why I hated human food. It was gross, and the texture was so off. I don't know how or why, but humans can take a simple tomato and turn it into a slime-covered bit of goo. I mean, just leave it alone. Don't touch it. Just put it in your mouth and eat it.

Humans eat weird food.

After I had cleaned the house, it became quickly evident that I needed to wash the lace tablecloth. After the finger-loss induced bloodletting, it was clearly required. Unfortunately, the dratted thing was bearing the label 'hand wash only'.

Hand wash only!

Whoever had created such stupid fabric needed to be shown a washing machine. There was a reason that washing machines were created, and that was so hand wash only items needed no longer exist. But, some fool decided to make an unnatural fabric that needed to be hand washed only. Then another silly fool—ah-hem, Talon—decided to buy a bright white tablecloth for his lovely wife—that would be me—made out of said abhorrence of un-natural fabric.

I took the tablecloth down to the old guards' chamber, the closest place that the freezing cold water of the underground spring ran. The dark gray stone of the cavern was jagged, unlike the rest of the tunnels we called home. The roughly hewn walls arched high above my head, the only light source was a small collection of magical orbs that floated and bobbed amongst the shallow cavities of the stone ceiling. The green light that blossomed from above gave the room a dark glow that cast hundreds of eerie shadows around me.

The underground spring ran through the lowest level of the tunnels below Prague—well, the lowest level that anyone dared to go to anyway.

This room and the ancient dungeon below were old relics of when Edmund had first declared war on all magic. In the beginning, the dungeons were used to house traitors, and Edmund's men that Ilyan had captured, but refused to kill. There had been at least ten of the Skřítek army in here at any time, guarding the prisoners in the rooms below.

That was what the Skříteks were after all, an army—an army with the sole purpose of guarding the wells that sat in the lowest points of these caves.

The wells of Imdalind, the center of magic.

Ilyan and Edmund were the last ones alive who knew the way through the labyrinth of tunnels that led down to the muddy wells, which is why it was so scary that someone could be letting Edmund's people in here. If Edmund got in, he could stroll right down to the source of pure magic as if he were walking into a Denny's.

Now, however, the dungeons were bare, the rooms below and the guard chamber I now stood in were only a reminder of how the war had started and how many magical beings there had once been.

Placing the tablecloth into the water, I scrubbed the fabric before letting the majority of it trail away with the flow of the water. I held onto the corner, letting the white lace swirl through the freezing water.

In only a few minutes, my hands had become a lovely red color, although I couldn't feel the burning tingle of the cold. If my skin was threatening hypothermia, I had no idea.

Everything inside me had heated when my skin touched the stone of the floor. My skin felt as though it was alive, the sensation hadn't really gone away since Talon had hit me with that attack. If anything it felt more alive. I hadn't told Talon any of it, not after that look he gave me. Besides, my personal explosion factor increased by ten when my skin was in contact with the stone, now. Although I had only managed to accidentally explode a door frame, I wasn't quite ready to tell him.

"NO!"

I jumped—like, full on jumped—at the disembodied voice that bounced against the stone around me. The high-pitched scream shot through my body in an electric surge that raised every hair on my arms to full attention, my heart rate jumping with the speed of a twenty thousand volt reaction.

"P-please, n... no."

The woman was back, which meant that whoever was torturing her was back, too. They were close, close enough to find me. Close enough for me to find them.

"You're mine, you fudging bastards." I dropped the wet wad of lace down to the stone floor and tuned my ears toward where I could only assume the voice was coming from.

"I... I... w-won't t-tell you!"

My head spun, the voice seemed to have moved from one area of the cave to another. This time, the voice echoed down a darkened hallway that led toward the dungeon. I looked at the dark cavern, my nerves mingling with fear. No way was I going down there alone. No way. For all I knew, that was exactly what they wanted. Last thing I needed was to run into someone in the dark and then accidentally collapse the cave with my magic. Yep, that would be just my luck.

Why did this voice, this woman, only seem to appear when everyone else was busy?

"L-leave me a... alone," her voice broke and stuttered as she once again begged for her life.

I turned, ready to take off toward the sparring hall where the pull of Talon's magic told me he would be, but my wet Chuck Taylors squeaked on the stone on the first step. I froze, expecting to be heard, but the crying remained. The last thing I needed was to scare her off before I could get Talon, and we could investigate.

I began walking again, moving slowly this time until the volume of the crying had lessened enough that I figured I was out of earshot, allowing me to take off on a dead run toward the training hall.

I barreled into the large hall and wove my way through the small groups of sparring Skříteks, each group covered by the shimmering orb of a shield. I worked my way through them, looking like a fool when I jumped at an explosion that rocked against a barrier near my head.

"Hi, baby," Talon said softly when I ran up beside him. His face dropped at the look in my eyes and the transmission of my panic that I was sure he felt through our bond.

"I heard her again. I think she is in the old dungeons."

Talon said nothing more before dragging me behind him out of the training hall and toward the underground spring.

His feet moved quickly, his gait and cumbersome shape unable to be quiet as we bounded through one dark tunnel and another before arriving in the same large cavern I had just left, the dark entryway to the dungeons staring at us hauntingly.

"Are you sure you heard the voice from down there?" Talon asked, his voice shaking. I had never been down there, but Talon had, hundreds of times. The place was probably full of more haunted memories than crazy, flesh-stripped skeletons. There always were in dungeons.

"Of course I am not sure, Talon. Her voice echoes around like an

Olympic game of Ping-Pong. She could have been a mermaid in the water for all I know."

"Don't be silly," Talon said, his voice still shaking, although less than before. "Mermaids don't exist."

Talon took a step toward the stairs, his magic surging as he put on a small shield. Dude, he wasn't thinking about going in there, was he?

"Talon?" I asked from behind him, my voice catching at the petrified anger on his face. "Baby, let's go. We can't hear her anymore; she's gone."

I pulled on him, but he didn't move. I waited, but he didn't respond. His eyes stayed glued to the dark opening as if they had been sewn there. It was creepy watching him stare at something so intently.

"What are you two doing here?" Ovailia spat with as much icy venom as she possibly could and we both jumped.

I whipped around to see her standing in the entry, her long arms folded over her slender torso.

"Staring down holes, Ovailia, what are you doing?" I loved prodding her, and she responded in kind, lips pursed. She looked like a puffer fish.

"That is no longer your concern, Ovailia," Talon said simply, his voice making it clear he didn't feel the need to elaborate. I didn't miss that he lifted his wrist, showcasing the ribbon.

I guessed that was the one good thing about growing up with Ovailia; he was used to her. When you can think of someone as a tantrum-throwing toddler with a stinky diaper, their fits as an adult didn't truly bother you.

"What?" Ovailia said, her voice airy with surprise. I had always assumed it would take pigs standing and walking on their hind legs to surprise her.

"I do not need to remind you of Ilyan's proclamation regarding who is acting in his stead, do I?" Talon wrapped his arm around me, pressing my shoulder into him.

"No, I remember quite well," she said snottily, the airy confusion in her voice gone now as she began to shift her feet.

I stared at Ovailia intently, the nerves in my spine jumping sporadically. Something about the way Ovailia shifted her feet was freaking me out. Her whole body was screaming, liar! Run! I couldn't tear my eyes from the icy blue of hers and the way her lips curled in warning.

"Speaking of Ilyan," Ovailia started, her voice hesitant, "how is my dear brother?"

"Wonderful," Talon answered, his voice pinched.

Ovailia smiled, but said nothing. Talon began to lead me out of the large room, the basket and wet tablecloth perched on his hip.

"Oh, and Wynifred," Ovailia sneered the moment we had passed her, "I wouldn't go poking around in corners if I were you."

"Why? Am I gonna find your old withered skin that you change into every night?" I hissed, my body pulling away from Talon as my magic surged angrily.

"There are worse things. Not that you would remember."

I wanted to lunge at her, but Talon's strong arm wrapped around my waist and he dragged me out and away from her punchable face. I didn't feel comfortable just leaving her there, but something in Talon's body language begged me to.

I complied, choosing instead to stick my tongue out at the stone wall that stood between us.

Yes, sometimes I was just that childish.

CHAPTER 25
RYLAND

"Again! You failed again!"

My head slammed into the bars as my father threw me back into my cell. I instantly curled into a ball, hands weaving through my hair as I tried to protect my head. All I ended up doing was tugging at my hair and rocking back and forth as I sobbed.

"Please don't. Please don't." I barely recognized the sound of my own voice.

"Pathetic." *'How did I ever think you could live up to my expectations?'* "I'm ashamed to call you son."

"Please don't." I just repeated the words, Edmund's snarl fading to laughter in my head.

"Oh, I will do whatever I please. Cail!" Edmund called to his lackey as he turned. I already knew what was coming. There was no escaping him now.

"Ryland," Sain hissed through the bars, I looked up to him, my panic calming a bit. "You have to fight him."

"I'm trying." My whisper turned into a scream and whatever Cail and Edmund had been hissing about silenced, both of them turning to us.

"Do you have something to say, Sain?" Edmund asked with that icy snarl of his, and weirdly, for the first time, Sain didn't recoil like he normally did.

"Only to advise you against this."

"You have advised me, you useless Drak, and nothing has worked.

Why do you think I would continue to listen to you?" Edmund stepped closer, his eyes on me as he hovered over me. He never looked away, even though he was clearly talking to Sain.

I shivered under the iciness of his gaze and continued to tug on my hair.

"Because you know I am right." Sain's voice was weirdly strong, but Edmund didn't care. He just laughed and reached behind him. Cail handing him the knife.

"You were just wrong, Sain, or did you not see us return from our failed attempt at finishing them?"

Edmund looked at no one but the knife. All of our eyes were focused on the sinister red of the blade that Edmund was now caressing. Not even Sain was breathing.

"We will break through love, with love. Broken twisted shards of love... Cail. If you will, we have a svazovat to gain control of." Edmund pet the blade as he kneeled before me, Cail swooping to my side and pulling my shirt up to expose my chest. I tried to fight, but Cail's hand slapped against my chest, covering my heart as his magic flooded through me, freezing me. I could only look from Cail to my father in a panic as my father gripped the knife, grinning in preparation.

"I want her, Cail. Location. Mind. Magic. I don't care what you bring me, but it better be good."

"Yes Master." Cail's voice was tight, my heart a thunder of panic as Edmund lifted the knife, preparing to slam it down, right into my heart.

'I told you not to fight me.'

Edmunds' voice was harsh in my mind as the knife swung down, as Cail tensed against what was about to happen, as I watched in horror as the knife descended, as Sain yelled and slammed his hand through the bars as though to stop the blade.

Instead it slid right through his flesh.

Before anyone could stop it, the sharp point of the blade slid through Sain's hand, and Cail's, and plunged itself right into my heart.

My scream mixed with the others, all of us screaming in the pain of the stab, the pain of the magic as it connected to our souls and sliced against them. The agony was a white hot brand that reached every inch of my flesh. Pain. Too much pain. I couldn't scream enough. I couldn't escape it. Just when I didn't think I could take anymore, the world slipped away again.

This time, however, it did not fade the black hell that Cail put me in when he took control of me. Instead, it faded to white.

Blissful, serene white.

A white so pure that it seemed to burn away the pain. It washed away the agony of what my father had done. My body didn't ache. My mind wasn't teetering on insanity. I was me.

I felt the closest to myself than I had in months.

And even better, I could remember everything. The good, the bad, and her.

"Joclyn." Saying her name without fear or confusion was the exact balm I needed.

I stepped forward, as if I could find her here. But there was nothing but a swirling white smoke. It shifted as I moved, dancing like a fog at dawn. Although this fog seemed to glow, all on its own.

"Ryland." I turned at the voice, ready to attack whoever was there. It was just Sain, although he looked nothing like he had in the cells. His beard was gone, his hair clean, his bright green eyes almost startling against the burnt almond of his skin.

"Sain?" I barely recognized him.

He nodded once, and I instantly turned, there was more than one person who had been stabbed by the knife. I had no interest in facing him here.

"He's not here," Sain said, answering the look on my face. "Cail controls this place. He will bring us into whatever hell he is creating when he needs us."

"He controls this place?" I repeated, millions of questions popping into my mind at the same time. "He controls the soul's blade? Is that what this place is?"

"I would assume so, he seems to have a tie to it. I cannot be certain, though, I have never been stabbed by a soul blade before. If I had to guess, this is our soul, connecting right to the soul that the blade is made up of."

"Is that why I can remember everything? Why nothing hurts?"

Sain turned to me, sending more of that smoke swirling. "Yes. That's good. It means that whatever they are doing to you hasn't reached your soul. Keep it that way."

He said that as if I could control it. I just nodded politely and turned, still looking for Cail. Or whoever else was here.

"I knew one existed, but I never expected him to use it." Sain mumbled to himself as he looked around, almost as though he was in awe of the whole thing.

I felt my stomach twist. I could never be in awe of something like this. Someone was tortured to create this.

"If we are here, then where is the person who was used to create the blade?"

"Rosaline." Sain repeated the name of the blade with a bit of reverence. I felt my stomach flip. "I would assume she doesn't want to be seen. Or perhaps she is doing more important things..."

I had been imprisoned with Sain since all of this began, but I had never heard him speak like this. Well, not unless he was in sight. He sounded like a monk, or a hoity-toity prince.

"Listen, Ryland," Sain suddenly turned, rushing toward me and surrounding us with swirling smoke. As he moved, the fog behind him parted, revealing what I could have sworn were trees. Odd, I hadn't seen those there before.

"Now that Edmund has control of our souls, he is not going to stop. You need to decide how hard you will fight, and how much you are willing to give."

The smoke moved all on its own that time, the trees having moved closer. Yes, those definitely were not there before. Judging by the panic that had overtaken Sain, I would guess that whatever Sain had planned was moving closer.

"Give to Edmund?"

"To Joclyn." He was frantic now. I, however, smiled. Being able to think of her freely was warming, even if the situation was dire. "This bond between you is dangerous, and it is breaking. It may be hurting her as much as it is you. What would you give to protect the bond? To protect her?"

"Everything. I would give everything."

"Good. Then promise me, vow to me, that when the time comes, you will do exactly that. And if you need, you will break the connection to her to save her. There are things she has yet to do. Things I have yet to gain from her. Promise me you will break the svazovat and the Zêlství if it meant it would save her."

I didn't need to think of my answer to that.

"I promise." I had barely spoken the words, when the white was sucked away, and a blood stained forest surrounded us.

CHAPTER 26
JOCLYN

One night without the dreams had changed something about them. The trees were taller, darker, and more sinister. Growling surrounded me, the one previous voice changing to an echo on all sides.

Growing closer.

Closer.

It was all too real. The sounds, the way my hair stood on end. I could have sworn I had been transported to this forest and was not just dreaming it. The dreams had never felt so real before, the change was frightening.

I stood frozen in the middle of the large clearing, trying to find out what else had changed, what I should do, which way to run. But where do you run if enemies were everywhere? I needed to attack.

Tightening my jaw, I let my magic boil, the heat swelling in my fingertips. Even that felt more real. My magic in the dreams had always felt foreign, but this was distinctly mine.

I would need it. I wasn't alone.

My chest heaved as I breathed in and out, my nerves coursing wildly as the growling grew and figures formed amongst the trees. Their black shapes shifted around the tall trunks of the forest, weaving through the trunks as they moved closer, forming a wide circle, trapping me.

The growls deepened into something more human and my magic shifted, preparing for an attack.

Preparing for him. I had felt this pull before, in Santa Fe. Which could only mean one thing: Ryland was close.

But I had never felt this pull in a dream before, even before Santa Fe. I couldn't shake the feeling that something was off.

All at once the growling stopped, the shapes disappeared, and I was alone. I stopped spinning, freezing as I faced the pull of my magic and tried to ignore the desperation my heart felt at its call.

"It's not him. It can't be him."

I closed my eyes and tried to wipe the feeling, but then I heard it, the one growl that had always begun the dreams. I listened intently, trying to decide if it would be Cail, Ryland, or Edmund. It was always one of the three.

"I bet you thought you were free. Free of these nightly terrors." I spun at the voice, my insides tensing at seeing Edmund standing at the edge of the tree line with Cail standing next to him protectively.

Edmund moved out of the trees, Cail following, as the dark shapes materialized again; dozens of Trpaslíks emerging from the woods. Cail stood apart from those around him, his dark eyes dancing with menacing joy. I shrunk away from him instinctively, waiting for him to pounce at Edmund's command.

"Did you really think you were safe?" Edmund asked, my insides freezing over at the wicked sound. He didn't sound as if he was enjoying himself anymore, he was simply angry now.

"It's a dream, Edmund. Of course, I am safe." I pushed my voice out as strong as I could make it, the sound bouncing around us. Cail smiled at my response while Edmund fumed more, his large frame becoming even more menacing.

"No. Not here, in Santa Fe. Did you think you were safe."

I narrowed my eyes at him, my heart rate accelerating. This was a dream...

"Yes." My voice was a squeak.

"Safe with your Protector? Safe with Ilyan?" Edmund spoke his name like it was acid. It was the polar opposite to how he spoke to Ilyan. The two-faced nature of this man was unsurprising, but still unsettling.

I didn't challenge him with a response. I simply faced him, eyes digging into his.

"He would rather hide you than face us," Edmund sneered. "Hide like a coward. Is that what you are, a coward?"

I straightened my shoulders and met him straight on. "No more of a coward than you are."

Edmund laughed, the sound deep and joyful, making the hairs on my neck prickle.

"Really? How am I a coward, Joclyn; can you tell me that? I never hesitate and I fight when needed. Not like some newly awakened half-breed I know."

I flinched inwardly and stepped back. Those warning lights were just getting brighter.

"At least I don't kill people for sport."

"You're right. You simply choose not to kill anyone." Edmund's eyes flashed and I took a step back. I had seen that look enough in these dreams to know when to be scared of it.

This time my reaction was visible, and my movement did not go unnoticed. Cail stepped toward me, his body coming precariously close as he came between me and Edmund. I moved away only to find a wall of henchmen behind me.

"You are scaring her, Cail." I couldn't miss the wicked joy in Edmund's voice.

"Let me do it now," Cail said as his eyes dug into me.

"Be gentle with her, Cail. I am enjoying this little game. I want to see how it pans out."

"Oh, but sir, she seems to think that her dear Protector is innocent," Cail said, his eyes never leaving mine. My magic flared, but I kept it inside. If I was going to attack him, I needed to wait for the right time.

"Even Ilyan has killed, Joclyn. He has killed hundreds of times. He even killed Wyn's mother. Your best friend's mother, and yet, you still trust him?"

My hands flexed at Edmund's words, strangely I didn't doubt for a moment that they were true. It bothered me, but not as much as it should have.

"Ilyan doesn't kill for pleasure unlike you." I tried to keep my jaw strong as I faced Edmund, but it was hard with how I was quivering.

"You know this for a fact do you?" Edmund continued. "Ilyan sure does seem to enjoy a battle, doesn't he, Cail? He just can't walk away from a fight. From a possible kill."

When Edmund smiled—his blue eyes flashing—I froze; I knew what he was referring to and it scared me. It was the face of power Ilyan always got; the look of pure, crazy joy.

"You're wrong." My voice caught as I spoke, causing Cail to laugh. The deep sounds made his youthful frame rattle. I turned my head to face Cail, my angry glare directed at his dark eyes.

"Oh, really?" Cail said, his tone making me cringe. "You know this for a fact?"

"Yes."

"Trust him, do you?" Cail moved closer.

"Yes." I kept my voice strong even though Cail's responses felt like ice down my spine.

"Trust him to keep you safe?" I nodded once and Cail's wicked smile deepened. I attempted to move away from him again only to be stopped by the ever encroaching wall of people.

"He can't hide you from me forever." Edmund said and Cail smiled evilly, a small laugh escaping at his joy for whatever was to come. His eyes moved from mine to a spot behind me, the wicked upturn on his lips growing.

"Besides, I have something you want." Edmund continued.

Something told me not to look, but I couldn't help myself.

Ryland was there, but not the dark eyed monster. It was the boy that was being dragged into the clearing by his curls. Ryland fought and kicked, yelling at his captors in sharp Czech that I had never heard from him. Edmund turned to me with a joyful smirk, and I took a step back, careful to keep my emotions under control.

This wasn't right. I had felt it before, but now I knew it.

The dreams had always been distorted bits of a memory or expanded portions of my worst fears. They had never deviated from my expectations. There were always memories of Ryland, enacted horrors of his death, torture, and visions of my own impending death. But this was different. This was something new.

Nothing about Ryland being dragged into a forest was a memory. Cail's and Edmund's taunting of me, yes. But not this... Ryland looked up to me, his bright blue eyes pouring into mine, and I stopped breathing.

"He remembers you, you know." I hadn't even noticed that Edmund had come up beside me. My whole existence had frozen at seeing Ryland, *my* Ryland, there. "After all of my hard work, he still remembers you."

"Jos..." Ryland gasped my name, his body barely strong enough to support himself when sitting. I breathed in a shaking breath, willing my feet to stay still.

"There is only one thing to do now, sir..." Cail's hand ran down my arm, but I barely noticed.

"I leave it to you, Cail."

"Jos... Run." Ryland whimpered and I took a step forward, only to have my progress instantly halted by Cail's arms around my waist.

The contact broke me out of my shocked reverie. I turned to Cail, my face hard, my magic flaring in preparation.

"Let me go." I snarled as I attacked him, letting my magic fly. It only seemed to bounce off his skin. He didn't let go, he just leaned closer.

"Oh, no, no, no," Cail said, his face impossibly close to mine. "You see, I have a message from Edmund for you." I spun to where Edmund had stood a moment before to find the space empty. Cail smiled and I felt my insides freeze. Everything seemed too raw, too real. I turned to Cail, my head held high, not wanting to give away that I was scared.

"You see Ryland there? Alive? His memories returned? You have exactly one month to turn yourself in to us before we dispose of him."

"No!" I turned toward Ryland in a panic, but Cail's arms held me securely in place. I fought against him, though his grip was too strong, his hold brutal against me.

"Don't listen to him, Jos. Just run!"

"Panicked now I see. A little worried?" He pressed his cheek against mine, his body moving with me as I fought his grip. "Well you should be."

"Joclyn, run!" Ryland screamed at me as the large man behind him produced a glimmering blade. The man didn't even hesitate, he just ran him through with the glowing red blade. Ryland screamed and fell to the ground, his body not even fighting its loss of life.

"No!"

"Now, now. Don't worry. This dream is only a shadow of what's to come after all. I'm sure you have realized by now that we can't really hurt you, just like you can't really hurt us. Magic doesn't work here. We can only wake you up. The same has happened to him, although I would *like* to kill him." He said condescendingly, the terrible tones snaking around my insides like slime.

"Let me go!" I screamed as Cail released me, and the extra force sent me hurling across the clearing toward Ryland's body.

I gasped his name, my heart breaking all over again as I held his lifeless body in my arms.

We were all shadows in a dream world. None of this was real. I repeated the fact to myself, trying to stop the heavy waves of emotions from overwhelming me. I felt my lungs reaching for breath and my heart's irregular beat speed up. I couldn't look away from Ryland; his bright blue eyes still burned in my mind.

"Oh, and one more thing," Cail said from behind me, "if you don't come in one month, you can give up hope of ever seeing Wyn again, too. I will finish what I didn't before." He sliced his finger across his neck, his lips curled in a wicked sneer.

"You'll never find her." I tried to sound strong, but I knew the panic had seeped into my voice.

"Like I never found you? Ryland's bond with you was so weak we could barely track you across one little city, and if we were already in the city, what does that say about how safe you are?" I opened my mouth to respond, but was silenced by his smile. "With or without Ryland, we can find you anywhere, Joclyn. It's all about who you know."

"Who do you know?" My voice echoed around the otherwise empty clearing. Cail only laughed.

"Really? You think I am going to give away information just because you ask? Tsk, tsk, that's not how it works, missy."

My magic surged uncomfortably under my skin thanks to the raw anger that coursed through me. I pulled the power together and shot it at him in a stream of fire powerful enough to do some real damage. It bounced off the same as it did last time. Shock crossed Cail's face for a second before the attack hit him square in the chest.

Cail looked at the spot on his chest before he began to laugh, long and deep. "Oh, Edmund's going to be sad he missed this."

I clenched my teeth and raised my hands, ready to fire something at him again.

"Now you are going to fight me?" Cail said, "Sure why not! After all, magic doesn't work here the way you are thinking, you can't hurt a shadow."

I felt the blood leave my face, I sent another attack. He didn't even flinch, but when his attack hit me it felt as though every muscle had been ripped from the tendons. I screamed, Cail's laughter echoing over everything as I fell to the ground.

"You're no fun," Cail pouted, kicking dirt in my face. "Kill her. I will tell my master it is done."

I didn't have time to register what he had said before I felt the blade plunge into my back. I felt the cold metal separate my flesh and grind against bones as it moved deeper into me. I screamed in agony as my body fell on top of Ryland's lifeless corpse.

I woke up in a panic, my terrified screams bouncing around our tiny space.

Ilyan's arms were already wrapping around me, his hand moving to cover my mouth. I didn't hear his comforting sounds, his song. I screamed into his hand, his warm skin muffling the sound.

I couldn't calm down. I couldn't shake the feeling of the dream. My mind kept replaying what Edmund had done, what Cail had said, and the feeling of Ryland's lifeless body beneath me.

Eventually, my screams died down, but my cries remained. Howls of despair broke from my chest as my breathing caught and shuddered. Ilyan held me until my sobs had stopped; his song finally seeping into my mind as he sang it over and over.

"It's okay, Joclyn. I'm here. The dream is gone." Ilyan's hand ran over my back, the touch triggering something in me. I pulled away from him in fear, wiping away the last of my tears. I looked beyond him to the large scorch mark on the wall and my insides turned to ice.

"They're not dreams," I gasped through the remnants of my sobs. "They are something far worse."

CHAPTER 27
JOCLYN

Ilyan pried the memory of the dream out of my head and replayed it twice before I made him stop. I couldn't stand to see it anymore. I felt like my heart had been ripped open and filleted. Reliving every emotion with Ilyan had been brutal; he felt every pain, saw all of my reactions.

The exertion from the dream mixed with Ilyan's brain foraging had left me exhausted. I stared as Ilyan fidgeted in the small space, mumbling in Czech, his face twisted in anger and fear. I couldn't even find it in me to ask what was going on. I wasn't sure I wanted to know anyway. His reaction had made one thing very clear, Ryland remembered me, and I had one month to save him.

"Ilyan," I spoke quietly, hoping he would hear me, but he kept speaking to himself. "Ilyan!"

He stopped and turned, his long hair swirling over his face. He fixed me with a stare that scared me. Not because I was frightened of him, but because *he* was scared.

"How is..." I stopped, I didn't want to know. "How do I keep them out of my dreams?"

"I'm not sure you can. I am not even sure how they are doing it. The only thing I can think of is that they are using Ryland somehow, but how..." he faded off, and I looked down to my feet. Great, my connection with Ryland was causing more misery.

I loved Ryland. I loved the person Ryland used to be. The way he held me, sheltered me, protected me. After the last few months, whenever I thought of him there was fear. I had yet to see the positive side to our bonding.

My pity party was cut short by Ilyan's finger dragging along the chain around my neck. I looked up, unsurprised to see him kneeling right in front of me.

"I need you to go to Ryland. See if the boy will tell you anything. If something is happening, he should know at least a part of it."

"But what if he doesn't tell me? What if he pushes me out like last time?"

Ilyan gathered my hands in his. "I need you to try, Silnỳ."

"Okay. But will you call Wyn while I am gone? Make sure she is okay? Tell her I will call her in a few hours." I pulled the chain out from under my shirt, letting the ruby settle on my palm.

"Of course. Tell Ryland his brother says hello." Ilyan smiled, but it was strained. I nodded my head once and settled back down into the bed before closing my eyes and walking into the Tȍuha.

I opened my eyes to the kitchen of the LaRues' estate and gasped. It was the same kitchen my mother had worked in—the one I had first met Ryland in—except very little was recognizable about it. Yesterday's deteriorating expanse had been replaced by the kitchen, or an echo of it. The same rot had taken over. The counters were dark and slimy. The sink was filled with dirty dishes and molding food. Chunks of marble flooring was missing. The once pristine cabinet fronts were burnt, or rotting, or worse; many were hanging off of their hinges. I jumped at the large rat that I glimpsed running from one food container to another.

I wanted to scream. This felt like a trick or a cruel joke, being stuck in the place where everything had started. A place that reminded me so much of my mother and Ry.

No one was in the kitchen, and I didn't hear any sounds. I looked hopelessly toward the door that would eventually lead me to Ryland's room. The front was grey and covered by what I could only explain as rotting marshmallow.

"And I thought the dream was bad..." I brought my magic up, unsure if I would need it, or if it would do anything, but I wasn't about to take any chances.

I had been told that Ryland remembered me. I just needed the boy to remember me, too. I needed him to tell me what was going on. I walked across the kitchen and swung the marshmallow covered door open wide to reveal the little five year old boy I had grown to love on the other side. The hallway behind him was just as deteriorated and neglected as the space I stood in.

He looked up at me with dark blue eyes and a hard set jaw. I had never seen any child look so angry.

"You can't have him," he said, stronger than I would have expected him to.

"Have who?"

"Your friend. The one you are looking for. The man told me you knew he was here, but you can't have him. I won't let you."

"My friend," I couldn't ignore the overdrive my heart was experiencing right now. "He's here?"

"You can't have him," Ryland spat, his little voice laced with hate.

"Why... why not? Ryland, you have to tell me..." I kneeled down to get close to him and froze, hate and anger were the only emotions that looked back at me.

"You can't have him. If I give him to you, then I die." His eyes grew wide when he said the last word. It looked more like he enjoyed it than he was scared of it.

"Who told you that?"

"The man."

"What man?" My nerves jumped once, something inside triggering me to run.

"The man with the black eyes. He told me you wanted me dead. That's why you want your friend. Because you hate me."

"I don't hate..."

"LIAR!" His yell rocked the air and I lost my balance, toppling backward into the kitchen. "You hate me. And I hate you, too."

Ryland took one step forward and looked down at me. I cringed away from him, seeing what he was planning a second before he did it. His little hand made contact with my cheek, the strike hard against my skin. I closed my eyes and turned away from him, knowing instantly that Ryland had pushed me out of our Tȍuha.

I opened my eyes to dim light seeping through the blackout curtain. I had only been gone a matter of minutes. Ilyan's weight was firm on the bed behind me as he talked on the phone.

"Tell no one where we are, Talon. You cannot tell Wyn or Ovailia. This information is for you alone."

I twisted on the bed to face Ilyan who sat with his back to me. He turned at my movement, his expression dropping at the look on my face, which I was certain told the story of what had happened.

"We will be here a week, then we will be moving." Ilyan's eyes dug into me as he silently asked me what had happened. "I will tell you our next location when we get there, Talon. The less information you have the better."

Ilyan reached out with his free hand and moved some hair that had fallen over my face, his hand resting against my cheek for a moment before he turned back to his phone call.

"I don't care how much damage she causes, she is officially out of the loop, Talon. She cannot be Ochrana on this. Call me if you find anything out. I don't care what time it is, just let me know."

Talon spoke for a few minutes before Ilyan clicked the phone shut and turned to face me. I stared at him, unsure of what I was going to say.

"How bad was it?" he asked, softly.

"Bad." I pushed myself to sitting, cursing this tiny space when I hit my head on the windowsill. I looked away from Ilyan before I began to explain it to him, not trusting myself enough to look at him.

By the end of it, Ilyan had frozen in place. I could feel the waves of his energy ripple around the room, the kinetic anger of it scaring me.

"First my dreams, and now the Tòuha? How is he doing it, Ilyan?"

"I don't think the question is how, I think the question is with who."

"Who?" I asked. I didn't like how he had phrased that. "What do you mean?"

"Ryland has made it quite clear he would rather die than hurt you, so I don't see him letting them use the connection much. Cail made that clear in the dream. He believes Ryland's bond is weak, but I have seen how strong it still is. Ryland is masking it somehow on his end, which means they would need a blood connection to increase its strength."

Ilyan paced as he spoke, his jittery movements making me feel more on edge than I already was.

"What do you mean, 'a blood connection'?" My stomach flipped. I wasn't sure I wanted to know exactly what this could mean. Visions of severed hands filled my mind and I cringed.

"You're an only child, right?"

"Yes," I said, my eyebrows rising in confusion.

"And you are sure your mother is dead?"

My insides froze at his question; I brushed away the pit of loss before answering him.

"She was crushed by a refrigerator and didn't flinch, Ilyan. I'm positive that she's gone." Ilyan sat down next to me on the bed, his hand reaching to rest on my knee. His eyes were apologetic, but not for what he had said, it was also for what was to come. My insides seized.

"What?"

"They have your father." I narrowed my eyes at Ilyan, waiting for something worse, but there was nothing. My father. The man had barely been part of my life.

"My father? But how..." I stopped and exhaled, trying to find the right words to fit my confusion. "He disappeared before they even knew about my mark. How could they have him?"

"I am afraid they have him for a completely different reason, Joclyn. How they found out he was your father, though, I have no idea. I worried about what had happened after he disappeared, but I never imagined..."

"What are you talking about?" I interrupted his rambling. "What would Edmund want with my Dad?" Ilyan's eyes locked with mine for a moment before looking away, his hand moving to drag through his hair. I reached out instinctively and grabbed his wrist, stopping him before he avoided me.

"No, Ilyan. You have to tell me now. I don't care if you don't tell me everything, but you have to tell me about my dad. You have to tell me this."

The pause between us was deafening. It dragged on and on as Ilyan and I locked eyes. The blue of his was shocking. I could see each fleck of gold move as he contemplated what to tell me. I kept my hand firm on his wrist, my resolve strengthening.

"Please, Ilyan." I was surprised when my voice broke. Ilyan nodded once before turning away from me, his phone moving to his ear. He hadn't even dialed. I saw the screen flick white as a call was connected, the system being overridden by Ilyan's magic.

"Thom." Where had I heard that name before? "They have Sain. I need to tell the Silný. Tell Dramin of our arrival. We will be there in two days."

Ilyan dropped the phone without even waiting for a response, the screen flashed white before returning to its screen saver. I looked from the phone to Ilyan, more confused than before. My body froze at the look Ilyan was giving me—bright and fearful—and the strength that was radiating off of him.

"Thom?" I asked, still trying to place the name in my memory.

"Thomas. He is my brother."

My jaw must have dropped a visible inch. Wyn had told me of him, of how he went missing years ago.

"But I thought he was missing, I thought..."

"I hid Thom after Cail found out where he was hiding. I couldn't trust anyone with the knowledge of his survival, it was easier to have them believe he was dead."

The explanation of Thom made sense, however it still left me confused, "What does Thom have to do with my father?"

"Thom had been your father's bodyguard for four hundred years until twenty-five years ago when they were found at a University in Ohio. Thom was able to wipe your father's memory and put him into hiding before he, himself had to run in order to pull Edmund off of your father's trail. We never thought your father would fall in love, let alone have a child. So when he found me in Prague with no memory of who he was, you can imagine my surprise. I almost told him of his past right then, but I could already see bits of the magic breaking away; parts of his memories seeping through. It was how he knew to find me; how he knew that something was wrong with your mark. I needed to break the truth of his past to him gently, and right then we didn't have the time. I needed to get to you first."

Ilyan ran his hand heavily through his hair in agitation. I couldn't piece any of it together in my mind. I tried to sit and listen, waiting for Ilyan to finish, but my disjointed questions kept flowing of their own accord.

"Wipe his memories?" I repeated, "Why would Thom do that?"

"It was necessary. Thom knew he could get Edmund's men to follow him, but your father had to stay behind. Your father's memories are more of a curse. It was essential to displace them in the chance that Thom failed and your father was found."

"But he..." I tried to form a question, but it didn't come. After all, I didn't want to hear this. What he was saying couldn't be true. There wasn't any way it could be.

"You're wrong, Ilyan. You have to be. I mean, I have grandparents, and uncles, and cousins!"

"The Despain's lost a son, Jeffrey, in a car accident. Thom put your father in his place, replacing their grief with a surrogate." My mouth dropped open in horror. So much of my life was a mystery, a lie. I felt so empty.

"But why..." I broke off, not sure what I wanted to know.

"I will not tell you everything, Joclyn, because not all of it needs to come from me. I will tell you this, however, by blending the blood of your father with the magic of your mate, Edmund has found a way to torture you, to infiltrate you from a distance. To try to stop you from what destiny has planned for you." Ilyan's strong voice ricocheted around the space, the power behind it seeping into me uncomfortably.

"But... my father?" I asked, still waiting for clarity. Everything was a jumbled mess in my head.

"His name is not Jeffery, it's Sain. He was bred from the mud to be one of the first of the carriers of magic. He was the first of the Drak."

I gasped, the quick intake of breath trapped inside of me as I froze in place. The Drak. That name I knew.

The Drak were beings who possessed the gift of sight. The magical creatures who had been massacred at the hands of Edmund LaRue. Well, not completely; my father was still alive. The last one.

My head reeled like I was inside an old cartoon, my eyes bugging out of my head unnaturally. I knew this was huge, and scary, but I didn't quite understand how it had happened or even what it all meant.

"So, if my father was the first of the Drak, does that mean I am a Drak, too?"

"No, you bear the kiss of a Vilỳ. You are one of The Chosen, nothing more." Ilyan placed his hand softly on my neck, his whole hand covering my mark. I looked up to him, my wide eyes reflected back at me through his own.

"Then why does Edmund want him so much? What was so important that he had to have his memories erased?"

"He is not just any Drak, Joclyn. Not only is he the first of his kind, he is the one who saw a child come forth to defeat an opposing power. He was also tortured at the hands of my father so that he could convince his own daughter to work for him."

"You're not saying..." I stopped as his meaning caught up with me. I wasn't panicked. I wasn't scared. I was in shock.

Ilyan nodded as I pieced the last of it together. I remembered this story. Edmund had tortured Ovailia's mate to get her to work for him. Sain, my father. My father had been Ovailia's mate. He was the one she had double-crossed in her rise to a supposed power. No wonder he wanted his memories erased.

"But I thought he was dead."

"Edmund weakened their Zêlství to convince her of that. Ovailia, believing him to be dead, broke their bond. Then for hundreds of years my father kept Sain hidden as he forced information of the future out of him until the day that Sain escaped with his memory mostly gone and his powers greatly weakened. I stopped Edmund's Vymåzat and put him into hiding. He was too hurt—too ashamed—to ever see my sister again. Ovailia still believes him dead and I will do everything in my power to keep the truth from her."

"So Ovailia doesn't know?" My stress lessened a bit, though not a lot. I knew I should be reacting more—crying, yelling, screaming—but nothing came. What Ilyan had said hadn't sunk in yet.

"No. She doesn't know he is alive. It is best kept that way."

"So, what my father saw... about the child... It's about me, isn't it?" My pulse thumped in my ears in fear of the answer I knew was coming.

"Joclyn, it is not my place to say..."

"Then don't tell me everything, Ilyan. Don't tell me what he saw. Don't tell me how, or why. Just say yes or no!" I moved to stand in front of him, making it clear I wasn't going to let him off the hook. He hesitated for a moment before answering, his eyes large and softer than usual.

"Yes."

I hung my head, my jaw tightening.

"I cannot tell you all, Joclyn, not yet. But soon. We are going to see Thom and Dramin in two days, and then you will know everything. And when they tell you... Joclyn, when they do, please do not hate me."

"Ilyan?"

"Know I am here to protect you as I was born to do; as I have promised you." He reached up and softly traced my skin from my jaw to the mark and back again, his eyes never leaving mine. I couldn't move. I didn't register the shiver that moved through me at his touch, either. I merely stood still, waiting for everything I had been told to settle into an understanding.

"I will do whatever I must to keep you safe." He smiled and my breath caught, which only seemed to increase his happiness. Ilyan inhaled before he stepped to the window, the pane opening as he approached it.

"Ilyan?" I wasn't sure what was happening.

"I am going to go get some food. I won't be long. Promise me you will stay inside these walls."

I nodded and he began to move, however I knew I couldn't let him leave without knowing one last thing. He wouldn't tell me everything, but I knew this one thing he could.

"Ilyan?" I asked again. This time he turned, hesitant.

"What does Silnỳ really mean?"

His answer came without hesitation; two words spoken before he exited the space, leaving me alone with a bit of his warm magic shielding me from the inside.

"Most powerful."

CHAPTER 28
JOCLYN

Most powerful.

I stared at the window where the last light of day was seeping in. My body was exhausted, but all the new information had left me feeling jittery and wide awake. I plopped down onto the bed, Ilyan's cell phone bouncing around next to me.

I grabbed it without thinking, flipping it open and staring at the screen saver. I missed my phone. I missed all the pictures of Ryland and me. I ran my fingers over the screen, repeating his number in my head as I traced it.

What I wouldn't give to be able to call him, to hear his goofy voice as he taunted me, or to feel his hand against my skin as he comforted me. I closed my eyes, willing an imaginary phone call; bringing his voice so strongly to the forefront of my mind that I could almost hear it. I could feel the leather seats of his Lotus as we talked about everything... anything. We could talk about my father, about what I...

"So, Dad," I sighed aloud to the empty space. "You cursed me, and you didn't even know it. You keep getting better and better."

The stress at what Ilyan had said was growing, but so was my irritation at continuously not being told everything. I couldn't talk to Ryland, but I could talk to Wyn. If anything she could help me get my mind off everything. I held down the number three and waited impatiently for Wyn to pick up the phone.

"Jos!" She yelled the second she picked up. "Oh, please tell me you are okay! I've been so worried since Talon told me what happened, and then you didn't call me at all yesterday. I knew I should have gone with you! This never would have happened if I had—"

"It would have happened either way, Wyn." I cut her off, worried she would run out to find us right now. "If you were here you would have gotten hurt, too."

"Too? You got hurt?" She sounded like she was going to bust through the phone and seek revenge on my hand. I rolled my eyes.

"Nothing a little magic can't fix." I heard her exhale through the line.

"I can still come out if you want; an extra pair of hands doesn't hurt."

"No!" I sat upright, nearly bonking my head on the windowsill again. "Stay where you are. You'll only get hurt if you get too close to me."

"Stop being dramatic," she scolded with a laugh, I rolled my eyes and fell back on the bed again. At least someone was calling me out on my crap. "Is Ilyan okay?"

"He's fine," I felt his magic pulse in my shoulder, as though he could sense us talk about him.

"Are you sure you don't want me to come out?" she asked again, her voice gaining back some of its normal, playful quality.

"I'm sure, but can you do something for me?" It was a silly idea, but I needed some of Wyn's silliness right now.

"Sure! What's up?"

"Sing me a Styx song." I smiled as she laughed, her voice echoing through the phone.

"You're a dork," she giggled.

"I can't help it, you've got me addicted."

"Addicted to Styx?" I could hear her disbelief, and I only smiled more.

"Yep." I rolled onto my side, bringing the blanket with me

"Alright then, when was their first album released?" I paused, leave it to Wyn to see through my little lie.

"1840." I said as confidently as I could, causing her to laugh harder at me.

"Liar." She obviously wasn't going to sing anything for me.

"Come on, Wyn, just sing me one of their stupid songs." Her loud gasp came through the line. I could almost see her offended face, dark scars and all.

"I thought you said you liked them?" Her voice was hard. Leave it to me to piss her off by offending her precious Styx.

"Please, Wyn." I let a little bit of whine seep into my voice. I didn't want to have to explain.

"I'm sailing away," she sang, "I've got to be free..." I smiled. Her choice of song seemed a little bit too perfect given the current situation.

She sang and sang, and I let the lyrics wash over me, their meaning becoming deeper the more I heard.

Her song faded away, although I knew it wasn't over, somehow the words had helped; the edge of my anxiety had dulled and I felt a bit more relieved. I was glad I had Wyn, I just wished she was closer.

"Thanks, Wyn."

"No problem. I've gotta go find my husband now, okay? I'll call you in a few hours."

"Sounds good, Wyn." The phone clicked off and I shut Ilyan's and placed it in my pocket before turning to the window.

I knew Ilyan had asked me to stay in the room, but I needed fresh air. I had been trapped inside for two days, stuck in the same clothes I had been attacked in. My hair was gross, and I was beginning to stink. Besides, I had his shield around me, not around the room. I could go anywhere. I shuffled my feet as I rationalized, hoping this wasn't going to end up being one of my stupidest decisions ever.

Although, I was starting to get a collection of those.

The crisp air of dusk filtered into the room as I opened the window, and I breathed it in, letting its heavy energy fill me. The chill undertone of it reminded me of home. I opened the window more and stuck my head out, a slight evening breeze tugging at my hair.

The steady warmth of Ilyan's magic surged through me. I focused on it as I pulled my body out of the window, moving to sit on the small eave right next to the casement.

The main street of the small town was directly below me. Most of it was occupied by houses and small businesses. I could see a small restaurant and a gas station, and I thought I could make out about three hardware stores.

I curled my legs into my chest, cursing the breeze and my lack of hoodie for giving me goosebumps up and down my arms. Even with the chill, though, it still felt nice.

I could already feel myself relaxing, even with what was going on, and all I hadn't been told. I was going to remedy that immediately. It was my destiny, after all.

"I thought I told you to stay inside?" Ilyan's voice wasn't mad; he was more amused than anything.

I didn't even open my eyes.

"I knew you would keep me safe," I said, patting my shoulder.

"Well, I am glad you have so much trust in me," Ilyan said as he sat down next to me, "but next time wait until I get back. You are lucky I was paying attention or someone would have seen you."

I blushed and looked at him. I was glad he wasn't mad at me, but I had a tiny bit of guilt for not listening to him.

"I couldn't stay in there any longer. I felt like I was going to collapse in on myself."

"I guess I did leave you at a bad time, but I couldn't..." Ilyan stuttered to a stop, something I had never known him to do before. I looked at him curiously. His head was leaning back against the house as he turned to look at me, his long hair glistened in the setting sun.

"I'm sorry," he said through the night air. "I never should have left you right then." He paused and exhaled, his hand reaching around me to rub the goosebumps on my arm away.

"It's okay, Ilyan."

"How are you coping with everything?"

"I don't know." I sighed and Ilyan squeezed me against him. "I'm not sure I understand everything, especially everything about my dad. It still doesn't make much sense."

Ilyan rested his head on top of mine, the weight awkward, though also strangely comfortable.

"It will in a few days, and then if you have any questions, I will answer them. I promise. I will keep you safe and help you through anything."

"My Protector." I spoke it like the term had become revered.

"Yes." Ilyan moved me closer into him, giving me a squeeze before he moved away. "Well, your Protector has broken a cardinal rule and brought you back a greasy, meaty, nothing-in-it that's-good-for-you sandwich for dinner."

I jumped away from him as he produced a brown paper bag from a fast food chain I knew all too well. I couldn't help the smile that broke across my face. There wouldn't be a dandelion leaf in the bag. I opened it greedily inhaling the smell of grease.

"Oh, I could kiss you!" I said, holding the bag against my chest.

"Um, I don't think that would be wise," Ilyan responded a bit too quickly, his words morphing into an uncomfortable laugh.

I looked at him wide eyed. I didn't know why his quick shut down of my offhand comment hurt, but it did. I sighed and looked back to my cheeseburger, my stomach swimming uncomfortably.

"Unless you were talking to the cheeseburger, in which case, I will leave you two alone." Ilyan laughed, my reaction obviously having gone unnoticed. Thank goodness.

I pulled the bag open and removed the haphazardly wrapped burger, silently thanking Ilyan for keeping it warm. The smell of meat, cheese, and mayonnaise wafted up to me. Right now I didn't care that my last cheeseburger had been the night I had to run from Ryland. I was happy for what could only be described as comfort food.

I took a bite and savored it, letting everything roll around in my mouth. I groaned and let my head fall back against the house in appreciation.

"Fat, burned meat, and dead veggies... and they get that kind of reaction?" Ilyan said, disgusted.

"Leave me alone, Ilyan, me and my cheeseburger are having a moment." I took another bite, ignoring the fact that he was staring at me.

"Do you want some?" I asked, waving the burger in his face. He cringed away from me, his face disgusted.

"No."

I laughed and moved closer, waving the smell toward him.

"That is far worse than mac and cheese and Vienna sausages."

"You know you want some," I teased, enjoying the fact that I could make him smile.

"I haven't eaten meat in five hundred years, Joclyn. I am not about to break that trend now."

"Don't sound so much like an old man, Ilyan." I smiled broadly at him before taking another bite of the cheeseburger, rolling my eyes back in slightly exaggerated joy.

Ilyan laughed at me as his phone in my pocket rang. I pulled it out and handed it to him, but he only turned it around to show me Wyn's name on the caller I.D.

"Speaker phone," I said through a full mouth, covering my face politely.

Ilyan laughed and rolled his eyes before answering the call, hitting speakerphone as he did. He didn't even get to say hello before the sound from the phone hit our ears.

Ilyan's face lost its smile and my cheeseburger lost all flavor as screams, yelling, and explosions filtered from the phone's speaker.

"Jos! Jos, pick up the phone!" Wyn's screech was loud above the screams, panic and tears lining her voice.

I swallowed deeply, the cheeseburger feeling like lead going down my throat. Ilyan stood in a panic, holding the phone in front of him as he yelled into it.

"Wynifred! What's going on?" Ilyan's voice was commanding and powerful, the waves of it spreading out from him.

"Ilyan? Oh, thank heavens!" There was a pause and more screams as Wyn panted through the mouthpiece.

I stood on the roof, my body tense as I leaned into Ilyan, trying to see the phone as if the screen would show me a play by play as to what was going on. Ilyan's arm wrapped around me, his muscles tense as he held me around my waist. I had the distinct impression he might launch us into the air at any moment.

"Wynifred? Where is Talon?"

"They got him, Ilyan. They took him. I think..."

Another pause and more screams. I swear I could hear Wyn whimper and scream in the background. I clutched Ilyan, my fist wrapping around the fabric of his black polo shirt. When Wyn spoke again, it was clear she wasn't talking to us; her voice seemed farther away as if she had dropped her phone somewhere.

"No! Please don't!" I cringed as she screamed, her voice cracking and breaking. Other voices yelled in the background, yet I couldn't make anything out. Ilyan's knuckles went white as he clutched his phone, his arm tightening around me.

"Father! Please don't! Don't let them hurt me!" I listened to her plead with Timothy. Timothy shouldn't be in Prague.

Wyn screamed again, her voice breaking and crackling though the phone's speaker.

"Ilyan!" Wyn screamed, her voice losing strength. "Run!"

She hadn't even gotten the full word out before the line went dead. Ilyan's knuckles were white and hard against the phone, his jaw clenching below his ice-like eyes.

"Ilyan?"

He stared at the phone as the screen flashed white and Ovailia's name popped up as he placed the call. It rang once, twice, and then a third time. We stayed frozen against each other until she answered, the same screams and explosions sounding in the background.

"Ilyan?" Her voice was frazzled and scared. I had never heard her sound so raw before. "Ilyan, where are you? Please tell me you are all right."

"We are fine, Ovailia. What is going on? Wyn called..."

"They took her," Ovailia cut him off, panting as she moved through whatever destruction was tearing through the space. "They took Talon, too. I don't know where he is, but Timothy dragged Wyn off."

"Who's they?" Ilyan's voice was hard as he spoke through his tightened jaw.

"Father. Timothy. There are hundreds of them." I cringed. I didn't need her to elaborate; I knew who they were now, Edmund's hundreds of Trpaslíks.

"I don't know how they got in. Our whole city… I don't know how many are going to make it out."

"Get out as many as you can, Ovailia. Meet me in Isola Santa in five days. Can you do that?"

There was a pause as Ovailia breathed, more explosions filling the air that was already rent with screams. The phone's speaker vibrated at its exertion.

"I can try."

"Be safe, Ovailia."

"And you, Ilyan."

The line went dead for the second time and Ilyan's other arm came to wrap around me. I could feel his heart hammer through his chest, his anger pulsing his magic through his veins, and in turn, through my shoulder. I was beginning to understand what Wyn had said about Ilyan's temper.

Wyn.

"Ilyan?"

"I know, Jos." I tensed at the use of my nickname. He had never used it before. "I will keep you safe, I promise."

"And how do you plan on doing that?" I jumped at Cail's voice, a hundred volts of emotion plunging through me. I clung tighter to Ilyan as I moved my head away from his chest to face the two still figures that stood in the street below us.

"I told you I could find you," Cail sneered through the dark. Black-eyed Ryland standing right beside him.

CHAPTER 29
WYN

Now that Jos had finally called it felt like a weight had been lifted from my chest.

This must be what mothers feel like, I had seriously been overly worried for her. Not that I needed to be, she had Ilyan after all. Ilyan wasn't going to let anything happen to her.

I was more scared about Ilyan sacrificing himself for her safety and leaving her stranded somewhere.

I wouldn't put it past him.

Something was clearly off, I mean why else would she have me sing Styx songs? I would have to bug Talon when I saw him. If I saw him; he was way too busy lately. I had curled up in the blankets like a guinea pig, waiting for Talon to get home so I could interrogate him. Instead, sleep took me, the blonde girl and the Henry the Eighth wanna-be occupying my thoughts almost immediately. I watched the girl dance and the man laugh as he chased her.

He laughed.

He had never laughed before. He had never talked. I had seen his mouth move every night, but no sound had ever escaped.

The image jumped and bobbed, the girl flashing from one side of the field to another, the man doing the same before he ended up right beside me.

"We should go," he said, his voice conspiratorially low.

I would have jumped at the sound of his voice had I been in control of my body. I wasn't in control, though, and the dream me smiled joyfully, while inside, I only felt more and more panic.

"Go where?" Dream-me said. At least I thought it was me. It came from me and sounded a bit like me, although the voice was different, more mellow, adult, not the electric youthful tones I had now.

Yet another reason I was starting to doubt these were memories. Maybe I was the girl and I just didn't remember.

"Away," he answered as he turned to look at me, his blue eyes smiling.

I tried to scream and push him away, but I didn't have control over my arms. My body didn't move. I could feel my lips smile, even though I didn't want them to. I could hear my mind think about his eyes, the eyes of his father, royal blue.

His father?

It was my thought. I felt it form inside of me, but it wasn't mine. It wasn't true. How could it be? How could I know, how did I know?

"We can't get away," that wretched voice spilled out from me again, even though I still fought to control the body.

"We can run." His voice was desperate.

I felt myself screaming, but the body I was trapped in didn't follow suit. Instead, the body smiled and touched his face. I screamed until my eyes flashed open, the silence of our dark room filling the air in the wake of my nightmare.

I wasn't sure what had woken me. Not the dream, surely? I always slept through those. Then again, the man had never spoken to me before either.

I lay still, my mind pushing away the images of the dream while still trying to recall pieces of it. Why would I want to recall that? It was a dream, and I was not a Drak. My dreams had no meaning.

"I understand." I jumped as the voice came out of the dark. Even though I recognized it as Talon's right away, I had not expected to hear it or the stress that lined the words behind it.

"Only a week? Is it that unsafe?"

I could tell Talon was trying to be quiet. The light from the phone lit up his face, making the deep stress lines look even darker. My heart clunked as his stress leached through our connection and into me.

So that was what had woken me.

"What about Ovailia? She has been asking questions—"

Talon's voice cut off as Ilyan interrupted him, his head bobbing in agreement with something Ilyan said. I pulled the blankets up around me as I watched him, fighting the temptation to go back to sleep. I wanted more information.

Only a minute later, he lowered the phone. The light from the screen went out, leaving us alone in the brightening yellow shades of dawn that seeped in through the vent in the ceiling of our cave.

"Is everything okay?" I asked, my voice startling him.

"I didn't know you were awake." Talon moved over to me, his weight indenting the bed enough to make me roll toward him.

"Yeah, someone's stress woke me up."

"Not mine, surely?" He smiled as he moved to sit next to me, his arms draping over me as if he was locking me in place.

He looked down at me, and my stomach twisted. I knew what the fire behind his eyes meant, what the deep surge of magic I felt tumble through me was leading up to.

I smiled back at him, arching my back as I lifted my face to meet his, my lips pressing deeply against his.

My magic surged violently at the intimate connection, our magic rejoicing as they met their mates and curled around each other.

Talon lowered himself onto me, his body heavy against mine. I sighed as his hand moved up my arm to cup my face. His tongue dragged against my bottom lip before he left my lips and peppered deep, longing kisses along my jawbone and neck.

I couldn't help the moan that escaped my lips. I couldn't understand where this was coming from, especially with the stress that had lined his voice only a moment ago, but I wasn't going to complain. I was enjoying this far too much.

Talon kissed my neck once more before he stilled against me, his breathing deep and ragged. I closed my eyes and savored the way our contact moved through my body, the way every nerve ending felt illuminated. I could have stayed like that for hours, but I could still feel Talon's erratic heartbeat.

"Are you okay?"

Talon shifted his weight, moving back to sit at the edge of the bed, his hand cupping my face. His dark eyes glistened as more light filtered into our room, the sparks of dawn igniting around us.

"Talon?"

"I think I know who the crying voice belongs to." Talon's bold statement made my arms and legs feel like lead. I hadn't expected that.

I sat up and leaned closer to him, my heart thumping, desperate for more information.

"Who?" I asked, my voice only a whisper, the sound swallowed by my jumpy nerves. I could feel my magic skitter around inside of my skin, ready for a fight.

"All day yesterday, only one person asked me about Ilyan's welfare—several times, each more desperate. It was very unlike her to care—"

"No!" I gasped. His statement combined with what he had said on the phone a moment ago putting the name in my head. "Not Ovailia! I mean, she's a jerk, yeah, but she wouldn't betray him. Not again."

"What would stop her from doing it again?"

I held my tongue. He had a point. Ovailia's personality was not one that lent itself to loyalty; she would go where the chips lay thickest.

"Besides, the crying we keep hearing, it is like she is fighting against the bind Ilyan placed over everyone to keep his location secret."

I could only stare and nod. He had a point. Ilyan had placed that little touch of magic inside of everyone when he first went on the run, hundreds of years ago. I shouldn't be surprised it was still around and strong enough to keep Ovailia's tongue at bay.

"I'm going to go talk to her," Talon said, his voice making it sound as if he was walking into a death camp, not simply speaking with Ovailia. I didn't want to face Ovailia, not in the slightest, but I couldn't let him face her alone. This confrontation would not be pretty.

"Let's go," I said, trying to ignore the foreboding pulse of my nerves.

I jumped out of bed and took the two quick steps to my dresser. I didn't even look as I grabbed random items of clothing in my rush to leave: Styx shirt, red skinny jeans, black converse.

Talon, now dressed himself, nodded once before moving toward the door, my converses squeaking as I followed him.

"You go to her offices," Talon commanded, pointing down one side of the long hallway at the end of rooms. "And I'll go to her bedrooms. If you find anything, send me a warning flare through our bond."

"No attacking first?" I teased, rising up on my tiptoes to kiss his nose.

"No attacking first." He was firm, he knew me so well.

We turned as one and raced down the hall, my shoes squeaking in the dead-of-night-silence that dripped from the stone walls.

After a few minutes, I began to hum my favorite songs, keeping me comfortable as I went from room to room, growing ever closer to her office.

I was about halfway there when I noticed it; Talon's magic was gone. The pull that told me where he was had vanished. It wasn't gone like when he shielded himself because even then, I could have felt something that would have led me in his general direction; this was just gone.

I froze; everything inside me turned icy with dread.

I turned, my heart beating angrily as my feet ran toward him, my mind moving from panicked to focused with each step. I reached Ovailia's room quickly and found the door ajar, several voices filtering into the hall.

The voices overlapped and bounced around the smooth stone of the walls. There was more than Talon and Ovailia's voices; I could hear at least two others in there, both male, their voices deep and scratchy.

I tiptoed toward the door, flattening my back against the dark stone of the wall as I closed my eyes and expanded my vision into the room. I had to work to press it that far, but what little I could see was enough to make the contents of my stomach turn and my heart thump against the thin bones in my chest.

My father and Edmund were in there.

It was not just henchmen that had made it in; *they* were here. Edmund and Timothy. I knew they wouldn't travel alone either; they never did. Somewhere, in the once safe halls of Imdalind, an army stood in waiting.

I clasped my hand over my mouth, trying to keep the panic stuck inside, my breath trapping itself inside of my chest. Everything inside me constricted, my body freezing in place even though my feet were threatening to run in and attack.

Don't move; don't let them know you are here.

Ovailia sat in one of her many large, carved chairs, filing her nails as if she was bored out of her mind. In the corner of the large room, a man was crumpled and chained, his own blood staining his clothes and dark beard. The beaten man moaned and rocked as his fingers clawed against the wood of Ovailia's floor, large scratches appearing as black sparks flew from his fingertips.

My father stood in the middle of the room, Timothy's short, squat frame barely enough to hold Talon's wavering form steady, his neatly trimmed beard glistening with blood I knew didn't belong to him.

My whole body jolted at seeing Talon. I saw him, but I felt nothing aside from my own fear. There was no magical pull alerting me to his presence, no surge that would have normally filled the air. What had they done?

Edmund paced the floor in front of Talon, his tall, muscular body draped in black as he smiled wickedly toward him. Edmund moved to slick his curly hair back against his head, and my stomach muscles tightened, his knuckles were bloody from having turned my husband's face into a punching bag.

I watched them for only a moment before my eyes narrowed, my back straightened, and even through the fear and stress, I knew what I had to do. The shield around me was strong enough to block me from sight as well as hiding any magical signature I might have been broadcasting.

I let one breath escape my lips before I walked into the room, careful to keep my steps silent, my eyes watching the reactions of all those in the room, wary of being noticed. No one reacted or even looked in my direction.

My chest loosened, although just briefly. I was not walking into a surprise party—I might as well have been walking to greet my death.

"Tell me what I need, Talon, and I won't hurt her." I froze at Edmund's words, his voice dark and chilling. I turned toward him, worried he had seen me.

His focus was not on me, however, it was on Talon, whose face was already swollen and bloodied at Edmund's hand. I restrained a shout as Edmund pulled his arm back, his fist glowing white, before a strong sucker punch to the gut winded Talon with one shot. I froze as Talon grunted in pain, my magic attempting to escape.

"What about the rest of your men, Edmund? What would they do to her? I know how your deals work." Talon's voice was broken and pained, blood spattering around him as he forced out the words.

"Oh, we won't kill her if that's what you are asking," Timothy said, my father's voice full of pure enjoyment. Edmund only smiled at his response before wiping his hand on a bright white cloth, smearing it with red.

I moved toward the back of the room, my magic crackling under my skin as it kept the shield in place. The angry energy rippled through me in a raw need to attack, but not yet. If I began an attack now, I would be dead before I could get within reach. It was all about the timing. Running in to face the three most powerful people in the world was only a death sentence. Hell, attacking them on my own was a death sentence. Still, I wasn't scared—a fool, yes, but not scared.

I stared at Talon's face as I moved. My conviction growing as my magic surged. I would protect him, just as he would me.

"And the others? Will you hurt them, too?" Talon asked, his voice continually fading.

I fought the urge to run to him, choosing instead to knot my fingers around each other, hoping the tension in the small joints would dispel the panicked anger that was building in my heart.

"Oh, what do you care?" Ovailia snapped from the chair she sat in. "It's not like you are their rightful leader anyway."

"Very well put, Ovailia," Edmund said with true pride in his eyes. "She was always my good child," he said, more to himself than to anyone. "Took us a bit to break through Ilyan's spell and get the information I needed, but we got there in the end."

"Will you hurt them?" Talon repeated, his jaw tightening.

"Save who you can, Talon. Don't worry about the others. They will be in capable hands, I promise." Edmund leaned down close to him, his lip sneering only millimeters from Talon's face.

"Give me what I need, Talon," Edmund snarled.

"You better make it look good, Edmund." Talon laughed deeply, his voice loud as he taunted him, while Timothy strengthened his hold at the sound.

Talon's eyes widened as he attempted to fight against my father's hold, yelling out. The struggle only lasted a moment before Edmund placed his hand against Talon's skin, his struggle for release turning to one of agony as Edmund's magic seeped into him, the powerful attack torturing him.

No.

I didn't know if this would work, I couldn't harness the power beyond busted door frames, but I had to try. I slipped my right shoe off, letting my skin come in contact with the floor of the cave. Even through Ovailia's carefully preened wood floors I could still feel the energy of the caves. It prickled up my spine and down into my arms. I smiled as it seeped through the rock of the cave and into me. It flooded me as the power controlled me.

For the first time. I felt as though I could control it. As though it was part of me.

Now. I stomped my foot to the floor, a rumble spreading out from me as I shook the wood and stone. Edmund swore as the energy hit him, the power rushing up into him. I focused as my magic spread from the floor and into Edmund and Timothy. They called out as their bones grew and vibrated, the pain of my attack sending them to the floor.

"No! It can't be!" Ovailia stood in fear as I took a step forward, each hit of my skin against the ground sending more ripples of energy across the surface and into Ovailia as well. All three writhed with pain as I lifted Talon with my magic and pinned them to the ground.

"Wynifred!" My father's voice yelled as he fought against the painful restraints my magic held him in.

I moved forward to grab Talon just as Edmund broke the magical bond that surrounded him. His voice howled as he stepped forward, blocking my path to my mate, his eyes boring right into where I stood.

I wanted to say he couldn't see me, but the way his eyes bored into me, I was sure he could. I froze, carefully calculating the possibilities and my chance of survival.

I knew it was low, but right then, I didn't care. Right then, I just wanted Talon, even if it meant we would die in each other's arms. Not that I wouldn't go down without a fight.

"You will live to see Talon again, Wynifred." I froze at the voice that rasped through the air, the familiar tones triggering some long forgotten memory. I didn't dare turn to see who had spoken. I trained my eyes on Edmund's fingers as they flexed and glowed.

Edmund sent a surge shooting toward me without even a flex of energy. I threw myself to the side, the heat of his attack warming my skin as it grazed the air beside me. I caught my scream in my throat as my body landed roughly against the wood floor, sending more ripples through the stone and everyone to the ground.

"Run!" The voice came to me again, the yell pounding into my head.

I didn't want to listen. I didn't want to leave Talon. I could hear each beat of my heart as it begged me not to. Hear the voice's statement echoing around my head. Talon would live. I wanted to believe him.

I needed to believe him.

I jumped to my feet before anyone else had a chance to find theirs. I looked one last time toward Talon, my feet feeling like lead as they carried me away from him. I ran down the hall, their screams following me as I bobbed and weaved through the web of halls.

I didn't look back. I didn't dare. I only had a matter of minutes before they would regain their strength. I needed to draw them off my path while I figured out what I needed to do next.

I attempted to slow my heartbeat as I ran, but it was no use. Edmund was inside the caves of Imdalind. Edmund had gotten past Ilyan's protections, and Ovailia was the one to guide him through.

Ovailia had betrayed us all.

My soul froze as screaming began to fill the halls. The sounds of battle exploding.

The cave vibrated as the battle increased, screams ricocheting around the stone halls as the battle broke out all around me. I changed my direction, charging right toward them.

Edmund's final execution had begun. Only one race stood between him and the wells of Imdalind, and if Edmund had his way, there would be nothing left by the time the sun rose.

Edmund had started a war, and I was not going to back down.

CHAPTER 30
WYN

I ran through the halls toward the screams, the shouts increasing the closer I got to the battle. I couldn't deny the throb that wished to run into my father, to end this before it even had a chance to begin.

Each step I took thundered through the underground tunnels, shaking lamps and doors, each step recharging my magic and sending my magical currents surging.

Flashes of light filtered along the dark stone, the screams chasing the shapes as they rippled through the once dark halls. I passed a raging fire, not turning to see what was keeping the blaze going as I ran, my feet taking me toward the loudest concentration of noise. But, as I turned into another hall, I froze in place.

This was where it had begun. I could tell by the splatter of red on the walls, the screams that still lingered in the air. I could tell by the lifeless bodies of my friends that littered the ground, left to die with no one to hold them.

I fought the panic that rose in me, the hopelessness that tried to take hold; instead, choosing to let my anger and conviction fuel me. I tiptoed around at least twenty of my friends; selfless people who had taken me in and loved me after my father had tried to kill me. My father.

He had brought enough Trpaslíks into Imdalind to begin and end a massacre in one swipe.

This couldn't be happening.

I raced into another hall as I pulled out my phone. My heartbeat was erratic as hate and anger fluctuated through me in a surge that only hyper-activated my magic.

The phone rang in my ear as I ran, the loud thrum vibrating through my head and mixing with the frantic beat of my heart.

"Pick up," I growled to myself, turning a corner as I made my way toward a seldom-used row of apartments. "Pick up, Jos! Jos, pick up the phone!"

"Wynifred! What's going on?" I had never been so happy to hear Ilyan's voice. I could have kissed him, cried into him, and thanked him for saving us; but I knew he couldn't save us. I wasn't calling for a savior; I was calling with a warning.

"Ilyan? Oh, thank Heavens!" I yelled into my phone, one knot in my stomach loosening while another one tightened.

"Wynifred?" Ilyan boomed, his commanding voice seeping into me through the phone. "Where is Talon?"

"They got him, Ilyan," I panted as I ran, my eyes threatening tears. I would not cry, not right now. "They took him. I think..."

I turned from the darkened hallway into a place that was never used, a place I had hoped I could hide, only to find my father standing in the middle of the dark stone-walled room. My words dropped off my tongue as I saw him there and I froze for a moment. It was a moment too long.

A loud crack echoed through my ears as a powerful attack impacted with my spine and sent me across the large room to collide with the rock wall in front of me. My head hit the wall, my bones and joints rattling hard enough to vibrate through me in a claw of pain. The pressure increased as I hung there, Timothy and Ovailia's laughter loud in the quiet space.

"No! Please don't!" I screamed, feeling them come right up behind me. The force on me increased and my scream followed, louder this time.

"Father! Please don't!" I shouldn't beg; I knew it was pointless. "Don't let them hurt me."

No sooner had the words left my mouth that I was flung through the air again, my hands sparking as I attempted to find someone, anyone, to attack. The movement was too quick, the flight too short, and before I knew it, I was stretched out on the hard floor, my father restraining my hands above my head and Ovailia standing over me in an oppressive straddle.

I looked away, desperate to see anything other than the wicked sneer of the blonde above me, only to see the still lit screen of the cell phone reflecting off the dark stone.

"Ilyan!" I screamed, knowing I might not be allowed to live after this point, and hoping that my last warning was not my final goodbye.

Ovailia's eyes went wide, her head whipping around in fear as I yelled her brother's name.

"Run!" I yelled. "It's Ovailia!"

It did not take her long to locate the light, one pulse of her magic destroying the small box. I only hoped my warning had reached them before the line had gone dead.

"Nice try," Ovailia said, her voice heavy with indifference and anger. "But sadly, I don't think it's going to work." She smiled, and her face lit up like a maniac. Ilyan would get the same light when going into battle, but instead of giving hope, this one twisted my spine and rippled through my stomach.

Cold fury was raging inside of me.

"You have no idea what you are up against," I snarled, happy to see her recoil.

"Oh, don't I now?" Her crazed energy came right back into her face.

My father laughed from above me, the pressure on my arms increasing as he pulled them, the tendons in my shoulders pulled to their brink. His magic flooded me, cold spike digging into every muscle, making it impossible to move. Even my magic wouldn't respond against the chill. I winced and Ovailia laughed right alongside my father, the ringing of her cell phone drowning out the noise.

"I think I know exactly what I am up against," she said as she pulled the phone from the pocket of her designer jeans. Timothy's hold on my hands lessened as one of his hands moved down to cover my mouth.

"Now, princess," he said, the once sweet pet name spoken with acid, "don't try anything stupid." His hand cupped the entire lower half of my face, the pressure arching my neck back and making it difficult to breathe as he pushed my head painfully into the stone floor. I fought against him, yelled against his palm. "It wouldn't take much to kill you, Wynifred."

Timothy increased his grip and Ovailia smiled at me before putting the phone to her ear, her face and voice changing the second the line connected.

"Ilyan? Ilyan, where are you?" Ovailia said, her voice thin as she pushed emotion into it. "Please tell me you are all right."

She began to pant as Ilyan spoke, the movement of her voice making it sound like she was running.

"They took her," Ovailia said sharply, her voice panicked. She looked at me before firing a stream of light into the wall of the room, causing a giant explosion that rocked the floor of the cave. "They took Talon, too; I don't know where he is..." She gasped, panted, winced and screamed softly, each action perfectly placed to make it sound like she was fighting someone.

I knew I had to fight Timothy. Ilyan hadn't heard my warning and she was leading him into a trap. My father's grip increased and I winced again, the sound of my scream adding to the web Ovailia was weaving.

"I wouldn't fight if I were you," Timothy hissed in my ear, the heat of his breath uncomfortable against my skin. "You wouldn't want something to happen to that mate of yours."

My body relaxed as if on a switch. I felt like a puppet, a foolish, little girl who could only do what her father said.

"...But Timothy dragged Wyn off," Ovailia finished, her false exhaustion picking up.

"Father, Timothy," Ovailia said, and I heard Timothy's faint chuckle from right above my head. "There are hundreds of them."

Hundreds. I knew it was true. I had seen the bodies, smelled the blood and the smoke. Edmund had planned this attack well. It was to be his final attack. He wasn't going to let anyone survive. He wouldn't stop until he killed them all.

"I don't know how they got in," Ovailia continued, giant crocodile tears rolling down her perfect cheeks and cracking in her voice. She smiled at me, the tears glistening as she flipped her hair.

My stomach clenched, and my magic crackled between my fingers as it fought against Timothy's hold. I hated her. I regretted never saying it before, never seeing who she truly was before. She was evil.

"Our whole city... I don't know how many are going to make it out."

I groaned and fought him again; I wanted to claw at her face, to stop this, no matter how futile it was. Timothy stretched his arm out and away from my head, pulling my arms until I felt the tendons in my arms pop. I screamed, and he released his hand from over my mouth just long enough to let the sound flow through the phone.

I panted as the tendons in my arms began to repair themselves, the pain lessening as my magic covered it.

"I can try," Ovailia said, her voice more disappointed than anything else.

She nodded once to Timothy who stretched my arms again. What little repair my body had been able to produce shattered as my scream rent through the air around us, the rumble of explosions overlapping with the sound of my pain.

"And you, Ilyan." Ovailia smiled and tucked the phone back in her pocket. Her wicked eyes never left mine as she bent closer. Her hair fell around her like a curtain, the effect increasing my terror at being trapped between the two of them. I sucked in breath as Timothy released my mouth, the hold on my hands loosening just enough to let my body begin to heal.

"We will destroy you," Ovailia said, her voice hard.

I just met her gaze. I had nothing to say to her. I could rebut. I could be scared and give her what she wanted. I did none of that. I did, however, choose to laugh. It wasn't the wicked laugh of my father or the taunting laugh that had just graced Ovailia's lips, it was light and joyful, the change in mood jarring.

They were already celebrating, and I felt my father's magic slip from me. Just barely, but it was enough. The fool.

Ovailia's face fell and she looked around, her shoulders stiffening in expectation. I took my opportunity and slammed my bare foot against the ground, the rippling energy moving around us again, sending Ovailia off me and causing my father to fall away. His hands released my arms as he fell into the ground.

I spun away, regaining my balance as quickly as I could, and stumbled away from them, arms still dangling as they tried to repair themselves. I sent another stream of energy toward them, hoping to restrain them before they regained their bearings, but Ovailia caught sight of what I was doing and blocked my weak magic with a powerful shield of her own.

I immediately moved to attack, sending a bright light toward them, only to have Timothy block it as Ovailia sent her own attack in my direction. I dodged and blocked a moment before the attack would have hit me, only to see another force in my direction.

"Come on, princess," Timothy taunted, "let your ol' dad give you a present!"

I blocked his assault, but just barely. I could feel the heat graze my shoulder as the muscles in my arms tensed, the warning of what my father's magic would do to me as clear as if he had said it. The attacks kept coming, one after another, and I knew what they were doing. With my arm still dangling lifelessly I wasn't fast enough, wasn't strong enough, to fight off one, let alone both of them. I could only hope to hold off their attacks long enough to give myself enough time to escape.

I fell to the side, heat swirling through the ground with my skin contact, the earth responding to my touch. I rarely had control over what my touch would do in these caves, but this time, I focused. I forced the magic into my desired outcome and watched as they crumpled to the ground, their mouths opened in horror as their bodies heated up from the inside.

I picked myself up and ran, stepping over them in my haste to get away, to find Talon.

I spun around the corner and slammed into the thick barrel chest of a man who smelled of death and smoke. I didn't need to look up at him to know who it was. I pushed my hand into his chest and sent a stream of fire into it, only to be met by a shield that blocked my pointless attack.

"My, my, Wynifred. You would think that after a few hundred years you would know better," Edmund hissed, his thick fingers curling around my tiny forearm.

I tried to pull away, but I wasn't even sure why I did. There was no escaping now. His fingers met the small indentation of my spine through the skin in the back of my neck, and the white-hot heat of his magic shocked into my spine. His magic surged, numbing each and every one of my nerve endings and muscles before I could move even so much as an inch. The ripple of the attack moved through me before everything went dead, my body going limp as I fell into his arms. He held me against him, my head lolling. My unfocused eyes came to rest on the bruised, bearded man Edmund had been dragging around by the chains attached to his wrists.

I couldn't even move my eyes, I realized. I just stared at the intense green gaze of the battered man as Edmund placed a smooth stone on my tongue, his magic pulsing just enough to force a reaction that would make me swallow it. The tiny stone slipped down my throat and toward my stomach. The further it traveled into my body, the more numb and unresponsive my magic felt.

An omezující stone. The rare rock that was given to prisoners as a magical restraint.

I felt it as it lodged itself in my stomach, my numbed body unable to fight it. I felt my magic slow to a stop, freezing in place before it traveled to surround the rock, where it would stay until I could find someone powerful enough to remove it.

Silent tears rolled down my cheeks, my body accepting my defeat without my permission, accepting my loss.

"Wonderful," Timothy said as he came up behind us. "I was hoping someone would grab the little whore."

Timothy grabbed my hair and pulled my head back, my eyes drifting to the roof of the cave tunnel, unable to focus on their own.

Edmund chuckled at my father's comment. His rumbling voice vibrated through my head as he hoisted me over his shoulder and carried me down the hall, my desire to find my mate pulling me in the opposite direction.

CHAPTER 31
JOCLYN

Cail and Ryland didn't deviate a millimeter from where they stood on the grass lawn of the house, their dark eyes were focused up at us with as much intensity as Ilyan stared down at them. Ilyan's arms stiffened around me, his magic flaring as his shields grew. Even with Ryland right there, I couldn't feel the pull of his magic through the shield. Which meant Ryland couldn't feel it either.

My eyes fluttered between Cail and Ryland, my heart beating stronger the more I looked. The last I had seen of Ryland had been in the dream, and in the dream he had been himself with his memories back. The man before me, however, looked up with black eyes and a menacing snarl as he plotted all the ways he could hurt me.

They both laughed and Ilyan pulled me closer. I was scared, and by the erratic pulse of Ilyan's heart, so was he. One of his arms moved away from me, his hand gently facing the two figures below us as he prepared to fight.

"Relax," Cail drawled in a falsely bored voice, "we are not here to kill you, at least not yet." He smiled as his teeth flashed in the dim light.

Ilyan's magic swirled angrily under his skin, the power of it growing hot in my shoulder.

"Then what do you want?" Ilyan yelled down to them, neither of them flinched.

"To give you a message. You must have heard by now that your precious safe house in Prague is gone. The wells of Imdalind are now ours. Imagine what we can do with all that power! And you, the last of the true Skříteks, have failed in protecting it." Cail laughed, Ryland's musical chuckle joining in. Ice ran over my skin. That laugh was almost identical to how it used to be.

It isn't him.

But he had been so real in the dream. Even now, his hair fell over his forehead the way it always did. I wished I knew a way to pry him out of his prison. I jerked forward only to move back when his black eyes met mine.

It isn't him.

"Then what is your message?" I heard the strength in Ilyan's voice rumble through his chest.

"It is for Joclyn," Cail said, and I reluctantly looked over to him. "We have found you, as I told you I would, and we have your little friend locked up where you will never find her."

"No!" I called out without meaning to. It was just like in the dreams, his smile. The taunting. Except now I could do something. My magic was already boiling. I was ready.

I tried to break out of Ilyan's arms, to soar down there and throw every air conditioner on the street at the two of them, but Ilyan pulled me back. Cail smiled at his panic, his eyes dancing in pleasure.

"Oh yes, and you still have one month to turn yourself in to us. Twenty-nine days to be exact, or your little friend is gone along with the love of your life. You can save him, Joclyn." He stopped as he placed a hand on Ryland's shoulder. My insides froze, terrified as to what he was going to do.

"Unless you don't need him anymore," Cail finished, his head turning to Ryland. "Look how cozy they are up there, Ry." As Ryland turned his head to face me, I almost expected blue eyes, instead I only saw the black. "It almost looks like she doesn't need you anymore, don't you think?"

"You're right," Ryland said. I tried to pull away from Ilyan when I heard Ryland, but Ilyan's strong arms kept me there. "Have you told her then, brother? Have you told her of her true purpose and what she is to you?"

"What is he...?" I began the question, only to freeze at the fury that dripped from Ilyan's eyes.

"Well then," Ryland said, "if you have, I suppose you won't be needing me."

In a flash of blue I saw a spark of light bounce off a golden sword that appeared in Ryland's hands. He spun it once before swinging it violently through the air only to plunge it into himself. Ryland didn't even flinch as the air streaked with gold as he prepared to end his own life.

"No!" I screamed louder and burst out of Ilyan's arms, halfway to launching myself when Ilyan pulled me down. Cail may be strong, but with the fury I felt flowing through me, I knew I was stronger.

"You can't, Silný," Ilyan hissed, his voice shaking. He was actually scared.

"Stop!" Cail commanded, Rylands sword stopping only millimeters from his body. "You haven't told her, have you Ilyan?"

"I take it Sain has told you then?" Ilyan yelled down to them.

"Oh! Bravo! You know we have him then. You figured it out. You will make your father so proud. He was beginning to think you had lost your touch. I sure hope it didn't take you the full three months to realize that we were controlling her dreams?" Cail took a step forward, his hands moving as he spoke. I couldn't take my eyes off of them, terrified he would attack at any moment.

"Not even close," Ilyan laughed humorlessly through his lie. "See, I know the full story, and no matter what you have done to Sain, I doubt you have managed to get it all."

"Sain may not have told us everything, but he has been a wealth of information both now and before. We have been waiting for her to make an appearance as long as you have, and we are willing to wait just as long to find the secret of how to destroy her. Another month or so and we will know everything."

"I wish you luck with that," Ilyan laughed, his deep joy rolling through the main road.

"At least you continue to make this whole game more interesting," Cail said.

"It's not a game," I yelled down to him, interrupting their banter.

"Oh, really?" Cail sneered, "I think it's a game. Ryland thinks it is a game. Edmund *knows* it is a game. Your *Protector* up there, seeing as he hasn't told you everything, he must be playing the game as well."

Ilyan pulled me back against him and my insides went numb. Cail's loud voice boomed as he laughed and the yard to the house suddenly lit up with artificial light as a door was opened. Cail's attention turned to a man in the doorway, his laughter stopping as his face went hard.

"What's going on out here?" I heard the old man yell shakily through the yard, Cail having obviously scared him.

"Nothing that concerns you, old man." I realized what was going to happen a moment before it did. Cail raised his hand and placed his palm toward the old man then, as he had with me the first time, he let the power grow. His amusement at scaring his target was stronger than his intent to kill. In that next instant, Ilyan left my side to intercept the ball of energy Cail sent toward the old man. Ilyan's powerful energy redirected the fire toward a field of trees off to the side of the house with only a thought. Cail's red light connected with the trunk of a tree, sending it into a roaring inferno that spread inhumanly fast to the other trees in the small grove. It was ablaze in seconds.

The man yelled out in fear and the door closed, the yellow glow leaving the yard with the click of the door as the flickering light from the fire began to take over.

Ilyan stood before Cail, his tall frame towering over him while I turned to see the family coming out of the other side of the house and running away from whatever altercation was about to take place. I calmed a bit, hoping they would get away from this.

"Do you really wish to fight me, Ilyan? I told you we were not here to hurt you. Not today." Cail's voice was strong, but I heard the fear that lay behind it.

"Then do not attack the innocent," Ilyan said, his magic growing and spreading through the Štít as his shield encompassed me.

Ilyan took off into the sky, presumably back to my side, before his body was pulled back down to the ground and restrained against the damp grass by Cail's magic.

"I will attack any that get in the way of my job for my master," Cail said.

"You serve the wrong man, Cail." Ilyan's body glowed with golden light before he burst into the sky, Cail's magical restraints flying off him. When he had moved enough to put himself between me and the two men on the ground, Ilyan flexed his fingers, electricity crackling between his knuckles.

"I guess that is a matter of opinion." I froze as Cail raised his hand toward Ilyan. Ilyan did nothing, though. He stood there as his hair danced in the wind, his muscular body lit by the firelight. I felt his magic surge through me.

Light exploded out of Cail's hand, and a half-second later, Ilyan sliced his hand to the side, sending Cail's magic uselessly into the already blazing trees. Ilyan flexed his hand as the ground exploded around Cail, showering the yard with dirt and rocks.

I shielded my face from the onslaught of dirt, only to come face to face with Ryland when I emerged. I didn't wait; I raised my hand to attack; but before I could do anything, his hand wrapped around my neck and forced me against the house.

"Now, now," he said, his wicked voice cutting into me. "You know your magic has no effect on me, and as fun as a scuffle with you would be, my job is not to attack you. My job is to keep you here."

He snarled at me and increased his hold, and my vision popped and swayed from the lack of oxygen. I grasped at his hands, my magic not responding to my mind's weak calls.

"Oh, sorry," he said, although I heard no sympathy. "I guess it would be better not to kill you yet. It was nice of Ilyan to leave you here for me to play with. I guess his desire to kill Cail is greater than his need to protect you."

Ryland smiled greasily as I squirmed underneath his hold.

"You're wrong..." I gasped, foolishly wasting oxygen as my magic continued to spark uselessly between my fingers. "Ilyan... he's... Ryland!"

Ryland released his hold enough to give me breath, though not enough to move, I let my magic swell at my increased freedom, one spark slamming into Rylands gut.

It must have tickled with how he laughed.

"Nice try," he growled through clenched teeth and slammed me against the house again, the impact ricocheting through my skull. He smirked, the look was the same one he had given me for years, but there wasn't any love for me in him anymore; not in his eyes, nowhere.

"Stop trying to fight me," he snarled, slamming my head against the house again.

"Never. I know... you're there."

"No! There is nothing you can do. You see there?" Ryland squeezed my neck tighter. My head was spinning from lack of oxygen as he then forced me to look toward the side of the house where a cluster of Trpaslíks had gathered in the shadows out of Ilyan's sight, their hands against the house.

"And there," he moved me roughly, this time to the other side of the house where even more Trpaslíks stood.

"They are going to blow you and this house clear into the sky while your dear Protector is in battle, too busy trying to kill Cail to save you." Ryland's black eyes were shining. I stared at him, my jaw working as if it was trying to bite the oxygen out of the air.

The house shuddered under me, the joined magic of the Trpaslíks congregating beneath us. The vibrating house continued to shake as I gasped for a desperate breath in my attempts to yell, to scream, to fight him. My voice was caught, though; my magic a limp spark. It wasn't enough.

"Oh, and I have a riddle for you. Straight from Sain's own mouth." I froze. My father?

"'Two brothers stand beside you, both know of your true fate. They each have love in their hearts, but different needs to gain. One seeks power, the other light. The one with light in his heart may love you more, but he is the foolish one, the one who will die first.' I will give you one guess as to who that one could be," he said, releasing my throat as the vibrating reached its peak.

I gasped for breath again, trying to regain use of my magic, knowing there was only a matter of seconds before the house exploded.

"Ilyan!" I screamed with all the air I could gather, hoping that he would hear my call or feel my pain in his magic that pulsed through me. What I didn't expect was Ryland's answer.

"Correct." My eyes widened as Ryland's smirk increased. I didn't get a chance to ask him what he meant before Ryland pushed away from me to escape the impending blast.

I fell to my knees as the house began to collapse in on itself and tried to push myself into the air, my body too weak to answer my call. Seconds later, Ilyan's arms wrapped around me as the house imploded. The heat of the explosion on my feet burned as the blast grew, the sound of destruction ringing in my ears. I looked back and knew we couldn't escape it.

"Hold on to me, Silnỳ, and whatever you do, don't let go."

Ilyan wrapped his body around mine, his hold tight as his magic rushed into me with more pressure than he had ever used before. The pressure broke through my barrier, but instead of making me feel as if I was going to explode, I experienced the exact opposite. My body was squished even further against Ilyan as the pressure melded us together. What little air I had gasped was pushed out of my lungs, and my body felt as if I was being forced through a toilet paper roll.

I was convinced that the blast had found us until, suddenly, the sensation left. My body crashed against Ilyan's as we fell to the ground, his arms going limp.

Frigid air swirled around me, my hair and clothes whipping through the winter storm that had come out of nowhere.

I sat up and looked around in a panic, confused at the mountain landscape I was surrounded by.

"Ilyan?" I asked, my body beginning to shake with cold. "Where are we?"

I looked at the tall, snow-covered peak that towered over us, my eyes scanning for some form of shelter. I turned toward Ilyan when he didn't respond. My stomach immediately dropped into the icy landscape.

Ilyan lay still, his body surrounded by snow while his blond hair whirled in the air, but he didn't move. His lips and eyelids were tinged with a sickly shade of blue, his body limp and still.

"Ilyan?" I couldn't stop the panic that seeped into my voice. I pressed my hand against his cold cheek, surprised not to feel the warmth that usually lay right below his skin.

I moved my hand to my shoulder, trying to focus on his magic inside of me, but all I felt was a weak and dying pulse of latent energy. I pressed my hands against his skin, pulsing my magic into him, trying desperately to figure out how to help him, how to heal him.

"Ilyan!" I yelled, frantic to get his attention. "Ilyan, wake up. Please. Ilyan, please don't leave me." I continued to yell at him, my fear having turned into a full blown panic. Ilyan was the last person I had. Ryland's mind was still trapped, my mother was dead, and Wyn had been captured and taken to who knew where.

"Ilyan please!" The wind howled around me as I yelled, taking my voice with it. "Don't do this!"

I pressed my hands against his cheeks, pulsing my magic into him in desperation to awaken him—to heal him—but not knowing how. I looked around, desperate for shelter, for help.

No one was there. Nothing but snow on the side of what appeared to be a mountain.

"Don't you dare leave me!" My body was shaking uncontrollably now, the cold freezing me down to my bones. I clung to Ilyan, my magic surging as I attempted to keep both of us warm, but I couldn't focus enough to keep the flow of magic going.

"Ilyan!" I couldn't keep the hopelessness out of my voice.

Somewhere deep inside I wished this to be a dream, whether or not it was controlled by Edmund. I wished that all of this was a fabricated nightmare. But I knew it wasn't.

I lay down next to Ilyan, my skin freezing against the snow and my arms clinging to his still body.

"Ilyan..." I pleaded, unable to deny the ache I felt for him. "Don't leave me..."

I had barely gotten the words out before a dark figure emerged through the snow, moving toward us.

The shape was huge. I cringed against Ilyan, and pulled my magic. I had never attacked a monster before, but there was a first time for everything.

As it got closer, I could barely make out the shape of a man as he lumbered toward me. I sat up, not daring to hope, but terrified all the same. The figure yelled out something into the storm, his voice carried away by the wind.

Soon, the shape towered over me, his sharp green eyes digging into mine. He was an absolutely hulking figure, mostly caused by layer after layer of large fur coats. He pulled down his scarf to reveal a cleanly shaven face.

"Silnŷ! Early! As I knew you would be. But, Ilyan? What happened?" The man was panicked. He reached out and grabbed my shoulders with his heavily gloved hands, bringing me up to eye level.

I stared at him, unsure of what to say. I didn't know who this man was, and his voice and manner were scaring me.

"Tell me! You are in safe hands, but I must know!"

"Thom?" I asked, hoping beyond hope that Ilyan had gotten us to safety.

"No," he said, his voice strained. "He is coming, though. Now, tell me, what has happened? Is everyone safe?"

He continued to look into me, and I felt my heart fall. No, no one was okay. Ilyan was hurt. Wyn was gone. Prague...

"Prague. They found them," I stuttered, trying to find the right words. "They found us. Ilyan..." My voice broke and I looked toward Ilyan's still form, scrambling out of the man's hold and back to Ilyan's side.

"So it has happened." I barely registered that the man had spoken, my focus back on Ilyan again.

"Ilyan is hurt," I said, pulling the man's attention away from his reverie, desperate for help.

"Do not worry over your Protector, Silnŷ, his energy was spent in getting you here. He will be well in a few days." He smiled, his face lighting up. I just scowled at him.

"We need to help him."

"Yes, yes, and we will. Thom!" he yelled into the blizzard that surrounded us before turning back and grunting a bit. "The poor lad moves slowly in the snow. My name is Dramin, by the way, but you can call me Uncle."

CHAPTER 32
JOCLYN

I leaned over Ilyan protectively, Dramin still smiling at me as if he was amused.

"Uncle?" I asked, my voice shaking as my body convulsed in the cold.

"Yes, didn't Ilyan tell you?" He leaned over me, and I moved away.

"Ilyan didn't tell me anything." I grabbed Ilyan's hand, my heart plunging at his lack of response.

"I told you, Dramin. Ilyan wouldn't do anything he didn't need to, especially when it comes to her." I turned my body toward the gruff voice, surprised at the other large shape that had appeared out of the snow. He was tall and appeared twice as wide as I was sure he was thanks to layers of coats he wore. I could just make out a long, brown dreadlock protruding from underneath his woolen hat.

"Put that on," the second man said, dropping a huge fur coat in front of me. "You don't want to freeze to death."

He leaned over me and I caught a glimpse of deep blue eyes as he shooed me out of the way, they were gorgeous against his dark skin. He picked up Ilyan's limp and unresponsive body with one big jolt and heaved Ilyan over his shoulder, covering him with a shaggy fur before turning to me, his stare piercing me even through the blinding snow.

"You look just like your father," he said before turning away and walking into the snow storm. I jumped up, moving to run after him, but my red shoes slipped in the snow, chilling me further. I grabbed the coat and attempted to put it on, moving after them as quickly as I could.

"Slow down, child," Dramin yelled after me. "You will be going nowhere fast if you continue at that pace. Let me carry you."

I glared daggers at Dramin and ignored his warning before continuing my trudge after Ilyan and the man I could only assume to be Thom. I could see Ilyan's blonde hair swinging beneath the heavy fur that Thom had covered him with, the snowstorm threatening to swallow them up. I continued to slip and slide through the snow and wind, desperation filling me as they vanished.

"Wait," I yelled, knowing my voice would be swallowed up by the storm.

"Don't worry, child, Thom is taking him to our shelter," Dramin said, coming up beside me.

I continued to move stubbornly forward, though I could no longer feel my toes. I had only made it a few steps before Dramin lifted me into his arms. I yelled and struggled away from him, only to land on my back in the snow.

"I've got to get to Ilyan. He has to be okay. I need..." No, that wasn't right. "He needs to shield me so they can't find me."

"Ilyan? He won't be helping you for a few days yet."

"No! I need him..." My heart tensed at what I had been about to say, and I clamped my mouth shut.

"You've come farther along than I assumed." Dramin said, but I barely heard him.

I was too focused on Ilyan, on the new issue that him being unconscious had presented. I was completely unprotected.

"You have to do it!" I yelled neurotically as things clicked together. "You've got to shield me or else they are going to find me!"

"Don't worry. You are safe. Ilyan is safe. No one can track you here." I locked eyes with him for a moment, my teeth chattering, before looking toward where Thom had disappeared with Ilyan's body. I could see nothing except snow.

"Ilyan," I whispered. I felt so lost without him, he had been so constant over the past few months, and now... I watched the space he had been carried into, growing more desperate with every frantic beat of my heart.

Dramin's hand pressed against my shoulder, his weight pushing me further into the cold snow.

"Do not worry. His mind will awaken when you call for him in your most hopeless state." His voice had taken on a frightening tone and I snapped up to look at him, only to inhale sharply. His eyes were fully encompassed in black, the centers glowing like the ember of a flame, staring off into the distance."

"It will happen after the sun has risen three times, after your heart has broken twice."

Slowly the blackness left his eyes, but I was still frozen still in the snow, my magic attempting to heal my frostbitten extremities.

"You're a Drak." He smiled at my realization, his face lowering to mine, his eyes back to their bright green color.

"Ah-ha. So, Ilyan *has* taught you something." Dramin smiled wider, but I screwed my face up in confusion. How could he be a Drak? I had been told they were all dead... but then there was the issue with my father...

"You're a Drak," I repeated.

"Yes, so now you can be calm that your Protector will live. Although I am sorry about the heartbreak part. I can't often control these things." He smiled at me, but I only stared at him, my confusion growing. "Hmmm, I can see the gears turning in your mind. You are wondering how I could be a Drak if your father was the one born from the mud, the first of his kind, and without any children except you of course." He continued to smile, but I did not know how to respond.

"I will make you a deal. Let me carry you out of this storm and then I will tell you everything. I will answer every question that is burning inside that little brain of yours. I am sure there is much. Knowing Ilyan, he saved the dirty work for me. You could also stay here, or worse, attempt to walk on your own, and I guarantee that you will lose a leg by morning." He talked about amputation with too much of a sparkle in his eyes, he clearly knew what I was going to say, not that I had a choice. He swept me up without waiting for my answer, cradling me like a baby.

"Nice shoes. Did Ilyan make them for you?"

"Yes." He smiled at my answer as we raced through the snow, the cold air brushing past my face and making my eyes sting. Reluctantly, I glanced toward my feet, wincing to see them as red as the delicate shoes I still wore.

Dramin continued to run as we approached a large opening in a cliff face. Just ahead, and disappearing through the opening was the dark mass that was Thom and Ilyan. Dramin followed right behind them, sprinting through the snow like a marathoner.

"Well, Thom, you got your wish. She is just as stubborn as her father." Dramin said as he came side by side with his friend. I looked around Dramin's arms to see Ilyan's head swinging as Thom walked, his eyelids still tinged with a deathly blue.

"Well at least she is not my responsibility this time," he grunted before moving off to the side, taking Ilyan away from me again.

Dramin walked in the opposite direction, moving us into a large, rounded cavern. The space had obviously been carved magically because each curve of the rock was smooth and perfect. Light filtered in through enormous, ornate sky lights and reflected off of bits of mirror and glass that were suspended in obscure places across the ceiling. What could instantly be dismissed as trash was turned beautiful by the light that glimmered off faded paintings that I could tell had once been masterpieces. Dramin set me down in a large, squishy armchair as a fire was lit in the middle of the large space.

The whole cave had been set up like the spokes of a wheel. In the center was the large fire, and surrounding that a circle of chairs and couches. Beyond that, was a ring that was raised up from the sunken center, which held about twenty bunks carved into the stone walls. Each had a mattress and a shelf. One was hidden behind a gold inlaid dressing partition and another had an ornately woven blanket blocking it from view. The rest were bare. I could almost guess which one belonged to Dramin and which to Thom. On first meeting, Thom didn't seem the type for inlaid gold.

I looked around until I found Thom gently laying Ilyan in one of the bunks. I watched as he carefully stripped off Ilyan's shirt before covering him with blanket after blanket of thick animal fur and placing his hands firmly on his face. I moved in an attempt to get up and go over to him, but Dramin stood right in front of me, placing a steaming cup of some foul smelling liquid in my hands.

"Thom will take care of him, don't you worry."

"I have to help him. He needs me," I said, shock filling me at my own words. It was natural to be concerned, however this level of worry was... unexpected. I shoved aside my doubt of my own emotions as I attempted to stand and move around Dramin, but he only pushed my shoulders back into the chair, his hand wrapping around the cup to ensure I didn't spill any.

"You need to sit right there, drink that, and let your magic heal your feet before you lose them."

Dramin placed a blanket over me; I could feel my magic moving sluggishly around my body, congregating in my feet and toes as it attempted to heal me. I let it flow freely, even though I couldn't stop my eyes from drifting to where Thom was healing Ilyan, my mind continually checking the Štít in my shoulder for any change.

"What happened to him?" I asked, trying to keep the fear out of my voice. It was hard to believe that Ilyan could get hurt.

"He's exhausted," Dramin said and began shedding his many coats, laying them gently in one of the many chairs that surrounded the fire. The more he shed, the smaller he got until he was nothing more than a tall, wiry man with square shoulders. His hair was a tangle of long brown strands, his green eyes looking into me sharply as he smiled. He looked vaguely familiar. Not like I had seen him somewhere before, but as if I had *known* him. Not that that was possible. He only appeared to be a few years older than me, whatever that was worth given how magical people seemed to age.

Dramin sat down in the armchair beside mine, his hand patting my knee. "Ilyan is one of only a handful of Skřítek who can perform a Stutter. It is draining enough with one person, I have never known it to be done with two people before."

"A Stutter?" I pulled my eyes away from Ilyan to look at Dramin.

"Yes, a tri-dimensional move from any given point to another. It happens in the blink of an eye." Dramin took a drink from another mug filled with the same foul smelling liquid I held in my hands.

"You mean, he instantly moved us from farmland in Ohio to..."

"High in the Alps, near a peak known as the Pizzo delle Saette." My eyes bugged out of my head and Dramin chuckled at me before taking another drink.

I looked away from Dramin to Ilyan; I had no idea anything like that was possible.

"It takes a spectacular amount of power to accomplish. Most people do not have enough magic to transport themselves, let alone another. I am surprised the effort did not kill him, but then, Ilyan is one of a kind. His heart is good, child. Without that goodness and light, he may not have been able to save you tonight."

"'One seeks power, the other light.'" I mumbled to myself.

"I'm sorry?" Dramin asked, but I only shook my head at him.

I didn't want to think of Ryland's words on the roof. I didn't want to consider the possibility of Ilyan thinking about me that way, or even Ryland using me. The thought gave me a jittery, butterfly feeling I wasn't very appreciative of. Ilyan had saved me. He was my Protector and that was why he had done what he did.

"And you're sure he is going to be alright?" I desperately wanted to run over to him and somehow help Thom, but I could still feel the tingling of magic in my toes. I wasn't sure I could stand on my feet yet.

"Never doubt the word of a Drak, child. He is resting. You will see him in a few days' time."

"After my heart has broken twice," I repeated. I turned to face him, unsurprised to see him staring at me. I shifted my weight in the chair, the look he was giving me making me uncomfortable.

"I am still very sorry about that, but don't worry. It will be for a good cause." He lifted his glass to me as if to tap it with mine, but I stayed still.

"So, you are a Drak, then?"

"Yes," he said. "Didn't we establish this already? Oh, wait, you are wondering how I can be alive, or even be here considering the position of your father."

"Yes, and you promised answers."

Dramin looked at me, his gaze making my inside squirm. I felt like he was looking into my future; which given his magic, he possibly could be. I wasn't sure I wanted anyone looking into my future, so I shied away from him, squishing my back further into the chair.

"Are you going to drink that?" he asked, gesturing toward the still full mug of steaming, dark-brown fluid he had given me. I swirled the mug around a bit, the thick fluid not moving around much.

"Probably not. The smell is making me a bit sick." I tried to move it away from me, but Dramin only smiled.

"It tastes better than it smells, and it is the best thing for awakening magic. If you drink that, I will tell you everything."

I pulled the cup toward me before looking at him, one eyebrow raised in accusation, "I thought our deal was you get to carry me here, and in return, you tell me everything."

"This is a new deal." He smiled and I smirked back, playing his game.

"I like the old deal better."

I locked eyes with him for a moment, hoping to stare him down. He only grinned at me and leaned forward, giving me the same look he had before.

I don't think I could ever win against that look.

My insides squirmed and I pulled the mug to my lips, cringing at the smell of the fluid before the sweet honey flavor hit my tongue. The second I swallowed I could feel everything inside of me speed up. My magic warmed and moved faster. I hadn't felt the current inside of me feel so alive since the morning after Ilyan had first centered me.

"Talk," I said, not willing to admit that the drink actually did taste good.

Dramin smiled widely before sitting back in his chair, turning to face the fire. The light flickered around the space, ricocheting off of the pieces of metal and glass that hung from the ceiling and giving the whole space a glittery feeling.

"In the beginning, the four types of magic were born from the mud, the magical well of Imdalind that sits far below Prague: Rinax, the Vilý; Chyline the Trpaslíks; Frain the Skřítek; and Sain the Drak. From the beginning they knew of their abilities, knew of the magic that flowed through their veins. They used it in the ways that their souls dictated of them; for good, for love, and for assistance to others. Magic was good in the world. Three went into the world, were married and bonded, and carried on their seed. So the magic grew; each mate—each child—bringing their own magic into the world, yet one, Sain, was alone. He walked the earth desperate to find someone that his soul would call to and bond with, but none came."

He paused, and I took another drink, worried he would stop if I didn't. Even though some of this I already knew, I had the distinct impression that this was how Dramin operated, from the beginning.

"In his loneliness, Sain went to the mud and begged for companionship. He cried into the well and from a slice in his finger, added two drops of blood. The well blessed the world with another Drak, but still Sain's soul did not sing. He took me from the mud, named me, and raised me as he would a son."

"You?" Okay, so that would be why he looked familiar.

"Yes, so you see. I am your uncle." He smiled brightly, and I almost choked on the dark liquid.

"Wouldn't that make you my brother?"

"I am a bit old to be your brother, child," he said with a smirk.

"And Sain is a little too old to be my father," I replied with a grin. Dramin chuckled and rested against the back of his chair, his feet lifting onto a large ottoman.

"Touché."

I ignored him and took another drink of whatever he had given me. It was delightfully warming, and oddly enough, the smell was growing on me.

"So, if he was all alone, how did he end up with Ovailia?" I cringed at my words. I wasn't sure I wanted to know. This was possibly the largest piece of my past—of my father's past—that I still couldn't quite make myself believe.

"Sain wasn't alone. He wasn't complete, but he wasn't alone. He thrived as the head of the Drak, the race surviving through my progeny. It wasn't until the day Ovailia was born—when he went to visit the newborn daughter of the King—that his soul finally sang. He held that child in his arms, and before the day had ended, was telling everyone that he had found his mate; that he would bond himself to her when the time was right. Ovailia resisted him at first, but after sixty years she finally consented to a bonding. Everyone was so happy for Sain—for both of them—but after the bonding, something changed. No one was sure what until the day that Ovailia betrayed him."

"Betrayed him?" I said, "But, I thought..." My voice faded off as Dramin shook his head, his eyes looking sadly away from me.

"That Edmund almost tortured him to death? That Ovailia made a pact with her father in an attempt to save him? It is all true, but her betrayal began before that.

"She delivered what little she knew about Sain's sight about you to her father. When Edmund heard it, he demanded to know who had spoken it. However Ovailia only knew that a girl would be born who could defeat an opposing power, nothing more. She didn't know when, she didn't even know who the opposing power was. Edmund needed the seeing Drak, so he could glean more information, and Ovailia eagerly sacrificed her mate for what she believed to be a greater good. It wasn't until Edmund began to torture him that she began to second guess her decision."

"It was too late." A deep, gruff voice spoke up from across the large space.

I looked up as Thom joined us, his long dreads swinging as he sat across the fire from me on a large, brown couch. I wouldn't have even recognized him as the same man if it hadn't been for the dreads. He was short and stocky, and his brown dreads looked out of place with his clean-shaven, boyish face. He swung his mukluk covered feet onto the couch and looked away from me, closing his eyes.

I looked toward the bunk where Ilyan had been laid, his body still with only his head visible from underneath the large amount of furs. I went to move, but one grunt from Thom stopped my progression.

"He's fine. You can go fawn over him after your feet are better." I turned hastily toward Thom, my forehead furled in a scowl.

"I wasn't going to *fawn* over him," I said a little too acidly; Thom only snorted at me.

"You sure she doesn't know, Dramin?" Thom asked, his eyes still closed.

"I'm sure." Dramin smiled and refilled his mug with a wave of his hand. "Now, where were we? Oh, yes, Ovailia broke the bond."

"How could they survive?" I asked the question more to myself than to him. I still remembered the pain, the way my body had attempted to rot from inside out after my bond with Ryland had been cracked. It still protested every time I stayed away from the Tȍuha for too long.

"It is the one who breaks the bond that walks away unscathed while the one who is broken will suffer and die. It was Sain who suffered to the point that he appeared dead. Ovailia was unscathed because she broke the bond and because she no longer loved him."

I looked down into my glass, hurting for Sain. Or, I guess, my father. It was weird to think of him that way, especially considering Ovailia was involved. I exhaled and drank deeply. At least my mother had loved him until the day she had been killed.

"In his anger Edmund massacred all of my posterity; my sons and daughters, thousands of my grandchildren and beyond, all murdered. All while Edmund kept Sain imprisoned, hidden from Ovailia, trying to glean more information about the sight. Sain never gave it to him no matter how much he was tortured, though. They never found out more than what Ovailia had told them. Which is why they never identified you until Ryland found your mark. For centuries Edmund used Sain's abilities for his profit. He kept him under a Vymȁzat so strict that, while it never completed, it was enough to keep control over him. He wouldn't let him near the Black Water that the Drak rely on, and so he weakened further." Dramin spoke quietly and I could tell how much he was affected by what he was saying. He closed his eyes and leaned back against the chair, his hands still grasping his mug.

"For centuries he was only given an opportunity to drink the Black Water when Edmund needed the use of his sight. He was as weak as a human, his ability becoming so reliant on the Black Water that he could no longer control the visions or interpret what he would see, so Edmund learned to do all that for him. Sain's body slowly learned to rely more on human food than his own resources. In many ways, the Drak in him died." Dramin spoke into his mug, his knuckles white against the pottery. I couldn't help but feel sick to my stomach at this new bit of information.

"How did he get out?" I asked quietly, my voice awed like I was being told a bedtime story and not the history of my father.

"I got him out," Thom said from across the fire, though his body did not deviate from its relaxed position. "I grabbed him, knocked my father unconscious, broke Timothy's arm, and made a run for it. It took me quite some time to get any information out of Sain as to where we were supposed to go."

Thom scowled darkly and moved his hands behind his head, his eyes shifting to look at me.

"Worst mistake of my life." Thom said, "I should have left him there. Having to spend the next three hundred years in hiding, trying to get your best friend back from the mess your father had created of him, only to see him end up captured with no memory is not something I would like to repeat."

"Tell me about it." For the first time I understood Thom's grumbles. I had too many in the same predicament. Wyn, Talon, Ryland, and now Ilyan. The list just kept getting bigger. Dramin reached over and patted my leg like a comforting grandfather, the action awakening something in me as I forced back a smile.

"So you were in hiding?" I asked, pushing myself out of my misery.

"I'm still in hiding," Thom grumbled, "My existence as well as Sain's has to be kept as much of a secret as possible. If Ovailia found out about us, there is no telling what she would do, and while Ilyan has his suspicions, none of us want to find out what Edmund would do with us."

"How did Ilyan find you in the first place?" I asked, not wanting to dwell on all the negative that had happened in the past few hours.

"We were in college, pretending to be seniors, and we were bored out of our minds. Then, one day, we saw him—Cail." I visibly froze, the malice in Thom's voice matching my own. He turned toward me, eyes narrowing a bit. "I hid Sain with a human family and erased his memory in case he was found then pulled Cail off his trail. I was only able to return when I knew it was safe, which was about ten years later, yet without a true memory of his past, he had married. I stayed nearby, but I couldn't see any signs of magic from you, so I left. Content to give him a normal life and return when the time was right."

I wasn't sure what to say. I ran through the story, the fact that my life had been a giant sham becoming more of an irritating reality. It was making me grumpy.

"How did you know Edmund had found you simply because you saw Cail?" I asked.

"When you see Cail, Edmund and Timothy are not far behind. Even if you don't see them, they are always there." Thom sat up all the way and leaned forward. His blue eyes shimmered in the firelight as he looked toward me. "When Cail was born, it was decided that Edmund needed a new bodyguard. So Edmund and Timothy both infused the infant with a Štít of their magic, however Edmund also placed his there to give Cail power. You see, Edmund placed his Štít right inside Cail's heart. From birth, Edmund's wicked power has influenced him, and from birth, Cail has been taught how to use Edmund's power as his own. All with the knowledge that if he steps one toe out of line, Edmund can kill him no matter where he is."

I gasped, my hand subconsciously moving to my shoulder where Ilyan's weak tendrils still swirled within me.

"Yes," Thom nodded, "I know that Ilyan has done something similar to you." I saw Dramin's head spin toward me at Thom's words, but I ignored it.

"I will admit I was shocked when I was healing him and suddenly my energy moved across the room, but Ilyan's Štít in you is different than what resides in Cail's body. Ilyan has placed his there to protect you. Besides, I doubt you could use his magic to your benefit. Even trying to hold Ilyan's magic inside of you would kill you." Thom laughed as if he had told a great joke and lay back against the couch again. I let my eyes flow away from him to Ilyan's still body, my heart rate speeding up.

But I had held Ilyan's magic. He had accidently pushed too much into me when placing the Štít, and I had survived. I was sure he had done it again when using the Stutter to get us here, too. How many things about me were going to prove to be 'impossible'. I shook my head and looked away.

"So Cail can use Edmund's magic?" I asked before drinking the last of the liquid from my mug.

"Yes," Dramin answered, "although I don't think he does very often. I am not sure he can without Edmund's express permission."

I nodded, I knew exactly when Cail was using Edmund's magic with his permission—every night when he haunted my dreams. I didn't dare look over to Ilyan. I wished I could talk to him, tell him I had figured it out. Even though I am sure he already knew, I needed to tell him... needed someone to understand. I shook my head and looked up, cringing a bit to see Dramin staring at me.

"Ummm..." I began before he could ask me anything, lifting the empty mug to make my intent clear. "Can I have some more?"

"I'll get it," Thom grunted from the other side of the fire, as he lifted himself up to a sitting position.

"Don't bother," Dramin said as he waved his hand, the mug filling with the dark brown fluid.

I smiled appreciatively and took a big swallow, loving how it was energizing my body.

"No," Thom was suddenly snarling, his eyes bouncing from me to Dramin as he stood in front of the fire. He moved so quick I was sure we were being attacked, and foolishly prepared to use my mug as a weapon, completely forgetting I had magic.

"What?"

"You didn't? Dramin!" No monster behind me, Thom was just raging at Dramin.

"I did. You can imagine my own surprise when my sight showed me what would come if I did." Dramin's voice was calm against Thom's outburst while I continued to look back and forth between them, my confusion growing.

"You could have killed her, Dramin!" I jumped at Thom's shout, my heart thumping.

"I wouldn't have done it if I hadn't been shown that it was the right path, Thom. Besides, she just needed to be woken up," Dramin said, still sipping on his own drink, completely unphased by Thom's outburst. I felt like my skin was crawling. "At least now we know and can work with it."

"Know what?" I practically shouted, I was over being left out of this conversation.

"He gave you some of the Black Water to drink," Thom said through his teeth, finally turning to me. "Your father's blood flows strongly in your veins. That should have killed you. Well, unless you are a Drak."

CHAPTER 33
JOCLYN

"Wait, what? A Drak?" I looked between Thom's panicked expression to Dramin's gleeful grin. Thom seemed more likely to tell me the truth, so I turned on him.

"You," I said, finger pointing as I stood. "Tell me what he did."

Thom's eyes narrowed at me as he grunted and sat back down on his couch.

"The Black Water is the water that the Drak use to cultivate the magic of sight. It is their main food source, and essentially the very core of their power. The water can only be held in a mug made from the mud of the outer rim of the Wells of Imdalind. It's why your father became so weak when Edmund kept it from him. If you keep the mugs away, you keep the Water away. The water is poison to any being other than the Drak. By giving it to you to drink, he could have very easily killed you."

"But I didn't die, so what does that mean?"

"You are one of The Chosen, correct?" Dramin asked before sipping from his cup.

"Yes." I nodded my head, waiting for him to continue. That in itself was a reason none of this made sense.

"And you have a mark?" He smiled at me from behind his cup. I nodded at him. "Can I see it?"

I looked at him for a moment before exhaling. I didn't see any reason why I shouldn't other than that I didn't want to, and that wasn't a very good reason. I closed my eyes before lifting my hair to reveal the small mark on my neck. Dramin exhaled sharply, which I wasn't prepared for, but I still kept my eyes closed.

"Look Thom, it's a dragon. How interesting." Dramin's tone made it sound like it was far more than just interesting. It made my skin crawl.

"What?" I dropped my hair and twisted back around. Thom was back to staring at me. "Does that mean something?"

"Hmmm?" Dramin studied me and I got the same feeling as before, like he was looking inside of me. I shivered. "Not yet, I think."

"Oh no. You are going to tell me. I'm over this." I leaned into him in what I thought was a threatening move. He just chuckled and drank from his own mug. I wasn't going to give up so easy.

"The important thing here, Silnŷ, is that you are in fact a Chosen, and yet you can hold the Black Water within your body."

"Which means..." I prompted him. Dramin smiled, Thom grunted from the other side of the fire, I guess I wasn't going to get answers from him this time.

"Which means that you not only have the powers that the Skřítek and Trpaslíks carry—which were awakened within you when the Vilŷ kissed your skin—but also those of the Drak as well." Dramin smiled like I was the most amazing thing in the world, but my stomach tied itself in knots.

"So... I can, like, see the future?" I asked, the disbelief heavy in my voice.

"Ohhh... You can do much more than that." Dramin's smile increased. Thom sat up again, swinging his legs to face us, the same disgruntled look on his face.

"Just spit it out, old man," Thom barked, obviously irritated. I was starting to think he was always irritated, I would be too with all the riddles and chuckling from Dramin.

"Tell me, Silnŷ, what does the Black Water make you feel like? What does it do to your magic, your body, when you drink it?"

I shifted my weight and took a drink from the mug in my hands. Both their eyes were on me as I swallowed the mouthful of Water.

"It makes me feel warm, stronger somehow. My magic feels a little more alive, a little looser." I looked up to find Dramin smiling more, if that was possible. He may never not be smiling. "Is that good?" I asked, worried that I had said the wrong thing.

"Oh, that's very good." Dramin stood and threw the heavy furs off of my lap. I sat there, staring at him, wishing I could put the blankets back on. My feet were now a normal color and I could feel all my extremities, but the cave was still cold.

"Come along, Silnŷ. I want to try something." Dramin pulled me up, carefully taking my mug from me as he did.

Carrying my mug in front of him, he pulled me along behind him. Thankfully, my feet seemed to be working properly, and not falling off in giant icy chunks. Which I was actually worried about.

"Where are we going?" I asked when I realized he was dragging me back toward the dark tunnel we had entered the cavern through. I looked back to Ilyan, nervous that I was being pulled away from him. The longing I felt scared me, though, so I shoved it away.

"I want to try something," Dramin repeated.

"Yes, I heard that the first time. Have any more information for me?" I asked as he dragged me forward. I looked back to Thom in hopes of an answer but he was still standing near the fire, his arms folded.

"I'll stay here," he called after us, smiling at my panic stricken face. "Someone's got to watch over sleeping beauty."

I opened my mouth to protest, but Thom waved his farewell and turned to his bunk. Dramin dragged me not into the dark tunnel that led outside, but into another round cavern that was connected to the first.

This one was not as nice nor as cozy as the room with the fire. In fact, it was bare. The large dome of the rock spread high above us, the stone void of paintings or dancing bits of reflection. It was only stone and a hundred blue, glittery orbs that Dramin had sent to the ceiling when we arrived in order to give us light.

While bare, it was still impressive.

"What is this place?" I turned to Dramin, surprised to find his smile faded.

"This was to be a home for one of my posterity, a young lady named Delia and her mate Chandle. They were killed in the massacre. Thom and I stay here because no one except Ilyan and I know of this cave's existence. Ilyan helped me to build it. It was to be a surprise." He smiled sadly, and I didn't know what to say so I turned away from him, trying to keep my own sense of loss at bay.

"The room we came from is the living quarters, this is the practice hall, and through that door there," he pointed toward a small opening on the opposite edge of the space, "is the Hall of Sight. It is a sacred room where the Drak can see and record their visions."

I looked toward the room, my heart turning into a one man band as I panicked between wanting to go in there, and being terrified of what I would find. I still hadn't settled with the idea that I was going to be able to see the future.

Just thinking the phrase sent a knot into my throat.

"So what are we doing here?" I worded my question carefully, hoping to take his attention off of the Hall of Sight.

"Did you know, Silnŷ, that only one magic can exist in a soul at one time? A Vilŷ can only ever be a Vilŷ, a Skřítek a Skřítek, a Drak a Drak. If the love is strong enough they can mesh in a bonding; it has been done in the past, but I am not sure Ovailia ever loved Sain. That was one of the reasons Sain and Ovailia's bond never held; their magic could never truly be one. The only form of magic that can intermingle is that of a Chosen, but to have two types of magic in one person prior to a Zêlství has never happened. It would be too much. The body, the soul, could not contain it. And yet, here you are. You have the magic of a Trpaslík and a Skřítek, as caused by the bite of a Vilŷ and the magic of the Drak from your father. All that, in one little body."

I stepped away from him, instantly feeling awkward. I didn't like the way he was insinuating that I was some super powerful being.

"The Silnŷ," he said as if on cue.

"Most Powerful." I translated for him. "Is that what it means? Is that what is in the sight?"

He nodded, "Part of it. A child with magic beyond comprehension."

The rock in my throat was growing larger. I would have to unpack that later.

"Are you saying I might be like Ilyan, like how he can't use the whole of his magic on one person?" Dramin's eyes narrowed at me as he began to step around me like he was surveying me. I held still, even though I wanted to move away from his hawk-like stare.

"No, not yet," he said. I could tell it was more to himself than to me, but it still peaked my interest.

"What do you mean, 'not yet'?"

"You are not yet ready to see all that you must see." He smiled again as he stopped in front of me, his body far too close for comfort.

"Bull crap. I'm ready. I need to know." I was firm, he just smiled and pushed the mug back into my hands, the warm Black Water still swirling heavily inside.

"The Drak drink the Black Water from birth. It is part of our very nature, part of who we are. You have drank the contents of two mugs. It is the start of your new life. You will find in a matter of days that you will no longer desire human food. You will not need to sleep as much. You will only need the Black Water to sustain you."

I looked into the mug uneasily; I already wanted to take another drink.

"Now, let's conduct a little experiment. I will shoot a target into the air for you. I want you to drink of the Black Water and then fire your magic at the target. Aim to kill."

"I'm still waiting for answers." Although, what he was offering was almost more enticing. My magic was already popping under my skin, eagerly.

"And you will get them. But first, drink." His eyes didn't leave mine as he lifted his hand and fired a dark, heavy shape from his hands across the large space. It appeared more cumbersome than the magic I had learned to control, it almost looked... weak.

I lifted the mug to my lips and drank greedily, loving the way the liquid filled me up. I lowered the mug and I lifted my hand, surprised by the response my magic had to that simple thought. Without having to focus, a ripple of brilliant violet flew from the palm of my hand faster than I had ever seen. It intercepted Dramin's dark target with a bang, a purple shower filling the room as my magic destroyed the target.

I didn't dare move. Ilyan had been training me in combat for months and I had never been able to obtain that kind of power, even after I had been able to shield myself from the drain caused by the necklace. Ilyan had always said how strong my magic was, but it had never responded. Not like that.

"Wonderful!" Dramin shouted as he clapped his hands enthusiastically. "Did you know that the Drak carry no defensive magic? So the fact that you can do that, and so well, is amazing."

I stared at him.

"Would you care to try it again?" Dramin waved his hand over my mug, the liquid refilling itself to the brim.

I looked at the Black Water before emptying the mug with one gulp. Dramin laughed as he sent another target into the dark cavern for me. This time I released the mug into the air where it floated as I sent a strong impulse from both hands. The bright green wave soared through the dark cave in ripples of light, disintegrating the target and leaving a long divot in the rock. I reached out and grabbed the mug from where it still hovered in the air, my hands wrapping around the smooth ceramic as if I was afraid I would drop it.

"Amazing," Dramin whispered beside me. I could only nod. Yeah, it was.

"How is that possible?" I asked, looking at my hand. "I have never been able to... I mean, I..."

"It appears the Black Water has opened up your true potential, Silnỳ."

"And what is that?" I turned to him, hair flying, and stared at him wide eyed. He met my gaze, eyes shining as they searched through me. Again. I shifted my weight.

"No, not yet."

"Then when?"

"When you have accepted who you truly are." His answer was simple, yet somehow impossible. I looked at my free hand, my eyes trailing back to the large dent that had rent the smooth surface of the stone.

"I am a Drak," I said. I could still feel the addictive way that the Black Water buzzed through my veins.

"Yes."

"But I am also a Chosen." My fingers grazed over the seldom touched skin of my mark, as if I needed the reminder

"Yes."

"But the two cannot exist together. 'Different magic cannot exist in one being without a bonding'."

Dramin nodded and stepped closer, those eyes sending a shiver up my spine. "It seems, Silnỳ, that in you, all things are possible."

CHAPTER 34
WYN

My body was numb. It felt weird without my magic soaring through it. Almost dead. This must be what it felt like to be human.

Except humans probably weren't likely to find themselves restrained to a wall in the dungeons below Prague with their hands chained above their heads, the chain extended so their weight was supported by their wrists. That would just be me.

I stared into the darkness and tried to stand again, but my legs were too weak. Everything was too numb. Even though I could feel the stone against the balls of my feet, I couldn't move my legs to try to stand against it. So I hung there, staring into the dark, cold space, the air heavy with the smell of wet and mildew.

To think, just yesterday I had been too scared to come down here.

Now I was trapped, alone, strung up against the cold stone. I hoped that the mysterious power I shared with the stone of these walls would awaken and ignite, but the rock Edmund had forced down my throat had done its job. I was powerless.

I stayed like this for hours, with only the darkness and an occasional whimper that echoed off the stone for company. I couldn't tell if the sound was from a rodent or the battered man that Edmund had been dragging around behind him.

I don't know if I had passed out or simply slept, but the clanging of chains woke me. I jerked awake, only to feel a subtle pressure of fingers against my spine.

Magic pulsed through me and the numbing that had occupied my body was stripped away, leaving me in agony. My shoulders were on fire, my wrists broken from supporting me for so long. My scream of pain echoed off the dark walls, it hung in the damp air even after a wide fist collided with my face, leaving more pain behind.

"What?" I taunted, gritting my teeth into the dark. "You think I'm going to cower?"

Another punch joined the first.

"I won't--" I had to pause to spit the blood that filled my mouth. "Cower."

Another punch, but this time I said nothing. I just scowled.

The chains that suspended me clattered again as they were moved higher, extending my body until I was on my tiptoes, my shoulders threatening to snap. I screamed at the movement and the same hand smacked my cheek, the face of the hand's owner swimming into view.

"Silence, princess," my father sneered, his lip curling underneath his large moustache. "There are consequences."

He slapped me again. My cheek stung, and my body screamed, but I refused to give him rise. I refused to let him win. I stared into his eyes, the irises as dark as mine, waiting for more. None came, and his smile only increased.

"Aren't you going to say hello to your father?" he sneered. "I think I have taught you better manners than this."

I stared at him in silence, eyes wide as I taunted him, as I dared him. If I was anyone else, I might have given in; but I couldn't, something deep inside wouldn't let me.

Timothy's eyes narrowed at my defiant gaze, his confidence wavering at my stubbornness. Good. He might kill me, but I was going to put up a fight until the very end.

"Say, hello," he sneered again, the stubbornness I had inherited from him forcing him on.

He shook the chains, fire burning through my arms and shoulders. My taunt was lost as pain settled in my spine. A groan escaped me as I fought back a scream, my jaw clenching painfully as I looked at my father with as much hatred, as much power as I could muster. I found the sleeping magic within me and prodded it, but nothing happened. My now mortal body was useless and strung up before my father for whatever torture he had in mind.

"Say, hello," he prompted again, his fists flexing by his sides.

I stared at him, my jaw clenched, ready for the impact to come... when he smiled.

"Don't you want to see your mate, princess?" he snarled, and my eyes widened. His smile only increased.

I hung my head, not wanting to let him win, but I had no other choice. He had Talon.

I couldn't feel even the slightest of pulls to signal to me that Talon was alive, but if my father was using him as a threat, he had to be. I had to keep him that way.

"Hello, Father," I growled from behind clenched teeth.

"Good, good." He grinned and nodded his head to someone in the dark; the chains loosened, sending me tumbling to my knees. My arms were still extended above my head, although not as painfully as they were a moment before.

"You do what I say, Wynifred. I do not care what deal Talon worked out with Edmund. You are my child, and I will do with you what I please." His voice was soft as he kneeled beside me, his finger pushing aggressively into the tender skin of my now battered face.

"You stay silent, you do as I say, and we may not have to do this anymore."

I glared at him, not willing to look away. I may not rise to him, but I refused to cower in defeat.

He took my silence as affirmation. "Good girl," Timothy said, his voice made it sound like he was addressing a dog. "Now, your brother has just arrived in Prague, and I am sure he has news, if not a heart, for your master." He smiled once more before disappearing into the darkness, the heavy sound of his footsteps on the stairs announcing his departure.

I tried to focus through the dark, squinting to see anything through the black. Without the aid of my magic, I saw nothing. I gave up and sank back into the wall, trying to ignore the fire that was thrumming in my shoulders and arms.

"Do what he says, Wynifred, and keep your secret safe." The voice echoed from the darkness where the whimpers had come from before, the sound deep and rough like sandpaper. I recognized it at once. It was the same voice I had heard in Ovailia's room, the one that had told me to run.

So, it was the battered man who was there.

"What secret? What are you talking about?" I asked into the dark, my voice broken and muffled thanks to the swelling in my face.

"No talking!" The warning from what could only be a guard was loud and powerful. I sunk into the stone, trying to prob that sleeping magic again.

For years, I had watched Edmund and my father drag Skříteks down to the pit of whatever house we lived in. I had heard the screams, seen the blood that they washed off their hands. Now I was on the receiving end. I didn't want to know what was behind the screams. I didn't want to see the blood being drawn.

Not that I had a choice.

The minutes stretched into hours and thankfully, my arms began to go numb again. My head swam as my blood flow got all muddled, my body calling for water, food, and above all, a bathroom. None of which, I knew, would be provided.

I shifted my weight for the millionth time, the chains rattling as my joints surged with pain before settling back into the burn of numbness that was becoming normal.

Still, sleep did not come, no matter how much I wished it would.

I jumped as steps sounded on the staircase, the loud thump of feet cutting through the icy silence. Tension built in my stomach as the feet raced closer, the flare of fear working its way up my spine.

"This guy is heavy!" The thick voice of a man filtered down the stairs, his voice deepened by the echo of the stairway.

"Stop complaining and use your magic." Another voice joined the first, causing my stomach to twist.

"This is ridiculous," the first man said. "Edmund is just going to kill them all anyway."

An impatient growl followed the first man's comment and a loud rumble of something being dropped on stone echoed through the cold, dark room.

"What is going on here?" A new voice, a voice I recognized at once, cut across the first two. All of the fear and tension I felt multiplied.

Cail's snarl was loud and angry as dozens of footsteps joined the first two who had clogged the stairwell.

My eyes were drawn to the only light I had seen in hours, a gentle blue light that grew stronger as the voices moved closer. I pulled toward it, like a moth, my desperation to see rippling into my spine. Soon, the glow was enough to filter into the prison, letting me see what hell I had been trapped in.

The prison was a long, wide hall. One half was broken up with thick metal bars that segmented us into five-foot by five-foot squares, there was not enough space to lie flat and straight in the cells. There were no windows, and it was obvious that nothing had been cleaned for centuries.

I had smelled the mildew before, but now I knew why. A glistening sheen of wet covered the stone, the bars, even the large padded stool where a lone guard had sat. All the cells were empty to my left; as well as all, but one, to my right—where the battered man I had seen before was chained by his hands against the wall. He caught my gaze as I looked at him, the bright green of his eyes startling even in the dark. His eyes pleaded with me from behind his unkempt beard and hair as he placed his finger to his lips. I only nodded; the need for silence was evident.

"Why aren't you two down there yet?" Cail continued, his voice rising.

"I'm sorry, sir," the first man said, his voice soft and pleading.

I couldn't help the twitch that moved through my spine as Timothy's voice joined the others. "Just get down there and do what you were asked."

"Yes, sir," the two men mumbled together, and the footsteps returned, the light increasing as they all moved into the prison.

The battered man's warning was lost the moment I saw them. The two men I had heard arguing a moment before carried with them a hulking form with a mess of sandy brown hair I knew all too well.

"Talon!" I couldn't help it; I screamed, I yelled, and I fought against my chains. The small space filled with my voice as I yelled for him, the rattling of my chains almost loud enough to drown out my panic.

Talon didn't respond. He didn't even twitch as they dragged him into the cell right next to mine, dropping him to the ground with a thud. They didn't even bother to chain him up before they locked him in his cell.

My body was on fire as I fought against the chains. Every muscle, every bone, pulled in agony. I barely registered the pain. My need to reach him was too strong. I needed to touch him, to feel his heartbeat, to prove that he was still alive. I screamed, battled, yelled and pleaded, knowing it was of little use, but still, I couldn't help myself.

"Will someone shut her up?" I heard Timothy yell above my screams. I should have seen someone coming, but I was so focused on Talon's limp body in the cell next to mine that I didn't know anyone had come into my cell until a foot collided with my stomach, the impact knocking the wind out of me and sending me back against the wall.

I stopped screaming as I groaned in pain, gasping for breath. The chains around my wrists clattered as I slid down the wall, my arms pulling back into their extended position above my head. I stared at Talon until a strong hand grasped my jaw; I winced at the pressure on the bruised chin as he turned me to face him. My jaw instantly tightened.

"Was this your handiwork, brother? I will make you--"

"Don't push me, Wynifred!" Cail sneered right in my ear before his closed fist hit me hard against my cheek.

I turned back to look at him, my eyes narrowing in fight and warning. It was a useless threat; there wasn't anything I could do to him. He smiled once before moving out of the cell to stand in the small hallway that lined the jail block.

"Ryland," Cail said, his attention turning from me to the black-eyed man behind him. My head whipped up as Cail spoke his name. I didn't know why I didn't expect him to be here. Ryland was just as much one of Edmund's puppets as my brother was now.

Ryland stepped forward, his face blank, his curls limp as they hung damp around his head.

"Go sit by Sain, and chain your legs together."

Sain? The first of the Drak? The one Ovailia betrayed? The one Edmund killed? But he was dead-- my shock silenced as Ryland walked into the cell with the battered man, sat down next to him, and chained his own ankles.

Sain.

Sain. It couldn't be; it just couldn't.

Sain looked at me with those bright green eyes of his, his one glance daring me to deny what I already knew. He was Sain. I had no idea how, or why, but I was sure it was him.

Ryland's movements were stiff, his vision unfocused as he followed Cail's odd demands. I looked between all of them; my brother and father who were focused on Ryland, Talon's limp body in the cell next to mine, Ryland as a shell of himself, and Sain. His green eyes still bore into mine, the power behind them evident even beneath the blood-soaked hair and the bruised face.

Timothy moved over to where Ryland and Sain sat. Sain lifted his chained hands up to him. Timothy removed one of the chains from Sain's wrist and reattached it on Ryland's. Sain did not fight, and Ryland did not move. The eeriness of it scared me. I didn't know what they were doing, and I didn't want to.

"Ready," Timothy said as he stepped out of the cell, closing the door to the tiny space behind him and trapping the two men inside. "Turn him off, son."

"Yes, Father," Cail said obediently, and for one split second, the prison was quiet except for the sound of my chains as I looked between them. They were waiting for something. The silence took one more breath before the air opened up with a scream so mournful that I jumped, my own tears threatening as my soul understood the absolute heartbreak that the sound encompassed.

I recoiled as Ryland began to writhe and fight against the chains that he had bound himself with. Sain's emaciated body moved around like a rag doll with each of Ryland's spasms as he fought against his own restraints. Ryland screamed and yelled and howled, his now blue eyes panicked as he attempted to claw his way out of the cell.

This was like no side of Ryland I had ever seen. This was not the compliant Ryland that Cail seemed to control. It was not the aggressive Ryland that had attacked us at the party, nor was he the calm and loving boy that I had seen with Joclyn before this all began.

He was desperate, emotionally unstable, and terrifying. It was the terror that affected me the most. That raw primal aggression was powerful as he repeatedly lunged against his chains, hitting his head against the bars in an attempt to move through them.

I understood that pain. I didn't know how, or why. But I knew it. Watching him was ripping something open in me.

I scooted as far away from him as possible. My arms stretched painfully as I moved toward Talon, knowing he couldn't protect me, but needing to move away from the scene in the opposite cell.

"Joclyn!" he screamed, his voice weak and breaking. "What have you done to her?" Ryland continued to scream and writhe as Cail laughed, his footsteps heavy as he moved to stand in front of Ryland's cell, right next to our father.

"I haven't done anything to her," Cail said innocently. "What you should be wondering is what you have done to her."

Ryland froze, his jaw working in terror. "What *I* did?" he asked, his voice barely above a whisper. "I did... nothing... nothing... I'm good. Not hurt..." Ryland rambled for a moment, his words disjointed as his head twitched around. "What did you make me do?" Ryland asked, the sporadic action disappearing quicker than it had come on.

"I didn't make you do anything, Ryland," Cail taunted, his voice heavy with malice. "Did you hurt her?"

"You made me hurt her!" Ryland yelled, his body pushing against the chains that bound him so tightly. What little relaxation my shoulders had found left as I tensed away from the anger in Ryland's voice.

"Made me hurt... made me hurt..." he repeated, his voice clicking through the mechanic repetition.

"Now, now," Cail taunted, his voice calm and condescending. "I did nothing of the sort. I didn't wrap my hands around her neck. Did you?"

Ryland's voice broke for only a moment before he answered in a hiss, "Yes... yes."

"Did I break her arm?" Cail asked, his back arching as he lowered himself to Ryland's eye level.

"No," Ryland repeated over and over again. His voice had weakened in desperation, his body now only barely fighting against the chains.

"Did she try to kill me? Did I try to kill her?" I froze, my breathing catching at Cail's words. I knew what they were talking about, but it didn't make any sense. Joclyn tried to kill Ryland? She hadn't said anything about this on our call.

"No." Ryland's voice was soft.

"Did you?" Cail taunted. It was not a question.

"Yes."

"Will you do it again?" Cail spoke to him like a psychiatrist, his words soothing, and yet, the intention behind them was heavy and as clear as day. "Will you hurt her?"

"Hurt her... hurt her... hurt her," Ryland repeated as he began to rock, the rocking stopping suddenly as he switched over again, his voice loud.

"No!" Ryland roared, his desperation coming back quickly. "No." Ryland yelled and screamed as he fought against the chains, pulling at the heavy link that bound him to the rock wall.

"Really?" Cail taunted, his back straightening as he stood. "But she hurts you in your dreams, doesn't she?"

"No. Nonono..."

"What about when she kissed me, when her hands were all over me," Cail paused, "that hurt, didn't it?"

Ryland said nothing, but looked around frantically, his eyes darting all over the dungeon as his breathing picked up, his fingers curling as he moaned a deep lament filled with agony.

Watching him was traumatizing. I was torn between pity, an insane desire to help him, and fear over the explosive nature of his moods. I tried to catch his eyes, hoping that maybe getting him to see me would calm him, but he didn't seem to notice anyone other than Cail. Sain, however, was still staring into me, seemingly oblivious to the exchange going on mere inches from him.

I returned Sain's stare, not knowing where else to look, not wanting to see Cail torment Ryland anymore. I looked at him, silently hoping that the strong gaze of the old man's eyes would fill in the gaps I was so obviously missing.

"Or what about when she tried to snap your neck?" Cail asked.

"It wasn't her."

"But you just saw her, on the roof top of that little farmhouse, clinging to Ilyan," Cail continued to taunt, his lips turned in a sneer.

Timothy chuckled wickedly at the look on Ryland's face.

"Nononononono," Ryland moaned, his fingers curling again as he rocked back and forth, his head hitting against the bars several times.

"Do you think he's kissed her?" Cail whispered, the harshness of his voice hissing through the damp prison.

"No." Ryland's voice was strong, but forced, his belief in his words wavering, his body still rocking as he fought whatever demons had been placed in his head.

"I saw Ilyan kiss Joclyn. I looked into the window of Sain's mind and saw her kiss him. Her hands wrapped through that hair of his as he touched her, loved her and *kissed* her."

Cail spoke softly as if to a lover, but the tone of his voice only triggered Ryland's violence. His voice cracked and broke as he cried out at Cail's words, and he pulled at his hair and clawed at the shackles around his ankles.

"And she kissed him back." Cail barely got the words out before Ryland lunged at the door to his prison, his hands shooting through the narrow space between the bars as he reached for my brother. Ryland's fingers moved and flexed, intent on clawing out Cail's eyes, but he couldn't reach far enough. Cail and my father only laughed.

Ryland's eyes were feral, his growl deep and menacing. I turned to the laughing men, a different kind of determination filling me. They did this. They would continue to do this. We had to find a way to fight back.

"She loves him, Ryland," Cail said, leaning toward Ryland's still clawing fingers. "Joclyn loves Ilyan more than she loves you. What are you going to do about it?"

"Kill... kill... kill." Ryland repeated, although I wasn't sure who he was talking to.

"What. Are. You. Going. To. Do?" Cail asked, each word stronger than the last.

"I'm going to kill him!" Ryland pushed and tugged against the bars, his voice deep through his clenched teeth.

"And what about her?" Cail asked, his voice still containing that menacing taunt. "Are you going to hurt her? Make her pay?"

"Yes!" Ryland yelled, and Cail smiled more. "Hurt her... hurt her!"

"She hurt you!" Cail yelled, his voice changing back into a taunt, and I knew at once what they were doing. Cail had gained full control of Ryland's mind. He was manipulating Ryland into believing things that he wouldn't believe otherwise. The lines of reality and manipulated horror were so blurred I could tell Ryland had no idea what was what anymore.

But how had he gained control of Ryland's mind like this? This wasn't a Vymåzat. A Vymåzat erased, this was a type of control I had never seen.

"Are you going to kill her?" Cail asked, the final brick in his bridgework laid.

"Yes!" Ryland yelled, his feral growling against the bars increasing before Sain's hand, unseen by both Cail and my father, touched his back. The touch brought him back down to earth. The frantic movements slowed. Ryland's body settled back onto the damp floor of the prison, his hands shaking as his fingers curled around his head.

"No," Ryland gasped, his face horrified at what had just happened. "Nonononono." His voice opened again into that same mournful whine, the deep hollow noise of heartbreak and betrayal.

"No?" Cail asked, even though his anger at the temporary glitch was obvious, his voice still held that manipulative tone. He didn't miss a beat, and Ryland began second-guessing himself.

"But she hurt you," Cail stated, moving himself closer to the bars again.

"It wasn't her," Ryland said, yelling as he tried to convince himself as well as Cail. "Wasn't her, wasn't her, wasn't her."

"How can you be so sure?"

"I know." Ryland lunged at the bars again, but Cail didn't even flinch, even though the raw aggression had returned to Ryland's face.

"The way she knows you didn't just try to kill her, for the second time?"

Ryland's jaw moved as he tried to get the words out, but nothing came. Finally, two words left him, the conviction almost gone from his voice, "She knows."

"How?"

"She knows, she knows," he repeated.

"Why don't you show her?" Cail asked, his lips twitching with a pleased sneer.

Ryland's eyes widened as Cail pulled a double-sided blade from his pocket, the metal of the blade bright red. It had only a broken strip of leather as a handle. It almost looked like a shard of jagged stone, sharpened to a point on both sides.

Ryland looked at it as Cail extended it to him through the bars, his fingers twitching as he slowly reached to grab it. I couldn't take my eyes off the blade. I had only heard of these, seeing one made my stomach turn. It was a knife made of blood and bits of soul. It was dark magic at its core.

And they were using it against him. No wonder he was so broken.

There was no fighting against this. I pulled against my chains, the metal clanking as I tried to move away, knowing there was nowhere to go. I couldn't take my eyes off the blade, my breath coming in short, little spurts as Cail held it between his fingers.

"Tell her the truth, Ryland," Cail whispered, the last words all Ryland needed to hear before he snatched the blade from Cail's hand.

Ryland held it confidently, knowing exactly what to do with it. He lifted his shirt to reveal his chest, the skin over his heart pock-marked with line after line of stab wounds.

Sain reached forward and placed his hand over Ryland's heart, the skin of his hand equally as scarred. I only got a glimpse of the scars, only barely registered what was going to happen before Ryland plunged the blade through Sain's hand and into his own chest. Both men called out in pain, and my screams joined them until the pair passed out, leaving my screams to fill the prison.

Timothy took the final steps to stand right before the now open door of my cell. I barely saw him. I couldn't look away from Sain and Ryland's frozen bodies. I couldn't stop screaming. I expected my father to punch me again. What I didn't expect was for him to unchain me.

"Why don't you join them, princess?" Timothy's voice was icy as he grabbed the chains that connected to the shackles on my wrist, one yank sending me to the ground as he pulled me over the cold, uneven floor.

I didn't have to ask what he was doing. I knew. I kicked and fought as he tried to take me toward them. My voice caught and screamed as I pleaded with him to leave me alone, to save me. It was useless. Timothy ignored my pleas as he threw my flailing body toward the collapsed forms of Sain and Ryland.

"Are we ready?" I barely heard Edmund's voice over my screams as my father pulled my hand toward the protruding edge of the dagger. I was so weak I had no chance to fight him, my screams were the only defense I had against what was coming.

"Almost, Master." My brother's voice was cold, distanced and almost excited.

My screams turned to pleas as I felt the sharp point of the dagger press against the skin of my palm.

"No," I begged. "No, Daddy, please no."

"Sorry, princess," he said, although he didn't really mean it. "But you'll like this, I promise."

Cail and Edmund laughed at his taunt as Cail placed his hand over mine, pushing our palms into the blade, my scream broke through the air as my soul was sliced apart.

CHAPTER 35
WYN

I was floating; gliding through mist and water. At least, I thought that was what it was. I couldn't be sure. After all, I wasn't sure where I was, or who I was. My body felt disconnected. Not separated from me, but separate. I couldn't tell where my arm extended to or where my leg was. I saw white and dark, and memories that I knew did not belong to me, or were pieces of a past I had forgotten. I felt happy and sad and scared and anxious, but none of the emotions were mine.

I was lost in a sea of everyone, a mist of white that gobbled everyone up and mashed us together. The dungeon was gone. The pain was gone. It was just me, floating through the endless mist.

The last thing I remembered was the feeling of the soul's blade plunging through my hand; is that where I was? Trapped within the blade, just another nameless face to all those already killed by the dark weapon?

Yes, I supposed I was.

I floated and let the bits of souls wash over me, my body of smoke and cloud taking it all in, my cares gone.

"Sain?" a voice cut through the cloud of white. I was sure it was Ryland's, but it seemed younger somehow.

I would like to say I turned toward the sound, but I was not sure I could with how I was swimming in sea foam.

"I'm here." My consciousness peaked at the voice, my awareness clicking into place. “They brought Wynifred here, too, Ryland.” That voice, it wasn't familiar, and yet, I still felt like it should have been.

“Of course they did,” Ryland replied, his voice floating to me through the damp, white cloud. “She is their bargaining chip now.”

“Wynifred?” Sain’s voice called out to me. “Don't be scared, child. You are safe here.”

I would have loved to respond to him, but I still couldn't figure out how to speak, what to say, or even if I had a mouth to use.

“You need to focus, Wynifred. Think about where your body should be, and it should appear for you.”

I gaped at Sain's words, the instructions foreign and awkward. I wasn't a body. I was mist. I was bits of everyone, and at the same time, nothing. How could I focus on a body if none existed for me?

I heard Sain sigh and Ryland laugh, the sounds rippling through me. Why did they seem so normal? Weren't they screaming only moments before?

“She's more stubborn than you were, Ryland,” Sain laughed, an impatient clip in his voice.

“I'm just lucky you were here, old man, or I would have wandered this place in confusion for days.”

“I don't know why you count centuries of torture as 'luck', but I suppose I will take your word for it.”

“Did you feel that?” Ryland interrupted, his tone deep and panicked.

“Is Joclyn falling asleep?” Sain’s voice was just as worried. “Is he here?”

“No, it's something else.”

The mist swirled around me, taking me with it before it pulled me, held me, and I felt small fingers on my cheek. A cheek. Once I felt my cheek, my body fell into place, my mind detaching itself from the mist as my legs connected and stepped onto something hard, my weight dropping to the ground as my legs chose not to support me.

My vision circled and flowed as colors took over the white, a forest floor crackling under my fingers. I had barely registered the pine needles before Sain rushed up to me, his hands moving to my shoulders as he inspected me for injuries.

“Are you all right?” I looked up to Sain, his face clean shaven, his hair short, and everything about him clean and well taken care of. I wouldn't have recognized him if it wasn't for his eyes.

“I’m fine. Just pissed.” And confused, but I wasn’t going to admit that.

"You will be safe," Sain said, and I couldn't help hearing the heavy infliction in his voice, the way his tone dipped and wavered into something deeper.

"So it is you?"

"Yes. I could tell you my life story, but we simply don't have time for it, nor do I think you want to hear my depressing tale right now." He smiled sadly, his kind eyes still searching mine. I couldn't return the smile; I was far too confused.

"Can you stand?" Sain asked, his hands wrapping around mine and pulling me up before I had a chance to respond.

"It can be disorienting at first, so don't try to make too much of it. We are only here for a few minutes."

"Where are we?" I asked, the mist retreating as I looked around.

"This is where we wait," Sain said as he steadied me. "He doesn't know we are able to materialize. He makes us wait before he uses us as his pawns."

"He?"

"Your brother." I winced at Sain's words. The memories of what had just happened mixing with the old and making Cail even more of a bastard.

"So what is this place? What happens now?"

"Nothing good happens now. What your father has done to you in the dungeon, that's just the opening act."

"I thought you said we were safe here," I said, looking around and still not understanding.

"Not here," he said. "Where he takes us afterwards. Just remember, it is only a dream."

I swallowed hard, the inflection in Sain's voice heavy with fact and warning.

"It's gone." Ryland's voice was loud as it broke our conversation apart, leaving my hundreds of unasked questions unanswered. "What was it?"

"You control this place, Ryland; you tell me. It's just my blood that makes the connection."

Ryland snorted and shook his head, his curls bouncing as he finally turned and acknowledged I was there. He stared at me intently, a million emotions set into his eyes.

"Is she all right?" he asked succinctly.

I leaned into Sain, not knowing what to say or how Ryland would react to the little I did know. While I would like to say he was safer here, more stable, I could still see the anxiety and the exploding anger behind his eyes.

"Don't worry, Wyn," He said, stepping right up to me and holding out the big paws of his hands out. "I'm alright here. Well, alright as I can be. Everything has gotten worse since my father started using the blade, but here, here it feels almost normal."

"Here in the mist?" I asked, turning toward it. It moved as though it was trying not to be seen and I could have sworn I felt those fingers on my cheek again.

"It's the closest he is to having his soul in one piece," Sain said, his tone far sadder than I expected.

"Out of here..." Ryland hesitated, his voice catching, my heart tightened right alongside. "Out there all I can remember is Joclyn, but the details are all fuzzy. And Cail makes it worse... so... tell me. I need the truth. How is she?"

It was an honest enough question, but even Sain was coiled in nervous energy. I had a feeling I still needed to tread very lightly.

"I don't know," I whispered. "She has been in hiding with Ilyan. I haven't seen her in months."

I watched as Ryland's jaw clenched, his eyes turning to the chilling color of ice. I could feel the anger radiating off him as he walked away from us, his fist colliding with a tree and then punching through it as the sturdy trunk turned to smoke.

"Calm down, Ryland," Sain ordered, his voice deep and fatherly.

"How can I calm down?" he yelled, his voice loud as he turned on us. I flinched, Sain barely moved. "It's been months, she says. Months! We have been tortured, used against her, beaten—for months. All while she has been on an extended date with her new boyfriend." I flinched at his words, taking a step closer to Sain. I really wished I hadn't said anything.

"That's not true, Ryland," Sain said, his voice a calming beacon that Ryland didn't seem to respond to.

"Ilyan is just protecting her--" I tried to help, but Ryland whirled on me, angrier than before. I guess I had chosen the wrong thing to say.

"No! He's not! He has his hands all over her!"

"No, Ryland, don't give in to Cail's games. You know he is lying," Sain pleaded as he stepped closer to him.

Ryland stepped forward, squaring his shoulders, but Sain didn't back down.

"How do I know that?" Ryland spat, his anger fuming as he moved and paced.

"Because I've talked to them," I tried again, watching both Sain and Ryland for clues on what to say. "Ilyan is protecting her, but she still asks about you. Talks about you. She got mad at Ilyan over you. She is training to save you."

Thankfully that time was better and Ryland's breathing slowed.

"She is going to save you, Ryland. And more. Remember what I told you?" Sain's voice was calm as he placed his hand on Ryland's shoulder, the touch once again triggering a calmness in him.

"Only Joclyn can stop my father." Ryland's voice was tight as he spoke, his eyes unfocused on something far beyond us.

"Yes, and who is the only one that can help her with that?"

The temporary calm that Ryland had found faded away as fast as a slap. His breathing picked up, and his chest heaved, his eyes darkening into a deep icy blue. "I can do it."

"Ryland, I—" Sain tried to interrupt him, but Ryland exploded, and I jumped away from him.

"I am strong, too. Stronger than him. The sight was wrong, Sain! It is me that can help her! I need Jos's power to stop him."

"No, Ryland!" Sain roared, causing Ryland to stop in his tracks. "You must not take her power. That was your first mistake—when you foolishly sealed yourself to her. At that moment, you were more in love with Joclyn's power than with her."

"Don't judge what you don't know! I love her!"

I was not one to hide by any means, but the volatility of Ryland's emotions was terrifying. I stepped behind Sain, who thankfully didn't protest.

"You did, Ryland, you loved her. But when you found out who she was, your love changed—"

"No..." Ryland interrupted, his voice airy and desperate.

I looked at Sain, this seemed like dangerous territory, but he plowed on. He was here with him enough that I would have to assume he knows what he was doing.

"You loved her magic more than her," Sain insisted, his voice calm and level. "You loved what her magic could do for you."

"No, I need her magic." Ryland sighed and shook his head as if clearing the thought from his mind. "I love her."

"That may be," Sain said, his voice still low and comforting, "but this bond has only caused her pain. We have talked about this; you are not helping her now. You must trust in the sight if you wish her to end this."

"You just want Jos to be with a king, not a worthless prince." Ryland spun to face Sain as he spoke, the anger deep in his voice as he hissed at the old man, his face only inches from Sain's.

"I want her to live up to her true potential."

I stayed one step behind Sain, trying to follow their strange conversation. I felt like I was only hearing one side of a phone conversation, however.

"And that is not with me?" Ryland asked, the deep root of his voice struggling to keep steady. Sain only shook his head.

"How do you know, Sain?" Ryland spat. "Have you seen something new?"

"You know I have no control over my sights anymore, Ryland. I see only what he would have me see." Sain's voice was a whisper against Ryland's outburst.

Ryland howled at Sain's words, moving away from us to smash his fist through several more trees that turned to mist at the impact. Ryland stood still after disintegrating his eighth tree, his chest heaving as he watched the white mist float toward the empty expanse of sky above us.

"Don't give in to Cail's taunts, Ryland," Sain counseled. "If you give in, then he has won. Use this time to clear your mind. It's the only time you are in control of yourself. Don't let Cail's words cloud you here."

"He's my brother," I interjected, stepping forward confidently. This I could contribute. "He's a bastard. He only lives to serve Edmund and hurt everyone who is against him. Right now, that means you."

Ryland stood with his back to us, his head bobbing once in understanding before he turned, his strides taking him right into Sain's arms. The older man embraced him, his hands wrapping around him tightly. They said nothing; the embrace was enough to convey all that was needed. Ryland moved away and came right over to me, his giant arms sweeping me up as he squeezed me against him.

"I'm sorry, Wyn," he whispered in my ear. "I'm sorry I got so mad. I just can't see the lies from reality anymore." He dropped me and smiled. "My brain is a mess. It's like a child is playing with crayons in there, and the colors got all muddled."

I wanted to laugh at what he said; I could tell that had been his intention, but I couldn't. I heard the honesty behind it, and it broke my heart. Edmund had tried to delete Ryland's mind, but somehow Ryland had fought him. So instead, they turned to manipulation and torture. I felt my stomach swim, the lack of contents adding to my nausea.

"If it wasn't for Sain, I would probably be more of a mess." He chuckled again, only for the sound to die as though it had been sucked through the air. He looked away, his hands tightening on my biceps. Both his and Sain's eyes turned outward as tree after tree began to vaporize, the white fog that surrounded us started moving forward, seeping through the trees much faster than was natural.

"Remember, it's only a dream, Wynifred... Brace yourself." I barely heard Sain's words before the mist took me, the white mass moving into me and breaking me up into a million pieces again. This time, however, the feeling of carelessness didn't take me. I was aware.

I was aware as different trees began to form around me and aware of voices in the distance, these ones hard and menacing. I was aware of the change in my body and the hands that wrapped hard around my arms, aware of the fear that gripped my heart.

"This isn't a game!"

Joclyn? Joclyn was here...

CHAPTER 36
JOCLYN

The forest.

These weren't just nightmares anymore, they were real. With nightmares you could at least count on waking, but with these dreams I was not so sure anymore. Plus, after seeing the scorch mark in the wall back at the farm house, I didn't even dare defend myself in these living dreams without the risk of hurting someone else.

I ran the second the forest materialized, darting through trees and jumping over rocks. My breath came in sharp bursts as I raced away from the men I knew would find me. I hadn't made it far when the growling started, the sounds matched by high pitched laughter.

The sounds chased me, increasing as my heart rate did, echoing as I jumped over a fallen tree and landed in the middle of a clearing. I uncoiled from my not so graceful landing only to find myself face to face with Cail. He stood in the center of the patch of dirt, inspecting his fingernails as if he was bored. Edmund stood behind him, but he was faded somehow, as if he was shrouded in fog.

"Tsk. Tsk. Running from me, Joclyn? Really? Are you that scared?" Cail mocked me, his slimy grin uncoiling as I planted my feet in the ground, my back straight as I prepared to fight him.

"Never. I just couldn't wait to smash your face in." It was a lie, no matter how confidently I raised my chin toward him.

Cail smiled at my taunt, excited at the prospect of a fight.

"Really? I would run if I were you. You haven't made us very happy, you know. Escaping from Edmund's trap yet again, surviving no matter how hard we try to kill you. It's not fair."

Cail gestured toward Edmund who smiled slightly.

"Make it good, Cail."

"Of course, master."

Both men sneered before Edmund's shape shimmered and disappeared from view. I flinched as a jolt of fear lodged itself in my chest. I clenched my jaw and ignored it. I refused to let him beat me down.

"I'm actually impressed, you know. How far you've come. So strong, and yet, so breakable." Cail circled around me, his eyes never leaving me. When his hand reached out and glided down my long hair, I pulled away from the touch, but he only smiled more.

"Did you come bringing another message, Cail, or is this the only way you can even get close to a woman?" my voice was hard as I glared at him, locking my jaw in what I hoped looked like strength.

It was harder than it should have been, facing Cail. The guy was just so freaky. Dangerous. I shivered.

Cail laughed, pulling my hair up to his nose. He inhaled the scent as I moved away from him, the strands falling from his grasp.

"Hmmm, no message. You already know my deal... twenty days left to bring yourself to me and save him. Until then, I just enjoy spending time with you." He kept his hand against his nose as he looked up at me, his intense gaze causing me to shrink away.

"Yeah right," I scoffed. "You only like spending time with me if it involves attempted murder."

Cail smiled wider, his body moving closer to mine. It took everything in me not to step away, I swear I could feel the slime of his soul rub up against mine.

"Or torture," he added, his smile growing.

"Is that what Edmund told you to do, Cail; to torture me?" He didn't answer. He just continued his advance into my personal space.

"Ryland tells me you know that Ilyan loves you. Is that true?"

"Ilyan doesn't love me," I shot back, side stepping him to move across the clearing. I didn't like how this was going. There was always more than this. More screaming, more crying, more pain.

This was too much talking for him. He was up to something.

"Not in that way."

"Oh, so he hasn't told you. Could it be that I know more than you at this point in time? Oooh, I would love to see your face when you figure everything out; what Ryland did, what Ilyan is keeping from you. This game gets more and more exciting." He clapped his hands, his eyes dancing in a way that made my insides squirm.

"This isn't a game!" I yelled at him, making my voice ricochet off the trees and reverberating through the clearing.

He froze, his face blank for a moment before the grin returned.

"Not a game you say? Well, what do you say we turn it into a game?" He came up behind me quicker than I had expected him to, his hands wrapping around me and holding me in place. He rested his chin against my shoulder, my insides squirming at the unwelcome contact.

"Why don't we see who has the upper hand?" His voice was soft in my ear, I moved my head away from him, but he followed, keeping his cheek against mine.

"Bring them out!" he yelled. I cringed against the sound, but his arms still held me against him.

My magic crackled in expectation of an attack, but I pushed it away. It wouldn't work here anyway.

Instead, I was frozen as dark shapes began to form. They were not the regular shapes of Edmund's henchmen, they were rounded trolls that were accompanied by the grunts, groans, and screams. My mouth opened in a silent scream as the forms broke between the trees. One after another they came, each of their broken bodies framed by two of Edmund's men. I looked to each of them, Ryland and Wyn fighting weakly against their captors, Talon weak and still on the ground, and a man I didn't recognize. The man lifted his gaze to mine and I knew at once who he was.

Sain.

He looked the same as I remembered him, the imprint of his features still strong in my mind. His hair, as black as mine, was longer than I remembered. It made him look older and more travel worn. He looked up to me with his rounded face, his strong jaw tight and defiant as he fought against the men who held him. His eyes were as green as mine were before they changed, the orbs glossing over with unshed tears. Thom had been right, I looked just like him.

I wasn't sure what to say or how to react to this man. He was my father, but I barely knew him. He had left me. My heart beat heavily against my chest as it screamed at me to run to him. Part of me wanted to, yet another part was too hurt to care.

"We hold in our possession two of your friends, your lover, and even your father. And who do you still have? A 'Protector'. Someone who hasn't even told you the truth yet."

I looked between them all, my heart breaking at seeing them there. I had to remind myself that this was only a dream. They weren't really here. I could not save them.

"Where is your protector, now?" Cail taunted, and my blood turned to ice.

He didn't know that Ilyan lay unconscious. I couldn't tell him. I couldn't tell him where I was, or who I was with. I needed to get out of here as fast as I could.

"Let them go," I snarled, swallowing the giant lump in my throat.

"Why? We have the upper hand. We. Are. Winning. And you, you don't even know what's going on." He smiled and I pushed against his strong arms. He just pulled me closer. Everything about him was vile.

"Now, now, don't go anywhere yet. We still haven't gotten to our game! You see, we have four people in front of us and you can pick one. One that you will not have to watch die right now. The others we will kill before you. You will not have to see the last die, but here is the clincher. Whoever you choose will have to watch you die before we will release them from this nightmare, and let them wake up."

"You're a bastard!" I fought against him, not wanting to hear anymore; not wanting to play his game.

"Oh, I am so much more than that," he whispered in my ear and I shivered. I could smell his breath. "Who do you choose, Joclyn? Who do you want to watch you die?"

I looked at each of them as they fought their captors. Each one had fought for me, and I for them. I fought the burning emotions behind my eyes as I looked between them, my vision stopping at my father. He didn't fight against those who held him. He met my eyes, nodding his head once in understanding. I inhaled deeply.

"My father," I said. "I choose my dad."

He nodded to me once more, my mouth forming the words 'I'm sorry', hoping desperately that he would understand.

"It's okay, Joclyn." A million childhood memories flooded me with his voice.

"Wonderful!" Cail sneered, his hold on me tightening, his hand tight against my stomach. I was going to throw up. "She's made her choice. Dispose of the rest."

"No!" I tried to look away, but Cail held my head as three swords plunged through the chests of my friends. In sync, each screamed and gargled as the life left their bodies. As Wyn's hand extended helplessly toward Talon, I tried not to cry. I tried to convince myself that they were not hurt—that it was only a dream—but the tears dripped down my cheeks anyway.

Cail laughed at me, holding my head in place for a moment longer as I watched their lifeless bodies sag into the forest floor.

Cail, thankfully, didn't let my eyes linger long before turning me to face my father, the men behind him holding him in place and forcing his eyes open so he didn't miss a thing. An instant later, I saw the flash of the blade to my side, praying that whatever Cail was going to do would happen quickly.

"I'm sorry, Daddy." I closed my eyes as I spoke, not wanting to know what was going to happen.

I felt the flow of the air as the sword moved, and then the pain filled me. I screamed at the impact, at the intensity of the agony. I continued screaming as Cail's arm around me disintegrated and the rough sheet of my bunk took its place.

I continued to shriek and writhe at the memory of the pain, waiting for the arm to wrap around me that would never come. I cried, and howled, and yelled in panic while, somewhere in the back of my mind, I knew that Thom and Dramin could hear me.

I screamed Ilyan's name until I had gained a little bit of control over myself. Still shaken, I replaced his name with his song. My shaky voice was louder than usual, the song ricocheting around the stone walls that threatened to swallow me whole. I sang Ilyan's song until my voice became a whisper and then faded to nothing.

I didn't dare move. I faced the cave wall with no desire to know if Thom or Dramin had witnessed my episode. When I was sure that enough time had passed, I turned, thankful to find no one except Ilyan's still body in the bunk across the common area from me.

I stood, my stocking-covered feet hitting the stone of the floor then grabbed one of my heavy fur blankets and ran across the space, prancing lightly from level to level until I stood before him. I had checked on him before I went to bed, but after the terror of my nightmare, I ached for him.

I hadn't realized how much I had come to rely on him—how much I needed him—especially in times like these. I hadn't realized how much he had come to mean to me.

It scared me.

It scared me even more after what Cail had said.

I climbed onto the bunk, worming my way behind him, making sure not to step on his feet. I curled myself into a ball, wrapping the blanket around me and leaned against the stone to stare at his calm, although blue tinted, face.

Calm, serene, free from this mess.

"So, Cail is using you against me now," I whispered even though he couldn't hear me. "I can't say I'm surprised. It was going to happen eventually, right?" I tried to laugh, but the sound came out strained.

"Ryland told me some stupid riddle about love and seeking power or light. He said it was about you." I lay my head against the stone wall, not daring enough to look away from Ilyan.

I didn't know what else to say. I didn't even know why I was talking to him. This stupid game that Cail was playing with my heart had me in knots.

Cail had spoken about love like I was being fought over and spoke of death like it was joyous; it made my insides squirm. I didn't like that Cail had dragged Ilyan into this whole mess or that he had become a weapon to be used against me, too. I knew I was being manipulated, but the thing that bothered me the most was that he had somehow crawled under my skin. I shook my head and swallowed, trying to find some stability.

Some strength.

Maybe enough for us both.

Ilyan was brave. He was confident. He was capable. But right then I couldn't help seeing how defenseless he was, how weak, and perhaps, even human he appeared. I closed my eyes at the confusion. The odd pulls and jerks that drew me toward Ilyan were making me uncomfortable.

I brushed away the emotion.

"I am going to be stronger, Ilyan. I am trying to face the nightmares alone. I think I can, but I still wake up screaming anyway." I couldn't just wish to be stronger. I needed to *be* stronger. I needed to be able to face everything and not be scared.

Ilyan wasn't weak; he wasn't defenseless. I didn't need to protect him, no matter how strongly I felt that I did right then. Ilyan was the strongest person I had ever met.

I didn't need him. I wanted him. More than I had ever thought I would, but I didn't need him to do everything for me. I was strong, too, and Ilyan had made me that way. He hadn't told me I couldn't. He had shown me how I could. He helped me be stronger because he believed in me.

I leaned forward, letting my hand brush his cheek, his weak magic swirling beneath the surface of his skin as it did inside of me.

"I saw my dad. He looked exactly the same. It was weird." I leaned my head against my knees, the pain from the nightmare still heavy inside of me. I left my hand against his skin for a moment longer before bringing it back inside the warmth of the fur blanket.

"You know, when he left I shut everything inside, and then Wyn asked me why I was throwing everything away..." I exhaled and looked away from him, my eyes scanning the large cave without really seeing anything.

"It was then that I decided not to. I'd always let Ryland in, but after that I *really* let him in. I gave him my heart. I gave him my magic, even though I didn't know it at the time." I dragged my eyes back to Ilyan's pale face, my finger moving to touch the dim blue of his eyelid without my even knowing.

"I let Wyn in, and I actually started to feel like I had a friend. I mean, even though she didn't understand me all the way—even though she didn't really know me—I felt like she could. Like she wanted to. Like I mattered to her." Everything had come out in a rush. I stopped abruptly, my voice catching on my last words while I sank back into the wall, my head hitting hard against the stone.

"And I let you in, Ilyan. First as a teacher, someone I could trust, and then, over the last three months, you became more than that. You have become my friend. Someone that... I mean... I could..." I stopped as my heart thudded, my eyes burning. I didn't know exactly what I wanted to say. I didn't know how to word it properly because everything was jumbled inside of me. Cail's manipulative taunts were still fresh in my mind.

"I hope you can't hear me, or else you're going to think I sound like a lunatic." I inhaled again, sniffing loudly. "I loved Ryland and they took him. I mean, I might not be able to get him back, but I am going to try. I am going to make Edmund pay. And Cail. So, you better wake up to see it..."

I was confident, my magic buzzing with the hope. But I couldn't stop that voice in the back of my head from hissing all of my fears.

'What if I'm not strong enough? What if I can't get there in time?'

I buried my head in my hands, cursing the tears that had finally broken through.

"I trusted Wyn, and they got to her, too. They took her, too." I wiped away the tears with the back of my hand. "And I..." I stopped, searching for the right words, but I wasn't finding them. "Ilyan, Thom says you're going to get better." I pressed my hand to my shoulder from within the warmth of my blanket, wishing his magic was stronger. "And I want to believe them, but there is so much that I don't understand, so much that I don't get. I am scared that everyone I care for is being taken from me."

I looked away from him again, my eyes moving somewhere, anywhere, at the same time that I tried to wade through the tangle of emotions inside of me.

"It's my turn to protect you now, Ilyan. It's my turn to be strong for you. I need you to wake up. I need you to come back. I… I need you." I stopped, trying not to give life to my nightmares; to Cail's taunts.

"I… I don't know how else to say it…" I think I did know how to say it, though. I wanted to say I loved him, however it wasn't the same love as I had for Ryland. It was the love of a friend—of a companion—and saying it would make my nightmares real. I couldn't let that happen.

"Don't die, okay?" I said as I moved to lay beside him, squeezing my body against his. I pulled the fur over me and snuggled into his neck. I knew I shouldn't be there. I knew I should be able to be stronger.

But right then I wasn't, and right then I could accept that.

It's okay to be weak, sometimes.

"Goodnight, Ilyan."

CHAPTER 37
JOCLYN

"Wake up, Silnẏ, you are in the way."

My eyes fluttered open at Thom's gruff voice. I knew at once why he had spoken, too. I was still lying in Ilyan's bunk with my arm draped over his torso. Two nights ago I had awakened uncomfortable with Ilyan's proximity, now I was doing the same to him. Great.

I sat up, head buzzing at the movement. Thom wasn't even looking at me. He was already moving blankets, his hands pressed against Ilyan's skin as he checked on him. I pushed a hand against my shoulder, saddened to find the same weak magic flowing through me.

"He's still the same?" I asked as I moved to the foot of the bed. Cramming my body into the corner of the bunk, I tried to keep myself covered with the heavy fur while Thom shook his head and kept working.

My body had that heavy, dizzy feeling it always had when I had stayed away from Ryland too long. I was surprised it wasn't worse given that yesterday's visit had definitely not been long enough to fully rejuvenate me. I leaned my head against the cold stone, letting the cool temperature take away some of the dizziness. I had forgotten how fast and strong these sensations came on. I knew it had been more than a day and that I needed to go see him, but I didn't want to. I traced the tip of my finger along the silver chain and sunk into the stone work.

Having to endure the aftermath of the nightmare on my own had weakened me both emotionally and physically. With Cail gloating over his control of my subconscious, I was afraid of what I would find if I went into the Tòuha. What once had been an amazing place for Ryland and me to share had become just another potential torture chamber.

I might be able to go in and come out in a matter of minutes, however I knew it wouldn't be enough. Or worse, what if something happened while I was in there? Ilyan wouldn't be here to pick up the pieces. I could already tell Thom wasn't the type to be willing to do that.

"Are you okay?" I looked up from my daydreams to see Ilyan was covered again, and Thom was staring me down.

"Yeah, just thinking about how to save the world." Thom narrowed his eyes at me, clearly trying to decide if I was joking or not. Too bad I had no idea.

"Here," he said, pulling over one of the large, ceramic mugs from last night. "Dramin left this for you."

I took the mug from Thom and smelled the Black Water. It almost smelled appealing to me now.

"Thank you," I said before draining the mug in one large gulp. The Black Water moved into me and I actually found myself feeling better. I still felt the body aches from my separation with Ryland, but they weren't as sharp and my head didn't feel as fuzzy. I sighed and leaned against the rock wall.

"Where is Dramin?" I asked, wishing I already had more of the Black Water.

"Shopping," Thom said, although I could tell it was more than that. He leaned forward and looked into the mug, his eyebrows rising to see the contents gone. "Does that stuff taste good?"

"Yes," I said, placing the mug on the shelf above Ilyan's feet. "It smells a bit funny at first, but the taste is nice."

"Well, I am glad it didn't kill you," Thom said gruffly before leaning against the side of Ilyan's bunk. He narrowed his eyes at me and I jumped. I knew that look; I had grown up with that look. It was the look every kid had given me when they were trying to figure out what was wrong with me.

"You looking for horns or something?" I shifted my hair around my mark, even though I knew I didn't need to.

"You are very interesting," he said. I waited a moment for him to elaborate. He never did.

"Thank you?" I was going to take that as my cue to leave, but Thom continued before I could move.

"You're nothing like your father. There is a lot of bitterness in your heart."

"Well that's what happens when said father abandons you, I suppose."

"Not all fathers abandon their children on purpose. Your father didn't abandon you," Thom spat, causing me to jump at his bitterness.

"Well he certainly wasn't there." My hackles were up, his tone setting me on the defensive.

"Sain only left you to do what was best for you."

"Oh, how would you know?" I spat the words as I shifted, suddenly glad I was tucked into the bunk and not facing him. "You're not a dad."

"Not anymore." Thom's eyes had suddenly gone dead, and my heart promptly dropped to my toes. The air suddenly felt like ice.

He didn't need to say any more. I could see the pain in his eyes, and I immediately hurt for him.

I opened my mouth to ask, to apologize, to say anything, but I couldn't decide, so I just shut my mouth with a snap. I was sure I looked like a fish.

The silence stretched, both of us standing there, staring. Thom broke the silence first. "Did you know I lived with my father for two hundred years before I left to join Ilyan?"

"No."

"Yes, I had seen many of my siblings go off and fight against Ilyan, leave to fight against my father, go back and forth until they would find their death, however I stayed on my father's side. I trusted him beyond anything. I didn't see a reason not to. I *knew* he was right. He was my father." Thom still leaned against the side of Ilyan's bunk, arms folded. "Your father showed me how wrong I was. That's why I helped him escape. I would have never pegged Ilyan for a good guy until the day I met him. I watched him heal Sain without question, and then he held me like a brother..."

He stopped for a moment, his eyes lingering on Ilyan. I followed his gaze, almost hoping Ilyan would be sitting there listening.

"I'm glad to return the favor," Thom said, more to Ilyan than to me before placing his palm against Ilyan's forehead.

"He's going to be alright then?" I knew he had said that before, but when someone has blue tinted eyelids you start to question.

"You can check for yourself, Silnỳ." He waved his hand over Ilyan's body as if in invitation, but I shook my head no.

"I don't know how." Thom's face was pure shock before turning into an awkward looking smile. "We mostly focused on defensive magic." I answered his unasked question, with a shrug. Thom didn't seem to notice.

"Place your hand on his cheek then," Thom said as he gestured over Ilyan's body.

"Excuse me?" I didn't know what Thom was getting at, but I didn't want to learn healing magic on Ilyan. I shook my head, hoping to get my point across.

"Most powerful, my ass." Thom grumbled.

"I can do it... it's just..." He looked at me like I was crazy, which granted I might have been.

Grow up, Joclyn.

Thom barked something that could have passed for a laugh as he pulled my hand out of the warm fur I had curled myself into. When he stretched my hand away from me to rest on Ilyan's cheek, I was forced to shuffle forward to keep from falling on top of Ilyan.

"You do know something about human anatomy, correct?"

"Yes," I raised an eyebrow at him, worried about where this was going.

"Good. Now, push your magic into him." This I had done before, so I obeyed while looking to Thom for instruction about what to do next.

"Think of his body as a body."

I stared at him.

"You know," he continued, irritated, "with a heart, and lungs, and bones, and muscles. Now use your magic to find his heart."

I looked at Thom for a minute, waiting for him to elaborate without actually expecting him to. When it became obvious that he wasn't going to help me anymore, I pushed my magic through Ilyan, trying to focus on where my power was in relationship to his body. My magic flowed through him, but nothing was really defined. He was like mush. Ew.

I could make giant gashes in rock walls after the Black Water, but healing was difficult. I shook my head and moved away, but Thom's hands moved over mine, keeping them in place.

"You have to actually try, Silnỳ." His voice was stern.

"I was."

"You won't find anything scary." It was the softest I had heard Thom speak and I looked away from him, closing my eyes in an attempt to focus.

I cinched my eyes together tighter and tried harder. I pushed more magic into Ilyan and let it flow right to the spot where I hoped his heart would be. It took me a minute, but before long, I could feel it. My eyes snapped up to meet Thom's. His eyes shining at my obvious success even though he did not smile in encouragement.

"Now, close your eyes," he instructed, "and use the interior eye of your magic to see his heart."

My lip curled in disgust. "Why would I want to see a beating heart inside someone's body?" My stomach turned at the thought.

"You will not actually see his heart, Silnỳ. Have you ever seen the Matrix?" Of course I had seen the Matrix, but the fact that he had seen it was a little odd.

"I'm going to see computer code?"

"No," Thom said, his patience wavering. "It's different for everyone, but it won't be a real picture."

I looked at him for a moment longer before closing my eyes to focus. Slowly, the red mass of what I could only assume to be Ilyan's heart came into view. It looked smooth and abstract, like a water color painting.

"Now, find the problem." Thom's gruff voice broke through the silence.

"What will that look like?"

"Hard to say. But find something that should not be there. It will shift depending on what is wrong."

I searched with my mind's sight before seeing a dark spot near the base. It wasn't as smooth as the rest of Ilyan's heart and looked like a burn. I opened my eyes, surprised when the image of Ilyan's heart stayed before my eyes for a moment longer.

"What's the black part?" I asked, surprised when Thom's eyebrow raised.

"That's the whole of our problem. When you arrived, his whole heart was covered, the exhaustion from your journey had burned him from the inside. I have been able to heal most of it. Once the last of it is gone, he should awaken within a few days." Thom moved closer, his hand resting on Ilyan's forehead again.

"What can I do to help?" I felt more of my magic flow into Ilyan of its own accord. "How can I heal it?"

"You can do nothing. In fact, it would probably be best if you didn't let so much of your magic mingle with his."

"Why?"

"Well, first, because of what you are, and second, because of who you are."

"Want to try something a little less cryptic?" I teased, and he made that same half bark half laugh sound again.

"You are one of the Drak, Silnỳ. The Drak do not normally heal those with different magic." I glowered at him for a minute, hating the limit that my supposed new species was placing on me.

"But, I am also one of The Chosen."

"Yes."

"So I should be able to heal others as well," I countered softly. "Unless it's something else."

"You are new to healing. I would hate for you to miss and kill him." That was all I needed to hear, I withdrew quickly and pressed myself into the back of the bunk.

"Okay, then teach me another way."

Thom narrowed his eyes at me before he placed the palm of his hand against the stone wall and pulled down, pressing hard against the surface. He brought his palm back to me, revealing a few shallow scrapes, one of them bleeding.

"Then heal me, start small."

"Well, at least it's not a stubbed toe," I shrugged and leaned forward, reaching from Thom's hand.

I pushed my magic into him, surprised at how quickly it flowed. I closed my eyes and searched through his hand for the cuts, smiling when I found the dark black amongst the pink watercolor strokes of his skin.

"Now what do I do?" I kept my eyes closed, not wanting to lose the shapes and colors of his injury.

"Think about how your body heals you, about how you can feel it knit your skin back together, and about how it straightens and repairs. Use your mind and your magic to do the same to me."

"Okay, easy enough." If I didn't watch it, all of this false confidence was going to get me in trouble.

Thom had said to think about how my magic knit me back together. That seemed to make the most sense so I focused on it, thrusting my magic into the black mass of his injury. I pushed the skin back together, laying it end to end before driving even more in the hopes of eliminating the wound all together.

"Incredible." I opened my eyes to Thom's hand, shocked to see that not only had the blood flow stopped, but the skin had completely put itself back together. I couldn't even see so much as a scar.

"Cool." I couldn't help but be proud of myself. Knitting skin together might not help me to kill Edmund, but it was still cool.

"I have never seen that work quite so fast before."

I couldn't help smiling at my accomplishment and how quickly I had managed it. Although it was still weird to be referred to as a Drak, the Black Water had undeniably unlocked my ability.

"Now I can heal Ilyan?" I asked, leaning away from Thom to sit next to Ilyan.

"No, Silnỳ, it is still not a good idea." I froze at his words, his tone making it obvious what this was about.

I should have realized it before.

"It's because of what my dad saw, isn't it? Because of who I am?"

"Yes."

"And, you're not going to...."

"No," Thom cut me off. "Dramin will decide when you are ready."

I leaned over Ilyan, letting my eyes linger on his dull blue lids before moving back to sit by his feet. As I crawled back across the bunk my body began to ache again. I shoved the pain to the back of my mind, determined not to go inside the Tȍuha yet.

"Do you normally sleep with Ilyan? We have some double bunks if it will help you to sleep better—"

"No!" I interrupted him loudly, Thom stopped midsentence his face tensing in confusion. "I don't sleep with Ilyan. I kind of sleep next to him for half the night after... after..." I let my words drift away as Thom continued to glare, aware that I had begun to ramble.

"After your nightmares," he finished for me. I turned back and nodded. I wasn't sure what made me open up even a little bit to him—maybe it was the fact that he had heard my screams—but it made me uncomfortable.

"Do they happen every night?"

"Yes."

"Dramin warned me. He said that you would wail, but the only one who was to help you was Ilyan."

I was grateful neither of them had tried to help. I had fought Ilyan when he had first tried, and my exertion against him had made it worse. I was sure I would fight them even more.

"And there is nothing you can do to stop them, a tea maybe?"

I looked at him and shook my head. Ilyan had tried everything in the beginning, but nothing had worked. Now I understood why.

"Cail controls my dreams." I said, looking back to Ilyan again, if only not to look at Thom.

"Cail?" His voice was scared, maybe even angry. I didn't blame him. He had every right to be. I was.

"Yes, he uses them to taunt me, to hurt me..." I rested my head on my knees, my eyes unfocused on the blanket in front of me. "I'm scared to go to sleep anymore, and now, without Ilyan..." I exhaled and stopped, not wanting to elaborate anymore.

Thom didn't say anything. He looked at me intently before pulling up a tall chair and sitting next to me. He didn't get too close. He didn't reach out to touch me. He just sat, looking around for a few minutes. Surprisingly, it wasn't uncomfortable. We both sat thinking about our own vices for a moment before Thom spoke.

"Have you ever seen the statue of the Greek Titan, Atlas, who holds the world upon his shoulders?"

I looked to him, confused as to where this could be coming from, or how it connected to Cail. I raced the story of Atlas through my brain. I knew it, however I couldn't find any similarities with what we had been talking about.

"Yes?"

"My father had that statue in our home when I was with him. He used to say that it was there to remind him of the best way to defeat your enemies. Those who hold the world can do nothing except struggle and cry."

"So you're saying that Edmund is doing this to weaken me, to keep me from whatever it is I am supposed to do?"

"Exactly."

"Well, he is succeeding," I mumbled to myself.

"If you think like that, then you have already lost." I snapped my head up to Thom, my emotions and my magic bubbling in irritation.

"He has taken everything from me, Thom; forced me into this life with its pain, and fear, and secrets. And I still don't even know all of it yet, in case you have forgotten." I was a little bitter, and I knew it, especially since Thom was trying to give me words of wisdom.

"You need to find someone to help you carry your load. That is where Atlas failed. He tried to trick others into taking it from him instead of asking for help."

"How can I lighten my load if he has taken away everything that's ever been a support to me?" I had calmed down, but I still felt my anger surge.

"You are speaking of your friends? Of your father?" Thom leaned forward in his chair.

"Yes."

"What of Ilyan?" Thom asked.

"He's kind of busy at the moment, isn't he?" I said, waving my hand over his motionless form. I could have sworn Thom cracked a bemused smile.

"You never know who may be supporting you from behind the scenes, Silnỳ. Even though Ilyan is ill, he is still with you. He has the strength to carry the weight of the world for you, and he has that strength for a reason. When he wakes, he will be there to help you hold it, and hold you up along with it if needed."

Ilyan had told me several times he would be there to support me, to help me and lighten my load. I knew he would be. I knew I could trust him. I just wasn't certain I was ready for him to. Ryland's riddle was still too fresh.

"I think I see what you're saying," I admitted. Thom said nothing, he only grabbed his chair, and walked away.

I slid off Ilyan's bed, my body aching as I stood by him, smoothing his long hair. Thom had said that Ilyan had his strength for a reason. I couldn't rely on him carrying all of my worries for me—I didn't want him to—but I didn't know if I had enough strength of my own. I didn't know which I wanted to be; strong on my own; or strong enough to ask for help.

I didn't know which I was supposed to be.

CHAPTER 38
RYLAND

The ache in my chest ignited as the blade was pulled from me. My muscles and skin knit together, instantly healing itself thanks to Cail's magic.

Everything else wasn't so lucky.

The blade wasn't embedded in me anymore, but I still felt cut to shreds.

Sliced. Diced.

'Broken. As you should be. This is what happens when you don't obey me.'

"No, no, no," I moaned, rocking against the wall as I pulled at my hair, trying to pull the voice out of my head. Something told me it didn't work that way, but I couldn't stop myself.

"Ryland, shhh..." Sain hissed in my ear. I could tell he was trying to be comforting, but the clang of chains, the harsh laugh of my father in my ear, the sobs from somewhere off in the distance... it all had the opposite effect.

'No. This is just how it should be. How it always should be.'

"No. I won't. You can't." I wasn't even sure who I was talking to anymore. I couldn't think straight. Not unless I was in the white space. Everything had gotten so much worse since my father used the blade. I couldn't even fight him. Or was I fighting him? I didn't know anymore.

'Me. Your father. Your master. Bow."

"Never!" I screamed, slamming my back against the stone wall as shiny shoes stepped before me. I didn't have to look up to know who was there.

Cail.

"Did you hear her, Ryland?" Cail said, the blood soaked blade still in his hand as he kneeled before me. I twitched and I moaned but I couldn't look away from the blade, the wet drops of blood and soul hardening against its surface. Making it bigger. "Did you hear how Joclyn wailed when I mentioned Ilyan. Mentioned that she loved him?"

I slammed my back against the stone, I already knew what was coming. "She doesn't. He doesn't."

"Oh, but they do," Cail continued to spin the blade over his palm. "Otherwise why would she have reacted the way she did. She's hiding something."

"No! No. No." I refused to believe it, refused to see. But it didn't matter, the moments from the nightmare pulled through my mind like a movie. Almost like Cail was controlling it.

'Yes,' the slime of my father's voice echoed in my head, the scene in my mind slowing down. *'Don't you see? She wants him. She loves him. She doesn't even look at you.'*

She didn't.

My heart tightened, all of those slices that cut into my body and soul deepening. Digging. Hollowing me out.

"Now do you believe me, Ryland?" Cail continued, rising to his feet so all I could see were his shoes and Sain's wide eyes. He shook his head no, begging me not to believe it, it didn't matter. I had already seen.

"Now do you see how she had betrayed you. She doesn't love you anymore. She is your mate. And she is using you."

She was. I had seen it. Cail had shown me. It was exactly as he had always said. Tears dripped over my cheeks, although I wasn't sure why. There was no room for crying. Not with what Joclyn had done.

She had done nothing.

She loved me.

'Loved you. Don't try to tell yourself otherwise. She used you, Ryland.'

"What are you going to do, Ryland?" Cail asked as heavier steps began to thunder down the stairs.

"Kill her!" The words screamed out of my throat, even as my heart screamed at me not to. "Kill her!"

"No, Ryland, no." I could barely hear Sain's moans.

"How did it go?" Edmund asked as he raced down the stairs into the dungeon. Bringing more light with him. I cringed against the yellow orbs that flooded the room, hissing and moaning as I turned from Sain to the spot in the cell next to me.

To Wyn, still desperately trying to reach Talon.

The same way Joclyn had tried to reach me in that fight.

When she had tried to save me.

Just like the last time.

Just like every time.

"No," I hissed as the memories began to flood me. All of the times that Joclyn was there for me. That she saved me. "No! I won't kill her!"

"Again?" Cail hissed, the door to my cell swinging open. Sain scuttled away as fast as he could. I sat, chained to the wall, my father's voice screaming in my head as I lifted my chin to Cail.

"I won't kill her." He kicked me in the gut before I could finish.

"Cail." Edmund drawled as though he was bored, the light dimming a bit. "I need him delt with."

"Yes, Master," Cail said, moving to kick me again. I managed to dodge it, even though my father's voice was now screaming in my head so loud I was having trouble hearing anything else. I couldn't see anything else but what they were showing me. Ilyan and Joclyn, clinging to each other on that roof.

Clinging.

Holding.

Kissing.

His hands all over her.

Removing her shirt...

'See. She doesn't love you anymore. She has betrayed you,'

"No." That one was more of a sob.

"I will handle this." Cail was beaming.

"Good. I expect a full report in an hour, as well as your suggestions as to how we will handle this. It's time we put an end to it. All of it. I am ready for this war to be over."

"Yes, master," Cail said as the might from Edmund's magic began to fade, and the dark began to take over again. "Consider it done."

He walked closer to me, his magic dripping from his fingers. Except, with every step he took towards me, he shifted. Until it was no longer Cail who was smiling and laughing. It was no longer Cail who was preparing to hurt me.

It was Joclyn.

"Joclyn, no..." I cowered against her, but she just smiled.

"It's all in your head, Ryland. It's not her." I heard Sain plea, but it didn't matter.

Joclyn had already lifted her hand to attack.

CHAPTER 39
JOCLYN

I pressed the mug of Black Water to my lips, a soft groan escaping as the liquid flowed through me. It was better than a cheeseburger.

I was worried I wouldn't miss them, either.

It had been weird when I had only wanted to eat a small amount of rice and vegetables for lunch, my body just didn't want it. The Black Water was all I needed. Dramin had been right.

"Do you need more?" Dramin asked from where he stood with Thom on the other side of the training hall, he had been supplying me with the drink since he had returned earlier that morning.

"Not yet. It's good this is just water, Uncle, or I might be worried I was turning into an alcoholic." Dramin chuckled, and Thom grunted loudly from where he leaned against the stone.

"Poisonous water," Thom amended, which only caused Dramin to chuckle more.

A grunt and a chuckle. I couldn't think of anything else that could explain the two men better.

"Well, if you don't need more," Dramin said, ignoring Thom as he stepped toward me, the sound of his shoes echoing over the stone. "Let's get back to work, shall we?"

I took another drink and let the warm energy pulse through me. Thankfully, the water was taking away all my aches from my avoidance of the Tŏuha. I enjoyed the feeling, but what I loved even more was that the Water had fully unlocked my abilities.

I had sparred with Thom this morning, and even through my sore and rigid body, I had been able to beat him in three matches. He may not be as powerful as Ilyan, but I had never beaten anyone before—without cheating of course. I may have been a bit excited, which may have led to some gloating, which may have led to Thom being a bit surlier than usual. I didn't care. It was worth it.

I was sitting on the floor of the large training hall, a giant fur cloak draped around me. Seeing as I arrived here without a change of clothes, or a coat, this fur had become the equivalent to my hoodie. That and it probably helped to keep my smell down. I hadn't actually seen a shower since Santa Fe and thanks to all this sparing, I was sweatier and rattier than usual. I had tried to smooth my hair at some point, but had given up when I realized I was fighting a losing battle. I would have to look a little bit derelict until I located a shower and a clothing store; both of which I had been informed the cave did not have.

Dramin stood about ten feet behind me, Thom slightly to my left. Even with my eyes closed I could see them. I had opened up my internal vision to include the whole room, much to Thom's dismay. He could only manage about a ten foot circle, and even though I could see the whole cave, I was sure I could manage more if I focused.

"Ready," I called out. Thom stretched his fingers and began to shoot objects away from him; real, magical, and conjured. I caught the real objects with my mind, setting them down by the entrance where they had started. I shattered the conjured objects with a pulse from my own magic, and intercepted each of the magical attacks with either an attack of my own or a wave of negative energy, turning them into bits of smoke.

The room exploded with color and action for the seconds it took me to do away with each of Thom's potential weapons. The ribbons of color snaked down to the ground last, only to fall in pools of glitter before they disappeared back into the stone. Through it all, I didn't move my hands an inch.

"Six seconds!" Dramin called out. He ran toward me as I opened my eyes, stiffly moving to my feet. "How many was that, Thom?"

"Twenty real, ten conjured, and five attacks." Thom didn't seem too pleased. "You probably could have gone faster."

"Thanks for the vote of confidence, Thom," I gave him a grin to go with my sarcasm, Thom rolled his eyes and moved away from us.

"Do you think you could do more, Silnŷ?" Dramin asked as he bounced on his heels.

I would say he was too excited for what was going on, but if he wasn't bouncing around like a hyper teenager, I would be. I had worked with Ilyan on this for months, and now I was finally making progress.

"More items or more magic?"

"Both," Dramin's voice was so eager, he reminded me of a five year old being offered ice cream.

"You read my mind." Okay, now I was bouncing alongside him, anyway.

"Well," Thom yelled from across the hall, "if you don't need me, I am going to go check on our invalid."

"Thom!" Dramin yelled after him, but Thom only waved his hand in farewell.

"Thom!" Dramin tried again, but Thom didn't even turn to look back. "You great lazy oaf! Get back here!" Dramin was still yelling, but Thom had already disappeared back into the main room where I was sure he was going to take a nap by the fire.

"Well, what are we going to do now?" I asked, before taking a nice long sip of the Black Water. Yep, I was definitely becoming addicted.

"How about we test your sight?"

So much for my magical celebrations. I looked at him out of the corner of my eye. I knew what he was talking about, and honestly, I wasn't interested.

"It's twenty-twenty thank you very much." I spoke as brightly as I could before smiling and strolling away, following after Thom. I may have Drak blood, but I didn't want to see any of the things the sight could give me.

"What's twenty-twenty?" Dramin asked, obviously not getting the reference.

"My vision." I provided, but Dramin sighed, his regular smile disappearing.

"I am talking about your sight, Silnŷ. Not your vision. There is no reason to be scared."

I froze, but didn't turn to face him. Instead, I looked up to the large gash I had placed in the stone dome the day before, not wanting to give him an answer. Of course I was scared. I had no interest in reliving my past, let alone seeing the future.

"There is no reason to be scared," Dramin repeated, his steps coming closer. "This is simply another step in the process. Without using your sight, you will not be able to summon the Black Water for yourself, and I will not be able to show you the sight that told of your true purpose."

"That's not a problem," I said, turning toward him. "You can come with me and Ilyan, and you can tell me what was said rather than show me."

I smiled brightly, happy when he chuckled. My thoughts of compromise were dashed when he began to shake his head. Of course he wouldn't make it that easy.

"I cannot follow you all around the earth while you fight Edmund, Silnŷ. I am also not going to travel with you on your honeymoon, or always be there when you are injured."

"Honeymoon?" I said, interrupting him. "Who said anything about a honeymoon?"

"You must call the Black Water on your own," Dramin continued as if I hadn't said anything. "And as for the sight, I have to show you."

"The sight?" I asked, folding my arms and bringing the fur cloak closer around me. "Like *the* sight. You're going to show me?"

"I do. I have seen it, Silnŷ. This is just another step in the process."

I needed the Black Water. I needed to know what had been foreseen about me. He had me there, and I hated it. I turned toward him, keeping the cloak around me tightly.

"Fine," I said grumpily. "Show me the way."

Dramin bounced once before turning and walking toward the large opening he had shown me the day before. I followed after him, my body aching with each step. I took a drink as I walked, the Black Water dulling the ache.

The adjoining chamber was different from the others. It was the same dome shape, the same raised stone work circling the walls, but there were no bunks or benches lining the platform. Instead, there were odd runes carved into the stone. A portion of the circular room was sunken, but you wouldn't be able to tell without looking closely. The sunken area was filled right to the top with an unmoving liquid that I could easily recognize as Black Water. Somehow, even though the water did not move, the room was filled with the rippling reflections of waves on a pond.

The waving light hit against the far wall revealing more carvings, more runes, and a delicate glass pane that revealed the outside where the blizzard still reigned. The light of day that managed to make it through the blizzard filtered into the space, mixing with the magical shimmers.

Even if I knew nothing about Drak, and Skříteks and Chosen; I would have known this room was magic. It shook in my bones.

I stepped around Dramin to walk around the large cavern.; the light ran over my face as I traced the rough carvings with my fingers. I didn't feel any peaks of my magic or strong sensations of what was going to happen, but I felt comfortable. The terror at seeing into the past or future had ebbed, leaving me with a jittery excitement.

I continued to walk, letting my fingers trace the shapes. I had all but forgotten that Dramin still stood behind me until he spoke.

"The Hall of Sight. This was the last one built and one of the only ones that remain. They can only be built in select places on earth where the magic seeps to the surface, the Black Water bubbling up for our use. While we can use the Black Water at any time because the Water resides within us, the larger, more important queries always require our sight to be used within this hall, and many times, more than one Drak must be present."

I barely heard him. My blood seemed to hum the more I was in the room, reminding me of when Ilyan had centered my magic.

"It has been many years since I have used my sight beyond the mundane. I miss the power very much. Someday perhaps I will be able to see with others again."

"Is it hard to do?" I asked, the question more to myself than to Dramin, my nerves having almost left.

"It is as easy as breathing, Silnỳ. The magic already resides inside of you. Once you have unlocked the door, the rest of your abilities will open to you." He spoke reverently, his excitement at what was about to happen clear.

"What abilities?" I turned from the runes to face him. He stood right by the water, the still surface reflecting nothing.

"The ability to recall previous sights, to provide yourself with the nourishment you need, and most importantly, to use your sight at will. After you experience your first sight, the Black Water will become a part of you."

I didn't want that. Or maybe I did, and I was just scared of it. The serenity of the room, and the calm on Dramin's face were sure helping to take the edge off.

I swallowed heavily as I stared into the smooth reflection-less surface of the water. I could feel my body pull me toward the surface, willing me to join it somehow. I took a step forward before moving back again, fighting my need to touch the water.

"Does it hurt?" It was a child's question, but I needed to know. I was beginning to realize that I couldn't avoid pain, but I could at least prepare for it.

"No, child, but your first sight will be the strongest you will ever experience on your own." I wasn't sure his answer helped. "As the water moves into you and becomes part of you, you will see the past, present, and future of yourself and those you hold in your heart," Dramin stepped right beside me, his voice a whisper. "It will come in a web, and it is likely nothing will make sense. It is only after, when you learn to recall your sight, that you will be able to make sense of the confusion."

Confusion like I wanted to jump head first into the pool.

"Are you ready?" he asked, his eager anticipation bleeding through him.

"Yes." My answer was instant. I still could not take my eyes off of the water.

"Then place your hand in the water."

"That's it?" I asked, turning toward him for the first time.

"Yes. For those who are not among the Drak the water will burn their skin, but to touch the water is essential for the Drak."

"Will it burn me?"

"No, Silnỳ. You are one of the Drak. Just place your hand in the water."

The prickling of my skin grew as I fell to my knees, the heavy fur cloak falling off of my shoulders. I reached toward the water, hesitating for one shaky breath before I pushed it beyond the surface.

I had barely registered the warmth of the water before my vision faded to the burn of a bright red ember, like the flame that I had seen in Dramin's eyes that first day. My head felt light and airy, everything swimming and swirling as I looked into the burning red color. Then the sight changed.

Shadows twirled and danced before me as an image of an infant being placed into my mother's arms began to form. The vision changed to a flash of blonde hair running down a hall I had never seen before as screams filled the air. The hair changed to a flash of me crying in my bed as my parents fought. A moment later, a vision of Edmund choking Talon against a wall came into view, Talon's face battered.

"Give me what I need, Talon," Edmund's voice rang out like an echo in my ears.

"You better make it look good, Edmund." Talon let out a deep chuckle.

Edmund's hand moved back in preparation for a strike before the colors washed away to be replaced by me running through the trees. Ryland's hand hovered over the ground as he formed a perfect ring of Pansies, which disappeared as soon as they grew, changing into Wyn and my father running through a dark cave, a man falling to the ground in agony before them.

"Was that really necessary?" my father asked, his voice tense and scared.

"He would have done the same to us," Wyn hissed without looking away from the body in front of her. "Don't like it, don't travel with a trained killer."

"As long as that assassin doesn't turn her skill on me, I think I will be happy." Sain laughed humorously as the vision changed to Ryland as a child, speaking to his mother through the bars of a cell, their hands intertwined.

"Don't cry, my little love, you are stronger than your father will ever be." Her voice echoed around the space as Ryland cried.

The sight changed again to Cail crying in the dark and Wyn wrapping her arms around him in an attempt to comfort him, a ripped t-shirt hanging off her shoulders. A flash of fire met my eyes before it faded again to me crying on a bed, older this time, screaming for help as Ryland moved toward me, his eyes gentle and blue.

"Jos?" Ryland said softly, "I'm not going to hurt you, honey."

"Go... Away!"

A quick change showed me an image of Ilyan running down a stone hallway, his hair short and dark with his face covered in blood and bruises. My heart ached for a reason I couldn't place. My head began to pound as the speed of my sight increased, some images barely registering, the voices beginning to overrun one another.

"Take him and use him for your benefit; maybe that will give you the upper hand." Edmund said as he spoke to someone I couldn't see, his hands pushing Ryland's weak body away from him.

It flashed again to Cail lying in a chair, Edmund and Timothy around him. "Make her break the bond, Cail, then the sight can never be."

The colors washed away to something else before Edmund had even finished speaking.

"If you touch her, father, I swear I will end you," Ryland was firm, but Edmund only laughed before they continued to spar in the basement of their estate.

The image of them sparring changed to Ilyan holding me against a wall, a building burning around us, his hand soft against my face. I could just make out tears flowing down each of our cheeks before it changed again to Ilyan walking into a large stone hall that I had never seen before, his hair short against his head. It then flashed one last time, a man's scream echoing in my head as it followed me back into reality.

I panted heavily as the vision left me, everything that I saw combined into a jumbled mass. One thing stood out, though. One thing was crystal clear to me.

I felt Dramin's arms come around me as he replaced the cloak, my breathing slowing down.

"It's okay, Silnỳ," he said softly. "It's over now."

I continued to gasp for air, my knees aching from being pressed against the cold stone floor.

"Dramin," I gasped, as I reached for Dramin, holding onto his wrist tightly. "I saw your death... I saw..."

I felt my head go light, my vision blacking out as the sight showed me his death again. He moved in front of what I could only guess was Ryland, the bright light of an attack shattering into the air. As I watched the scene unfold, my voice spoke in an oddly dark and monotone way. I should have been scared, but my heart rate never increased, my mind accepting my new power.

"Betrayed by your brother in the last hour of light, you will save one who has lost more than you. It will come at the dusk of a powerful death before the blood red moon will herald a birth."

My voice faded out as my vision returned, Dramin's surprised face coming back into focus.

"Uncle?" I asked, alarmed at having seen his death.

I expected him to be more concerned, for panic to spill out, but instead he only nodded.

"I know."

CHAPTER 40
JOCLYN

I sat back in the large, squishy armchair, letting my magic pull the fur tighter around me. The cave was cold, even with my magic keeping the fire strong. The orange light casting odd, eerie shadows around the empty chamber, they probably would have been scary if it wasn't for the howl of the wind that echoed down the long tunnel. The sound of the blizzard was deep and relaxing and I sunk further into the chair, willing myself to stay awake.

Dramin had carried me back to the main hall after my first sight, I had been too weak to get back here on my own. He had draped me in blankets and talked on and on about the significance of what had just happened, and what I had seen.

He talked on and on about how to understand the subtle changes for sights of the past; such as the dirty quality of the image or the tinny distanced voices of the subjects. I was too tired to remember much, though. I was going to have to ask him to go over it all again in the morning.

Which I was sure he would.

He wanted to see everything.

I was trying to forget.

The image of Wyn comforting Cail upset me the most. The image was crystal clear, so it wasn't a sight from the past; it made me anxious to know what it could mean. Or why after everything Cail had done she would be comforting him.

Dramin had tried for about an hour to get me to use my recall to view the sight again and in further detail, or to even be able to call the Black Water myself, but it was no use. I was too tired and my mind too unfocused.

I knew why. I had a feeling that Dramin knew too, but I wasn't going to say it out loud, nor was I going to visit the Tȍuha to remedy the matter.

I was scared.

I was as scared of the Tȍuha as I had become of my nightmares.

"Stupid." I hissed, knowing I was being ridiculous. I was sure Ilyan would tell me as much. He was my protector after all.

My Protector.

I turned to where he lay, my heart twisting. It was odd to think of all that the words had come to mean to me; all that he had come to mean to me.

I wiped the thoughts from my head and turned back to the fire, not wanting to dwell on something that would ultimately lead me to replay my nightmares and riddles.

Which unfortunately was the best thing to do when you were avoiding sleep.

I sighed; I couldn't avoid it any longer, my eyes had already started drooping. I drained the last of the mug and shuffled to my bunk, body groaning and head spinning.

My feet barely carried me across the cold stone floor before I collapsed on my bunk, the layers of furs smothering me as I landed hard on the pile of furs that passed as a mattress.

"Don't be a wimp, Joclyn," I moaned to myself, the sound echoing around the tiny alcove my bed sat in. A few days ago I had been desperate for my own bed, and now I wanted anything but.

I let the blankets and furs swallow me and closed my eyes. It only took seconds for sleep to overtake me and the dream to come.

I stood in the middle of the clearing as always, the eerie branches stretching and swaying around me.

"We've been waiting for you, Joclyn." Cail's voice was loud and right behind me. I fought the desire to spin around to face him, instead keeping my body still as I stubbornly looked toward the trees.

"Have you?" I pushed as much snark into my voice as I could.

"I take it you thought that if you stayed awake you could avoid me?" He ran his hand down my hair, the weight pulling at the long strands.

"It was worth a shot," I said a little too honestly. I attempted to keep my voice light and airy, but my fear was too severe.

Instead of replying, however, Cail laughed. The sound bounced around the clearing and reverberated inside my head.

"Oh, Joclyn. Sweet Joclyn. How I enjoy our time together." His words were endearments, but his voice was like ice. It ran up my spine and sent an unpleasant shiver through my shoulders.

He had come around to face me, his dark eyes even darker in the dim forest as the red of his hair disappeared in the night.

"Well, that makes one of us. I would rather rot in hell than spend time with you." I leaned in, well aware I was sending spit flying over his face. He deserved it.

He looked at me with his wicked smile, his hand coming to wrap tightly around my wrist; pain shoot up my arm as he squeezed.

"You know better than that," he said as he yanked my arm and pulled my torso into him. "You can't escape me, and you can't beat me." He laughed like it was a joke. I pulled my arm away sharply, my magic boiling through me.

"You wanna bet?" I spat. I took one step back, twisting around to hit my hands hard against his chest. Even though my magic surged with the contact, the dream dampened it. It was still enough.

Cail looked shocked as he stumbled back to slam roughly into one of the trees. When he had steadied himself, I prepared myself for his attack, but he wasn't angry. He wasn't going to fight back. He simply laughed.

"It's a good thing your magic doesn't work here. With a temper like that, you'd be an awful lot of fun. I sure hope you don't throw magic at Ilyan like that." He clicked his tongue at me and walked closer, his strut making my stomach flip in disgust. "There he is, sleeping next to the one he loves, and you go ahead and kill him!"

Cail laughed with all the humor he could muster and my stomach tensed uncomfortably, my eyes narrowing. How did he know where Ilyan slept, and that my magic presented in the waking world? He couldn't. He had to be playing with me.

"Ilyan doesn't love..." I began to say confidently, but Cail clamped his hand over my mouth and pinned me to his side, his eyes flashing dangerously.

"Don't say it. You're going to take away all of my fun, and we haven't even gotten to our little game yet."

"I'm not interested." My insides flipped at the mention of yet another game. I tried to get away from Cail's firm grip, but he increased his hold, his hand turning into a claw against my face.

"You don't have a choice. You see those trees?" He jutted his chin toward the line of trees directly in front of us. I followed his line of sight, my eyes widening to see two bright-red trunks creating a doorway into the shadowy forest behind them.

"I have hidden two very different things in there, and I am going to send you to find them." I tried to fight him, but his hold continued to increase, his grip plastering me against his body.

"One of them will kill you the second you are seen and the other will rejoice at your arrival. If you find the one who would kill you first, then the game is over and you will wake up. If you find the other, you have until I find you before your time here is over. So either way, it ends in your death." He spoke lightly, my stomach dropping at what he had implied. I couldn't take my eyes off of those trees.

"Ryland." I couldn't stop the name from escaping. Cail couldn't have been more pleased.

"Yes, but which one? I am going to give you a ten minute head start." I swallowed hard as Cail released me from his grip and sent me stumbling toward those red trunks.

"Go."

I didn't wait. I ran into the trees, my heart racing at the thought of finding Ryland. The real Ryland.

The forest was quiet, the silence making the dying landscape even more terrifying. Desperate to get away from Cail, I ran for a while before realizing that my hurried steps would give away my approach.

Magic may not work as a defensive tactic here, but it could work to my benefit. At least I hoped it would. I took off into the sky, thankful when my magic supported me as I sped through the trees.

It wasn't long before I caught a glimpse of something dark ahead of me and I slowed to a stop, my heart hammering in my chest as I hovered directly above Edmund. He stood tall in the middle of the forest, his dark curls slicked back. He didn't move, nor did his eyes waver from the direction I had just come from.

Cail had sent me into the trees on a direct route to Edmund, practically a guarantee that he would be able to torture me and send me back. I didn't doubt that Ryland would be here as well, but he would be hidden.

I found him about a hundred feet behind Edmund, his body limp and leaning against a tree. I dropped from the air, barely able to catch myself before I hit the ground.

I moved toward him, stopping at the bright-blue eyes that met mine. He smiled at seeing me, his hand coming up to rest against my face as I knelt beside him, his thumb lightly tracing my bottom lip.

I wasn't even sure it was really him. This was a dream and not a Tòuha after all, but I couldn't ignore the fire that was steadily moving through my veins.

"Is it you?"

"I don't know," Ryland's voice was forced, his tones strained. My heart dropped as I fought the need to run away. "I think it is. I remember a lot, but not everything. My brain's messed up. I..." He stopped as his eyes met mine, the blue looking deeply into me.

"It's okay." I said, placing my hand on top of his, leaning into his touch. I didn't feel my magic pulling toward him as it always did, but part of me didn't care if it was him or just another way to torture me.

"I love you, Ry," I whispered. "I miss you so much."

"I miss you too, sweetheart." He pulled me into him, his arms draping over me limply. He lacked the strength to hold me to him.

"I'm going to save you." I pulled back, all of my magic flaring in determination. I couldn't do it before, but I could do it now. I wasn't foolish enough to tell him how strong I was now or where I was hiding, but I could tell him that I was going to save him.

"I wish you wouldn't."

"What?"

"I don't think you can, Jos, and I don't want you to get hurt. Please, stay with Ilyan. He will protect you."

It was the rebuttal he had given me since the beginning, but it broke my heart to hear him say it again. Both of us had been through hell. If there was a chance I could save him, I was going to take it. Especially since Edmund and Cail were using him to manipulate and torture me every chance they got.

"I can save you. I can't let them hurt you anymore."

"While they what? Give you beautiful dreams and magical fantasies in our Tòuha? I won't let you go through it anymore. I'm going to break the Zêlství. I am going to break our bond." Ryland's voice had gained some confidence, but his body was weak. Breaking the connection would probably kill him. It could kill us both. Maybe that was the point.

"No, Ryland, I can't let you do that. If you do, you will kill me. Do you understand that?" He balked at my words before sitting himself up, his hand reaching forward to grab mine.

"Not if we do it at the same time."

"No." I pulled my hand away, disgusted with what he was saying.

"It's the only way to save you, Joclyn. I have to do it. They are going to keep torturing you, can't you see?"

I stood up and moved away from him, shuffling my feet into the ground. This couldn't be him. Ryland had sacrificed everything to complete the connection. He would never suggest breaking it.

"No," I said. "This isn't you, Ry. This isn't..."

"Besides," Ryland interrupted me, his voice even stronger than before. "It probably won't even hurt you. You don't truly love me anymore. If I break the connection, it won't even affect you."

"What are you saying?" My voice was barely even above a whisper. "You can't be... Ryland!" I dropped to my knees feeling pain so strong I couldn't breathe. "Don't say that. I do love you. Why else would I have gone through all of this to get you back?"

Ryland shook and mumbled something I couldn't hear before he pulled me against him, his arms gaining strength as he pressed his lips into my hair, kissing me softly. I moved at his touch, desperate to feel his lips against mine at least one more time. He looked at me right before he kissed me, seeming to decide if I wanted him to or not. I waited, my breath caught in my chest for the moment before our lips met.

This was not a Tõuha, it was only a dream. There was no electric connection, yet my heart still stuttered with the feeling of ecstasy that washed through me. I clenched my hand around his shirt, pulling him closer to me, and inhaled deeply as his tongue wiped against my lower lip. I groaned and leaned into him further. My body was begging him to deepen the kiss, but instead of answering my need, he pulled away, his eyes boring into me.

"We need to say goodbye, Jos."

"Not yet." I tried to kiss him again, but he recoiled.

"It's okay if you don't love me anymore, Jos. I don't blame you. Our connection has done nothing except cause you pain and misery. If anything that will make the severing of our bond easier."

My jaw dropped at his words. "Don't play like that, Ryland. You know I love you. I..." I noticed a minute too late that his eyes were dimming to black. "No!"

"Oh, yes." I froze at the voice.

Edmund snaked his arm around my neck and pulled me up; my feet left the ground as he flattened me against him, his strong arm cutting off my air supply. I gathered my strength and produced a large chain to wrap around him, but the magic turned to smoke in my fingers.

He laughed in my ear as I sputtered, his strong arm causing my vision to pop much faster than I would have expected.

"Watch your mate die, my son," he said, his voice deep. "Oh, no,

Joclyn. It doesn't seem like he is too concerned. I guess he wasn't lying. He doesn't want you anymore."

I looked to Ryland, gasping out his name with my last breath, but he didn't move. He just sat there, his body too weak to do anything, his dark eyes dim and unfocused.

He didn't even move as I gasped for air; as everything went black.

I woke up in a start, gasping for breath as the panic at what had happened worked me up into a terrified state. I wasn't screaming as I had been before, this time it was a howling sob. The sounds I made were those of heartbreak.

I cried and called out to Ilyan, to Ryland, to anyone that would help me, but no one came. No one was there. I wasn't sure if I was upset that no one came or glad that I had been ignored. I couldn't have Ilyan or Ryland, and there was no one else I wanted to calm me.

I turned in my bunk, my body calling out in pain as I moved to face Ilyan's bunk where he continued to lay in his dimly lit hollow, his hair fanning over the edge of his stone bunk. I looked at him until my howls had died down into gentle sobs. I desperately wanted to go to him, but one move of my arm told me how impossible that was. Pain shot through my shoulder and my back, eventually traveling into my head. I gasped through the tears at the new pain.

I was alone. Ryland, if that had really been him, was determined to break the bond. Wyn was gone. My parents were gone. Ilyan...

I was supposed to be the most powerful of all, destined to do something huge that I didn't even understand. It was as Thom said, I was like Atlas, holding the world on my shoulders, and try as I might, I would never be strong enough.

I stopped; my pity-party halting in its tracks. Atlas. I had missed the whole lesson behind what Thom had tried to tell me. I had been too caught up in my self-loathing to have fully taken in what he said.

Atlas had possessed plenty of strength. He had just been too proud to ask for help when he had needed it. It wasn't strength that I lacked, it was stubborn pride that I had too much of.

I didn't need to be strong all the time. I needed to get over my insecurities and start to have faith in someone else to help me through it. I needed to stop hiding silently behind my pain and throw the emotional hoodie away.

I was strong.

I looked at Ilyan. He might be the one who could help me do that. At the very least, he was definitely the one I wanted.

CHAPTER 41
WYN

Ryland was screaming again.

All he did was sleep and scream.

After we had all been released from the blood magic, we had been bound alone in our cells. Sain sat still in silence, Talon remained unconscious, and Ryland transferred between periods of waking and sleeping. His waking moments were spent screaming in agony about Joclyn, even strangling the bars of the cell as he attempted to kill her. What little he was awake, and not screaming, he always sat, rocking back and forth, as he mumbled promises to himself to both kill and protect Joclyn.

It had only gotten worse after the last time they had forced Sain and Ryland to open up a blood connection, trying some weird plan that Edmund had. Ryland had spent two hours muttering that he didn't love her anymore, that she didn't love him, before he had finally given in to the torture Timothy had forced him to endure and became silent.

Ryland had been driven mad by torture, the Vymàzat and Cail's manipulation. If it wasn't for Sain and his support, I was sure Ryland would be much worse. They had been imprisoned together for over three months. Ryland had only been let out when Edmund needed his magic to track Joclyn—when he needed him as a weapon.

And Sain... Sain's magic was weakened to nothing by years of Edmund withholding the clay mugs. Without the mugs, Sain could not produce Black Water. Without the lifeblood of his magic, he was left weak and useless.

We all were in the dark, both literally and figuratively, confined in small spaces, food never provided, a bathroom a thing of the past. The only luxury we knew anymore was the daily glass of water. One glass of filthy water and I dreamed of it as if it was wine.

The whole room smelled of vomit, human excrement, and the heavy mildew smell I had noticed on my arrival. The odors hung in the air, heavy and physical. It seeped into our tattered clothes, our hair, and lingered in our nostrils. I would like to say that I had become immune, but the smell stuck to me. I had given up begging for water and food. I had given up begging for a bathroom. Each time I opened my mouth, my father would appear, the back of his hand at the ready and my query forgotten.

We were in the middle of another of Ryland's fits, and I could hear Sain whispering through Ryland's screams as he tried to calm him, to silence him before someone came down.

"Shut him up, Sain," I hissed, my eyes peering through the darkness toward them and then back to where I knew the staircase was. I listened intensely in the fear of footsteps.

Sain whispered more, and I shifted my weight, the chains of my shackles rattling as I turned my body toward Ryland's cell.

"Shield him," I hissed, but Sain said nothing. It was a foolish idea anyway. They had already heard him, and if they found out Sain still used what little magic he had left, we would all be in trouble.

"Ryland," I whispered, my voice joining Sain's. "It's okay. Joclyn's okay."

Ryland only howled more, and my heartbeat froze as footsteps sounded on the stairs, the pace fast and quick. I shuffled back to my wall, my hands directly above my head, as a blue light floated down before Cail came rushing in, his face hard and angry.

"Shut up, dog!" he yelled, the door to Ryland's cell swung open without Cail having even touched it. Cail blinked once, and Ryland screamed in agony, the magic attacking him from the inside. I looked away, not wanting to see the physical blows that were sure to come. They always did. We all had our fair share of bruises and broken bones, and with no magic to heal us, we sat, useless and mortal in the dark prison.

I pressed my face into my shoulder as the sound of flesh on flesh echoed against the stone. Ryland screamed until his cries turned to sobs, his sobs turning to whimpers, and then silence.

Cail laughed, while the grind of the metal as the cell door closed echoed around the rock. Then, there was nothing. I didn't move. I didn't flinch. I kept my head rolled into my shoulder, my eyes staring at Talon's sleeping form, silently begging him to wake up. I wasn't sure if Talon waking up would take away my terror or add to it. I didn't know what I would do if they beat him in front of me. I knew I wouldn't be able to keep my mouth shut.

I tried to focus on something good as I waited for Cail to leave, the prison silent with expectation. He didn't leave, though. His breathing picked up before the squeal of the door to my cell sounded, the door opening slowly.

"What did they do to you?" he questioned, I almost didn't recognize his voice.

I couldn't help it; I looked up as Cail walked in, and I recoiled. I wanted to plead with him that I had said nothing, that I had remained silent, but I couldn't let the words filter to my tongue.

My brother looked at me, the hard line of his jaw gone, his eyes soft. There was a look of hope in his eyes that I only remembered in the shadows of my memory. I glimpsed the look of the love and dedication that he had shown me as he raised me.

"Does... does it hurt?" he asked as he kneeled in front of me.

I couldn't trust this. Brother or not, Cail only hurt those around him. Always. Every part of me recoiled as he kneeled in front of me, his hand moving up to touch the metal bands around my wrists. I gasped and moved myself into the wall in an attempt to get as far away from him as possible. The metal clicked as the shackles opened and my hands fell into my lap, my weak and pained shoulders unable to support them.

"I'm sorry, Wynifred. Dad is mean sometimes." I froze, my eyes wide as my breath caught, tears threatening. This was familiar, this voice and those words. I couldn't remember much, but I knew that this was the brother I had known as a child. He reached forward, and my breath stalled in expectation of a hit, but nothing came. Instead, his hand was soft as he reached out and it rested against my cheek.

I stared into his eyes, the pressure against my cheek soft and gentle, and waited for my breathing to regulate. I couldn't seem to gain control of it. Everything screamed at me to attack him, to run. Deep down, I wondered if that was what he wanted. If this was all a game to give him a reason to attack. Cail wasn't like that, though. He didn't need a reason. He just liked to cause pain. I couldn't trust this, I couldn't.

My breathing calmed and my heart rate slowed as he looked at me. It took me a minute to figure out what was going on. Without my own magic to alert me to the change, I had missed the fact that Cail was calming me.

"It's okay, Wynifred," he said, his voice only a whispered breath against my skin. "I'll make all the bad go away."

I couldn't breathe. I couldn't force myself to inhale. I was too shocked, too scared. The pain in my shoulders lessened, the fire in my wrists left and my brother smiled at me, his face twitching.

I wanted to reach up to him, to comfort him, but before I could even move, his hand flew to the skin over his heart. He clenched his fingers around the fabric of his shirt as his face screwed up in pain. He backed away from me, his back hitting the bars that separated me from Talon, his eyes wide as he clutched his shirt, tears flowing down his cheeks.

"Cail?" I asked, unable to help myself, not understanding what was happening.

I heard Sain gasp, in warning or curiosity, I wasn't sure, but it barely registered. My brother was crying in front of me, his hand clenched over his heart.

"Save me." He hissed the words, and I froze as everything went on high alert inside of me.

"Cail?" I had barely moved before the back of Cail's hand connected with my cheek, the smack sounding loud and clear in the dark room.

"Shut your mouth," Cail snapped, the hard lines of his face back, his eyes hard.

He looked at me once more before he left my cell, the door closing with a loud snap before he ran up the stairs, the light going with him and leaving us in the dark again. I looked toward the staircase, my eyes slowly adjusting to the lack of light.

"What was that?" I whispered into the darkness when I was sure that Cail had gone, not daring to say more and hoping that my voice hadn't traveled beyond my own five foot square.

I exhaled shakily, rubbing the tender skin on my wrists, and then it hit me that I was unchained.

The footsteps were long gone, but I still dreaded the darkness, the possibility of someone waiting just beyond the black, out of sight. My breath picked up, and finally I scooted across the small space toward the cell where Talon lay, my arms stretching through the bars as I reached for him. I clawed through air until I grabbed what I was sure was a shirt. I traced the fabric until I felt his skin, the warmth shooting through me as it always did, but without the magic behind it. Only my heart responded this time, the beats heavy and excited.

I didn't dare say anything until Sain gave the all clear. I wasn't stupid enough to risk talking without Sain's help. Ryland only howled because he couldn't help it, or perhaps because Cail made him; either was a possibility.

Why had my brother been so gentle with me? I wanted to find a rational excuse, a reason for what had just passed between us. Even as a form of torture, it made no sense. Why leave my hands free? Why give me what I want? This was absolutely what I wanted.

I traced down the skin of Talon's arm until I found his hand. It was limp, but I intertwined my fingers with him anyway, desperate for the connection. There was no wild flaring of joined magic when we touched. The omezující stone had done its job, but I didn't care. The touch of his skin, the feel of his fingers was enough for me for now.

A dim, green light flared from the other side of the prison, and I turned slowly toward Sain who sat with a tiny orb settled in his hands.

Sain's magic wasn't restricted; Edmund needed the use of his sight, so restricting it was useless. Sain was also weak and Drak's were mostly powerless besides their sight, so he couldn't do much more than give us some light and shield our voices anyway.

I kept my hands intertwined with Talon's as Sain looked up at me, his eyes barely visible from beneath his mat of hair.

"Are you all right?" he asked, his voice calm and low so as not to breach the shield.

I nodded once. "Was that a trap?"

"Cail?" Sain asked as he leaned over to check Ryland, his chest shaking as he struggled to breathe.

"Yeah."

Sain exhaled, the sound as shaky as Ryland's labored breathing. "Your brother is complicated, and strangely still with a conscience."

I exhaled, not really knowing what that meant, but Sain only chuckled.

"You will see what I mean soon enough, Wyn." Sain moved his hands through the bars of his cell as he reached for Ryland, his own chains rattling as they hit the thick bars of the cell.

"Have you seen something, Sain?" I asked, fully aware I sounded like Ryland. In Ryland's brief moments of lucidity, it was always the only thing he asked, what Sain might have seen.

"I have," he said simply. "I always see. I see you now sitting right in front of me. I see my daughter in a place of power. I see Ryland in his rightful place, and I see Cail finding his peace. You will see some of that, too."

He was always so cryptic. I had never been around a Drak before. I wasn't sure if I had been born before their extermination order was given, but I wouldn't remember anyway. I wish I did, Sain was fascinating. I wasn't sure if it was just his way, or an attempt to keep us all safe by keeping us in the dark.

I leaned my head back against the bars, keeping my hand entwined with Talon's.

"You will make it out of here safely, Wynifred."

I turned toward Sain, but he had already turned back to Ryland. I wanted to smile, but I couldn't find it in me. I couldn't smile in a place like this, with my wrists and arms covered in blood, and my husband passed out beside me. Call me pessimistic, but I just couldn't do it.

It hadn't escaped my notice that Sain had said nothing of Talon.

"Ryland?" Sain asked softly as he ran his hands over Ryland's side.

Ryland shuttered at his touch, his body racking with even bigger sobs.

"No more." Ryland's voice was more of a cry than actual words.

"No more what, Ryland?" Sain asked, his endless patience enduring.

"No more pain. She hurts me... hurts me... hurts me..." Ryland wrapped himself up in a ball, his fingers clawing at his curls.

"I hate seeing him like this," Sain sighed as he attempted to stop Ryland's frantic movements. "It's so much easier when his mind is clear, before Cail started using the blade."

"She hurts me... hurts me..." Ryland continued to pant, his pained groans pulling Sain's attention back to him.

"No, Ryland, no. She doesn't hurt you. It's all in your head, remember? It isn't really her." Sain reached up and touched the boy's hair, his fingers soft and gentle as he attempted to calm him. It had the opposite effect.

"Let me kill her!" Ryland's voice roared through the small, rock room, his body fighting against his chains as he moved from one barred wall to another; clawing, kicking and grabbing at the bars in his attempt to escape. "I'm going to kill her!"

I moved into the bars I was huddled against, my hands squeezing Talon's as I pulled him toward me, desperate for some comfort.

"Not kill, Ryland. Save. You have to save her," Sain pleaded, his volume increasing as he fought to convince Ryland otherwise. I could see his furtive looks toward the main door, his fear evident. Ryland's voice was going to break through Sain's weak shield, making our noise audible to those above.

"It's okay, Ryland. Calm down," I pleaded. Ryland didn't seem to hear; he kept rattling the bars like a caged animal. He looked at anyone he could as he yelled for Joclyn's death, his hands clawing and grinding through the air, Sain's soft voice barely audible from behind him as he tried to comfort him from his own cell. He needed to calm down, I wasn't certain he could take another beating so soon.

I looked toward the staircase, terrified that someone would hear him and come down, but no one came. So far, Sain's shield was holding. It was obvious we didn't have much longer as Sain's orb of light began to flicker and dim.

Ryland's eyes began to droop as Sain's muttered comforts began to sink in. His movements slowed until he dropped to the ground, his breathing still erratic and labored, but his voice now silent.

"Save her," he whispered, his voice strangely dead and monotone.

"No!" Sain suddenly yelled, the light disappearing. I stiffened at his outburst. I didn't know much about Sain, but I did know this, he did not yell. He did not get scared.

He was both.

I froze, my hands still intertwined with Talon's as loud footsteps sounded on the stairs. I didn't move as I attempted to regulate my breathing. I didn't know what was happening, but Sain was scared and that was enough to terrify me. I lay down and rested my body as best I could, hoping that feigned sleep would be enough to keep them at bay, praying that they would not notice me.

Part of me wished I could re-shackle my wrists, thinking this was Cail's game the whole time, but it was too late to fix it now. So I lay still as voices began to filter down to us.

"I like this plan, master," Cail said as he addressed Edmund, my insides turning to ice even more. "Now if only we can accomplish it."

"Is there a problem?" Edmund asked, and their footsteps froze.

A dim, yellow light filtered through my eyelids, but I kept them closed in the hope that they wouldn't notice me.

"There has been more weakness. I am not sure I can--" Cail began, but Edmund's voice cut him off quickly.

"Use what you need Cail, and stop making excuses," Edmund finished, the sneer on his lips evident in his voice. "I need this done."

"Yes, master."

Their voices were cut off by the deep grinding sound of a cell door opening. I tried to keep my shoulders relaxed.

"Get out of there, old man." I heard a kick and a grunt after Cail's words.

I closed my eyes tighter, not even wanting to imagine what might have just happened.

"So compliant now, Sain," Edmund said, his voice full of the same taunting malice I had heard in Cail's. "It's no wonder. You want some of that delicious water, don't you? You can't wait until I give you the mug."

I heard a groan of deep guttural need come from Sain as they locked him in with Ryland.

"Will you do something else for me, too? Do this and I will let you eat tomorrow."

I tensed in the silence, every nerve in my body on alert as I fought the desire to turn and find out what was going on. I squeezed Talon's hands as silence fell only to jerk at the ear splitting scream that cut through the silence.

I recognized the scream at once, the same scream I had heard when Sain and Ryland had been forced to use the blood connection the past two nights, obviously this one was no different.

The two howled, and I moved myself into the bars, my arms desperately grabbing at Talon as the screams died off.

"When will we end this, master?" Cail asked, his voice almost sounding bored. Perhaps even tired.

"Ovailia is due back in a few days," Edmund said, and my shoulders tensed on their own. "Let us see what she has to tell us and then we will make our final decisions. I still have many more tricks up my sleeve after all," he chuckled. "Now, let us go make the little girl pay."

"Yes, Master."

I let their words wash over me. Something infinitely more important was taking all of my attention. Talon was squeezing back.

CHAPTER 42
JOCLYN

I knew the moment I attempted to sit up the next morning that I was in trouble. My back felt like it had broken all over again, causing me to fall back against the bed with a groan as everything spun. I couldn't wait any longer. I reached for the chain and pulled the necklace out, letting it rest in my palm.

"Don't let this be a total mess," I mumbled, glancing at where Ilyan still lay, reminding myself I was not alone before plunging my magic into the necklace and closing my eyes.

I opened them again to the same disgusting kitchen as last time, everything rotting and falling to pieces.

The memories this kitchen induced and what the destruction seemed to mean felt like another knife to the heart. If the trend of my last few trips to the Tòuha held true, Ryland would show up and push me out of the space. So I held still, hoping to make my time in here last as long as possible and rejuvenate my body as much as I could.

It was ridiculous, coming to this traumatizing hell and hiding. Maybe Ryland was right...

I closed my eyes and shook my head, trying to banish the thought. When I opened my eyes again it was to a very small, very angry Ryland.

"I told you not to come back," he spat, his little voice dripping with hatred.

"You know I can't do that, Ry." I tried to keep my voice level in an attempt to calm him and hopefully lengthen the Tõuha, but I could tell it was a pointless effort.

"I don't care about you anymore!" he yelled before shoving me abruptly. I let him. I didn't know how to fight him, and even if I did, the very idea of fighting to stay in such a terrifying place did not interest me.

I opened my eyes to the carved stone roof of my bunk. The light that was reflecting through the chamber seemed brighter than before, but I knew I couldn't have been gone long considering I hadn't been in the Tõuha for more than a few minutes. I certainly hadn't been gone long enough to do much good. Everything still felt heavy and painful, just not quite as bad as it had been before.

"Well, a little strength can go a long way." It was wishful thinking, I should probably just roll over and go back to sleep.

Or not.

"Good morning!" Dramin's bright, sing-song voice echoed over me as he woke me up. The happiest alarm clock there ever was.

"Morning." I tried not to groan too much as I sat up to face him, happy the worst of my aches had disappeared while still wishing that all of them could have left. Dramin stood beside my bunk with two mugs in his hands. He held one out for me, and I took it gladly, grateful for the Black Water that would take away the last of the pains.

"Thank you, Dramin." I sighed as the water buzzed through me.

"You seem to be doing better today," he said over the top of his mug. "How is your mate?"

Of course he knew. I shouldn't have been surprised.

"He's fine."

"Hmmm." Dramin could see through my lie like it was wet paper. I just didn't know how to explain all that was going on. I chose to ignore his silent question by draining my cup of Black Water.

It flowed through me and I wiggled my toes, relishing the sensation. Dramin leaned over to look inside my cup, chuckling to see it already empty.

"You have the appetite of a child," he said, smiling. "It's quite refreshing."

I smiled back at him, handing over my cup. My body was already calling for more.

"Oh, no," Dramin smiled. "Not anymore, your body is healed. Your Drak magic awakened and tied to the wells. You can do this on your own."

He grabbed my hand and placed it firmly over the top of the mug.

"Think of the water and how you would like to see it; warm, cold, or maybe iced. Now pulse that thought into the cup."

"So, it's like ordering at a drive thru?" I raised an eyebrow at him, looking more confused than I felt. He just continued to laugh at me.

"It's easier than it sounds. It is second nature. Give it a shot." He smiled and I nodded my head at him before closing my eyes.

"I would like hot Black Water... ummm.... Please?" Warmth filled my hand, a tingling spreading over everything. When I opened my eyes to look at the cup, the steaming liquid filled it right to the rim.

"Good job! Although you don't have to speak your order, just think it." He winked at me and I blushed. "Now, if you will go into your Tȍuha every day, you will continue to have the energy to sustain yourself."

Dramin took a drink right after he spoke, his eyes digging into me from over his mug.

"How *did* you know?" I asked softly before taking another sip.

"The question is not how I knew, child—for that should be obvious—but, why are you avoiding your mate?"

I couldn't look at Dramin so I chose to look at the thick contents that swirled inside my cup instead. I guess if I had to confide in someone while Ilyan was indisposed, I should. Besides, I had started opening up to Thom, and that had turned out well. I supposed I needed to be more trusting.

"Well, for one, Ryland keeps pushing me out. Two, I am pretty sure Cail is controlling them." I sounded so dejected, I tried not to cringe at the sound of it.

"You mean he is controlling the Tȍuha as well as your dreams?" I had been beginning to think there was nothing that would surprise Dramin, yet I couldn't miss his shocked tone.

"Yes." I was suddenly feeling very cramped in the tight bunk. I slipped off my bed and walked right past him, my mug still clasped between my hands.

I moved to the large chairs that surrounded the fire, trying to avoid looking at Thom who was busy healing Ilyan.

"But how do you know?" Dramin asked as he came up behind me, already sinking into his chair.

"Ilyan pieced most of it together, but what you said about Edmund's Štít inside Cail, it kind of fit it all together for me." I sat down and draped one of the many furs that were piled around the chairs over my legs.

"But what does he want from you? Does he know—" When Dramin

finished abruptly, I lowered the mug from my lips to raise an eyebrow at him in question. "Does he know that you are one of the Drak?"

"No, I don't go screaming out random bits of information for them to hear. I am a bit smarter than that. Mostly, Cail enjoys messing with my mind." I tried to keep the tone of the conversation light, but I could already feel the desperation creeping into my own voice. "He finds different ways to torture me. In the dreams he plays little games or makes me relive bad memories. In the Tȍuha he has been telling what is left of Ryland's mind to get rid of me. They are trying to get me to break the Zêlství."

Dramin dropped his mug to the stone floor where it promptly shattered. I jumped at the noise, startling even more when I saw his face. For a moment I was worried he was lost in a sight.

"Who has told you this?" Dramin asked, panicked. His jaw was open and his eyes wide, the bright green thankfully still there.

"What?"

"Who asked you to break the connection?" I sunk away from his panic, keeping the mug tight in my grip. I didn't want mine to break.

"Ryland asked me in the dream last night, but I'm not sure it was him. There was something off about him."

Dramin nodded enthusiastically. "And in the Tȍuha?"

"What's left of Ryland's mind in the Tȍuha doesn't know enough, but I can tell someone is trying to break us apart. Ryland told me the man with the dark eyes told him to get rid of me."

"And you're sure he means Cail?" Dramin leaned forward eagerly, his eyes boring into mine.

"Either Cail or the Ryland that they are controlling."

"Or Edmund," Dramin provided, his voice oddly eager. It sent a chill up my spine.

I nodded, not wanting to give him an answer. I emptied my cup and refilled it, hoping that Dramin's excitement would dissipate.

"Are you going tell Ilyan of this?"

I glanced toward Ilyan's bunk at Dramin's words. Thom had disappeared somewhere, and my heart dropped to see him still unconscious.

"Tell Ilyan, what?" I asked, unwilling to rip my eyes away.

"That someone is trying to convince you to break the connection between you and Ryland."

"I suppose I will. I tell Ilyan everything."

Dramin paused before speaking. "I am not sure that is the best idea in this instance."

I narrowed my eyes at him. I had decided I wouldn't be like Atlas. I would swallow my pride and ask for help, but Dramin sat there, telling me that it might not be the best idea to tell Ilyan something that was already eating at me.

"You will know why before the day is over, child."

My eyes bugged out, I knew what he was talking about. The sight. The sight concerning me. He was finally going to tell me.

"But not yet," he finished before I could get too excited, and I leaned back into the chair. "You need to decide for yourself if you will break the connection. I believe you will, but not until the time is right."

"I'm not going to break the Zêlství."

"I know," Dramin was still calm, even though I suddenly felt as though I was going to explode. "But until you know for sure, trust in your sight. Your sight will lead the way."

"I don't like the sound of that."

"You must get used to that. It is the way of the Drak." I didn't know how he could smile right then, but his grin was broad as he settled into his chair.

My team seemed to be getting bigger. First, Thom; now, Dramin. Perhaps someday soon I would have the support of Ryland, too. My Ryland, with his memories intact.

I still had three weeks until Edmund's deadline to when he would kill Ryland if I didn't turn myself in. With my newly unlocked abilities I was feeling a bit unstoppable. Maybe it was the Black Water flowing through me, but I might be getting a bit cocky.

I was going to knock Edmund on the pavement.

I laughed at the thought, ignoring Dramin's raised eyebrow by taking another deep drink of the Black Water.

"Well," Thom announced as he approached the fire. "He should be awake in a few hours."

My back straightened, my eyes flying toward Ilyan's bunk in expectation.

"Relax, Silnỳ, I said a few hours not a few minutes. It could still be tomorrow."

I exhaled heavily and slumped back in the chair. Thom grunted at me in greeting before setting a blueberry muffin on my lap. It looked delicious, but I didn't want it. I eyed it for a moment before picking it up and setting it on the small side table next to me.

It seemed like such a simple act, but it had immediately caught the close attention of both men.

"Aren't you going to eat that?" Thom asked, alarmed.

I looked to the muffin and bit my lip, nervous about their sudden interest.

"No, I don't think I am." I didn't meet the eyes of either of them, although I knew they were both staring at me. Instead, I took another drink before placing my now empty mug next to the muffin.

"You are ready." I froze at Dramin's words, my hand coming back to rest in my lap.

I turned to him, nerves and excitement getting all jumbled up in my body.

"Are you going to show me now?" Dramin nodded his head once in response to my question.

"I'm not sure I am ready," I answered honestly, my voice quiet.

"You are, Silnỳ." I turned to Thom, even he was nodding his head in encouragement.

"But... Ilyan said... Will I really hate him?"

Dramin smiled in response to my question, but his face was sad. "Ilyan has worried for the past eight hundred years if what he said in the Hall of Sight was the right thing. That is eight hundred years of nerves. Of course he is scared. But know this, all that you are about to see will happen; you cannot change it. You are ready to accept that, and that is why you are ready to see the sight."

Dramin stood, his frame towering over me.

"But what if I am not ready, Uncle?" I had practically demanded to know what was in that sight for months. Of course now I would get the jitters.

"I am afraid, child, that you no longer have a choice."

Dramin placed his hand against my head. But instead of pulling out my memories as Ilyan had done, I felt my head go light and airy as Dramin put them in.

CHAPTER 43
JOCLYN

I recognized the room as a Hall of Sight the moment everything came into focus. This one was bigger and more ornate than the one in our cave, though. Carvings and beautiful panes of stained glass were set into the walls. It almost looked like a cathedral. The same sunken pool of Black Water filled the center of the room, but instead of the raised shelf that surrounded it, a number of chairs and thrones had been carved out of wood and placed in a circle facing the pool. In each of the thrones a man or woman sat. They did not speak, they sat with their eyes closed, heads bowed with their features obscured by large, woolen cloaks. I knew what they were doing, I could feel the magic of sight run over my skin like feathers.

I didn't know what I was doing here, and I was still shaky about the details of what Dramin had done to me and how he was showing me this. Even if I knew everything about the process, I didn't think I could shake the nerves connected with what I was about to see.

I was about to learn everything.

Ilyan's plea for me not to hate him echoed through my head. After all he had done, how could I hate him? I mean, he laid unconscious after risking his life to save mine. I didn't know what could negate that, but I guess I was about to find out.

"He is coming, can you feel him?" I turned toward the voice, surprised to see that one of the still figures had stood. His head moved from his bowed position to one of strength. I must have audibly gasped —though no one seemed to notice— I had come face to face with my father. His face and body seemed younger, if that was possible, and his hair was shorter. He was powerful and strong, so much more so than I had ever remembered seeing him. The change was startling. I could tell he was the patriarch among them. He was respected and revered, his commanding voice guiding all of them.

"We can feel him." The remaining Drak in the hall stood in unison as they spoke as one, their voices echoing around me. I jumped, unsure if the sound was awesome or super creepy.

"He wishes to know," Sain said, his voice deep and rumbling.

"Know of his future," said another.

"Know of his heart."

"Shall we tell him?"

"Shall we give him sight?"

"He is the only one who can see, the only one who understands."

"That is why he has come, come to see us."

I spun around as each voice spoke, their voices coming in quick succession. Each of the Drak stood still, their black eyes ringed with the glowing embers as they looked beyond their own sight and into the Black Water.

This would have been much creepier if I hadn't seen it before, and felt it in me.

"He has come." I turned toward my father at his announcement. All of the Draks' eyes shifted from black to their normal, multi-colored array. I looked around them, unsurprised to see Dramin standing to the left of my father.

I waited, my nerves on edge, wondering what they were talking about, or who was coming, but no one in the Hall of Sight moved. Their eyes were focused on the door behind me, their gaze deep and unwavering. I heard the creak of the oversized door as it was opened, another gasp escaping me when Ilyan walked through.

I shouldn't have been surprised.

He looked different, but I knew it was him. I would recognize him anywhere. I suddenly realized why this all seemed so familiar; I had seen him walk into this room in my first sight.

His hair was short and cut above his ears, the blonde strands darker and waved slightly against his head. I had seen his hair short once before, but somehow this look was different. The change was becoming, his features more defined, and dare I say it, he looked... gorgeous.

Not that he wasn't gorgeous with long hair. He was.. But this... I shouldn't be thinking like this...

He walked in quickly, his features both strong and yet nervous. He wore the same clothing I had seen him wear for council; the long tunic, high boots, and ornate jewels all firmly in place. Yet I had the distinct impression that this was not some special attire, this was the clothing of the time.

Dramin's words of Ilyan having waited eight hundred years echoed through my head. My jaw dropped as the numbers sprang to life in my mind; eight hundred years ago would make it around the year 1200, and Ilyan would be a little over two hundred years old.

Sometimes his age smacked me upside the head, like now.

Ilyan marched in before falling to one knee, his head bowed as he waited. He, the king, was bowing to them. I might have underestimated my father's role in the world of magic. Ilyan stayed like that as all of the Drak looked at him. I was frozen in place, my eyes glued to Ilyan's back. Finally, after a few minutes, Sain stepped off of his throne and approached Ilyan, who still did not move.

"Welcome, My Lord." Sain greeted him warmly, the Drak's pleasure at seeing Ilyan echoing around the large cavern. Ilyan rose at Sain's words, and I was surprised to find his eyes bloodshot.

"You know why I have come?" Ilyan asked, his head rising about a foot above Sain's.

"How could I not?" Sain smiled sadly and took Ilyan's hand, leading him toward the pool of Black Water that stood in the middle of the hall. I reluctantly followed, my skin prickling with nerves.

"Tell me, how did you survive for so long?" Ilyan's voice was so pained that it cut straight into me. Sain patted his hand with the same sad smile in place.

"You of all people know that I did not manage it easily. If I had then we would not have my lovely Dramin, and I would not be bonded to your sister. My life is full now, but only after many centuries of waiting." Sain's voice was not sad as it echoed around the stone chamber, if anything it was full of acceptance and comfort. It was a voice from my childhood; I had heard it with every scraped knee or tumble. This voice reminded me of home.

"I know, but still..." Ilyan trailed off and hung his head, looking into the still water that did not show him his reflection. None of the other Drak moved, their eyes remaining focused on Ilyan and Sain.

"You are lonely," Sain finished for him confidently. Ilyan nodded once, his eyes glistening with tears, which he tried in vain to hold back.

"I feel lost. My heart breaks for someone I have never even met, someone who may never exist. I cannot weave my magic with someone without causing them injury. I am beginning to believe that the joy of a Zêlství will never be in my future."

I took a step toward him, wishing I could console him somehow until I reminded myself that this was a memory. Ilyan wiped the tears from his face before turning back to Sain, who wrapped his arms around him comfortingly.

"Would it help you to know that I have felt your pain?"

"That is why I have come to you, Sain. I knew you would understand."

"And yet you still wish to use the sight to see into your future?" Sain asked, his tone curious and worried.

I found myself growing concerned about what exactly I was about to see. I had been told this was the sight about my true purpose, but Ilyan was asking about his love life. Cail's words about Ilyan's feelings for me shot through me, my body freezing in realization that the two things might be connected.

"Yes. I would gladly wait until the end of days if only I knew that she would be waiting for me, that someday I would be with her."

"The future does not always hold hope, Ilyan. What would you do if no one ever came into this world for you?" Sain moved away from Ilyan, walking around the pool before facing Ilyan from the other side. The Water began to ripple between them, yet their reflections still did not shine on the dark surface.

"I would do what I have been doing, Sain. I will continue my work with Man, but at least I will know to stop looking."

Sain studied him for a moment before coming to a decision. He nodded once and moved back to place his cloak on the throne he had originally sat in. He was dressed in the same tunic get-up as Ilyan, although his was not the gold and white of Ilyan's; but black and red. Returning to the pool, Sain knelt next to the water which rippled deeper.

"Bare your chest Ilyan. This is a matter of the heart, and not one that the Black Water will take lightly. My soul tells me that this is more than it seems." Sain spoke loudly as he leaned over the water, each of the Drak kneeling beside the pool as he did.

Ilyan did not hesitate before removing his tunic, the fabric falling into a heap on the ground near his feet. He moved right to the bank of the pond, wearing only thick tights and high leather boots. His chest was smooth and scar free. I had grown so used to seeing the scars that seeing him without them was odd.

"Do you wish to use my sight to know the matters of your heart, Ilyan, son of Edmund, heir to the throne of our King?" Sain's voice was loud. It had taken on that strange dead quality I had heard in my voice when I used my sight.

"I do."

"Then show him," the voices of every Drak in the hall spoke at the same time, their voices hollow as well.

"Tell me of what you desire." Sain extended his hand until it hovered right above the Black Water, his fingers barely skimming the surface.

I inhaled sharply, my nerves bubbling as much as the surface of the water.

"I wish to know if the fates have designed a mate for me—be it now, or in the future. I must know if one will be born who is strong enough to hold my magic." Ilyan's voice ricocheted around the space, growing louder with each word. My muscles stiffened, my body reacting to what I knew was to come. What I didn't want to hear.

"So let it be." All the Drak spoke together as Sain plunged his hand into the water.

The moment his hand was submerged, the water seemed to come to life. The ripples of before became a torrent as they bubbled over the surface in an angry boil. The bubbles continued to grow until the water sprouted vertically into a pillar of thick darkness. I could no longer see my father where he knelt on the other side of the pool. The only thing left visible to me was Ilyan's back as he stood before the pillar of water, his muscles flexing in anticipation.

Once the Black Water had grown to a height above his head, Ilyan called out in pain, his yells loud as they cut through me. I ran over to him in a panic, needing to help him. I stopped in place as I saw what was happening; streams of Water flowed away from the pillar to drag themselves along Ilyan's chest. I inhaled sharply, remembering what Dramin and Thom had told me; Black Water was poisonous to any other than the Drak, but contact with it was necessary for the Drak to use their sights for others.

Ilyan yelled out, his voice restrained as he tried to hide how much agony it was causing. He clenched his jaw as tongue after tongue of roving water dragged itself over his chest, his flesh turning an angry red as it bubbled. He yelled and screamed, but he did not call for them to stop. I could see the determination in his eyes, his fervent desire to know guiding him.

It took far too long for the Black Water to stop slicing away at Ilyan's flesh. His screams died as his magic healed him, his power taking away the pain. Ilyan squared his shoulders and looked straight ahead as the Drak began to mumble, their voices overriding one another until they became a roar.

The sound was both deafening and terrifying. I cringed into myself as the sound grew in caliber. It ricocheted off of the walls as the water exploded even further, the pillar extending violently up to the ceiling.

The Black Water began to swirl and ripple as colors passed over it, the sights from the Drak reflecting onto the water so that Ilyan could see them. Flashes of red moved together before forming a tangible image of fire, of destruction.

"There is one among us..."

The Drak spoke together, their voices so precise it sounded like one loud voice. The power of it filled me. Even though I knew this was a memory, I could feel my own Drak blood calling to them.

"...who seeks to change the magic. Someone who seeks to kill the magic."

As the Drak spoke, the fire in the vision was joined by the faint sounds of screaming, the image within the pillar changing to running feet, explosions, and above all, Edmund's laugh.

"He seeks to kill the magic for his own personal gain. We see him as he fights, as he sheds the blood of us, as he sheds the blood of others. We see him as he stops the reign of magic, as he stops the time of ours."

As the Drak spoke, more sights of the early destruction caused by Edmund flashed through the water. The screams of children and families rang out around us as the flashes of misery continued. I cringed away from them all, I had seen enough of what Edmund was capable of in my own life.

"Is this now?" Ilyan asked, his voice raised above the constant noise that filled the chamber.

"The time is now, My Lord," The Drak said together. "You alone will be brave enough to fight him. Where others will lose their lives, you will prevail."

More sights flashed before us as the Drak continued to mumble. Ilyan and I looked at the pillar as images of him fighting against unknown foes were replaced by his stripped body strung up on a tree as he was beaten, and then it returned to a sight of Ilyan victorious against at least ten men.

I looked to Ilyan curiously, surprised to see his shoulders squared and jaw set, almost as if he was ready to plunge into battle at any moment.

Looking at him right then, I could understand why he always fought; why he relished battle. It wasn't a thirst for blood as Edmund would have me believe, though. It was a pure desire to help, to be good, and to protect. It was light.

"In a time far ahead, near the end of the world..." Flashes of war after war, all raged by man, filled the pillar of Black Water. I ached at seeing all the destruction humans had waged in such a raw way.

"...in a time when everything is changing and everything is new..."

The water showed us visions of my time and I watched Ilyan's eyes bug out of his head at the sights of high-rise buildings, cars, and the everyday modern life he was being shown.

"...there will come a child."

The same sight from my own vision flashed on the water; that of my mother being handed an infant, me. My heart beat rapidly, my mouth had gone dry.

"A child, an infant, a child that we see. We see her when she's born. We see her when she's grown. We see her now, and we see her then."

Visions of my childhood flashed through the water in quick succession, I recognized moments of triumph sprinkled through the many images of loss, pain, and anger that made up me. Ilyan clutched his heart, his sadness at my life evident. I had to look away as the images continued, each heartbreaking memory hurting more. Then they began to change. I was smiling more. I was laughing. And I knew why. Each of these sights were when I had been with Ryland. Even though he was never shown, I knew without a doubt he was there. My spirits soared thinking about him as he used to be; before the pain of his insistence that I break the Zêlství had crushed my joy.

"She is of The Chosen. Marked by the sign of the creature of fire, she has smoke in her eyes."

More visions flashed, showing us snippets of when I received my mark, my eyes before and after, and of how I had tried to hide the mark over the years. I reached up and covered my neck, suddenly feeling very self-conscious.

"A Chosen just for you." Their voices reverberated through my head as the pillar showed a sight of Ilyan and me. His arms were entwined around me, his body soft against mine, his lips pressed firmly against my own.

"No," I gasped silently. My stomach turning at what I was seeing. I had known from the beginning what was going to happen, but I refused to believe it. I didn't want to accept what Cail and Ryland had said as truth.

The vision continued and I looked toward Ilyan, his hand extended longingly toward the passionate kiss we shared. I could see all the longing in his eyes. He had waited so long. This wasn't supposed to happen, it couldn't happen. Yet I still found that knot in my stomach turning to an ache.

"For in this child is power, power beyond belief."

The sight of our kiss faded to an image of me, strong magic flowing as I fought several Trpaslíks at the same time. I was shocked to see that I was winning.

"She is the most powerful. She will be The Silný, the one who protects us all."

The sights continued—one after another—of me fighting, my power prevailing. More often than not, Ilyan was by my side, his magic battling right beside me. The visions continued before ending with Ilyan defeating an unseen assailant, his arm wrapped around me securely. I recognized that one because it had already happened. It was from the night we had fled the LaRues' mansion, the night we had failed to rescue Ryland.

"Her life is nothing other than misery, for everything she touches is ash and in her heart is only pain."

More images of my childhood. My heartbreak as my father left. My pain as I was bullied through every year of school. My misery at finding my mother dead, only to be thrown out of a window. I gasped as I saw my fall, the impact never shown, though the pain on my face was heartbreaking.

"Only you can help her and fill her heart with love."

They spoke as more sights flew through the water. I looked, expecting to see some startling way that Ilyan would make me love him, but all of these had already happened. I felt my heart loosening toward him in that moment just as it had then. They showed Ilyan caring for me, holding me as I lay dying, tenderly making shoes for me, and holding me every night as I cried. Seeing it from this angle—watching his actions as I slept and screamed—changed my perspective. I saw the tears I never knew he had shed over me, and the love he had kept hidden.

"Only you can save her and keep her for her true purpose."

A sight formed again, this time of Ilyan gently laying me on the bed in the attic, his finger running along my jaw as I fell asleep. It showed him then lean down to kiss me. A forbidden kiss; a kiss I had never felt. I gasped as I saw the action. I was angry that he had kissed me, and yet... and yet...

"For you were born and you were bred only to protect her."

More images of Ilyan and I floated past, his arms always around me, protecting me from those who would hurt me. Some I had lived through and some I had yet to experience.

"It is your future, Ilyan. Now is your time to see her. Then your place will be near her. It is your purpose to protect her. But beware, even as your heart longs for her, she will love another."

My heart clenched as the sight replayed my first kiss with Ryland, our magic exploding as Ryland sealed himself to me, completing the Zêlství. This time it was not my turn for heartbreak. Ilyan reached longingly out, his voice calling out in disbelief. I could hear his heart break and it fractured something inside of me. I shook my head, basking in the memory of the kiss instead of the trauma I had been facing.

"Your heart will long for her, but she may not be yours to take."

More sights of Ilyan; more visions of secret kisses, intimate moments when we sat with our arms around each other, as we laughed and joked. Finally, when he had attempted to teach me to Salsa dance. I couldn't help but smile at the memory. Even though I didn't want to accept all that was being shown, I couldn't keep out the joy that tried to seep its way into me.

"You must find your strength to protect her—to be near her—for it is only by your side that she can find her true purpose; that she will find the strength to kill those that would end the magic of the world."

The images in the water changed again, this time to show Ilyan standing by me as I fought, his presence strong as he supported me from a distance. I could tell what was happening. I was using his magic. The knowledge of that rocked through me and my jaw dropped. There were only two ways in which that could happen, through a bonding, or through the Štít. I clutched my hand to my shoulder. He had known.

I understood the look now, the look he gave me when he spoke of the Štít for the first time. It was heartbreak. His heart had broken because he had known that he could never have me and that the Štít was the only way he could be close to me. Then, when I had held his magic, all of it, he knew that a bonding truly was possible, but also that it would never happen.

I had come to love Ilyan, maybe more than I could ever fully accept. I felt my soul rent with the realization of his pain and heartbreak. I longed to help him—to protect him, to make it okay—yet I knew I couldn't. I was bonded to Ryland, and Ryland had protected me, too. Ryland loved me, too. And even though Ryland's protection might end by a severing of our bond, I didn't know if I could ever move beyond that.

"It is only when she is with you that she will be able to accomplish all that she must. It is your place to protect her until the day that she passes from this world and into the next."

"No." Ilyan and I said together at the vision of him holding my body, his arms wrapped tightly around me as he howled and cried in agony, explosions filling the space surrounding us.

"This child is power." Sain spoke alone, his voice loud and powerful. "Power that is strong enough for you."

More flashes of my ability raced across the pillar. I couldn't tear my eyes away from them. I couldn't comprehend that I could be so strong.

"For you," the Drak repeated together, "for you, for you."

Their voices reverberated eerily as image after image of Ilyan and I together filled the space. Sights of intimate kisses, intertwined bodies, beach houses, and children flashed one right after another. They came faster and faster until they were a blur and the water went black, the pillar falling into the pool again. I ran to it, gasping at the smooth surface and the reflection of myself that was now staring back at me.

"You will love her," Sain said with the deep, deadpan voice of a sight. I looked up to him, unsurprised to see him standing, his eyes covered with blackness and lit only by the glowing embers the Black Water gave him.

"But you cannot have her." The Drak spoke as one, each of their eyes also covered. They stared out, unseeing, the glossy blackness calling to me.

"You will protect her," Sain said.

"But you will fail," the Drak continued, their voices coming in quick succession.

"The one bred to change the world of magic," Sain lifted his hands as if he was seeing something, but the hall stayed still.

"The one bred to die." I froze at the words of the Drak.

"What?" I said aloud to the empty space, even though I knew no one could hear me.

"She is the only one who will come to this world," they continued together, "the only one your heart can hold."

"The only one?" Ilyan asked, my insides tightening to hear how defeated he sounded.

"She is here," Sain announced, his voice deep and reverent.

"Do you feel her?" They all spoke together again, the addition of Sain's voice doubling their intensity. "Do you see her?"

"I do." Ilyan's voice was right in my ear right before his arms came around from behind me and pulled me into his newly scarred chest.

CHAPTER 44
JOCLYN

My heart thumped, my soul screamed, confusion and shock and wonderment blended together as I stood against Ilyan, his arms wrapped around me.

Ilyan's arms tightened as he pressed his cheek softly against mine. I didn't lean into his touch, but I didn't shy away either. I froze, my heart aching for Ryland, my soul rejoicing at Ilyan.

It only added to the confusion.

"Do not be afraid, mi lasko." I relaxed at Ilyan's voice, so soft and familiar in my ear. "I know you have seen everything, and I know you are scared, but do not be. I can feel you inside of me; I can feel your soul inside of mine. Know that I am here to protect you, to save you, and to love you. Even if you will never love me, I will still be here, right by your side."

He turned me gently in his arms so that I could face him, his arms still held me against him. I looked up to him; he was so different, and yet so much the same.

"You're beautiful." He sighed the words like a prayer, his fingers coming up to trace the lines of my face. "I promise to always keep you safe."

He leaned down and my heart froze, but instead of kissing my lips, he pressed his lips against the Vilý's kiss on my neck, his lips soft and gentle.

The touch of his lips against my mark sent a jolt through my whole body. I had only felt that electric response to Ryland before; the jolt that preceded bonding. Ilyan sighed as the jolt ran through him, his body relaxing at feeling something he had been longing for.

I, however, was working myself into a panic.

"I love you." He said softly, his words true and honest. I could tell he meant what he said, but I didn't shy away from it, either—not as much as I should have—and it scared me.

"I... I love... No!" I yelled out in a panic. My voice echoed around the great stone chamber as I pushed my hands against Ilyan's chest, pushing myself out of the memory and into my usual chair in the cave.

It was obvious that a whole day had passed; the light from the skylights in the ceiling was coming from an angle that suggested it was already night. Thom's partially eaten lunch still lay on his couch, but neither Thom nor Dramin were anywhere to be seen. Even though I had done nothing but sit all day, I could feel the exhaustion of a full day dragging me down.

I exhaled deeply, my chest shaking before I reluctantly looked toward where Ilyan lay. I was glad Thom and Dramin had left me to myself. I needed the time. To think. To feel. Dramin must have known, too. After all, he had known from the beginning all that had been said; all that had been seen.

Ilyan had known, too.

Ilyan had known for eight hundred years about me; he had known my face, known some semblance of a future with me. And yet, he had said nothing. Even when I had struggled and pined for Ryland—even as he had trained me—he'd said nothing of the future he longed to have; the future he dreamed of with me. He had never tried to talk me out of it. He had never tried to place himself in a better position. He had let me do what I had longed for. He supported me in every way that I needed.

Suddenly, the look that Ilyan had possessed the very first day I had seen him standing against the wall in English class made sense; his intense gaze, his look of frightening awe. After eight hundred years of waiting, I had been sitting right before him. I cannot imagine the heartbreak he must have felt, or how the knowledge of what he could never have must have eaten him up inside.

I stood to face him, still and calm on the bunk, his long hair falling gently over the side. I couldn't decide if I was angry with him, agreed with him, or accepted what he had done. Everything lay numbly inside of me as I stood staring at him.

My Protector.

He had been born to protect me—born with magic strong enough to do so—and yet, too strong to give him companionship. He had borne it willingly, his actions showing his strength. Although he loved me more than he could ever love any other, he had held his tongue and let me follow my own path.

He was truly a better man than I would have guessed. How could he ever worry that I would hate him? I shook my head before walking toward him, my steps slow and controlled. Thom's words of his imminent awakening sounded in my head. I had wanted him to wake up, now I needed him to sleep. I needed to process.

I had been born to defeat Edmund—born to usher in a new age of magic— while Ilyan had been born to protect me and bring me to serve my true purpose, even if it ended with my death. An image of him from the pillar, his heartbreak as he held my dead body, entered my mind and I stopped a few steps away from him.

I clutched my hand to my chest as the pressure in it built. I knew the second heartbreak Dramin had predicted was coming and I knew why. I had fallen in love with Ilyan.

I loved Ilyan, but it was a different love than with Ryland. Ryland was passion and a history of friendship. Ilyan's love was built on something else... something deeper.

It scared me.

"I'm sorry, Ilyan," I whispered to his sleeping body, my voice catching on my tears, "but I can't give you what you want."

I turned and ran before I had finished speaking. My feet stumbled as I tore across the large space in tears, only to lunge myself into my bunk. I covered myself with as many of the large furs as I could, hoping to dampen my sobs before they escaped my lips.

The sight had said that everything that I touched would turn to ash, and this seemed to be no exception. I was in love with and bonded to my best friend. A boy who had been tortured by his father for loving me, who may or may not remember me, and whose very bond with me terrorized my waking and non-waking existence. Ryland meant the world to me, and yet he desired to break our bond. Even thinking about his words, about his promise to sever the Zêlství, brought more heartache.

Nothing about my bond with Ryland brought joy, and that in itself was painful for me. I longed for him while, at the same time, I was scared of him.

I howled at the loss of him, which only opened up a deeper chasm in my heart. It rent open the feelings I had been hiding even from myself. The feelings I now knew Ilyan shared.

Everything around me was crumbling again, the weight on my shoulders too much to bear. Bred to die, born to fight, raised to be broken, and always the cause of pain for those I cared about most in the world.

"I'm sorry Ilyan," I said between my tears, wishing he was here. I needed his strength, his song. I needed the reminder that it was all going to be okay.

He was the one my heart called to. I don't know if it was because he was the only one that was left or because he was the only one I wanted. He was my Protector, and right then, that was what I needed.

"Ilyan!" His name mixed with my tears, my sobs becoming an uncontrollable monster inside my chest. It clenched, and clawed, and burrowed into me, increasing my howls and my pain.

I writhed in the foolish hope of getting rid of the pain, but it didn't help. I could find no comfort. The blankets of security I had placed around me had become a prison.

I had not even felt the covers lift when long, sinewy arms I knew all too well wrapped around me, a strong chest coming to rest against my back.

I turned in his arms, my tears changing from those of despair to some of hope. Ilyan lay right next to me, his arms wrapped around me tightly, his magic flaring as he calmed me. I looked into his bright eyes, my heart beating much faster than it had ever done before.

He smiled as he moved my tangled hair out of my face, his eyes never leaving mine. They had that look I had seen during the sight; a burning love that incapacitated me.

My tears had slowed to nothing as I reached up, carefully placing my hand against his face, touching him in a way I had never done before. His skin was soft and smooth.

"You're all right," I gasped out, the words almost washed away with my tears.

"I am all right," he affirmed, his accent thicker than I had ever heard it. Ilyan pulled me to him, his lips pressing roughly against my forehead before he buried me into his chest. The scarred chest.

"I will never leave you, Silnỳ." His voice caught and I could tell he was crying, too.

We stayed like that, my tears falling over his chest while his mingled into my hair, our joy at seeing one another again settling in.

Slowly I began to come back to myself, the rough scars on his chest coming into my line of sight.

I reached up to trace the lines with my fingertips, my heart unsure about such close and intimate contact.

"I'm sorry that the water hurt you." I continued to trace the raised scars, the skin rough under my fingertips. The white scars zigzagged over his chest, no longer as angry as the red they had originally been.

He stiffened underneath me.

"So they showed you then?" His voice was taut and I could hear the fear behind it. I didn't want him to be scared. I pushed my head against his chest, the wild thumping of his heart fluttering in my ear.

"Yes."

His heart continued to pound as he hesitated; as he decided what to say to me.

"I am glad I have them, the scars. They have always been a reminder of what I may someday have."

"I know." My voice was soft.

"And... you are not mad at me?"

I hesitated. I wasn't sure how to phrase this; how to say what needed to be said. I pulled away, my eyes meeting his as he searched mine for any signs of what was to come.

"I'm not mad," I said, as I reached up—hesitant to touch his face, to trace his features—before withdrawing again, leaving him untouched.

"But why not?" I could understand his confusion, however there was something very important that I needed him to understand.

"Because I love you too, Ilyan." His face lit up, yet my heart only cinched tighter at what I was about to say. "But it doesn't change anything. We can never be together."

I thought for sure I would have shattered his heart. Instead, the radical light that emanated off him grew, his magic flaring until I could feel it push against my barrier. His smile grew and he pulled me back into him, his arms wrapping me tightly to him.

"I know, Joclyn. I know it doesn't change anything. I know I can never have you. I am alright with that. I expect nothing from you, but hearing you say it, even if it is only this once, that is enough for me. I can live the rest of my life knowing that you love me, even if nothing else will come of it, because I know I am not alone in this world."

Ilyan sighed heavily and I felt his tears fall against my skin, my own not far behind. I could still vividly recall his heartbreak as he had talked to my father, his longing as he had watched the images of us; the images that would never be. I wanted to soothe him, my soul longing to heal those pains.

"You are not alone, Ilyan," I whispered. "Not anymore."

"Thank you, Joclyn."

I buried my face into his chest, his warmth and his heartbeat surrounding me. My heart swelled at the comfort he gave me. Thom had been right, I needed someone to help me to hold the weight, and there, in Ilyan's arms, I actually felt stronger—like I could accomplish anything. Besides, even though nothing could ever happen between us, I knew the devotion we held for each other would be enough.

Until the day I died.

CHAPTER 45
RYLAND

"If this is what you had to show me, Cail, then I already approve."

I recoiled against my father's voice, the deep boom grinding against his incessant laughter that always lived in my head. I winced and pressed myself into the corner again, not wanting Cail to turn on me again. My body ached just sitting here, and everything was fuzzy thanks to the swollen skin around my eyes. I didn't think I could take anymore.

'Why do you think you have a choice?'

"Whatever you have done to him is beautiful." He stepped closer, his fingers pressing painfully against the swollen skin. I winced and I clung to the wall more, which only caused the two to laugh. "It is beautiful, Master, I agree, but it is not why I have called you here."

"What is it?" Edmunds voice darkened as he rounded on him, both of them leaving me to cry and sob on my own.

"I have found the way to complete your plan."

"You have?"

The greasy Trpaslík was smiling now. "Yes. I have breeched the svazovat. The way to the Tȍuha is clear."

Tȍuha? What was he... oh god... no.

No...

'Yes.'

I winced, trying to pull my magic inside of myself, trying to cover the line that I had tried so hard to keep protected. Even when I didn't know what it was I was protecting I had kept it safe. But this time I couldn't reach it. I couldn't shield it.

Cail's magic was everywhere.

I chanced a glance up to the two men, both of them smiling, both of them looking right at me, towering over me like the monsters they were.

"I am glad, Cail." Edmund said, his eyes still on me. "But what does this give us beyond what the soul's blade has? We already have a connection to her."

"Yes," Cail clicked his tongue and my body and mind shifted, his magic controlling me again as everything became fuzzy and I was forced to stand. "But with the two of them together, master, we will not only have a connection. We will have control."

"Control? Explain."

I stood there, watching the two as they stared at me with the same look they always did. Like I was their shiny new pet.

"You want to break her mind as we are breaking Rylands. And while I can with just the use of the blade, it will take longer. With both the Tȍuha and the blade, I believe I can control her the way I do Ryland. I can not only infiltrate her mind. I can bring it to us."

I wanted to fight them. I wanted to scream and rage and tell that they couldn't. I wouldn't let them. But the words couldn't come. I couldn't even move. I just stood there, staring, slowly forgetting who they were talking about anyway.

"Wonderful."

EXTENDED RUBY EDITION

SCORCHED TREACHERY

IMDALIND SERIES BOOK THREE

REBECCA ETHINGTON

CHAPTER I
JOCLYN

Ilyan did not move from my side all night. We lay in each other's arms until we drifted to sleep; Ilyan was there when I woke from yet another nightmare, his song soft in my ear.

He was awake. He was alive. He was well.

That alone pulled me into a deep sleep, having him there just made it better.

I woke up the next morning with his arms still around me, our legs intertwined comfortably. I knew I should move away. I knew it was wrong for us to be lying like this, but I didn't care.

I twisted in his arms and smiled at the serenity in his sleeping face. Even though he was asleep, I could feel his magic's strong presence in my shoulder, the gentle lull of it as small tendrils weaved throughout my body. He would be there for me no matter what. If the sight had not given me enough proof, what I was feeling now was more than enough

I sighed heavily and shifted closer, cursing my sore, creaking joints. I hadn't entered the Tȍuha yesterday because of the sight; if I didn't go in now, today would be a miserable day.

I pulled the necklace out from underneath my torn shirt and let it rest in my hands. I knew whatever I found inside would not be pleasant, but even a quick trip would help my body and then I may not have to worry about it for a few days.

I grasped Ilyan's hand in my own and leaned into him again before I pushed my magic into the necklace, closing my eyes to enter the Tȍuha.

It was all the same; the same kitchen, the same mold, the same deathly silence. My heart beat erratically as I stood alone, suddenly wondering if Ryland would do something to shove me out or if 'the dark-eyed man' that Ryland had told me about could find me there. Either way, I needed as much time as possible in that wretched place.

I moved further into the kitchen before ducking down and sliding myself underneath the counter by the bar stools. My knees slipped on rotting food and a couple of small mice scurried away, but I barely took notice.

Had it come to this? Had the Tȍuha really become nothing more than a vessel for energy? Ryland's voice echoed in my head, his promise to break the Zêlství; his gentle words begging me to do the same.

And yet here I sat, hiding from him underneath a counter amongst garbage, terrified about what was going to happen in this place that joined me to my mate, just so I could keep the connection. It seemed ridiculous even to me.

What was I doing?

"I thought I told you not to come!" Ryland yelled.

I could only see his foot as he attempted to kick me. I was sure the contact would send me back so I dodged, scrambling through rotten food and broken glass, sending barstools side-long into the kitchen.

"Get out of here!" he yelled as he chased after me.

"I'm not going to do that, Ryland. Not yet." I continued to crawl away, my hands and knees covered with filth and dirt.

"No one wants you here anymore!" Ryland yelled again, still kicking after me. I looked back to him as I reached the end of the counter, my stomach dropping to see his angry little body swinging a bar stool right toward my face.

It made contact and I howled out in pain, the impact sending me right out of the Tȍuha. I sat up automatically, my hand flying to my nose. It felt as if it had broken.

"What the heck?" I hissed, grabbing at my nose as my magic flared. I froze when my fingers touched the warm wetness of my own blood. I stared at the blood on my fingers, my breath coming faster than usual.

Pain had never followed me from the Tȍuha like this before, not like it did with the nightmares. Even with the nightmares I was never truly injured. In the Tȍuha, however, it seemed that I could be.

"Joclyn?" Ilyan asked softly. My panic had obviously woken him up. He placed his hand on my back as he traced up and down my spine. "Are you okay?"

"I'm bleeding."

Ilyan was up in a flash, one arm wrapped around me while the other held my hand before moving to inspect my face. His fingers pushed softly against the skin, his face filled with deep worry lines.

"What happened?" I wasn't sure if he was furious or worried.

"Ryland threw a chair at me."

Ilyan froze, his hand still pressed against my face. His other hand tightened against my hip, his magic swelling in frustration.

"In the Tòuha?" The heavy restraint he placed on his words made me tense.

"He has become very aggressive in getting me out of them." I looked away from him, the same question as before bussing in my ear. Why was I doing this?

"But... to hurt you?" Ilyan's fingers pressed against the bridge of my nose, his magic healing me quicker than I could heal myself.

"I'm not sure it's coming from him." I looked up at Ilyan as the skin knit back together, the tips of his fingers tracing over the tender skin as he raised his eyebrow at me, prompting me to continue. I swallowed hard.

"Cail made it very obvious that he is in control of my dreams. I think he is manipulating the Tòuha as well." I picked at the hairs of the furs we were covered with, uninterested in looking at him.

"I am not surprised. I had my assumptions after what he said before. Has he hurt you?" Ilyan's magic surged into me in a flood, as if he was expecting hundreds of broken bones.

"No, he likes to mess with my head, which is super fun considering I have to go into the Tòuha, and I can't control if the dreams come or not."

Ilyan's body stiffened, his breathing shallow against my hair. My new injury, mixed with the fact that Cail was controlling my dreams, was bringing all of his protective rage right to the surface.

"I only went into the Tòuha once while you were gone."

"How long was I gone?" he asked, his voice soft as he pulled away to look at me.

"Three days." Ilyan's hand moved down my face to lift my chin up to look at him.

"And the nightmares?" I looked back down to the scars, trying to ignore that my heartrate had turned into a drum at just the mention of the dratted things. Ilyan's fingers tightened on my back, I guess he heard. "I will fix this. I will make the Tòuha safe for you to go into. I will never let it happen again."

I pulled his hand away from my face, holding onto his fingers tightly.

"You don't have to fix it. We can fix it. But I am going to need your help. Nothing about this is going to be easy."

Ilyan pulled me against him, his hand still wrapped around mine. "I know. We will figure it out together."

He held me against him, his heart beating in my ear while I traced his scars with my free hand, his grip pressing me against his chest.

"I will never leave you," he whispered in my ear before he kissed my mark. The jolt I had felt only twice before shot through my body. First with Ryland at the party, and then With Ilyan in the hall of sight. And now again. Here. I stiffened at the sensation, looking up to Ilyan in a panic.

"You feel it, too?" His voice was awed, his eyes glossing over.

"Yes. I felt it before when you... in the sight, I mean..." I let my voice trail off uncomfortably, unsure of how to phrase it.

"You felt it then?" Ilyan's voice was quiet and unsure. I had never heard him without his confidence, it made me soften against him. "I have always wondered—since that day all those centuries ago—I always wondered if you felt it, too. If you heard what I said."

I nodded once and his face relaxed, his confidence almost instantly returning. It was interesting, seeing that hidden side of him, the gentle kindness that I saw in Santa Fe. That I saw now. It was like I was seeing the real him.

Sometimes it felt like Wyn and I knew two different Ilyan's. Maybe we did.

"I did. I heard every word." He smiled again and I looked away, my face heating as I turned into a giant ball of blush and nerves. "I meant every word," he whispered as he kissed my hair line, his body warm and close against mine. "I will always love you, but I will never force you to be with me. I will never stop you from being with Ryland. He is your mate, Joclyn. I will always respect that."

Ilyan gently placed his hand against my face, and lifted me to meet his gaze. He looked at me softly, his eyes full of the golden specks of light I had seen before.

"Thank you."

"Of course," Ilyan let his finger trail up my jaw to rest on the mark on my neck, the jolt shooting through my body again. Ilyan smiled; I am not sure he could help it.

"Ilyan, what does it mean?" He only shook his head, his face confused and yet so hopeful.

"It means," Dramin began from behind us, his voice making me jump, "that the Silnỳ has come to accept what you mean to her, My Lord."

Ilyan sat up at Dramin's arrival, his face breaking out into a wide smile. Dramin returned the smile as he set down a heavily laden breakfast tray before embracing him like a brother.

"Welcome back, my old friend," Dramin said, his voice cracked. "It is so nice to see you alive and well. You had us worried."

"I highly doubt that," Ilyan chuckled, "but thank you for taking care of me and Joclyn. I cannot thank you enough."

He clapped Dramin heavily on the shoulder, however Dramin only looked at me curiously.

"So, Joclyn, is it? That is a very pretty name." He smiled and I instantly felt awkward. I hadn't realized I never told them my name. I might have been a bit too concerned about Ilyan and sights and coming wars.

Whoops.

Ilyan looked at me, his eyebrows raising in confusion.

"They never asked." I shrugged and reached out to grab a mug out of Dramin's hands in an attempt to ignore the look he was giving me.

The cup made it half way to my lips before Ilyan hollered in a panic and hit the cup hard. It sped away from me, spilling the delicious Black Water as it clattered and spun over the stone floor.

"Stop! Joclyn! Do you know what that is?" I turned to Ilyan, my stomach tensing at the panic in his face. He didn't know. I mean, how could he, he had been asleep. I turned to Dramin who was clearly trying to hide his chuckle as he chugged water from his own mug.

Some help he was going to be.

"Actually," I began, extending my hand as the mug flew back into it. I took a deep breath and placed my hand over the rim, my eyes never leaving Ilyan's as it filled. I knew there would be no easy way to tell him.

"Yes, Ilyan, I know exactly what it is." I tried to ignore my nerves as I drank from the mug, Ilyan's face melting from horror to amazement. My insides loosened and I took a breath. I had been half afraid he would react like Thom, or worse.

"You're amazing," he said, his hand moving softly up my arm.

"If you think that's amazing," Dramin chuckled, "wait until you see what else she can do."

CHAPTER 2
JOCLYN

I stood in the middle of the training hall, the three men facing me from where they stood against the far wall. Dramin bounced on his toes in eager anticipation, Thom stared off into space with his signature bored-as-hell scowl, and Ilyan looked into me with a deep-rooted mix of confusion and anticipation. Having them all watch me like that was making me uncomfortable, I had done this enough, but not with Ilyan here. His presence was making me nervous for a whole different reason.

My magic buzzed in eager anticipation, at least it wasn't nervous. I firmed my feet against the ground, took another deep drink of the Black Water, and prepared myself.

"Now, Ilyan," Dramin said, "remember, you cannot help her. As much as your body calls for you to do so, she will not be able to show you all that she has accomplished if you do."

Ilyan nodded once before turning back to me, the intensity of his gaze increasing. I felt my pulse quicken.

"Great, Dramin!" I yelled back to him, my sarcasm weakened by the shake in my voice. "Now if I mess up who is going to come to my rescue?"

Dramin laughed and Ilyan looked like he had swallowed a toad.

"What's the score again?" Thom asked as he flexed his fingers and shook his head, his dreadlocks swinging clumsily.

"Six seconds for thirty-five attacks," Dramin said with a hint of pride. I let out a deep breath and took another drink.

"Sounds good. You ready?"

I nodded in response to Thom's question and closed my eyes. My mind opened up completely, letting my mind's eye see the room in detail. The second I closed my eyes, Ilyan shifted his feet. Poor guy was getting nervous. I better make this good.

"Go!" Dramin's voice rang out in my ears and Thom rained hell in my direction.

Rather than send things flying around me as we had done in the past, he sent each and every object flying directly toward me. I hesitated for less than a breath before clapping my hands together and forming a large orb around me. The objects began to hit my shield and the fireworks started. The magical arsenals hit the barrier with an explosion, conjured objects vanished, and with one flick of my mind, I sent each of the furniture pieces back to line up along the side of the room in a neat little stack.

Everything went quiet.

"Joclyn!" Ilyan's voice was panicked from the other side of the smoke wall, but I didn't move. With my eyes still closed, I could see Ilyan barreling through the mess to try to reach me. His magic was flaring through my shoulder as he desperately checked for injuries. The second he broke through the smoke, he stopped, his eyes practically bugging out of his head at seeing me standing there unharmed.

"Four seconds!" Dramin yelled, his excitement evident. Thom swore loudly, but I was frozen under Ilyan's gaze as he slowly walked toward me.

"Don't look at me like that, Ilyan. You're making me feel like I am going to sprout an extra head."

He stopped his advance, his face breaking out into a smile rather than the oddly reverent face he had before.

"You're amazing."

"So I've heard." Now it was my turn to chuckle.

"I'm not sure you need me anymore." He was clearly joking, which was good because his words made my stomach drop to my toes.

"Haha. Very funny, Ilyan. Don't forget, I have seen the sight. I know what was said, what you said." He blanched at my bluntness, before his face broke out into a wide smile. I stepped forward and grabbed his hand, pressing it between mine.

"I know, mi lasko." Ilyan said, his finger tracing to my mark. The jolt moved through me again and I shivered.

"I heard you, too, you know. The night you came to me while I slept," he said softly leaning in so his words whispered over my neck. "I heard you."

Oh... I hadn't expected that. I blushed and moved away as Dramin came bounding up, grinning from ear to ear.

"See, Ilyan, I told you. Turn the girl into a Drak and suddenly the world opens up to her."

Dramin grinned at me, but I turned away from him still waiting for the blush to go down in my cheeks.

"It's a little weird, I must admit," Ilyan said, "the fact that she can see into my future, although the extra power is nice. It makes my job a little easier."

Ilyan smiled widely and rubbed his fingernails against his black polo like he had just taken credit for something spectacular. I glared at him and smacked his arm, which only caused him to smile more.

"Well, what do you say? Do you want to fight her?" Dramin's eyes sparkled as his voice bounced through the cave.

"I'm not sure," Ilyan said, looking me over as his magic flared through the Štít. "Are you ready to lose, Jos?"

My stomach twisted pleasantly at the use of my nickname. That made two times he had used it. My nerves melted, only to flare again at his confident smile.

He didn't know what he was getting into, I had beaten Thom twice after all. Ilyan would be much more of a challenge, but I was up for it. I knew I would at least be able to mark him without cheating, and that in itself would be a miracle.

I swiped my hand through the air. A large, ornate sword appeared, only to fall gracefully into my hand. Gone were the days of the grungy metal 'T' shape. Ilyan's eyes popped before settling into an impressed smile.

"I'm sorry, what were you saying about losing?" I knew my attempt to trash talk him was useless, but I didn't care. It was kind of fun to do.

Ilyan smiled before producing his own sword and swinging it through the air. I rolled my eyes at him.

"Magic and conjured weapons, first person to five wins unless I take you down first." I announced confidently.

"Wait. Magic and conjured weapons, Joclyn? Are you sure?" Worry built behind Ilyan's eyes, but it just made me more excited to show him what I could do.

"I'm sure. Will you keep score Thom?" I yelled back to him, but he only grunted in reply. I took that to mean yes and squared my shoulders once before attacking Ilyan. I wasn't going to hold back.

I swung my sword wide while simultaneously shooting a wave of fire toward him from the other angle. Ilyan swore loudly as he turned to stop the magical attack, my sword hitting his arm.

"My point." I couldn't restrain my glee. I had never done that before, of course, that just meant Ilyan was going to come back at me harder.

I jumped back, spinning through the air to land twenty feet away from him. I held my sword up, my head low in preparation. Ilyan froze and stared at me in awe before his jaw set, his eyes lighting up in eager anticipation.

I winked at him before exploding into the air. He jumped at the same time, meeting me mid-air where our swords clanged, the force of our collision sending both of us back. Ilyan was content to glide back down to the ground so I quickly changed directions, shooting myself toward him like a bullet, sword ahead of me. I met him as he landed our swords clanging loudly as we met blow after blow.

I closed my eyes and continued to fight him. Me closing my eyes must have freaked him out and he lost his nerve, his motions slowing. It was only for a moment, but it was enough. I swung wide, sending a strong burst of wind into him; it knocked him into my sword before he was slammed into the wall with a dull thud.

"Two points," I said as I smiled at him. He returned my smile and lunged at me, his eyes determined and dangerous.

"You're going to keep trying, Ilyan?" I asked as he swung wide, his attack blocked not by my sword but by my magic.

He didn't acknowledge the block. He continued to move, going from one attack to another as he got into his stride. Okay, so he had been holding back. He moved so fast he was a whirlwind, his magic strong as it rocked against the cave. I would have been impressed if I wasn't the one to fight him. I only had enough in me to barely match him, even with my new found power.

I sent another attack toward him and he spun away, the movement of his hair revealing tiny drops of sweat near his hairline.

"You're looking a little tired, Ilyan? Are you doing okay?" I asked lightly, he turned quickly, blocking my sword as he smiled inches from me, our swords crossed between us.

I should have known what was coming, but his move blindsided me as he twisted behind me, his arm wrapping around my waist to bring me flat against him.

"Did I ever tell you how beautiful you are?" he said softly in my ear. He released me and I spun away from him, my feet faltering. He took advantage of my stumble and hit my leg with the flat side of his sword. "My point."

"Once," I replied, not going to give him the credit of admitting his dirty trick had worked. I had done the same thing to him, after all. "Several hundred years ago. You were very sweet about it, too." I gave him a saccharin smile as I circled opposite him, watching my steps.

"Of course I was sweet. My mind was filled with images of kissing this beautiful girl I had been told I could never have." He smirked and I could have sworn the air was sucked out of my chest. Saying it like that made everything much more real.

He took advantage, swinging his sword toward me, but he was not fast enough. I jumped and swerved, my body moving faster than I had ever been able to accomplish before.

"You're right," I taunted him, trying to ignore the kicking in my chest. "You can't have her."

"Yet."

I balked in confusion at his one simple word. "What do you mean, 'yet'?"

Ilyan only smiled wider.

"I'll tell you in a hundred years or so."

"Not fair." I pouted and pushed two waves at him from opposing sides. He grabbed me and shot us up into the air, his instincts to protect me kicking in.

"You don't need to protect me here, Ilyan." I smiled before kicking hard off of his chest and sending him flying back into the wall. I spun and flipped to land carefully on the ground of the cave.

"My point," I said as I watched to make sure he was okay.

Of course he was.

Ilyan jumped up and sped toward me, his body like a bullet through the space. I threw my sword to the side, the conjured weapon vanishing into the air as I jumped before he met me, my arms wrapping tightly around his neck.

"Sorry, Ilyan," I whispered in his ear. I kissed his cheek before spinning us around and pinning him to the ground, my sword appearing in my hand and pointing right at his heart.

"I win." We stared at each other for a moment longer, his eyes holding that same fiery look of desire that I had seen before.

That same look from the sight. From this morning.

It settled in my stomach and brought all of that bubbling swirling confusion back to life.

I jerked myself away from him, sending the sword back into the air.

"That was amazing, Joclyn!" Ilyan exclaimed as he jumped up. Who knew he would be so happy to lose? He hugged me tightly before stepping away, making it obvious he was giving me space.

"Of course; you always knew she would be, Ilyan," Dramin laughed as he walked up, a reluctant Thom following him over to us. "You did see her in the sight after all, and a sight is never wrong."

He smiled and looked between us, and I knew what he was getting at, all those images of Ilyan and me. Kissing. Laughing. More kissing...

"What do you mean, 'a sight is never wrong'?" I asked in alarm, the happy feeling in my gut instantly evaporating.

"A sight is never wrong, Silný." Dramin's eyebrows arched precariously high, Ilyan looked worried, and Thom looked as though he was preparing to settle in for a show.

"Now, that's a matter of opinion, Dramin." Thom interjected, his voice hard.

"Not in the opinion of the Drak, Thom." Dramin glared sternly at Thom as he spoke.

Both men stared each other down, jaws and fists clenching. Ilyan's hand snaked around my waist protectively as he pulled me against him. I had the sudden feeling that a box of baby tigers had just been unleashed.

"He understands that, my friend," Ilyan said, Thom's scowl increasing as the tension built. "He is only talking about the few times where sights have never seen fruition."

"We do not speak of the zlomený." Dramin snapped.

"Well I am speaking of it." Thom spat, his shoulders tensing as he prepared to stand down the Drak who was drinking nonchalantly from his mug. "The sights which never came to pass."

"It is hard for a sight to be infallible when the one who gives it is being tortured," Dramin said, his face inching closer to Thom's.

"And what about the one who was tortured after? What about her?" I had only seen Thom mad once—when Dramin had given me the Black Water for the first time—and that outburst had been nothing compared to this. The air around him seemed to ripple, his dreadlocks shook, and his fists were clenched firmly by his sides.

I looked between them, their faces tight with nerves and frustration. I felt my shoulders knit together as their anger seeped into me.

"What happens when a sight is wrong and everyone dies? She should matter, Dramin!"

Ilyan pulled me into him as Thom continued to rage. I just stood in confusion.

"That is not the fault of the Drak."

"How would you know. They were victims of the same lie."

"I'd take the word of a Drak over a stubborn Prince any day," Dramin jibed, his smile falling away for the first time.

"I'm not a prince anymore, Dramin."

"And my sight is never wrong." Dramin tried to smile, but it was strained.

"Well, I hope you're right, Dramin." Ilyan interjected in an obvious attempt to break them up, although he didn't seem as worried as I did. "Because tomorrow we will find out exactly what we are facing."

"What happens tomorrow?" Thom asked, still glaring at Dramin; his anger was only barely masked.

"Well," Ilyan said. "I've been told I was asleep for three days. And if my sister has made it out of the onslaught in Prague, she will be meeting us in Isola Santa tomorrow."

"What!" Thom bellowed, his anger quickly returning. "You are bringing that bitch here? For what purpose? So that she can come here for a happy family reunion?"

"For information, Thom. She still resides under my care." Ilyan looked toward him, his face making it obvious that he was willing to stand his ground.

"You would bring her to our door? You would meet with her?" Thom shouted, his voice threatening fire and his fingers twitching with static magic. "After what she has done to me? To Dramin? She destroyed my best friend and betrayed her love. She is single handedly responsible for the murder of every last member of Dramin's family, of Joclyn's family!"

Okay, that was new. I had only heard of what happened with her and Sain. But to say she was responsible for the death of the Drak?

I looked at Ilyan, but he was focused on the others, all of them locked in a death stare. Ilyan's magic surged through my shoulder, a shield rippling out around us.

"Do we need a time out?" I asked with a humorless laugh. They all ignored me.

"You know she was tricked. She was used." Ilyan spat, his arms trying to pull me behind him. "It was not in her full control."

"To what extent, Ilyan?" Dramin spoke, his voice strained as he tried to keep it level. "Even after everything, she still fought with him for hundreds of years."

"As did Thom." Ilyan's patience was gone. He roared and I cringed into myself, suddenly wondering if I needed to get myself out of here. Ilyan must have sensed my discomfort because his hold on me increased, his breathing leveling out as he gained control. "She came to me beaten and bleeding. Her heart has been in the right place for the past four hundred years. She has proven that to me."

"Then why don't you trust her, Ilyan?" Dramin asked, the tone of his voice controlled.

"I trust her."

"Not completely." Thom's loud voice ricocheted around the cavern and Ilyan flinched.

"I have forgiven her the same way I have forgiven Thom. I must trust that." Ilyan's voice had almost taken on a pleading edge, like he was trying to convince himself of that. He had told me himself that he wasn't sure if he could trust Ovailia.

"And yet, you still dare to bring her here?" Thom stepped forward, Ilyan said nothing.

"You are a fool." It was not Thom but Dramin who spoke, his voice like venom.

"Do not say such things!" Ilyan roared, that royal tone returning to his voice. I hadn't heard it in months. I pulled away, glaring all of them down.

"Calm down. All of you." I couldn't help myself, I was yelling too. Their fury was infectious. "I'm clearly missing something, and I fully expect to be filled in later, but right now will you all calm down? You are freaking me out, and if you keep yelling like this you are going to cause a cave in."

"This cave can't collapse, it's held up by--" Dramin began, but I silenced him with one glare.

Dramin and Ilyan backed down at my request, Thom however, was fuming just as much. He stepped forward slowly, his jaw hard.

"Ovailia would happily see us dead, Ilyan," Thom began, his voice laced with fury. At least he wasn't yelling, but the firmness in his voice was nearly as bad. "You have hidden our existence from her for centuries because you yourself do not trust her, and now, you would bring her into the one place on earth we have to hide, the one place in the world that is a sanctuary. When she turns this information over to your father then where do we hide? Where do we go?"

No one spoke. I looked between the three men, my nerves accelerated as my breathing increased into a panic.

No, it wasn't a panic. It was me. I felt my head grow light, my vision blur, and I knew I shouldn't fight it. I clung to Ilyan's shirt as the Black Water took over, the sight filling my mind and my eyes burning with the embers within me.

I gasped as I saw her, Ovailia carrying Ryland out of the LaRue estate. She did not fight. She simply walked past those who should attack her. She moved quickly as she dragged him, her head held high, her nose crinkled as if she was carrying out the trash.

My voice came in a wave, the monotone sounds rippling through the cave.

"A tryst has been set in motion, one you cannot ignore. The father of the four is using his seed, one against another, and in the end none will fall until two lives are lost. It cannot be stopped. Beware where your trust lies."

My sight faded back to the cave, the three men staring at me as I stood trying to catch my breath.

Okay, so Drak power was going to take some getting used to. But right now we had bigger problems.

"Thom's right," I said, my voice thankfully back to normal as I turned toward Ilyan. "We can't trust her, Ilyan. We have a problem."

CHAPTER 3
JOCLYN

I yawned and took another long drink from my mug. It had been hours since my sight, hours since I had replayed it for all of them with Dramin's help, hours of them bickering... and they still hadn't come to a decision. The bickering had gone on and on. Part of me wished I could use my sight and then tell them what to do, but Dramin had informed me that it didn't work that way.

So I sat and drank deeply of what was now my only food source, letting their conversation roll around me as I avoided sleep, yet again. Although this time it wasn't all my fault. I highly doubted I could sleep with all the noise they were making.

"I'm telling you Dramin," Thom snapped. "If she shows up in Isola Santa and no one is there, she is going to think both of them have died."

"I don't see the problem with that," Dramin countered, his usual chuckle strained.

"There are two problems with that, old man. First, Edmund has control of the wells of Imdalind. If he thinks the Silnŷ is dead, he will do whatever he wishes with the power without fear of repercussions. I don't fancy trying to clean up that mess, do you?" Thom paused, glaring Dramin down, but the man said nothing. "And second, if Ovailia is working with them she knows every secret Ilyan has trusted her with. We don't want Edmund knowing where we are, he has been after our heads for centuries." Thom finished with a theatrical wave and sat back down on his white couch, his dreads swinging wildly.

"You are forgetting the biggest problem of all, if Ovailia is working with Edmund again, then she knows about Sain. Which means she knows that Ilyan has been lying to her," Dramin countered, he gestured wildly and spilled some Black Water which Thom glared at evilly.

"Only if she is working with my father," Ilyan countered, his words seemingly unnoticed. I wanted to remind him what I had seen, but I had done that a few times already. Ilyan was stubbornly holding out hope that Ovailia hadn't completely betrayed him. Again.

"So she knows about Sain," Thom said, his hands writhing as he stared into the fire. "If she knows about Sain, then she is going to go above and beyond the things she would normally do for Edmund, just to seek revenge."

"And with Ovailia that is the issue." I had to agree with Dramin on that. Ovailia on a regular day was a pill. I would hate to see her unleashed.

"At least we are on the same page now," Thom barked and leaned back, as if somehow their agreement had solved the issue.

"We?" Ilyan gave a harsh laugh and I almost rolled my eyes. "Why are you including me in this? I am not even sure she has 'crossed over' as you two so eloquently put it."

"Of course I am including you in this, Ilyan," Thom snapped. "You're the one who kept Sain from her for hundreds of years. If it wasn't for you then this whole mess may not have happened!"

They were talking in circles; they had, yet again, gotten themselves off topic and were focusing more on mud-slinging than the actual problem. This fight was not helping anyone.

"Oh, placing blame, are we? Don't even get me started on your little debacle at the university!"

"At least I was able—" Thom began.

"Will you guys shut up?" I yelled loudly, stopping Thom in his tracks. They all turned to me as I glared them down. Someone needed to stop them and get them back on topic, all this bickering was driving me bonkers. "Listen, what if we used the sight to our advantage? What if we made it happen by giving her a job? Something important to do for Ilyan. Then she wouldn't realize that we know... might know that she is a traitor, and then, if she doesn't know we know, she wouldn't go out of the way to do anything, but we could get what we need anyway. Besides, if she has a job, we can use it to our benefit."

"What in the wells of Imdalind are you talking about, child?"

Dramin's eyes narrowed at me in confusion. In fact they were all looking at me like I had lost it.

"Okay, so hear me out--"

"We will as long as you make sense this time." I gave Thom a look before I continued.

"In the sight Ovailia was carrying Ryland down the hall in the LaRue estate, no one was stopping her."

"Yes, yes, you have showed us this, mi lasko." Ilyan said, although he was thankfully calming down.

"Well, if she is working for them in the sight, and we assume she is now, we just ask her to get Ryland out for us now? We know she gets him out, so what if she brings him to us? It's an important job and is something that Ilyan would only ask someone loyal to him, and strong enough to do..."

"We feed her ego," Thom said, catching on.

"Then not only can she bring Ryland to us so we don't have to worry about rescuing him on our own, but she is proving to us that she is on our side, even though we know she really isn't. She will think that we believe she is, so she will also think we trust her, and then..."

I stopped; they were all looking at me like I had cats growing out of my head.

"Well, that's a brain twister if I have ever heard one," Dramin chuckled after a moment.

"Look," I continued pursing my lips at Dramin before running my hand through my gross, greasy hair. What a stupid habit to have picked up from Ilyan. "We know she carried Ryland out of the estate, and if she brings him to us then we can save him. We get what we want, and she thinks she gets what she wants. Everyone is happy; some more the others," I added softly, knowing what it would mean for Ilyan to not only lose trust in his sister but to have me back with my mate again. Not to mention the fact that Ovailia would get nothing other than double-crossed in this plan.

Which, you know, wasn't exactly tearing me up inside.

"It could work," Ilyan said softly, his hand squeezing mine.

"I know it will."

"Joclyn and I will go to Isola Santa tomorrow to meet with Ovailia. We will instruct her to get Ryland and tell her where we are going..." Ilyan stood up as he spoke and began to pace, but he didn't get very far.

"Why does she need to know where we are going?" Thom jumped to his feet, alarmed. I put down my mug on the side table; so much for calming everyone down.

"Well, if she gets Ryland, she has to be able to bring him somewhere," Ilyan argued. Thom just continued to fume.

"It's risky." Dramin remained sitting, but I could hear the uneasiness in his voice.

"Of course it's risky! Having Ovailia anywhere near us is risky! She is going to kill us!" Thom spat, the fire growing abruptly as his magic surged, causing everyone to jump.

"Tomorrow we will go to Isola Santa, we will find Ovailia, tell her to get Ryland, and tell her where we are going to meet her. We will all go there, all four of us. After all, she will soon find out you are alive anyway."

"I don't want to go anywhere; I would prefer to stay here. It's nice, warm, and claustrophobic. It suits me here." Thom sat down, his body language practically closing the deal.

"Thom," Ilyan whispered. "Please, I may need you."

The room went quiet, everyone staring at Ilyan.

"Not right now you don't." Thom snapped, jumping up again. "But when you do, you know how to contact me, and when you call me, I'll come running to your rescue. Right now, however, I am fine here." He sat down and turned away, his eyes closed as he ended the conversation.

"Thom."

"I have spoken my peace, Ilyan. I am staying here." And I thought Ilyan was stubborn.

"Dramin?" As Ilyan turned to his old friend, I felt my insides clench, I didn't want to witness Ilyan being undermined by two people in one night. I was surprised he hadn't pulled out his 'king' voice yet.

Dramin didn't answer right away; he took a long drink before lifting his eyes to meet mine, then turning to Ilyan.

"I will come with you because she will need me." His voice was darker than usual and I felt my magic spark up my spine in warning.

"Well, that was awful cryptic. Care to elaborate?" I narrowed my eyes at him. He, of course, chuckled.

"Ah, child, sometimes one's sight is for personal use alone." Dramin grinned before he continued to drink from his mug, his unfocused eyes staring at the fire. My uneasiness grew.

"I don't like how that sounds." I gave him one last stare down, but he wasn't going to budge. I knew there was a way that I could pull the sight out of his head, but Dramin hadn't taught me that yet.

I had a feeling that oversight was done on purpose.

"Well, at least now we have a plan." Ilyan sighed before he too moved to sit back down. At least everyone had finally calmed down. "Worst case scenario, Ovailia doesn't bring Ryland, betrays us all, and we are dead by morning. Best case scenario, she brings Ryland, isn't a traitor, and everyone lives happily ever after."

"Don't forget Ovailia brings Ryland, still works for Edmund, brings his army right to us and kills us all," Thom grumbled from where he was still pretending to ignore us all.

While I was happy that we were finally going to have a chance of getting Ryland back, I couldn't help feeling a sense of loss at what we were going to be leaving behind.

And who I had forgotten in this grand plan.

"What will happen to Wyn if we take Ryland?" I asked, my heart tightening. "She was their bargaining chip. You don't think they'll...?"

"They have Wynifred?" I jumped at the startling panic in Thom's voice. The guy had jumped off the couch so fast he nearly knocked it over.

"Yes? Do you--"

"Thom, we can talk about this later," Ilyan interrupted me, that thick royal tone streaming into his voice.

"But, she said..." Thom pleaded, his hand waving wildly between Ilyan and I. Okay, now I was really confused.

"I know Thom."

Their eyes locked daggers. I looked between the two of them before looking to Dramin for answers, but he wouldn't even meet my eyes.

"They will not hurt Wyn," Ilyan stated firmly. I wasn't certain if he was assuring me or Thom. "They will still need a bargaining chip to get you to turn yourself in. Without Ryland, Wyn is the best they have."

Thom nodded and sat down, Ilyan followed suit as he grabbed my hand. I looked at him in confusion. Wyn had told me that she'd never met Thom, but Thom's reaction clearly stated otherwise. Ilyan shook his head, like he thought that was enough of an answer. I would get answers later, besides it wasn't just Wyn they were holding captive.

"And what about Talon and my dad?"

"One thing at a time, child," Dramin said, his voice low and comforting. "You saw her carry Ryland, so we know she will bring him. Maybe the others will be mentioned tomorrow, but at least we know of one who will be returned to us."

I just nodded. This was war; there were always casualties in war. I already knew I was going to be one of them. My anxiety peaked at the thought and Ilyan's magic instantly moved to calm me. He looked at me out of the corner of his eye, but I ignored him.

"We will get them back, Joclyn." Ilyan leaned forward, his voice low and meant only for me. I knew the others could still hear him, but I didn't care. I was grateful for his comfort, his support. "But if we don't, please do not forget what you and I have seen. No matter what happens, I will always be there for you."

"Well then," Dramin interrupted loudly. "If that's all settled, I am going to bed. I have been awake for seventy-eight hours, and my body is a little tired. Seeing as Joclyn's eyes are dragging, I don't think she is ready to face a full two days without sleep."

Dramin stood and made his exit, his long black bathrobe dragging on the stone floor.

"More water, child, more water!" he called as he walked away toward his bunk.

"Good night, Dramin," I yelled after him before taking an obligatory sip.

"Well, if Dramin's leaving then I sure as hell don't have to be here to watch this gush fest." Thom didn't wait for anyone to say anything. He stood and strode away; his hands plunged into his pockets.

"Goodnight, Thom," I called, although I knew he wouldn't care either way.

"Whatever." He grunted as he disappeared behind the blanket he had hung over his bunk.

I watched the blanket for a moment before turning back to my Black Water, letting it warm me.

Ilyan sat silently next to me, watching me as I took sip after sip. After a few minutes, I began to feel uncomfortable, mostly because I knew he was aware of what I was doing. I took another long drink, staring him right in the eye.

"Are you ready?" he asked, softly.

Honestly, I would never be ready. I looked back to the fire and set my mug down with a gentle clink.

"After so long, you would think that I would be more ready," I whispered, not wanting anyone but Ilyan to hear. "You would think that I could plunge into the nightmares and take Cail down like a bad wrestling match. Not that I haven't tried..." We both gave a half-hearted chuckle at that.

I watched the fire, the magical flames burning and crackling in a rainbow of colors. I kept my focus on the flame, not wanting to meet Ilyan's eyes.

"But every time I close my eyes, I am still scared of what Cail is going to do to me. I'm scared of what he is going to make me witness. It's the same with the Tȍuha. I'm scared of it, too. I never know what Ryland will do to me the next time or how long he will let me stay in."

When I turned to Ilyan and extended my hand, he grabbed it eagerly, wrapping my hand in his. He leaned forward, his torso close to me as he absorbed my words.

"I wish I could control it." Ilyan's magic surged through my shoulder and I smiled.

"I understand, Joclyn, and when you wake tonight and your heart is aching and your mind is screaming, I will still be here." I leaned toward him and wrapped my arms around him, the chair awkward in between us.

"I know, Ilyan. Thank you," I whispered in his ear, surprised when he lifted me up and swung my legs up over his other arm.

"Plus, if you punch Cail in the face, I will be the first to cheer you on." We both laughed at that, the sounds echoing over the stone as Ilyan carried me to my bunk and sat me down softly, his hand sliding up to rest against my neck. His finger touched my mark and the now familiar jolt shot through me. I closed my eyes at the touch, my heart hammering, unsure of what I felt or what I wanted to feel.

"That is why I am here," Ilyan whispered, his lips millimeters from my face. "That's why I was born. I have waited the last thousand years so I could protect you."

I closed my eyes and exhaled softly, his proximity making it hard for me to focus.

"Someone has to help me hold up the world." I spoke softly, more to myself than to Ilyan, however Ilyan smiled anyway.

"Ah, you've been talking to Thom." He smiled and moved to sit on the side of the bunk. He pulled the heavy blankets over me, his hand resting softly on my knee.

"It took some doing to get it out of him, I'll admit."

"He is a very smart man. He just has a lot of pain in his heart – a lot of regret." He shook his head, his own pain pulling down his lips. It was the same frown as his brothers when I had mentioned Wyn.

"How does he know Wyn?" I asked.

"He doesn't." His eyes darted to mine, his voice strained. "He knew her mother."

"Oh." I guess that made sense, but that had been quite the reaction he had produced earlier for someone he didn't even know.

Ilyan looked at me, my eyes drooping further the longer he stared at me. Finally he shook his head and gently helped me to lie down, his hand smoothing over my hair. I was suddenly very worried that he was about to leave me.

"Sleep well, Jos." I smiled at his use of my nickname before panic set in.

"Ilyan." My hand shot out to grab his, desperate to stop him from leaving. "Will you stay with me, just for tonight? I don't mean... but I... Someone's got to celebrate with me when I wake up with a broken hand from punching Cail."

Ilyan smiled as he came back, his fingertip tracing the lines of my face.

"I'll be right here to break out the champagne."

My eyes began to droop again at his touch; at the gentle magical pulses that he weaved through my body. His finger left my face as he moved, my eyes opening as I watched him shift to the foot of the bunk, his strong arms hoisting him up to settle near my feet.

"I will stay here, Joclyn. Sleep now."

I felt his magic grow in my shoulder, the strong energy moving through me as he put me to sleep. I didn't even fight him. I gave in, letting the world of sleep and the horrors that it held take me.

"Good night, my love."

CHAPTER 4
JOCLYN

Isola Santa was a tiny tourist trap of a village in the high Alps of Italy. It consisted of one restaurant, a small hotel, and the few homes of those who worked in and ran the small businesses. Each house was made of grey brick with the trademark alleys and small walkways that were the signature of the renaissance. The whole thing was nestled up against a beautiful lake, the high mountains surrounding us on all sides.

It was exquisite. I looked around in wonder as I sat in one of the many outdoor tables of the town's café and forced down my perfectly sautéed mushrooms. I was sure to anyone else they would taste delicious, they were making my stomach turn. The crisp mountain air breezed through my hair, moving the clumps around awkwardly. I just hoped I didn't smell too bad, I didn't need many more of the tourists cringing in my direction. I had already had a few.

Ilyan looked around uneasily before his magic surged through me. Even though I could now easily manage my own shield, Ilyan wasn't going to take the risk. It was probably better anyway, I could already feel my body ache from being outside the Tȍuha so long. I should have been calm and collected in this beautiful place, but instead I was so on edge that I could barely function.

Ilyan looked as he had that night in Santa Fe. His hair was pulled back in a braid and he had aviator sunglasses on. Although his jeans were a little more ripped and dirty, it was nothing compared to the disarray I was in. My clothes were filthy, my hair greasy and matted, and I was certain that I looked like a messy beggar that Ilyan had picked up along the way.

I kept placing the Ilyan in front of me against the image of him from the sight. With short hair, his jaw line popped more.

Ilyan caught me looking at him and I looked away quickly, causing him to laugh.

"What?" he asked, his accent rolling.

"I think I like you with short hair."

I spoke my mind and instantly regretted it. His eyes widened and a smirk played on his lips as he connected where my comment was stemming from.

"Not like before, not dark. You didn't look good with dark hair."

"But short..." he interrupted me, "like in the sight."

I nodded and looked away. I didn't know why the conversation was making me uncomfortable, but it was.

"Maybe I will cut it for you," he mused, leaning in with that gorgeous smile that was starting to do weird things to me.

I ignored him and went back to staring at my mushrooms, contemplating if it was worth it to try and eat another. It had been decided that morning that it was imperative that Ovailia not find out that I was a Drak, which meant that I needed to at least attempt to force down normal food. But the taste was so bitter and the texture so gritty that I was having trouble making it look like I was enjoying it.

"Are you okay?" Ilyan asked from beside me. He sat back in his chair sipping at his wine, his eyebrows arched in question.

"I'm swell," I grumbled, poking at a mushroom. "You know, I am just chilling in a beautiful Italian village, dressed like a hobo, forcing down strange food, and waiting for your sister—who is, in a strange way, my step-mother—with the hopes of begging her to go save my boyfriend." Ilyan's smile at my discomfort grew, I scowled and decided to ignore him.

"How did I ever eat this stuff?" I asked a little grumpily, but Ilyan only laughed deeper.

"I think they are delicious." Ilyan leaned over the table and plucked one of the perfectly golden mushrooms from my plate. He plopped it in his mouth and smiled heavily as he leaned back in his chair.

"Better than a hamburger," Ilyan said with a smile.

"Ew." I cringed at the thought and Ilyan laughed harder. I rolled my eyes at him and forced another mushroom into my mouth.

"It is kind of endearing, this new side of you." Ilyan swirled the wine in his glass alluringly as he leaned in, his back arching him forward.

"Why? Because I don't eat meat now?"

"Well, there is that. It is everything, though; all of it. How strong you are, how confident, and how powerful." He was genuine, and my stomach swooped, which of course meant I chuckled awkwardly. "You're amazing, Joclyn."

My heart thumped into a restart, however I ignored it.

"At least you don't think it's creepy. The last thing I need is for you to think I'm some kind of freak."

Ilyan reached forward and grabbed my hand, his thumb rubbing over the ridges of my knuckles.

"Never, Joclyn."

"Well, aren't you two cozy." I jumped at Ovailia's voice, my aches surging through me.

Ilyan stood at her arrival, his arms wrapping around her without question.

Ovailia looked the same; perfectly poised, not a hair on her head out of place. She embraced Ilyan awkwardly, looking thoroughly out of place in jeans and a silk top.

"Ovailia!" Ilyan finally released her, but he kept a hold on her shoulders. "I'm so glad you are well. I was so worried!"

Ilyan's voice was so pained, so relieved. I felt bad. Especially given what the situation was. The planned double-crossing suddenly felt like acid on my tongue.

"You, too, Ilyan. You have no idea. When I saw them... in Prague..." Ovailia broke off, and I was suddenly worried we were going to hear a play by play of what had happened. I wasn't sure I was ready for that. I didn't want to hear traumatizing accounts of what had happened to my best friend and what she had gone through because of me.

Ilyan pulled away from her and brought up a chair, prompting her to sit down. The waiter approached and Ilyan ordered something in Italian before sitting. The entire time, Ovailia kept her face down in an emotionless mask. I couldn't take my eyes off of her, the sight of her carrying Ryland down the hall still fresh in my mind.

"Ovailia," Ilyan said as he sat down. "I need to know what happened. You have to tell me who betrayed us."

Ilyan's voice boomed with his normal, regal air; a sound I hadn't heard in quite some time. It was obvious he was putting on the front with Ovailia in an attempt to get the information he needed from her. I tensed as I turned toward her, my body stiffening in expectation of whatever truth or lie was going to spew out of her mouth

"It was Talon." I gasped at her words, her head whipping around to glare at me.

"Talon?" Ilyan asked, his voice just as stunned as I was.

"Yes," she said as she held back what I could only assume were tears. She sounded like she swallowed a frog. "I don't know how and I don't know why, but he was leading them down the hall. There were so many. I don't know if anyone else escaped, Ilyan. I couldn't find anyone else."

"No one else got out?" Ilyan asked, his voice loud in his heightened fear. The waiter jumped at his outburst as she came up behind him, placing another glass of wine and another plate of mushrooms on the table. Ilyan apologized in Italian before turning back to Ovailia.

"No one?" He repeated, his voice catching as the emotion of this new reality pushed its way up. I reached my leg out toward him from underneath the table, pressing my calf to his. He looked up to me gratefully, his eyes shining.

"I couldn't find anyone. I was too scared to stay. Father was there and I... I..." Her voice tensed to a stop and Ilyan reached out gently to take her hand.

"Why would Talon do that, Ilyan?" I asked softly, "It doesn't make sense. Why would he do that to Wyn?"

"She was screaming to her father when we last spoke with her, it must have been his call. Besides, I don't see Talon allowing them to kill her. She had to have been taken." Ilyan's logic made sense, but something still did not fit.

"But Ilyan, I saw..." I stopped myself, having been about to reveal something I had seen during my first sight.

"Oh, what would you know about it?" Ovailia snapped, her icy blue eyes digging aggressively into me. "And what in the world gives you the right to call him by his given name?"

I opened my mouth to reply, but then closed it quickly. I needed Ovailia to believe me weak and incapable still.

"Ovailia," Ilyan scolded soundly, "Joclyn is as much of a piece of the puzzle as we are now. I do not keep anything from her, and as for the name, she is free to call me anything she chooses."

He smiled at me and I looked away, placing another of the gritty mushrooms in my mouth. They were vile, but I needed something in my mouth to keep me from saying something I shouldn't.

"So, you have told her everything, then?" Ovailia asked, her voice awed. I kept my gaze away from her, fully aware that her eyes were boring into me.

"I have."

"Odd. She doesn't seem worried, and you don't seem to be as hands on as I thought you would be."

"Unless that is due to her hygiene. I had assumed you knew how to take better care of yourself, Joclyn. Though this look does suit you, it's disgusting."

Well, I needed this reminder as to why I did not enjoy Ovailia's company.

"Be polite, Ovailia," Ilyan scolded her loudly, his leg pressing against mine. "We've been hiding in terrible places since someone ratted us out in Santa Fe. There hasn't exactly been a shower available."

"And yet, you stay perfectly poised."

I ate another mushroom. It was that or yell at her that Ilyan had been unconscious for three days whereas I had been working and training almost nonstop. I hung my head forward and let the clumps of hair fall around me. I was beginning to realize why Thom had kept his hair in dreads.

Ilyan and Ovailia spoke in Czech, their tones quick and irritated, before I felt Ilyan's hand on my chin.

"I think she is beautiful," he whispered, his voice soft. My head spun, fully aware that Ovailia was staring right at us.

"Not now" I reminded him, my voice caught between pleading, worry, and joy.

"Not yet," he replied, his hand dropping back down to the table.

"And speaking of that," Ilyan mused, turning back to his sister who was looking at us with a mixture of disgust and irritation. "I need you to go and get Ryland."

"What?" Ovailia burst to her feet. The table shifted with her movement, causing most of the remaining wine to spill from the impact. Heads turned toward us at the sound and I shrunk away, well aware that people were wrinkling their noses at me.

"Sit down," Ilyan hissed, yanking her arm back down toward the table.

Ilyan's magic flared in me abruptly, his power pressing right up against my barrier as he turned his head to either side, looking for something. I closed my eyes and expanded my vision, but I didn't see anything out of the ordinary.

Although, to be fair, I wouldn't know what I was looking for anyway.

Ovailia sat down with a pout, her descent making almost as much noise as her outburst.

"Get Ryland?" she hissed, leaning over the table. "Why in the world would I want to do that?"

"Because our father has given Joclyn a one week window to save him, but she is too weak to do anything, and because I am commanding you to do it." Ilyan's voice was authoritative and far too loud. Multiple heads in the tiny café turned to us. I hoped they didn't understand English.

I saw Ovailia calculate things in her mind. Her eyes narrowed toward her brother before darting to me and back again.

"The last thing you commanded me to do, you ended up handing over your most valuable piece of information to a traitor. Why should I trust you, Ilyan? How do I know you're not feeding me to the wolves?"

The two locked eyes, their blue gazes so different, yet so similar. I couldn't breathe as I waited for her answer. I knew she would do it, but at the same time, I couldn't help thinking that I was signing Wyn's death certificate.

"Let Joclyn come with me," Ovailia finally said, folding her arms as she leaned back in the chair.

Ilyan's magic flared and I gasped as it pushed roughly against my barrier, though Ilyan didn't seem to notice. He was staring right into Ovailia, his eyes narrowed and angry.

"Why would I let you do that? Not only is she mine to protect, but I told you she is too weak to fight." Not to mention that she hated me—probably more than ever if she knew about Sain—but I wasn't going to bring that up now.

I ate another mushroom.

"She knows the interior of the mansion better than anyone. Not to mention, I am going to need her there to get Ryland to cooperate." She spoke as if it was the plainest thing, but I saw her flaw immediately. My head spun to Ilyan in the hope that he had heard it as well, however his jaw stayed tight and firm, and his gaze never left Ovailia.

"Ilyan?" I asked; ignoring the glare Ovailia gave me at using his name.

I felt his leg press against mine and I held my tongue.

"How do you know he is in the estate? They took over Imdalind, why wouldn't they be there?"

She shrugged, although she had begun to tap her toe in the air nervously, her bright red heels glinting in the light.

"I worked with him longer, Ilyan, I know his ways. Let Joclyn come with me."

"Ryland's mind is erased, Ovailia. How would Joclyn be able to help?"

"If Ryland's mind is erased, then why does Joclyn want him back so much?"

The two continued to stare at each other, neither of them spoke and I got the feeling they were very carefully dancing around each other in a game of chess. Each one was plotting their next move. Each one was tracking the movements of the other and waiting for a misstep.

"I want him back. He is my brother," Ilyan said slowly, leaning back to grab his magically refilled wine glass. "I need a pawn to play with as well. They have Wyn and Talon. I want Ryland on my side."

"That boy would kill everyone the first chance he got, including her," she said as she pointed toward me absently, her eyes never leaving Ilyan's.

"I can handle it," Ilyan said.

"Have a death wish do we?" Ovailia spoke slowly, her long fingernail pushing around one of the mushrooms delicately.

"Most definitely." Ovailia raised an eyebrow at Ilyan's affirmation, the mushroom sliding away from her touch. Ovailia seemed to make her decision and stood as Ilyan placed a small envelope on the table.

"Our next location. Bring him there." Ilyan said, his eyes turning away from Ovailia to face me.

"Stay safe, brother," Ovailia said as she picked up the envelope, placing it in her back pocket without even looking at it.

"And you."

Ovailia turned away from us and began walking down the small alley, her hair swinging as she moved.

"Oh, and Ovailia," Ilyan called out, his eyes not leaving mine. "Don't do anything that you will regret in the morning."

"Same to you." Ovailia turned and continued down the street. Ilyan's eyes finally left mine as he covered his face, leaning his head over the table.

"Ilyan?" I whispered his name, reaching over the table to grab his hand from off his face. He looked up at me, his eyes glistening.

"You were right, Joclyn. She simply can't be trusted. Just once I would like one of my siblings to stand by me. I want them to believe in something good and not to be taken in by his lies. My father only leads to hate and heartbreak." He was so sad. He had held out hope until the end, only to have his faith in his sister completely dashed.

I reached across the table and grabbed his hand, instinctively pushing my magic into him in an effort to calm him, I could feel his heart stutter and pulse as my energy wrapped around it, his muscles relaxing as extra oxygen flew to them. My actions must have caught him off guard because he looked up to me with wide eyes, his expression startled. The look made me uncomfortable so I pulled away.

"Sorry," I said softly, dearly hoping he wouldn't make me elaborate or say something gushy.

"Don't be. No one has ever done that to me. Not since my mother." His voice was so soft that I barely heard him.

"Healed you?" I asked, confused. After all, Thom had been pushing his magic into him all last week.

"Comforted me," he clarified, his eyes boring into me. I looked away, my heart pumping much quicker than normal.

CHAPTER 5
WYN

I laid on the floor of the cold dark prison under Imdalind and stared into Talon's eyes, his beautiful, brown eyes. His thumb rubbed across the skin of my hand as his other caressed every inch of the skin on my face, my neck. I wished I could move closer, I wished I could whisper in his ear, but we weren't alone. A guard paced in the dim blue light near my head, his steps the only sounds besides the deep breathing of Sain and Ryland as they remained stuck inside the blood magic. I shifted my weight and moved closer to Talon, my hands clenching his.

Talon's eyes had opened only moments after Edmund left. Cail, Ryland and Sain were still in the cell, though none of their consciousnesses were present.

I looked into Talon's eyes, my shaky finger pressing to my lips as I begged him to be silent, my eyes pleading with him to wait so I could answer everything under the protection of Sain's shield.

I could see the fear in his eyes, the terror at the first thing that I was sure he noticed. There was no magic flowing through his veins. No fire as our skin connected, and although I watched him try several times, no Tòuha for us to retreat to.

I wanted to tell him it was okay. I wanted to promise him that I was alive, and that was all that mattered, but my lips remained closed, the words trapped in my throat as we spoke with the subtle movements of fingers. A kiss—a promise. A glance—a vow. Soon, the language of touch was not enough to say what we wanted to say, so we settled into each other, content to hold hands and stare, happy to simply see each other again.

I flinched when I heard the gasp, the groan and the subtle laugh that escaped from my brother's lips as he returned to reality.

"Well, that was fun," he sighed, and Talon's hand clenched against mine. I stared at him, begging him to say nothing, do nothing, praying he would get the message and that he wouldn't even try to battle through the weakness in his body.

I lay still as I listened to stumbling feet and the grind of iron as Cail opened doors and shifted bodies around. Shackles were replaced, doors closed, and a flash of red splashed over the wall as the soul blade reflected off the blue light.

"Anything interesting happen?" Cail asked, his voice moving closer to where we lay. I closed my eyes, hoping Talon followed suit, praying that we would simply look like we were sleeping.

"No, sir."

"Good. Come along. Let's go join the bonfire and say goodbye to the last of the Skříteks." Cail chuckled, and my shoulders tightened. I didn't want to think about the end of the massacre that was occurring only a few levels above us.

I waited until I was sure that they were far enough away before opening my eyes, unsurprised at the absolute darkness surrounding us.

My fingers fumbled away from Talon's hand until I found his face. I knew what was coming, and I had an extremely brief window in which to act. My fingertips pressed into his cheek, the pads of my fingers following around his jaw until I moved him closer, pressing his face against the bars as my lips found the hollow cup of his ear. He winced at the pain that my movements had given him, his lips parting in a subtle gasp.

The pain passed, and I felt him tense, waiting for me to say something. Still I waited; this had to be perfectly timed. I didn't need to risk being heard. I waited, Talon's heartbeat pulsing against my hand as I kept my palm against his neck.

A groan and an exhale. Sain was awake.

I could count it like clockwork if I tried, but I didn't wait.

"Don't make any noise," I whispered into his ear, hoping that he could understand me, that they could count my whispered mutterings as Ryland's groans. "They beat you if you talk. I am okay. I love you."

I wished I could have said more, but my window closed as the scream of agony I had grown used to opened up through the jail. The sound echoed and grew, Sain's whispered pleas adding to the noise as Talon clung to my hand, his fear at the sound evident.

"It's okay," I said through the yells, hoping it was loud enough for Talon to hear, but no one else.

"She's okay, Ryland. No one is hurting you. You are safe. She is safe. Joclyn is safe. She loves you, Ryland. It's okay." Sain repeated the phrase continually, but I knew it wouldn't be enough. The footsteps were already approaching, and Sain's words halted as he backed away from his friend.

The grind of metal, the whimpering, the crying and the sound of flesh on flesh, I heard it all, and I felt Talon's tears as he heard it for the first time. As silence took over the cell, Ryland's breathing equalized, the whimpers leaving him and unconsciousness took over. The grind of metal repeated and then there was silence, the long silence that stretched into the black.

I clung to Talon as Ryland's breathing changed to the deep pulse of sleep. Sain joined him, and reluctantly, even I fell into sleep, the darkness giving me no other option. The brutal reality of my life gave me no other escape.

It was the first night I dreamed since I had been imprisoned. I would have expected the dream to focus on the brutal torture of the little girl, but no, it was the meadow again. The girl danced through the daisies and poppies, her dress spinning as she twirled.

I watched her as her image moved from one scene to another before it shifted to an old-style market. I fought the urge to laugh, my dreams taking me to a medieval fair. The girl ran before me, her hair laced with wildflowers as she weaved her way through the crowd, her body jumping around as if I was watching a scratched DVD.

"Mama!" she yelled happily, and my heart clenched. Her voice was beautiful, so sweet and innocent. "They have chocolate, Mama! Papa, Papa, come see!"

The image jumped. The Henry the Eighth wanna-be flashed as he smiled at me, his lips moving, but once again, no words came through. He suddenly appeared several feet in front of me, standing next to the little girl, pieces of chocolate in his hands.

Papa? Mama? That couldn't be right. I couldn't have had a child. I wouldn't have forgotten that. Why would I have forgotten that? I pushed the need to know more aside and just focused on the girl, desperate to take something beautiful with me from the dream.

"Here, Wynifred." The man was suddenly closer as he handed me a large piece of chocolate. He smiled, and I felt my cheeks turn up in a laugh. No, no laughing. I wanted to look back to the girl, but I couldn't, there was only the man. Once again, I had no control.

The vision jumped again. This time the man was by my side, the girl back to dancing in the meadow.

"We should go," he said, his voice repeating what I had already heard. This scene, those words, this imagery, I had already had this dream before.

"Go where?" my voice asked. I tried to fight the words, but they came automatically, whether I wanted them to or not.

The image of the girl jumped, her dancing moving statically as she appeared and reappeared.

"We can run." I felt his hand on my shoulder. My body turned to face him, the pleading in his eyes cutting through me, but I knew the emotion wasn't my own. I wanted to yell at him for taking my eyes away from the beautiful girl again.

"He would find us," my voice was simple, defeated.

"He will kill her if we don't."

"I know."

My vision flashed once, twice, and again and again. The images changed from the market, to the man in the meadow, a walk by the lake, and more—flash after flash.

I wanted to scream for it to stop, but I had no control over these memories. The flashes continued until I woke up, screaming.

My own voice filled the dungeon, Sain yelled something over my screams, and then Talon's large hand clasped over my mouth. He pulled me against the bars, the gritty texture of his skin and the pain of the bars against my back alerting me to where I actually was and what danger I had just put myself in. My scream stopped as quickly as it had come.

It was not my scream we had to worry about now. My yell had awakened Ryland. His animal instinct took over, and his wails filled the air that mine had so recently vacated. Talon tensed as Ryland yelled and howled. He clanged his chains against the bars and rammed his head into them repeatedly.

"Let me at her!" he screamed, the sound of the metal mixing with his panic. "Hurt... hurt... hurt..."

Talon grasped me tighter, his arms weak enough that it only felt like a gentle tug. He had heard Ryland scream before, but it had been nothing like this. Ryland's panic at being awoken had opened up into a full blown attack. His messed up brain had unlocked, and he rambled and mumbled and pleaded and yelled.

"I have to save her," he howled, his chains colliding with the bars of his cell loudly. "Protect her... I have to hurt her..."

"Leave him," I heard Sain hiss through the dark, and my tension grew. I watched what little movement I could make out, Talon's arms encircling me and holding me close to him, when a bright, yellow light suddenly ignited the prison.

The light burned my eyes, and I shied away from it, my hands moving to cover my face in an attempt to keep the light out.

"Who woke him up?" Cail hissed, making me withdraw into myself even further.

No one answered him, Ryland's continued screams ate up the sound.

"Who screamed before Ryland did?" Cail asked again, the wicked pleasure in his voice evident even above Ryland's screams.

"You hurt her," Ryland screamed through the silence of Cail's unanswered question.

I waited for the clunk of a chain, the hinge of a door. Nothing, but Ryland's continued howls filled the damp air of our prison.

Talon's fingers dug into me as he tried to move me closer to him, the bars digging further into my back at his attempt.

"What?" Cail asked, the mock disbelief in his voice unnerving. "No one is going to answer me?"

"You killed her!" Ryland roared, the metal of his cell clanging once more before his screams turned to sobs. "Killed her... she's gone... dead... dead..."

"That's all right," he trilled, the wicked pleasure dancing in his voice. "I'll find out anyway. More importantly, we have a new arrival in Prague. Did you know that?"

Ryland had all but stopped now. His sobs turned to whimpers as he rocked himself back and forth with his hands clasped through his long hair. I could hear each step of Cail's shoes against the ground as he paced in front of us, the sound blending with the gentle clicks of his tongue as he contemplated what to say next.

"Oh, yes, our visitor has just come back from seeing Ilyan *and* Joclyn." The single word woke Ryland up again.

He jumped up, his hands hitting against the bars as he lunged for Cail.

"Joclyn! Where is she? I need her! Let me kill! Love her... I love her..."

"Ovailia just saw Joclyn, Ryland, and I guess Joclyn wants you back...

do you want to go?" Cail's voice was quiet as he turned to Ryland, and I felt my entire spine solidify. No. Cail was about to succeed, he had built a weapon and now was able to let it go.

"Yes!" Ryland yelled, his voice cracking in desperation.

"What are you going to do when you see her, Ryland?" Cail asked. I curled inside of myself, not wanting to hear what was coming. "What are you going to do when you see her, when you see Ilyan's arms around her?"

Ryland's breathing picked up as Cail spoke, his breath coming in deep heavy spurts as he threatened hyperventilation. I listened as the sound of his breathing turned into yells. The word 'kill' repeated over and over.

"Good," Cail sneered, the pride at a job well done evident in his voice. "Everything is coming together."

I heard the click of Cail's foot against the bottom stair, the sound barely audible over Ryland's panic attack and continued panting. That one click clenched inside of me, my body rocking in on itself before it snapped, sending me to my feet. Talon gasped at my movement, his body too weak to follow, to defend me.

"I won't let you do this, Cail." Ryland stopped repeating his words, and Cail turned around, his dark eyes meeting mine as a sneer appeared on his lips.

"Oh? And how are you going to stop me?" We stood facing each other, Cail's dark eyes taunting me, warning me of what would come if I opened my mouth and did what I was planning. I knew better; he would do it anyway. I took the warning, magnified it, and sent it back to him, my eyes narrowing.

"I won't let you."

I could hear Talon's whimper, feel his weak fingers on my ankle, but I ignored them. For my idea to work, it had to be me against Cail. I needed to get the knife, and we needed to warn Joclyn.

"Won't let me do what?" Cail was already enjoying this game. I plowed on.

"You're going to let him go and make him kill her, aren't you?" I asked, keeping my voice as loud as possible. "You're going to chicken out and make Ryland kill her for you."

Cail moved off the step and back in front of the cells. His hand wrapped around one of the bars of the door to my cell, his face pushed awkwardly against the narrow opening as he glared into me. His lips curled, and narrowed.

"I don't 'chicken out' Wynifred. Would you like me to remind you of that?"

My heart clunked to a stop, the wretched thing forgetting to beat in its sudden panic. I ignored the pain in my chest and the desperate grab against my ankle. I ignored my better judgment and stepped forward, placing my face only millimeters away from his.

"You're weak, Cail," I spat, saying the one thing I knew would always be his trigger, the vice that Edmund had implanted him with. "You are nothing without Edmund. You can't even kill a little girl on your own."

I took another step forward, my hand extending toward the pocket of his jeans as he pressed himself against the bars, the door rattling ominously as his anger shook through him.

"I can kill a little girl, Wynifred. Or do you not remember?"

I sneered, careful to keep his focus on my face and not on what my fingers were slowly maneuvering out of the pocket of his pants and into my own.

"Can you really?" I taunted as fear and hunger shook my legs. I knew I wouldn't be able to stand much longer, but that was okay, I had done what I needed to do.

Cail's lip curled as he shook the bars, his anger so close to the surface that even he could barely control it. I wanted to congratulate myself on my accomplishment. I had pushed him to this brink several times, but before, he was my loving brother. He would have never followed through then. Now, I was his enemy; I would be a punching bag.

"Prove it."

I wanted to scream as the door swung open, his shaking body rushing into the cell. I held still, ready to take what was coming. Cail's hand clasped around my neck as he pushed me against the wall, my feet lifted off the ground as he held me there. The strong grip of his hand against my throat cut off the airflow, the blood flow, and started to cut off my life.

I heard Talon scream, and Sain plead. I heard their voices for one minute before the static took over, the blackness seeping into my vision.

It started slowly on the outer edges, but all I could do was smile. I didn't know why, but all I saw was the image of the beautiful girl. I heard Talon's voice whisper that it was okay.

As the black took over and zeroed in on Cail's face, I saw my brother, the boy who had practically raised me. I saw the soft lines of his face, the dark purple sheen of his eyes. Strangely enough, I still loved him.

CHAPTER 6
WYN

"Wynifred?" Talon's voice was soft in my ear, his hand warm against my cheek.

I moaned and tried to roll over, but my body wouldn't respond. I stayed limp on the floor, my cheek pressed into the ground, and my eyes slowly opening to the green light that Sain held in his hands.

"She's awake," Sain sighed, his voice quiet as he tried not to wake Ryland up.

I blinked, letting my eyes adjust as I looked toward Sain. The intensity of his stare scared me. I wanted to look away. I wanted to move away from that look. But I couldn't make my body do anything.

Everything hurt.

Talon grasped at my shoulder frantically, the pads of his fingers slipping on wetness and sending little pinpricks of pain down my spine.

I tried to move again. This time, my body allowed me to roll onto my back. The movement was only half managed though and I landed hard as I half fell, half rolled onto the stone. I groaned as the impact sent a wash of agony through me. My teeth clenched in an attempt to keep the pain out of my voice. I wasn't sure there was a part of me that didn't hurt.

"What happened?" I managed to squeak out, my voice catching on what felt like sandpaper lodged in my throat.

"Cail beat you unconscious after you punched him, Wyn." Talon's voice was strained, the tone rough, making it obvious he had been crying.

"I punched him?" I asked, the words barely escaping.

I didn't remember punching him. I only remembered being pinned against the wall and then blackness.

I looked away from the filthy ceiling toward Talon. He lay on the floor of his cell, his body still pressed up against the bars, a new purple bruise forming on his cheek. I wanted to reach out and touch the dark mark, but couldn't get my sore fingers to respond. Just seeing it there told me the story I knew Talon wouldn't. Talon had yelled out, pleaded with Cail to stop hurting me, and in turn, he had been beaten, too.

He looked at me with glistening eyes and moved his arm closer. His face screwed up in pain as he moved, his arm only making it halfway before it dropped to the stone, his body not strong enough to support it.

"Yeah... and then he..." Talon's voice caught, his hand still reaching toward me, not quite able to reach. "Are you okay?"

I moved onto my side and pushed myself toward Talon as I heaved myself up to sit against the bars. Everything hurt as I moved, every joint, every bone, and every inch of skin that covered my body. Pools of wetness slipped over my skin, my own blood washing over me and leaving glistening trails of bright red to swirl around the jagged lines of black.

I leaned against the bars where Talon lay, his arms wrapping around me. His lips pressed against my bare arm; wet from the tears of relief that moved down his face.

"Why did you do that?" Talon hissed, his voice panicked and weak as he leaned heavily against the bars in an attempt to be close to me. "He could have killed you, Wyn."

I cringed as I leaned my head against the bars, the simple movement igniting yet another inferno of pain.

"He's going to kill, Joclyn," I said simply, hoping that my statement would be enough to pacify him, but knowing it wouldn't be.

"And you wanted to join her?" Talon asked; Sain's chuckle strangely out of place.

"No, I wanted to save her." I cringed as I shifted my weight, a loud groan escaping my lips as I pulled the long, red blade out of my pocket. I held it up, letting Sain's dim, green light reflect off the surface, shattering a wicked prism of red around us.

"No," I heard Talon gasp, his fear and disbelief at what I held in my hands haunting.

Sain, however, moved forward, his hand grasping the bars as he tried to push through them, desperate to get through and reach what I held in my hands.

"You can go in and warn her," I said to Sain, his eyes widening as they flashed from the blade to me.

"I can't on my own," he said simply, the energy not leaving his face. "But without Cail to meddle with his mind, Ryland might be coherent enough to get the message across. He has tried before, without the blade, but it has never worked."

I nodded my head once in understanding before moving forward, my body screaming as I moved. Talon remained silent as I shifted away from him, the blade stretched toward Sain as I gripped it in between my fingertips. His hand wrapped around it, his hand encompassing it as he held it against him like a precious stone.

"Thank you, Wyn. We might be able to save my daughter now."

I nodded briefly and slowly moved back to rest against the bars of my cell, Talon's arm wrapping around me from where he lay, too weak to pull himself to sitting.

"My shield might be able to keep the scream at bay as we go in, but not as we exit. Just pray it holds."

I said nothing, I only watched as Sain lifted Ryland's shirt, moving his hand over Ryland's heart. He hesitated for only a moment before plunging the blade through, the two men screaming in unison before they blacked out, the green orb of light extinguishing the moment their screams did. I froze in the darkness, waiting for footsteps, knowing they would come eventually, but hoping the shield had masked the noise enough not to draw immediate attention.

We had no guarantee that Joclyn would be sleeping. For all we knew, it was the middle of the day and we had hours to wait. Ryland and Sain needed all the time with her that they could get.

"Please let them find her soon," I said to myself, unable to keep the thought from entering my mind. "Please don't let this have been for nothing."

We waited in silence, with no shield to give us the ability to speak and with no light to see. I shifted down to the cramped floor of my cell, letting my arm entwine with Talon's through the bars, a silent prayer for safety on my lips.

Thunk.

I felt the ripple of movement before I heard the sound of footsteps on the staircase that led down to the jail cell. The heavy tread was followed by Cail's loud voice as he sang happily while he made his way toward us. I moved away from Talon, ignoring his frantic grasping for me to stay, and shuffled across the floor to what I hoped was my original position.

Cail's voice grew louder as the light he brought with him brightened, his voice moving from song to speech as he stepped into the prison area.

"I have great news, Ryland. We get—What the hell?" He stopped mid-sentence and everything inside of me turned to ice, my heart pounding loudly in my chest.

I listened to his footsteps, to the iron grinding as the door opened, another loud exclamation from Cail and then silence.

Silence.

I waited and waited. I could hear Talon's labored breathing behind me, the shallow breathing of those on the other side of the bars and then screaming.

All three men hollered as they were pulled back to reality. Ryland screamed in agony, Sain in fear and Cail in anger. The sounds joined each other before the only scream left was Ryland's, his scream morphing into wails of agony.

"Where did you get the dagger?" Cail yelled, his voice loud and oppressive.

"I didn't..." Sain muttered as he frantically backed his way into the stone. "Ryland..." Sain's voice cut off as his body hit the rock of the wall.

"Don't lie to me!" Cail roared. Ryland's screams picked up at the increased volume of the room.

All I could hear was Ryland's screams, his mumbling pleas and the bang of his head against the bars. The sound loud, until it left, leaving us in silence.

"Sit down, Ryland," Cail commanded, and I stiffened.

Cail had reattached himself to Ryland's mind, turning him back into the black-eyed monster. I should be happy for the lack of screams, but I still remembered Ryland's cold and aggressive behavior from when we had tried to rescue him. With that one action, Cail had placed another enemy in the prison, in the jail cell right next to me.

Right next to Sain.

"Now," Cail continued, leaving a long silence and keeping his voice calm. "Who gave you the dagger?"

"Ry... Ryland," Sain panted, his voice tensed. I fought the urge to open my eyes. I really didn't want to see this played out.

"Don't lie to me, Sain! I don't like being lied to, and you have done it an awful lot recently." Cail's tongue clicked impatiently, the sound followed by the clang of a chain, the groan of defeat.

"First, you lie to Ovailia and then to us about your first vision. Last, you lied about who your daughter was. Here I was thinking I was going to get to feed you today."

"No!" Sain begged. "Please, I need water."

"Then tell me who gave you the knife."

"Ryland," Sain's said before being cut off with a loud thunk as Cail pushed him into the stone wall at the back of his cell.

"Ryland, you say?" he asked, his voice heavy in warning.

"Yes."

"Interesting." Cail's voice echoed right outside of my jail cell, followed by the creak of metal as he leaned against the bars, causing them to jerk against their joints. "Very interesting."

Sain's screams filled the darkness as Cail attacked him, but it was not an attack of physical blows. Cail was attacking Sain with magic. Sain's body jolted in pain as Cail laughed, the dry sound mixing with Sain's screams as it all echoed around the jail.

I curled up in a ball and pushed my fists into my mouth, desperate to stop myself from yelling out. I needed to fight back, to save him, but I had nothing to fight back with. I did not know if I could survive another beating. I didn't know if Sain could either. Everything tightened inside of me as guilt seeped into my heart, tense anger washing over me.

I could save him, I should. I just couldn't make my voice come. I stayed still, waiting for the screaming to stop, while dry tears seeped from my eyes. I waited for it all to end, my shoulders finally relaxing when it did.

"Don't lie to me, Sain, or I will do it again! Who gave you the knife?" Cail asked, his voice loud above Sain's gasping breaths.

"It was Ryland, I swear it," Sain begged, his voice pained.

"Then I hope Ryland can give you the water you need, Sain, because you won't be getting any from me." Cail laughed, the loud sound making me jump.

"No!" Sain roared, the power behind his weak voice surprising. "I need water, Cail, please. It has been too long."

Sain was begging, and I knew at once that Cail had won. Cail knew it, too. I could feel the change in the electrical current that flowed through the air, the oppressive mood that Cail always brought lifting slightly. I tensed; I didn't know what to do. I couldn't move. I couldn't run. I could only lay there and listen to Sain as he whimpered my name into the damp air. I listened as Cail thanked him, his voice almost passing for genuine gratitude.

I focused on breathing in and out evenly, keeping my chest from shaking, although I was sure that was impossible. Each of my ribs ached as they moved and my lungs were on fire as oxygen hit them with every breath. I listened to the methodical steps as Cail moved closer to me, the sound of the latch of my cell door unlocking, the squeak of the hinges and still I did not move. I was frozen in fear as I silently pleaded for mercy, pleaded that Talon would keep his mouth shut during whatever was to come.

"I can't say I'm surprised. It only makes sense that my pretty, little sister helped you." Breathe even. Don't rise to his baiting. Stay Still.

"N... no," Sain stuttered. I could hear the regret in his voice, the plea for forgiveness. I wanted to tell him it was all right, that I deserved it after not speaking up before, but I couldn't find the words.

I heard one tap of Cail's foot near my head and then my body flew through the air, Cail magically lifting and restraining me against the wall. I screamed as I was slammed against the wall with such force that my vision went black. The movement of my body ignited every single new injury in a pressurized pain I couldn't focus through.

My eyes opened slowly, the bright light that Cail had cast on our prison illuminating everything. My eyes burned, and I tried to look away, but Cail's magic kept me so perfectly restrained that there was no hope of moving. I stared at Cail as he came toward me, his arms folded as he sneered.

"Hmmm, say, pretty, little sister, did you help them?"

"I helped Joclyn." I met his eyes, squared my jaw and locked my eyes with his, wishing he would back down as I fought the shiver of fear that wiggled its way up my spine.

"It was Ryland," Sain gasped uselessly from his cell, his guilt making him take a regrettable back step.

Please don't, Sain, don't push him. I could see it in Cail's eyes; he was going to take everything out on me.

For one split second, his face softened, his hand moving up to cup my face. Then it was gone, the gentleness I had seen before leaving as the hand on my cheek turned into a slap.

My arms flew above my head as his magic whipped through me, my shoulders stretched painfully as the shackles wrapped themselves around my wrists and the chains lifted until my feet left the ground. I felt my big toe release from the ground just as Cail's magical restraints left me; leaving my shackled wrists to support my own weight. I refused to scream, even as my body weight pulled against my shoulders and the heavy metal cuffs cut into my wrists.

"Leave her alone!" Talon's weak voice echoed around the stone walls, making him sound much stronger than he actually was.

"Talon. No." My head snapped up at the sound of his voice, my eyes opening at him, pleading with him to just lie down and stay out of it, to save himself.

I knew he wouldn't.

He was slowly attempting to pull himself up, but his arms gave up halfway, sending him down to the ground. Cail moved away from me to squat down in front of Talon, the large, slimy bars of my cell the only thing between Cail and my husband.

"I guess I need to teach you a lesson, too." Cail didn't even move; he stayed squatted with his hands hanging limply in front on him when Talon started to scream.

"Leave him alone, Cail!" My back arched as I screamed and tried to fight my way toward him, sending my body bouncing against the stone wall, my screams changing to my own agony at each impact.

Talon screamed as his body shifted on the ground, his weak muscles not giving him an option to fight back. Cail was hurting him without skin contact. I didn't want to start thinking about what else he might be capable of. I knew it wasn't his own magic he was using there—it was Edmund's. And Edmund was capable of just about anything.

Talon's screams died, and Cail's eyes widened.

I froze, my eyes stuck on my husband and on the limited movement in his chest.

"Talon?" I gasped, not caring about the consequences.

I stared at his chest, at the stillness of it. I couldn't tell if he was breathing or not.

"Talon!"

"Shut up, sister!" Cail yelled as he pulled himself back to standing. "He's only passed out. I wouldn't kill a perfectly good body, not when there are so many other chances to torture him."

He looked at me and smiled. I tried to control my breathing, I tried to settle down and scowl at him. I wanted to show him that I wasn't afraid, but I couldn't. For the first time, I was scared.

"Well, it looks like my work here is done," Cail said as he strode out of my cell, leaving the door wide open.

"I'll go get your reward, shall I, Sain? Be right back." He spoke like a friend, but his words were more of a warning than anything.

I watched him as he left, leaving his light behind to brighten the disgusting prison we were trapped in. My shoulders were on fire, and my head was spinning slightly as my body attempted to give into the pain.

Please let it give in soon.

CHAPTER 7
JOCLYN

I walked into the cave late the next day feeling clean and refreshed, if not a little awkward. In the last four months I had been trained to fight, lost a battle, chased by my boyfriend, beaten by my best friend's brother, and attacked by all of the above. So, when Ilyan had taken me to a nice hotel after our unfortunate encounter with Ovailia I had gone right to the shower. It had been amazing to have running water and cotton sheets, maybe almost normal. Almost. My life wasn't normal anymore; it felt odd to have normal things.

It had taken two hours to clean the obscene amount of dirt off of me, only to get out of the shower to a perfectly folded pile of clothes. I had breathed in the fresh smell and rubbed the cotton against my skin, thankful for something clean to wear. Who would have guessed that I would ever feel so much joy over a simple pair of khaki pants and a blue t-shirt?

I put them on and ran out to thank Ilyan who then convinced me to let him braid my hair. He had done it so gently, his finger rubbing over my mark as he braided. Each time sent a jolt up my spine.

So, when I walked into the cave, hair pulled away from my face, my mark revealed, and Ilyan's hand was wrapped firmly around mine; I felt the cleanest, most awkward Drak in existence. We walked in to find Dramin holding two large mugs. He handed one to me and I grabbed it greedily, thankful for his preparedness.

"You wouldn't be so needy if you would go into your Tòuha when you are supposed to." Dramin said, his scold lost amongst his chuckle.

"Don't judge me, Uncle," I growled between gulps.

"Next time you take her anywhere, Ilyan, remember a mug. This poor girl is ravenous."

"It wasn't worth the risk," I said as I came up for air and refilled my mug. "I am sure Ovailia would have found out." Another gulp. "And we don't want that."

"Yes, starvation is always more preferable."

I moved the mug away from me to scowl at him, but Dramin only chuckled more while Ilyan smiled down at me before placing his arm around my waist and leading me right to the same squishy arm chair I had been using for the past few days.

"Ah!" Thom yelled at us as he came around his bunk's partition. "You're back! And alone I see."

"Were you worried, Thom?" Ilyan asked as he covered me in several furs before turning to his brother and embracing him, fists pounding on backbones.

"I was."

"Well," Ilyan announced as he pulled away and moved to a large table laden with fruits and leaves. "You didn't need to be. You were right."

Thom stopped in mid-sit, hovered for a second and fell onto his couch in shock.

"So she is a traitor then?" Thom said excitedly.

"Yes. Perhaps." Ilyan said, causing Thom's excited face to drop dramatically. "I am still not convinced about that." I turned to him, Ilyan hadn't said anything about this to me last night.

"But you just said I was right." Thom was already getting wound up. I rolled my eyes and went back to my mug. I was going to need more information about what Thom had against Ovailia, because this fight clearly wasn't going anywhere.

"And you were. She can't be trusted. I am sure she is working with our father." Ilyan's voice was heavy, his heartbreak at the news still evident.

"Yet, somehow not a traitor?" Dramin spoke, putting words to the confusion we all felt.

I looked up at Ilyan, my eyebrows raised nervously; I had a feeling about where this was going, and I didn't like it.

"No," Ilyan said, his eyes meeting mine with deeper sorrow. "Joclyn, you told me you saw my father with Talon in your first sight."

And I was on my feet. Screw the pain in my joints, I had a dog in this fight now, and I wasn't going to back down.

"She wasn't telling the truth, Ilyan. She was lying to you to throw you off the trail." I pleaded with Ilyan as he returned to the fire with a small stone plate covered with what I could only assume to be dandelion leaves.

"I'm not so sure of that." The regal tone was creeping into his voice, but I just balled my fists.

"You have to be. Talon had nothing to do with this. He wouldn't have done that to Wyn."

"Talon?" Dramin and Thom's voices blended together in differing levels of alarm. I ignored them, still glaring down Ilyan.

"There is no reason for him to side with Edmund, Ilyan." I reached for his hand, plunging my magic into him. I wanted to believe he was blaming Talon to try and take the blame off of Ovailia, but I knew it was deeper than that.

"The Silnŷ is right, Ilyan. Talon has no reason to double-cross you." Dramin said, but I wasn't sure Ilyan even heard him. His eyes never wavered a millimeter from my own.

"The sight, Joclyn. Show me the sight."

I sighed before closing my eyes and pushing that portion of the vision into his mind again.

Edmund held Talon against the wall, his hand tight around his throat. Talon's face was bloodied and battered.

"Give me what I need, Talon," Edmund's voice rang out like an echo in my ears just as it had last time, though this time it had a longer, tinny sound that signified a sight of the past.

"You better make it look good, Edmund," Talon let out a deep chuckle, which echoed around my head. I pulled the vision back, not wanting Ilyan to see too much. Ilyan's face swam back into view, his jaw set hard.

"I can't be..." I couldn't finish. I knew what it looked like; I had known from the beginning. I had always assumed that it was just Talon egging him on because it had seemed like something he would do. At least I thought it was.

"I do." The look of ultimate betrayal on Ilyan's face mixed with furious anger in a way that terrified me.

"Wait," Thom said loudly, "Talon is the traitor?"

Ilyan nodded once.

"How is that even possible?" Dramin said. It was obvious no one except Ilyan believed this line of thinking.

"I'm not sure, but I will figure it out," Ilyan replied.

"I can't believe it; he wouldn't do that to Wyn," Thom began, his body leaning forward as his dreads shook. "Talon doesn't make any sense. Ovailia, however, does."

"I will give you that, Thom. If it is not Talon, then it is Ovailia."

"Really?" Thom's voice hit an octave that I wasn't sure was possible for him.

"Now you're surprised. You were sure of her guilt forty-eight hours ago," Ilyan laughed.

"Oh, you misunderstand, Ilyan. I am not surprised she is a traitor. I am surprised that you are admitting it."

"Only partially," Ilyan admitted and sunk into his chair.

"So did she agree to it?" Dramin asked, heading off the bickering. "Is she bringing Ryland to us?"

"She did," Ilyan said confidently. "Not without revealing her true nature, but she agreed to do it."

"So, she's a traitor," Thom said happily. I was already sinking back into my chair. Nothing about this was sitting right with me.

There was no way Talon could have betrayed Ilyan. Sure, I didn't know him well, but I knew him enough. There had to have been something in the sight we were missing.

"So she knows about Sain?" Dramin asked, leaning forward.

"Without a doubt. If she is working for Edmund, then he has shown her. Especially if he is hoping it will fuel the fire of her anger against me." Ilyan's voice was firm.

"Oh, she must hate you," Thom taunted, his feet moving back and forth in joy.

"And yet, you do not think she is the one who betrayed you?" Dramin asked, his eyebrow raising as he ignored Thom.

"You have seen Joclyn's sight, Dramin. You know what it looks like." Ilyan's voice was tight and strained. He leaned forward in the chair as he pleaded angrily.

"I have." Dramin said calmly as he sipped at his Black Water. "But sometimes things are not what they seem. You know this better than anyone. Do not discount one, simply because you hope for another."

"I agree with Dramin." I said quickly, my back creaking as I sat up. "Ovailia knew about the house. She tried to get me to come with her." Thom was back on his feet at that. "This isn't really up for debate, Ilyan."

Ilyan gave me a pained look before he exhaled deeply and sat back against the chair, his jaw tight. I had never seen Ilyan like this. He was so angry and betrayed. I reached out awkwardly and placed my hand against his cheek.

"You are not alone." A weight seemed to lift off him as I spoke.

"Not anymore," he repeated, his hand covering mine. I suddenly felt very awkward and tried to pull back. But I couldn't move.

"So," Dramin spoke loudly in an attempt to pull focus. Thom was staring at us with the tiniest of smiles and my stomach sagged to my toes. I resisted the urge to hide underneath my furs for a while. "Where is she bringing him?"

"The Rioseco Abbey."

"In Spain? The same one..."

"Yes." Ilyan cut him off in an obvious attempt to stop him from saying something.

I looked at Ilyan curiously, begging him to elaborate, however Ilyan only shook his head. Unfortunately, the exchange did not go unnoticed.

"Tell her, Ilyan," Thom moaned as he sat up on his couch. "Deep inside she wants to kiss you anyway, so you might as well let her know when and where it's going to happen."

I froze, an onslaught of images from the sight ramming into my brain. Not yet, maybe not ever. I repeated it to myself, although I couldn't ignore the excited heart slamming I was experiencing. My breathing picked up before Ilyan's magic surged into me, calming me almost instantly.

"Not yet." Ilyan spoke quietly in an effort to calm me. It worked until Thom spoke again.

"Get it over with, brother! Kiss her! You almost did. We just watched you!"

"Thom!" I hissed, sure I had turned and unattractive shade of red. "Shut up!"

"Not until he tells you, and trust me when I say I can keep this up all night." Given the look on his face, I didn't doubt it.

"You're right, Thom," Ilyan said, his voice light as he stood, already walking toward his brother. I froze. "Would you care to practice with me?"

"I would love to," Thom was already on his feet, something Ilyan clearly wasn't anticipating. I had never seen him go so white.

I couldn't help it, I laughed so hard that I squeaked. They all turned to look at me and just laughed harder.

"Now, now boys," Dramin said with a smile. "You can battle it out in the hall in a little while, goodness knows you need a bit of a testosterone release, but now is not the time."

"Next time, brother." Thom huffed dramatically and put his feet back on the couch, his hand moving to rest behind his head.

"If you do, I want to watch," I said, the thought of them battling out their manhood was almost too good to pass up.

"Kiss or fight?" Thom asked, already back up.

"Fight!" I squeaked before Thom got any more ideas. I don't think I had ever seen him this light. It was endearing.

"You can join in, too, Joclyn," Ilyan teased as he popped a berry into his mouth.

"In the kissing or the fighting?" Thom teased, even Dramin was laughing now.

"No, thank you," I laughed as Ilyan turned to me and winked. I looked away, as my stomach began to do its usual somersaults.

"Why not?" Thom said, sitting up. "You can be on my side. Together we can take him."

Thom rammed his fist into his open palm and I almost choked on the Black Water I had just swallowed.

"Number one," I sputtered as I tried to clear my throat, "I have already defeated him on my own. And number two, I can probably take both of you with my eyes closed, thank you very much."

Both Ilyan and Thom stared at me open-mouthed as if I had seriously undermined their manhood while Dramin only laughed.

"Of course you can take them with your eyes closed, Silnỳ, your mind's sight is better than your vision."

"Is that a challenge?" Thom said, standing up as if Dramin hadn't even spoken. "Ilyan and I can beat you!"

"I'm not joining in on this," Ilyan said, already backing down.

"Don't be a chicken, brother. You are doing this with me."

I knew Ilyan wasn't one to back down from a challenge, he was declining for reasons that I could feel pulse through my spine as I tried to shift my weight.

"Maybe tomorrow," I said and twisted in an effort to relieve some pressure. Ilyan's magic flooded into me more.

"Tomorrow? I say now!" Thom had obviously been a little too cooped up in here.

"I'll spar with you tomorrow, Thom, I promise" I said from behind, Ilyan, who had gone into full protector mode at Thom's outburst. "I'm too weak today."

Ilyan turned, his body dropping to my level, his face instantly concerned.

"Is it too much? We can do it today." I smiled at how he instantly knew what I was talking about and at his willingness to fix it. I felt his magic surge as he tried to repair any current damage that was being done to my body.

"Not today," I cringed. "I can wait one more day."

"Are you sure? It's already been two days." Ilyan asked, his finger tracing down my neck. I jumped involuntarily when the shock sped down my spine at Ilyan's contact with my mark.

"Yes," I said somewhat breathlessly. Ilyan smiled at my reaction.

"Let me know if you change your mind."

"Ugh!" Thom groaned loudly as he flailed around on his couch in obvious frustration. "Will you two get a room? With a door?"

I blushed and looked away. Ilyan stood and moved away from me to stand before Thom, the two beginning to fist fight each other playfully. Dramin took a long drink of his Black Water while I did the same as I sighed and sunk into the chair.

I watched the two men fight, their odd banter bouncing back and forth as they jumped around the large space. Dramin chuckled at their play. I sunk back further, and before I knew it, I had fallen asleep.

My eyes opened to Ryland standing alone in the middle of the clearing.

"Jos." He whispered my name before running to me, his body strangely strong and whole again. His dark curls bounced as he came to me, his bright blue eyes cutting into my soul.

"Ryland?" I didn't dare hope, but right then I was so happy to see him after everything that he had said before that I needed to know.

I opened my mouth to ask if it was really him, but I never even got one word out. His lips covered mine as he pressed into me, encompassing me with a kiss I could have never imagined would come from him. It was deep and needy in a way that made my toes shake. I sighed as a spot deep inside my belly spun with joy.

He pulled away, his eyes gazing deeply into mine. His look was suddenly desperate and panicked.

"Ryland?" I asked, growing worried.

"You know I love you, right?" he asked, his eyes darting frantically over my face. "More than anything?"

"Yes," I answered breathlessly.

"And you know I would do anything to save you, to protect you. Right?" My veins turned to ice. I didn't like where this was going.

"Ryland?" I asked, not willing to give him the answer to his question.

"Break the connection, Joclyn. Now. Have Ilyan show you how. Do it the second you wake up." He grabbed my hands tightly and pulled me down to the forest floor, my knees crunching against the dead leaves.

"Ryland, why are you asking me to do this?" I could barely get the words out, my throat felt so tight.

"It's the only way to keep you safe, Jos. I should have never completed the Zêlství. I thought I was strong enough, I thought I could..." He shook his head and looked away from me. "I thought I was right for you. But I knew I wasn't. I just... you're my best friend."

"Ryland?" I didn't know where he was going with this.

"You have to break the connection, Joclyn. Hide the necklace. All of it. Don't wait."

"I can't. Ryland... I can't." I clung to his hands tighter, pulling him into me. "I need you."

"No, you don't!" he yelled loudly, his voice reverberating off the trees. "I can't save you. I can't protect you. I never could. It wasn't my place."

"Ryland," my voice was a squeak, my heart thumping wildly in my chest.

"You have to break..." He stopped and his eyes went wide as his gaze strayed somewhere beyond me, the panic evident on his face. I went to turn, terrified at what I might see, but Ryland forced me back to look at him. Quick footsteps were coming up behind me; a hand grabbed my hair and pulled me to standing.

"Break the connection, and don't go in..." Ryland's voice was silenced in my ears as I felt a body behind me at the same time a knife was thrust against my throat. Cail's wicked laugh echoed through my head before I woke up clutching my neck. My breathing came in sharp, panicked spurts, but I did not scream.

I stared at the roof of the bunk I had obviously been moved to as I waited for my breathing to calm, my mind playing Ilyan's song for me inside my head. I listened to it until the panic was gone, most of the vivid images of the nightmare fading into the netherworld that existed between sleep and waking. I curled into Ilyan's chest—partially wondering why he was already in my bed—before I drifted off to sleep again

CHAPTER 8
WYN

"Is he all right?" Sain asked, his voice a whisper. I gaped at him, shocked he had the balls to say anything, and risk them coming back down to hurt us. Not like that mattered anymore.

"Yes."

I could see the gentle rise and fall of Talon's chest, so slow it might not have been there at all. My heart rate picked up, the sharp staccato overriding the pain in my body. *Please just be knocked out. Please.*

"Are you all right?" Sain whispered from the other side of the jail, the regret I saw in his eyes earlier just as heavy in his voice now.

I was beginning to hate that question. I hated what it meant. I hated that it was the first thing we asked one another. I missed asking someone how their day was, or even talking about the weather. God, how I missed talking about the weather.

I didn't answer Sain. I rested my head against the rock wall, my arms tight against the skin of my cheeks.

"It will be soon," Sain said, and this time I looked at him. Something about his voice was different.

"What will be soon?" My voice creaked in worry, the muscles in my throat burning as I forced air through them.

"When that life is lost, there will be a moment when you can do anything." His voice was strangely deadpan, his eyes focused on Talon and not on me.

"Sain?" I asked, ignoring the throbbing of truth that was burning through me. His words seeped into me and rattled my bones with a sob that wouldn't leave. I pushed it to the side. I locked it away as my pride, and my fear, took over.

"No, Sain," I pleaded, not wanting him to continue.

"Follow the light, and you will escape. Follow the pain, and you will die."

"Sain! Stop it!" I screamed at him, not caring if I was heard, not caring what beating might follow. I just wanted Sain to take his words back. I didn't want to hear them.

Sain turned his head to me, his hands wrapped around the bars as he looked at me with dark eyes. I barely made out the crinkle of a smile before footsteps thundered down the stairwell.

My father bolted down the steps and right into my cell, right to me. His hand collided with my jaw, dark eyes staring into me wickedly. He was daring me to challenge him, daring me to speak back, glare, anything. I couldn't. I couldn't see beyond the blinding words Sain had just unleashed on me. They leached out of the air like a poison and zapped all the fight out of me.

"Good girl," Timothy said, his lips turning up. He raised his hand and the chains that suspended me loosened, my body dropping to the ground as much as the chains would allow, leaving me in a weird squat that was almost worse.

"Don't cause any more problems," Timothy spat as he walked away, just as more feet and voices echoed down to us.

"Oh God, what is that terrible stench?" Ovailia's icy voice cut through the air, adding to my fear.

"The smell of fear and oppression, my dear," Cail said, laughing as he walked back in. Ovailia, Edmund and one of their guards followed him in.

My father turned at Edmund's arrival, bowing slightly as Edmund surveyed the prison. I stared at Edmund, knowing that defeat was evident on my face, knowing it didn't matter anymore.

"Lovely," he said, his voice stiff as he tried not to inhale. "I think you two have done a wonderful job."

Edmund paced in front of us, his hands clanging each of our cells as he moved past.

Ovailia followed her father, Cail right beside. As she moved past me, I caught her gaze. I didn't care that everything hurt, that I couldn't fight her. I gave her my biggest grin.

"You're looking well, Wynifred." She smiled, and Cail laughed at her taunt before grabbing her hand and dragging her to the cell against the far wall.

To their true prize.

"Hello, Sain," she said as she kneeled down before Sain, the sharp points of her high heels stuck out precariously, the glistening of the black leather caught in the low light. I looked at the shoes, wishing I could grab just one of them. It would make a spectacular dagger.

"How are you doing, dear? Did you miss me?" I could hear the laugh in her voice, the taunt, but Sain only smiled, his eyes crinkling in joy.

"I never missed you, Ovailia." Even I could hear the lie and the heartbreak that his voice held.

"You never were a good liar, Sain," Ovailia sneered. "I have a gift for you."

Ovailia lifted her hand, and the servant that had followed them down put a large, brown mug in it. She lowered it down so that Sain could see, and he jumped, his body pressing against the bars. Sain's chained hands reached for it, his desperate fingers unable to gain contact.

"Water," he gasped, the need revealing a primal urge that I hadn't been aware he possessed. I watched as he grasped for the mug, his fingers reaching as Ovailia's smile increased.

"Thirsty, are we?" she asked, and the men behind her snickered.

"Calm down, Sain," Edmund said, he was almost bored. "You know our deal."

The old man backed down, his chains grinding against the floor as he retreated to the corner of his cell.

"What would you have me see?" Sain asked, his voice distanced as he recited words I was sure he had said a million times before.

"Ilyan wants Ovailia to give him Ryland," Edmund said. I moved against my chains, trying not to call attention to myself, but wanting to hear everything. "We need to know if the boy is ready for the job we have prepared him for."

Sain nodded once in understanding and then Cail swung the door to his cell open, letting Ovailia walk in with the mug in her hands. She walked right to him, her heels clicking as she spat in the mug, her saliva dripping down the inside wall of the cup before she handed it to him with a wicked smile. He clenched it greedily, his fingers shaking as he held it against his chest.

"Not yet, Sain," Edmund said as he, too, stepped into the tiny cell. I could barely make out Sain from behind the forest of legs between us.

I watched in silence as Edmund took out a tiny silver dagger, cutting his daughter's finger and then his own, adding their blood to the mug before stepping out.

"Don't you want to try some, Ovi?" Sain asked, causing Ovailia to turn, her heels clicking to a stop.

"I never did, Sain," she sneered, folding her arms, her hair swinging as she glared at him. "I only told you that so you would think I loved you." She smiled and exited the cell, thinking she had won, but I could see the crinkle around Sain's eyes.

"You only lie to yourself to decrease the hurt, Ovi. Don't deny what you have felt for me."

Ovailia turned to lunge at him, but three pairs of hands held her back. Sain had already pressed the mug to his lips and was drinking deeply of the disgusting mixture of saliva, blood and Black Water. He drained the mug quickly, resting his head on the wall as he sighed in appreciation.

Sain opened his eyes, the large orbs of green now the purest black, the very center glowing with the red heat of a fire before extinguishing to deep black like the rest. I gasped. I tried not to, but it came out anyway. Thankfully, no one looked my direction; no one seemed to hear.

Sain had opened his mouth, a deep moan releasing before he began to speak, the deep, unnatural sound I had heard before taking over his voice. "Two men stand, one will fall. Blood will drip. The game is played, and those with the most pawns will take the stage. Take your man and play the game, but be careful where your trust is laid."

The same deep groan filled the halls as his voice faded out, his keening continuing as the voices of our captors overlapped each other, trying to decipher the sight.

I didn't hear them; I didn't even try to break words out of the mess of sound. I just stared at Sain, his eyes now back to their usual bright green. I wanted to make sense of the stories in those eyes. I wanted to hear the explanation and know what he had seen behind the black. He only stared, the sadness telling me all I needed to know. He had seen something, and it wasn't good.

"Stop." Edmund's lone word broke through the bickering, and my focus went right back on them. "If I send him, I could lose him. That was always an option. I don't think Sain's sight says that however. Cail has used the same terminology about pawns with Joclyn, this is a chess game, and it is all about foresight. The pawns are certainly in our favor."

Edmund turned and looked over each of us, his eyes lingering for a moment on mine, the only one of the captives who stared right back. He smiled, the hatred in his face looking through me, as though he saw someone else. I could see the need to control me in his eyes, the same look he had in my dreams as he hurt the beautiful child. No one should be able to hold that much hate in their heart.

I looked away as he smiled, wishing the conversation would just end, and they would leave us, taking the suffocating hate with them.

"But, Master," Cail said, "it also said one would fall. What if that one is Ryland?"

"Then let him fall," Edmund hissed, Timothy laughing at his outburst. "He was always just an expendable piece of property."

"Is he strong enough?" Ovailia asked as she walked up to his cell, bending at the waist to get a better look at Ryland. "He doesn't seem to be doing much."

"Cail is controlling him, Ovailia," Timothy said, his hands writhing together in excitement.

"What can he do?"

"Turn him off, Cail," Edmund said. I stiffened, knowing what would come after, my breath catching in my throat for one solid minute before I was able to pick it back up. "Let my daughter see what all of your work has done for us."

"Thank you, Master," Cail breathed, his voice awed and humbled. He bowed slightly before moving forward, his hands wrapping around the bars of the cage.

I couldn't look away from Ryland, from the calm way he sat until the first whimper escaped his lips, his hands already moving to claw through the air around his head as the hold Cail had on Ryland's mind dissipated.

"Joclyn," he moaned, the grip of his fingers increasing as he began to rock back and forth, his mumbling increasing.

"This is your weapon?" Ovailia asked. "A weeping child?"

"No, Ovailia, it's what the weeping child does that is the weapon." Edmund smiled and clapped Cail on the shoulder, his action making him look like a proud father. "Go on, Cail."

"Ryland," Cail taunted, "Ovailia's here. She saw Joclyn."

Ryland looked up, his whimpers turning to a howl as he stood and rammed at the cage, his voice opening up into a wail that only increased as Cail went on. I pulled against my chains, I wasn't scared of Ryland, but I didn't know what Cail had planned for his little show-and-tell, and that worried me.

"Joclyn?" Her name was a groan on Ryland's lips, his hands gripping the bars in front of him so tightly that his knuckles had turned bright white.

"Yes, Ryland. They had a nice dinner together, and do you know who else was there?" Cail asked, turning to Ovailia who smiled broadly and stepped up to the bars.

"Ilyan was there," she said simply. Ryland's grip tightened as he yelled, slamming his head into the bars over and over again.

"Yes, Ilyan was there, Ryland," Cail continued, raising his voice enough to be heard above Ryland's yells. "He was holding her hand and touching her face."

Cail stopped as Ryland's howls opened up, his body pulling against his chains repeatedly as he tried to get through the bars to them. Cail smiled as Ovailia squealed with joy, her hand hitting the bars loudly in an effort to excite Ryland, his howls getting louder.

"He kissed her hand, Ryland," Ovailia said, her icy voice eager to jump in on what she obviously viewed to be a wonderful game. "He traced her lips with his finger. He touched her neck—"

"I'm gonna kill him!" Ryland howled, his voice rising with every beat of Ovailia's hand against the bars. "I'm going to make her pay!"

Edmund stepped forward to view his son better, his eyes full of pride as he watched his own flesh and blood writhe with torment and agony. "Perfect. I never thought I would say this about him, but he is perfect. If he cannot fight beside me, then I will use him as a weapon. With the power he has, and his lust for Joclyn, he is the perfect weapon."

Edmund reached through the cage as Ryland continued to fight to get at them. His hand ran along his son's face, a wicked gleam shining in his bright blue eyes.

"Are you going to go kill your brother, son?" I froze, my eyes flashing to Sain who looked just as shocked as I felt.

"I'm gonna kill him!" Ryland howled, his head knocking against the bars. "Kill... kill... kill..."

"And what of Joclyn?" Edmund asked, his hand leaving his son's face to curl around the chain that attached to his wrist. "Are you going to make her pay? Pay for hurting you?"

"Hurt her!" Ryland howled, his fingers clenching and unclenching in a halo around his head. "She's hurt me... hurt... she's gonna hurt..."

Ryland hit his head repeatedly in his agony, and the group in front of him laughed.

I couldn't watch anymore, I couldn't. I couldn't watch the beautiful boy who had been destroyed by his own family and turned into a weapon against the only person he ever loved, the only person who had ever loved him back.

I tried to drown out the sounds of his suffering, the sounds of his torment, but they kept coming. Ovailia's squeals of joy, Edmund's chuckles of pride, and Cail's constant taunts broke through the general cacophony.

I wished I could cry. Ryland needed someone to mourn over what he had lost, what he could never get back. I wished I could do that for him; there weren't many left who would.

"Let's finish this," Edmund announced and the iron-barred doors opened simultaneously, the grind of the metal closely followed by the clatter of chains.

"Are you ready to go kill your mate, son?" Edmund asked, the chains rattling as Ryland was led, writhing and screaming, out of the prison and up the stairs.

"Kill!" Ryland screamed. "She... she has to pay!"

"Come on, Sain," Ovailia spat, her voice so full of hate I could taste it on my own tongue. "I want to show you what I should have done to you in the first place."

"I hold no hatred for you in my heart, Ovi," Sain said calmly as he stood.

"Don't call me that," Ovailia snapped as she led Sain out of his cell, his hands still shackled and chained.

"I am happy to see your love life has improved," Sain said, his voice light, as if he was talking to a long lost friend and not his former lover. "Cail is a much better match for you."

"Anyone is better for me than you were." Ovailia turned on him, her finger sparking as she shoved one long-nailed pointer in his face. I would have expected Sain to flinch away, but he stood still, his eyes focused on her and not the warning that flared only millimeters from his face.

"I quite agree; Angela Despain was a remarkable woman."

Ovailia's finger sparked; her face hardening as she jerked on his chains. His torso jolted down until her finger pressed against the skin between his eyes.

"Leave my love life alone, Sain."

"Then leave my daughter alone," he replied. Ovailia released her hold on Sain's chains. I would have assumed the strength in Sain's voice to startle her, but I knew better.

"Haven't you been listening?" she asked, moving her face closer to him. "Ryland is going to take care of her for us. Well, after he kills Ilyan anyway."

"We'll see," Sain whispered, his calm voice not missing a beat.

"You act like you actually control your sight, Sain." Ovailia laughed at the idea and left the cell, dragging the old man behind her.

"Oh," Cail scoffed once the sound of Sain's chains had ebbed away to nothing, "I almost forgot."

He laughed and threw something at me as the light began to fade. I stared at the loaf of bread he had tossed into my cell, unable to move toward it, my stomach rolling with need.

"Bon appétit, Wynifred," Cail spoke from the steps, his body already disappearing around the bend in the stairs. The shackles around my wrists opened, sending me tumbling down, and I landed on my chest right in front of the dinner-plate sized loaf of bread. The stale, mostly green surface was crawling with maggots.

Bon appétit, indeed. I reached toward the loaf, my weak fingers curling around what was sure to be the only food I would see for another week.

CHAPTER 9
RYLAND

"No, don't make me! I won't! I can't!" I tried to fight them, to pull against the hands that dragged me toward the center of the room and the four chairs that were set up around a hospital-type bed. A bed with straps.

I knew what was happening. I had heard them talking about it. I had tried to warn her just hours ago, I had told her to leave. Begged her. I never should have done made the svazovat. I never should have thought I was strong enough. She needed to break the connection.

I hoped she listened, because as much as I was fighting, I knew I wouldn't win.

'You'll never win against me. You'll never get away.'

We were out of time.

"You can't have her!" My entire world shook as I screamed, my words rumbling as the guards continued to drag me closer to that table, Cail already standing there, grinning.

"Have who, Ryland? Joclyn? You can't have her either. Ilyan has taken her from you." His words were slime in my head, the imagery working like an infection that snapped something inside of me and what little control I had slipped away.

"Ilyan!" I screamed, fighting the guards for a different reason, now. "I'll kill him. I'll kill them both."

"Then come here, Ryland, and you can." He patted the table and the voices inside of my head screamed. Some in victory. Some in panic. I was fighting again.

"No! I won't! You can't make me!" I tried to bite at the guard to my left, he punched me instead.

"Shut him off, Cail, I can't even think with all of that racket." My father drawled as he followed us in, his shoes tapping loudly as he and Ovailia circled to stand by Cail at the table.

"Yes, Master." At Cail's words the blanket of his magic swarmed over me, my mind, my thoughts, my body, my magic. It all became numb. The guards stepped away as I relaxed, and walked confidently towards Cail's grin.

'Good boy, so nice to see you beaten down. As you always should have been.'

"I bet you are going to be glad to be rid of him." Ovailia crooned, twirling Cail's hair as he forced me forward, my body mechanical as I laid down on the table.

No. I shouldn't be doing this. I needed to get away...

I needed to...

"No." The word was more of a hiss than a shout as I lay there, all of them strapping me in.

"Yes," Edmund leaned over me, my father's eyes sparkling as he smiled. "I told you, son. For years I told you. Stop fighting me. And now, here we are. I have won despite it all."

"No." The word was stronger that time, but still not enough to do anything more than trigger an echo of laughs around me.

"Yes, Ryland. You are going to give Cail what he wants, and then we are going to unleash you." He was proud. For the first time in my life he was proud of me, and I couldn't feel worse.

This was not what I wanted.

"No."

"Bring Sain!" My father called, ignoring me as the door was opened again and Sain's shuffling steps entered the stone hall.

"Edmund, this will not end in what you desire. Your son may be part of your downfall," Sain began, I tried to twist in my bands to see him, but I couldn't move. "There are other ways to make yourself strong. I have told you this before."

"Don't worry, Sain, I am following all of your advice. You have been invaluable to me, as I know you will continue to be."

"Yes, so invaluable," Ovailia laughed at her response to our father, Cail joining in as the wicked stabs of their glee sliced against me.

"I need you to do this last thing for me," he continued to drawl as the last of the straps tightened me against the table. "Break your daughter for me."

Sain said nothing. I was forced to watch as they gathered around, hand after hand placed over my heart. The blanket of Cail's control slipped away and I began to fight. Began to scream. Began to plea. I tried to grab at my magic to stop them, to save her.

But it was not enough.

Nothing was enough.

The world went black as the blade plunged into my heart.

"Who are you?"

I opened my eyes at the voice. I expected Sain to be standing there as he usually was, instead, it was a girl with blonde hair to her waist and eyes so dark they could have been completely black. She couldn't have been more than ten.

"Who...? What...?" I gasped as I whipped around, this space was different then where I had normally gone.

"Who are you?" she said again, stepping forward.

"Who are you?" I echoed the question, looking around into the void. I had never been in this part of the blade before.

But I think I had an idea who the girl was.

"You are his son," she said, not answering my question. "I know that. You look like him."

"Yes?" I asked it like a question, still looking around as I waited for Sain to arrive.

"You are the one he is hurting. I asked him not to hurt you, but he doesn't listen to me. Sometimes he doesn't remember me. I've been trying to help. But it's been too long." I turned back to the girl. She was still looking at me curiously. She seemed familiar and yet I knew I had never seen her before.

"Who are you? Are you Rosaline?"

"I asked you first," she replied, forcing a smile that time.

"Ryland." She nodded as if she had known all along and she stepped forward, her hand wrapping around mine.

Her skin was soft, and warmer than I had ever felt in this place. Just the touch of her tiny hand against my own sent everything buzzing and rumbling. Pain and fear and hope and love all swirled through me, the feeling was the same as every time I stepped into the world the souls blade created.

My eyes widened.

"I figured." She moved closer, the black eyes looking up to me with hope. “You have his eyes. I didn’t, that’s why he didn’t like me. It’s why he put me here. They tried to save me, but no one could stop him. But I will help you, for as long as I can. Whatever they are planning, you have to stop it. I don’t have the power to do so. You have to.”

“Rosaline?” I asked again, but she didn’t smile. She just squeezed my hand and turned into smoke, right as I felt that line in my heart explode.

The line of the Zêlství.

They were taking us right to Joclyn.

CHAPTER 10
JOCLYN

I woke up the next morning and almost yelled out. My body was filled with the aches of having avoided the Tȍuha for so long. I shifted my weight in Ilyan's arms and my back seized, the muscles calling out in protest.

I knew I couldn't wait any longer to go into the Tȍuha, but I was still scared; more so after last night's dream. Dramin had told me to wait to talk to Ilyan about breaking the bond until after I had decided what course to take, but I was clearly out of time. It scared me the way Ryland had begged me to break the Zêlství right then, and then there was Cail...

Cail lived off of his taunts—his torture—but he hadn't even hesitated before killing me. The lack of his usual games made my teeth clench.

I shuddered at the memory, my heart rate accelerating until my chest felt like it was pressed under a hundred ton weight. I rolled over to face Ilyan and moved the hair that had fallen over his face, his mouth slightly open in his sleep as usual.

I knew what I had to do. As much as I didn't want to, as much as it hurt, I needed to break the connection. I had thought I needed Ryland. Ryland had protected me as I had grown up. He had loved me and taught me how to love when I hadn't been sure I knew how to anymore. He had protected me from his father and used his body to shield me, and now he was trying to protect me by breaking the connection.

I loved him more than I ever thought I could love someone. That's why it hurt so much every time he asked me to break the connection. I didn't want to lose that. I didn't want to lose the last normal thing from my old life.

But I wasn't normal anymore. I wasn't normal. And I don't think the relationship I had with Ryland could ever be what it was.

Besides, once that connection was broken, I would be free. Free from the torment. Free to become what I was born to be.

The Silnŷ.

"For it is only by your side that she can find her true purpose, that she will find the strength to kill those that would end the magic of the world." I whispered the words of the sight to myself, still staring at Ilyan's sleeping face.

I knew it was true, and although part of me shattered at the thought, I knew it needed to be done.

I needed to break the connection.

"Ilyan," I said his name loud enough for him to hear me, my hand on his bare chest.

His eyes opened sleepily, blinking a few times before he fully registered where he was.

"Jos," he sighed, his voice heavy. He reached up and placed his hand over mine pushing it into his scarred chest.

"No nightmares?" He was so hopeful, I only smiled and shook my head. After all, that would be the last one.

"I am so glad." He freed my hand from his chest to pull me into him. I cringed at the pain the movement and pressure caused. He stopped immediately, his magic flaring abruptly as he searched through my body. He looked at me alarmed and I knew he had found something.

"I have to go in," I whispered, my voice as weak as my body felt.

He leaned over to me and gently kissed my forehead, his lips soft against my skin.

"I will be here the entire time, Joclyn. Be quick." I smiled at him and nodded. When I got back I would tell him. I would need strength to break the Zêlství anyway.

I pulled the necklace out from under my shirt and pushed my magic into it before leaning into Ilyan's chest and letting his arms wrap around me.

I closed my eyes only to open them to the same dilapidated kitchen and instantly started hyperventilating. Cail stood right before me. His face was pulled into a wicked grin, his eyes blacker than I had ever seen them.

The dark eyed man.

"Why hello, Joclyn," he said. "You don't seem happy to see me."

I stared at him, unsure of what to say.

"What are you doing here?" His twisted joy grew at my fear.

"Why, Joclyn, isn't it obvious? I've been here all along." He smirked and stepped forward, causing me to step back instinctively. My foot hit the table leg and I stopped, trapped, as he continued to move forward.

"I was here when Ryland showed you the Vilỳ, I was the one who told him that you didn't want him, and I was the one that took away the pretty overcoat Ryland had given this place." He gestured around him to the rotting kitchen, but I couldn't take my eyes off of him.

"This is what your mate's mind truly looks like; destroyed, rotten, forgotten. There is no love here, which is why you don't belong here. Or maybe you do. You don't love him anymore, either."

He continued to move toward me, but I couldn't move. The memories and fear of every encounter with him weighed me down.

"You're the one who has been telling him to force me out." I gasped, letting the fact free from my fears.

"Now, that's an interesting thing. I actually have not been telling him to do that. It would ruin my fun, after all. Ryland's mind is an interesting place. Not only does he remember enough about you to realize you're in danger, but he also risked everything to get into your dream last night. He was desperate to get you to break the bond to keep you from this mess. Thankfully, you didn't listen."

Cail emphasized his last words, each syllable shooting through me like I had been slapped. Ryland had been trying to protect me all this time. I felt the wind suck out of my lungs.

"And, now," Cail continued, "here you are. Trapped."

"Trapped?" I repeated the little air that I could hold in my lungs gasping out.

I spun around to look for the black door that I had always been able to exit through. My heart dropped to see a tall man standing in front of it, his eyes boring into me dangerously.

I took a step forward, my hands raising toward the tall guard, I was getting out of here. I felt my magic crackle between my fingers, it felt more alive than in the nightmares; more powerful.

"I wouldn't do that if I were you," Cail taunted, freezing me in place. "Everything you do here, you do in the waking world, remember? You attack him, or me, and you will throw that weapon at Ilyan. I bet he sleeps right beside you, holding you. Protecting you. It would be a shame if you killed him. An absolute shame."

Cail came up behind me, his hands moving to rest on the table on either side of me, pinning me in place.

"Now, I bet you are thinking," he continued as he leaned into me, his voice wickedly soft in my ear, "that you could just find a way to fight him and leave, but then, Ryland hit you with that barstool last time, and I bet when you woke up you were bleeding."

He let his words drift off, his hand moving to trail up my arm. The touch shot through me and I spun around, grabbing his arm and twisting it awkwardly into the table. He yelled out as my strength pinned him down. His discomfort lasted barely a minute before I felt his magic surge and a conjured knife appeared in the palm of his free hand. He motioned me away from him. I gasped and jumped away, the memory from my last dream still fresh. My movement only caused Cail's joy to increase, his smile widening.

"Did Ilyan heal you when you woke up? Do you think he could heal you if you didn't wake up?"

I looked toward the man who stood in front of the door, his eyes following me greedily as he flexed his fingers, red energy crackling between his knuckles.

"What are you saying?" I immediately regretted asking, but I couldn't help it. I silently prayed he wasn't saying what I knew he was.

"This is not like your dreams, Joclyn. You attack me here, you attack Ilyan there. You conjure weapons here, you do the same there. You will not wake in the arms of your true love if you die here, you will simply die."

I gasped and he smiled more. He grabbed a rotten apple and balanced its weight in his hand for a moment before throwing it against one of the teetering cabinet doors. The door fell to the ground as the apple exploded.

"Boom!" Cail yelled joyfully, causing me to jump. "Dead. Gone! Which in all honesty is how we want you. But I figure, and Edmund agrees with me, why not have a little fun first? Why not play a little game?"

"No," I gasped in panicked desperation. I clutched my shoulder where Ilyan's Štít lay; I felt nothing.

"Oh, yes." He smiled and my breathing picked up. "If you try to get through that door," he pointed to my normal exit, "he will kill you. Which means the only way out of this room is through that door."

Cail grabbed my shoulders and moved me to face the door that led into the mansion.

"Now, through that door is the depths of Ryland's mind. In there, he may remember you, he may not, or he may hate you enough to kill you himself. But do not fear, I am not sending you in there after him, I am sending you in there away from me. Because when I find you, I will do away with you in the most painful way I can think of. It's the greatest game of all."

I cringed as he produced his knife and rested the blade against my chest. I tried to move away from him, but he held me tighter.

"Don't worry, I will give you a head start. It's only fair after all." He dug his fingers into my shoulders, causing me to gasp at the pain. "But don't forget, whatever magic you do here, you do in the real world. Though if I do my job right, in a matter of hours you won't even remember you have magic inside of you."

"Let me go," I snarled as he continued to hold me. I stumbled when he released me with a little push, surprised he had done it so quickly.

"If you insist," Cail said. "But you'd better run, your ten minute head start begins now."

I spun around to face him, Cail stood with his face screwed up in manic excitement.

Cail had trapped me in here with the full intention of torturing me in a way that would only end in my death. I needed to get out of here. I knew there had to be a way. I could already feel my soul call to it, a promise of showing me a way out that would not end in my death.

My eyes darted to the guard who stood in front of the black door, blocking my exit. I knew I could defeat him easily, but I also knew that Ilyan still lay right beside me, his arms wrapped around me. Anything I would do in a fight, would go right into Ilyan.

Cail caught my eye, his lip curling as he interpreted my thoughts, knowing his plan was working.

"Run." Cail said, and I didn't wait. I turned and ran into the pits of the house, which was all that was left of Ryland's mind, my heart slowly breaking.

CHAPTER 11
ILYAN

Joclyn's voice had been a treasured memory from the first day I had heard it, eight hundred years ago. The rise and fall of her tone, the way she said her Rs—it was an accent I wouldn't hear for hundreds of years after the day I had received the sight.

I had dwelled on her voice for centuries, allowed the memory of her to be my light in my darkest times, and hundreds of years later, I had basked in her voice when I heard it in my ears again.

"Ilyan."

I was so used to hearing Joclyn's voice in my dreams that when she woke me up by a simple call of my name it always took me a moment to decide if it was a dream or reality. It felt like a dream. Every morning, when I woke with her in my arms after so many years of waiting, it all felt like a dream.

I didn't even care what Talon had warned me about anymore. Perhaps he had been trying to keep me away from her anyway; I had no way of knowing. All I knew is that the last few days had been less torture and more wonder. Although, I was sure the torture would come.

The warmth of our body heat was trapped under the layers of furs, a stark contrast to the cold of the cave against my cheek. Her hand was pressed softly against my bare chest, her warm breath flowing over my skin. I could have died right there from the joy I felt.

"Jos," I sighed, happy at being comfortable enough to say her name so familiarly.

She smiled at me, but the smile was sad, the pain behind her eyes stronger than it had been last night. Something was bothering her: a decision, a choice. I couldn't tell what. I had missed something.

My muscles tensed in alarm. I should have never let her wait so long between Tȍuhas.

I pushed my magic through her, letting the warmth slow her heartbeat. She looked at me with those sad eyes before the look began to fade.

Calm washed through her before I registered the light in the cave. It was morning. She had slept all night. My soul felt light at the thought. Finally, she had gotten some rest.

"No nightmares?" I was hopeful. How could I not be?

"I am so glad," I whispered at the shake of her head, pulling her into me and wrapping my arms around her. The small movement must have triggered a million aches inside of her because I felt her back seize as she gasped.

My heart clunked heavily in worry and I did the same thing I had done for months. I plunged my magic into her as I healed her. I wrapped her spine in energy as I repaired the tiny fractures that lined her bones. Hopefully Ovailia would bring Ryland back soon and then she wouldn't have to endure this anymore. I needed her whole. I couldn't bear to see her in pain, even if his return would take her away from me.

I was only serving as her safe harbor until Ryland was able to return to her.

"I have to go in." Her voice was so soft, so fearful. Not for the first time, I wondered if I should have prompted her to break the bond in that first month.

I leaned forward and pressed my lips against the skin of her forehead, her warmth shooting through me like lightning. I pulled away, much sooner than my heart begged me to. I had to remind myself that she was not mine for my heart to claim.

"I will be here the entire time, Joclyn," I whispered to her, my soul lost to the doubt and fear that flashed through her silver eyes. "Be quick."

Something deep inside of me begged me not to let her go. I didn't want to see the pain on her face, or find her bleeding when she returned. But I couldn't stop this.

She pulled the beautiful necklace my brother had given her out from underneath her shirt, the jewel glimmering as she plunged her magic into it. I could feel the power emanating from the immaculate stone, the strength of Ryland's magic swelling in the air. The jewel sparkled as his heart stayed with her, his magic surging through her as he protected her.

She didn't look at me as she pushed herself into my chest again, my arms wrapping around her. Her body was stiff against mine before she relaxed, her mind leaving to connect with that of her mate.

I ran my hand over her hair, the thick braid I had placed in it only the day before all ruffled and frizzy from a fitful sleep. Neklidný spánek?

No, that couldn't be right. Joclyn had said that she had had no nightmares and the few nights without them, she had always slept so still, so soundlessly.

I reached up to wind a thick strand that had come undone back into place, and her body shuddered against mine. The small movement was almost that of a sob.

"Jos?" I pulled her limp body away from me, but her eyes were still closed, she was still in the Tǒuha.

I had almost pulled her back into me when she shook again, this movement heavier. Her head jumped and lolled before coming to rest on my arm. The world seemed to freeze.

She had never moved like this during a Tǒuha. It was always the nightmares that racked through her body and brought the seizures and agonizing movements. Tǒuhas were gentle. I had seen so many of my kind enter them through my life span. The gentle way their bodies lay, the glowing, ethereal beauty that would overtake them as they visited such a pure eternal place.

Joclyn twitched again, her fingers sparking slightly. I brought her against me, my hands fanning against her back as her heartbeat fluttered in fear.

"Jos?" My back stiffened when she didn't react, my hands moving to clench her to me, my muscles tensing.

Someone was hurting her. Anger pulsed through me, the need to protect her taking over my better judgment. She had only been gone a matter of minutes, but that was much longer than she had visited recently.

Her body shook again, her chest heaving as she gasped and coughed into the skin of my chest. Warmth from her breath spread over my chest, leaving behind a wetness that stuck against my chest. I froze as I smelled it; the earthy scent of blood.

I pulled her away to reveal a bright red patch of her blood on my chest. It continued to drizzle from her gaping mouth and onto the sheet of the bed we lay in.

"Ne," I gasped. *No.*

Blood trickled down the side of her mouth, the bright red vivid against her pale skin. My fear flowed into my bloodstream, igniting my fury, my anger.

Someone was hurting her. Someone was going to pay.

My magic pulsed in search of the connecting thread of the Tȍuha, ready to get her out of there, but I felt nothing before she began to convulse.

She shook violently, moaning and gasping as if she was being strangled. Her rough movements grew as I attempted to steady her. The more I tried to grab her, the more she writhed, sending my hands away.

"Joclyn!" My voice broke as I yelled at her in a foolish attempt to wake her up.

She continued to writhe and seize, the moans turning into agonizing yells. My magic pulsed through the Štít, I knew she could hold the power if the barrier broke, but nothing budged. My jaw locked in fear, my magic bubbling high above the power I normally held in reserve.

I attempted to move closer when she shifted, hands flying forward as her magic pulsed into me and sent me skidding across the cold floor of the cave. I stood in one jump, immediately running back to her.

I yelled as I squared my shoulders, fully prepared to battle my way through her seizure and save her… until her hands began to glow.

If I wasn't so focused on her, I might have missed it.

Magic exploded out of her, an electrical current so strong it would have buried us all in the mountain in a matter of seconds. My magic burst away from me in a shield that cocooned its way around Joclyn, trapping her in a lightning storm of energy.

Her magic crackled and boomed within the shield, flashes of light shooting over the dark walls of the cave. My fear grew as the onslaught I had trapped her in got worse, and I realized the possible danger that she could now be facing alone.

I ran to her, keeping the shield strong as my magic pushed through the Štít in its desperate attempt to get near her. I couldn't break in, but it didn't matter. We had bigger problems. The powerful barrier I had placed around her was no match for her magic.

I could already feel it giving way, my magic straining as her attacks kept coming.

"Dramin!" My voice was barely able to rise through the cave before the shield shattered. The loud crack of her magic hitting the stone resounded through the cave in a fearful rumble.

The sound rattled in my ears, the danger calling right into my gut. I tried to stop her attacks, but I was powerless against her. I was no match for the power that Joclyn held inside.

Dramin's footsteps were barely audible above the destructive sound of Joclyn's magic as the uncontrolled streams of her white hot magic poured from her fingers and tore through the mountain, the impact shaking the ground beneath us. A rumbling sound ricocheted through the cave, echoing off walls as it intensified and the mountain began to fall apart around us.

Thom and Dramin called out from somewhere behind me when the shaking sent us all to the ground, our feet unable to stay steady inside of the rumbling cave. The current ripped the rock of her bunk apart, pieces of it falling around her, falling from the ceiling as it threatened to entomb us all.

I didn't think. If I had, I wouldn't have moved. My soul just stepped in, moving me forward in an attempt to save her. I dodged the falling stones as magic crackled in the air, yelling as one long tendril sliced deeply into my arm.

Dramin and Thom were yelling behind me, begging me to stop, warning me of the danger, but I didn't listen. I ignored the blood that flowed freely down my arm. I ignored their voices. I could only focus on the girl who was fighting for her life right in front of me. I reached her just as the attack stopped and her arms went limp. I grabbed her body and brought her safely into my arms, the bunk shifting into a mass of rock and debris as it collapsed over where she had been only moments before.

The rock settled, Joclyn's magic finally calming as I held her. Everything was silent just long enough for us each to take a breath.

The groaning of stone turned into a crack of thunder. I turned toward the two men behind me to see my own fear mirrored in their faces. Thom looked around as the groans increased and Dramin's head whipped around as a loud bang sounded through the cave as the roof began to collapse on itself.

"Get out of here! Jdi!" I yelled loudly in Czech, fully aware that I had placed the magical stream into my voice that would require them to comply. I knew that neither Thom nor Dramin could perform a stutter, and I was not going to leave them here to die alone.

Both men turned and ran, their speed increasing as more groaning echoed and cracked. I held Joclyn's body to me, praying she did not continue to attack her unseen assailant before I could get her to safety, or at least out of the cave that would kill us all.

The floor shook and the ceiling continued to fall around us. The sizes of the stones increased as the mountain shifted. Groans echoed as we ran, the deep moans from the mountain warning us of the end.

Thom's long dreads bounced around his shoulders as they ran, Dramin's night robe flying behind him like a cape. Joclyn's continued jerks and spasms were masked by the jostling movements of my run as we dodged around falling rocks and dirt. The intricate stonework of the cave crumbled around us, the beautiful iron work that once hung from the ceiling crashing to the stone floor only to crinkle like paper left too long in water. We darted through obstacles as the noise grew until each of us had made it into the hall that would lead us out, only to find it blocked.

My heart plunged, Thom and Dramin looked to me, fear and anger lining their faces.

"The training room." My commanding voice barely resonated above the groaning of the mountain, but even without the magical pulse weaved inside of it both men quickly obeyed.

The sound of the collapsing mountain had grown so loud that I could barely hear anything above it. I shifted Joclyn's body up, leaving her dangling over my shoulder as we ran, praying that the space where we were heading would be free of the horrors we had just left.

It seemed intact enough to keep us safe.

I turned to face what little was left of the beautiful cave. The palms of my hands came to rest on the cold stone that lined the dark hallway, the strong pulse of natural magic whirled, pulling at me before being sent back to speed through the mountain alongside my own. I closed my eyes as I focused, my magic pushed into the rock, shoving it away. There was no way I could stop the destruction, but I could slow it down, stop what hadn't already happened.

I felt the shifting of the rock slow, the mountain answering to my call. I continued to push against it, sweat forming underneath my long hair as I forced the mountain to do what I wanted.

Boulders moved back into place, rocks piled up against others, and I heated and fused the rocks back together in a desperate attempt to stabilize the mountain. My mind moved each hulking mass quickly, stopping the fall in one place only to have it start in another. Even with the speed that my ability gave me, I wasn't going to be able to do enough to keep our way out free of more obstruction.

I refused to give up.

Slowly, the groaning stopped, the crashing of rocks ceased, and quiet filled the air. I kept my hands flat against the stone as my magic moved back inside of me.

I didn't dare move, not yet. I stood still, waiting for the groaning to return. I could feel Joclyn's jolts against my back, her frantic movements cutting at my soul.

"Ilyan?" I didn't even move at Dramin's voice. I remained still, waiting, needing to know that the mountain wasn't going to continue its attempt to bury us alive.

"Is it safe back there?" I asked through gritted teeth, still not looking toward him.

"Yes."

I felt his body only a step away from me, his energy pulsing through the air. I focused on his energy, my nerves tingling as I felt his arms rise, presumably to lift Joclyn from my back.

"Leave her." My voice was hard.

Dramin's arms dropped, but he did not move. The minutes ticked by until I was sure that the mountain had ceased its implosion.

I shifted Joclyn's weight into my arms, her head lolling over my elbow as I walked passed Dramin, his eyes hooded with concern and fear as he followed me into the bare cavern. Before, it had been used for training, now it would be used as our home. At least, until I could find us a way out of here.

"What happened?" Thom yelled in a panic the moment I walked into the room, his words followed by profanities that no man should be aware of.

"Napadli Joclyn." *They are attacking.*

"What do you mean *they* are attacking her, Ilyan?" Thom yelled, his anger boiling out of him. "Your girlfriend just tore apart the cave and trapped us underground!"

I could feel the confusion and anger emanating off both of them as their magic peaked and their stress heightened the magical flow inside of them.

I wasn't focused on the gentle flow and pulse of Thom and Dramin right now. I was focused on the fact that I felt nothing from Joclyn. Her undercurrent was there, but the actual strength seemed smothered. It was more than when Edmund had been limiting her power through the necklace and worse than when her magic was dying. The thrum I felt now was weaker than when I had first felt her magical pull before her powers had even awakened.

My magic pulsed into her through the Štít, and thankfully this time, it flooded her. The strong barrier that had prohibited me from so much as calming her before was now weak and breakable between us like spun candy.

I scanned her body for the thin connecting line of the Tòuha, my body freezing when I found nothing. I pushed into her, letting my magic fill her to every corner, the full extent of my power was enough to kill any other, I knew it should at least cause her pain. Joclyn just lay there. I searched for the bridge to her mind, for injuries, for warning signs, for spells and curses—but found nothing.

I dropped to my knees, keeping her body in my lap, keeping her close.

"She is being attacked in the Tòuha," I provided, knowing I had to give them some sort of explanation as to what in the world had just happened.

"Ryland?" Thom accused, his angry voice bitter.

"No."

"Then who?" Thom's voice faded off as he asked the question because he knew. We all knew. We had all heard her retelling of Ryland as a black-eyed man, of how Cail was controlling her dreams. This wasn't a dream, however, and I didn't know how to wake her up. I didn't know how to help her. Somehow, Cail's control had moved into the Tòuha.

"So, she attacked him in the Tòuha and almost killed us?" I couldn't tell if Thom was angry or concerned. "Is she going to do it again? Can't you just wake her up?"

"I can't find the bridge to her mind, Thom. I've been looking."

"How long ago did she go in?" Dramin asked, the confusion in his voice triggering my own.

"Ten minutes," I provided, knowing the short amount of time would sound silly. It did to me.

It wasn't just the time that she had been in there that had triggered my alarm; it was her actions, what had happened to her body. I felt my lungs constrict in stress as I looked at the still wet specks of blood around her mouth.

My hands pressed one of hers against the blood on my bared chest, against the dozens of scars that lined my skin. The pain flared through my chest at the pressure against the scars, the same way it had always done. I looked at our hands before dragging my eyes back to her face.

"How is he doing it?" Dramin asked, letting the unspoken name float between us.

"I don't know. But I will find out." I looked up to the two men, looking from the deep sea green of Dramin's eyes, to the crystalline blue of Thom's—the color our father had cursed us with, the color of royalty.

The necklace Ryland had given Joclyn still hung around her neck, the large ruby glistening. *No, not a ruby,* I reminded myself. A diamond. I touched the stone lightly, knowing what it meant to her, but right then, I hated it. I hated what it had come to represent.

It had been the bridge to his mind.

My heart rate increased as I stared at the jewel, my breathing stuttering as I attempted to control myself. Before I could stop myself, I wrapped my fingers around the necklace, breaking the clasp as I ripped it away from her neck.

I waited, waited for her to wake, waited for the bridge to make itself known, but she stayed as still as ever, the necklace dead and cold in my hands. I pocketed it quickly, returning my hand to her face.

"Why didn't that work?" Dramin asked, his voice making it obvious that he had already known it would not.

"He has been controlling her dreams through a blood connection, but a Tȍuha? I didn't even know that was possible. I have never seen anything like this before, Dramin." I gave them as much of an answer as I felt comfortable giving, keeping my voice an emotionless mask.

"I have."

CHAPTER 12
JOCLYN

I ran into the mansion without looking back. I knew Cail was serious. I needed to get away from him as fast as possible and figure out a way to get out of here before Cail found and killed me.

A few steps into the house, I tripped on broken bits of carpet that had been pulled up, burned away, or maybe eaten by some form of rodent. I caught myself, picking my feet up in my run and quickening my pace. I sped through the house, taking the path I had traveled almost every day of my life until last May; the path that would take me to Ryland's room.

Sparks of my magic dripped from my fingers on my command, little bits that I would hope would give Ilyan warning to what was happening.

What was coming.

I was going to need to use my magic, and if I could get him away from me I could have a chance. Although, knowing him, he would just move closer.

Damn him! The chivalrous bastard! Why did he have to be so... good...

My heart thumped loudly as something told me to stop, my breath catching at the overwhelming sensation. I stopped dead, clutching my shoulder, hoping to find Ilyan's warmth inside of me but still finding nothing. I kept my hand there as I thought through what I was doing, what I was going to do, something unsettling deep in my gut telling me to hide.

I had gone right to where Cail would expect me to go; which means this would be a trap. I backed up a few steps, I needed to figure out what to do before I came face to face with him.

I dropped my hand from opening the door to Ryland's hall and instead sunk into what I knew would be a supply closet. Cail had given me a ten minute head start, surely five of that had already passed. I had five extra minutes to hide or five minutes to find my way out. That was, if Cail chose to wait the full ten, which I doubted.

I closed the door to the closet behind me as softly as I could. I would know in a few minutes if Cail would come right here in his attempt to track me down or if he would begin his search elsewhere. It all came down to how well he knew me.

Or thought he did.

I needed to be smart about how I handled this, the faster I got out of here the better. I sent out a few more magical sparks, still trying to warn Ilyan. Without being able to use magic to defend myself, I was limited as to what I could do and how fast I could leave. If Ilyan was paying attention to the sparks I could just go back and blast Cail's dumb guard on his head. I just didn't know if it was worth the risk.

My eyes were trained on the dim light that was filtering in through the crease in the door while I attempted to keep my mind off the scurrying feet and other noises that were filling the small room. I had only waited a minute before heavy footfalls filled the air, the impact of them rattling bins and boxes of who knows what in my hiding space. The sound grew louder as Cail ran down the hall, tracing my exact steps. I slunk away from the door, holding my breath in terror. My back hit against a shelf, causing moldy towels and mouse feces to fall over my head. My mouth opened in expectation of a scream, but I shoved my fist heavily into it, desperate to keep myself quiet.

If I was going to fight, I needed surprise on my side.

His footsteps stopped, and I knew I had made too much noise. As quietly as I could, I shoved myself into a corner, placing my body as much behind one of the large shelving units as possible. I cringed as my foot stepped on something soft, and I closed my eyes, not wanting to think about what it could be.

As soon as I had moved myself into the corner, the door flew open. I flattened my body even further against the soft, damp wall, hoping that I was back enough that he wouldn't see me. The light from the open door caught the eyes of more than a dozen large rats, each lifting their head in expectation.

The light illuminated the stacks of molding towels and mildewed sheets that were dotted with feces and cleaning supplies which had rusted through their containers leaving glistening patches of dried chemicals underneath them. Everything lit up as Cail stood with the door open, his breath flowing through the room in silent puffs.

I kept my breath trapped inside me, focusing on random objects around me so as not to think about the pain that was seeping through my chest. My eyes widened when they came to rest on a long, rusty length of pipe hidden in the piles of rot.

I kept my eyes on the pipe as I listened to Cail's breathing, trying to ignore the earsplitting pressure from my lungs. My body screamed at me for air, and I screamed back that he would kill me.

The door slowly closed, the sound of the hinge grinding through my brain and making the movement feel even slower. I waited to breathe, but his footsteps did not retreat. He was standing right on the other side of the door waiting for me. He knew I was in here.

Cail was playing his game.

Everything inside of me was begging for air. I took a step forward, my feet soft against the floor, and reached out and wrapped my hands around the pipe, the metal cold and slimy underneath my fingers. I gripped it firmly, moving it up like a bat as I surged my magic through it. If I couldn't use my ability as a weapon against him, then I would use it to increase the power of a weapon.

I closed my eyes.

Please don't let Ilyan still be next to me. Please don't let this actually move through into the real world.

My breath released as I swung the pipe forward, aiming it where Cail would be standing on the other side of the door. My magic filled the metal, making it grow red as it prepared to explode through the door and hopefully Cail.

The shadow of Cail's feet shifted as the pipe made contact with the door, the rotted wood falling away from the impact. I had expected to hit Cail, but instead the pipe sliced through empty air. My eyes widened in confusion before a long-fingered hand wrapped around the pipe, and with one pull, yanked it through the door, my body following as I futilely held on.

I stumbled through the shards of wood, my feet barely keeping me upright before the hand moved from the pipe to my arm, the grip digging into my skin as Cail pulled me against him.

"Joclyn, Joclyn, Joclyn. You are going to make this far too fun, aren't you?" I cringed away from Cail's brittle breath in my nostrils.

"I wouldn't call this fun, but if that's the word you choose..." I gritted my teeth and moved closer to him, hoping to catch him off guard.

Cail's eyes widened in excitement before I slammed my knee in between his legs, his body toppling over me before I grabbed the pipe and hit the metal against his back with as much force as I could muster.

I didn't wait to see if I had done any damage. I turned and ran from him, the pipe in front of me like a sword. I had just begun turning a corner when I felt Cail's magic wrap around me, his power dragging me back and slamming me against a wall.

I cringed as Cail limped up to me, a string of profanity flowing from him as he rubbed his neck. His magic held me tightly against the wall, rendering my pipe useless. I racked my brain for options as he moved toward me. I had already been trapped inside of the Tȍuha for the last twenty minutes by my best guess, meaning it had only been a few minutes in the real world if my math was right. I sent up a few more sparks, letting them look like threats to Cail.

Cail came up beside me, his one hand resting against the wall by my head while the other massaged his neck where the pipe had made contact.

"You naughty little girl," he said, his lip turned up a wicked grin. "Now I see what Ryland was talking about."

"What? That I am strong enough to defeat you?" I raised my eyebrow, hoping to sound confident even though I knew that the shake of fear in my voice gave me away.

What little bravado I had used for my façade faded away as Cail began to laugh, his loud voice ricocheting around the hallway.

"No," he taunted, my muscles tensing, "that you need to be trained."

I sent out the tiniest bit of an attack toward him, my hands open as my magic exploded, only to die when the pipe collided with my stomach. The impact raced through my body, vibrating up my spine and ricocheting through my skull. I screamed out at the impact as Cail's binds left me, and I collapsed to the ground.

I didn't have time to run or even move before the pipe impacted my spine. Once. Twice. It sent me sprawling. I screamed out and little flecks of blood flew from my mouth, splattering the ground with glistening red.

"Will you look at that?" Cail mused as he kneeled beside me. "Blood. I bet Ilyan is having a conniption. I can almost hear him, 'Oh, my love! Why are you bleeding!'" Cail's voice went high as he mocked Ilyan, I barely heard him. If I was bleeding in real life, Ilyan wouldn't be by me. Ilyan would be running for Dramin.

I didn't wait to think. I focused my magic on the floor right below Cail, sending a pulse directly at it. The floor exploded at the impact, sending him hurtling through the fissure I had opened.

I struggled to my feet, limping around the hole as I raced back toward the kitchen, terrified that Cail would return before I could get out.

Silently, I prayed that Ilyan wasn't hurt; but thankfully that attack should have been enough to warm him. I could get out. I just needed to get back to the kitchen.

Cail's scream echoed behind me, and I dodged into Ryland's room, hiding in the shattered remains of Ryland's kitchenette. I sat still, letting my body heal me so that I could run, so that I could fight and get out of here. I let my magic run through me, feeling more than one broken bone.

So, fighting him may not have been such a good idea. While I was more than powerful enough to do away with Cail, I still needed to be careful so that I didn't collapse the cave...

"What are you doing here?" My head snapped up at the voice, relaxing to see Ryland towering over me.

"Ryland?" Everything in me relaxed until I registered the panic on his face and the anger lines on his forehead.

"I warned you, Jos. You've got to get out of here." He grabbed my hand and pulled me up, not saying anything before dragging me behind him and out the door.

We moved back toward the main kitchen, our feet slipping and catching on debris. Before we had gotten too close to the kitchen a loud rumble shook the floors ahead of us. Cail was already there. Ryland deviated, pulling us out of the servants' quarters and into the main living space.

Large, rumbling bangs sounded through the house as we moved. It reminded me of when we had fled this place leaving Ryland behind during the battle. I had just caught sight of the main ballroom before Ryland dragged me into a large office, shutting the door behind us.

The door had barely clicked shut before he turned back to me, the anger on his face now mixed with fear.

"What are you doing here? I told you to break the bond." Ryland's hand shook as he moved hair away from my face, his eyes staying on mine for a moment before darting around the room. The movement of his eyes and the shake of his hand put me one edge, his paranoia contagious.

"I know, but I had stayed away too long--"

"I told you not to come back." His hands dug into me, his grip pushing me against the wall.

"Why didn't you break the bond?"

"I was going to, after..." I reached up to touch his face, my hand stopping halfway at the look in his eyes.

"You waited, and now it's too late. He's going to kill you, Jos! Do you know what I risked to warn you? What they did to me? To Wyn? To your dad? We risked it all and you didn't listen." His anger cut through me. I could only stare at him wide-eyed as I tried to make sense of what he was saying.

"I didn't know... I'm sorry. I--"

"Being sorry means nothing!" he yelled, slamming his fist into the wall by my head.

I jumped and tried to move away from him, but his hands kept me restrained.

"What do you want from me, Ry? I'm trying, okay?" I couldn't help but yell. The anger and fear inside of me bubbled out, directing itself at Ryland.

"Trying to what, Jos? Not Listen? I'm trying to save you and you can't even let me do that. Why did I even bond myself to you?" His words were loud and echoed around the empty room. I wanted to sink away into nothing. I had asked myself the same thing a million times because of the doubt that I had felt, the hopelessness that the Zêlství had caused me... us. Because of the pain, the torture; I had felt it all and asked the same question, however hearing it from him still hurt.

"Why did you?" I asked, my voice soft.

"Because I can't live without you! I couldn't see you with someone else, ever. I was hoping I could take Ilyan's place if I sealed myself to you!"

"Take his place?"

"You can't love him, Jos. He's not the one for you. I am."

I stared at him, my mouth hanging open. I loved Ryland, but he stood there admitting that he had known what I had been born for. He had known what the mark meant, and he had still bonded himself to me. I didn't know if he had done it because he wanted to protect me, or because he really did love me, or because he wanted the power.

"*I* love you," he said, his hands strong against my forearms.

"Love me? Then why did you do it? You knew what I was. You knew I was meant for Ilyan. What did you have to gain?" My words trailed off at the memory of the riddle about the two brothers that Ryland's possessed body had told me on a rooftop. It couldn't be...

"No!" I yelled, pushing him away from me.

Ryland couldn't have bonded himself to me for his own gain.

I repeated it to myself, almost willing the words to be true.

"Leave me alone!" I yelled as I turned away from him, his fingers curling around my forearm like a vice and stopping me in my tracks.

"Is that what you want? For me to leave you alone?"

"Yes!" I spat, ignoring the knife-like stab in my heart.

"Wish granted!" He pushed me away from him as I stumbled, my head spinning as the room shook. Another explosion sounded, this one closer and more aggressive than the last, Ryland swore loudly before grabbing my arm and dragging me through the manor.

We didn't get far before he shoved me into a closet just as footsteps approached. I moved my body into the corner as Cail yelled out, his voice loud in the tiny space.

"No!"

"Yes," Ryland taunted him, his voice deep and menacing.

"How did you get here?" The level of fear in Cail's voice was shocking to me. Why did Ryland's presence scare him so much?

I felt the small paw of a rodent press against my shoulder before the full weight of the creature transferred onto my collar bone. I opened my mouth in horror, not daring to move, while my body unwillingly took in a shaky breath that I prayed was not audible.

"It is my mind, Cail." Ryland said, the smile evident in his voice.

Everything froze as the rat walked across my back, his body tangling itself in my hair. I tried to keep my panic under control and another shaky inhale silent as he made his passage.

"Not for long."

The tiny closet shook as an explosion rattled the space sending books and baskets onto me. I screamed and covered my head, hoping my voice was not heard through the fight that was being waged right outside the door.

My breathing picked up as the explosions moved further down the hall, Ryland leading Cail away from me and giving me a chance to escape. I wiped away the invisible tracks of the rat, my shoulders shuddering in disgust as I broke out of the closet and took off back the way I had come. I turned into a hallway I had never entered before, hoping the two locked in battle had not seen me flee.

I was at a disadvantage here. I only knew parts of this mansion. I knew how to get to Ryland's room and most of the servants corridors of the upper levels, but the main living space and all the lower rooms were foreign to me. I needed to retrace my steps to get back to the kitchen.

I continued to run down the hall, my feet slipping on decaying carpet as I bolted down one corridor, then another.

I hadn't gone very far when a loud crash echoed in the space around me, causing light fixtures to shake and pieces of plaster to fall. I stopped in my tracks, my pulse surging heavily as I waited; as I tried to figure out what course to take.

"Don't stop moving," I whispered aloud to myself, but I still couldn't move. Slowly I pried my feet off the floor and shifted into a run, knowing that a moving target was harder to catch. I kept going until I came to a split flight of stairs; one side leading up, the other down. The kitchen was on the ground floor, I needed to go down.

I picked up my pace as I headed down the stairs, my hand lightly grazing the dirt and mold covered railing. I turned corner after corner as I descended, each level becoming more infested, more deteriorated, and more blood covered. Even though I knew that was what it was, I begged my mind to believe it to be paint. It was splattered everywhere.

The more I moved through the silence, the more I became aware of every noise and twitch in the air. I jumped at every creak, at the steady thumping that came from somewhere over head. I would pass doors which lead to floors of the estate, sure I heard voices on the other side, only to stop and have those voices turn into the squeaking of mice or ripping of paper.

I stopped abruptly when I had moved down about six stories, my heart thumping wildly at the pool of red liquid that occupied the landing of the steps below me. The smooth, red fluid swirled aggressively as if it was being disturbed; as if something around the next turn was moving through it.

I gasped as my muscles tensed, my panic growing. This wasn't right. I was too low. I had gone too far. I didn't know where I was. I needed to go back. I turned as quickly as I could, running up the stairs, desperate to get away from whatever was deep within the pool of blood.

I had gone up far more floors than I had gone down when I realized that nothing was changing. I should have moved back into the manor by now, but the walls still remained red and glistening. My eyes darted around wildly before I turned to retrace my steps.

Two steps down, I howled in horror as my foot plunged into the warm pool of fluid. I looked at the bubbling pool of blood, fear pulsing through my ears. I had left this pool behind me, at least ten flights of stairs down, and yet, here it was.

As I watched, the liquid lurched, growing a step and splashing against my foot. I screamed and grasped the door knob to the nearest floor, flinging my body through the door, not bothering to check if anyone was waiting for me on the other side. My only thought was to get away from the pool of blood.

To find the kitchen, even though something was telling me that it was gone.

CHAPTER 13
ILYAN

"What?" I turned to face Dramin, his words melting into my panic.

"I have seen something like this," he repeated, not quite meeting my eyes.

"Where?" I asked, trying to keep my voice level, the anger and regality seeping out without me wanting it to. "Was it a sight, Dramin, or at some point in your living life?"

He hesitated, and I instantly knew why. Last night he had spoken in his usual guarded way about being needed; it was his reason for consenting to come to the Rioseco Abbey with Joclyn and me. I hadn't thought twice at the time, how could I? For hundreds of years, guarded words and cryptic answers had been the way of the Drak. I had no reason to think that would have changed. I felt Thom's magic surge dangerously as his temper rose.

"You have seen this in sight, haven't you, Dramin?" My voice was level, the regal tone I had tried to keep restrained for most of my life seeping through.

Dramin didn't answer. He simply extended his hand toward me, his face pained as he gave me permission to use the full extent of his recall.

I placed Joclyn on the cold, stone floor of the cave to grab Dramin's hand and place it against my forehead. My eyes closed to blackness before the vision filled me. I could see myself, standing over Joclyn, the stone walls of the Rioseco Abbey clear in the background. Her body was still, limp, and yet I was yelling at her, panic evident on my face. I watched as Dramin walked into the room, his face calm before he, too, panicked. Before I could see any more, Dramin removed his hand from my head, the vision leaving with it.

There was no sign of her waking up in the sight, only her limp body, my pain, and panic. That sight could be in a week or in five years—I had no way of knowing. I re-ran the vision in my mind as I inspected every aspect: different clothes, my usual shorter haircut, the Rioseco Abbey.

"Why didn't you tell me, Dramin?" I ran my fingers through my hair, pulling hard on the long, uncomfortable strands.

"Tell you what?"

"Tell me what would happen! That something was wrong, something is..." I stopped, not knowing exactly how to finish that sentence. "We could have stopped this."

"What could you have done, My Lord?" Dramin's voice was deep and accusatory. I could already hear the regular rebuttal of his kind on his tongue—the lack of knowledge, the inability to interfere with things to come.

"You could have told me," I said, knowing my reasoning would be lost on him. "I could have stopped her from going into the Tȍuha—"

"How was I to know it was Tȍuha?" Dramin asked, his voice rising. I straightened in front of him, my height and heritage pulling at my temper. Anyone else would have recoiled, but he was so used to me he didn't even move.

"I showed you all that I have seen, Ilyan. There was no way to know—"

"Zastavit." *Stop.* I spoke loudly, prickling agitation moved up my body in a ripple. I let it take over for one weighted minute before I released it; unleashing my temper against Dramin would solve nothing.

"Does she wake?" My voice was a whispered breath.

"Yes." My head snapped up at Dramin's answer, hope running through me.

"Then we will wait. We will go to Rioseco, and we will wait." I was firm, confident, but all that left when a feminine moan pulled me from Dramin and back to Joclyn. I spun around, part of me desperate to see her eyes open, her bright smile.

She was the same.

I dropped to my knees, pressing my hands against her arms as my magic flowed into her.

"Ne," I gasped when I found it. She had a broken bone in her leg. The break was clean and ran right through her tibia. I was sure she had not had it when we entered the training room.

"What?" Thom knelt next to her head, and strangely, the anger in his voice was leaving, concern seeping through in a slow trickle.

"Her leg is broken," I said, not willing to accept it myself.

"Broken?" Dramin leaned down beside me, his hand moving against her head. His magic moved into her alongside my own, the heavy tendrils of the Drak magic cold. He gasped when he felt it and withdrew his hand, his magic leaving with the loss of contact.

I wrapped the bone in a hard layer of my magic, giving it a strong internal cast to help heal it. I didn't know how long it would take with her strangely vacant magic unable to do most of the work itself.

"What is he doing to her, Ilyan?" Thom moved away, his fear at the power of our father obviously affecting him.

He had seen too much of our father's games. I just didn't like to lose, and Edmund had upped the stakes in this game.

Edmund was torturing her, hurting her, intentionally. He had done the same to me more than a dozen times—every time he had somehow managed to capture me. It was his favorite game, causing pain.

He had tortured and killed mortals in front of me, hoping to break me or drive me mad. Now he was doing the same to Joclyn. He had found a way to hurt her, really hurt her, in a place I could not follow.

Or could I?

"I need to get in there." I stood quickly, ignoring the confused glances from the men on either side of me, my focus only on Joclyn's body.

"What do you mean, *get in there*?" Thom asked.

"I mean, go into the Tȍuha and get her out. Wake her up." I squared my shoulders, still unwilling to look away from her.

"Is that even possible? You said you could not find the bridge." Dramin's voice was quiet.

"I will find it when I join my mind with hers, Půjde to?" I clenched my jaw, my mind working in preparation for what I was suggesting.

"This is ridiculous, Ilyan," Thom pleaded. "Tam jít tam, you would only be stuck in there. Dramin has seen her wake. We just need to wait."

"Wait?" I scoffed at Thom's reasoning. A few minutes ago, I had been content to do the same, but now her leg was broken. I would not let Edmund get away with this. "Two hours there for every twenty minutes here. She has been trapped in that prison for six hours. They have broken her leg and hurt her enough to make her bleed internally. I can't leave her in there. Who knows what else they have done, or are going to do? I don't have time to wait."

"I can't let you do this, My Lord." I turned at the sound of Dramin's voice, the desperate plea catching me off guard.

"I don't know what else to do. You are her brother, Dramin. As her brother, would you stand by while someone tortured her?" I didn't need him to understand, I could do it on my own. He was one of the first of his kind, and Joclyn's blood.

"He's her brother..." Thom said just as the thought crossed my mind. I could see what he was thinking, I knew where this was going, and I didn't like it.

"No, Thom," I said sternly, hoping to stop the thought in his mind before he found his voice.

"It's what our father is using to control the nightmares, correct?"

"Yes, but—" I began, but Thom swiftly cut me off. I could feel my spine prickle at the lack of respect, but I ignored it.

"It must be what he is using to control the Tȍuha." Thom's face was growing in maniacal intensity. I watched him closely, knowing I would have to put a stop to it soon.

"Using a blood connection is not an option," I hissed through gritted teeth.

"I don't see why not, Ilyan. It's what Edmund is using against her. So, we can use the same technique to save her."

"No, Thom. I won't let that happen, not ever. It's wicked, evil. You should know that better than either of us. Do you understand?" I spoke deeply. Blood magic was dangerous. The cutting open of hearts and souls was inhumane.

"It's just a blood connection, Ilyan. It is how Edmund is able to control Joclyn's dreams. They have Sain, but we have Dramin—"

"No. I will never allow you to cut open my heart or sever my soul in an attempt to save her. This is madness, Thom." Even Dramin was panicked.

"Then what do we do?" Thom whispered, his shoulders sagging as he gave in.

"We get out of this cave," I said, knowing there wasn't another option. Not anymore. "Once the rock settles we will begin. Thom will you check the extent of the damage or the cave? I need to be with Joclyn."

We all nodded in understanding before I moved away from them to Joclyn. My fingers ran over the lines of her face as my magic swelled through her, my touch moving over eyes, her cheeks, and across the soft skin before her ear.

I lay down next to her, my body pressing up against hers as it had only an hour before. She was so warm compared to the chill of the stone.

I pushed my magic into her, confident that I would not hurt her. Her magic pushed against mine, but the strength of it still seemed to be missing.

"Come back to me, Jos," I whispered, hopeful that my voice would flow to her as hers had to me. It wasn't fair what fate had planned for us; to take us from one hell to another, to tear us away from each other, to tear her away from her mate.

I let my magic settle inside of her before I moved it toward my target, fusing parts of myself with her, my magic connecting with nerve endings in an attempt to contact her. I let my finger slide down to connect with her mark, the jolt rocking through me as it always had, every day that I had touched it from the first. Even when she had felt nothing, I had always felt the surge. I sighed at the sensation and closed my eyes, letting my mind fuse with hers.

I would have yelled at what I found, but I was too scared to see the emptiness of her mind.

There was a reason I could not sense her power, her emotions or her soul. Nothing was there. Her body was an empty shell. I gasped at the emptiness, at the confusion and loss I felt from finding her gone.

There should have been memories, dreams and visions, but I saw nothing but blackness, the velvety color clear and dark.

If she had left to join her mate in some expanse of eternity, would it leave an empty shell behind? I was foolish to think that this would work, that even a blood connection would work. It couldn't work because there was nothing to attach to. There was no bridge to bring her back.

Edmund must have attached himself to Ryland before he used the connection and pulled her through to him. Before he locked her away. That was how he gained control.

I let my mind linger inside the black realm that Joclyn had left behind, searching for any way to bring her home.

As I searched, I sang. I sang the song I had written for her all those hundreds of years ago.

The song that was only for her.

I left the song inside of her head, hoping that it would, at least, welcome her home.

CHAPTER 14
WYN

No one came back to the dungeon. Not Sain. Not Ryland, or even Cail. They had all left a week ago, and not even the guards had returned for more than a moment.

At least, I thought it had been a week. There was no easy way to track the passage of time when you spend all of it in the dark. I had slept six times, and someone had brought the daily glass of muddy water seven times.

One glass, not two, just like there was only one maggot-covered loaf of bread.

Just like Talon hadn't woken up.

A week alone in the dark, with only my husband's limp hand for company. I slept next to him, my arms around as much of him as I could reach as I dreamed of the beautiful girl and Henry the Eighth, but never of the torture. I was glad that the dreams of torture had left. I had enough torture.

I still hurt from what Cail had done to me a week ago. My joints still ached, and my skin was tender to the touch. At least I could move, although not a lot and not very fast. I ambled between the glass of water and Talon, not like there was anywhere else for me to go.

I clung to him in the dark, a high-pitched wheeze occasionally escaping as his chest slowly rose and fell, his skin getting hotter and hotter. The fever that had appeared two days ago was increasing by the hour.

I ran my fingers over his skin, the heat feeling like hot stones in summer. With very little water to cool him and no magic to heal him, I didn't know how to get him to cool down. I was trapped in a nightmare of torment, and all the while, Sain's words still echoed in my head.

It will be soon.

I shifted my weight and crawled toward the filthy glass that sat in the corner of the cell. My fingers clutched at the stone floor, moving over sand, dirt and bits of what I could only assume were rodent bones, until they gently hit the hard surface of the glass. I fidgeted through the air until my hands wrapped around it, the grit on the glass feeling like slime. I clutched the glass to my chest, the small amount of fluid that was left in the bottom as precious as gold.

I shuffled back to Talon, my knees screaming as my weight rested on them, the water held against my chest. I felt in front of me for the bars, terrified of going too far, of losing my balance and dropping the glass. It took a few tries before I found him again, the warmth of his skin heating the air.

With shaking fingers, I scooped the water from the glass and pressed it against his skin. I trickled it against his lips and into his mouth. Over and over, I moved, pressed and sprinkled the water, only to have it evaporate into the damp air the second it touched his scalding flesh. I held my damp fingers against him, hoping to keep the water there longer, hoping the chill of my own skin would serve as an equalizer.

Something deep inside of me was pleading for me to accept that this was hopeless, begging me to save the water for myself, but I couldn't. I couldn't abandon him. I would sacrifice myself for him until the very end. Half for me and half for him. Always.

"I love you," I whispered, my voice barely audible. It was all I could risk, but it was the most important thing to say.

The now empty glass clattered to the stone floor, my body giving out to collapse against the bars and slide across the slime covered surface to reach Talon, my hands clinging to him as I attempted to fall asleep.

I would have, if it weren't for the footsteps somewhere above me, moving toward me. I didn't know if it was the whisper, the clatter of the glass, or the groan as I had hit the floor, but something had reminded them of my existence.

The footsteps were faster than I had ever heard and the voices behind them louder, angrier. I clung to Talon, my overgrown fingernails digging into him as someone began their decent down the stairs.

"It's only been a week, sir," Timothy said, slightly out of breath. "You can't expect him to have finished her off by now?"

"I can expect anything I want, Timothy," Edmund spat, the footsteps stopping as he spoke, "Don't make me put you in your place, old friend. You have been with me from the beginning, but that does not mean you are on the same pillar as I."

There was a pause, a pause that lasted an eternity of heartbeats and tingling nerve endings. I had no idea what they were talking about, and I didn't care. The only thing in my mind was how close they were.

"Sorry, sir," my father gasped, the footsteps resuming almost immediately. Everything clenched as they came closer, my brain panicking in fear of why Edmund was coming down.

"I gave him a deadline, and I expect results. If he needs a little persuasion, then so be it." Edmund's voice grew louder as a bright light blasted through my closed eyelids. I held as still as I could, knowing that no matter how much pretending I did, it wouldn't stop them. The mere fact that Edmund was down here spelled danger for me.

"But are you sure this is the way?" Timothy asked, disgusted.

"You should have seen his face when I threatened to unbind the curse," Edmund said. "This is the way."

Their voices were right outside my cell now, their conversation ending as iron bars grated together.

"Put him in that end cell down there and then you can go."

Footsteps, the grinding of iron, and the rattling of chains. I heard Sain grunt and I fought the urge to turn toward him, my arm jerking on its own before I could stop it. They had brought him back. Ryland was not with him, which could only mean that they had sent him with Ovailia. I needed to get out of here. I needed to find a way to warn them.

"Get up, Wynifred."

My father's voice was deep with warning. I knew I needed to obey, but didn't want to face whatever Edmund had in store for me.

"Come on, Wynifred," Edmund coaxed, his voice sweet and condescending. "Listen to your father."

I didn't want to listen, but I also didn't want to push it. I moved a bit and began to push myself up to sit, my weak arms shaking as I lifted myself. My joints groaned and I gasped before letting my body weight rest against the bars, my head flopping back as I looked at them.

"Hello, Father," I said with as much ire as I could, but my weak voice swallowed my pride.

"Why, Wynifred," Edmund said, ignoring my comment to my father, "you are looking well. Better than I think I have ever seen you." He smiled at me as he squatted, bringing himself to eye level.

I clenched my jaw and scowled at him, not wanting to know what was coming.

"Not going to say hello?"

"No. I'm not." I narrowed my eyes, daring him to continue, begging him to finish me.

"Not going to ask after my welfare?" His voice was still irritatingly calm.

I stayed still, my jaw clenched. A feeling I could not place was forming in the base of my spine. It was pure irritation blended with spite and it created an emotion I had never felt before.

"Hmmm, no matter," Edmund continued and smiled. "By the time I am done with you, you will be begging me to say 'hello'."

I didn't flinch. I didn't move. I just stared at him as the door to my cell opened and he took a few steps in to tower above me.

"Stand, Wynifred." I almost laughed at him. It was a miracle I was able to move myself to sitting. Standing was out of the question.

"Not going to obey your Master?" Edmund asked.

I flinched, words that I knew I should never say to his face tumbling off my tongue before I could stop them. "You are not my Master."

"Well, not *anymore*..." He smiled, his hand patting the top of my head harshly. The weight of his touch sent me sliding down against the bars. "...but once upon a time."

I wanted to say something, but I couldn't. He was right. Or, he could be. I didn't remember my past.

But he did, and he knew something that I was beginning to think I didn't want to know. I looked away from his towering form, burying my face in the bars to look away from him. Instead, my eyes fell on Talon, my eyes seeing for the first time what the darkness had not shown me.

His eyes were sunken in, and his skin was pale and covered with a thick layer of sweat. His eyes twitched as he lay still, his lips moving as he mumbled in his sleep.

"Years ago, you would do my bidding with only a smile and a swish of your hips." I ignored him and kept my focus on Talon, listening to the tap of Edmund's feet against the stone. "Well, until you betrayed me."

Betrayed him?

My mind was swimming.

Edmund stooped down before me, careful to balance his weight on his toes and not touch the filthy ground. I kept my sight on Talon until

Edmund's long fingers turned my head toward him, forcing my gaze to him and his greasy smile. I would not give in to him. I glared right back at him.

"Tell me, how long did Cail help you? How did you help him to block the Štít?"

My confidence broke, confusion weaseling its way into my expression as I looked at him. I knew he was talking about my past, but I couldn't fathom how what he was saying was correct.

"I have no idea what you are talking about," I said, refusing to place myself inside of his trap.

"Did you do the same to Ryland?"

I waited, his eyes digging into mine. He glared into me, his patience leaving as he slammed my head into the metal bars behind me.

"Answer me!" he roared, his hand pushing me back into the bars again.

I howled at the pain, my hands moving toward my head in an attempt to ease the pressure. They had only made it halfway before the heavy iron shackles snaked through the air to wrap around my wrists. The large bands jerked me away from the bars, dragging my body against the stone as the chains pulled me against the wall, arms extended above my head.

"What did you do?" Edmund roared, his face coming within inches of mine. I looked away from him and toward my father, who stood by the stairs with a wicked smile turning up his lips. I turned from him to Sain, who sat against the bars of his cell, his green eyes narrowed at me in both warning and expectation.

"I didn't do anything," I answered, my voice strained.

Edmund's eyes narrowed at me, his face moving in close until his nose was only an inch away from my face, his polar blue eyes the only thing left for me to focus on.

"Don't lie to me," he warned. "Tell me what else he did when he stopped your father's curse and tried to save your life. Tell me what happened when he put those pretty marks on your skin." Edmund dragged his finger along the dark marks as he spoke, his finger pressing painfully against my bruises.

I cringed against the pain, my eyes narrowing at him. Cail didn't try to save my life, he had tried to kill me. Just as my father had, but the curse misfired and instead marked my skin.

"N... no," I managed to stutter out, my confusion growing.

"What secret did Cail hide inside your pretty, little mind?"

"What?" I gasped, unable to keep my confusion at bay any longer. Edmund only smiled as he closed the gap between us and pressed his cheek against mine. I felt the uncomfortable warmth of his skin and the iciness of his blood pulsing just underneath the surface.

"Don't worry, Wynifred; you will remember everything soon." He smiled and moved away from me, the chains around my wrists tightening, lifting me up so I could only balance on the balls of my feet.

"I'm sorry, sir, but what exactly are you saying?" I guess I wasn't the only one who was confused. My father looked between us as he, too, tried to fit together the missing pieces.

Edmund, however, seemed to be enjoying keeping more than one person in the dark. He smiled as he turned to face me again.

"You remember that night, don't you, Timothy?" Edmund taunted, his eyes feeling like warm lasers cutting into my brain.

"Texas, 1867. A simple assignment—kill Thom. After four hundred years of flawlessly killing every person I commanded her to, Wynifred here missteps. She tells me Thom is in Texas and not in Italy as I had already ascertained. So off she goes to Texas, to kill the father of her child. But I see through it, and I follow her..."

My mouth opened automatically, my jaw working in disbelief. Four hundred years of working for Edmund, a child, Thom...? None of this was my life.

"That never—"

"That never happened?" Edmund asked, his cynical voice twisting the meaning behind my words. "You don't remember it? Then tell me what you do remember."

He arched his eyebrows, his lips curling in a wicked half smile as he waited.

That night. The night when I got the marks, I remembered it perfectly. The flash of light, my brother's face, the yelling. I remembered feeling scared. I remembered... I didn't... what was said?

I knew my past had been wiped away, but why was so much more missing?

My jaw worked its way open and shut like the jaws of a fish as my brain tried to find the words to answer his questions.

"Don't remember what happened? How about your childhood? What happened then?" He had moved closer, but I barely noticed. My childhood...? I couldn't remember. I could see faces, feel emotions, but exactly what happened... how... there was nothing there.

"Can't remember, can you?"

"What are you saying, Edmund? We've always known about her memory loss—"

"Yes, but what if her memory loss, her change in personality, what if it wasn't a result of Cail's attempts to bind your curse. What if he did it intentionally to hide something?" Edmund ran his finger along my jaw, his eyes still boring into me.

I wanted to deny everything he had said. I wanted to tell him the truth. I just couldn't. I couldn't say something I couldn't remember... I couldn't remember...

What did I know?

I was Wynifred, born in about 1795, exiled in 1867. I had a father, Timothy, and a brother, Cail. Ilyan killed my mother in... He killed her because... My father gave me the marks because I was caught giving information to Ilyan... They caught me in... Texas?

Except that wasn't what I knew. That was what I had been told.

My eyes grew wide, Edmund's smile following suit.

"What secret did Cail lock in your mind, Wynifred?"

My eyes fluttered around the room, from Talon's still body, curled on the cold ground, to my father, to Sain, looking for anyone to give me a different explanation. Sain looked at me and nodded once.

"Time to open the lock, Wynifred."

Edmund smiled as he placed his hand against my skull, his magic rushing into me. I screamed as the pressure moved into my brain, the heat flooding through me as the force increased. My own scream echoed in my ears as Edmund's powerful magic threatened to rip me apart. It opened up my mind and let everything out.

My head throbbed and pulsed as things I had long since forgotten filled me. Memories that I had wanted to stay locked away came flooding back—the beautiful child's screams and the Henry the Eighth wanna-be suddenly made sense.

Everything made sense.

Because I remembered it.

CHAPTER 15
JOCLYN

I pressed my back against the door as it closed, my eyes widening as I came face to face with the longest hall I had ever seen. The hall extended for miles, the walls lined with doors. There were too many doors to count, all of them in differing states of decay and damp. I almost expected Cail to come bursting through them in search of me.

I tried to control my panic, but I knew it was no use. Cail had trapped me in the worst nightmare I had ever experienced. This was a million times worse than every time he had chased me through the manor, hunted me through the forest, or murdered me into waking. I could feel my neck twitch in fear as I fought the urge to collapse into myself.

I began to sing Ilyan's song in my head as I walked down the hall and into the unknown realm I had entered. I moved as silently as I could, jumping over open gaps in the floor and tiptoeing around small animal carcasses. Every other step would trigger a sound far down the hall and I would freeze, staring ahead as my fingers tingled. I was ready to face whatever would come for me.

But nothing ever did.

I kept moving, my pace slow as I trudged forward. Jumping over the floor. Dodging around bones. Singing. It became a pattern as I moved endlessly forward, the motions running in repetition as I tried to find a way out.

A way out?

That was what I was down there for, right?

I froze, staring down the endless hall as my heart rate peaked. Everything was fuzzy, like the recall in my mind had been broken. I shook my head, twitching as that sound echoed again.

Yes, I wanted a way out of the Tòuha. Cail had trapped me here.

I can't have been down here so long that I would have forgotten.

Two hours in the Tòuha for every twenty minutes in the waking world. I wanted to say it had already been two hours, but it was hard to tell. Maybe it was more. I had been walking down the hall for far too long. Somewhere in the back of my mind I wondered if Ilyan might know how to pull me out of here. I knew he would try, but I still had to get out.

There was a door that would take me there.

But where was it?

My thoughts were cut off as heavy footsteps began to sound behind me. These weren't like the other sounds, these were rough and heavy. I knew those steps. I stopped, turning toward the black hallway behind me before I picked up the pace, my panic infecting every inch of me.

I jumped over open caverns, leaped around bones and feces, but the steps grew closer. The sound grow louder. I took one last leap before fiddling with the knob of one of the many doors along the hall. It swung wide and I jumped inside, slamming it loudly behind me before turning to face the room. But it wasn't a room. It was yet another long hallway with more blood, more bones, and more pits into an endless abyss below.

At least I was safe from whoever was chasing me. I turned, and froze. The door was gone. It was just more hall.

An endless hall and rattling footsteps that had followed me here.

I ran and immediately began opening doors, racing through them so I could get away. I moved from one hallway to another, running as the steps followed. Louder. Quicker. Just like the sound of my heart in my ears.

One door. Then another.

Another.

Doors.

One of them had to lead somewhere I would recognize. One of them had to lead to... to...

Where was I going?

I stopped as I moved through the fifth door in the third hallway, or was it the twelfth door in the ninth hallway? I couldn't tell. This hallway looked like all the others. Was there something there I was trying to find?

Yes.

But what?

I closed my eyes, racking my brain and trying to replay the last few minutes.

The way out.

I was looking for a way out.

Which was behind a door. I just had to find the right door.

This space was messing with my mind. I immediately turned around and went back through the door I had entered, back into another identical hallway when I froze.

More doors.

I had no way of knowing which one I had come through. I was so concerned with getting away from whatever was following me, that I had gotten myself lost; lost in this house. I wasn't even sure how I had gotten here.

Ryland's mind... I was in Ryland's mind.

I sunk down to the ground. Tears burned my face as they trailed down my cheeks, I tried to restrain the noise, unsure if Cail was down here or if he was even still trying to find me. I sucked in my tears, letting Ilyan's lullaby take their place. I sang the song aloud, whispering the words in the desperate hope that no one would hear me while still needing the comfort.

Slowly my pulse began to slow. My breathing evened out, and I let the song fizzle away. I wasn't comforted. I wasn't safe. I was still trapped in this hell that Cail had designed for me, but things didn't seem so desperate. I needed to find...

What was it again?

That was right.

Home. I needed to go home.

I stood and walked across the hall, reaching for yet another doorknob. I froze, my hand still poised over the knob.

There were voices on the other side of this door.

The voices seemed familiar, but I couldn't place them.

"It's been hours. How is the progress?" The older man's voice boomed. He almost sounded bored, as though he was looking over paperwork.

"It is coming, Master. I have guided her to where we want her and begun the process as you have asked."

Master? Why did that phrase sound so familiar?

Suddenly the voice of the younger, scared man clicked into place—Cail. Which would make the older man Edmund. I shook my head in an attempt to clear the fog. How could I have forgotten them?

"Have you? Already?" Edmund sounded shocked now, pleased.

"Yes."

"Very nice, Cail. I'm impressed," Edmund said, "They have already begun to break their bond, I will continue the process before she finds her way back."

Break the bond? That sounded familiar. I moved one step closer to the door, pressing my eyes against the small opening, desperate to see. Cail stood before Edmund, who sat in a large ornate chair with his legs crossed as he played with an elaborate ring on his finger. Edmund looked wrong somehow, though; almost like he was faded or covered in wax paper.

"I have set a web to trap her inside my mind." Cail said, his voice breaking with tension. "There is no way to find a way through it without guidance." Edmund didn't even look at him.

I stepped away from the door to look around me. Cail's mind. He had told me it was Ryland's mind.

Ryland.

The bond.

"She has been brought here through the bond, meaning Ryland could find his way inside and lead her out. Break the bond and destroy the path that got her here. She would be trapped, her mind lost inside of yours with no way out."

Everything clicked together and I covered my mouth. Something in me was screaming trap, danger, warning; but I still couldn't quite remember why they would do all this to me.

"Are you sure you are up for the challenge, Cail?" Edmund asked, yet Cail only laughed in response.

"I am sure, Master. She is putting up quite an enjoyable fight."

"You better give me a good show, Cail. Finish quick, otherwise I will unbind that little curse you put on your sister."

I pressed my eyes against the opening again at the mention of Wyn, surprised that the recollection of her name had come so swiftly. I didn't like how fuzzy this place was making my brain. I needed to get out of here.

"No!" Cail's voice was loud, panicked, and unexpected. I would never have expected such terror to come out of him. Cail had taken a desperate step forward, the action causing Edmund to look up.

"Oh, yes, imagine all that poison weaving itself away from her skin and into her blood stream..."

"Master, you..." Cail began to interrupt him but was silenced with one look from Edmund. Cail's hand flew to his heart in panic.

"Cail." The strict tone of Edmund's voice was like ice down my spine.

"Yes, Master." Cail spoke quietly—dejectedly—before his back straightened and his head turned to look right at me. This time I was sure he had seen me.

"Yes, Master," He said again as his lip curled. "Let the games begin."

"Oh, good. I will give you one month, Cail." I barely heard Edmund's voice over the heavy thumping of my heart. Cail turned and was walking right toward me, his eyes boring into mine. I couldn't move. I had frozen in place, my hand still clinging to the doorknob.

I knew I should be looking around for some form of weapon or trying to get away, but I couldn't tear my eyes from his black stare or the sneer on his lips.

"Run, Joclyn." I barely registered that someone had spoken before a hand wrapped around mine, another person dragging me down the hall.

I stumbled along for a few steps before turning toward whoever was pulling me away. My heart jumpstarted at the mop of dark curls bouncing in front of me.

Ryland led me from hall to hall, the long passageways changing to smaller rooms, and even apartments complete with kitchens. Everything about the space we now moved through was familiar, like a place I had lived in or visited once. I looked at them all in brief intervals, unwilling to take my eyes off of my savior for long.

Ryland could get me out of here.

Couldn't he?

But what had Cail said about Ryland's memory, or was it his mind?

I couldn't remember.

Everything was tangling together again.

Finally Ryland came to a stop, his large hand pressing me against a damp wall as he looked back around the corner, obviously worried we had been followed.

I clutched his hand, wanting to cling to him—to apologize—but I couldn't think of why I needed to apologize. Had something happened?

"I think we're okay," his voice was relieved, yet when he turned to face me, I audibly gasped.

It was Ryland, but something about him was off. His eyes weren't as blue, or maybe his forehead was higher. I couldn't place exactly what was wrong. I shook my head, maybe I just wasn't remembering him right.

That must have been it. I sighed and pushed myself into him, relaxing as his arms wrapped around me.

"Oh, Jos. You have no idea how happy I am to have found you." His hold increased, it was almost like he couldn't get close enough.

"I know," I said, my body shaking much more than I would have expected. "I thought Cail was..."

My voice cut off as Ryland's grip got tighter again, choking the air from me.

"I thought I would never see you again." He said deeply, his tone becoming monotone while his grip continued to increase.

I gasped and sputtered, hitting him as I pounded at his back, but he didn't respond until the last possible minute when his hold loosened and his eyes lowered to look right at me.

"I'm sorry, Jos. I got scared."

I looked in his eyes, desperately trying to figure out if it was him or not. All the times in the Tòuha, all the dreams, every encounter with Ryland's possessed body had made it so I couldn't tell the real Ryland from the fake Ryland anymore. I didn't know if this Ryland would hurt me or protect me. The old Ryland—my Ryland—was now becoming a fuzzy memory of someone I wasn't even sure existed. I didn't trust the Ryland that held me. I didn't want to be near him.

With that one thought, everything that I had felt before was shattered. I didn't feel the love I had once felt for him and it scared me.

"It's okay," I said, my words stopping as the heavy footsteps from earlier filled the space, the cabinets and bottles in our current refuge rattling with each impact.

Ryland clutched me to him, his nails digging into me at each beat. I barely noticed. My muscles jumped at each footfall right along with them.

Before I knew what had happened, Ryland had grabbed my body and thrown me across the room. I sped through the air, screaming at the unprovoked action, before slamming into an empty bookcase. The second my body made contact with the moldy shelves, the thumping stopped.

"You brought them to me!" Ryland yelled, his voice echoing around me.

"What are you talking about?" I picked myself up to face him, body aching. His eyes were wide and his fists balled at his sides. I stared as he yelled at me before hunching his shoulders and charging at me.

"You cursed me!"

He had made it about halfway across the room before I ran through the first door I could find, Ryland still yelling behind me. I swung the door shut, though I did not halt my progression. I ran from door to door, hallway to hallway, until I thought that I had put enough space between us.

I looked wildly around the room I had entered to see cabinets, a hospital bed, a dresser, and a filthy toilet. I recognized this place, but like all the other rooms, nothing made sense. The walls that had once been solid had deteriorated enough that you could see through them in many areas, but only enough to see what was coming.

It was a lookout.

A hiding place.

I ran over to the toilet and wedged myself between the filthy bowl and what was left of one of the walls, an old hospital bed perfectly placed to block me from view.

I moved my legs into my chest and clung to them, my eyes wide as I looked around and tried to figure out my next move.

Next move?

Why was I here anyway?

Did I live here?

No.

That wasn't right.

I clung tighter to my legs, rested my head on my knees and tried to ignore the smell of the toilet, the scurrying feet of large pests, and the

drip

drip

drip

of water that was falling on my head.

A strange heat slowly began to spread through me. It began in my shoulder and soon reached every part of me. I screamed and jumped up, expecting to see blood trickling over my skin, but I found nothing. I looked around in a panic, knowing my yell had given away my location and that Ryland would be right behind me.

I ran my eyes over my skin, still looking for some form of injury, there was nothing there. Just warmth.

The warmth seemed familiar, comforting, wanted. I just didn't know why.

I had the distinct impression I was forgetting something.

Or was it someone?

CHAPTER 16
ILYAN

My stomach growled with the lack of food, but I ignored it. I had gone longer without eating. I had been living in comfort for too long, my body had become used to consistency. Being trapped in a cave for the past few days had not provided my body the food it now felt it needed.

I laid my head against the back of the cave, ignoring the hard, cold stone and focused instead on the soft warmth of the girl that was curled against me. At least I could make Joclyn comfortable. I pulled Dramin's robe around her, tucking the edges under her in an attempt to trap her body heat.

Her heartbeat was steady. It hummed against my skin as it followed the rise and fall of her chest. I focused on it, waiting for her body to seize again.

I had slept with her here for the past few nights. Tonight, though, I could not sleep. I didn't know what was going on in the prison she remained in, but her body had twitched and moved more than usual. Only an hour ago, her knee had been hurt so badly that the tendons had been ripped away from the muscle. I repaired it dutifully as she slept, wrapping it in heavy bindings as she twitched. Through it all, I sang my song to her. I let the words fill her mind, my voice imprinting inside of her whether she was there to hear it or not.

It had been the same pattern for the past four days—heal her and sing to her. Then, after every time, I connected with her mind in an attempt to find her. I would keep trying everything I could to save her, to bring her back to me. I would wait forever if that was what it took.

Her body seized again, and her chest racked as she coughed, more blood drizzling from her mouth. I wiped it with the back of my hand and then onto my jeans. With nothing to clean her with, my pants had become stained with a warm, red hue, her blood deepening the color every day.

My fingers clung to the once soft fabric of her shirt, pulling it down just enough to check the skin on her shoulder where the Štít lay inside of her, the dark red scratches deepening in color as I watched, a small trickle of blood appearing on the surface. I replaced the shirt and held her against me, rocking as I clung her to me.

Desperation, it was a feeling I had rarely felt in my long life. I had never really been hopeless enough to feel it. I was always the one in control, powerful and resilient. I laughed at battle and found joy in an impending death. With Joclyn's injured body in my arms, though, I only felt desperation.

If I had ever believed in God, now would be the time I would call to Him, beg Him to save her, to bring her home. I still didn't know if such a God existed, and whoever had called my kind to come forth from the mud had always been strangely silent.

"Have you slept?" I didn't move at Dramin's question. I kept my head curled against Joclyn, my hair falling around us.

"No," I whispered loud enough for him to hear me. I knew my voice would carry through the cave. "Last night was bad." I didn't dare elaborate.

"Any new developments?" He knew there would be none, just as I did. We were still trapped in the cave, and Joclyn was still trapped in the Tȍuha.

"I can stay with her again today, if you would like? Thom can shift rock on his own for a while; it would give you time to rest." I knew he meant well, but I didn't need to be coddled. Resting while Joclyn writhed was not a possibility. I would rather shift rock with Thom as I did every day. At least then, my mind could focus on other things.

"I see you braided her hair again," he commented when I didn't answer him. I nodded at Dramin's question, waiting for what would come next.

I had braided her hair after some of her blood had dried in it. I had been able to repair the head injury easily enough, but the dark mass of curls needed to be washed. With nothing to clean it with, I resorted to re-braiding, weaving the clumps into the intricate five strand braid. I hadn't even realized what I had done until it was finished.

"The wedding braid is an interesting choice." I ignored him. "To match the shoes, I take it."

I leaned my head back and looked at him out of the corner of my eye, almost daring him to continue.

"You can imagine my surprise when she showed up here wearing those things on her feet. They are excellent workmanship."

Dramin let his unasked question linger. I could feel it swirl around us, the intensity of it growing the longer I left it unacknowledged.

I knew I owed him no reply; it was not my place to allow insight to my every thought. But, Dramin did not ask as a curious servant, he asked as my friend and Joclyn's brother. In that regard, I owed him an explanation.

"I made the shoes as a gift," I finally admitted, refusing to look at him and instead focused on Joclyn's heartbeat.

"She had lost something I couldn't even fathom; I wanted to give her what was due her. What her husband should have placed on her feet on the night of the bonding."

"And so, with him gone, you tried to take his place." I could hear the accusation clearly, but instead of making me angry it only made me laugh.

"You know, that was never my intention, strangely enough. I made the shoes as a gift from her newfound brother, a wedding gift. Part of me fully expected Ryland to return, to fight Edmund and reappear as if nothing had happened. But then, when she wasn't recovering, when Ryland never came, I knew he was gone. Then, I had begun to make them for an entirely different purpose."

"As a gift from a husband to his wife."

I nodded. I knew it was a foolish line of thinking, and one I still resented ever having, but if that last visit into the Tòuha hadn't cured her, I would have replaced Ryland's bond with one of my own. I knew that would have saved her because I had seen it done before. I would have gladly taken that role if it was necessary, but it wasn't.

"It is not my place, Dramin."

"Not yet," he said. I could only smile, letting the beautiful visions of the sight from so long ago wash over me.

"She is bonded to my brother, Dramin. That is a sacred connection and one I would never take advantage of. I will protect her for him. I will keep her safe as my soul calls for me to do, but I will never take her from him. She is not mine. I love her more than I have any other. I love her enough that I would rather see her happy than in my possession. My time will come."

I didn't doubt that any of my words were true, and it wasn't the fickle truth of having convinced myself to believe something. I truly believed it. I had felt it from the beginning when I had first seen Ryland swing her around on the grass at her school. I knew then that I could never take that away from her, that connection. It wasn't my place. Besides, doing things like that was not who I was.

"But she loves you, Ilyan." Dramin's voice was deep, almost as if he was trying to convince me I was making a wrong decision, but I could only laugh at him.

"I know, Dramin. She told me so," I whispered, my fingers moving to run over the soft skin of her face. "And those words flow through my head every night as I keep her safe in my arms, holding her until the right arms can take my place."

She sighed as I held her, almost as if she heard me. I smoothed my hand over her hair and the soft skin of her face. Her deep breathing seeped into me, relaxing me as well. The heady beating of my heart slowed, the uncharacteristic relaxation making me feel more in love with her than before, if that was possible.

"It will be harder than you think, handing her over to him."

"I know. Trust me when I say I have already been warned." I couldn't help it, my muscles tightened around her, bringing her against me tightly. I knew Dramin was right, but no matter how hard, I still would not interfere. Even though there was a very loud voice in my head that cursed me for not doing it before.

"You are a better man than I thought you to be, Ilyan." Dramin sat up slowly, his back leaning against the cold wall beside me.

I looked at him curiously, not sure if his words were that of a compliment or not. He just looked at me with pride and knowledge lining his handsome face.

"All those years ago," Dramin explained, "when I first saw the fate of what was to come for you, I was happy for you, so šťastný. But the heartbreak at her being with another... I thought you would purposefully tear them apart to get what was rightfully yours. I am sorry I ever thought badly about you. You are a man beyond words."

I smiled, but chose to say nothing. For years I had thought the exact way that Dramin had. I had been possessive, needy. She was mine, and no one was going to take her away from me. After all, I had waited for hundreds of years, what could one mortal do to stop me? He wasn't a mortal, however; he was my brother.

My brother who had stood up to our father and refused to torture me; who had fought him to give me a chance to escape. Ryland who had been poisoned at such a young age, a mere science experiment to our father. A boy who had known no love in his entire life had found that love, that sanctuary, in a girl I had been waiting for the majority of my life. I could not take that away from him, from either of them.

Once that realization had occurred, my heart no longer ached for her. It still longed, but it no longer ached.

"Sain's going to love you, Ilyan," Thom's voice came out of nowhere, and we both jumped. "Of course, he had no idea it was his own daughter he was showing you when the sight was first delivered. Noble Ilyan, so kind to his only daughter."

"Am I detecting a touch of resentment in your voice, Thom?" I asked as he came to sit across from me, the light in the cave increasing.

"Oh, always, Ilyan. As my perfect, older brother, I will always resent you." We both smiled, but it was strained. The bonds of family were always tense between us, between all of our father's children.

"Well," Thom began, leaning back on the palms of his hands, "I'm tired, bolák, hungry, and dying of thirst. What do you say we get out of here today?"

Dramin and I turned toward him, confused. And yet, I couldn't stop the fire of hope that ignited. We had been shifting rock at the mouth of the cave since the collapse first happened. We had almost made it out yesterday, but another small collapse had hindered the process.

I knew why Thom wanted to get out. We all needed food and drink; I could already feel my skin prickle with dehydration. Acting rashly wasn't going to get us out of here any faster; it was just going to get us killed.

"Brzy, Thom," I said, hoping to convey that a rush was not needed.

"Dnes, Ilyan," he countered, his inflection so modern it brought a smile to my face. "I don't want to wait anymore. We almost made it through last night. If we had used all three of us, we might have been able to do it."

"What are you saying?" Dramin asked, leaning toward him. He wasn't actually going to give Thom's idea his support, was he?

"If we all work together, we can make a hole big enough for us to escape through. Ilyan can carry the Silný, and we can all be in Rioseco by nightfall." He paused, and we just looked at him. I had to admit, part of what he was saying made sense. The small collapse from last night made me worry, however; the rocks might not have had a chance to settle.

"Just think about it," Thom prompted, "Skutečné postele, food and mugs for Dramin's poison..."

The silence stretched through the cave; it stretched between us until Joclyn moaned, her voice soft. Everyone's attention pulled to her as she twitched, blood seeping through the shirt over her shoulder. A quick check revealed that besides the scratches, she had a small skull fracture. I winced. I needed to help her, and being stuck in this cave was not going to give me that opportunity.

"Who knows, maybe feeding the Silnŷ some of that poison will cure her." Thom let his words linger in the air, no one saying anything as Dramin and I exchanged a look.

It was the one thing we hadn't tried. The one thing we couldn't here. The pool in the hall of sight had drained with the collapse of the cave, leaving Dramin as starved as everyone else. I couldn't ignore the desperate need I felt. I needed to try it. I would try anything for her.

I leaned down to encompass her with my arms, my cheek pressing against hers as I mended and braced the new break in her skull. Her body was so broken. So many of her bones were covered with magical casings, so many tendons were still trying to join back together. If we were in the mortal world, she would be in a full body cast by now.

As I sat there, I felt my magic shift. My power swell and scream. It took me a second to realize what it was. The bind that Cail and I had placed on Wynifred had broken.

Edmund had control of her magic. We couldn't wait here any longer.

I only nodded once, knowing they were waiting for my approval, knowing there was no way I could say no. It might not have been the best decision, but for the people around me, it was the right one, and I couldn't lead them astray. Those were the requirements of my position.

My inheritance.

CHAPTER 17
ILYAN

We walked down the stone tunnel slowly, my ears attentive toward any sound. My fear of another cave-in was strong, much higher than it should be to attempt something like this. This area wasn't like the training room; this small, claustrophobic space could collapse at any time. We could be crushed to death in an instant.

I straightened my back, Joclyn held in my arms like an infant, my magic peeking into the rock with each step. Although I couldn't do much with such a weak connection, I could at least give us warning if something was coming.

The light from the glowing orb that Dramin held in his hand flickered around the walls of the tunnel, the shadows moving and swaying like living hands coming to tear the rock down around us.

"I heard what you said back there," Thom said from beside me, his voice calm. I looked toward him, but he wasn't looking at me, obviously uncomfortable about what he was going to say.

I waited for him to continue. Knowing Thom, he was going to be overstepping with what he was going to say, but I wasn't going to pull out any haughty orders, not right now.

"You really aren't going to force Ryland and the Silnỳ apart?"

"No." I kept my answer short, my voice making it clear I wasn't going to elaborate. He had already heard what I said. I saw no reason to continue.

"I always wondered why you didn't after you discovered Cail was controlling her nightmares," Thom stated, and I tensed.

"I would never break her bond with another without her permission." I raised my voice a bit, letting my tone set the end of the conversation. If only Thom had picked up on it.

"Did you even ask?"

I tried not to fume at his off-hand comment. I kept my eyes ahead, and my fingers curled around Joclyn as my magic pulsed through her.

No, I had not asked. I was afraid to hear what she would say, afraid that she would get the wrong idea and think my intentions impure. Asking her to break the bond was the equivalent of sentencing Ryland to death. I could not ask that of her. I could not ask that of myself.

I chose not to respond to Thom, instead hoping—once again in vain —that he would understand that our conversation had ended.

"What if the bond is what is keeping her in the Tǒuha?" he asked and I felt my muscles tighten. This wasn't a new thought. I had felt this line of thinking crossover my mind several times before.

"What if by breaking the bond, you would release her?" Thom continued when I didn't respond. "She couldn't be hurt anymore. You could save her."

"I have thought of it," I said, holding Joclyn closer to me. "But what happens if you break the bond and her mind is still trapped... Co se stane potom?"

He hadn't experienced a bonding, as I had not, not that neither of us had not desired one. Both of our loves were just out of reach.

"She would be gone." Thom sighed after a moment, his own desperation showing in his voice.

Dramin's light bounced off the rock, casting flickering shadows on the boulders that had begun to obstruct our path. We weaved our way around them, the path becoming more of a single file labyrinth full of jagged stones and loose rocks.

We had been working in this tunnel for the past few days. Thom and I had shifted, melted and moved the rock to make the narrow path we now traveled down, but it wasn't enough.

"There," Thom announced when we had reached the solid wall of rock that covered the exit. He pointed toward a small space between two large boulders near the upper left side where a small gap could be seen between them. The space was large enough for no more than a mouse to go through, but big enough to let in some of the fresh air from outside.

"Tight fit," Dramin observed with a chuckle.

I looked at him curiously, only to see him smiling widely. Leave it to Dramin to find humor and joy in any situation.

"We aren't going to crawl through there, Dramin," Thom sighed. "The crack is a start. If we work from there out, we should be able to shift the rock enough to escape."

I could smell the snow and feel a million different energies carried on the wind from that small crack. My muscles tensed, stretching tight over my chest. I could sense the crack through my connection with the mountain, but what I was sure Thom could not feel was the instability of the large boulder above it.

As large as a house, the mass rested on the crack, but the majority of its weight covered the roof above us. One wrong move and the rock would shift, crushing us in an instant.

"I am beginning to doubt if this is a good idea." I kept my voice low, suddenly aware of the danger this cave had now become to us. Chances were high that we would never make it out of here, not with the instability of the boulder directly over our heads.

Only Thom had returned yesterday after the collapse to assess the damage. If I had known the instability of this space was so bad, I would have never consented to bring us back here. I held Joclyn's body against mine, terrified we would have to run at any time.

"It's the only idea, Ilyan," Thom said quietly. "What would you have us do, sit in a cave until we all waste away?"

I narrowed my eyes at him, watching him as he pleaded with me. I didn't know what to say.

"What other option do we have? This is our chance; if we don't take it, then you have doomed us to death already," Dramin whispered. I knew what he was feeling. I felt it, too. Thom was right, as much as I hated to admit it.

I said nothing as I laid Joclyn's body down against the smooth rock next to me, her body settling into an unnatural position. I moved past them, their focus on me as I approached the opening.

They watched as I placed my hands against the stone. I held my kouzlo there, ignoring my heartbeat that was racing in a desperate plea for me to stop.

The energies of the three bodies behind me thrummed through my bloodstream. This decision, to move the final rock, was dangerous. The selfish part of me begged to just stay, to find another way, but the leader I had been raised to become could not deny the needs of those with me and all those who still lived on the other side of our stone prison, few though they might be.

I needed to do right by them as well.

My magic surged into the rock, the powerful energy flowing away from me as I surveyed the rock more carefully. I tried to formulate a plan for the highest chance of success. The rock shifted and moved at my touch, the living elements within the stone responding to my very thoughts.

The shifting mass felt like a part of me, an extension of my own mind as it obeyed my commands, as it yielded to my power. Then I felt it, the tiny shift, the start of what I had feared, what I had known was going to happen.

The mountain was coming down on top of us.

The large rock just above our heads, the one I had been fearful of since the beginning, began to shift away from the larger mass of the mountain. I grunted as I released more of my energy into the rock, hoping that I could shift it enough to fuse it more securely to the mountain it nestled against.

A large groan echoed through the cave, the sound loud enough to drown out the loud profanity that had spewed unbidden from my mouth.

Thom and Dramin raced from where they had been standing to either side of the cave, their hands flying to the rock as they, too, moved to assess the damage. Now that the rock had shifted, it only took a moment for them to find the weakness and for their magic to move alongside mine as the three of us heaved the giant boulder back into position.

My voice echoed around the cave as I yelled out, my strained magic weakening my body enough to cause me physical pain. I could feel the muscles in my shoulders knit together as I pressed against the rock. I pushed as if I alone was holding it up, attempting to make it move, my heart thundering in my chest in fear and panic.

I glanced to Joclyn, she looked so peaceful. For one moment, her body didn't twitch, and her shoulder didn't bleed. Although I was sure the horrors she was trapped within were still a terrifying prison, right then, she was peaceful, beautiful. Just looking at her set the beat of my heart into a steadier rhythm.

I needed to get her out of here.

I knew what needed to be done. I always did, from the moment I sensed the boulder above our heads, I knew. As with all right decisions, there was a sacrifice to be made, wrong steps to take first. There always was. Making the right choice was never easy, but making it was required, and it was what I was raised to be.

A king, a leader to my people.

"I am going to blow the rest of the cave open," I announced, my voice loud above the incessant growling of the cave. I could see Thom and Dramin's heads turn to me in a panic, but I didn't acknowledge them. "I will be able to hold the ceiling for enough time for us to get out of the jeskyně."

"Ilyan... I—" I stopped Dramin's words with one stern look.

I knew what Dramin was going to say. I could hear the words on his tongue; feel the doubt in him. Doubt wasn't going to help us. I had run all other options through my head, each one enacted within my mind's eye as I watched Joclyn's sleeping body curled up against the rock.

"When I say go, vypadni odsud, and don't stop until you get to Rioseco. No matter what happens, do not stop." I kept my voice deep, the tones laced with the magic I always attempted to restrain within me.

Each man nodded in agreement, fear lining their faces.

"And, Joclyn?" Thom asked, his voice soft.

"I will carry her. She is my responsibility." I turned to her, sending one small strand of magic toward her, lifting her body into the air and bringing her right into my arms. What would normally only take less than a thought, drained me. So much of my concentration and magic was focused on keeping the boulder, and in turn the mountain, off our backs that even the smallest magic used could be felt deep in my bones.

I shook my head, sending my blonde hair swinging as I focused back on the rock in front of me. I forced my mind off the people I was surrounded by, the people who were now fully relying on me to save their lives. I let the feeling of Joclyn's skin on mine move into me, the power of her touch lighting my soul on fire as it had always done. The contact increased my energy, the fire within me burning bright enough to take away the aches I had begun to feel.

I couldn't help the smile that spread across my face at the sensation. The light of the fire spread through my soul, igniting the rest of me, and I couldn't wait. I replaced one hand on the wall, wrapping the other carefully around Joclyn's head as I cradled her against me. I hovered my hand over her mark, the dark dragon shape staring at me through the dim light of the cave.

"Teď!" I yelled at them to go a second before I let my finger touch the raised skin on her neck, the magical connection between us supercharging what remained of my magic.

I took the surge of power and sent it out in an explosion so great that I felt the floor underneath us rock with the energy.

The rock that had lined the exit exploded out in front of us, white snow suddenly visible only a few hundred feet out. Our feet moved before the smoke had begun to clear. I could hear the grunts and pants of Thom and Dramin as we stumbled and slipped on rubble in our desperate attempt to escape.

The cave filled with loud, resonating groans as my magic left the rock above us, the sound extending beyond the blast. The rumble grew as the rock shifted, the sound of our footsteps lost in the sounds of falling rocks and the groan of death that was coming down on top of us.

Thom and Dramin were ahead of me, their frantic movements coming into sight as the smoke began to clear. The white sheet of freedom was blanketed with rocks from the blast, the rubble heavy between us and freedom.

The deep sound of the mountain grew as rocks just behind me began to collide with the ground, the air thick with the sounds of destruction. There was a heavy crash directly to my left, the impact rocking the ground and sending Joclyn and I sideways toward a wall.

One misstep and I had secured our death. I looked toward Thom and Dramin's retreating forms for one fleeting second before I pulled Joclyn to me, our bodies still falling toward the wall. I felt the tick of each moment like a death toll in my heart, every footfall ricocheting inside of me.

It was dangerous to take her with me through a stutter again so close to my recovery. I knew that chance of my survival was low, but I held in my arms the one person I would willingly die for, and I would do anything to save her life.

I didn't think, I just moved us into the heavy realm of the sub-dimension, moving our bodies away from the rock that would otherwise destroy us and, hopefully, into the warm sanctuary of the Rioseco Abbey.

CHAPTER 18
WYN

I remembered everything.

"What do you mean, '*he wants us to have a baby*'?" I spat, turning toward Thom.

Thom stood in the middle of my large room, that awful hat twisting through his fingers. Curse the ridiculous British king for such a style. It made Thom look like a peacock.

"Just that, Lady Wynifred. He has commanded it." I gaped at him, my mind working just enough to let me turn away from him.

I could see him through my mirror, his bright blue eyes boring into me from underneath that curly hair he had inherited from his father, and the sandy color that had come from his mother. He narrowed his eyes and went back to twirling the hat. The poor boy looked absolutely traumatized, and I didn't blame him. What was King Edmund thinking?

"You are sure this message is for me?" I asked, the laugh barely disguised in my voice.

"Yes." He was continually turning that hat in his hands. Round and round it went. I shook my head and looked away, not wanting his stress to leach into me.

"Are we to be bonded then?" My voice was as uninterested as I could make it, my focus more on the ornate hairbrush Cail had given me for my birthday than on the prince behind me. It wasn't the first time Edmund had tried to force me into a bonding, but to use his own son this way was a little surprising.

"No."

"No?" I wasn't sure if I was more relieved or upset. This was the oddest request His Majesty had ever given me. You didn't often send executioners into a wedding bed, especially without a wedding. I guessed it was one of the perks of being a woman and under Edmund's control. He thought he could tell me who to sleep with as well as who to kill.

"Does this upset you, Wynifred?" I smiled, Thom's usual haughty demeanor coming back strong. It was unsurprising; men hated it when you insulted their masculinity.

"Be with a prince, but not be branded as a princess? Of course it upsets me." I glanced at him through the mirror before continuing my morning preparations. "Give me a name, Thom, let me take a life. That is what I am good for, what I thrive at, not this nonsense."

"Perhaps he wants you to have a challenge." Thom moved closer to me, the strength in his voice not leaving that time.

"Hmmm... Then let me kill his first born." I smiled, pleased when a bloodthirsty light flickered in Thom's eyes.

"Ilyan's mine." He grinned and I couldn't help returning the smile. Everyone wanted to kill Ilyan, but no one could get close enough to even attempt it.

"Why me, Thom?"

"You are the most powerful of the Trpaslíks, the only one who still possess the fire magic-"

"And he wants his blood blended with that strength?"

Centuries ago, the fire magic that the Trpaslíks had been born with began to disappear. It wasn't until my birth, over a hundred years ago, that the fire magic had returned. It was only me, though. It never moved beyond that, making my blood, my magic, a highly sought after commodity and one that Edmund greatly desired.

Thom nodded in answer to my question, the hat in his hand finally stopping its incessant spinning. I smirked and turned toward him, leaning against my dressing table.

"What of you, Thom? Does he want you to be stronger as well?" I stepped toward him, his eyes lowering as he looked me over.

"I think it is his hope."

I could only smile, of course it wasn't. If Edmund wanted Thom to be stronger, he would have insisted on the bonding. Then, at least, Thom would inherit my unique power should I die. No, Edmund wouldn't do that. He wanted my power for himself. He had tried to punish me after I removed his finger in warning when he suggested I bond myself to him.

It was then that he had placed me as one of his assassins rather than his bodyguard, but I rather enjoyed the post. Not to mention, I was good at it, taking out a whole herd of useless Draks by myself had been much easier than I would have assumed. No, he wouldn't be so foolish as to give that power to one of his children. This forced pregnancy, however, was a different story.

It only took him seventy years to figure out a new punishment for my treachery. It was almost enough to make me regret burning off his finger in the first place, however.

I wondered how difficult assassinations would be with a bulging belly. If this were Edmund's new punishment, then I would gladly shove it in his face.

When it was all said and done, I had expected to hand the child over to Thom and walk away back to my blood-soaked career path. What I hadn't expected was the reaction I had at holding a small wriggling infant in my arms. One look at the dark eyes of the beautiful baby girl and I was changed.

Rosaline.

Of course, she was cursed from the beginning. Her eye color was not the royal blue that Edmund demanded. He had killed so many of his children when they were born without the bright blue of royalty that a grandchild wouldn't make him bat an eyelid. I knew at once that she would be destined for the same fate if she didn't possess my magic.

Fury would not be a word I would use to match Edmund's anger at his failed attempt at biology. It was much worse.

I was the one who would be punished. While Thom was left to raise our precious daughter, I was sent out on assassination missions, each one more difficult than the last. I continued to track the last of Draks with the forced sight of Sain. I tracked and murdered all of Ilyan's extended family, and even the family of his precious, clunk-headed bodyguard, Talon, in an attempt to flush him out.

Through all the blood on my hands, it was the moments with my little, blonde-headed girl that meant the most to me.

"Mama!" I turned at Rosaline's voice. Her rosy cheeks, her dark eyes, everything about her seemed to glow as she ran toward us, her hair flowing in the wind. "Mama! Will you bind these flowers in my hair?"

"Of course, baby, why don't you go pick some more?" Rosy smiled at me and danced back into the meadow, her hair flying behind her like ribbons of silk.

"She's like you." I turned at Thom's voice, his smile wide as he winked at me before turning back to our beautiful dancer.

"Are you training her in hand to hand combat while I am gone, Thom?" I asked, waving to my eager child as she plucked dozens of long-stemmed daisies.

"Oh yes, choke holds are her favorite." We both laughed, but it was strained, the truth of his words held a dark edge. "What I meant to say is that she does what she wants. She doesn't care what people think of her."

"Well, that *is* like me."

"Incredibly." Thom smiled at me before following after Rosy, scooping her up and swinging her through the warm summer air.

I had never had a friend before. Thom was my first. He taught me to care for my child. He taught me to laugh. He taught me to enjoy life. I had been raised to kill, raised to hunt people. It was all I knew, but Thom changed that. He turned me from a weapon into a person.

With him, I spent sunrises in meadows, evenings playing cards, days at pubs, and nights at gypsy parties. He showed me the world in a different light. I was amazed that so much life could be inside of someone.

I watched him kill men with my own eyes, but he was able to turn around and find something to smile about. I had never been able to do that before. I had always just dwelled in my cynical life, relishing it.

Part of me wished that Edmund had never changed that by bringing Thom into my life.

Our child had been born without the royal eyes and, what was worse, without my unique ability for fire magic; Edmund's great experiment was useless to him. Useless things were disposable. Thom had tried to prove that she wasn't useless, that she was powerful, but Edmund never saw it. So, we made plans to escape, to take our child and run.

It would have worked if Edmund had not caught wind of our plan. As punishment, our child was tortured in front of us. My own father gladly took part in the hideous act.

I couldn't get her screams out of my head. Edmund had finally found a punishment that suited me; he had found a way to make me pay. He had done more than punish us, however; he had lost our loyalty. If only he would have guessed what we were truly capable of, perhaps he would have rethought his actions.

Thom left. I would have gone with him if it weren't for Cail's constant supervision. He never left me alone; his worry over me was paramount.

He held me as I mourned the loss of the first beautiful thing, the first person, I loved.

I thought I would never recover, until Ilyan found me.

He stood before me, his face screwed up in a strangely alluring smirk. His sandy hair sheared short against his head. He balanced his weight on an ornate walking stick, looking like he had just been caught taking a stroll on his enemies' land.

I was one touch away from murder, my hand posed above the trunk of the tree, ready to send a million shards of wood into his skin; but I didn't, all because of that stupid hat. The hat he held in his hands—Thom's hat. He held it gently in his fingers, offering it to me.

"Thom asked me to give this to you," he said quietly in Czech. I looked around the forest that surrounded Edmund's estate, wondering how he had gotten in here. A large shape loomed behind him, probably that hulking bodyguard of his attempting to hide behind a tree.

"Thom?" I asked, the fabric of the cap soft in my fingers as I took it from him.

"Yes, he and Sain are in my care. I came to offer the same asylum to you." I clenched the hat in my fist, the feather turning to ash as my magic flared. I wanted to say yes. Oh, how I wanted to leave right then, leave the giggles that haunted my dreams and the perfectly laundered children's gown that still hung in my closet. I just couldn't. There was one thing I couldn't leave.

"I can't," I sighed, my own words stinging my throat.

"You want revenge." My head shot up, my heart thumping at his words. I wanted to ask how he knew, but I could see that he shared the same aspiration.

"Yes." My voice was a wispy gasp of desire; it dripped off my tongue and into the air in need.

"Then work for me." He smiled and moved the walking stick in front of him, where he leaned on it like the village boys would against a fence.

"Work for you?"

"Yes, I have something you want, after all." He smiled and leaned forward, making me fight the urge to slap him. His eyes were so much like Thom's. Thom, who had left me behind.

I laughed lightly, using the tinkling sound of my voice to draw him in. "What could you possibly have that I would want?"

He smirked, but it was different from the smirk that most men gave me. It wasn't a smirk of desire, the light in his eyes only showed strength.

"I can offer you a way to betray the man who betrayed you."

He kept his eyes on me, his fingers clenching and unclenching on that walking stick of his. I arched my eyebrow, my hand dropping just enough that my threat was lessened, but not enough that the danger was gone.

Then again, this was Ilyan; my threat to him might have never been present. I had watched him rip the arms off a man and wipe the mind of another only a decade before, all while still tied to a tree. There was a reason no one had done away with him yet.

There was also a reason my heart was thudding in my chest.

"What do you have inside that pretty head of yours, Ilyan?" I trilled, bringing my hands to the hips of the scandalous red peasant dress I had chosen to wear that day. "What would you have me do?"

He hesitated, his breathing level as he studied me. Part of me wondered if he was scared of me as well. The sheer tension of the situation made me smile. I popped my hip and raised my eyebrows at him before stepping forward. Ilyan stayed still, his hand still resting on the long staff in his hands.

"What do you want from me?"

"I don't want your power, Wynifred."

"You don't?" I laughed. I found that hard to believe. "What of your silent companion? Would you have him take my power to better protect you?"

I saw the hulking mass stiffen behind the tree. At least my words seemed to be affecting someone.

"Talon does what I bid him, Wynifred. If it wasn't for that, he would be driving you through."

A wicked smile spread across my lips at his words. Ah yes, Talon. So it wasn't my power, or even the fact that I was a woman that was affecting him, it was the murder of his younger sister not more than five years ago. Probably best not to mention how she moaned for him before I snapped her neck.

"So, that's a no then?" Finally Ilyan smiled, his teeth flashing briefly before hiding themselves behind his lips.

"That's a no." Ilyan shifted his weight, his walking stick moving to rest against his hip, his long boots shifting as they crunched the pine needles of the forest floor.

"So if you don't want me for my magic, then what do you want me for?"

"Information."

"You wish me to spy?" I was flabbergasted. Yes, I wanted to make Edmund and my father pay for what they had done, but he was not only asking me to pass on information, he was asking me to put my own life in danger.

"Oh, this is not simply a request for a spy, Wynifred. You are my father's top assassin. You kill anyone who puts a toe out of line. Good or bad, you kill them all. And you do it well."

"I am good at it for a reason, Ilyan." I smiled, taking his compliment to heart. "It's not just death. Anyone can kill. Anyone can remove the beating heart of a magical being." I lowered my voice alluringly as I moved closer to him, wanting to test the boundaries of Ilyan's bargain. I was pleased when his jaw tightened uncomfortably. "No matter how much I enjoy it," I continued, "it's more about finding information, and I can do that above all others."

"Then find information for me." He lifted his chest, his eyes flashing dangerously. I smiled.

I liked this game of cat and mouse, but what I liked more was the very real possibility of destroying the carefully placed web that Edmund had created. My adrenaline surged at the very thought. I would make him pay.

"What type of information?" I asked coyly. I still needed to play my cards right to make this arrangement benefit me.

"His plans, his weakness, what he knows about the sight." My head snapped to his, my eyes narrowing, but he only smiled. "The name of your next target and everyone following."

I stopped my pacing. All of that was doable; I could tell him most of the information now. The name of my target, though? Ilyan wasn't requesting that so he could do the job for me, he was requesting it so he could save their life.

My job didn't entail just destruction; Edmund required proof of the job's completion. He wanted the still beating heart of the victim. Edmund wanted their magic. If I were to turn the names over to Ilyan, then I would have no way of handing the hearts over to him. I would have no way to prove the job had been done.

"What would you have me tell my Master, Ilyan, if I suddenly stopped bringing him the hearts of his enemies?" I was careful not to let my eyes leave his. We might have been in the beginnings of a bargain, but I did not trust him, not yet.

"You will think of something," he smiled, and I couldn't help returning it. He was right, I would. I had already begun to think of possible ways to disguise mortal hearts as those of magical beings.

"Besides, he is not your Master anymore."

"And you are?" my voice snapped as I spun to face him, the fabric of my skirt dragging through pine needles.

"I am no one's Master." His voice was hard. Odd, he almost seemed offended by my comment.

"I think your muscle would disagree with that." The shadow shifted at my words, and I found myself drawn to it. Perhaps it was because Ilyan wasn't responding to any of my advances, and I needed someone to confirm that my techniques were still usable.

"He is free to come and go whenever he pleases."

"Then maybe I will steal him from you." I smiled, but Ilyan's face only hardened.

"Only if you wish to make acquaintance with his sword," he said through gritted teeth. I could tell right then that he would never trust me, even if he consented to what I was about to ask of him.

I stood still as our eyes locked, each one weighing the other. He was wondering if he could actually trust me, and I was wondering why he hadn't done away with me already. I had killed more than half of his army with my own hands, and yet, he let me live. I didn't know if it was pity or desperation that had brought him here, but part of me wished he would plunge me through already.

"Information?" I asked when the silence had become too much.

"Yes." He swung his walking stick once, slamming it into the ground as if to accentuate his words. I didn't even flinch.

"And not my magic."

"No."

I shouldn't have felt stung, but I did. It was not because all of my physical advances had yet to be effective, but because everyone wanted use of the last of the fire magic.

Everyone.

They all wanted my power and the upper hand it would give them, but the leader of the Skříteks stood in front of me saying he wanted none of it. I would be lying if I said I wasn't at least a little bit suspicious.

"Am I not appealing to you, Ilyan?" I popped my hip, testing him, watching him, needing to know for sure.

"I'm taken."

"So it would seem," I laughed, eyeing the shadow of the man who still stood guard behind him.

Ilyan said nothing, he only stood, jaw tight, his weight balanced on the narrow stick in his hands.

I stopped my movement, letting my hair fall down my back as I looked at him. So far, I liked this deal, but we still had my requirements to discuss.

"I will do this for you, as long as you give me everything I ask." Ilyan's eyes widened, his shock melting as he settled in to listen to my requests, a small head nod prompting me to continue.

"I will give you the information you need for as long as I can. I only ask one thing, after I am caught, you get me out alive. You give me asylum and wipe my memory."

His shoulders tensed at my last request, the muscles moving further toward his ears before relaxing down again. He didn't like that last part, not that I blamed him.

"You ask me to put a lock on your mind?"

"Yes, I don't want to remember anything. I don't want to remember Thom, my child, or the thousands of drops of blood that litter my hands." I held my palm out to him as if proving my sins, but his eyes didn't leave mine.

"I don't erase memories, Wynifred. That is a form of torture only my father uses."

"You can and you will if you want me to do this for you." I smiled, knowing I had caught him. "It is not a matter of power, Ilyan. I know you can do it."

"I can also bury you alive ten feet underground with one thought, but I don't." He smiled. "Or maybe I will."

I smiled back, but I wasn't going to relent on this. It was the one piece that I really wanted. I would gladly do all he asked for nothing, but then I would walk away with only my haunted memories for company. It was not a life I wished to lead. I would rather meet my death at my father's hands, but then I would gain nothing from this arrangement. I did nothing for free.

Even Edmund offered me his own form of payment.

"My memory, or my death, for your information."

He exhaled, his muscular chest heaving as he contemplated my request.

"What would you do, Wynifred, once your memory is gone?"

"I'm not sure. Walk the world, discover a new land, perhaps I will join a nunnery."

The laugh that filtered out of his lips startled me, the humor heavy in the air. I didn't see the joke.

"You are not the type to join a nunnery."

"Oh, how would you know, Ilyan?" I snapped. "Once my memory is gone, I can be any kind of person I want to be."

That was the key, right there. I could be anyone I wanted to be, not what Edmund or my father wanted. Me. I could make my own decisions.

"Make your choice," I prompted, pulling a slip of paper out of my pocket. The white slip contained the name of the man I was on my way out to kill when Ilyan found me.

I twisted the paper as Ilyan eyed it, my actions forcing his decision, giving a good show of faith.

"We have a deal," he said, his hand extended toward me.

I closed the gap between us, his hand closing around mine.

"I will honor my deal with you as long as you honor mine, Wynifred. You have my word."

I froze, the sincerity of his voice shocking to me. No one had ever spoken so simply to me. Well, no one since Thom. I could hear his honesty, the commitment and the promise in his voice. Normally, I would have shied away from such emotion, but Thom had affected me in that way as well.

"You have nothing to fear, Ilyan."

"What is his name?" Ilyan asked, pointing to the paper that was still in my hand.

"Dramin, son of Sain," I said, ignoring the shock that lined his eyes and handing over the piece of paper to prove it. "There is reason to believe he is in the East."

"Good." He smiled, thrusting his walking stick into my hands. I clutched it automatically, the heavy wood igniting the magic in my blood.

"This will connect you to me. Use it whenever you have news for me."

I nodded once in understanding; Ilyan's smile the acceptance of my promise to him.

He said no more. He simply vanished into the air before me, leaving me alone with his shadow.

No wonder no one could ever find him.

CHAPTER 19
WYN

Thomas Král

The name on the paper was moving, but I knew it wasn't the ink. It was because of the blood that was rushing to my head in my panic. My eyes couldn't seem to focus.

Thom had been sighted, and Edmund would have me kill him.

The sound of hammers and horses washed over me as I stared at the name. The construction of Edmund's new estate was progressing quickly after I had assisted Ilyan in burning down the last one. Why Edmund had chosen the American West as his new base, I still wasn't clear on. I now spent more time traveling over oceans than anything else.

"Is there a problem, Wynifred?" I looked up to see Edmund jump down from the carriage we had just been sitting in, the dust from the ground kicking up around us as he landed.

"Nothing is wrong, sir," I said, keeping my voice bored and defiant.

"Good," Edmund sighed as he wrapped his arm around my waist to help me down, bringing his lips to rest against the hollow skin under my ear at the same time, "because I want his head."

"His head?" I asked, moving myself away from him. "What would you want with that ugly thing?"

"Think of it as a trophy, Wynifred. Sometimes a man wants more than a heart." He smiled and my insides froze at all that was said behind those eyes.

"Besides, I think it is about time you prove your loyalty to me."

Another smile. What did he know? "Find him and bring me his head before my child is born. That should give you about a month. And if this one is born with eyes the color of mud like the last one, you can do away with it and its mother as well. Sounds like a full month for you."

He moved away from me and strode toward the new house before I could move at all, which was probably a good thing. The desire to kill him right there was too strong, but Ilyan had warned me not to take him on. I didn't know what reason he had for doing so, but I was more likely to trust Ilyan than Edmund at this point.

After three hundred years of espionage, I had seen more than my fair share of bad and had even developed what some may call a conscience.

"Where is my brother?" I asked one of Edmund's goons that was standing around, surprised my brother wasn't here to follow him around like usual.

"Try the bar," he said before shouldering me out of the way. My jaw dropped as I watched him go, my fingers buzzing with energy and a need to teach him a lesson.

No one dared treat me that way, not unless they wished for death. I would have asked what I was missing, but I already knew.

I strolled away from the construction site, my skin prickling with energy as the dirt seeped through my shoes and heavy stockings.

I didn't look back. I didn't dare. I walked right to the small tavern in town, where I knew my brother would be.

His back was to me as I walked into the bar, downing yet another tequila.

"Another!" he yelled into the empty space, it was far too early for the honest men of this town to be drinking.

"Make that two," I spat as I sidled onto the stool next to him, the bartender eyeing me as if I had asked him to hand over the deed to the place. "Now," I added when it became obvious that he wasn't going to pour the drink anytime soon.

"You seem to be in a bad mood," Cail commented, not taking his eyes off the small, dirty glass in front of him.

"Did you know about this?" I spat, not caring who heard me.

"Know about what?"

I slapped the paper down on the bar, letting my magic spread the paper flat until Cail could read the words. His eyes grew wide, and I felt the shield go around us. He held out his hand, and I took it, placing an even more powerful shield around his heart. His face relaxed the moment the Štít was covered and his mind and body became his own.

“Of course I knew,” was all he said, the small statement boiling my anger closer to the surface.

“And you didn’t tell me?” I was furious. Cail had warned me of difficult assignments and helped to disguise the hearts of my victims for the past two hundred years by implanting some of Edmund’s own magic within them, but this time, he had dropped the ball.

I couldn’t disguise a head.

“It’s a trap, Wyn.”

“Of course it’s a trap!” I spat, grabbing and downing the tequila the bartender had just set down in front of me. “He wouldn’t send me after him otherwise.” I swirled the empty glass around out of habit, refusing to look away from it.

“To death!” Cail toasted before emptying his glass, his head dropping to the table the moment he had drained it.

I whipped around to face him, my eyes narrowing dangerously.

“To death?” I asked, surely he hadn’t given up on me quite so easily.

“Ah, yes,” he said, sitting up to pull a paper out of the pocket in his vest near his pocket watch. “You see, you are not the only one who has been given an assignment.”

Dramin, Son of Sain

It *was* a trap, for both of us. I looked away, the buzzing in my ears growing briefly before I dispersed it, my jaw clenching as I shook my head and let out an irritated breath.

“Come with me.” I didn’t give him time to question me before I pulled Cail by the hand I still held, away from the bar and up to the long line of rooms above.

“Hey!” the bartender called out after seeing our ascent. “You can’t go up there!”

“I’ll pay you for the room after, old man, and it will be very worth your while.” I smiled seductively over the banister and the old man paled, a small twitch in his lips telling me all I needed to know.

I towed Cail after me before closing the door to the small room behind us, my magic expanding to place a stronger shield around us while still keeping the one around the Štít in Cail’s heart.

I pulled the small stone that Ilyan had enclosed in his walking stick out of my undergarments and held it in my hands, the stone growing warm for just a moment as I said his name, calling him to me.

“Do I really need to be here for this?” Cail asked, the irritation heavy in his voice. “I only help you, not him, after all.”

“By helping me, you are helping him,” I reminded him, but he only ignored me, sitting back on the bed and putting his muddy feet on the clean bedspread. Great, I didn't want to see the bill for that.

"What is he doing here?" I spun at the thick voice, surprised to see not Ilyan, but Talon standing in front of the door.

"I might ask you the same question?" I said, my eyes narrowing at him.

"Ilyan is indisposed, so he sent me in his place." He stood straight and tall, his eyes focused on the opposing wall, anywhere but on me.

"You can stutter?" I asked, the impressiveness of that feat heavy in my voice, even I could not stutter.

"No."

"Then how did you get here?"

Talon narrowed his eyes at me briefly before glancing at Cail. His message was clear. He might trust me, which I doubted, but he did not, under any circumstances, trust Cail. There were not many who did.

"Why did you call for us?"

He still wasn't looking at me, a small detail that I wasn't going to push. It had taken him a hundred years to come face to face with me and another hundred not to draw his sword every time I was near. This was a marked improvement.

I handed over the papers silently. Talon took one glance before looking back to me, his eyebrow raised.

"These are the names of our next assignments."

Talon's eyes widened. "But Dramin was the first."

"Yes," I said knowingly, cocking my head at him. That was the point.

"And Thom." He crinkled the papers in his large fist before shoving them in his pocket. "Does Edmund know where they are?"

"I am not sure," I answered, looking back to my brother who was dutifully ignoring us with a newly lit cigarette in his mouth, the ugly American Cowboy hat laid low over his eyes.

"He knows," Talon said, his deep voice quiet. I wasn't even sure he had meant to speak aloud.

"Excuse me?"

"They travel together, with Sain. It isn't a coincidence that these names came up together."

Lovely.

"So, your position with us has been discovered?"

I could only nod.

"Then you need to come with me." He reached forward and placed his big hand around my forearm, his grip too tight, hurting me. I zapped him, the small shock sending a warning, and he dropped me quickly, his eyes narrowing dangerously at me.

"We had a deal, Wynifred." Why was he pleading with me? That seemed a little out of character for him.

"What of Cail, Talon?" I spat, not even trying to keep the acid from my voice. "He has risked just as much for you and Ilyan, and one of those names was delivered to him, not to me."

"The deal did not include Cail," Talon said, his shoulders squaring as he went back to staring beyond me.

"Then I want to make a new deal," I said after a moment, twisting to face him.

"What could you possibly have that Ilyan would want?" Talon looked at me, and I stepped back. I wasn't one to step away from the man, but something in his eyes had changed, the subtlety of it catching me off guard.

"The fire magic."

"What would I do with that?" Ilyan asked from the corner behind me, causing me to jump, my hand covering my heart as I turned to face him. He sat on top of the high wardrobe, looking as thoroughly American as Cail tried to be, except the rugged look actually suited him. The limestone dust was a little much. There was authenticity and then there was trying too hard.

Limestone.

They were working on the estate. I couldn't help but smile at the ingeniousness of it all. What better way was there to gain knowledge of the layout of your enemy's fortress than to build it?

"I don't need your magic. I have no use for it," Ilyan said as he moved down to the floor, his tall frame towering over me.

"Then bind it, it is my payment to you for saving my brother," I pleaded, taking a step toward him.

"What if I don't want to be saved?" Cail's voice was loud from the bed that sat in the corner of the room, causing us all to turn to face him. "What if I like where I am at, because, no offense, Ilyan, but I don't trust you. You killed my mother in cold blood. Why should I trust you?"

"It wasn't cold blood, Cail. You know that as much as anyone."

"Yes, revenge is just as good as a reason." Cail lifted his hat to look at Ilyan, the metal of the bed frame squeaking as he sat up. "She breaks up your parents' bond, and you kill her. Seems honorable to me."

"She was your father's pawn," Ilyan said simply, his voice level. I looked between the two of them. Cail had always been good at triggering emotions from others, but Ilyan seemed immune to his taunts. How interesting.

"That, too."

"This is a strange game you are playing, Cail," Ilyan said, turning to address him directly. "Your sister has offered a sacrifice to give you asylum and to take the Štít out of your heart, and you don't seem to want it."

"I don't," Cail said simply, his eyes not leaving Ilyan's.

I took a step back, right into Talon's stiff chest. I moved away from him automatically. How could Cail not want this? He had been helping me for a century, and to what end? He was now going to walk away, give us up to Edmund? My jaw clenched in frustration without me even realizing it.

"Why is that I wonder?"

"Simple," Cail said, his eyes still not leaving Ilyan's, the contest of wills and power strong between them. "With no one left on the inside, who is going to stop Edmund from coming after her?"

"I promised her asylum, and I will deliver that."

"You will? Against Edmund and all his men? You think you will face them all when they come to retrieve her? Impressive." Cail nodded as he moved to the window, everyone's eyes following him. Talon tensed, making it clear he would do anything to stop Cail if he made a move to leave. He couldn't risk anyone finding out about Ilyan's location or breaking their cover.

"He is my father, Cail. I know his strength. You do not seem to see mine."

"Then you know about the Vilý?" Cail turned, his back against the window, blocking some of the light that was able to come in through the dingy, bottle-glass window.

"The what?" I didn't miss the confusion, the need in Ilyan's voice. I had to hand it to my brother; he played his cards well.

"Make me a deal, and I will tell you."

The room was silent except for the clicking of Cail's nails against the windowsill and the constricted breathing from Talon's chest as he fought the desire to protect Ilyan from my brother. I half expected them to just disappear and leave us both hanging, but they didn't.

"What deal?" Ilyan breathed out, his eyes narrowing.

"Protect my sister," Cail said without hesitation, his fingernails still clicking against the wooden frame. "When the time comes, I will stop the zánik curse that my father has already begun infecting her with."

I inhaled roughly. Cail had been holding back. No wonder he had been handed a death card. He knew far more than he had been letting on. Even Edmund had never used the zánik curse. That level of pain and suffering was reserved for the ultimate of traitors, which I supposed I was.

"The zánik curse?" Ilyan asked, a wicked glow lighting up his face. "My my, you *have* gotten yourself in some trouble, Wynifred."

"If you take her now, he will kill her before even you will have a chance to stop it," Cail said, fear lighting up his eyes even though his face was still hard. I wasn't sure anyone else would have caught his panic, but I could see it. "But, let us walk into their trap, and I will bind the curse and take my father's control from it. Then you can take her."

"Why wait?" Ilyan asked as he leaned toward Cail in an obvious attempt to establish authority.

"Now, Ilyan," Cail taunted smoothly, "do you really want to give up a chance to attack your father? Besides, if we wait, I will not only be able to bind the curse inside of Wynifred, but I will also be able to siphon the curse through me using Edmund's power. I may be able to send the curse back into Timothy and curse him instead."

Everyone eyed Cail curiously, my breathing increasing at what he was saying. I was sure my eyes looked ready to explode from my face. What was he saying; siphon the curse? That wouldn't just kill our father; it would kill him as well.

"No, Cail. You can't." I was firm.

"It will come at a cost," Cail continued, ignoring me. "You will have to remove her from my care quickly."

"What are you saying, Cail?" I gasped, my words lost in my panic, the hard edge that was always in my voice all but gone.

"I may lose my mind."

To use so much magic that his mind would crack—I couldn't let him take that risk. What was more, if he failed, then Edmund would live knowing that Cail had attempted to use his magic without permission. That alone was a risk I couldn't allow him to take. The Štít was there for control; he had been warned about what would happen if he utilized it any other way.

"Cail, you cannot do this," I pleaded, knowing he wouldn't listen, even if he heard me.

"Don't show your emotions, sister; it is incredibly unattractive," Cail spat. I stepped back, my disgust still evident on my face. "Once my job is done, keep me from her. Then, on the day the curse fulfills itself, when

Timothy has died and when my mind has returned to its own, then you will get me out."

"Sounds fair enough," Ilyan said at once, my gasp of surprise echoing around us.

"There is only one hitch," Cail continued, finally stepping away from the window. "If I can only bind the curse, not send it into Timothy, and I die before my father, then the curse will be unbound and it will be unstoppable and Wynifred will die. To save her life, to save both our lives, my father must die first."

"That does complicate things," Ilyan said, his hand dragging through his hair as he contemplated everything in front of him. The minutes dragged on as we waited. I tried to catch Cail's eyes, to plead with him not to do this, but he avoided me, his focus only on Ilyan.

"I will agree to your request, Cail, if you both consent to my terms. Cail will bind the curse, with a future promise of sanctuary, and Wynifred will give up her fire magic."

"Deal," Cail said at once, his hand extending in an attempt to seal the promise.

I could not move. Cail was risking everything for me, putting his life on the line in a crazy attempt to get me to Ilyan and hopefully into safety. I could do nothing more than return the favor, even if it would be years before he could redeem it. I would do anything to save my brother, just as he would obviously do anything to save me.

"Deal."

"Tell me of the Vilŷs," Ilyan said the instant the word was out of my mouth.

"Edmund has found a way to make a Vilŷ strengthen his magic," Cail began, and everyone stiffened. Everyone knew that Edmund had captured the little things, but even I didn't know what he was doing with them.

"There are cages of Vilŷs he hides underground, harvesting their poison in the hopes of someday creating a child more powerful than you. He plans to inject his next child with enough poison to either kill it or turn it into a weapon. He also keeps a Vilŷ by his bedside, letting him bite him every night on his mark, in hopes of increasing his power."

Ilyan swore loudly in Czech, all of us looking at each other in varying shades of panic. Nothing about that was good, and here we were planning treason.

Everything washed over me, the onslaught of memories coming in such a rush I couldn't help the wave of bile. My stomach emptied itself, the dull splat of liquid against stone echoing through the cave as my vision swam, the cold prison coming back into focus.

The two men exclaimed before Timothy laughed, his joy making the sound high pitched and girlish.

"Feel better?" Edmund asked. "Remember everything?"

I didn't respond. I just hung my head between my arms, the lack of muscle strength giving me reprieve.

"Now, tell me Cail's secret. Why will he do anything to save you?" I just looked at him, not willing to give him the information, knowing deep down that soon I wouldn't have another choice.

"Tell me what I can threaten your brother with, Wynifred." His fingers pressed against my spine, his magic jerking into my spinal column as he moved to take the information by force.

"If Cail dies first, then I die. If Timothy dies first, the curse unbinds itself." My voice was dead as Edmund forced it out of me.

"There now," Edmund sneered, the smile wide on his face, "That wasn't that hard, was it? Come along, Timothy. It looks like I have a job for you."

He moved away from me then, the door swinging shut behind him with a clang before the shackles around my wrists vanished, sending me to the ground in a heap.

CHAPTER 20
ILYAN

I could not thank Ovailia more for her foresight in adding modern bathrooms to the ancient chambers at Rioseco than I did right now. The room was still steamy from the prolonged shower, the air heavy with the mist of the okouzlený bush. I breathed in the heavy flavor of the wood, savoring the way it relaxed my heart and cleared my lungs.

I had let the water run for much longer than was strictly necessary as I cut my hair back to the short cut that Joclyn had said she liked, letting the steam move out into the bedroom where Joclyn lay on the large, soft bed. She looked so peaceful, and although I knew the magical properties of the bush would not wake her, I hoped they would somehow travel to her.

Thankfully, we'd had no more injuries since arriving at Rioseco. I still couldn't believe we had arrived safely, my heart whole and unscathed. Magic like that had never been accomplished before, and to do so twice in such a short time... I had not expected to survive it. I did not look at this accomplishment as one to boast of. If anything, it only increased my ability to protect her.

Cleaned, cut and shaven, I walked out of the bathroom of my large suite into the bedroom. Joclyn lay still underneath the heavy white covers of my bed; the bright white looking out of place against the ancient stone walls. Generally, I preferred white. I preferred the serenity, the hope and the reminder that you could always start again that it offered me. So many of my rooms were decorated with it, but here, in the ruins of the first abbey I ever lived in, I could not cover the brick I had laid with my own hands with such a trivial thing as paint. These walls reminded me of starting over in their own way.

Joclyn's clean hair fanned behind her like a dark stain of spilled ink against the white. My magic flared inside of her, moving to reach every corner of her body in an instant, the once powerful barrier now nowhere to be found.

Thankfully, her body was whole, but the absence of the barrier still worried me. I knew the absence meant something, but what it was, I couldn't place.

With all my training, all my power, this problem had stumped me.

We had one thing left that we could try. Being at Rioseco had given us access to the mugs that could hold the Black Water, just as Thom had reminded us in the cave. As Joclyn's only food source, the Black Water might possibly be the key to awakening her.

I laid down beside her and held her to me, allowing my mind to wander inside of hers, my song filling her mind, my words lingering as they echoed through her soul and vibrated through the tender muscles of her heart. I left them there, within her, before withdrawing from within only to hold her to me, her body pressing up against me.

"Jos, my love," I whispered to her, begging that she would hear me. "Whatever happens, please know that I will always hold you in my heart. I now know I was not the one to save you, as much as my heart longs to be. But I will protect you, until the one who can awaken you returns."

I leaned forward and kissed her cheek, the warmth of her skin shooting sweetly through me in an electrical current that caught my veins on fire.

Before I could let my heart linger on my words, a soft knock filled the room, echoing off the stone walls.

Not a moment passed before Dramin walked in. As much as I hated the ritual bows and formal speeches, there were times when I missed the formalities my position usually accounted me, this was one of them. Although, I don't think Dramin had ever been good at knocking.

Dramin smiled as I stood to face him, a mug of Black Water balanced in his hands.

"You ready for this?" Dramin asked, his dark green eyes looking at me over the mug.

I nodded once. Dramin needed someone to hold Joclyn still and upright. I had agreed without complaint, although it meant that I might get some of the poisonous water on my skin. The thought caused my muscles to tighten. I could still vividly remember the pain of the water as it lashed against my chest, the internal burning that plagued me for years afterwards. They still hurt whenever anything rubbed against them. It was worth it, as this would be, since it was done for Joclyn's sake.

Dramin set the heavy mug on the ancient table beside the bed. I shifted Joclyn onto my lap where Dramin would need her.

"You are a good man, Ilyan."

I only nodded at him, unsure how to respond. His statement was loaded with the implications of both past and future. I let the ire wash over me before arranging Joclyn on my lap, her head lolling against my chest as Dramin placed a towel beneath it. I only hoped the flimsy fabric would catch enough of the Water to prevent too much of an injury.

Dramin moved to the side of me, his jaw tight as he shifted her head. I held her head where Dramin had placed it, my skin warm where it made contact with hers.

"You can't move, Ilyan, even if it burns you. You move, and it will only burn you more." Dramin lifted the mug, and I cringed as the putrid smell of the deep brown fluid hit my nose. It smelled like rot, the heavy death smell of the body pits that had littered my home while the black plague ravaged Europe. The images of the time floated to mind, their suffering still fresh, even though the travesty had happened in my youth.

I closed my eyes against the memory and held Joclyn's body closer, everything tense. Thom had suggested we just restrain her magically, but I had swatted the idea away, wishing instead to be near her, wishing to help her physically. Now, I was second guessing my decision.

Dramin placed the mug against Joclyn's lips, his thumb and forefinger pressing against her mouth to open it slightly, the sag of her jaw making her look deathly and vacant. I looked away, not wanting to think of her being that way, and instead stared out the high stone archways that led to my wide balcony and to the misty Spanish countryside that lay beyond that. It all looked the same as when we had built this beautiful building. This place was like stepping back in time for me, one of the only places that felt like home. Of course, it didn't hurt that so many of the images in the original sight took place within these very walls.

In the sight given by Sain all those centuries ago, I had seen Joclyn battle powerful enemies. I had seen her bloodied and beaten, and I had seen her crying—tears streaming down her face before she kissed me. The images flashed before me now, and I could tell where each of them would occur, what corner of the ruins of the abbey she would stand in, many of which were only a few steps away.

The beautiful images were stolen from me as the deep, burning sensation of the Black Water shot across my arm. I called out, my voice loud and deep as I tried to keep my body still. I yelled and swore, the rough Czech words bouncing off the stone as I remained still as Dramin continued to work.

The burn moved deeper into me, the acidic fire burning into my bloodstream where it ignited and moved all over my body in a matter of minutes. The pain was not as intense as I had remembered, but still it caused my muscles to tense, the deep magic reacting with my blood. My magic tried to heal me, but it wasn't fast enough to fight the burn that shot through my veins.

"H... he will... willl t... tear usss ap... apa... apart." The quiet, feminine stutter rocked through me. The hope that I felt filled me faster than the burning pain had. Dramin stepped away, the mug returning to the ancient table. Joclyn's body twisted easily in my arms, falling down to my lap as limply as she had been before. Was she coming back?

Her eyes were open, the endless black depths seeing something neither Dramin nor I could see. The pain and fear in her voice was strong, and I hoped the timbre of her voice had more to do with the sight than whatever was happening where she was.

"Jos? Mi Lasko?" My fingers curled against her skin, desperate to pull her to me, but also afraid of missing her awakening or that the sharp movement would hinder whatever progress was being made here.

"If... if... y... you w-w-wish to ssseeee th... the end, g... give m-me y... your heart."

"Jos?" I whispered as her eyes closed, hoping she could hear me, hoping that she would not return to her prison, but nothing happened. She stayed limp in my arms as her mind returned to the hell she was trapped in.

"He will tear us apart. If you wish to see the end, give me your heart." I had almost forgotten Dramin was standing behind me. "What do you think it means?"

"You're the Drak." I could only shake my head at him. It was obviously a sight as shown by the blackness of her eyes, and not the rambling nonsense that could happen while people dreamed. This meant the words were meant to guide.

I pulled away from her, my eyes widening at the large burn on my arm. My skin was raised in an angry, red welt where the water had touched me. The water that could unlock her sight; the touch of the water against my flesh, one that would trigger it.

Dramin saw me looking at the welt on my arm, his inhalation confirming that my thoughts were headed in the right direction.

"It's for you." His voice was awed. The water had called her from a dark place, and my sacrifice had been the one to do it.

"He will tear us apart. If you wish to see the end, give me your heart," I repeated the words softly, the tender words sounding like a message rather than a warning.

A message from her; from Joclyn.

She was still in there somewhere. I just needed to find her.

CHAPTER 21
ILYAN

I was out of bed before I had registered what had happened. I had heard the soft knocking in my sleep and sat up, my body tense and ready as if expecting battle. I could still feel the warmth of where Joclyn's body had been pressed against mine, the heat leaving as the chilled night air that came in through the open archways on the veranda swirled against my skin.

The knock sounded again, the taps soft against wood. A familiar energy seeped through the door, and my body relaxed.

I made it to the door in two steps, throwing it open to reveal a very disheveled looking Thom. His dark dreads were pulled back into a ponytail. The earbuds of his iPod were hanging out of his shirt, where I could hear the occasional twang of a guitar. Normally I would laugh at seeing them there—Thom always kept his love of country music hidden—but the concern on his face trumped the humor.

"Thom?" I questioned when he didn't say anything.

Thom looked over my shoulder to where Joclyn lay in the bed before looking back to me.

"You need to come with me."

It was very strange how one sentence could put each nerve in my body on high alert. My muscles tensed as I stood taller; my back straightened in an inadvertent attempt to challenge him.

Thom reacted, but not in a way I would have expected from him.

"Shield her, and follow me."

"Thom? What has happened?"

Thom's eyes darted around uncomfortably, the action only adding to my heightened awareness. My muscles tensed in expectation. I looked down the hall behind him, expecting Edmund to be standing right there.

"I found something outside." His voice was so soft and unsure that I barely heard him.

"What?" I asked, Thom jumping at my voice. His uncomfortable jitters seemed to be growing rather than receding.

"I want you to see."

I looked at him sternly for one minute before backing off. I would receive a clearer understanding of what was happening by following rather than demanding answers.

"Následuj mě." *Follow me.* Before I could say more, Thom had begun to walk away, his steps short and panicked, suggesting trouble. Everything prickled inside me in warning, but I wasn't one to second-guess Thom.

I glanced back at Joclyn before her body vanished from sight; the heavy shield I covered her with smothering her.

Thom's steps were short, the sound muffled by his quick, soft movements. I followed him in silence as we moved from the renovated space on the northern side of the abbey to the ruins that existed on the far south. What had once been a beautiful cathedral was now reduced to a few exquisite arches and some tile work, most of it destroyed by war, neglect and tourists of the later 1800s.

"You better shield yourself," he whispered as he stopped to face me.

My back straightened as he looked at me, my eyes boring into him in a silent threat. He shook his head, ignoring me and instead disappeared underneath a shield.

I began to follow him, my steps mirroring his. We raced through a large, open area. I could see the tree line of the forest that surrounded the abbey clearly and the moon that hung above the trees, the face of the sleeping man I had grown up whispering my secrets to so clear on the textured surface.

As I followed Thom's lead, my magic peaked at some distant power I could not place. I fought the need to stop and investigate the new, unwanted energy that was buzzing through the air, but continued on. I could usually determine anyone I had met before by the feeling of their magic, but this was either too far away, or someone I didn't know. I brushed the feeling away, my nerves readying themselves for an attack.

Thom tiptoed through rubble as he led our way to the only remaining turret in the area. The tall pillar of stone still housed the large cathedral bell. The tower worked best as a guardhouse, which is what Thom had been using it as. My muscles tensed as we climbed, the silence dragging on and on, leaving me to worry about what Thom had found.

I could desperately grasp at the hope of seeing Ovailia burst through the trees that surrounded the abbey, Ryland's body in her arms, but I knew better. Thom would have given me more information if it was good news.

The large, wooden door at the top of the spiral staircase opened of its own accord, and I felt Thom move up onto the large platform above. I followed him up; moonlight filtered through the rounded stone opening, casting confusing shadows on the walls around us. The ancient bell hung from a wound rope the width of my arm, dust sprinkling down around it as the rope creaked and moved in the breeze. I stood against it, looking over the fields and forest that surrounded us.

"Are you there?" Thom whispered, his reluctance to be heard flushing through me like ice.

"Yes."

"What do you see?"

I scanned the trees, the dark shapes barely visible against the night. I looked above them in hopes of finding what he was talking about when a bright yellow light popped through them.

The yellow-gold flickers of a fire were nestled between the trees, casting a shadow through the dark stumps and making long, bright fingers amongst the strips of black. Several bodies cut off the light as they moved around the fire, making the intimidating shadows flicker and move.

I watched the light for a moment, trying to make sense of it when another light flickered through the trees. One after another they appeared, disappeared, and re-appeared as bodies and objects moved in front of them.

There were dozens of them.

My heart thumped heavily in my chest as I watched the lights flicker, the magical pulses going on and off. The magical current I had felt before washed over me again, the strength of it tingling up my spine. The magical flow wasn't one I recognized, not against the familiar cold spikes of the Trpaslíks.

"Ovailia has brought her army, I see?" I couldn't help the wicked smile that spread across my face, the pulse of my magic as it alerted me to its wish for battle.

"Are you really surprised?" Thom was smug. I ignored him.

"How many camps?"

"Eight," Thom began, his frustration seeping into his deadpan voice. "They weren't there when we first arrived, so they must have come sometime in the last few days."

I sighed heavily. We hadn't been keeping as heavy a guard as we should have been. Our first two nights here we had taken turns at watch while the others ate and slept, but last night we hadn't posted one at all.

I watched the lights before turning to leave, using my magic to pull Thom behind me. I moved quickly, my steps were much louder than they should have been but I was keen to put some distance between the assembling army and us. They knew we were here, after all, no amount of tiptoeing could keep them from pounding down our door when the order was given to attack.

The second we moved past the open stretch of rubble, I released my shield, bringing my body back into sight.

"So, now that you know Ovailia is good and truly a bastard, what do we do?" I didn't turn at Thom's voice, the hardness of it expected. I could feel the same anger rippling through my body, just under the skin.

I turned to face him, my taller than average frame towering over him. He looked up to me, his eyes, so much like a child's, wide and pleading.

"There is not much we can do. We stay here. We wait for Joclyn to wake and hope that Ovailia brings her mate to her."

"Ovailia? She has brought an army to surround us and you want to *wait* for her?"

I nodded once before turning away from him, my steps taking me back the way we had come.

"Why, Ilyan?" he said as he came up beside me, his legs working double time to keep up with my longer strides. The muscles in my neck tensed. I really didn't need to explain myself to him, but his question was understandable given their history.

"Because she will have Ryland," I said, keeping my voice strong and distant. "Ryland is the key to waking Joclyn. Once Joclyn wakes, we will be able to face the Trpaslíks that surround us."

I smiled, the visions from the sight flying into me. Saying it aloud somehow sealed her fate, making her the one that would defeat my father and assuring that she would become the beautiful warrior I had seen.

"Why can't we just attack them now?" Thom asked. I couldn't help but laugh, the hearty sound of my voice sounding odd against the tension that still rippled off both of us.

I stopped again to face him, the door to my suite only a few steps away. I could already feel my heart pull me toward the door, my magic stretching to ensure her safety.

"You would attack twenty or more Trpaslíks with only you, me and a Drak?" I raised my eyebrow at him, the dare for him to answer evident.

While I might be able to defeat more than half that amount on a wet day, I knew Thom had always struggled with his ability. Being the son of an un-bonded mortal had always made him weaker than the rest of us. Dramin would prove little help at all. Draks had no defensive magic. There was no other way to put it. It was the reason my father had been able to exterminate them so easily.

Thom shook his head and looked away from me, his answer evident in his eyes. I ignored the bristle I felt at his lack of respect, but kept it at bay, reminding myself that my role as a ruler had died with my people. Not like I had taken it seriously in the first place.

"We will watch them. We need to set a more consistent guard—which between the three of us may prove impossible, but we must do what we can." I set orders as I always had, Thom's back straightening in preparation to obey. "If we can make an adequate map of where their camps are, it will help us to attack without incident when the time comes."

Thom nodded once in understanding, the nervous energy that was flowing off him receding with my words.

"Thom, get some sleep. I will watch from here, dnes večer, strengthen our shield, and develop a clearer plan."

Thom nodded in respect as he turned from me, the thick strands of his hair swinging as he walked down the hall toward his room. I watched him put the tiny buds back into his ears before he turned the corner, leaving me alone in the dark corridor.

I couldn't ignore the thrum of my heart any longer, the pull moved against my skin like the crawling of a hundred emotions washing over the surface. My shield released from around Joclyn as I entered the room, bringing her back into view.

A few more days and she would wake.

If Edmund had already sent Trpaslíks after us, then Ovailia couldn't be more than a day behind. Soon, I would wake her.

No, Ryland would wake her.

If Edmund had sent Ovailia with him at all.

I straightened my back and walked away from her, toward the window. I could still feel the need to be near her, but for now, I needed to prove that I was stronger than my desire.

The breeze that came in through the high arches of the windows swirled around me, the mingled magic of the men who stood around us in preparation for attack evident to me now. The power was weak, but it was there. I could feel their anticipation, the nerves and excitement.

The hairs on my arms prickled as my energy rippled over my skin, my alert power tingling, desperate to be used. I always kept so much of my magic restrained for safety reasons. It was only in battle that I could freely feel my magic flow through me, that I could be free. My energy rippled now; the maniacal energy setting me on fire in eager anticipation.

The danger had followed us to our door once again. The time was coming, closer and closer. I could feel the tick in my blood, beating like a clock, signaling its arrival.

We just needed Sleeping Beauty to wake.

"He will tear us apart. Rozdělí nás. Jestli chceš vidět konec, dej mi své srdce.." I spoke the words of Joclyn's sight silently, the words sounding like a deep prayer of mass when whispered in Czech.

Give me your heart.

Hadn't I done that already? Hadn't I promised her every beat that it possessed when I first held her in my arms during the sight eight hundred years ago?

Yes, but I had also taken it away.

I had taken away her claim on me when I made the decision not to break the bond between her and her mate. My brother. Could I break that bond now, after all I had sacrificed, after all I had promised her? No, it was not in me to be so cruel.

My back was still toward her as my heart beat for her; love and confusion swelling inside of me. I didn't need to look at her to feel my conviction continue to cement itself within me. I could see her beauty, her strength, her power. I could see her weakness and the hold it had on her vanishing slowly every day. I could hear her laugh and see the way she wrinkled her nose. I could see the flash of her silver eyes when she was upset.

She was amazing.

I would do anything to protect her, to help her, to let her become what she wanted and needed to be. I would give her my heart, she had it until it beat its last.

The tops of the trees reached toward the moon, the shadows dark and deep. I loved this view, the natural beauty of the world that modern man had destroyed. There were so few places on earth where you could find that peace anymore. Places that I had walked through, loved, worshiped and explored through my hundreds of years had all been overrun with what others were calling progress.

The energy of the earth radiated from the ground, the natural force strong here; whereas, in the cities of the world, the natural power was covered and poisoned until it no longer existed.

The thought came to me before I could stop it, the desire to hold Joclyn as we looked out at this beautiful view, as we felt the magic of the earth together, because I knew she could. So many of our kind never could, but she would. I wanted to see her face when she did.

I wanted to show her the beauty in the world, not just the sadness.

I wanted to give her my heart openly, and I wanted her to take it.

CHAPTER 22
RYLAND

Everything felt fuzzy, and yet the world was in sharper focus every day.

I still had outbursts. I still had fits of panic. But the further from Cail that Ovailia took me, the more his hold on me decreased. I could remember more, and so many of my thoughts were my own.

There was one thing that I hadn't been able to get away from.

'And you never will. You will always be mine to control. Otherwise you are useless. To everyone.'

I flinched at the voice and sat back in the hard chair that Ovailia had commanded me to sit in. I didn't have it in me to complain. I was too tired for nearly a week of being on the road.

Besides, I knew where we were. Ilyan was close. I just had to get to him, then Ilyan could help me.

Ilyan had her.

'He's kept her. He's claimed her. She's no longer yours.'

"No!" I snapped at the voice, causing Ovailia's head to twist to mine from when she paced on the other side of the canvas tent that the Trpaslíks had brought us to.

I hadn't seen much of the camp that was hidden in the Spanish forest before we had been tucked into the tent, out of the sight of the Trpaslíks who wandered through the camp and guarded muddy brown tents dirtier than I had ever seen.

It was an army camp, and in the distance the high turrets of what looked like an ancient castle.

I had to assume that was where Ilyan was.

'Where you will kill him.'

"No!"

"No what, Ryland?" she crooned in that sugar-sweet voice, bee-lining for me as I began to rock and pull at my hair.

'You will never get me out. Just like Ilyan will never get me out. He has taken everything from you--'

"NO!" I screamed that time, jumping to my feet as though I was going to find the voice and destroy him. Instead, I tugged and ripped at my hair.

"No?" Ovailia asked, piecing it together as my father's voice in my head laughed. "You still think you won't do exactly what we want when the time comes?"

'You will. You will kill her. You will kill both of them.'

"No." I wasn't so sure that time and I sat back down in the hard chair, going back to rocking and tugging as the flap to the tent opened and Timothy strutted in, flanked by two Trpaslíks.

"Ovailia! We didn't expect you for another week!" He crooned, arms opened wide. His usual three piece suit was flawless. He didn't look as though he had been leading an army in the middle of nowhere for weeks on end. Well, except for the mud that was caked on his shoes. I stared at it as I rocked, the normalcy of it pulling me back down to earth.

"Well, we had something come up." She stepped aside, revealing me as I rocked on the chair. His eyes went dark.

"You are sending him in?"

"Yes. Before I do, we will need to go over plans and prepare for the attack lest something goes wrong. Then I will take him in." They were both looking at me now, both smiling.

"Are you sure it is wise, you taking him in? I have many others who would take him close. Let him stumble in on his own." Timothy asked, suddenly nervous.

"How else are we supposed to gather intel on their situation? Although, I don't anticipate Ilyan letting me stay longer than it would take him to question me and find me a traitor, but I have every intention of getting as much information as I can before I leave Rioseco and return here."

I looked up from the mud on Timothy's shoes, Ovailia stood facing the stalky man, looking every bit an elegant Skřítek against the squat

Trpaslík. Her sheet of blonde hair fell down her leather jacket, her shoes still red and unmarred. Timothy looked up at her with his dark eyes, the two staring each other down.

My mind slipped into deeper clarity for a moment, more of the tent coming into focus as Timothy stepped closer.

"Is that the only reason you are here, Ovailia? Where is my son?"

"Doing what my father, your master, has asked of him. He is placing his own pawn, and once he is done, he will join us here. How are the preparations coming?" Ovailia shook her head, sending her hair shimmering and the guard's eyes turning. Timothy wasn't deterred however, he was looking right at me, eyes narrowed.

'See, even he doesn't trust you.'

I moaned at the voice and began to rock. Timothy's stare only grew more intense.

"How do we know we can trust him? Is he still attached to Cail."

"Don't you worry your little insignificant head about that," Ovailia said with a flick of her hand. "I have it all under control. Don't I Ryland?"

"No, please no." The words snaked out in a sob as she stepped closer, long nails tapping on her jeans as a few sparks of magic flew out.

"He may not be connected to dear, old Cail; but he is still going to do exactly what we want. One look at Ilyan... holding Joclyn. Loving Joclyn. Kissing--"

"No! I'm going to kill him!" I was up, heart pounding, vision swirling, what little control of my mind that I had slipping away as I prepared to lunge through the flaps of the tent. I was ready to take off into the air, soar right to the castle and rip Ilyan's head off.

Before I could move a step, Ovailia flicked her finger and chains wound around my ankles and wrists, snapping me back down into the chair.

'Soon. Soon you will do the only thing you are good for. You will make Ilyan pay.'

"Pay." I repeated the word, my mind flooding with images of Ilyan's head being removed from his body. It was beautiful.

No... it was wrong...

I couldn't do this. He was the only one who could help me.

'Help you what? Do you think you are worth helping?'

"Yes," I moaned, slamming my back against the chair. "Yes."

'No. You are worthless, and the only thing you are good at is making Ilyan pay.'

"Pay."

'He took Joclyn from you. Hurt him. Hurt her. Make them pay.'

"Pay! Kill! Kill Ilyan!" I yelled and fought against the chains again, pulling both Ovailia and Timothy's focus from some war plans that they had been going over, and I had missed thanks to the insanity in my head.

I only barely got a glimpse of the large map of where we were, and the hundreds of dots surrounding that old stone, before it was rolled up and carted away by the two Trpaslík guards that had followed Timothy in.

"I told you that you shouldn't worry," Ovailia said with a smile. "Everything is going to plan."

"Plan? Ilyan won't let him anywhere near him if all he does is scream about how he wants to kill him." Timothy was skeptical. Ovailia was victorious. I continued to slam my back against the chair.

"Don't worry. I have a plan for that too. Now leave us. I have a few items of business to attend to before we deliver our weapon to my dear older brother."

Timothy gave Ovailia a scowl, but did not complain as he left, the tent flap falling quietly back in place, leaving Ovailia and I alone.

She smiled as she looked at me, as she stepped closer. I recoiled under her gaze, pressing myself into the chair as the sounds of the camp bled through the canvas.

"Why are you scared, Ryland?" Her voice was calm, and I wanted to trust her. But truth be told, I didn't know her. She was my half sister, but since I had met her she had done nothing but hurt me. Just like all the others.

'Because it is all you deserve.'

"I'm... I'm..."

"Aren't you excited to see Ilyan?"

Again, that one word sliced through me, any hope of recovering even a piece of my sanity slipping away.

"Kill!" I screamed, raging as Ovailia smiled.

"Timothy is right, you know, they won't let you get close to him like this. Good thing I have a plan." Ovailia kneeled before me, her eyes not leaving mine as she reached into her pocket and pulled out a scrap of cloth.

I didn't need her to unwrap it, I already knew what it was.

I could feel it.

I could feel the pain. The suffering. I could hear her screams. I could hear my own now too. My soul was part of the blade as well now.

"No! No!"

"Yes." She pinched the blade between her fingers, looking at it with a grin that would haunt dreams before she pressed it against my side, and stabbed me with it, pressing the blade all the way in, and embedding it inside.

"There are other ways to control, Ryland. And dear old Rosaline can help me do just that, whether she wants to or not."

She stood, the blade deep inside of me. I could already feel my magic close the skin around it, feel my soul breathe as part of me was returned. I felt closer to me, the shadows not so loud in my head.

I was me. I was free.

And then everything got so much worse.

CHAPTER 23
ILYAN

For hundreds of years, this abbey had housed the brethren that came to worship their own silent God. They farmed, they prayed, and they worshiped until the year the troops drove them away, leaving my beautiful home abandoned. It had been ransacked, the stained glass windows were destroyed, the gorgeous pews burned, and the stone walls carved with crude declarations. What had been my home, my personal place of sanctuary, was now only a discarded, forgotten place.

I could see one of the carvings now, a roughly drawn heart and an unintelligible figure carved amongst it. It was bright against the stone in the evening light, the last of the day's sun bouncing off the angles of the ruins like glittering jewels. I stared at it as I sat on the rubble strewn floor, my legs crossed in front of me in a style more common amongst the Chinese worshipers.

I had always intended to restore this portion of the building, giving life to the ancient arches and restoring the glass back to what it had once been. Now, it seemed to be too late. What could be rebuilt would only be ruined and destroyed within a matter of days.

I breathed in the smell of earth that lingered heavily in the air, the density of it filling my lungs before dispersing throughout my body, the heavy earth magic lingering with my own.

My feet had brought me here after the nerve endings in the base of Joclyn's neck had been severed from her spine. I had felt them snap, one by one, my magic working tirelessly to repair them as her heart began to go into cardiac arrest. If I hadn't been singing to her at the time, I would have missed it. She would have died in my arms as I slept.

My heart longed to stay next to her, but I couldn't. I couldn't look into her face and not blame myself for being unable to release her from her prison.

Ten days.

For her, it had been more than a month, more than a month of what I could only assume would be consistent torture.

My hands lay on my knees in meditation, my thoughts focused on the desires of my heart while my power focused on the natural magic that surrounded me. It was the only religion I knew, the only deity I had found in this world—the magic in the earth.

I had to hope it was enough. I breathed it into me, pulling the heavy ancient power through me only to transfer it to Joclyn, to move it through the Štít and into her.

When I first came to this place, almost a thousand years ago, my heart was heavy, broken and guilty. I had taken a life, and part of me felt power in that. A wicked ribbon of black that I could feel attempting to infect my soul. If my father had gotten his way, it would have. But I had seen that maniacal light in his eyes then, the joy at what I was able to accomplish, and the look scared me. If I had any wisdom at the time, I would have seen what he was capable of then, and I would have stopped him, but I was only a child.

A child who ran away from home, ran from what I was supposed to become, to build a monastery and find inner peace. I was still not sure I had ever found it.

"Ilyan?" I kept my eyes closed at Thom's voice, his magic adding its own ebb and flow to the air.

Thom's steps crunched against the destroyed bits of the chapel, his magic heavy with insecurity and yet steady, always steady. He sat down next to me, and while I still did not move, I opened my eyes, hoping the small gesture could be taken in greeting.

"Dramin told me what happened." I could only nod, not sure I wanted to talk about it, not sure what to say. "He's on guard now, but... I wanted to see if you needed anything nejdřív."

I kept my vision forward, although my magic flared to Joclyn, covering her through the Štít as I reconfirmed her safety. She still slept, her body continuing to heal as she lay.

I couldn't be mad at Dramin for leaving her, although part of me wanted to be. If we didn't keep someone on guard at all times, we would soon be overrun. Trpaslík camps had been popping up every night, each one bringing our enemy closer to us, each one giving us less time before they would attack.

"Ilyan? Můj Pane?"

I sighed and looked at him out of the corner of my eye, one quick glance before returning to stare at the graffiti on the wall. He obviously wasn't going to leave me alone. He was worried, but I couldn't help feeling his worry was misplaced. I could handle my own issues.

"I'm fine, Thom. Já jen..." I stopped. I never opened myself up to anyone. It exposed too many weaknesses, too many weapons that could be used against me. I had heard the mortals use the phrase 'skeletons in the closet' for hundreds of years, and that was sometimes how I felt—as if I had skeletons in my closet. Except it wasn't one or two hung up on a coat rack, it was an armada. If I could ever control them, I could take over the whole world.

I had surprised myself when I had begun to open up to Joclyn, when I had told her of my past. The only people who knew such things about me were those who had been present my whole life: Dramin, Ovailia, Sain and Talon. Even they did not know the whole picture, but Joclyn, I wanted Joclyn to know everything. I wanted Joclyn to understand me, to trust me, so that when the time came for her to rely on me and trust in my judgment, she would do so without question. I didn't want to have to command her magically as I sometimes did all the others. I had done so once, after she had first lost Ryland, and I still regretted it.

Thom continued to look at me expectantly, his eyes burning into me. I stayed still, my vision forward, my breathing even. As much as I trusted Thom, as much as I loved my brother, I didn't want to let him inside my head.

"You'll find a way to get her out." I couldn't help but smile at Thom's words, at his easy confidence. After all, he had been so set on simply destroying her not long before.

"You believe that, do you?" I could almost feel him twitch. I had overheard him talking to Dramin last night, his fears about the inaccuracy of sight spoken aloud. It might have been wrong to eavesdrop, it might have been wrong to bring up what I had heard, but my regal blood demanded one thing, while my logic another. The distinction was never clear to me anymore.

"You know I only fear our father," he said, the wavering in his voice surprising.

"Vím že." *I know that.* I suddenly felt bad for bringing it up. "I do, too, which is why I am still alive and why I can't bring myself to look past the terror that Joclyn is trapped in."

My muscles tensed; the words had come unbidden from my mouth, and now I was to face the consequences.

"Do you remember Rosy?"

Thom's quiet voice caught me off guard, the subject matter startling. Rosy was never spoken about, least of all by Thom. I had never met her, but I had heard the story, saw the terrors from Thom's memories. Unsurprisingly, Thom was now looking intently at the crude carving in the stone before us.

"Ano."

"When she was three, Wynifred and I used to take her to visit the serfs in the countryside." Thom's voice was distant, his mind lost in his memories. I could feel my heart tense at what was coming. I might not know the whole story, but I did know the outcome.

"It probably wasn't the best day trip for a child," he laughed, "but she enjoyed playing with the other small children. I could watch that smile on her face for days. She looked so much like Wynifred. Those crazy dark eyes; they would shine more than you would ever think possible."

I cringed, but stayed silent. Edmund had not allowed Thom to bond himself to Wynifred, and they were left separated for much of the time.

"I loved to watch her dance. She was so graceful—we all thought so, even Edmund. His first grandchild. He was so proud. Except..."

Thom's words faded as the memory grew darker. I could see everything in my head, everything Thom had told me when he arrived under my protection. Rosy was the way he had to explain his allegiance for me; the pain over the torture and murder of his small daughter the reason for his defection. In coming to me for help, he had also given me something more, a link to Rosy's mother. I knew she would stop at nothing to get her revenge. I still remembered my anxiety at meeting face to face with Wynifred for the first time. I sighed heavily, the reason for Rosy's death almost too simple to even comprehend.

"She didn't have his blue eyes," I finished for him.

"I was so lost in what our father was doing to her, to my child, that I couldn't see beyond it. I couldn't focus. It became just another way for him to control me, but I didn't see it before it was too late. Suddenly, she was gone, my willpower tied to her life. When she was gone, all I had left was my anger, and it covered me. If it weren't for Sain, I would have been killed, too. The way..."

I knew he was about to mention Wynifred, how he had left her behind. She couldn't leave Rosy's memory behind. Her soul had been tied to what Edmund had done and he had left without her.

I reached up and clapped him hard on the back, needing to comfort him as a brother, not as a leader.

"He's doing the same to you, Ilyan," Thom said, looking straight at me.

"I know, bratr." I couldn't say much more than that, the tight restriction in my chest wouldn't let me.

"Don't let him."

"You are a wise man, Thom," I said, feeling humbled by the strangely perfect lesson I had just been taught by my younger brother.

"I've had a lot of years to perfect it."

I could only nod. After all my years on this earth, after all my lessons, studying, and worshiping, my younger brother had become wiser than me. He saw the world in the way I always wanted to.

"Well, you've done well."

"Not really," he said, surprising me with a rare laugh. "Sometimes, the things you need to hear have to come from others. You can't give yourself good advice, after all."

I turned to him, stunned. He looked at me for only a moment before looking away, obviously embarrassed.

"You've done it again, Thom."

"Whatever," he said grumpily, the modern word sounding odd in Czech.

He stood, his stalky frame unraveling awkwardly. I looked back toward the crudely carved heart as Thom's ebbing magic signaled his departure, his direction making it clear he would sit with Joclyn until my return.

He left without another word from either of us, neither knowing what to say. Someday I would thank him for everything. I would find a way to help him seek his revenge, to let him find a way to fill the hole in his heart.

He deserved that, we all did.

CHAPTER 24
JOCLYN

The words were funny, but they calmed me. The strange words belonged to a song, a beautiful song that warmed my heart. I sang the song, the melody one that still lived somewhere deep inside me. I sang it to put myself to sleep every night in the only place I knew. In this room, against the toilet; I stayed here because I could see when they were coming for me. It was the only safe place in this terrifying space.

Ryland was hunting me.

He was determined to kill me. He tried to every day. Every day for forty-two days, I had made marks on the floor by the toilet to track the days, all the days he hunted me. The lines of my blood told me how many days he had hurt me. Forty-two days.

Forty-two days of Cail taunting me before Ryland came. Ryland hurts. Cail didn't hurt; Cail warned.

Cail came first.

Cail always came first.

I felt the drip, drip, drip, against my neck, and that strange warmth flared again. I clawed at it, the same way I had for weeks, the skin now raw and broken in places. I scratched again, trying to get it out of me, but only my own blood ever came.

Blood wasn't comforting. Ryland showed me that every day.

But this warmth was supposed to be comforting. I knew that somewhere deep inside of me.

I knew.

It was like the song; the one with the funny words. I knew they were the same. I knew because of how the song made me feel; how fear slowed when I heard it. I knew the warmth was supposed to be the same.

I knew I was missing something.

If only I could figure out what it was, then I could get out of here.

Go...

Clunk

I froze.

He always tried to find me at night, but he hadn't found this place. Not yet. The only place I was safe was in here. I had hidden here every night during the times I should have been sleeping. Nights, I sat. Days, I ran.

Forty-two days.

Like the marks on the floor.

I had forgotten why I was keeping track. Why did the days matter? I had forgotten what the lines meant, yet still I marked them. Every day a new line. Every day a new mark. I was sure they were supposed to mean something, but I had forgotten.

I forgot everything.

Except the song.

Clunk

I knew he was close. The clunk was closer. I had to move. If he found me here, I would have nowhere to hide.

I stood and ran, not willing to see if he had found me. My foot dragged. It didn't work right after encountering Ryland yesterday. I held onto walls, keeping myself steady, and moved as fast as I could.

I ran from the safe place, through the hall of doors, through the door that led me to what looked like a school, and beyond that a library. The biggest one I had ever seen. I could be safe in the library, but I kept going.

I jumped at all the noises. I cringed away from the rats that watched me run. But I kept going until I reached the room where the desk was. I hid underneath it, hoping it was far enough.

My heart beat loudly, and my breath came hard. I couldn't stop the pounding in my ears. I knew Cail was right behind me.

The door opened before I could stand and find another spot. Cail's heavy footfalls entered. I hid behind the desk, trying to ignore the deafening sound of my pulse in my ears.

He had found me.

I tried to keep my breathing even, yet I knew it was no use. He was looking right at me. I stood slowly, my hand slipping against the side of the desk.

"Y...y...you ca...can't have m...me." I stuttered the words out slowly. It only increased his smile. He shook his head at me dejectedly, looking at me like I was the disgusting filth I knew he saw me as.

I moved my chin toward my collar bone, my nerves catching at his stare, my eyes not quite willing to leave him. I began to twitch and his smile grew.

"Oh, Joclyn," he mocked. I had to remind myself that he was using my name.

"Don't you think this has gone on long enough? Can't you give in? It's already been over a week."

I twitched at his words, my eyes darting around. A week? Wasn't it longer? It felt longer, much longer. Forty-two marks, weren't those the days? I looked at Cail questioningly, but he only smiled more.

"No one is coming for you, Joclyn. It's time to end the game."

Was I expecting someone? I couldn't remember. The warmth in my shoulder grew again, and I instinctively moved to scratch at it.

"Wh...wh...who?" I managed to get the one word out, but I could instantly tell that Cail was playing with me. There was no one there to help me, there never was.

"You can't even remember? I wonder what you *can* remember. I wonder what you are holding onto." He looked at me again, and I twitched away.

Clunk

I jumped and Cail smiled at my movement. More noises could only mean one thing. Ryland was coming. Ryland hurt. I knew nothing other than pain from Ryland. Somewhere deep inside me something yelled at me that there had once been more, but I couldn't remember what it was anymore. It had been forgotten like everything else. Only one thing mattered.

Ryland hurt.

I knew I needed to run. I moved out from behind the large desk, my eyes getting wider as the sound increased. I jumped at each thump, my eyes so wide they burned. My leg dragged from where they had caught it in the doorframe yesterday. I could see Cail smile when he saw it still hurt.

I didn't wait.

I just moved. I went through the door that would take me through the apartment, then the hall with the fingers. Cail watched me as I went. Cail never hurt.

He just came first.

CHAPTER 25
WYN

"Why didn't you tell me, Sain?" They were the first words I had spoken since waking up, since Edmund had left with the last piece of the puzzle, the thing he needed to prompt Cail to kill Joclyn faster and give him even more power over my brother.

I had sat in silence, the dull, green glow of Sain's light keeping me company as I thought through the experiences I now possessed and let who I had been blend with who I had become in a mashed up jumble of personalities and experiences.

I couldn't even bring myself to touch Talon. It wasn't because he had lied to me about my past, it was because I had murdered his family, and the guilt was eating me up inside. I didn't understand how he could have forgiven me for something like that.

So I sat with my back against the cold wall as I let everything wash over me. I tried to find balance.

"Would you have believed me if I did?" Sain whispered from across the prison.

The answer to his question was clear; no, I would not. I had known I was missing my past, but I could have never guessed it was that... horrible. I had been an assassin, a whore, a keeper of magic stronger than any other of my kind. And I had somehow become a fun-loving friend. Fun-loving, Thom had taught me that and Talon had perfected it.

"Who am I?" I asked the question more to myself than to Sain, but he laughed nonetheless, his answer coming quickly.

"You are Wyn."

I fought the urge to roll my eyes, to groan, to yell, to threaten, or seduce. Every single emotion was there, every desire, and they blended together so seamlessly that it wasn't confusing, but somehow, it all made sense. Sain was right.

I am Wyn.

I smiled at the thought, the wicked sneer I had long forgotten sprouting on my lips as I looked at Sain from beneath my eyelashes. He was right; I was Wyn, and I would not just sit here and take this.

Sain returned my smile, his own power shining from beneath his eyes, the silent conviction we both shared strong and defiant.

Then Talon groaned.

I heard him and my heart called out, my guilt forgotten. I was at his side in an instant, my hand wrapped around his. His burning flesh scorched my skin, but I held on anyway, pressing his hands between mine as his eyes slowly fluttered open.

"Talon?" I whispered, but he didn't shift, his eyes remained unfocused on the ceiling. I heard Sain's chains rattle as he attempted to move himself closer, desperate to see.

"Talon? Baby?"

His eyes were still unfocused, but his lips had begun to move, the limp movement subtle.

"W... Wyn..." he said, finally able to get my name out after several false starts.

"I'm here. I'm here." Slowly, his focus slid toward me, the color of his eyes clouded over as he looked through me.

"I thought... I hoped you had gone," he gasped, his voice wheezing as his chest struggled to give him enough air.

"No, baby, I would never leave you. I'm here," I whispered, my hand clinging to his.

He coughed a bit, small drops of blood lining his lips. My eyes widened. *No.* I squeezed his hand between mine, the warmth painful, and yet, somehow comforting.

"It's going to be okay." It was an empty promise. I knew it. I had heard Sain's proclamation as clear as day, and now, with my memory returned, there was no way I could deny the words. I knew Sain's power.

"It's going to be okay," I said again, trying desperately to ignore the tightness in my chest.

Talon said nothing; he only looked at the air behind me as if he was seeing my face there, his eyes drifting in and out of focus.

"Wyn?" he asked, his voice faltering after only one word.

I breathed in slowly, my emotions causing my chest to shake and my eyes to burn.

I grabbed his hand and placed it against the filthy skin of my cheek, needing to feel him, to be close to him. His skin was fire against mine, his palm flat and strong before it went limp again.

I clung to him, watching his eyes drift before they finally came to rest on me, a small smile playing on the corner of his lips.

"Wynifred..." Talon began, his eyes coming into focus. This time, the clouded irises met mine.

"I love you, so much." *No.* I couldn't let him say this. Not now.

"Don't start, Talon. Please," I said, but he didn't even hear me. He plowed on.

"I never thought I could love you..."

"Talon, no."

"I want you to always be happy."

"Talon." My voice was lost in a sob, my hands shaking around the palm of his hand that I held against my face.

"I want you to laugh every day. I want you to find a reason to... to..."

I tried to speak. I tried to talk. I tried to control the sobs that racked my body. Nothing could escape the shaking that had taken control of my lungs. Nothing could escape the panic that held me together.

I clung to him, holding on to his hands as tightly as my frail body would let me. I pushed myself against the bars, desperate to be closer to him, to hold him.

"Clara." His voice broke as he said his sister's name. His vision moving beyond me, his eyes on something that no one else could see.

His sister. She had come to take him home.

"No, Talon. No." I pressed my shaking hand to his, my words distorted through my sobs.

"Be safe, Wyn," he gasped. "Be happy."

He paused as he wheezed, his breathing stopping before picking back up, my hand shaky against his.

"You've done so well, Wynifred. You amaze me."

I sucked in breath, my voice shaking as the sob released it in an almost inaudible burst.

He smiled. "You know when I first loved you? When I knew?"

I couldn't answer. I couldn't try. I just sat and cried.

"When you gave up your magic to save your brother. I had seen the good in you for years, but that's when I knew."

I gasped at the knowledge, my sobs racking through me as I tried to get the three words out. The three words that were the most important ones I could say, the ones I wanted him to hear before it was too late.

"I love you. I love you, Talon."

"Clara."

His voice faded to nothing, his eyes drifting out of focus for the last time, and the heat of his flesh left me as his hand dropped to the ground.

The air was silent, my sobs forgotten, the wheezing in my husband's chest gone.

He was gone.

"No!" I cried as everything exploded. I sobbed as I yelled. I clawed at him through the bars, trying to pull him toward me, but his body wouldn't come. I couldn't reach him. The bars of the prison that had killed him still kept me from him.

"Talon! No!" I shook the bars, hitting myself against them in vain, willing myself to be strong enough to reach him.

My heart ripped open, pouring out loss and grief as I felt everything, raw and fresh as if for the first time. The loss of Talon and Rosaline burst together in a mixture of sorrow so deep it threatened to incapacitate me.

I didn't care if someone heard. I didn't care if they came. I didn't care if this was the end. I screamed out my pain in a keening moan that ripped open my throat and rattled my vision.

Edmund had taken them away from me. My father had taken them away from me. They had taken everything from me.

Everything.

No. Not everything.

I could already feel the boil of my magic as Talon's soul left him and his magic released from his body. Free from the omezující stone, his magic found its mate for the last time, the strength of him rumbling through me as it joined with my own. A new emotion roared through me, a new power, a new strength.

Talon's magic filled me from my toes to the tips of my fingers. The feeling was so foreign, so forgotten, that my body almost rebelled against it. I keeled over onto my hands and knees as my stomach heaved. A steady stream of pain ran through me, my body fighting against the magic, against the pain.

I opened my eyes to a pile of sick on the floor only to gasp at the small, black stone that rested amongst the disgusting mess.

Talon's last gift to me.

He had banished the omezující stone.

His magic settled into my blood, taking its rightful place as my own came back full strength. The power that rippled under my skin was strong and painful. I hadn't felt power this strong since Ilyan had bound it inside me. I had almost forgotten how powerful I felt, how powerful I was.

Edmund had made one giant mistake. When he had unbound my memories, he had also unbound my power.

He had unleashed me.

I gasped as the sobs left me. My anger squashed my anguish and turned it into something violent.. I was ready for it. I needed it.

"I love you, Talon," I whispered against the skin of his hand, the last contact I would ever have with my mate, the only closure I could ever hope to receive.

Talon's hand fell to the floor as I stood, my fingers wrapping around the small stone on the floor, clenching the slippery surface in between my gritty fingers. I felt my body heal as I stood, my magic knitting muscles, bones and skin back together. I felt bruises disappear.

I flexed my fingers as my determination took over.

I didn't care who came.

Let them come.

I opened the doors to each of the cells, the shackles that still bound Sain's wrists falling to the ground with a clatter as I released him. I watched him stand in my peripheral vision, his feet bringing him straight to Talon.

He kneeled down next to him, closing his eyes, and then he kissed his forehead. Any thought of my doing the same was forgotten as the footsteps that had begun thundering above us came nearer.

"You ready?" I asked, surprised at the deep timbre of confidence that had come back to my voice.

"We will need to get to the Rioseco Abbey," Sain said as he came to stand by me.

"I don't suppose you know where that is?" I asked, trying to keep the irritation out of my voice.

"It is in Spain."

Great.

Spain. Half a continent away.

I didn't look toward him. I stood still, unwilling to move as the footsteps thundered down the stairs.

The strength of the earth flowed through me, the fire magic building to a flame. When the guard appeared at the foot of the stairs, his eyes wide and confused as to what had happened, I didn't move. I just let the magic surge, turning the man into ash. He didn't even register what had happened until he tumbled to the ground in specks of grey glittering snow.

I smiled. I couldn't help it. I had forgotten how addicting taking a life could be.

"Was that really necessary?" Sain asked, his voice torn between disgust and humor.

"He would have done the same to us," I answered as I began to move forward, Sain right on my tail. "If you don't like it, don't travel with a trained killer."

"As long as that assassin doesn't turn her skill on me, I think I will be happy." He wasn't worried. His voice was light and airy, and I could tell at once that he had seen something.

I took one last look at Talon, at the body of the man I loved, the only one who was strong enough to love me back. My heart beat once in silent farewell, the heavy pulse thick against the fragile skin of my chest.

Goodbye Talon.

I ignored the sadness and let my anger fuel me as I raced up the staircase and into the thankfully empty guards' room. The room looked the same as it had the day I washed the sheet, the eerie light bouncing off the jagged edges of the stone.

I let my magic surge outward, searching for anyone nearby. No one else was close, but it wouldn't stay that way for long.

"We should move," Sain spoke from behind me, and I didn't challenge it.

I walked out of the room and into the first of many dimly lit halls with Sain on my heels. I kept my magic alert, each step of my bare feet against the rock on the floor giving me a clear map of where we were in relation to everyone else within the mountain.

There was a clear path laid out that would lead us right to the exit—to freedom. As it stood, we wouldn't run into anyone, we could simply leave.

I was already moving us in that direction when I felt it, the gentle tug of a magic that I knew all too well. It surged through my feet as it called to me, the magic of the earth making its presence known. Cail and my father were tucked away somewhere deep in the caves.

Cail's warning ran through my head. Kill Timothy first. I raised my left hand and stared at the marks on my skin, the jagged edges where the zánik curse was bound strong. My brother had done that and in doing so had severed his mind into two halves. He had done it to protect me, in the hopes that he would someday be saved in return.

I had two paths before me, one to certain freedom, and one in the service of my brother.

With the power in my veins, the only thing that could stop me was Edmund, and he was safely tucked inside the bowels of the caves in search of the wells of Imdalind.

Imdalind.

I don't know how, but he hadn't found them yet. I could stop everything before it even began.

"Which have you chosen?" Sain asked. "The path of light or that of dark?" The reference to his sight was jagged and unwanted.

"I don't know what you are talking about, old man," I said, my voice hard. "I am choosing the path that makes the most sense."

I tapped my toes once against the ground, a surge of power and energy rushing away from me. It flowed through the rock before it exploded into the large cavern that held the orchard, the whole thing going up in flames with a loud explosion that shook the entire mountain.

I couldn't help but smile at the surge of power, while Sain jumped at the distant noise. His sharp intake of breath increased my smile before he laughed, soft and joyful. I guess that meant I made the right decision.

I tapped my toes against the stone once more, confirming that my father had moved away from Cail in his attempt to find out what had happened. My jaw clenched as I felt him move closer, the wicked desire to kill that I had lost when my memories were bound coming back strong. I was ready. Timothy would be walking in front of us in three... two... one...

His quick steps moved him through the tall doorway of an adjacent hallway, but he didn't even make it past the archway before my magic had grabbed him and pulled him into the darkened space Sain and I hid in, flattening him against the rock.

He caught sight of me and opened his mouth in a scream that never left his throat. I placed my hand against his mouth, my magic pushing the small, black omezující stone into his belly before my power flared and burned his vocal cords to a crisp. He didn't even have time to draw breath.

"Hello, Father," I taunted, cocking my head to the side in amusement.

His eyes widened as he tried to move against my bindings, the strength incapacitating him. I smiled, my eyes flashing at the sudden reversal of roles.

He deserved this. My blood pulsed strongly in expectation and my smile grew.

"What? Are you not going to say hello?"

Timothy's pupils dilated in panic as he looked at me, the scream of pain and fear that he could never muster lost somewhere deep inside of him.

I placed my hand against his stomach, my palm pressed against the fabric of his shirt. His eyes widened as I pushed against him, my magic shooting a blade of fire into him. My eyes flashed with glee and then I pushed harder, dragging my hand against his belly as my magic sliced a large gash through him, the heat of my magic cauterizing the wound instantly.

"Choose light, Wyn." I froze, the advance of my hand stalled at Sain's voice.

Fine, I would choose light, but that didn't mean I would leave him unaccountable. I would not leave him free to repeat his same sins. He could die alone in the dark. The way he deserved to.

"Goodbye, Father," I spat before sending his body flying back toward the empty room we had just come from, his back snapping as he impacted with the wall. He slid down and fell into a heap, his lack of magic immobilizing him.

I didn't look back.

"This way," I hissed, grabbing Sain's hand and pulling him behind me.

One step against the stone and I could see a quick layout of the caves, my magic pulsing at the realization that Edmund was moving directly toward us. It was no surprise. The man was smart and he knew me well, too well. I altered my route, pulling Sain into a connecting hallway I hadn't planned to use in an attempt to get away from Edmund.

If only the hall had been empty. Four of Edmund's guards were running through the hall in their attempt to get to the blazing orchard, their feet stopping the second we came into view.

Crap. I had been so focused on Edmund that I hadn't noticed them.

I pulled Sain behind me as each of their faces registered our presence, their hands rising in unison. They looked between each other and then back to me, their faces lighting with an eager anticipation. They thought they were going to take me down.

Poor little bastards had no idea what was coming.

"You aren't going to try to kill little, old me, are you?" I asked, a little pout entering my voice. Each of their faces fell. Now they knew. Most of them were old enough to remember what I had been capable of, what Edmund had trained me for.

The Trpaslík at the back wasn't going to risk being near me. One look and he took off in the other direction, trying to escape before I unleashed my full power on him.

Let him run, it wasn't as if I wouldn't face him eventually. Besides, I had three more to play with.

I smiled, waiting for them to attack, letting my magic surge as I prepared to breeze past them. The one in front raised his hand, his fingers shaking as he tried to pull together enough strength and confidence to attack me.

It was pitiful to see, and if I hadn't squashed down all my emotions until I had time to deal with them properly, I would have felt sorry for him, but I didn't. I reached my magic out toward the wall of the hallway, the cold stone warming under my fingertips. The heat inside my body grew as my magic moved into the stone and I liquefied it, the rock heating and melting into a stream of molten lava that seeped away from the wall and over the floor toward the guards.

The man that had come to the front screamed as the fast moving molten rock covered his feet and began working its way up his body. Pain incapacitated him as he was smothered, the rock hardening over him in a coffin of stone.

"Whoops," I whispered, sending the last of the guards running in the opposite direction, tripping over their own feet in a panic to get away.

"Don't say anything," I whirled on Sain before I pulled him past the molten man, making our way toward where I hoped Cail still was.

My feet picked up pace, knowing the fire in the orchard would only keep them busy for so long. Edmund was already onto me. I could deal with his minions, but I didn't want to test my newly remembered strength against him directly so soon, if I could help it.

I ran forward, trying to focus on where Edmund might be, but he seemed to have disappeared.

The halls grew darker the closer I got to Cail's magical imprint. The normally brightly lit lamps were covered and dark, the yells from the orchard fading into nothing.

I rounded the last corner only to come face to face with Edmund. I had hoped we would beat him here; obviously, I had been too optimistic. He stood between my brother and me, his arms folded over his black leather jacket as he looked me up and down. Cail was on a large bed behind him, the jagged red blade protruding awkwardly out of his chest.

I had seen the souls blade so many times over the last few weeks, but now that I had my memories back it gnawed at my heart until it ached.

That was my daughter. That was Rosy. If I wanted to free my daughters soul I would need that blade. Looking at it now, it seemed smaller, more fragile.

Just like Rosy when Edmund had killed her.

I clenched my teeth as I glared at Edmund, hoping my face would be enough to issue a warning, but he only smiled, my challenge greedily accepted.

"Out of my way, Edmund, or you're going to lose another finger," I growled, my magic moving through the rock toward him eagerly.

"You really think I am just going to let you leave after I worked so hard to dispose of everyone else in these halls?" Edmund's voice was deep, a wicked gleam playing in his eyes. "You are the last one, and you are going to die, just like the rest of them."

"Move, Edmund." My fingers flexed as I watched him, unwilling to look away for a second. I wasn't going to step down. I would not back away, not after I had come this far.

"You would risk everything for him, wouldn't you?" he asked, my warning rolling off him like water. "Just as he would do the same for you?"

"Out of my way," I snarled through my clenched teeth.

"Very well," he said casually, shifting to the side and giving me a full view of the stone room at the end of the hall. I glanced at Cail's sleeping body, my feet ready to take me forward, when a man moved to stand beside him, a large knife poised in his hands. I took one step forward without thinking, my blood pulsing with desperation.

"Nonono," Edmund taunted. "Remember, he dies first and then you die, and if I am not mistaken, Timothy still lives."

Curse Sain for talking me out of killing the old man. I was a fool to have listened to him. I should have known better. I should have expected Edmund to play this game.

My jaw clenched, my eyes glaring at Edmund before moving back to where Cail lay on the bed. Choose light, Sain had said. What was he thinking? Light and dark. I thought I had chosen correctly. Had I really chosen the wrong path? I wanted to say no, but I could hear the footsteps of Edmund's army surrounding us, and I felt Sain cower by my feet, his practically useless magic no help to me.

That was fine. I had enough power for both of us.

I narrowed my eyes at Edmund, my lips turning up in eager anticipation. I felt the army surround us as their magic surged through the stone. The large stone cavern was now protected from every angle, trapping us in place.

For the moment.

Forgive me, Cail.

I surged my magic into the rock below me, sending Sain into the air as I tapped my toes to the ground, a deep rumble spreading out away from me like a ripple on water. The rock shifted as it opened up and swallowed those around me to the waist before solidifying again, trapping them in the stone. I didn't wait, I knew I only had a matter of minutes to use this diversion, and we needed all the head start we could get. I took off into the air, grabbing Sain around the waist and cutting our bodies through the air toward the exit.

Yells and explosions echoed behind us as the rock I had trapped everyone in was blown apart.

"Wynifred!" The ripple of Edmund's magic traveled through the air behind me and I twisted and dodged, afraid of what he might do to us.

It was too late anyway. There was only one way in and out of these caves, through the gate. You couldn't even stutter in or out, Ilyan had seen to that.

The massive reflective carving that served as the gate into the underground circuit of caves towered above us—the large man sitting astride his horse, surrounded by a large intricate arch.

I angled us toward the carving, toward what appeared to be a wall of solid rock. Without stopping, I pulled us through the rock and into the large canyon on the other side, right into a large group of tourists that had hiked through the moss-covered trench to see the mirror image of the carving that we had just passed through.

Shouts of surprise echoed around us as a few tourists at the front witnessed our miraculous appearance from the stone.

I pulled Sain behind me as I plunged into the thickening crowd of people, the initial shouts drawing others from nearby. I didn't care about their mortal worries right now, I had bigger problems on my heels. Like the fact that we were attracting too much attention, and I knew Edmund and his guards couldn't be far behind us. I shielded us quickly, the decision only causing more screams of fright to echo round the canyon as we disappeared from view.

I moved us through the horde of tourists that had congregated around the ancient carving at the end of the damp canyon. The carving was known as the dwarves' door to the tourists, but was known as the gates of Imdalind to my kind. It was those gates I needed to seal.

At this point, I did not care about the upset I caused. If I had, I might have been more careful, but my only goal was to get us in position before Edmund could find us. I needed him out of the cave before I could block the opening and seal him away from the wells of Imdalind.

I pushed people out of the way, causing more fear as people reacted to being manhandled by an invisible entity.

We reached the end of the line of tourists and moved around the edges of the crowd back to the side of the ornate carving.

My heart thumped in anticipation as I locked my jaw. The tourists had begun to settle down, forgetting what they had seen quickly, as is the case with magic—their fully mortal brains unable to process what had happened. There were a few others, the ones with un-awakened abilities in their blood, who were still so worked up that they were lingering on the edge of panic.

I watched and waited, trying to control my breathing as I placed my hands against the rock face. My magic surged under my skin, the pulse of it matching the hectic beat of my heart. I felt the magic surge again as it prepared to burn the rock and destroy the portal. I needed to find him first.

It was only a matter of minutes before I caught sight of him, my chest tightening at seeing Edmund in the middle of the crowd. He had appeared there, having shielded himself to get through the gate, but unable to maintain his cloak as he moved through the panicking tourists. Edmund was out. Timothy and my brother were still inside.

I narrowed my eyes and let my magic swell, filling the rock as I melted and morphed it with my power, as I urged it to shift. I was careful to keep the labyrinths of mazes intact, careful to keep Cail safe. I moved the rock until I was sure I had covered the entrance, hoping to block Edmund from the wells of Imdalind. Of course, I was also trapping Cail inside, and I was leaving Talon's body behind.

Perhaps forever.

CHAPTER 26
WYN

I stood beside the fused rock and took one moment to breathe. I risked more than I should have in closing my eyes to say goodbye. I looked into the blackness behind my lids and said goodbye to my brother. I thanked him for what he had given up to help me and then silently prayed he would be alright and that I would see him again. I said my final goodbye to Talon, the man who had loved me no matter what and had protected me from myself for a hundred years, helping me grow as a person and learn to love life. I placed my hand against the cold stone of the mountain and felt my magic surge, the heat behind my eyes growing as I fought back the tears.

Then the moment was gone. I shoved the pain and loss into the black pit of my icy heart and opened my eyes to the crowd of tourists. They snapped pictures of the carving, made crude signs in front of their cameras and complained about their lack of water. I heard them, but let it all wash over me as my eyes scanned for what I was really looking for.

My magic ran through the ground, serving as my sensor. My magic did not work as Ilyan's did; it did not alert me to any power nearby. I had to scan through the ground.

My eyes narrowed as I found him near the edge of the crowd, surrounded by at least twenty of his men. Edmund stood still, presumably looking through the crowd for me.

My jaw set in a scowl as I looked at him, my magic pulsing in excitement.

I could take out at least three of Edmund's guards before he could do anything. If the tourists surrounding them didn't notice the men turning to pillars of ash right beside them, however, I would eat Thom's ugly hat. I wasn't sure that causing trauma for innocent bystanders was really my thing anymore, anyway.

I didn't want it to be.

I needed to get to Ilyan and to Joclyn, so that together we could end this. As much as regaining the fire magic had benefited me, Joclyn was the only one that could stop Edmund. Fighting was not an option for us here, no matter how much I wanted it to be. Our best chance was to fly toward Ilyan's ancient evacuation tunnel hidden in the catacombs of St. Vitus Cathedral in downtown Prague.

There were a few problems with this plan. First and foremost, it was in downtown Prague. We were currently tucked away in the mountains, and it would take me at least fifteen minutes to fly us there, if Edmund didn't track us right away.

The Cathedral also sat in the middle of one of the busiest squares in the old town, and at this time of year, it would be flooded by tourists. I would have to be careful. I couldn't let Edmund follow us, too many people would die. Too many people already had.

"St. Vitus." Sain's voice was a whisper next to me. I had almost forgotten he was there. I turned to face him, not daring to keep my focus off the crowd in front of me for too long.

"Excuse me?" I asked, alarmed that he had somehow seen into my head, which given who he was, probably wasn't too far off.

"We are going to St. Vitus, but we need to go by the Orloj where Kadan put his clock. I must retrieve something or this escape will have been in vain." His voice wasn't normal. It wasn't like when he was given the Black Water, but more like when he had told me of Talon's death. Considering what Edmund had done to him over the centuries, it was amazing his sight was still part of him at all, but if this was how the remains of his power chose to make itself known, then I would take all the help I could get.

I grabbed Sain's frail hand and held it in my small one. Our best bet was to fly, and if I could do this without detection, it would be a miracle. Digging my bare toes into the loose dirt, I let the power inside me build. It bubbled and boiled until my body felt like it was vibrating; the anger and power bleeding together in a torrent that flooded out of me. It raced through the dirt, and into one of the large wooden benches that someone had placed on the side of the path.

The second the power had filled it, I sent a pulse, one strong surge of magic that boomed through the air in a violent explosion. Fire filled the sky as the tourists screamed, the noise barely audible above the echo of the blast that bounced around the small canyon.

People raced down the canyon in their mad attempt to escape the blast. They ran into each other, children and women racing away as frantic men trampled over them. I could just make out Edmund as he turned toward the explosion, his eyes scanning the crowd for me.

I wasn't stupid enough to expect him to run toward the blast. He was smart, and hundreds of years of working with him had taught me his weaknesses.

I dropped the shield around us, the lack of security making us visible to him, but making it easier for me to merge with the crowd. I didn't wait to see if he had noticed us because I knew he would.

I took off running toward the now destroyed bench, my hand tight around Sain's as I weaved us through the terrified hoard that was fleeing the scene.

Please don't let anyone get hurt.

I shielded us again, hoping that our brief stint of visibility was enough time for Edmund to have noticed us and then sent my magic into a bench on the other side of the canyon.

This time, I didn't wait for the pressure to build. I just sent the pulse into the wood and sent the shards of wood into the air in a fiery explosion.

The effect was instantaneous. The remaining tourists screamed and turned to run toward the narrow opening in the canyon that had led them here, the only way to truly escape. They panicked and screamed as they ran, and I was swept up with them as they fled toward safety, their exodus taking Sain and I along for the ride.

Edmund and his guards were forcibly separated as the crowd intercepted them, dragging them toward the bottleneck that was forming in the crowd.

At any other time, I might have expected Edmund to attack. He saw mortal life as useless, but they were his cover as much as they were mine. He was being smart.

So was I, and I couldn't wait any longer.

I stomped my foot into the ground, sending out a pulse of energy that shook the mountain. It rippled away from me and sucked the energy out of the legs of all those within range. Mortals fell as the power surged through them, their primitive minds signaling an earthquake as they screamed in fear.

I kept the shield strong around us and took off into the sky, Sain's body unsupported as he dangled below me. I couldn't risk bringing wind to support his weight as that would be much easier for Edmund to detect. Sain would have to wait until I was sure we were not being followed.

Edmund and his men had fallen to the ground with everyone else, but they recovered quickly, and instead of searching the people on the ground, he was scanning the skies.

Crap.

He lifted his hand, his magic soaring through the empty skies. It would only be a matter of seconds before it would intercept with me, signaling to Edmund exactly where we were.

I felt his magic wash over me. It was the sign of the end, but I wasn't going to give up without a fight. I turned abruptly in the air, changing course, hoping that he would assume I had continued in the same direction.

"Are they behind us?" I asked to still dangling Sain, careful to keep my voice low and controlled. "Are we being followed?"

"I don't know..."

My jaw clenched. Of course, we were being followed. It was a stupid question really. My only hope was that they were following the wrong glare of the sun, the wrong gust of wind.

We sped through the air as farmland turned to city. The red-roofed buildings of Prague looked up at us as I soared over the narrow, cobbled streets and right to the center of the city, the small bend in the river serving as my compass.

I set my jaw and increased my speed. I could see the cathedral now and the clock was just on the other side of the river.

We were almost there.

"Wyn! Look out!" Sain screamed, his voice ripping me from my focus on our goal and straight to the car that had exploded from the ground below us, the large heap of metal making a beeline right for us. I screamed and blinked once in reflex. The car exploded in the sky.

"Well, if there was any question of where we were before..."

I swore loudly and spun out of the way of the explosion, drawing wind to support Sain as the exertion of my power caused my shield to evaporate. Not like it mattered, they obviously knew right where we were anyway.

I twisted my body through the air, searching for them, only to see Edmund streaming toward us, about three hundred feet behind. For one stupid second, I rejoiced that it was only him, but then reality caught up.

Crap. Edmund was right behind us.

I sent my hand out, my magic surging into a line of fire that worked itself into a wall, a barrier that I hoped would slow him down. The wall moved toward him, the attack lingering in the air as I dropped us toward the crowded streets below.

"Is he following?"

"What kind of question is that?" Sain yelled as we landed in a large courtyard before an ornate fountain, cherubs and snakes shooting water behind us. "Of course he is following us."

Tourists scattered and screamed at our arrival, but it was only a horrifying backdrop as Edmund prepared to land right before us.

"Your magic... Can you help me?" I asked Sain, my eyes trained on the wicked man who was set on killing us both.

"Not unless you want to know what you are going to have for breakfast."

I couldn't help the smile that spread across my face, the wicked gleam floating up to Edmund who only smiled more.

"Get to the clock, then meet me at the Golden Gate."

I didn't wait for his response, it wouldn't matter if he could get to the clock and back if I didn't stop Edmund after all. Or at least slow him down.

That was realistically the only thing I could hope for.

I swung my arms wide, sending what was left of the tourists and residents away from me. They slammed into buildings and landed in the fountain, but I didn't care. If I didn't get them away, something far worse was going to happen to them. Broken bones they could recover from, melting skin they could not.

I let my magic surge through my feet. It connected with the magic of the cobbled street and grew as it rushed through the stones, shaking me as the road vibrated. The cobbles that had been laid thousands of years ago rattled and pulled themselves out of the ancient plaster they had been set in. They hovered above the ground as my magic seeped into them, heating them, melting them.

I watched Edmund's hands rise toward me, his palms growing white as he prepared to rain down acid through the air around me.

He had his trick, and I had mine.

The molten rock flew toward him as the white light grew in his hands. I shielded myself from his attack as the lava intercepted with him, the molten clumps of rock colliding with his powerful shield. His shield flashed and flickered as the boiling hot earth wove its way through it. The stones splattered against his hands and face, sending him to the ground as the white magic disappeared.

His agonized yell of pain rang over the courtyard. He was definitely injured, possibly weakened from the attack. For one moment, I thought that I might be able to turn him to ash, not just a single finger as I had done once before. I knew better, though; he would recover quickly thanks to the Vilỳ poison he infected himself with every night.

Now was not the time to fight him. It was not my destiny to end him, no matter how much I wanted to.

I turned and ran right to the river, the steeples of St. Vitas on the other side. I ran through the narrow streets of Prague, the beige rock fronts of the buildings a mellowing calm over the frantic beat of my heart pounding in my chest.

My feet padded against the stones, and with each step, I let my magic flow through the rock, tracking where he was. I had only barely turned the corner before his signature disappeared from the ground. He had already recovered and was chasing after me.

I shouldn't be surprised.

I brought my magic to me as I raced and weaved through the crowd. I pushed people out of my way, throwing them into walls and small cafes in an effort to keep them out of danger. Each step increased my fear, my expectation, but still Edmund had not reached me.

I could see the break in the buildings, the grey of the river, and the Úřad vlády České just on the other side.

I had just turned the last corner toward the river when his warm body collided with mine, the force of the impact sending me headlong into the white bricked wall I had been running next to. A loud crack echoed in my ears as the impact split the stone.

I felt my skull crack, my magic congregating at the wound as everything swam, my vision going double. Edmund turned to face me. I couldn't help smiling at the red welts of blistered skin where the scalding rocks had hit him.

"Wynifred!" he howled as he slammed his hand into the wall by my head, another crack joined the first as he pinned my arms above me.

"Yes, Edmund?" I said causally, as if we were just enjoying a romantic stroll.

"I am glad to see you're back to yourself, now stop attacking me and get back to work." He moved his other hand to rest against my cheek, and I smiled. I smiled at him the way I had for centuries before letting my magic flare through my cheek and into his hand.

He yelled out in pain, his grip on my wrists increasing as his own anger flared.

"You can't have me, Edmund. I will never submit to you." I smiled at him, narrowing my eyes in defiance. He howled in anger before he threw me away from him, my body tumbling through the air only to land in the middle of the murky waters of the Vltava River.

My body hit the water with a loud slap that seized through me in an agonizing ripple and cut all sensation from my muscles. I sunk into the cold water, kicking my way back to the surface when a warm hand wrapped around my neck. The strong hand pressed roughly against my water-filled windpipe as it pulled me up through the waves and held me just below the surface of the lapping waves.

I looked into Edmund's face from where he held me under the grey water, my last breath held in my chest, his crazed face mad with victory. I attempted to fight him, but the lack of air made it difficult.

"Think you can escape me and go back to that little half-breed? I will never let you win. Never!" His voice bellowed from above the water, sure of his imminent success. Had he really forgotten me so easily? There was no way I was going to let him win.

The bubbling energy of my magic moved through my veins, boiling within me. I could feel the fire magic taking over.

I smiled at him from beneath the murky water.

His face paled, his crazed energy flickering. He was still fighting when the light from my body grew, reflecting off his face as I gazed at him from underneath the murky waters.

The water boiled around me, the river turning into a hot pot around my super-heated body. Edmund yelled out and attempted to release his hands, but I held them in place, feeling his flesh heat.

"No!" he spat, his voice muffled through the water. I felt his hands pulse with an attack, and my body convulsed underneath the water, the electrical attack frying the tips of my nerve endings.

My mouth opened as I yelled in agony. The sound waves of my scream reverberated through the water as they burst from me, the water splashing away and splattering Edmund's face with the scalding heat. Edmund yelled again as the attack hit him, but he flattened his hands against my skin and sent pulse after pulse of paralyzing energy through my body.

I let go of his wrists as I screamed in pain, Edmund laughed maniacally, believing his attempt to kill me was succeeding.

He really was a fool.

My lungs burned for air as my hands flew toward Edmund's face. Anyone else would have turned to ash, but with Edmund the best I could hope for was a few lost fingers, maybe a singed ear lobe, and the time to get away.

He yelled out as the pain hit him, my energy a pulse that sent him flying through the air away from me.

My magic took over as I threw myself out of the water and into the air. I hacked and gasped as I flung myself through the sky like a ragdoll, only to right myself and quicken my pace as Edmund's yells behind me increased.

I turned toward the green copper roof of St. Vitus cathedral, the arches of the south entrance glittered at me in the distance. The tall, stone arches sparkled in the sun, the sandstone appearing as bright as gold in the setting rays of light.

Edmund yelled from somewhere behind me, the sound increasing as he got closer.

Please let Sain have made it to the gates already. I didn't have time to wait, and I was going to have to seal the gate once I passed through it. I just wished I had enough time to complete the process.

I dropped my body closer to the earth, my heart beating quicker when I saw Sain standing near the large golden stone work, a large earthen mug clutched against his chest.

"Run!" I screamed when I was within distance.

Sain looked up at me, confused for only a moment before he turned and bolted down the hall, toward the large chapel.

I didn't slow my speed for landing. I flew right into the courtyard, bricks exploding into the air at the rough impact. I straightened myself and turned to face the courtyard just beyond the gates.

Edmund was right behind me.

I set my jaw and raised my hand, a shimmering shield flowing from my fingers to cover the large opening of the golden gate.

My magic surged as it spread in a curtain between the giant arches. I looked through the magical barrier to see Edmund change his course in order to intercept me.

He was almost here, and the shield had not set yet. I pushed harder, my teeth clenching as I grunted through the pressure, yelling as the exertion hit its maximum and my magic pushed and pulled to escape from me.

My mouth opened as I screamed, the shield setting itself into the stone the moment Edmund's body hit hard against the barrier. The impact of his collision rumbled through me, shooting me away from the shield and slamming me into the high wall behind me.

I straightened myself the same moment Edmund did, his jaw as set as mine as he turned to face me. Our eyes met, the whites of his eyes were blood shot with anger and power. I had never seen him this worked up. I could tell at once that this shield would only hold for a matter of minutes once he decided to come at me.

Edmund uncoiled his body as he faced me, his hand lifting to his face. A large chunk of his arm was missing, the edges blackened with ash. Even with all of my power, that was all I had been able to accomplish against him.

He smiled at me as he lifted his finger, the one I had burned off all those centuries ago, the replacement forcibly taken from one of his many servants. He bit down on it and pulled, the flesh separating slowly, his hand dripping with blood as he ripped the finger from his hand.

"I have a present for you, Wynifred," he sneered, his breathing shallow as some power-based insanity threatened to take over him.

"Keep it," I spat, turning from him. I didn't want to be on the receiving end of whatever he had to give me ever again.

I had barely turned my back on him before I heard the heavy clang of an attack against the gate.

I didn't turn to see what he had done. I let the angry yells that Edmund filled the air with wash over me as I ran.

I overtook Sain quickly, his pace was quick in the panic, but his body was not up to the strain.

"You will have to seal the door to the tombs. Otherwise, we will not have enough time." Sain's voice was low as he spoke, his pace not nearly fast enough for us to get away.

"You think I don't know that already?" I grabbed his arm, knowing he was too weak to move fast enough, and pushed him forward through the ancient chapel.

I would have loved to walk quietly through the massive space, bask in the ancient architecture of the buttresses and stained glass windows I had known since I was a child. However, the manic yelling of the man behind us was a heavy reminder of the desperate situation we had found ourselves in.

The calm heads of the pious people turned at our frantic movements and the yells that followed us in. I saw the ancient priest step forward in his long black robes, his hands extended in welcome and worry.

He was sweet and kind. All of these people were, and I knew Edmund would kill him.

"Utíkej!" I yelled to the old priest. His face opened in horror as the high screech of my voice broke through the relative quiet of the cathedral.

He wasn't moving. Fine, I would make him.

I lifted my hand as we passed him, his body lifting ten feet into the air before I sent him tumbling into a confessional.

It was enough.

Edmund's growing screams mixed with the new fear of those in the chapel. I saw people cowering against walls, hiding under pews, and a select few darted toward the main door.

I didn't wait to watch them hide. I kept my attention in front of me. There were only a few rooms to go before we would reach the catacombs, only a few minutes before we would reach Ilyan's tomb. We could make it.

We could.

Sain and I turned at the ancient pulpit at the head of the chapel to dart through the heavy, wooden door to the left of one of the many sandstone statues. The door slammed behind us, and for one brief moment, we were trapped in silence. I listened to my labored breathing, Sain's panting, and felt the tightness of my chest adding to the panic I felt.

"To the door," Sain whispered.

I nodded once before continuing to drag him behind me.

My heart beat and sputtered as we moved through the small, bare hallways of the offices and apartments of the clergy before coming to a lone, black, stone door at the end of the empty hallway.

The catacombs.

My hand touched the ancient knob as the door several halls behind us opened, releasing the screams we had trapped in the main chapel back into our ears.

He was coming.

I caught my scream in my chest. The door swung open and I shooed Sain into the dark, damp space in front of us, closing the door behind us as quietly as I could.

The smell of ancient death hit my nose. The long forgotten smell of loss ignited my panic even further.

I sealed the door, my magic closing the cracks and melting the stone together into a solid slab of rock.

It was pointless really; Edmund knew where we were going, but anything I could do to slow him down, I would.

CHAPTER 27
WYN

Our breathing escaped in a rush as we raced down the winding stone steps and into the depths of the tombs.

"Faster," Sain panted. I didn't know if he spoke to me or to himself, but I took it as a warning and let my magic flood through both of us, increasing our pace.

We flew down the staircase as the air grew even more damp, the light dimming as it welcomed us into the home of the dead. We reached the base of the staircase, the dark expanse of the tombs a vivid reminder of the prison we had just left behind—the prison I had left my mate in.

I couldn't think that way.

Death filled my lungs as we moved past the large, dark stacks of bones that made up the walls of the labyrinth. Skulls smiled at us, each one a casualty of plague or war. The bones served as a warning to grave robbers, but it was not one I needed to heed. We were going into a tomb, not taking things out of one.

My magic heightened my sight as we moved through the maze of bones, while Sain's green light once again shone brightly in front of us as it led the way. We moved quietly, following the deathly green hues as we waited for the sound of the door exploding off its hinges.

The sound never came.

My heart beat wildly. I was having trouble keeping my focus. Edmund should be here by now, something was wrong. My nerves prickled as my heart called out 'trap', putting me on high alert.

Sain stopped in place, our intertwined hands pulling me to a quick halt in front of him. I gasped at the sudden stop, the sharp intake of breath echoing around the open space that surrounded us.

"He is here," Sain whispered, and my whole body turned to ice. "Do not fight him, or we will not survive."

We stayed still in the labyrinth of bones as Sain's words settled into my mind. Edmund had moved beyond the door.

The sound of our breathing joined with a drip of water that was falling somewhere around us. The sounds bled together as they bounced off the bones and amplified themselves.

I took a hesitant step forward, the heavy thump of my heart against my ribs causing me physical pain.

We took one step after another, my bare feet against the stone floor flooding with magic as we moved through the labyrinth of bones at a snail's pace. I peeked around each corner, dragging my feet through puddles of stagnant water in an attempt to keep my connection to the earth's magic.

I shivered as we moved into the main hall of the catacombs, the ceilings higher, the stone darker. The roof was speckled with small windows that let ribbons of light into the ancient hall. They fell over crypts and statues that were in even more of a maze than what we had just come from.

"Where is he?" I hissed as I searched for him. But I felt nothing, saw nothing. I wanted to believe that Edmund was not here—but I felt Sain's tense body beside mine.

Sain said nothing in reply, the quiet that surrounded us only interrupted by the occasional echo of a drip of water. I turned to face the old Drak, his eyes wide as he focused on the bright white coffin that the mortals had buried Ilyan in when he resigned as their ruler, faking his own death more than six hundred years ago.

I turned toward it, expecting to see Edmund standing right beside it, but the large hall was still empty. The room was silent except for my ever-increasing breathing.

I took a step toward the tomb, Sain following as he cowered behind me. My bare foot accidentally slapped hard against the smooth stone of the floor, the sound echoing around us. I froze. If Edmund was down here, I had just given away our exact location.

"Ruuuuun," Sain breathed out, his voice shaking as his whole body began to convulse.

His words were lost as my pulse quickened. I turned toward him, only to see his body shake, his eyes darkening into black and then fading back into green. Sain's eyes widened as if his whole face was being stretched.

"Ruuuuun," he repeated again, his voice deep and hollow.

The word sank in; it ignited inside of me and sent my feet moving in a panic. I dragged Sain behind me as he stumbled in a blind attempt to follow. Our feet hit heavy against the floor, our breathing mixed with the hollowness of our steps as we made our way toward what was now our only chance of escape.

"I'm going to hurt Cail, Wynifred." I froze at Edmund's voice, my feet coming to a stop only inches from the tomb that would lead us to safety.

"I'm going to rip his body apart, piece by piece. Hundreds of years of disloyalty needs to be punished after all." His voice echoed all around me, his heavy breathing making the desperation, the madness, heavier in his voice.

I could have sworn I felt the same. I fought for control. I fought to recall the words Sain had said only moments ago.

"I am going to make him pay."

"If you can get in," I said simply, unable to control my mouth as I took the last few steps toward the tomb.

"You think a little fire can stop me? I will be back in there before nightfall, you little slut. Then I will do to Cail what I did to Rosaline. I will remove his soul from his body, as slowly and as painfully as I can."

"No!" I couldn't help the shout that ripped from my throat, my chest aching. I turned around to face him, my fingers clawing at my thighs with the need to rip his eyes from his face.

Edmund stood at the entrance we had just come through, his eyes flashing joyously as he watched me, his dark hair loosened from its usual tightly gelled style, his hand dripping blood from where he had ripped the finger from his body.

This had been his plan. He knew I wouldn't back down from this threat; he knew and so did Sain. Sain wrapped his arms around me as he attempted to keep me back, to stop me from attacking.

"Do not fight, Wynifred," Sain hissed in my ear, the reminder of his sight barely grazing the surface of my panic.

"I will rip him apart, limb by limb, until there is no more blood to shed, until his soul has given up." Edmund continued as he stepped forward, his words a hot poker against my soul. "And then I will take his soul, Wynifred, and I will use it the way I use Rosaline's. I will keep it in a place you will never find it. Not that you will be alive much longer than he is."

"NO!" I fought against Sain, his weak body using up the last of his energy in an attempt to keep me at bay.

"I would do the same to Talon... if he was still alive."

I could hear Sain mumble behind me. I could hear him gasp as my magic surged under my skin, burning him on contact. He didn't budge. He endured the pain as he attempted to keep me safe.

Stay safe, Wynny.

My fight left me as Talon's voice echoed through my head, his words joining Sain's in a jumbled mess that pulled the fight out of me.

I stopped struggling against Sain's hold. I looked down to the stone floor of the catacombs, my eyes scanning over the tombs that littered the floor before I raised my head to Edmund.

Edmund smiled at the look in my eye, at the way my lips pursed. He believed he had won, that I would fight him now and he would win.

I wasn't who he still thought me to be.

I was Wyn.

My eyes locked with his as I sent my magic surging through the floor of the tomb, the ancient magic in the stone connecting with mine to supercharge the pulse, which hit in a surge that shot him straight into the air.

Edmund yelled as he impacted with the roof of the tombs, my magic still burning through him. I pulled Sain with me as I turned, the lid of Ilyan's coffin lifting just enough to allow us passage inside.

Edmund's screams died as we slipped ourselves through the opening, the magical barrier of Ilyan's protection washing over me as I moved through it.

There was no way Edmund could follow us here. For the moment, we were safe.

"Wynifred!" Edmund yelled and I turned, peering at him through the gap in the lid. "I will make him pay."

"I will retrieve both of their souls, Edmund, right before I rip your heart from your body. You will pay."

He balked at my statement, his face going white before the lid to the coffin dropped, enclosing us in the dark space.

I listened to Sain's breathing equalize alongside mine as we waited for a sign that Edmund was trying to follow us, as we waited for his attempt to break through the barrier Ilyan had placed around the tomb.

But none came.

A deep green light flared in Sain's hand, giving just enough light for us to see. We just looked at each other, neither of us having the words for what had just happened.

Sain turned toward the tunnel that opened up behind him, the long, dark abyss that would lead us safely underground and right into Italy. His light flickered along the walls of dirt and stone until the tunnel faded into an endless stretch of claustrophobic black.

In any other situation, I would have been scared at seeing an endless enclosed space. Instead, my heart relaxed at the promise of safety it held for us.

"We'd better hurry," Sain whispered as he stepped into the tunnel, the first step of a long journey.

I rushed to catch up with him, his words sending ice down my spine.

"What do you mean?" I asked, dearly hoping he hadn't seen anything else.

"We don't have a lot of time." Sain didn't look at me as he spoke; he simply continued walking, his slow pace taking us straight forward.

"Is he coming?" My voice slithered over my tongue, the fear rushing right back to the surface.

"No," Sain answered as he turned to face me, "but you have less time than I originally thought."

Sain reached forward and grabbed my left hand, lifting my arm to eye level. I looked at him in confusion, trying to make sense of his words. But he was focused on my arm.

"Edmund has plans for your brother. We must get you to Joclyn before it is too late."

CHAPTER 28
ILYAN

The large map of the grounds that surrounded the abbey took up the majority of the expansive table that we had set up in the middle of the long kitchen. I stood over it, facing the crumbling stone ovens and fireplaces that had once been used by the monks of Rioseco for food preparation.

It had been seven days since the first eight camps appeared. Now we could see twenty-two. Each one was marked by a small, red dot on the map, the number of how many we assumed to be in each camp marked in quill pen beside it. The camps kept coming, and still no Ovailia.

Joclyn had been trapped in the Tồuha for almost two weeks—three months for her. For three months, Edmund had been torturing her. I had healed her after every attack, but the injuries kept coming. Last night, they plagued her over and over until, in the end, I had to restart her heart, my magic manually pumping it in an attempt to keep her alive. Futile, that was how it felt.

My only hope for her now was Ryland.

I scanned the map, trying to find a rhyme or reason to the pattern, but once again finding nothing. That didn't necessarily mean anything though. It could simply mean that the Trpaslíks did not follow instructions, which was common.

I snatched a strawberry out of one of the bowls that held down the massive paper, moving around to the other side of the table, hoping another angle would help.

"One new camp last night," I said as Dramin walked in, his energy slow and lagging from having just woken up. He came up beside me, and I pointed to the newest red dot, the ink on the number six still drying.

"One is better than ten," he chuckled, his reference to yesterday's surge making me cringe.

Yes, one was better than ten, and after they had come so steadily, it only left me worrying about what was still coming. I stretched my hands out to hover above the map, trying another view, but nothing jumped out at me.

"Do we have a plan yet?" Dramin asked, but I only laughed humorlessly at him.

At this point, if Joclyn didn't wake, it would be me against upwards of a hundred Trpaslíks with a little help from Thom. While I had defeated that number before, it was not without grave injury, something that would take time to recover from. Even then, I had been alone at the time. This time I had people to protect.

"Does the battle happen before or after Joclyn wakes?" I asked.

"Does it matter?"

"It might," I prompted, careful to keep my voice light. "When does she wake?"

"Soon." Dramin grunted as he sat down beside me, his hands already wrapped around a full mug of Black Water. I stared at the water as if it had offended me. We had given Joclyn the water for the past four days and nothing had happened. No waking, no more sights. She stayed still every time, laid out on the wide couch that had been placed in one of my side rooms years ago.

I sat down heavily next to Dramin, my eyes still focused on the poison in his hands.

"Myslíš, žeif," I began, careful to keep my voice level. I didn't need to set Dramin on his guard. "*Do you suppose* we could give her another sight, she might wake? We could pour the water over my skin first."

I cringed internally at the idea, the pain from my last burn still hadn't fully left. Most of the time it was just a dull hum of an ache, but sometimes it would flare up in agony, especially when anything touched it, much like the scars on my chest. Those still ached, so I didn't see these going away any time soon.

"I'm not sure what that much Black Water inside of anyone other than a Drak would do," Dramin said simply, but his words set me on high alert.

"Uvnitř?" *Inside?* My voice must have sounded much deeper than I thought because Dramin chuckled, his youthful face turning toward me.

"Yes, Ilyan, inside. Why do you think it still burns? It will burn until your magic has changed it enough to let it flow comfortably through your veins. Even then, it is still Black Water. It's just more you than Imdalind at that point."

I stared at him wide-eyed. I was raised to be King, raised with all the knowledge of our kind so as to be able to lead them. But this? I had never heard of this before.

"I just entrusted you with our only secret, Ilyan. You better keep it that way." Dramin smiled at me, but it was sad, his eyes were shaded by something... Regret? I couldn't see Dramin ever regretting anything, but then, he had just released a secret the Drak had seen fit to keep from everyone since the beginning of time.

"So what does that mean for me?" I asked, my eyes narrowing at him. Dramin only laughed at me, his usual joyful timber coming back into his voice.

"You have had Black Water flowing through your veins for eight hundred years and now you worry? Nebojte se," he said as he patted my hand in a grandfatherly way, an action that did not match his appearance. "You will be fine. All I said was that I did not know what would happen. If there was a threat of an additional head sprouting on your shoulders, we would have never consented to give you, or anyone else, access to sight."

He laughed and everything relaxed inside of me. He was right. I had feared the possibility of a greater ability. I did not need more power. I already feared the strength of the magic that flowed through my veins.

"Well," Dramin began before draining the last of his mug, "I'll go get Joclyn ready. Come to her after you finish with Thom."

"Thom?" I questioned, not understanding.

Dramin nodded once before standing, the sound of Thom's excited yell echoed around the stone hallways.

"Ilyan!"

"I guess I'll go see what he wants, shall I?" I laughed alongside Dramin as we both left the kitchen; Dramin leaving toward my suite where Joclyn slept, and I toward Thom's frantic yells.

Thom's voice ricocheted around the stone hallways. To anyone else, the bounce of his voice would have made it impossible to know where he was, but I could sense his magic. His deep earth energy was strong with excitement as he moved closer to me, the excitement mixing with panic the closer he got.

I had almost reached him when his odd mix of emotions hit me hard, setting me on high alert. I moved faster. Curiosity and panic mingled inside of me with each step.

Thom turned the corner at a dead heat, his feet sliding as he caught sight of me. His face was wide and alert in excitement, but I could hear the rapid rate of his breath in my ears, the pace too quick to be purely excited.

My curiosity left as fear took its place, a million possibilities leapt to mind, but deep down I knew—they were attacking. My heart pulsed once in desperation, begging me to simply take Joclyn and fly away—to save her. The thought was only a breeze from a bird's wing before it was gone, before inheritance and responsibility took its place.

"Come, Ilyan!" I picked up my pace, following him as he turned back the way he had come. It wasn't until he turned toward the large garden on the west side of the chapel that the fear in me shifted.

The camps were arranged on the north side. Had we missed something? Something new, bigger?

Everything thumped in time with my footsteps, my heart beating in my ears and my breath moving in time with my steps.

Without thinking about it, I moved my magic to check on Joclyn, shielding her as much as I dared.

We turned one more corner before Thom stopped, my feet halting right behind him before I collided with him.

This was not what I had expected, it was worse.

Ovailia stood in the middle of the hall, her hair down to her waist and a smug smile in place, as if she expected me to praise her for a job well done. However, it wasn't a job well done. It was a nightmare.

Ryland stood right next to her. *Stood.* His eyes were bright blue. His hair was damp with sweat, making the dark curls longer than usual. He looked at me with understanding, with knowledge, and with eager anticipation. He was awake, and he remembered me.

"Where is Joclyn?" Ryland's voice was eager, panicked. I could feel his need and longing as it settled deeply into his voice.

I would have gladly taken him to her right then, except that Joclyn was still asleep, trapped in a Tȍuha that she supposedly shared with Ryland.

But Ryland wasn't in the Tȍuha.

"You're awake." I couldn't help the panic that edged into my voice. As much as I needed to be the royal leader right then, I just couldn't. I saw Ovailia's brow furrow, but she said nothing.

"Yeah." He took a step toward me, ready to plead his case, ready to see her.

"But, the Tòuha?"

"Dad broke our bond... last week... I..." Ryland's voice trailed off as my soul turned to ice.

I said nothing as I turned and ran down the hall. I didn't know what to say. I didn't know how to explain. How could I when I had no idea what was wrong?

Footsteps echoed behind me, I barely heard their worried questions, Ovailia's snarky shouts as she raced behind. I could only hear my panicked breathing. I could only feel my heart clunk against the frail bones in my chest. Everything was falling apart inside of me.

I passed the ancient architecture, passed the ornate window I helped set. I passed it all without seeing. I ran without knowing. I followed the beat of my heart, the pull of my soul. My magic had already gone to her; it filled her completely, checking for something I might have missed. She couldn't just be a shell, she couldn't.

I slammed the door into my suite open, not bothering to close it, not bothering to say anything before moving into the small side room. Joclyn's body was still and small on the large couch. She didn't move, didn't turn. Could she not hear my heart beat for her? Could she not feel my terror?

When I entered, the room was empty except for Joclyn. Dramin had obviously gone for something, leaving the large mug of Black Water on the table beside her. I grabbed it without thinking, my fear and worry taking over my better judgment.

"Mi lasko!" My voice was loud. The panic in me, scared me. I had never felt this afraid.

I moved to sit over her, my legs on either side as I lifted her head. My hand moved to her face, my finger tracing her lips for only a moment before I opened her jaw, her mouth sagging. I placed my fingers just inside, cupping my hand before her mouth, like a bowl, a bowl for poison. I tilted the mug, focusing on the determination in my soul and the steady beat of her heart before I poured the water into my hand, the slope of my skin forming a ramp into her mouth.

I screamed with a howl of agony and misery. The sound hit stone and glass before bouncing back to me, but I barely heard. I kept pouring, burn on my palm growing into to a blister. I continued to howl at the agony that was threatening to incapacitate me.

This pain was worse than the brands on my chest, worse than the accidental drip on my arm. This was torture. I howled as I collapsed onto her, my body tensing as it attempted to manage the pain. I held her to me as every muscle seized, as my throat burned with the howls that escaped from me.

The water tugged at me, pulling something out of me and took it into her. The heavy strand of magic moved the pain through me and centered it over the Štít, over our connection. I could feel her more acutely than I had ever done before, her heartbeat bounced in my ears, her breathing moved over my chest. I felt her inside of me as well as alongside me, my mind aware of her as if I was her.

The connection pulled stronger and stronger, unlike anything I had ever felt before or anything I had ever heard of. It was all I could focus on; her body, her soul, the thin thread of her consciousness that trailed far away, and next to that... the thin thread that connected her to the Tȍuha.

"Mi lasko! Snap out of it! Get out of there!" I could feel her, somewhere deep inside. I could still feel that thread, the clarity of it shining at me like a golden ribbon.

Joclyn's heartbeat increased inside of me, the sound of my voice increasing the tempo for only a moment before she relaxed again. At least, I hoped it was my voice she was reacting to. *Please let her hear me.* I said the words to myself, a silent prayer to a silent deity.

"Joclyn! Come back to me!" My tears flowed as I looked at her still body and felt the slow ache when her heartbeat did not respond. "Joclyn!"

I could feel the bridge that the water had created between us leaving, the strength of the connection moving away from me. *No! I couldn't lose her!* I pressed my hands to her face, the angry burn on my hand pressing itself against the soft skin of her cheek.

The strong pulse of her magic surged through the raw skin. It rocked through me and my spine straightened, the power rough and violent.

I could feel the warmth of her body, the silky texture of her skin, but more than that, I could feel her again. I could feel *her* inside of me. Somehow the water had bridged me to her, connected my body with hers.

"Dramin!" I yelled his name, knowing he wouldn't know what this was, or how to keep it, but he would have water, and perhaps the water could strengthen the connection again. The water had brought the clarity; I needed the water to keep the clarity strong. "Dramin! Bring the water!"

Dramin ran into the room before I could even finish talking, his face calm before he saw me kneeling over Joclyn and the tears on my face. I could only imagine how I must have looked, how desperate I must have seemed because I felt it inside me. I could feel the pain, the anguish, the desperation.

"What in land's name is going on here?"

I looked at him with all of my weaknesses on my face, no façade, just me. He looked at me for one minute before the realization hit him and his own panic took over.

"Ovailia has returned. It was just as Joclyn said... Ryland's here." I tried to keep the emotion out of my voice, tried to regain my composure, but it didn't want to take. "He's awake."

"What do you mean he is awake?" Confusion was clear in his voice, and it made sense. Joclyn was sleeping, so Ryland should be, too.

"Joclyn!" I yelled. "Ovailia brought him. He is fine. But the bond is gone. Edmund broke it weeks ago."

My voice bounced around the room before I looked back at Dramin, hoping that he would understand me by the desperation in my eyes. He only stared at me, his heart breaking. I didn't want to think about what that look could mean, what that pain was for.

This could not be allowed to happen. It was not the end. I had seen my path, and my path was her. I had seen the end, seen my love for her and hers for me. I had seen everything. It was her. She was my everything. I would wait a thousand more years to experience those sights, but they would come to pass. They could not just be a zlomený. I wouldn't allow it.

"But, she is still sleeping... She's been sleeping for two weeks..." My eyes looked away from Dramin; I couldn't stand to try to explain something that I didn't understand. "How can she be..."

Dramin came to stand next to me, his hand moving to lay against Joclyn's face. His touch was soft against her cheek as he filled her with his magic. My eyes moved to glare into him as I felt his magic surge, the power of it right up against mine. I had never felt Dramin's magic so strongly. It wasn't the same deep magic of the Drak I was used to feeling; this was bright and strong. It almost felt powerful.

Dramin looked at me in wonder, the gleam in his eyes making it clear that he had found my new connection to Joclyn. He had known what the Black Water would do inside my veins after all.

I turned my hand toward him, showing him the angry welt that covered my palm. My face cringed as I let the pain show through my eyes, my chest still locking the rest of my pain inside.

Dramin's eyes went wide as they stared at my hand in silence. With one nod, he pushed more of his magic into her, the flow wide and strong. The burn on my hand had obviously opened up something inside me. It was more than the connection with Joclyn; I could feel the hidden strength of a Drak now.

I could feel something else too. The heavy black mark that had hidden the thin strand of fine gold ribbon that her mind had followed to enter the Tồuha.

I found it.

I found *her*.

"It's a Vymằzat."

"What?" Dramin's hand pulled away from Joclyn's face, the mug in his other hand dropping to the floor in surprise. "How did you miss that? You tried everything—"

"I didn't miss it. It was hidden," I said as I pushed my magic into her, feeling it move through her as it would in me. My awareness of her body swelled. I felt everything. I felt the thick ridge of the curse inside the hollow cavity of her mind. The curse had spread like spider webs over her skull, so thin and fine, it was no wonder I had missed it. Whatever Edmund had done to her, he had hidden it well. Just not well enough.

I kept pushing my magic into her, my body beginning to feel weak and heavy as my power smothered her. I pushed as I worked to reverse the Vymằzat, to remove it from inside her.

"Ilyan, you can't possibly be saying what I think you are saying..."

I surged my magic violently through it until the thick strands of my father's curse began to break loose, the bands loosening away from her spinal column. It was there, with the sensation of her within me, that I felt her mind coming back.

Joclyn's mind, her soul, was clicking back into place as the Vymằzat loosened its grip on her. Her mind moved back into her, like a child playing with dominos—one piece falling after another as they moved into place. I could feel the heavy threads of her thoughts, the increased panic of her breathing, the elevated rate of her heart, and her hand against my shoulder.

CHAPTER 29
JOCLYN

I screamed as the bone cracked.

It always cracked.

And then healed.

Always healed.

"Come back here! Let me finish what I started!" Ryland was angry, always angry. Always hurting.

I dragged myself to the room with books. I could hide there until it healed. I heard him behind me, he was too close. He wanted to end it. He wanted me gone.

He had told me so.

He'd said it had been too long. Over Two weeks.

No, eighty days. Was that two weeks?

I had lost track, I didn't know which made sense.

Lots of lines on the floor.

Which day? How long?

I didn't know how long.

I clawed at the warmth in my shoulder, my fingers wet with blood. The warmth was there all the time now. It was nice; I liked it. If I got it out, I could see what caused it. I could hold it in my hands.

I got to the books and pulled myself into the corner where the rats lived. They let me in. They sat on my lap.

Song.

Song.
No more words.
Words were gone.
Only the song.
I rocked, the rocking helped. The rocking felt nice.
Like the warmth, the warmth so strong.
Song.
Song fading.
I was fading, too.
I could feel it.

"Snap out of it, Joclyn!"

That voice.
I knew it.

"Mi lasko! Snap out of it! Get out of there!" The voice was close.

The warmth was strong. So strong it hurt. I looked up to find the voice, but it was not a voice. It was a girl on a bed. A man was kneeling over her. He was strong. His face was strong. He was tall with bright blue eyes and short blond hair. He was the one who was yelling, but he was not angry like Ryland, he was scared.

Seeing him scared me, too. I moved into the rats, but the rats were gone. They were scared.

"Joclyn! Come back to me!" he yelled again. I could tell he was crying. He placed his hands on the girl, but his hands didn't hurt. His hands were gentle.

I didn't know someone could be so nice.

The warmth inside me grew, but I didn't claw at it. I didn't think I was supposed to.

I couldn't stop looking at the man. I knew this man.

"Joclyn!"

That was my name. He called the girl my name, but the girl was not me. This girl was clean. This girl was beautiful.

I moved to look at the girl.

"Dramin! Bring the Water!" he yelled. Another man entered. This one was tired, but he was kind, too.

"What in land's end is going on here?" The new man was worried.

I walked around them. I couldn't take my eyes off the sad one.

I knew him.

Something was familiar about him, but something was off.

He couldn't see me.

Why couldn't he see me?

"Ovailia has returned. It was just as Joclyn said.... Ryland's here. He's awake."

I spun in fear as the new one said his name, but he was not here. Pain was not here.

"What do you mean he is awake?" the sad one said. There was fear in his voice. He looked back to the girl.

"Joclyn!" he yelled again, but the girl did not respond.

"Ovailia brought him. He's fine, however the bond is gone. Edmund broke it weeks ago."

The sad one was still scared. The new one looked scared now, too.

The warmth. It grew again. It was hot now. It hurt.

"But she is still sleeping... She has been in the Tòuha for weeks. How can she be..." The sad one's voice was heavy. He placed his hand softly against her head.

They were both so nice. Could people be so nice?

"It's a Vymåzat."

"What?" The new man dropped a mug he was holding, the dark liquid seeping into the floor. "How did you miss that? You tried everything..."

"I didn't miss it. It was hidden."

The warmth was so hot it hurt. I clutched my shoulder, my teeth grinding with the pain.

"Ilyan, you can't possibly be saying what I think you are saying..."

Ilyan.

I knew him.

My Ilyan.

The song.

My song.

He sang me the song as I lay dying, when I woke from nightmares, and when I was sad.

I remembered.

Everything.

The sight. The sight of the Drak.

My sight. It must be how I was seeing this.

I looked to Ilyan as he continued to yell at the girl, no, to yell at me. Was this happening now, or had it already happened?

"Ilyan?" I yelled his name in a panic, words were foreign on my tongue after not using them for so long. He didn't respond. He looked at the girl, his hair short on his head. I liked it. Now it was the way it had been in the vision. Was that why he cut it? Was it really him?

I waved my hand in front of his face, but he didn't turn. The warmth continued to grow. The warmth that was Ilyan's magic.

Magic.

I walked around them, watching their movements, trying to figure out what to do, and why I was seeing this. It had to be for a reason. It was my way out. I knew it.

My heart thumped at the possibility, my body twitching the way it had for however long I had been trapped in here. One hour to every ten minutes. Weeks. I twitched again. It had been so much longer to me.

I yelled to Ilyan, screaming at him as his panic grew; as he and the new one, Dramin, yelled back and forth. The room was full of sound as they yelled, each person's panic adding to the noise. Without thinking, I reached out to place my hand on Ilyan's arm.

My hand made contact.

Ilyan's skin was warm underneath my icy fingers. He looked up, and I was sure he could see me. His eyes widened in horror before moving back to the beautiful girl he still sat over.

Everything clicked together as Cail walked through the door, his wicked scowl fading at the scene before him.

And then it hit me.

I had magic.

I placed my hands firmly on Ilyan, shoving him out of the way and directly onto Dramin. Both men fell onto the floor in a heap as I raised my hands; the sleeping form of myself raising hers as well.

I could feel the crackle in my skin, the power congregating before I released it right into Cail's chest. Cail screamed and jumped to the side, the powerful burst flying into the soft, blood soaked wall behind him.

"No!" I could only smile at his outburst, the fear in his voice making me feel more powerful.

"How do you remember?"

I looked at the group to my left. Cail obviously couldn't see the vision as I could. "I am stronger than you would have ever assumed, Cail. My father made me that way."

"No! It can't be!"

Cail moved to attack, but I stepped to the side, my brain able to determine the weakness of his weapon early on. I did not wait for him to regroup. I did not wait to find a weakness. I needed to get out of here, and Cail was keeping me trapped. I moved my energy into him, and let the power burn him away.

His eyes grew wide at the first of the energy and at the pain my attack was causing him. Soon his legs gave way and he sunk to the ground; his life ebbing away.

"Wyn." His final word was a whisper of his sister's name. My best friend. I didn't have time to make sense of it. I didn't have time to rejoice.

It took only a moment for me to realize my mistake, though. I was trapped inside Cail's mind, a mind I had just destroyed.

Everything around me began to shift and fall as Cail's consciousness disintegrated into nothing. I screamed as the ceiling peeled away, doors fell off of their hinges, and red liquid poured into the room from behind every new opening. I would drown in it. Drown here, in Cail's mind. There was no return path out of here. I would die here.

I turned to Ilyan, knowing this was the end.

My breath caught as Ilyan looked right into me, his eyes seeing me as I stood in the melting room, the floor shifting as it attempted to give way.

"Goodbye." My voice caught as I reached toward him, my fingers twisting around his newly cut hair. I wished I could tell him that I liked it. I liked how young it made him look, how strong. I smiled, trying to ignore the tears on my cheeks. "I love you."

"No!" Ilyan's arms wrapped around me, his body bridging the gap between worlds. His magic flared and filled me so quickly I couldn't stop it.

I screamed in fear at the pressure before I realized the change.

My body seemed more real, and my brain was clearer. Ilyan had somehow brought me back.

I looked around wildly not knowing what to expect. I was lying on a bed; my body twitching, and my breathing ragged.

"Joclyn?" Ilyan's voice was wild, his eyes wide.

I didn't know how to respond to him. I didn't know if I could. I reached up and placed my hands on his face, my eyes boring into his. I had his eyes memorized; every speck of gold, every vein. Those memories came back stronger than I had ever experienced, and for one fleeting moment, I felt my heart calm.

It was him.

"Ilyan."

I pulled him to me, placing my forehead against his as I clung to him, basked in him.

And then everything changed.

The door to the room I was in flew open and Ryland walked in. His blue eyes were wide and scared as he searched for me, but it didn't matter.

He was pain. The reaction was branded into my soul. I couldn't stop it.

My reflexes took over, my breathing picking up as my body moved into a panic. Except now I could fight back. Now, I had magic.

I lifted my hands as something deep inside of me yelled at me to stop. My brain screamed at me, but I couldn't focus through the fear. The response that I had been trained to display over the past two months had become far too strong in me now.

Somehow—in the recesses of my mind—I knew I had seen this scene before.

Still, I aimed to kill.

My magic flew away from me and Dramin stepped in front of Ryland as he did his best to shield him. I knew why my mind had been screaming.

I had seen this before.

And now I knew where.

The screaming of everyone in the room intensified as Ilyan's magic ran through me. I once saw a flicker of Dramin's slow descent to the floor before Ilyan's magic put me to sleep.

CHAPTER 30
ILYAN

"Ilyan." Her voice moved through me with the strength of a tidal wave. It crashed into my soul and took the breath out of my chest.

I looked into the silver sheen of her eyes, my soul undeniably lost to her, my heart belonging to her more than it ever had. Just as her sight had said.

She wrapped her hands around my neck and brought my forehead down onto hers, the contact of her skin igniting my blood. I could feel the fire of the Black Water speed up in my veins, its burn deep and yet so pleasant.

I would have gladly stayed there for hours, staring into her eyes, her skin against mine, but I could feel them coming. My magic had been so focused on Joclyn that I didn't feel their pulses until they were right on top of us.

I turned toward them as the door opened, stepping away from her in a panic, unsure as to how Joclyn would react at seeing Ryland.

He was the first one in the door, his blue eyes blazing as he searched for her. I looked toward Joclyn, expecting to see the heart-stopping joy I had seen light up her face before, but it was not there. The look of pain and fear that I had seen on the haggard girl's face had taken over Joclyn's beautiful features. Panic and fear ravaged her before her hands raised toward him, a pulse shooting through the air with more power than even I could conjure.

The glowing mass exploded from her hands with enough energy that the air rippled behind it, the deep earth magic reacting to Joclyn and strengthening the attack.

Time slowed as I watched the flame burn through the air, everyone slowly registering what was happening.

I shielded Ryland quickly, knowing that her energy pulse would burn right through. The mass barreled toward Ryland's chest faster than a bullet. I could tell by the look on Joclyn's face that this wouldn't be the last attack. She was angry and terrified. Her eyes held more hatred than I had ever seen.

I surged my magic through the Štít and into her tense and frantic body, my magic soothing her mind to sleep as quickly as I could, just as Joclyn's attack made contact.

I expected the impact. I had yelled out against it, but it never hit Ryland. It hit Dramin.

He moved in front of Ryland in silence, his eyes hooded and sad. He was not panicked at what was about to collide with him, he was accepting. Dramin looked at Joclyn as her magic hit him, his face full of pity before he collapsed to the ground.

Everything froze in place as I felt Joclyn fall into sleep beside me, my magic plunging her into a deep, dreamless sleep.

Joclyn's body sagged as Dramin's did, but it was Dramin's body that held my attention this time. The dull clunk of his head against the wood echoed through the quiet room, Thom's yell breaking the silence.

"Dramin! No!" Thom collapsed to the ground by his friend, his hands shaking as he reached for him, plunging his magic into him.

All other thoughts left me as I dropped to Thom's side as he howled, my own yells joining his as he held onto his friend. My friend. All the times I had hidden him, protected him, and now he was just another one to fall.

"Dramin," I gasped, my voice inaudible above Thom's moans. "No... No... Dramin!"

I placed my shaking hands against Dramin's face, my magic moving into him in an attempt to find some evidence of life inside him, to find anything that would give me some hope.

I let my magic flow, my panic making it hard for me to regulate the strength of my magic. I explored every inch of his body, my power covering him in my desperation to find something.

If it wasn't for the deep tick of the Black Water that would forever flow through me, I might not have felt the small spark that was hidden in his heart.

"He's not dead," I said firmly, the regality coming back into my voice as I fought the hopelessness that Dramin's injury had filled me with.

"What?" Ovailia's surprise mirrored my own, but the bitter sound within her voice was stronger than usual.

I grabbed Thom's magic that now snaked through Dramin's body to direct him to the spark of energy that I had found.

"Focus on that," I instructed him before pulling away.

My magic left him as I brought it back inside of myself, my heart thumping against my chest at what I was about to do.

"Please don't let me kill him," I spoke more to myself than anyone else, but I knew that everyone had heard me, that everyone knew what I was going to do. It was what I had tried to do to my friend, Sarin, before I killed him a thousand years before. It was what I needed to do now in order to save Dramin's life.

My hands pressed against Dramin's as I breathed in, bringing my magic right to the surface, before breathing out and surging it into him. I let in just enough to jumpstart his entire body and hopefully, ignite his magic, but not enough to kill him—or so I hoped.

I looked up at Thom expectantly, hoping to see him looking at me, but his focus stayed on Dramin. The spark had obviously not ignited; his magic was still not strong enough to sustain his life.

I needed to perform the ozdobit třásněmi one more time.

I repeated the process, careful to keep my magic at just the right caliber inside of his body. This time, a small groan escaped Dramin's lips, his hand twitching in response to my jolt. My heart froze for one terrible moment before I gently pushed my magic back into his body, stretching it right to the small spark I had found, pleased to now find a fire.

I exhaled with a shake, the knot in my back loosening. I looked up to Thom, his eyes meeting mine.

"He's alive?" he asked in awe, his voice a heavy rumble over Ryland's mumbling voice behind us.

"Sotva." *Barely.* I answered Thom, careful to keep my voice low. Even though Ovailia was now standing next to Ryland and Joclyn, I knew she was listening.

"I've never seen anything like it," I gasped through the tense feeling in my shoulders.

"Me either," Thom said, his voice awed. "Even when we sparred back in the cave, after she gained full use of her power, she was never able to produce something that strong."

I sighed and ran my hand through my hair, forgetting that I had already cut off the long strands.

"Try to keep him alive, Thom," I pleaded, trying to make it plain that I needed his help.

"I will, but there is only so much I can do. With his magic so weak..." Thom's voice drifted off as he placed his hands against the skin of Dramin's face, his head shaking in worry. "Why did she attack Ryland like that in the first place? I thought she loved him."

"She did. She does," I corrected myself, ignoring the heavy thumping in my chest. I looked toward Ryland, he and Ovailia now standing on either side of Joclyn as Ovailia hissed something to Ryland. That could be anything but good. I needed to get over there. "Something must have happened in the Tȍuha," I continued, bringing my focus back to Thom. "He must have been attacking her somehow."

"Ryland was attacking her?" Thom asked, the alarm in his voice igniting the heavy Black Water inside of me again. I cringed against the burn, against the anxiety that was flaring in my chest, and stood.

"I believe so."

"Is Ryland even safe to have here?" Thom's eyes darted over to where Ovailia hovered beside Ryland.

"Safer than Ovailia is at this point."

Thom's gaze darted away from our siblings, his eyes narrowing at my words, almost daring me to say what he wanted to hear.

"I need you to watch her."

"You need me to watch Ovailia *and* heal Dramin..."

I sighed and straightened my back. Thom had put into words exactly how terrible our situation was. I had foolishly thought that Joclyn's awakening would solve all of our problems, but now, somehow, she had only increased them.

"Ano," I said simply, knowing I was already asking too much of him. He only looked at me, nodding once in understanding, his own stress staring right back at me.

"Take him to his room, Thom. I'll be there shortly."

I stood as Thom carried Dramin's body out the door, the knot in my heart relaxing. Dramin would be okay if the spark of his magic stayed strong. I wasn't sure what Joclyn had hit him with, so I wasn't sure if what I had done was enough.

I turned, Ryland was still hovering over Joclyn. I could feel Ryland's magic inside of her, the foreign power infusing her through the edge of the Štít. I dutifully kept mine on the other side of the Štít, even though keeping it there was a physical pain to me now.

Ryland's voice filled the air around us, the English words sounding out of place as he whispered to her.

"He will live." I spoke more to myself than to the room, needing to hear the words for my own benefit.

"Honestly, I was surprised to see him alive in the first place." Ovailia's voice was high and filled with fury.

I had known I couldn't avoid this confrontation for long. Instead of walking into the ruins of Rioseco to find just Joclyn and I, Ovailia had found two others—both of which she had thought to be dead. Thom and Dramin, one her brother and the other the son of her former mate.

Given where she had just come from, this conversation could easily be used to my advantage, something I definitely needed in this game of cat and mouse that my father had set up.

I carefully fisted the burn on my hand, keeping it out of sight. Ovailia had laid her cards in front of me. I needed to play mine right. If I was going to get us out of this, then everything to do with the Black Water needed to stay hidden for my round to play out properly. Joclyn being a Drak was our greatest asset at this point, it was not information I would ever willingly hand over to Ovailia. Each of us continued to weigh our options as we danced around each other in a silent tango.

"Is she alive?" Ryland's accusatory voice was barely louder than a whisper, but it broke the tension between Ovailia and me.

"Yes, I just put her to sleep."

"Why isn't she waking up, Ilyan?" Ryland's panicked voice cut through the silence as he shook her shoulders.

I turned toward him, my frustration flaring at his questions. Had he not noticed what had just happened? Did he not care that the man who had saved him was fighting for his life?

I brushed my irritation at his selfishness away. His hands were wrapped around hers as he whispered to her. I thought I had been prepared for this, but I was surprised by the uncomfortable thunk that sounded deep within my ironclad heart.

Torture.

"I am keeping her asleep, Ryland."

"Wake her up!" he demanded, his desperation making him edgy. "I need to see her."

Ryland ran his hand over her hair, his fingers touching the skin of her face as he looked at me, waiting for me to act.

"I am not sure that is wise." Ryland's eyes widened at my response, my curiosity at his odd behavior peaking. "She just tried to kill you, Ryland."

He looked at me for only a minute before moving down to place his forehead against hers. I felt the pressure against my own head, and shook it off, surprised the bridge was still there even though I no longer had contact with her.

"She didn't mean it." Ryland's voice was heavy and low, his words spoken more to Joclyn than to me.

I looked toward Ovailia, expecting to receive some support, but she only looked back with a wicked gleam in her eye. The shine in her eyes prickled at my better judgment in warning.

"She woke up only a moment before you came in—"

"I know," Ryland interrupted me. "Thom told us she was sleeping before. She was just confused. She didn't know she had woken up. I need to tell her she is all right, Ilyan. Please. Let me do that."

I felt my protective instinct flare at his words, the desire to push him away from her strong and growing. "Why would she have need to attack you in a Tòuha, Ryland?"

His eyes widened, they drifted from Ovailia to me uncomfortably, as if he was unsure what to say or how much he was allowed to reveal. The gesture made me wary, my fear rising quickly within me.

I had always counted on Ryland standing with me. He had gone out of his way multiple times to save me, to save Joclyn. He knew what her purpose was in this life, and yet, I could see the doubt in his eyes when he looked at me. He doubted that he could trust me, that I was telling the truth. The look triggered my own doubts about the situation, and I looked toward Ovailia, my eyes hardening.

"What is going on?"

Ryland's body stiffened, the large muscles in his shoulders bulging beneath his blue polo shirt. My body prickled as my magic flared in expectation of an outburst.

"She wouldn't... I mean..." Ryland's fingers began to dig into Joclyn's skin, his grip tightening with every word. "If you saw what he made us do... I mean... YOU CAN'T HAVE HER!" He roared, making the glass in the window rattle, his magic erupting out of him. The whirlwind of power circled through the room, ripping blankets, pictures and ornaments out of their places.

"SHE'S MINE!" Ryland yelled only a second later as the torrent continued, his hands digging into her, little drops of her blood trailing at his fingertips.

That was enough. Seeing her blood was all it took for my instincts to kick in, for my heart to thump for her safety. My magic surged as I threw him away from her, slamming him into the stone wall of my suite where I restrained him.

The second he had left her side, I had gone to her, my arms resting over her in a physical shield.

Ryland looked at me in a panic, his eyes wild as he fought against me.

"Don't ever touch her like that," I snarled, aware that my composure had left.

"My, my, Ilyan," Ovailia soothed as she came up beside me. "Having trouble letting him near Joclyn, are we?"

"He was hurting her."

"That doesn't matter. He's her mate."

"That bond was broken. Or have you forgotten what it takes to break a bond, Ovailia." I let my hard voice plague my words as I turned to face Ovailia, allowing my height to tower over her dauntingly. She met my hard gaze with a glare of her own, her lips turned up in that wicked, little half smile.

"Oh, now, how could I forget? No matter how much you wanted me to." She smiled wider, and I froze, my face in its hard mask.

I wanted her out of here, out of this room and out of the abbey. If I forced her out now, she would only instruct the Trpaslíks to attack. My father's plan was clicking into place now, his carefully woven web settling in around us. Like all webs, there was always a hole.

"I'll just take him to my suite for now, shall I?" Ovailia asked, the gleam in her eyes making it obvious she knew she had me. "I'll calm him down and then he can come check on Joclyn in a few hours."

Ovailia moved toward Ryland as my magic released him, letting him slide to the floor.

"I can't leave her. I don't care what you say, Ilyan. I need her. I can't..." Ryland's voice was so weak, so pained, and I couldn't ignore the desperation that lined it.

"I know, Ryland. I will let you see her again soon. I promise."

Ryland opened his mouth to say something, but Ovailia stopped him. With one whispered word from her, his face hardened, his eyes dark as he followed Ovailia out without a word, his eyes never leaving Joclyn's sleeping body.

I had no choice, but to let them go, to leave Ryland in Ovailia's hands and let her manipulate him right in front of me. I could already feel the pieces of a larger game fall into place. Joclyn's sight from only a few weeks before rang in my ears, the words strong beside the vision that she had shared with me. The vision of Ovailia carrying Ryland down the hall.

'A tryst has been set in motion, one you cannot ignore. The father of the four is using his seed one against another, and in the end, none will fall until two lives are lost. It cannot be stopped. Beware where your trust lays.'

For once I needed time on my side, but in only a matter of minutes, time had already effectively ruined our chances.

CHAPTER 31
JOCLYN

A thump of a knock pulled me out of a fitful sleep, the sound mixed with the whisper of voices and my mind kicked into overdrive. I spun out of the bed, landing on the floor as I looked around the unfamiliar space in an attempt to get my bearings.

This was not the cave from months ago. It was not the old moldy bathroom that I had been trapped in since.

This room was old, with several large, stone arches that sat to the left of the king-sized bed I was in. Each one opened to a beautiful, star-filled sky. The whole room was made of dark stone and even darker wood. Any other time I might have called it beautiful. Safe.

I couldn't even find the word.

This space was too open. I was too exposed here. Pain could find me.

That was a word I knew. A person I knew.

Besides the arches that opened into the night sky, there were two doors. I could hear voices behind one, so I crawled to the other, holding my breath in case I was heard. There were no sounds behind this one. I could hide here, at least until I figured out what was going on. I slipped inside, my eyes burning at the dim blue light that rippled over the walls.

Slowly my eyes adjusted to a modern bathroom built out of porcelain and glass. Everything was clean, polished. I had almost forgotten that bathrooms could be this clean. I looked around for another way out but found nothing.

You're safe. Nothing is going to get you.

I tried to convince myself of it, but the blood-bathed rooms of Cail's mind were still too fresh. I could feel everything; the torture, the running, the fear. Still, I could see Ilyan's face as he'd rescued me. And Dramin...

My heart tensed and I slid myself between the toilet and the sink just before the door on the other side of the room creaked open, the whispers from before becoming audible.

"I can't do everything, Ilyan. Ovailia is already eyeing me, and I am not sure how much I can do for Dramin." Thom's voice was loud. Desperate. The depth of the sound shook through me and I twitched, my hands flying up to tangle in my hair as I pressed myself into the toilet.

"We need him, Thom." Ilyan was calm, so calm. I took a shuddering breath, trying to release some of the stress. Please let me be safe here. "The faster we know if he is going to pull through, the better. I cannot produce the Black Water and Joclyn will be needing some very soon..."

"But that's just it, Ilyan," Thom interrupted him. "It's almost as if he saw this coming. His room is covered with at least fifty mugs, each filled to the brim with that poison."

"What?"

"I know, and if he saw that, then what else did he see? Especially with how Ovailia is acting."

"Is she still not letting him out of her sight?"

"No. I don't trust her, Ilyan." Thom's voice was heavy, hurt. I had never heard so much fear in him. Something was wrong, but I couldn't think past my panic enough to know. It was as though I was trapped between two worlds.

"I don't trust her, eith—" Ilyan stopped talking suddenly and then swore loudly in Czech. I flinched again.

"Where did she go?" Thom asked, his question fading as Ilyan closed the door.

I didn't hear Ilyan's footsteps, I only felt his magic grow inside of me as he tracked me. His energy moved through me, strong and panicked; the absence of my barrier giving him free rein. It was the same warmth from before, when I was trapped... I gasped and moved closer to the wall, hoping to disappear behind the toilet.

Ilyan's magic lessened as the door to the bathroom opened and he approached me, crouching in front of me. He had obviously been sleeping; his short hair was tousled, his chest bare. Ilyan's eyes were soft, wide, and shining. My heart rate settled at his gaze. It hadn't felt this normal in months; the pain from the incessant thudding lessened.

"H-Hi." I whispered as my voice caught, I was scared to say more than that.

"Hi."

I stared into those eyes, relishing the steady beat, the calmness that he was bringing me. I hadn't even noticed his hand was moving until it came to rest against my cheek. I jumped at the unexpected contact before settling back, my shaky hands moving to cover his.

I clung to Ilyan, holding his magic deep within me as he healed me, comforted me. Part of me was still scared he would disappear or that this was all a trick; that he would hurt me, too.

I leaned my head against the base of the sink—my hair falling over my face as I moved—Ilyan gently moved it away, his finger touching my mark as he placed the strands behind my ear. I jerked at the jolt that moved down my spine from Ilyan's touch, the single jerk morphing into a million twitches.

"Shhhh, mi lasko, shhhh." Ilyan's hands were firm against mine, his voice soft. It was just what I needed. I exhaled with a shake, forcing the world to calm.

"Is-is Dr...Dramin... d-d-dead?" I tried so hard to keep the stutter out of my voice, but it didn't work. It seemed to have followed me here. Ilyan's eyes widened at my voice, and I realized I hadn't spoken more than his name since my return to this world.

"No, he had a shield around him, but your strength was still too much for him. He is alive, but we do not know for how much longer."

My heart felt as though it was being cleaved in two. I had done this. I had seen Dramin's death in my sight, the unknown magic flying toward him. So to have seen it replayed in life, with my magic as the death blow, I knew what that meant; Dramin would not recover. I cringed, pushing my terror away as I clung to the cool porcelain.

"It's not your fault, Joclyn," Ilyan whispered. I turned toward him, my eyes wide. I couldn't tell him how wrong he was. I may not have been in my right mind, but it would never be anything other than my fault.

"Ryland had a shield around him..." Ilyan's sentence was drowned out by my screams.

Just hearing his name brought every single memory that I had been trying to restrain to the surface. They cut into me like a blunted knife; tearing through me in slow agony. I cringed and howled, my eyes darting as I looked for him, expecting pain to come through the door at any minute and hurt me. Break me.

"N-n-no!" I howled. Ilyan's eyes widened as he tried to figure out what was going on; why I was reacting this way.

"H-he ca-can't f-find m-me." I clawed at the toilet in an attempt to push myself further back against the wall, I clawed at the heat that was flaring in my shoulder.

I was back in Cail's mind again. Nothing had changed.

"Jos... love... calm down..." Ilyan's hands fluttered around me as he tried to figure out what to do, his panic clear.

"H-he wi-will hurt-t me." I grabbed his arms, desperate to make him understand the danger I was in. My twitches flowed freely even as I tried to control them.

My body was waging a battle with itself. One side desperately wanted to run, to hide. The other pleaded with me that I was safe, that Ilyan was here and the nightmares were gone.

"No, love, no," I focused on Ilyan's words as his magic flared, my heart rate slowing at his command. "He will never hurt you again. I will keep you safe."

He looked deeply into me, my nerves continuing to unwind.

Safe. Ilyan would keep me safe. I knew it was true. I focused on him and willed the calm to overtake me, willed my brain to believe his words.

"What happened to you?" I could tell the question was more to himself than to me, but it still startled me. I didn't want to relive it all.

I looked at him—his magic moving through me, his hand wrapped around mine—and wished I could tell him everything, but I didn't want to see it. I didn't want to say it.

I uncurled my hand, the fingers stiff and bent, and felt the strength of my magic under my skin; the strength of Ilyan's magic that moved alongside mine. I knew what to do.

Without a word, I placed my hand against Ilyan's forehead and let my magic surge into him, his eyes closing as I pushed the memory into him. For one sparkling second my body relaxed, the flinching stopped, and my heart rate normalized. As the memory left me to play inside of Ilyan's mind, I felt like myself again, like everything was okay.

I could see Ilyan and Ryland clearly. I could feel some of what I had once felt for Ryland; the feelings that months of torture at his hands had taken away from me. The clarity didn't last.

Ilyan's eyes opened and the memories came flooding back into me, the twitches and fear returning with it. I moved further back against the toilet, the sudden return heightening the emotions.

"Mi lasko?" Ilyan said softly, but I could hear the heartbreak, the blame he was already placing on himself.

"It... it's n-not your f-fault."

"You are safe, Joclyn." Ilyan shifted closer, his heavy voice right against my ear. "No one is going to hurt you, not anymore."

I wanted to believe him, I longed for it, but I couldn't make my reality calm down enough to do so.

"For two weeks I couldn't figure out what was going on. I couldn't get you back. I tried everything..." Ilyan dragged his hand through what was left of his hair, his eyes shining with tears that he was trying so hard to hide.

I looked at him, I wasn't sure I wanted to hear what he had to say, but I needed to. I needed to know that I was safe and why.

"It's no wonder I couldn't. They had taken you through the Tȍuha and into Cail's mind, leaving no trace. Your mind was disconnected from your body. It's a miracle I got you back... especially without the connection of a Zêlstvί."

"Wh...what-t-t d-do y...you m-m-mean?" I struggled to get it out of me, my internal mind still screaming at me to run.

I'm okay here.

I repeated the words to myself, trying to keep my panic in check. I already knew it wasn't working. I could feel the panic taking over.

"Edmund broke the Zêlstvί between you and... and..." he hesitated and I knew he was trying to tiptoe around Ryland's name, "your mate, in an effort to trap you in Cail's mind."

I stared at him, not sure how I was supposed to feel. Strangely, I wasn't as sad or heartbroken as I probably should have been at hearing about the loss of my bond with Ry. I wasn't even sure what I felt. When I thought of him, instead of love, I only felt fear. I was still scared of Ryland coming to find me, scared of the pain, of how he would hurt me.

But more than that, I was relieved.

I was free.

No more nightmares. No more torture. No more.

I opened my mouth to say something when a knock on the bathroom door sent me jumping. Ilyan calmed me before opening the door just enough to look out while still keeping me out of sight.

"Yes?" Ilyan asked, his voice level.

"He said it took about a week to adjust, but he's not sure what was done, so it may take longer." Thom's voice was quiet on the other side of the door.

"Was it this bad?"

"No," Thom said, "but you know how Ryland was raised... she's not used to that."

His name was a trigger. I flinched and gasped, sobbing as I once again tried to find a place to hide. I didn't care that a tiny voice inside of me was screaming that I was okay, that I was being irrational. I couldn't stop. My pulse picked up again and Ilyan's magic flared in an attempt to calm me.

"No," I moaned, "no, no, no."

"Jos," Ilyan soothed, "It's okay. He's not here."

"He...h...he's g...going t...to f-f-find me. Hurt, hurt, hurt me." I instinctively began clawing at my shoulder, the warmth of Ilyan's magic triggering the learned response.

"No, mi lasko, no. I'm not going to let that happen, remember? Remember it wasn't really Ryland in the Tòuha."

"I-i-it wa-was him. P-p-pain. No, no m-more."

Ilyan's magic flared, causing my consciousness to dip enough for me to get a grip on my panic. I exhaled, my chest shaking as he grabbed my hand, holding tight as he rubbed his thumb over my skin.

"You're okay."

"I-I'm okay."

Ilyan's jaw clenched and I tightened my shoulders as he turned back to the door, expecting Ryland to burst through the door.

"What else is it, Thom?"

"He's asking to see her again." Thom's voice was laced with more worry than I had ever heard.

"No." Ilyan's tone made it clear he did not want to elaborate.

"When?" Thom asked, although I was sure he didn't care.

"A week, a month, maybe never. I don't know. You heard what happened when you said his name. I'm not sure what I am looking at here yet." Ilyan looked at me and I glanced away.

"Well make it snappy, we spotted two more camps this morning...."

"I know, Thom," Ilyan interrupted, making it obvious he was hiding something. I simply didn't care.

"Are those for her?" Ilyan asked, gesturing to something that I couldn't see.

"Oh, yeah, I brought quite a few with me now, in case she breaks some." Thom brought a tray with about five mugs of Black Water into the room, Ilyan scowling at him as he looked toward me. His eyes widened at seeing me there, hiding against the toilet.

"Hi, T...T...Thom." I tried to sound as normal as I could, seeing as I was hiding against a toilet, but still couldn't keep the stutter out of my voice.

"Hey, Silnỳ," he said, a deep vein of pity lining his voice.

In his eagerness to spy, he dropped the tray a little fast and one of the corners snapped against the tile floor before Ilyan could catch it.

I jerked so fast my head slammed into the side of the sink, my hands coming up to cover my ears as I began to rock back and forth, Ilyan's song humming on my lips.

"Good Gravy!" I heard Thom exclaim, "What did he do to her?"

"Out, Thom!" Ilyan roared as Thom left, the door clicking a little too loudly behind him.

I groaned in panic and pulled my head down into my knees. Ilyan's magic surging through me as he sang alongside me, the words to his song pulling me back to reality.

For now.

CHAPTER 32
ILYAN

I hadn't slept since I had pulled Joclyn from the hell Cail had trapped her in. My name had been soft on her lips before she attempted to murder her mate. *Former mate.* I had to keep reminding myself that the bond was broken, broken by my father without their permission, their love tarnished for his wicked agenda. It made me sick to think about.

My experiences over the last two weeks had been only a small touch of what Ryland must have felt while separated from Joclyn for so long, constantly praying for her health and safety. Every day was filled with worry and panic. Then to see her again and have her attack you...

I shook my head. Part of me wanted to bring Ryland to her now, to let him be there to comfort her and protect her, while another part of me wanted him to stay far away.

No matter what I wanted, he couldn't come back. It wasn't safe for him here. Joclyn had proven that as she huddled against the toilet yesterday, her panic seeping into my soul. I had felt guilty leaving her alone since then, so I had left while she was asleep and chose to keep my visits with Thom and Dramin short, the ones with Ryland and Ovailia even shorter.

While her sleep was kept dreamless thanks to my magic, my waking hours were a nightmare. Joclyn had shown me the memories of the months she was trapped inside Cail's mind. I had felt every bone break, every impact of her body against stone, walls and cement. I had watched in terror as she ran through bloodstained hallways, only to come face to face with a Ryland who never ceased to find new ways to hurt her.

It wasn't really Ryland. It was a close enough likeness that even Joclyn had been fooled, but it was just a projection. A projection of Ryland that Cail had placed inside her mind to hurt her, to torture her, so that in the event she did escape, she would only be a weapon against him.

To be killed by your own mate; it was my father's sickest form of torture.

I replayed the memories as I dissected everything, but mostly the way Cail yelled for Wynifred with his dying breath. Guilt filled me that I had not been able to keep my side of his bargain. A secret for a life, and he had lost his life anyway. I could only hope that Wyn was all right.

Anger bubbled up inside me like oil left too long in a pan, slow and smothering. I wasn't mad at Cail for what he had done. I wasn't even mad at Ryland for not getting her out in time. I was mad at myself for not protecting her, not demanding that the bond be broken before this could have happened.

I should have kept her safe, broken the bond when I had the chance, and protected her mind from the terrors that had changed her. I hadn't, though.

My choice to give her the joy of her first love had only led to a terror I could never fathom.

I shook my head and continued down the halls, back toward my suite, back to where Joclyn still lay. My magic surged through her, keeping her asleep until I could return from checking on Dramin.

His room had been bare except for the Black Water. Mug after mug of the stuff. He lay on his bed, his body was still and cold as if death was unwilling to let him go. That was what I had thought when I first walked in—that he was dead. His magic was still strong inside of him after the restart, but everything else had seemed to shut down.

"Ilyan?"

I jumped at Ryland's voice, swinging around to face him. No one had snuck up on me in centuries. I could always feel everyone's magical impulses, I could hear their breathing in my ears; and yet, Ryland stood in front of me, nothing flowing off him, not a wave or a whisper. I had felt the deep green waves of Ryland's energy before, first when he had released me from our father's torture chamber as a child and again when I had seen him with Joclyn for the first time. Now, nothing was there.

"Yes?" My eyes narrowed in confusion, my magic surging as I tried to figure out how he was restraining his magic to the point that I could not sense him.

"I... I thought you would come get me by now." I arched an eyebrow at him, not following. "To see Joclyn."

Ah yes, I should have known. It was wrong of me to keep him from her, but I worried. Worried what he would do to her and worried what she would do to him.

"It's not safe, Ryland, not yet." I kept my voice soft, hoping to speak with him like a brother, not a ruler.

"I can decide what is safe," Ryland snarled as he squared his strong shoulders. So much for a calm talk between brothers.

I kept my posture straight, while still trying to maintain my calm façade.

"She tried to kill you, Ryland. That has not changed. When Cail trapped her in his mind, he used a projection of you to torture her. Right now, she doesn't see the difference."

Ryland's eyes widened, the distrust showing in the furrowed lines of his forehead. I couldn't help the deep sigh that escaped me. Ovailia and our father had already set their framework against me; getting him to see things differently was going to be difficult.

"She doesn't see the difference because you won't let her." Ryland's voice was deep and angry.

"That's not true, Ryland." I planted my feet as he began to pace, his agitated movements alerting me to the fact that something much darker was dwelling within him.

He paced and mumbled, talking to something or someone as that darkness took control.

"Ry?" He spun at my voice, as if he had forgotten I was there. His eyes widened in anger, and his hands began to shake, even though he had stopped pacing.

"Don't call me that." I stepped back, the snarl in his voice keeping me on high alert. I wished I could feel his magic, know what was coming.

"Only Jos can call me that. She's the only one..." His fingers flexed in agitation, his hands glowing with power as his eyes darkened—and still I couldn't read him.

"All right," I said slowly, hoping to alleviate the pressure that was obviously building inside of him. "I didn't know that, Ryland. I won't do it again."

"She's all I have. I... She's mine." He snarled the last statement again, his hands continuing to open and close as his anger fueled his power.

Nothing.

"I know that, Ryland. She knows that. She risked everything to see you. Even when the dreams hurt, when the Tŏuha—"

"Then don't keep her from me!" I flinched as he snapped and his pacing returned, the agitated movements increasing in his arms.

I had to remind myself that he had only been released from his Vymăzat a week ago. If his horrors were anything like what Joclyn had been forced to endure, then he had made amazing progress.

There was hope for both of them.

"I'm not keeping her from you, Ryland. She is afraid of you. She wants to kill you. I am protecting you from her, as well as protecting her." I watched him as he moved, alert even as I tried to calm him. I could have turned myself into a giant teddy bear, I doubt it would have done anything.

"I don't believe you." He didn't even look at me as he paced, his eyes darting anywhere but at me.

"I would never lie to you, Ryland. You are my brother. You released me from our father's imprisonment. You saved my life. Now it is just my turn to return the favor."

"You don't know what he did to us!" he yelled, the palm of his hand moving to smack against his head in frustration.

I could already tell there would be no controlling Ryland's anger. It was too new. He reminded me of Thom when I had first met him, how the anger had been all that he had, what he held onto. It took Thom decades, and Sain's guidance, to see how wrong that anger could be. I doubted we had the time this time around.

Ovailia had obviously led him to believe that I was keeping Joclyn from him. He needed to see that I hadn't taken her away from him, that I had no intention of holding them apart.

"I may not know what he did to you, but I know what he did to Joclyn," I whispered, my voice just loud enough to freeze him in place.

"He hurt her."

"Yes. In every nightmare. You were there, weren't you?" He shook his head; I tried to ignore the surge of pride at my lucky guess. "He hurt you, too."

Ryland looked up at me, his eyes calming as his breathing regulated. The moment his eyes met mine, I felt it. It was weak and only there for a moment, but his magic surged through the air before retreating again. I smiled and wondered at the fact that he could control himself so much that he could hide all of his power from my detection.

"They used me to hurt her." I visibly flinched at Ryland's words, at the way he clenched his chest as if the pain of the blood magic was still fresh on his mind. "I didn't want to, but when I fought them, when I warned her... Hurt Me!" His last words flew out in an angry rush, the disjointed nature of them alarming.

"I know."

"Hurt... hurt... hurt..." he repeated before hitting himself hard against the head with his palm again. As quick as it started, the deranged anger on his face left.

"I don't want to hurt her," he whispered. I nodded to him once, afraid of what speaking might bring out next. Ryland's hand moved to clench over his chest again, his eyes drifting back to me.

I didn't know how much Ryland remembered of the Vymàzat, or how much of what had been done was his own choice, but one thing was clear. He had suffered as much, if not more, than the rest of Edmund's children. If only for that, he deserved my patience.

"It wasn't your fault, Ryland. He has done it to all of us." I moved toward him slowly, keeping my voice level.

I needed Ryland on my side, I needed to regain the trust he had lost in me. Ovailia had moved him into position as a pawn, but he wasn't a pawn; he was a person. My brother. He was someone I cared for. If I could save him, I would.

"Everyone?" Ryland looked up at me from beneath his long bangs, the wicked gleam back in his eyes. I didn't know what was said to trigger his anger, but with one statement, we were right back where we began.

Fine. If he wanted to be angry, I would let him. I would not, however, let his foolish emotion affect me or my choices. I would fight fire with fire. My skin prickled the way it always did in anticipation of battle, my magic surging as I smiled. I knew the wicked gleam was back in my eyes. I didn't try to hide it; I let it shine in warning. He stepped back.

"Yes, Ryland, everyone. Most everyone has died at his hands. Zetta was killed at birth because of her brown eyes. Sylas was forcibly mated only to be killed when he never produced an heir. Mym tortured all her young life, turned into a five-year-old weapon. She never knew love until I rescued her, but even then, she struggled. How can you learn to recognize love if you've never felt it? Thom watched as his daughter was tortured and murdered at the hands of our father. He smeared her blood on his face."

"Thom?" Ryland asked, the timber of his voice changing to one of sickened pity. Had no one told him yet? Had he not placed it together?

"Yes, Thom. He is your brother, too. Only the four of us remain. Some have escaped the horrors, others let them engulf them, and they are turned into heartless monsters. Joclyn fights her horrors every day; what will you do?"

"Joclyn..." His voice revered her, as if she was his deity. The anger was gone from his eyes now, his head hanging between his sagging shoulders. Right then, I could see the child who had saved me. He was scared, but so brave. In that moment, I knew that his strength was still there; it was the line between right and wrong that had been blurred.

We just needed to draw it again.

"I have kept her safe for you, Ryland. Just as I promised you I would. But I need to continue keeping her safe until she realizes that she doesn't need to be afraid of you."

Ryland's eyes looked up to me, and I felt my heart beat uncomfortably as it tried to escape the prison that I had trapped it in, as it tried to stop me from enacting on my heritage.

"She still loves you, Ryland. I can see it in her eyes. I saw it every day that she would talk about you, in the way she held out hope. She told me every day, Ryland. Her heart belongs to you."

Ryland's body relaxed, his eyes softening as he listened. He walked toward me slowly, his magical impulses finally released from wherever he had held them prisoner, the waves calm in the air.

"I will make this right and return her to you whole." I smiled, my face pulling up uncomfortably as my heart protested against my words.

"Thank you, Ilyan." Ryland's voice was soft in my ear as he embraced me. I pulled him closer.

"Samozřejmě, bratr. I will let you see her as soon as she is ready."

Talon had been right. Thom had been right. From the very beginning. Handing her over was going to be harder than I had ever imagined.

It was my duty, my role, to do what was right. There was no question that this was the right thing to do. I could not lead the few of us that remained if I was not honest and right.

And doing this, this was right.

The choices we make are not always easy, but it is the ones that are hard that matter. I could tell, looking into his eyes, that this was the one that mattered. This was the one that would make a difference.

This was the one that needed to be done; no matter how much it hurt.

CHAPTER 33
RYLAND

'Did you see the way he sheltered her? The ways she looked at him?'

No. It's not like that.

I was trying to fight the voices, but they had grown so much worse since that tent in the middle of the battlefield. They never stopped, not unless Ovailia let them. And she never let them. He almost kissed her.

'I could see it in his eyes. She's kissed him. That's why she doesn't want to see you.'

"No... no... no..." I moaned, my hands moving to cup my ears in an attempt to keep the voices out, but you couldn't keep out what was already inside of you. I couldn't keep the shadow of my father's voice, of Cail's voice from tormenting me.

I tried... I tried....

'It's why she attacked you.'

No. That wasn't her. Just like this wasn't me. I needed to control this. I needed to calm down. "No... no... hurt her..."

'And what did she do? She tried to kill you.'

"Kill... kill... kill"

'Are you going to kill her?'

"Kill... kill... kill her..."

The words repeated over and over, over and over. I felt my hands claw at my head, I felt my body move as I thumped my body against the wall over and over, over and over, over and over.

Bang.

'Are you going to hurt her?'

Bang.

'Kill her... kill her...'

Bang.

My eyes darted around as I tried to find something to focus on, to help pull me out of the nightmare. There was nothing but stone. Ovailia, her heels tapping as she made her way over.

"Are you going to kill Joclyn, Ryland?" She asked in that fake-sugar voice of hers as she squat before me. I wanted to say no, but I couldn't find the words.

'Kill her... kill her... make her pay.'

"Kill!" The word exploded and I slammed myself against the wall, and then against the magical barrier Ovailia had trapped me in. I needed to get out of here, I needed to find Ilyan and get his help. I needed to attack her. I needed to hurt her.

I needed... I needed...

"I don't know what Cail's problem was. I can do anything with you with that blade in your side. He clearly wasn't using it to its full potential." Ovailia smiled as I rammed into the barrier, over and over, over and over. She kept me here, like a caged dog, it didn't matter how much I fought.

I was trapped.

If I could get away from her, away from her magic, I could think clearer.

But she never left.

I hit my body against the invisible barrier again in an attempt to escape, to fight, to kill, the color shimmering with each impact. My magic flared and the barrier left, disintegrated to the ground like millions of falling stars.

"Shall we go see her?" Ovailia asked, her voice burning like a flame through me as I looked up to her in confusion.

"Ilyan won't let me." I growled.

"He won't let you?" She asked, and I hit my back against the wall.

'He's keeping her from you. He wants her for himself.'

"No... no... no... kill..."

"He doesn't want you to see her," Ovailia sneered, "He's a bad man."

Was he? Something said he was good. That I needed him. But I couldn't think straight with Ovailia's eyes on me. Everything was too muddled. Too broken.

"Bad... bad... bad..."

"I know where she is." I froze, my hands shooting out to grab her, to demand she tell me, to take me there, but there was no need. "I'll take you there."

She smiled and stepped away from me, her long hair swinging as I followed behind her.

"You will take me there?" I asked, not daring to hope.

"Yes," she smiled, as she watched me, her eyes hard. "Shall we go there now?"

CHAPTER 34
ILYAN

I woke up with Joclyn in my arms, her body pressed against mine as I sang to her, my words flitting between Czech and English. I had finally fallen asleep at some point last night after making one last check on Dramin.

I had slept dreamlessly, but at some point, the restraint I had against her waking had slipped off and she woke. She was scared. I could tell by the unsteady beat of her heart and the way her hand pressed against me, as if she was trying to move into me. I tightened my arms against her, hoping the pressure would help to relax her.

I had seen her need for security and the way she had come to get that from pressure as she wedged herself in between the toilet and vanity the other day. I had felt her need for the strength of something else when she could not find her own in the memories she had lent me.

Joclyn stiffened at my touch, a small flinch that shivered over her shoulder blades. Her breathing picked up and her heart rate increased, but I kept my arms tight around her, not willing to let her move into herself, not wanting her fears to take over. I pushed my magic into her, calming her, settling her frayed nerves.

I stayed silent as I held her, as she calmed. I wanted her to decide when she felt safe enough to speak. I wanted her to feel security come from me and then be able to find it in herself.

"Joclyn?" I kept my voice soft, my lips speaking gently against her dark hair. "Are you okay?" I ran my hand over her hair, feeling the soft strands between my fingers.

She nodded her head against me, the subtle nod not one I hadn't expected. She was okay. Even though I could feel her fear, feel her panic, she still felt okay.

My heart beat in one wild thump before settling again, my hold on her lessening. I kept her against me as I ran my hand over her hair, my other coming to press her back into me. I surrounded her in security, keeping her broken mind safe for just a moment.

I hummed the melody of her song, our song, into her hair. She relaxed at the sound, her breath escaping in a warm rush against the skin of my chest. I smiled as I sang, and she calmed and breathed against me. I could still feel the stutter in her breath, the small half beat of her heart, but for one small moment I didn't hear that, I couldn't feel the tightness on her back, the tension in her joints. She was just Joclyn, in my arms once again.

She didn't know it now, but she was stronger than the demons that had filled her soul. I could feel it in the way she relaxed, in the steady strum of her heart. She could overcome this. She would become bigger than it. I would help her find that path. To help her figure out how to put it behind her, to prove her own strength to her. I would help her find herself again.

I sang as I watched the sky lighten through the large arches of my room, the stars fading as the light of dawn took them. Minutes turned into hours but still we lay, her body against mine, my song providing the calming security she so desperately needed.

I moved away from her slowly, surprised when she jerked as if the movement had been a lightning strike. I didn't dare go too far, only far enough to be able to look at her, to see her beautiful eyes stare into me. I had missed them, and in the morning light, they seemed to shine, the light of her soul sparkling through them.

My hold on Joclyn loosened as I lifted my hand, the sun catching on the angry red burn that covered my palm and the inside of my fingers. The skin was red and raw, the moist flesh raised as if it had been partially eaten and cast aside.

It had taken centuries for the burns on my chest to heal, and the burn on my arm was still angry and red. This burn seemed much deeper than the others. The pain was definitely stronger and uncontrollable. I could already tell it would take much longer for this burn to heal, if it healed at all.

The connection that had been triggered by the touch of the Black Water had left me, leaving me feeling strangely empty. Even with the magic of a bonding, such intimate connections weren't possible. To feel her heart, her body, within me, that wasn't something that had ever happened.

I just wished I knew what that connection meant. With all my training, with all the knowledge that had been demanded of me, the Drak's choice to keep this information hidden was one that would affect us in ways I didn't think I could ever understand.

Without analyzing the thought, I pressed my scarred hand against her cheek, a gasp escaping my lips as the connection restored itself. With one touch, my awareness of her increased. Her heartbeat was strong within me, and I could feel the steady thrum of her soul moving alongside mine.

I couldn't help it. Even though I knew I shouldn't and my brain begged me not to, I let my finger trail down her neck and onto the raised skin of her mark. As my finger connected, the jolt that I had always felt shot through me, supercharging my magic in a surge of energy. It buzzed through me like the most addictive drug.

I was surprised when I felt her heart seize as her own jolt shot through her, the shock of our joining magic strong in her body as well as my own. Before she could panic, before her heart rate could increase much further, she controlled it. She forced the fear down, forced the beat of her heart to keep a steady beat, even without my help.

She was amazing.

I couldn't keep the look of pure joy out of my eyes as I looked at her. She would never cease to amaze me. Everything that would be thrown at her she would overcome. I could tell that now. I was beyond honored to be the one to keep her safe, to be allowed to love her.

Her eyes looked into mine. Confusion and happiness intermingled with each other before she gasped and moved into me; her hot breath against my chest sent waves of energy shooting over my skin.

I pulled her into me, my hold tight against her. I wanted so much to stay like this, our arms locked in each other's embrace, but it could not be. It was not right to dwell in a joy that was not yours, and sadly, that was just what I was doing.

"I'm going to go get you some Black Water. I'll be right back," I whispered in her ear before I pulled away, my muscles aching at the loss of her warmth.

Joclyn curled herself into a ball as I left, the loss of contact already affecting her. I needed to hurry. Clear my head and come right back.

I moved swiftly out the door, careful to close it silently so as not to trigger any more of her panic attacks. The last thing I wanted was for her to panic without anyone there to calm her.

My magic surged through her as I raced to Dramin's room, grateful for his foresight in placing his chambers so close to my own.

Thom stood over Dramin, his hands on his head as he worked over him, healing his body and removing the burns that plagued his organs.

"Any change since last night?" I asked through the silence, but Thom only shook his head, a small sag in his shoulders telling me all I needed to know.

"Nothing."

"Keep trying, Thom. We can't lose him." I grabbed one of the full mugs before turning back to the pair, Thom's head hanging over his friend, his dreads making him look like he had been trapped in a cage.

"We can try to give him some Black Water later, perhaps it will help." I raised the glass toward Thom, causing him to look toward me, his eyes shielded by his usual mask.

"At least that poison is good for something." He forced a laugh, the sound causing the lingering tension in the room to grow.

I opened my mouth to reply when a flare of my magic moved away from me and into Joclyn. Her panic had pulled it to her and I could feel her clinging to it like a lifeline. As it filled her, I felt the erratic beat of her heart and the pressure in her joints. The fear I had worked so carefully to remove from her had come back tenfold. Someone was there in the room with her.

I said nothing to Thom as I placed the mug back on the table and ran toward her. Fear was growing within her, the panic turning into a yell.

The sound of her scream vibrated against the stone hallways as I turned the last corner to find Ovailia leaning against the large wooden door to my suite. She looked at me with her usual smug smile, her eyes flashing with a sheen of red I hadn't seen for hundreds of years.

"So, brother. Are you going to tell me what happened to your hand?" It was such a normal question, I couldn't believe that she would ask it here, in the hall, while she guarded the door that she had obviously let Ryland through.

"I cut it," I lied, pushing my way closer to her.

Ovailia didn't move. She stayed where she was with her long frame leaning elegantly across the door. She looked at me with that wicked gleam she had perfected long ago, and I could tell at once that this would not go as planned.

"Get out of my way," I commanded, careful to keep my magic out of my voice.

"No. He deserves to see his mate. Unless you have taken her for yourself. Did you ruin his mate, brother? Tsk. Tsk. I knew you couldn't keep your hands off her." She spoke as if she was relating facts, not disgusting lies. I could never do something so vulgar. By the look on her face, I could tell that she had already spread the seed of doubt in Ryland's mind.

"Don't spread such lies!" I yelled, fully aware that the power in my voice was shaking the door she still leaned against.

"Then why can't he see her?" She raised her voice to match mine, the increase in volume obviously only meant to fuel whatever was happening inside the room.

"Because she will kill him!"

"Oh I doubt that, but if she does, it doesn't matter. It's what Father would want. They are both weapons, created only to kill each other." She sneered, the little twist of her lips identical to our father's, the action fueling my rage.

"Out of my way!" I roared, and with one flick of my magic I sent Ovailia flying away from the door, her body hitting the wall opposite as the door flew from its hinges unveiling Ryland, Joclyn and the horrors on the other side.

CHAPTER 35
JOCLYN

Laying in Ilyan's arms was the return of something that could now be described as normal. I curled into him before the panic could start, pressing my face into his chest and his scars. His smell made me light headed in a pleasant, comforting way. I hadn't remembered Ilyan having a smell, especially one as strong as this; wildflowers and smoke. Was the smell new, or had I chosen not to acknowledge it until right then?

With his arms around me and his song on repeat, I could feel the panic and despair leaving me.

I could feel normal.

Almost.

Ilyan pulled away enough to look at me, the gold specks in his eyes reflecting the morning light. He moved my hair away from my face, his finger grazing against my mark. The jolt of magic shot down my spine and I fought the panic that tried to break free, my eyes glued to his as he smiled. His face was a mixture of pride, worry, and most of all, love.

I knew, as well as he did, that it was now only Ilyan's touch that could cause such a reaction.

"I'm going to go get you some Black Water. I'll be right back." His lips brushed my hairline before he was gone, leaving me under the covers, trapped with his heat.

The heavy, wooden door opened and closed. I stretched my hand out over the cotton sheet, laying it flat on the warm part where his body had just been. My heart rate stayed steady even though he had gone; the warmth almost a promise of his return.

Almost.

I wasn't sure, and that worried me.

I didn't even have time to think about it before the door opened again, this time closing with a thunk before heavy footsteps moved toward me. I jumped at the noise, my body instantly rolling into a tight little ball. I tried to convince myself that it was just Ilyan coming back, but I knew better. I knew that gait. My brain had memorized that breathing. I peeked out from behind the covers, not wanting to see.

Ryland stood before the bed, his hands calmly at his sides, his dark curls falling over his bright blue eyes as they had always done, but my mind didn't see that.

My mind replaced the happy smile with a wicked grimace, dark curls with greasy strands, and even the wall behind him began to turn red in my panic.

My breathing picked up as I scuttled over the covers away from him, pressing myself against the headboard as though I could move through it. I panicked and stuttered, his eyes growing wide at my reaction.

"Jos? Sweetheart? What's wrong?" His voice was kind and gentle, but I didn't trust it. He had played this game on me before, only to end up hurting me.

"G-go a...a...away." I tried to make my voice strong, knowing from the start that it wouldn't work.

"Jos? I'm not going to hurt you, honey," Ryland pleaded as he leaned against the foot of the bed, prepared to crawl towards me.

I howled as he moved onto the bed, my voice making noises that had no recognition in any language in an attempt to get him away from me.

"It's okay, sweetheart. It's okay. I had to see you. I had to know you were all right. After everything that Cail did..."

"Go. Away!" I was surprised at my own voice, but tried hard not to let it show.

I balled my fingers into fists, grateful my fear kept me from attacking him, but not knowing if it was the right choice. I wanted to attack him.

I wanted to fire my magic at him and end him. Make him pay for what he did to me.

"Jos! I'm not going to hurt you!" he yelled in frustration. He was practically on top of me now, my heart felt like it was going to beat right through me with how hard it was thumping in my chest.

We were both silent at his outburst; my breathing ragged, his heavy.

He didn't remove his eyes from mine as I watched him calculate what to do with me. Then we both heard it, yelling voices in the hall.

I recognized them both immediately. I had heard them enough. Ilyan and Ovailia. My eyes widened as Ryland looked at me, a million different puzzle pieces clicking into place. But the picture still didn't make any sense.

"Ovi...Ovailia b-brought y-you hee...here?"

"Yes. Ilyan wouldn't let me see you. I needed to see you, Jos. You are all I think about. One of the only memories I have left." I could see the heartbreak in his face, and for one moment, I almost pitied him. I almost understood him. But even if I had wanted to, I couldn't trust him. I still waited for him to hurt me even as I continued to fight the desire to hurt him.

"Ilyan p-protec-cts me." I had wanted to explain to Ryland how safe Ilyan made me, that he was doing what I needed, but Ryland's face changed.

His eyes grew dark, and I watched his body shake. What little calm I had been able to find was washed away.

"Ilyan hides you from me!" He rose up above me, his shoulders squaring dangerously.

"N-no!" I tried to move further away from him, but his legs had pinned me down. I was trapped.

"Yes! He wants you all to himself as he feeds you lies about how dangerous I am; how mean I am! Even though I would never hurt you. Ilyan made you break our Zêlství!" Ryland's yell rose as I continued to panic.

"N-no!"

"Ovailia was right." He roared at me, and I almost missed what was coming. His fist pulled back as the skin of his hand glowed red, his magic fueling his anger as he moved to punch me.

I couldn't move. I couldn't make my magic respond. I stared at him, tears flowing down my cheeks. The part of me that had held out hope that this was not the Ryland who had hunted me died when he did what I expected him to. Hurt me.

He punched me.

I howled at the impact. My voice rising up as burning pain spread through my skull, as I fought to get away from what Ryland would do next. Before either of us could make another move, a gust of wind flew through the room and lifted Ryland off of me. I didn't look to see who had rushed in, I only howled as I rolled off the bed onto the ancient stone and slid myself underneath the heavy, wooden bed.

Hiding was my first defense now. It felt safe here. I could feel the pressure of both the bed and the floor pushing against me. I tried to keep my breathing and cries to a minimum in the hope of not being found, but I was not sure it mattered. Ilyan and Ovailia's shouts had entered the room, the screaming match in Czech intensifying.

"But he didn't hurt her did he?" Ovailia yelled as she transitioned smoothly to English.

"Ovailia, he punched her when I came into the room!" Ilyan moved toward me, his stocking feet coming into view as he guarded my hiding place.

"I didn't see that." Ovailia lied, I heard Ryland chuckle next to her and my insides stiffened.

"He's going to lie anyway, Ovailia. He's been feeding her lies. Just as you said." I stuffed my fist in my mouth at the sound of Ryland's voice to keep from screaming.

"What lies have you been telling *him*, Ovailia?" Ilyan asked, the amount of fear in his voice alarming.

"Nothing much. Two can play at this game, Ilyan." Her voice was sweet as honey, but I knew better because this wasn't a game; no matter how many times Cail had told me that it was.

Cail.

Without warning I began to howl again. My safe place suddenly felt like a prison. I could hear Ovailia laughing beyond my screams.

"I want you out, Ovailia! Leave the Abbey and take your games with you," Ilyan roared above my yells. I could just make out Ovailia's laugh as Ilyan removed her and placed the door back in place.

It took a second before his face appeared in the gap under the bed, his hand reaching to help me out. I couldn't see through the fear enough to respond, though. I was frozen there.

Ilyan's magic flared inside of me, his warmth moving through me as he steadied my heartbeat. Ilyan reached forward again, but I just looked at him, not quite willing to leave the security the bed provided me. Ilyan waited another moment before lying down on the ground beside me. His body stretched out on the floor while mine was crammed under the bed.

"I'm sorry, Jos." His voice was soft, and while I could feel some of my panic edge away, it wasn't quite enough. "I will make you safe. I will make you whole again."

I stared at him, my eyes wide. I tried to convince myself that what he said was true; that I was safe, that I would be whole again, and that I would no longer feel this panic and pain that controlled my body.

But I didn't know if I could believe him. I wasn't even sure if that was possible.

Ilyan wedged himself under the bed; his tall, wiry frame moving right up against me. I could feel the warmth radiating off of his skin.

Without thinking, I reached up and pulled at one of the short locks of hair that covered his head. He smiled. "I cut it for you after what you said in Italy. When you couldn't wake up... I was..." his voice caught, and I could almost swim in the emotion that was emanating from him, the fear and the terror. I knew what he must have felt because I had felt it too when I had first been trapped in the Tȍuha.

I curled myself into him as he lay beside me, his body wrapping around me tightly. I laid my head against his chest as the space around us filled with his song. Ilyan whispered the words roughly, the sound surrounding me in comfort.

I stayed stiff in his grip as he sang, his hand rubbing over my back, his lips heavy against the skin on my temple. All the while, deep inside I was still waiting; waiting for someone to attack, waiting for blood to come. Waiting for Ryland to hurt me; Ryland, who wasn't even safe in the real world anymore. I knew that place was gone. I had made it out, right to where I wanted to be.

Where I yearned to be.

I was where I had held out hope that someday I would be again. It was the reason I had never forgotten his song. My heart had held onto him. As he clung to me, as he soothed me and held me, I felt everything begin to relax.

My heart opened me up, taking me away from the panic that still clung to my body and hid deep inside my muscle tissue. The panic, fear, and anxiety deep inside of me continued to be there. I knew it wasn't gone, yet somehow Ilyan made it better. He made my heart calm.

My heart.

Love.

It was so strong. It filled me, consumed me. If I focused on it, I could almost feel normal. Normal. No twitches, no stutters, no rats scurrying through my brain. I could easily remember every moment of my life, every heartbreak, every joy, and every fear. Every moment I'd shared with every person that ever meant anything to me. I saw it all with perfect clarity, the emotions sharper than I had ever remembered them. They weren't as raw as the terrors I had escaped from, they were just me, and with only those thoughts inside of me, I could just be me.

Just a girl in Ilyan's arms.

Slowly I uncoiled my body, my arms disentangling from against my chest to wrap them around Ilyan. My fingers dug into his shirt, wrapping the fabric around them. I pulled him close to me, and he enveloped my body with his own, keeping me close, keeping me safe.

Danger was everywhere. Heck, danger was now tucked deep inside my brain. I knew without a doubt I would be haunted by it for the rest of my life, but right there—right then—I was bigger than it. Ilyan helped me be bigger than it, helped me be stronger than it.

Ilyan made me stronger, and there in his arms, I felt everything open. Every magical vein in my body was alive, surging with fire—with power.

I wasn't as scared anymore. I wasn't as confused. I could do anything.

I was also certain of where I was going to start. I didn't know if it was based in fear, or pain, or revenge for what he had done to me, but one thing was clear...

I was going to start by killing Ryland LaRue.

CHAPTER 36
WYN

The Abbey was ahead of where we stood in the Spanish forest, the crumbling stone of the bell tower peeking out from over the tops of the trees. Ancient brick that I had seen a million times before was illuminated by the bright lightning that cracked above us. The decrepit building looked like the Taj Mahal after what we had escaped from.

Now, we only needed to get to Ilyan before it was too late.

Although, judging by the masses of Edmund's army that surrounded the ancient space, we might already be.

Figures.

I get my memories and the fire magic back in time to wipe out an army. Part of me wouldn't have it any other way.

Bring it on.

Telling Ilyan what had happened to Prague, to his people, wasn't a conversation I was looking forward to having. Neither was the 'Oh, by the by, I have all my memories back, and your best friend is dead' conversation.

My heart pulsed painfully at the imagery of Talon's hand against mine for the last time, of Rosaline, of everything that I had chosen to forget.

"We are almost out of time. We must move quickly."

I tried to restrain the eye roll at Sain's raspy voice. He had repeated the same phrase since the lid of Ilyan's tomb had enclosed us into the tunnel system under Prague. He had repeated the words every night as I tried to sleep, each day as we walked toward Rioseco. Each time the phrase rolled off his tongue, his eyes moved over the lines that covered the left side of my body.

Seeing as I had killed my father, I would have assumed the marks to vanish—as Cail had promised—but still, they remained, staring at me as dark as my sins.

"We must move quickly." Sain's whispered warning echoed again through the chilled air; and this time I rolled my eyes, looking back up to the tower again.

"Something is wrong." I turned to the old decrepit man, his eyes wide as he stared at me.

"I know." I couldn't even fight that one. I could feel it in the way the magic pulsed in the Abbey, the way that the weak magic flared and the strong pulsed. It wasn't a castle full of strength and power that I had been expecting. Something was off. *Something is wrong.*

Suddenly, I wasn't sure if the addition of my magic would tip the scales in their favor.

It was a blow to my pride that I wasn't interested in accepting.

Lightning ripped above us, the thunder following right behind in a roar that caused all the Trpaslík in the camp before us to jump.

They were the last of Edmund's men who separated us from the tall bell tower of the Abbey, our destination.

"We are almost out of time," Sain gasped again.

"So, you've said, Sain," I nodded and pulled him from the security of the trees and into the drunken hoards that Edmund controlled.

Our heavy footfalls were abrasive in the still air, the obnoxious laughter of the Trpaslíks barely enough to cover the sound of crunching leaves and snapping twigs. I supposed it was good they couldn't hear that, anyway.

The trees ahead flashed white as the sky did, showing the line of refuge only moments away. I reached toward them, expecting the thrill of calm that our destination promised, the relief of security. The moment my fingers made contact with the jagged edges of the tree's bark, however, my magic pulled in the opposite direction.

An electric shock snapped through my tense muscles. Pressure swelled like a massive balloon as it pressed against my bones, against my lungs, through my skull. I gasped, trying to take in air as the pressure grew, as my magic tried to fight against it, to stop whatever was happening to me. It was no use.

Even though I already knew.

My eyes opened wide in horror as I stared at the dark, jagged lines that stood out like flames against my pale skin, flames that licked and moved against the skin.

Moved.

I kept the scream inside, kept my breath steady and fought against the pressure that consumed me, the pain that, try as it might, my magic couldn't defeat.

I had felt fear before—fear when I was chained in the bowels of Imdalind, fear when I had worked as Ilyan's liaison for two hundred years. But, this fear ... This fear was bound in agony and heartbreak. It rumbled through the earth with such supremacy that I was amazed I hadn't felt it before, that I hadn't understood. Sain hadn't been speaking of the battle that was coming. He hadn't been warning me of the camps that surrounded us.

He had been speaking of me.

I was almost out of time.

"If I can only bind the curse, not send it into Edmund, and I die before my father, then the curse will be unbound, and it will be unstoppable. Wynifred will die. To save her life, my father must die first."

Thunder drowned out the whisper of my voice as I repeated the words that my darling brother had said so many centuries before, the day he had made the promise to keep me safe, the day Ilyan had made the promise to keep him safe.

Neither had happened.

Now Cail was dead. Dead before my father.

Dead before Ilyan could save him.

And the curse was unbound, and I was to die like all the others.

But how?

I had killed my father, bound the stone into his belly, fused his throat shut, and thrown his body into the pit where I had lost the only man who had ever truly loved me. He should be dead. The curse should have unbound itself days ago. I should have been set free, which could only mean one thing.

Cail had been wrong.

Even if Timothy was the first to die, I would still die. The Zánik curse would always unbind itself, and I would be cursed to face the traitor's death, to literally be burned from the inside out.

The thought, the knowledge of what was about to happen to me, wound up my spine in a ribbon of horrific, agonizing fear.

I called out in pain as I collapsed against the tree, my hands wrapping around the rough bark as I tried to support myself, my whole body seizing under the attempt.

I turned toward the old man who looked at me with sad eyes that echoed the truth I now understood. I was going to die. And, judging by the dark, hooded look he gave me, he had known all along.

Was he really so heartless that he just stood there? In my pain I could have sworn he was smiling.

"We are running out of time."

"Sain?" My voice was a gasp as I reached toward him. My fingers were distorted and broken as the lines snaked over my skin, a heat I hadn't expected burning against my skin as though they were on fire.

The curse was seeping it's toxin into me, slowly killing me. I tried to fight it, to press my magic against it, but I already knew it was no use.

"Sain." The word was a whimper, a plea, a promise. It was the last word I would speak before the heat grew into an agonizing peril, before my legs gave out underneath me, and my vision faded to black.

I wasn't sure if I had fallen. I wasn't sure if he had caught me. For all I knew, I had fallen through the earth and was trapped between layers of rock and stone.

The world around me had become nothing except pain and pressure. Heat wound its way through me like knives and rope.

I tried to fight it, but the magic that had always been so powerful, had always been so capable at destroying was gone.

"We need to get you to Joclyn," the words flitted to me through the darkness I was trapped in, the voice distorted by my own screams, by the television static that cut in and out like the signal was broken, but the only station that was coming in was that of my own agonizing shouts.

I didn't want to listen, anyway.

Somewhere, deep inside, something screamed that I was giving in, that I was letting the curse destroy me. Not that I had a choice.

CHAPTER 37
ILYAN

"SAIN!"

Joclyn jumped in my arms as her father's name ripped through the silence, her silver eyes looked into mine in longing and fear, the pupils growing as Ovailia's shout rang out again.

"SAIN, YOU BASTARD!"

"Stay here," I instructed quietly, the words causing her heart to thump wildly. "Stay under the bed. I will shield you here and keep you safe."

She said nothing, and for once, I wished she would. I wished she would snap back at me about how I couldn't tell her what to do or make a joke about the ridiculous situation. But nothing came but a slow nod of understanding.

I looked into her eyes for one more second more before another scream tore through the air.

"I love you, and I will always protect you." It was foolish of me to say, and I shouldn't have done it, but I couldn't stop myself. Hearing Sain's name echo through the Abbey only triggered a million warnings of what was coming, and I wanted her to hear it. I wanted to leave her with something beautiful.

I was gone before she could respond. I left the shield over her body as I took off through the door, only to signal for Ryland to follow me. We flew out through the window, speeding through the air to land in the large courtyard, the camps of the Trpaslíks glittering in the forest behind us.

Dirt and rocks exploded into the air on my landing, the ground rocking with my anger at what was unfolding before me.

Ovailia stood in the center of the garden ruins, her exit out of the Abbey leading her directly into the path of two coming in.

I almost couldn't believe my eyes when I saw them.

Sain and Wynifred.

Sain was on the ground between Ovailia and me, his hair long and shaggy, a long beard plastered on his face. He looked even more haggard than when he had sought me out to tell me of Joclyn's existence. He cried toward Ovailia, pleading with her in Czech, French, and Mandarin only for Ovailia to counter each plea angrily, her arms moving around and tossing a small, weak-looking figure through the air with each gesture.

Wynifred screamed as Ovailia flung her around, her body writhing in pain as she flopped through the air. Wynifred was weak, her clothes dirty and bloodstained, but it was the marks on her skin that yelled danger to me. They were what was causing her pain, not Ovailia.

The jagged spirals and flares had begun to move and shift, the dark black shifting over her skin like a living infection. I knew at once what had happened. When Cail had died his lock on the zánik curse had been removed. The marks were releasing their poison into her body, and after a hundred years, the curse was going to complete itself and end in Wynifred's death.

Once again, I was going to fail in my task to save someone. After hundreds of years working for me, Wynifred's sacrifice was going to be for nothing.

"Ovi! Let her go!" Sain's voice broke through the night air, his back to me as he yelled, his body doubled over as if he had just been attacked, which, judging by the look on Ovailia's face, I wouldn't doubt.

"Wyn! You're hurting her, Ovi! Stop!" Sain pleaded as I walked past him, Ryland stopping to help the old man.

"Oh, hello, Ilyan." Ovailia spoke as if she was simply weeding a garden, not holding Wyn's body limply by her side. "Look what I found. She looks like she's hurt, and strangely, I think she remembers everything."

She held up Wynifred's small frame as the girl yelled again. I moved toward her slowly, careful to keep my steps even, my face strong. Ovailia had snapped. I was going to have to tread lightly. I needed to get Wynifred away from her before she did something stupid.

"It looks like someone hurt Cail. After all his hard work too... poor Cail. Daddy won't like that." She smiled at me, her hold keeping Wyn's body dangling as she yelled.

"Daddy doesn't like it when you keep things from him. I don't like it either." She smiled, her eyes darting between Sain and myself. I knew what was coming. She had no need for a cover; I had thrown her out of the Abbey. Now she could say what was on her mind. I waited for the onslaught, waited for her to retreat so I could move closer and help Wynifred.

"Don't you?" I couldn't keep myself from answering. I didn't even try to keep the cutting edge out of my voice. At any other time, I would have at least tried, but Ovailia was preparing herself for battle, so I let my maniacal power overtake me for a minute, making Ovailia flinch when she saw the look in my eyes.

"I thought you didn't like to wake the dead?"

"Maybe you should have let me die," she yelled, her face coming within an inch of my own.

"I didn't make that decision for you, Ovailia." My voice was hard and distant as I took two more steps nearer her.

"Well you will," she smiled, "Because, I am coming right for you, with your worst enemy on my heels," she said, her face glowing with the expectation of victory.

I just stared at her as she smiled, her warning mixed with Wyn's yells, ringing in my ears. I couldn't wait any longer.

With one blink of my eyes, I sent her flying, Wyn's body fell before I caught her and brought her into my arms. Ovailia's yell rang in my ears as she righted herself, her posture strong as she defiantly faced me.

"Goodbye, Ovailia." It was all she needed to hear, her smile increasing before she stormed off to disappear into the forest.

I never saw her go. I never took another look at my sister; I just turned toward the Abbey, Wynifred cradled in my arms. Her yells broke through the night as she writhed, the marks continuing their decent into her soul.

I seeped my magic into her, only to be burned by the powerful magic. The slow death her father had cast against her all those years ago had only become stronger. I withdrew my magic, not even able to numb her pain.

"Ian." I looked down at her, surprised to hear my code name from the centuries she had spied for me.

"Tell Thom I'm sorry." She barely got the words out before she cried out incoherently again.

"He's here, Wynifred." I was not even sure she could hear me, but I needed her to know that her last moments would not be alone.

Sain rushed forward intent to help her in any way he could, evident on his face. I knew it was no use. The curse was too strong, there was no hope.

I raced into the Abbey, Sain's pulse joined in my wake, Ryland's falling right into step beside him as I began to run, Wyn's body hanging in my arms.

I could feel the pulse of Thom's magic in his room and I knew at once that that was where we needed to go.

My magic pushed open the door to Thom's room before we had even arrived. I could see him turn, his hair whipping around at the unexpected movement. The movement alerted him, not the yells. He pulled the tiny ear buds of his iPod from his ears as we entered, the heartbreaking fear slamming into him as he registered who I was carrying.

"Wynifred!" His yell broke through the air like a knife.

I laid her down on the bed, her eyes closed as she writhed and yelled. The marks continued to snake across her skin, their number decreasing as they finished the work they had been sent out to do so long ago.

Thom was at her side, Ryland and Sain flanking him as all three of them placed their hands on her, all three withdrawing as the supercharged curse stung their magic.

"That is dark magic," Sain said, his voice shaking as he cradled his hand against his chest as if he had been burned.

Thom sighed and looked up to me, begging for help. Neither of us said anything, my face telling the whole story – there was nothing to be done.

Thom dropped his hand dejectedly, his shoulders sagging as he looked at Wynifred as she yelled and writhed.

"Her memories have returned," I whispered to Thom as he clung to her hand.

"Cail?" he asked, his voice panicked.

"Joclyn must have killed him when she escaped the Tòuha. I didn't think so at first, but only Cail's death could release Wynifred's curse. It was either Joclyn or Edmund who killed him."

"It barely matters now. Can you bind it again?" I only shook my head.

"Talon?" Thom's voice was a whisper.

I could only shake my head, I didn't know.

"He's gone." My head snapped over to Sain, his voice scratchy, like sandpaper, against the loud chaos of the room. "He passed five days ago."

I was sure that my heart had stopped beating. Talon had been my best friend for as long as I could remember. We had been raised together, and he had been my guard until the day I dismissed him, on the day of his bonding with Wyn.

I wanted to destroy something. The pain that my loss was creating consumed me, wanting to turn the Abbey to ash, run rampant and rain death through the Trpaslík camps.

I sucked in a breath, willing my soul to move past the pain, to hold the loss deep inside with all the others.

"Wynifred." Thom's voice was calm as he spoke to her, her eyes growing wide with recognition.

"Thom?"

"I'm here," he whispered as she shifted her weight, her jaw clenching as she tried not to yell, but failed.

"Am I dead?" Wynifred's voice was deep and strong again, the way I had known it for centuries. She spoke the words through clenched teeth as she cringed against the pain.

"Not yet, sweetie. But I'll stay here until the end."

I could feel the sting in my eyes as Thom spoke to her, as he prepared her for what was coming. He clung to her, his hands wrapped around hers as he soothed her the only way he could. His focus was only on her, as was everyone else's. Ryland and Sain could only stare with tear-stained cheeks.

It was with a strained heart I realized what I was witnessing. Sain, Ryland, and Wyn had been imprisoned together. They had suffered together. Ryland and Sain's tears suddenly made sense; they too were watching their friend die.

"Talon?" Wyn asked, her voice getting weaker.

"He will be there waiting for you. He's going to be right there...and...and you know who is going to be with him?"

"Rosaline?"

"Yeah, sweetie, she is going to be right there. Right there with Talon. She's been waiting for you, waiting... for her mommy." Thom's voice caught, and I had to look away, I couldn't think about what he was saying to her, what he was promising.

Instinctively, I pushed my magic toward Joclyn, needing to feel her, to feel her magic, to know that she was still okay. My eyes opened wider as I felt her presence right outside the door.

I looked back at Thom's goodbye to his best friend for only a minute before I moved out the door, finding Joclyn curled up in a ball against the floor, her hands wrapping around her knees and pulling her into a tight fetal position. I dropped to the floor, Joclyn snapping up at me, her wide silver eyes blazing into me.

"Wyn." Her voice didn't shake as she said her friend's name, the intensity of the word making it clear what she wanted.

"She's dying, Joclyn." I ran my finger over her cheek, not knowing how to comfort her or even if she needed it.

'I can save her.'

I heard her voice in my head. My eyes widened in surprise, but her eyes continued to stare into mine, as if what she had just done was the simplest thing in the world.

"Ryland is in there." I tried to keep my voice level, not wanting to send her into a panic with the shock I was feeling at just having heard her voice in my head.

'Don't let me see him. I will kill him if I see him.'

I balked at her words, my jaw loosening in shock. I could hear the truth behind them, the conviction in her tones. She truly believed what she was saying. It couldn't be. I wished I could blame her misplaced intentions on what the imitation of Ryland had done to her in the Tȍuha, but I had heard Ovailia's words. Edmund had intentionally marred them both, making them weapons against each other. Joclyn's words only confirmed it.

I struggled to keep my anger restrained. The pain of hearing Wynifred's screams, of losing Talon, mixing with the anger I felt at what Edmund had done to Joclyn and Ryland before it threatened to explode.

"Joclyn..." I began, unsure of what to say.

'I can do it. Take me to her.'

Joclyn only looked at me for a second before closing her eyes, her hand wrapping firmly around mine as she stood, her body bent and crippled from the torture her mind had gone through.

Wyn yelled again, and I knew I couldn't wait. I wrapped my arm around Joclyn, bringing her close against me as I led her through the door.

Sain and Ryland stiffened when I brought her in, both men taking a step toward her in longing. Both men drawn to her for different reasons. I shook my head at them frantically, hoping they would understand. Ryland still attempted to move toward me, but Sain wrapped his hand around Ryland's strong bicep, bringing him back against him.

"Do you remember when we took her to the beach?" Thom's voice was soft as he tried to keep Wynifred calm with memories of her long forgotten past. He didn't notice us until we were right in front of him, Joclyn's body moving toward Wynifred as if she sensed exactly where she was.

Thom sat back as Joclyn fell on top of her friend, her torso draping over Wynifred's, her hands extending to cover the moving marks on her arm. I could feel Joclyn's magic surge at the touch, the air around her sending a powerful aura right into me. I felt the surge a moment before everyone else could see it.

The air around Joclyn rippled as her magic swelled. She pulled the magic out of the air, the stone, and the earth. She brought it into her, using the power as she would her own, her control, above any I had ever seen.

The air continued to ripple visibly, the breath of everyone held in place as they watched. Silence filled the room as Joclyn's body and magic smothered Wynifred's pain. Even with the energy Joclyn was channeling, the marks still moved on Wyn's arms, the curse still seeping into her heart in an effort to kill her.

"N-n-need m-more." Joclyn's voice was quiet, her magic straining as she began to sweat.

I moved closer to her, my body hovering over hers as I leaned down to whisper in her ear. I could see Ryland shift uncomfortably at my close proximity, his intent to injure me obvious. Without Sain and Thom there to restrain him, he probably would have.

"Use me, take it through the Štít," I whispered softly, not wanting Ryland or Sain to hear.

I began to push my magic into her, the full strength of it filling her before she grabbed it and pushed it into Wynifred. As soon as she did, I could feel Wynifred, feel the curse, but I could also feel that my magic was not fully mine. I could feel it. I could recognize what it was doing, but it was Joclyn who controlled it.

"M...more...Il...Ilyan..." Her voice dropped as she began to pant, the work involved in healing Wyn becoming too much for her.

I looked away from her to the three men at the other side of the room. They watched our actions, fear, amazement, and anger spread across each of their faces. I knew what my next action would mean to Ryland, to Sain, but it had to be done.

I moved Joclyn's hair out of the way, shifting it around her neck to reveal the raised dragon shaped brand on her neck. The kiss stared at me from her smooth skin as I unwrapped my bandaged hand, letting the smooth covering fall to the floor and revealing the angry red scar of the burn.

I didn't hesitate. I didn't look to the gasps that sounded as they each recognized the angry red marks that covered the palm of my hand. I lowered my body to press against Joclyn's back, my palm hovering over the mark for just a moment before I lowered it onto her skin.

The razor sharp jolt sprung through our bodies simultaneously, the connection the Black Water had forged between us coming to life and combining with the jolt from her kiss. Our voices called out in harmony as the connection forged between us. I could feel Joclyn's exertion, her weakness, and her mad need to heal her friend. But more than that, I could feel our mingled magic surging strong through Wynifred. The amount of power rushing into her should have been enough to kill her instantly, but somehow Joclyn controlled it. Joclyn maintained the magical pulse and Wynifred's life in perfect harmony.

The black marks on Wynifred's arm that had been moving into her heart were fast, but strangely, Joclyn was faster. She moved in a way that even I would not have been able to. Her power was obviously beyond even that which I had been born with.

I opened my eyes; the three men staring in amazement as Wyn's marks not only stopped moving, but also began to fade from her skin.

'Hold me.'

I didn't need to be told twice. I looked away from the three pairs of eyes that stared at us and wrapped my free hand around Joclyn's waist, keeping my scarred hand against her mark as I brought her body against me.

No sooner had I pressed myself against her back than both girls began to scream, their voices matched in pitch, the sound ringing out like a song rather than the agonizing pain I could feel mirrored in my own body.

The scream ended only moments after it had come. Joclyn gasped for breath before she rocked away from Wynifred's body and threw both of us away from the bed.

Wynifred's yell lasted for a moment longer before her mouth opened wider, her jaw extended like a cat on the hunt. She writhed on the bed, her back arching eerily before her body released a plume of black smoke. It spewed from her gaping mouth like the steam from an engine, the blackness rising and curling dangerously into the air before it vanished.

I held Joclyn's body against mine, my eyes darting down to Wyn, whose body was relaxed and her marks all but gone. No one dared to move, least of all me. We all knew just by looking that Joclyn had done something even I couldn't.

'Cover my eyes.'

I did as she asked, recognizing the change that was coming over her. Her body stiffened as her head spun, her breathing picked up as her mind was filled with a sight, her spine tensing as she spoke.

"T-take th...the l-left." Her deep voice filled the room. Thom barely looked at her before rushing back to Wyn's side.

Sain's eyes widened as he pieced together what had just had happened, but Ryland hadn't seemed to notice, he just looked at her with that desperate longing in his eyes again. I'm not even sure he realized that there was something different in her voice.

I looked at Sain, pleading with him not to say anything, to keep this secret. I still wasn't sure I could trust Ryland. I needed to keep Joclyn safe, and letting this get out would not help her.

Sain nodded once in understanding, the action letting my muscles relax.

"She's fine." Thom's voice cut through my silent exchange, bringing us all back to what had just happened. "Joclyn healed her."

I couldn't help but smile as I brought her body into mine, keeping her close to me.

'I told you I could.'

Her eyes were still closed, and her face was pressed against my chest. She could have been sleeping. I slowly removed my finger from the mark, allowing the connection to begin to fade from my mind. I wished I knew how she was doing that, how she was filling my mind with her voice. No one had ever managed anything past crude pictures – not since the first were born from the mud. But to hear her voice, without the stutter, inside my mind... It was as beautiful as she was.

She was amazing.

'Thank you.'

CHAPTER 38
JOCLYN

Fireflies.

When I was growing up, I thought fireflies were magic. I thought they were like fairies. I would try to catch them in jars and take them home to convince them to grant my wish.

I was four when I caught my first one. I had put him in a glass jar and watched him glow as he fluttered and banged against the glass. He was going to grant my wish. My father had sat with me and ran his finger over the glass, the firefly drawn to him. When my father's finger was there, the firefly didn't bang his head against the glass anymore; he just followed the line my father traced.

Dad asked me what my wish was, but at four all I could think of was a pony, a pony and the ability to fly. My father smiled and told me that magic was inside of you, not in bugs. I asked him if I had magic then, and he got that face that parents get when they are caught in a lie. I knew it then, that magic wasn't real, but I didn't care.

I had laughed as we set my little firefly free, sad for the loss of a wish but happy for the bug.

It was one of my only happy memories of my father.

Then, many years later, I found out what magic really was. And just like the firefly, I wished I could just open the jar and go free.

I still wanted to think of fireflies as magic. I watched them as they danced outside the window of Ilyan's room, and I wanted to dance with them, but I couldn't. I couldn't move my body out of the heavy blanket I had wrapped around myself, the thick wool keeping me warm as I sat against the stone. So, I watched the fireflies, and I felt my magic surge and flow through the air, the power wild and unrestrained within me.

My magic flew away from me as I sat there, desperate to be out of the small container my body provided it. It flowed through the air and over the yards of the Abbey like water. It fanned away from me and brought back signs and signals from everyone around me.

I could feel the armies that surrounded us and their eagerness for a battle that they knew was coming. I could feel Thom's joy as he sat next to Wyn, closeted up in his room where I had left them only a few minutes before. I could feel Wyn's sadness at losing her mate. I wished I could tell her that I could still feel Talon inside of her, but I didn't dare speak. Not yet.

I had sat with them as Wyn woke up, my eyes closed as I hid myself in Ilyan's chest. I could feel them all around me. I could feel my father's magic, I could feel everything. But in that tiny room, I was trapped.

As soon as Wyn woke, the questions came, the voices all sounding at once. They asked questions and demanded answers, their voices growing louder and panicking me. The touching followed, my father's hands on my skin in excitement, Thom reaching out to me in thanks, and though I understood their desires, my body curled into itself. I couldn't stop the sobs.

I wasn't ready to talk to any of them. I wasn't ready to look into my father's eyes and relive all that had happened since he had left. So instead, my father had hugged me as I sat on Ilyan's lap and he whispered in my ear how much he loved me. Ilyan had passed on my words to him before taking me from the room.

I had crawled to the balcony after Ilyan had left me here to rest, unable to resist the buzz of magic that was out here. No matter how confusing everything was. I needed to be here.

Everything was getting clearer, but I still hadn't broken free.

I could feel the pulse of Ilyan's magic from where he stood with Sain as they healed his son, my brother. I could feel Ilyan's emotions, the heightened connection giving me access to loose pieces of his thoughts. Ilyan was nervous about me, he wanted to leave, but he was fighting it, knowing he needed to stay there too. He had responsibilities that he could not ignore.

Ilyan's anxiety pulsed as Sain began to tell him all that had happened. His anxiety triggered my own; my magic surging through him as my own peaked, confusing me as to whether I should calm him or myself.

If I focused, I could hear their conversation. I could pretend to be well enough to be around them but they weren't alone. There was someone else with them. I knew that if I heard his voice, I couldn't be sure what I would do.

'Ilyan.'

I let my magic grow and sent my voice into his head, the word traveling through the Štít and into him. I wasn't sure how I had done it the first time. I had sat huddled on the floor as Wyn screamed, and I could feel my magic grow into something that it hadn't been before. I looked into Ilyan's eyes and my soul had told me what to do. It didn't take more of a thought than that.

I felt Ilyan's excitement increase at my message, his thoughts changing from stress over what he was being told toward me, his thoughts heavy with worry.

'I'm fine, Ilyan.'

A moment passed as he talked, but soon his thoughts were torn between wondering what I needed and trying to focus on what Sain was telling him.

I didn't know what had caused me to call to him; I knew he would come when he was done. Until then, I had my fireflies to keep me company.

My body shook the longer I sat, my hands twitching underneath the blanket. I could feel the anxiety rise, the uncertainty taking over. I focused on the panic, trying to calm it, but knowing it would come no matter what I did.

Before it could grow too loud, Ilyan's song filled my mind, the thought flowing from Ilyan into me, my own lips following suit as I whispered the words to myself.

The song ended as the door creaked open as he entered. I knew it was Ilyan, but I couldn't stop the tension from filling my joints or the way my head moved toward my chest. I kept my body still against the stone wall as Ilyan moved closer to me, the ebbs of his magic growing as he calmed me.

I turned my eyes as he sat next to me, his legs crossed beneath him, just far enough away that I couldn't touch him easily. I could hear that part of me scream for his contact, but the jitters begged otherwise.

Even through the fear, I still wanted to touch him. I pushed the thought away, choosing instead to focus on his blue eyes and how they dug into me, the way his fingers twitched in desperation to touch me, and the way his lips turned up in a calm joy when I looked at him.

I watched him, and I felt the tension leave, my heart rate slow. Not for the first time, just the sight of him calmed me.

"Ilyan," I breathed, my voice calm. I wasn't sure I could manage more than that one word though.

He smiled at the sound of his name on my tongue, his magic surging in response.

"Are you talking now?" he asked, his voice a cross between amusement and worry.

'No.'

I sent the one word into his mind, but instead of sadness, he only smiled. I didn't see what was so funny, but he obviously did. I wrapped my hands around myself, my body tensing at what that smile could mean. It was nothing. It had to be nothing but happiness.

'I will only talk to you.'

Ilyan smiled again, his gaze darting away from mine to his hands before coming back to rest on me, the soft blue light of his eyes glossed over.

"And, I will cherish every second of your voice that you give me."

He smiled again, the warmth of his face seeping into me, soothing my nerves. My tension loosened a bit, and I couldn't help but let my own small smile filter onto my face. A smile. It felt weird and foreign. I had forgotten what happiness felt like.

"Y...you w-w-will?" My smile left as the stutter took over, the shake of my voice taking my newfound happiness away.

"I will," he sighed, shifting closer to me. His knees pressed against the heavy blanket I had covered myself with. I focused on the pressure, leaning into it. I leaned into the warmth I felt from his touch and the ripples of heat coming off his body, my body hovering precariously away from the pressure the alcove provided me.

"How are you feeling?"

'I'm not sure if I am fine or if I am broken.'

"It's okay to be both, Joclyn," he sighed, his hand moving to rest against my cheek, but it wasn't skin I felt. I turned my head toward him in confusion, my eyes narrowing at the heavy bandage he had covered his hand with.

My heart beat quickly at seeing it there. Ilyan had hurt himself. How had I missed this? For the first time, I worried about what had happened while I had been trapped in hell, while I had been tortured. Ilyan had been injured.

Ilyan's heart quickened as I removed the covering, my breathing shaking as the angry red marks came into view. The red welts stood up from his hand like a burn, but the skin was still wet in places.

As though from water.

'What happened?' I asked, my fear for him overriding my personal demons for the moment. He didn't need to tell me. I could see the moment replayed in his head, the horrors of those last moments in my hell a swirl of color and fear in his eyes.

'This is how you brought me back? The Black Water?'

He nodded once, and I pulled the hand toward me, my back arching as I brought the scars against my face, another mark that Ilyan would bear forever, another scar he had taken for me.

'Thank you.'

"Haven't I told you enough? I would do anything for you."

His voice was so soft I barely heard him. I leaned toward him as I pressed his hand against me, his magic pulsing through me. It was so warm and delicate within me. I could feel it reach into every part of me, cradling me as if I was something precious.

I could feel his emotions whisper it to me now. I could feel his heart ache; his love for me that was always held behind the strict barriers of what he felt was right, broke through, and bared between us.

Then, something changed. He second-guessed himself somewhere along the way, his emotions withdrawing and his insecurities taking their place.

As his doubts and fears took hold, they also seeped into me. I moved away from him. I wanted that feeling back, that love that I had felt emanating from him only a moment ago. I felt my heart hunger for it, need it.

'What's wrong?' I asked, unable to keep my worry locked inside.

Ilyan looked at me with pain in his eyes, his mind pouring out his sadness before his mouth even opened. His first word brought the panic I had kept at bay until this point.

"Ryland has asked me..."

"No!" My voice caught him off guard, his eyes widening at the power behind my one word.

I couldn't stop the panic that flowed through my body. I moaned as I curled into the blanket, every nerve ending tensing in agony, in fear of what was to come. Ilyan's magic surged, my own magic joining his as I attempted to calm myself, to take the fear away.

I could see Ilyan's thoughts in front of me, his worry for his brother and his friend and his desperate need for me, and I could hear Ryland's words in his head.

'I will not see him.' I answered the unasked question inside his head. *'I will kill him if I see him. I* want *to kill him.'*

I narrowed my eyes at him, my jaw tensing at the calm agony his eyes showed me. I curled into the wall, my mind fighting against my better judgment as it begged me to run away.

"You won't kill him," Ilyan said as calmly as he could, and I felt my anger rise and my magic pulse. For one fleeting second it was stronger than the crazed anxiety that still overtook me.

'I will.'

"No, Jos," he whispered, and I couldn't help the thunk of my heart at my nickname on his lips. "You don't want that, not really."

'I do, Ilyan.' I begged him. I begged through the panic, the fear. I needed him to understand this. To understand the anger that was a fire inside of me, the need for revenge fanning it ever higher. *'He hurt me... he...'*

My thoughts stopped as Ilyan's hand moved against my neck, the sharp jolt as his skin made contact with my mark stopping my words. I sighed at the sensation, at the pleasurable heat it gave me, before staring into Ilyan, knowing it had been his intention to stop me.

"You don't want to hurt him. You don't want to kill him. It's not really *you* that feels that way. You think it is because you are still so scared and confused at what has happened. You were hurt, Joclyn, but not by him."

His eyes dug into me as he plead with me to believe him. But I couldn't. I couldn't see beyond the panic and pain. It consumed me. A part of me wanted it to. In some ways, the pain and the anxiety made me remember that I was alive.

'It was him.' I spat as I pushed Ilyan away, as I let the anxiety mix with the hate. I could feel my magic surge and pulse, but it wasn't like when I had healed Wyn; this was uncontrollable, like I myself was the danger, as if I would explode.

"No, my love," Ilyan said calmly, his eyes scanning me as I continued to try to move into myself and my breathing picked up. "It was a farce, a projection in Cail's mind meant to confuse you so that you would kill him if you ever got the chance."

Ilyan's magic moved into me and took away the frayed edges of my panic. I wanted to hold it to me, and relax in the pain, but I couldn't. I couldn't tear my mind away from what Ilyan was saying, what he was trying so foolishly to get me to believe.

I couldn't. Ryland needed to pay for what he had done to me.

'It was him, Ilyan. I know...'

"How do you know it was?" The desperation in his words stopped me, my eyes widening. Why did he doubt me? Why was he pushing me? What had Ryland told him? What had my father said?

I had shown Ilyan everything; I had filled his mind with those memories. Why couldn't he see that I knew? I knew by the way that he had walked, the way that his hair curled. I could have admitted that there had been something different about him, but I couldn't tell what it was. I didn't want to.

I pressed myself into the wall as I tried to keep the fear at bay, as I tried to hold onto reality.

'How do you know that it wasn't?' I countered, my voice snide in his head.

Ilyan closed his eyes for a moment, and I could hear the replay of the last hour in his mind, the conversation he had had with Sain. I didn't want to hear it. Even though I could tell he was trying to give me the thoughts, I wouldn't let them in.

"They did the same to him, Jos." He sighed, his breath exhaling as he lifted his eyes to look at me again. "They turned him into a weapon to hurt you. It's why he punched you. He still sees you as the enemy they haunted him with. He is trying to fight it, but I am not sure he can."

I just stared at him, the words sinking into a place deep inside of me that I wanted so desperately to ignore. Ilyan's eyes were soft, the truth behind them penetrating. I sighed as I leaned my head against the wall.

'How do you know that I am meant to be a weapon now?'

Ilyan stared and moved closer, his body folding as he leaned toward me.

"It's what my father does, Joclyn." His fingers twitched in desperation to hold me again. "It is what he has always done. You know this."

I did. I had seen it even before he had done it to me. I had seen it in Thom, and I had heard the stories of my father. I had no reason to doubt any of them.

"You need to let go of that anger, Joclyn," Ilyan continued when I said nothing, his hand finally moving to rest against the blanket that covered me. "You can't let the pain control you."

'I can't, Ilyan. If I let go of it, then there is nothing left. I have nothing behind that. It's all I am anymore.'

"That's not true," Ilyan said, his hand caressing my knee through the blanket.

'It's all I feel.' I sighed, pulling the blanket around me tighter. The jagged edge of that anger sliced against me, threatening to turn into panic. I pushed it away as I buried my face into the wall, refusing to look at him.

"You have to look beyond it, my love," Ilyan whispered, his voice soft as his hand moved from the blanket to the skin of my face.

'There is nothing behind it.' I said, the voice in my head breaking in my sadness.

Ilyan sighed, and his hand moved over my skin before he dropped it, before he leaned away. The movement scared me, and I looked toward him. But when I did, his eyes were looking right at me, the bright blue shocking as they raged with a heady emotion that took my breath away.

"My father hung me from a tree shortly after it became obvious that I was the one challenging him. He caught me, whipped me, and burned my skin with irons. I thought I would go mad. But I didn't."

I had always excluded Ilyan from the pain Edmund had caused his children. I didn't know why, but Ilyan seemed untouchable. Now he was telling me that he had been hurt. He had thought he would go crazy. But he didn't

'How?'

He smiled at my question, and for the first time since I met him, I could tell he was nervous. I could feel the anxiety in his mind; hear the thump of his heart.

His heart called to me, and I leaned toward him, the heavy blanket moving away as I reached for his hands and wrapped my hands around his.

"Ilyan?" I asked aloud, loving the way his name felt on my tongue.

"I thought of you, of the vision. I basked in the way you felt in my arms, the smell of your hair. I thought of every vision I had seen in the sight and I knew I was bigger than the pain. I looked beyond it, and I found love."

Love.

The look in his eyes, the way his magic felt within me, none of it was wild, none of it was scary. Everything about Ilyan was calm. He was love.

He was light.

He wasn't love simply because I knew he loved me. Because I did know that. Without question, he had proved that to me again and again. No, he was love because I loved him.

I loved him.

"What is beyond your anger, Joclyn? What is your pain hiding?"

I stared at Ilyan as I leaned into him, my hands untangling from his to trail up his shirt and over the skin of his neck.

I held my breath as I touched his face, the soft skin I had never touched before. I ran the pads of my fingers over his eyebrows, his defined cheek bones, and through the hairline of his short cut.

My heart pulsed wildly inside of me as I let my fingers trail over the scruff from a beard I had never seen, prickly and sharp, before dragging to his lips. I froze.

I froze at the sound of my pulse in my ears. I froze at the calm that had overtaken me. I froze at the desire that circled through Ilyan's mind and the willpower he was exerting to keep it there.

I watched his breathing. I felt the heat of his breath against my fingers, the pulse of his magic hot under his skin.

What was behind the anger?

"Ilyan," I said again, his eyes opening slowly to me, "you are behind my anger."

I smiled, my heart thumping even more at the clarity those precious words brought, at the way each syllable formed perfectly. Ilyan's lips upturned underneath my touch, the skin parting as he kissed the pads of my fingers, the wetness of his lips soft against my skin.

"I always will be," he whispered as my fingers fell from his lips and I moved closer.

As I kissed him.

WYN

My screams continued to cut in and out like a bad signal, until they were joined by something else.

The sound of voices.

Other voices.

Familiar voices.

They cut through the pain and static in languages I didn't comprehend, even though I knew I should. I knew the knowledge of them was inside of me. I just couldn't access it through the fire that was eating me alive.

"I thought you didn't like to wake the dead?" I jerked at the sneer, my body twisting as a hand wrapped around my arm, throwing me around like I was made of nothing more than fabric and a little bit of stuffing.

My eyesight flitted in and out as the courtyard of the Rioseco Abbey flickered through the dark, streaks of what I was sure was blonde hair adding to the visual cacophony.

Words plowed through the static like a steamroller as I was thrown about, my screams coming loud as the pain swelled and sucked me into the void again. The brief moment of understanding brought back a hope that I desperately needed. I tried to fight against the pain, to fight against the curse, to force my magic to battle, to force myself not to give up yet. I didn't want to, though I couldn't make anything come.

"I didn't make that decision for you, Ovailia." I knew that voice. I knew the depth of that accent. I knew the sound. It was so familiar. Familiar enough that it pulled me out of the disconnected world.

The sound of thunder rumbled through my bones as air moved through my hair. Then strong arms wrapped around me as if I had done nothing more than fly into them.

"Goodbye, Ovailia," the voice came again, the memory pulling at the name I had used so often it almost became more real than his actual name. The name of a king who had saved me so many times I could barely count.

"Ian." I wasn't sure if I had spoken aloud, if I had been able to control my mind enough to work over the screams.

The static came back and smothered Ilyan's voice as we ran. I could only hope that Sain would be able to tell him of Prague, that he had told him of whatever he had seen. If I was lucky, they were taking me to Joclyn. I could say goodbye before it was too late.

I almost wished it would hurry up.

"Wynifred." *Thom?*

I had hoped Ilyan had been taking me to Joclyn, that Sain knew how to heal me, but this? Hearing his voice? I wasn't sure if I was already dead, if he was really there, or if this was just more torture.

"Wynifred," the voice came again, breaking through the static like a battering ram. The sound of his voice was so embedded in my memory that, even if my mind had still been bound, I was sure just the sound of his voice would have broken the cage wide open.

I could still feel the pain. I could still feel the heat and the way my body tried to rip itself in two. Strangely, though, I didn't care. For the first time since the heat had taken me, I could focus beyond it. I could feel the heat of his hand against mine. I could feel his fingers as they ran against my face, my tears as he caught them.

I still could not see him, but I didn't care. If this was what I heard, what I felt, before I died ... There was nothing I wanted more.

"Thom?" I was sure I had spoken this time, even though my voice was broken and airy.

"I'm here." His hand tightened around mine at the shattered emotion of his words. The memory of how he had looked when he cried still so clear inside of me. The way his eyes pinched together, his hand instinctively moving through his short, brown hair, much the way that his brother did.

Everything was so clear, the memory so fresh, that for a moment, the pain didn't seem to matter. For the briefest of moments, a joy I didn't think I could feel again took over. The emotion was so backward from the agony that still ripped through me that I was sure the curse had already done its job.

That I had already passed from this life.

"Am I dead?"

There was only *dead* and *not dead yet* now. I couldn't ask if I was going to be okay. I didn't have that luxury anymore.

"Not yet, sweetie, but I'll stay here until the end," he said with an exhale, his voice shaking even though I could tell he was trying to be strong. I could tell in the way he held my hand, the way his hand pressed against my cheek, even through the shake of his nerves, of his heartbreak.

It made me ache. It made my muscles twist and writhe. It made my heart beat reawaken with a painful pulse of regret and longing.

In the last moments of life, I felt more alive than I think I ever had. I focused on that, focused on the heat, focused on the hand that held mine. And, for the shortest breath of time, the pain didn't seem to matter, the fire didn't seem so destructive, and the blackness that surrounded me fell away.

It faded to a dimly lit room and a man who, even though he had changed—even though his hair was in long dreads and his skin more worn, his eyes slightly dimmed—it was still the man who had taught me so much about life and love.

It was still Thom.

I looked at him, the pressure of his hands tight against mine, and saw him for the first time in centuries. I saw him for the last time.

I didn't dare say anything. I didn't have anything to say. He had heard it all before, felt it all, lived it all. I held his hand, staring into him as the world around him began to shift, as the black of the curse threatened to take me.

I waited for it to come, watching the grey seep into the world, only to have a courtyard materialize before me, the world waving and blending together as my mind took me to a place that I hadn't seen in what felt like years—the beautiful, perfect world that Talon and I had created inside our Tȍuha.

Even though I was sure I hadn't moved, even though I could still feel Thom's hand around mine, I could see the sanctuary that my bond with Talon had created. I could see every brick, the bench we had spent so much time on, the shadowed body of a man leaning against the wall.

"Talon?" My voice was soft with longing as I stared at the shadowed shape. I was sure he had turned toward me before the entire scene vanished into smoke and left me staring at Thom's tear-streaked face, his eyes deep with understanding.

My heart pulsed at seeing him there, torn between two worlds, two realities.

"He will be there, waiting for you," Thom whispered as he leaned close to me, the brilliant blue of his eyes devouring me. "He's going to be right there ... and ... and you know who is going to be with him?"

The pulse in my chest became a stab of memories, of reminders of the life we shared, of the life I had so willingly chosen to forget.

Never before had I regretted my decision to forget, not because I had turned my back on a life that had been so good, but because I had turned my back on Thom, a man who, for the first time, I realized, was still mourning the loss of our daughter as I was. He was still filled with pain and agony. We had both chosen to run away, although in different ways.

"Rosaline?" The word dug into me, my back arching with fire and gut-wrenching agony that I had thought I had escaped.

You can't escape something that is wound so deeply in your soul, however. I knew that now. I knew that in the way Thom's voice pulled me from the pain of the curse and the way Rosaline's memory bound us together.

"Yeah, sweetie, she is going to be right there with Talon. She's been waiting for you, waiting ... for her mommy."

Everything ached at his promise, the pain from the curse seeming to come back full force as he turned away in his own pain. I gasped at the fire, struggling against the scream that tried to rip itself out of me, the blackness that wanted to take me away again.

In a way, it would almost be more preferable, but I didn't want to lose this, lose these last moments. If only I had a choice.

I stared at Thom as my vision began to waiver, the same courtyard materializing around me, the same shadowed figure tucked off into a corner. Except, this time, he wasn't quite as shadowed, he wasn't quite as far away.

He stood, his body distorted as though I was looking at him through a fog, like I was only seeing him through a veil of life and death. That was exactly what it was, I realized. He was dead, and I was not. Not yet. He was standing there, ready to take me into his arms, ready to hold me in death as he had in life.

"She will be there," Thom's voice came to me as if he was still sitting right there, but I didn't see him anymore.

I couldn't seem to look away from Talon. Part of me desperately hoped he would step through the fog to take me, while part of me dreaded the moment when he would.

"Do you remember that big smile she had after she lost her first tooth? How she would always push her tongue through the little gap?"

I knew Thom wanted me to answer, but I wasn't sure I could. I wasn't sure I wanted to. I couldn't look away from Talon, my heart thundered in my chest as I waited for him to do something.

"She's not responding..." Thom's voice was broken, but until right then, I hadn't cared. I had only cared about the man before me, about what he was there to do, even if it scared me.

"You have to choose." The voice cut through the fog, deep and heavy. It resounded through my head in such a way that I knew it had come from inside me. While the deep, haunted rumble of the sound was unfamiliar, it was still comforting, its message clear.

Talon stood before me, shrouded by death. I could choose to be with him. I could choose to die.

How could I choose? You couldn't choose to live through this, through this curse. I was going to die. There wasn't a choice, only a reality.

"Just keep trying," Sain's voice cut through the distanced thoughts, attempting to bring me back. I stared at Talon's shadow, the distorted body shifted as it came closer, as a hand reached toward me through the fog.

His fingers moved through the cloud and became more than a shadowed distortion. They became real. They were skin and calluses and a scar I recognized at once.

They became Talon.

I looked up, expecting to see his smile, but he was still cast in static. His body was out of focus, as if I couldn't see him quite right, as if my eyes weren't powerful enough to see.

"Do you remember when we took her to the beach?" I could barely hear Thom now. It was almost like his voice couldn't move through the fog.

"You have to choose," the deep voice came again, rumbling through me.

I wanted to tell it I didn't have a choice, that someone had already made it for me. I couldn't seem to find the words, though.

It didn't matter, anyway.

Talon stood with his hand extended, beckoning me home.

I reached toward him, everything felt light and warm as I stepped closer, the pain of the curse almost gone now. I wanted to rejoice that it was gone, that I had left it behind. Left life behind. But, I couldn't.

Something was pulling me back.

No, not something—someone.

"N-n-need m-more." I recognized the voice at once, even through the broken stutter and the fear that trembled underneath it.

It was Joclyn.

It was her magic that moved through me.

It was her power that was trying to heal me, to save me,

I looked up to Talon, to his body so clear I could reach out and touch him. I wanted to.

I also knew that I couldn't, not yet.

Sain had seen this. He had seen every bit of this. His need to get me to Joclyn had been so sure, right from the start. He hadn't said goodbye before, either. They still needed me.

What was more, I still needed them.

I still needed to live.

"I'm sorry." I couldn't get any more out than that.

Talon smiled, wide and clear, as if he knew what he had done, as if he had been planning it for years and was proud of it. Seeing that look, seeing the playfulness in his eyes, a look that was so distinctly him I couldn't have a hope of recreating it within my subconscious, I knew it was him. I knew it was real.

All of it.

"Be happy, Wyn," he whispered, his voice soft as Rosaline's laugh echoed around us, the sound bringing joy and hope unlike any time before. Light and warmth seeped into me, moving through me in a wave of calm that took the heaviness of the dream away.

I remained still as the warmth left my skin, a chill moving over me. The smell of damp air and sandalwood permeated everything.

I tried to turn toward Talon, to move a little, to say goodbye. But he had already gone, and I was left with the heavy weight of exhaustion and pain. I knew at once I wasn't going to be moving anytime soon.

A deep groan escaped my lips and a relieved gasp filled the air, a gasp that was not mine.

My eyes snapped open in alarm, my heart beating a million miles an hour as they worked to adjust to the dimly lit space. The heavy buzz of agitated voices filled the air as my eyes went to the man who hovered above me, his cheeks stained with tears and long ropes of his hair pulled away from his face.

"You're awake," he gasped as the loud buzzing of voices disappeared into nothing. His lips twitched into a smile so rare I was sure no one had seen it in centuries.

I stared at him—at his eyes, his dimples, and the face that I had memorized hundreds of years before. My heart pulsed once in an emotion so strong it almost felt out of place given what I had left, what had happened, and the way my soul and heart and life had been split into two pieces of me.

Be happy, Wyn.

"Thomas."

GLOSSARY

Skřítek - /skr̝̊iːtɛk/ - Meaning Elf in Czech; these people are similar to the common Fae and hold a type of magic that pulls from the energy of the earth. They tend to be tall and fair and have a rich culture of fighting and protection. Bonded and mated pairs wear their hair long and in braids. These creatures have been hunted to near extinction and their dwindling numbers still protect the source of all magic: Imdalind.

Trpaslík - /trpasliːk/ - Meaning Dwarf in Czech; these people hold a type of magic that pulls from the dark fire energy that pulls from the center of the earth. They strive best in manipulating rock and elements. They tend to be shorter in stature, but do not hold many physical differences from the mortals of the world.

Víly - /viːlɪ/ - Meaning Fairy or Sprite in Czech; these small winged creatures have jewel bright skin and stand no taller than a grown man's forearm. Their magic dwells in the souls of the world and can affect emotions or feelings. Their bite also awakens magic in mortals. These creatures have been hunted into extinction by King Edmund.

Drak - /drah:k/ - Meaning Dragon in Czech, these people hold the magic of sight. They survive off 'Black Water' that is poured from the source of magic in Imdalind. They also use that water to see in the future and the past of those who seek answers. These creatures have been hunted into extinction by King Edmund.

Silnỳ - /sil:nee/ - Meaning powerful in Czech, this is the name that was given to the person that was shown in sight by the Drak to be the one to end the war over magic.

Drevo - /drey:vo/ - A type of magical poultice that is a Trpaslík magic that when eaten can connect and embolden magic to assist in healing.

Vymàzat - /vee:mah:zaht/ - A type of magic burn that connects two people and allows the person who has used the magic to control the other. Once the burn is set, only death can break the control bond.

Zêlství - /zɛl:str̝̊iː/ - The Czech word that is used in the magical world for when a pair is bonded or mated. For the Skřítek there is a ceremony that involves braiding and the connection or sharing of magic to complete the bond. For the Trpaslíks it is the sharing of earth and blood. The Drak's complete the ceremony through sharing of sight and water.

Tòuha - /to:hah/ - A plane of existence that connects two people who have completed a Zêlství. This place can only be accessed through the magic of the bonded or mated pair.

Zmizêt - /zmiːzɛt/ - A shield that is used by all magical people to not only protect themselves or others from magical attacks, but for many Skříteks and others with strong magic, can bring invisibility.

Svazovat - /svah:so:vaht/ - This is a type of magic that allows a person to be present or keep awareness on an object by leaving a piece of their magic within it. For a more complex presence in the object the person may leave a piece of magic and self within the object. Sometimes referred to as a souls bind, the name is deceiving as a piece of a soul is not necessary to complete the magic. Rather, it simply needs to be something precious and meaningful that will connect the two.

Další v příkazu - /dalʃiː v pr̝̊i:kah:zoo/ - Meaning Second in Command this is the title for those who the second or the hand to the king of the Skříteks and of Imdalind. This is also the name of the crimson ribbon that denotes the title and authority of the wearer. As the další v příkazu is traditionally a married male this has been woven into the mating braid of the possessor.

Štít - /st:i:ht/ - The 'good magic' counterpart to a Vymàzat. A Vymàzat controls, a Stit simply connects magic and supports and protects... or it's supposed to.

Zánik - /zah:n:eek/ - A fatal curse that uses ones own magic to consume and destroy the one who is cursed.

Zlomený - /zlo:me:knee/ - The name for sights that do not come to pass.

Omezující stone - /zah:n:eek/ - A stone that is found in high mountains, when consumed it can restrict the magic in **Skříteks** and **Trpaslíks**

About the Author

Rebecca Ethington is an internationally bestselling author with millions of books sold. Her breakout debut, The Imdalind Series, has been featured on bestseller lists since its debut in 2012, reaching thousands of adoring fans worldwide and cited as "Interesting and Intense" by *USA Today's Happily Ever After Blog*.

From writing horror to romance and creating every sort of magical creature in between, Rebecca's imagination weaves vibrant worlds that transport readers into the pages of her books. Her writing has been described as fresh, original, and groundbreaking, with stories that bend genres and create fantastical worlds.

Born and raised under the lights of a stage, Rebecca has written stories by the ghost light, told them in whispers in dark corridors, and never stopped creating within the pages of a notebook.

Find me online
www.rebeccaethington.com
contact@rebeccaethington.com

Also by Rebecca Ethington

THE WORLD OF IMDALIND

The Imdalind Series

Kiss of Fire, Imdalind #1

Eyes of Ember, Imdalind #2

Scorched Treachery, Imdalind #3

Soul of Flame, Imdalind #4

Burnt Devotion, Imdalind #5

Brand of Betrayal, Imdalind #6

Dawn of Ash, Imdalind #7

Crown of Cinders, Imdalind #8

Spark of Vengeance, Imdalind #9

Flare of Villainy, Imdalind #10

Imdalind Academy

The Gauntlet, Book One

Rogue Royalty, Book Two

Broken Renegade, Book Three

The Through Glass Series

Book One: The Dark

Book Two: The Blue

Book Three: The Rose

Book Four: The Cut

Book Five: The Light

THE IMDALIND SERIES

BOOK ONE: *Kiss of Fire*
BOOK TWO: *Eyes of Ember*
BOOK THREE: *Scorched Treachery*
BOOK FOUR: *Soul of Flame*
BOOK FIVE: *Burnt Devotion*
BOOK SIX: *Brand of Betrayal*
BOOK SEVEN: *Dawn of Ash*
BOOK EIGHT: *Crown of Cinders*
BOOK NINE: *Spark of Vengeance*
BOOK TEN: *Flare of Villainy*

www.ingramcontent.com/pod-product-compliance
Lightning Source LLC
Chambersburg PA
CBHW020720310726
48979CB00004B/1004

* 9 7 8 1 9 4 9 7 2 5 7 9 7 *